Popular Romances of the West of England; or, The Drolls, Traditions, and Superstitions of old Cornwall;

The Giant Bolster strides from the Beacon to_____ St Brea
— A distance of six miles —

POPULAR ROMANCES

OF THE

WEST OF ENGLAND

OR

The Drolls, Traditions, and Superstitions of Old Cornwall

COLLECTED AND EDITED BY

ROBERT HUNT, F.R.S.

WITH ILLUSTRATIONS BY GEORGE CRUIKSHANK.

THIRD EDITION, REVISED AND ENLARGED

London
CHATTO AND WINDUS, PICCADILLY
1881

"' Have you any stories like that, guidwife?'

"' Ah,' she said, ' there were plenty of people that could tell those stories once I used to hear them telling them over the fire at night, but people is so changed with pride now, that they care for nothing.'"—CAMPBELL.

PREFACE TO THE THIRD EDITION.

DURING the last few years a new interest has been awakened, and the West of England has attracted the attention of many, who had previously neglected the scenes of interest, and the spots of beauty, which are to be found in our own island.

The rugged granite range of Dartmoor, rich with the golden furze; the moorlands of Cornwall, with their mighty Tors and giant boulders fringed with ferns and framed in masses of purple heath; the stern coasts, washed by an emerald sea, quaint with rocks carved into grotesque forms by the beating of waves and winds, spread with the green samphire and coated with yellow lichens; are now found to have a peculiar —though a wild—often a savage—beauty. The wood-clad valleys, ringing with the rush of rivers, and the sheltered plains, rich with an almost tropical vegetation, present new features of interest to the stranger's eyes, in the varied characters of the organisation native to that south-western clime.

The railways give great facilities for visiting those scenes, of which the public eagerly avail themselves. But they have robbed the West of England of half its interest, by dispelling the spectres of romance which were, in hoar antiquity, the ruling spirits of the place.

The "Romances of the West of England"—collected into a volume which has served its purpose well—gives the tourist the means of restoring the giants and the fairies to their native haunts.

The growing inquiries of those who are desirous of knowing something of the ancient Cornish miners,—of the old peasantry of this peninsula, and of the aged fishermen who almost lived upon the Atlantic waters,—have convinced me that a third edition of this volume of folk-lore has become a necessity.

While correcting the pages for a new edition, a scientific friend, who was deep in the cold thrall of positivism, called upon me. He noticed the work upon which I was engaged, and remarked, "I suppose you invented most of these stories."

In these days, when our most sacred things are being sneered at, and the poetry of life is being repressed by the prose of a cold infidelity. this remark appears to render it a humiliating necess'y, to assure my readers that none of the legends in this volume have been invented. They were all of them gathered in their native homes, more than half a century since, as stated fully in the Introduction to the volume.

For this edition some necessary corrections have been made; and additions will be found in the Appendix, which it is thought will increase the interest of the volume.

ROBERT HUNT

March 1881.

CONTENTS.

First Series.

B

Second Series.

Contents.

INTRODUCTION.

THE beginning of this collection of Popular Romances may be truly said to date from my early childhood   I remember with what anticipations of pleasure, sixty-eight years since, I stitched together a few sheets of paper, and carefully pasted them into the back of an old book.   This was preparatory to a visit I was about to make with my mother to Bodmin, about which town many strange stories were told, and my purpose was to record them.   My memory retains dim shadows of a wild tale of Hender the Huntsman of Lanhydrock ; of a narrative of streams having been poisoned by the monks, and of a legend of a devil who played many strange pranks with the tower which stands on a neighbouring hill.   I have, within the last year? endeavoured to recover those stories, but in vain.   The living people appear to have forgotten them ; my juvenile note-book has long been lost : those traditions are, it is to be feared, gone for ever.

Fifteen years passed away—about six of them at school in Cornwall, and nine of them in close labour in London,—when failing health compelled my return to the West of England. Having spent about a month on the borders of Dartmoor, and wandered over that wild region of Granite Tors, gathering up its traditions,—ere yet Mrs Bray* had thought of doing so,—I resolved on walking through Cornwall.   Thirty-five years since, on a beautiful spring morning, I landed at Saltash, from the very ancient passage-boat which in those days conveyed men and women, carts and cattle, across the river Tamar, where now that triumph of engineering, the Albert Bridge, gracefully spans its waters.   Sending my box forward to Liskeard by a van, my wanderings commenced ; my purpose being to visit each relic of Old Cornwall, and to gather up every existing tale of its ancient people.   Ten months were delightfully spent in this way ; and in that period a large number of the romances and superstitions which

---

* Mrs Bray collected her " Traditions, Legends, and Superstitions of Devonshire " in 1835, and they were published in 1838   This work proves to me that even at that time the old-world stories were perishing like the shadows on the mist before the rising sun. Many wild tales which I heard in 1829 appear to have been lost in 1835

are published in these volumes were collected, with many more, which have been weeded out of the collection as worthless.

During the few weeks which were spent on the borders of Dartmoor, accidental circumstances placed me in the very centre of a circle who believed "there were giants on the earth in those days" to which the "old people" belonged, and who were convinced that to turn a coat-sleeve or a stocking prevented the piskies from misleading man or woman. I drank deeply from the stream of legendary lore which was at that time flowing, as from a well of living waters, over

> "Devonia's dreary Alps," [*]

and longed to renew my acquaintance with the wild tales of Cornwall, which had either terrified or amused me when a child.

My acquaintance with the fairies commenced at an early date. When a very boy, I have often been taken by a romantic young lady, who lives in my memory—

> "So bright, so fair, so wild," [†]

to seek for the fairies on Lelant Towans. The maiden and the boy frequently sat for hours, entranced by the stories of an old woman, who lived in a cottage on the edge of the blown sandhills of that region. Thus were received my earliest lessons in fairy mythology.

From earthly youth accidental circumstances have led to my acquiring a taste for collecting the waifs floating upon the sea of time, which tell us something of those ancient peoples who have not a written history. The rude traditions of a race who appear to have possessed much native intelligence, minds wildly poetical, and great fertility of imagination, united with a deep feeling for the mysteries by which life is guided, especially interested me. By the operation of causes beyond my control, I was removed from the groove of ordinary trade and placed in a position of considerable responsibility, in connection with one of the most useful institutions of Cornwall.[‡] To nurse the germs of genius to maturity—to seek those gems "of purest ray serene," which the dark, though not "unfathomed caves" of the Cornish mines might produce—and to reward every effort of human industry, was the purpose of this institution. As its secretary, my duties, as well as my inclination, took me often into the mining and agricultural districts, and brought me into intimate relation with the miners and the peasantry. The bold shores of St Just—the dark and rock-clad hills of Morva,

---

[*] Carrington's "Dartmoor" [†] Coleridge.

[‡] The Royal Cornwall Polytechnic Society.

Zennor, and St Ives—the barren regions of St Agnes—the sandy undulations of Perranzabuloe—the sterile tracts of Gwennap—the howling moorlands of St Austell and Bodmin—and, indeed, every district in which there was a mine, became familiar ground. Away from the towns, at a period when the means of communication were few, and those few tedious, primitive manners still lingered. Education was not then, as now, the fashion. Church-schools were few and far between; and Wesleyan Methodism—although it was infusing truth and goodness amongst the people—had not yet become conscious of the importance of properly educating the young. Always delighting in popular tales, no opportunity of hearing them was ever lost. Seated on a three-legged stool, or in a "timberen settle," near the blazing heath-fire on the hearth, have I elicited the old stories of which the people were beginning to be ashamed. Resting in a level, after the toil of climbing from the depths of a mine, in close companionship with the homely miner, his superstitions, and the tales which he had heard from his grandfather, have been confided to me.

To the present hour my duties take me constantly into the most remote districts of Cornwall and Devon, so that, as boy and as man, I have possessed the best possible opportunities for gathering up the folk-lore of a people, who, but a few generations since, had a language peculiarly their own,*—a people, who, like all the Celts, cling with sincere affection to the memories of the past, and who even now regard with jealousy the introduction of any novelty, and accept improvements slowly.

The store of old-world stories which had been collected under the circumstances described would, perhaps, never have taken their present form, if Mr Thomas Wright had not shown the value of studying the Cyclopean Walls of the promontory beyond Penzance, popularly called "The Giant's Hedges,"—and if Mr

---

* "The Cornish dialect, one of the three branches of the old British, bears greater affinity with the Breton or Armorican dialect of Brittany than it does with the Welsh, although it properly forms the link of union between the Celtic dialect of France and that of the Cambrian hills The nature of its inflexions, both in letters and in tenses and cases, is, generally speaking, alike, allowance being made for dialectic variations arising from the nature of the country in which the dialect is spoken " The above quotation is from the remarkable book published by Bagster & Sons, "The Bible of every Land . A History of the Sacred Scriptures in every Language and Dialect into which Translations have been made " Preceding the above quotation, I find it stated that "Dolly Pentreath, who died at Penzance in 1778, aged 102, was then said to be the only person in Cornwall who could speak the aboriginal idiom of that province of ancient Britain " This old woman died at Mousehole, and was buried in the churchyard of Paul Over her grave Prince Lucien Bonaparte has recently placed an inscribed granite obelisk Polwhele and some others have doubted the statement made by James Barrington, that Dolly was the last person who could speak Cornish As they contend, many other men and women may, a hundred years since, have known the tongue, but no writer has produced good evidence to show that any person habitually spoke the language, which Barrington informs us was the case with Dolly Pentreath

J. O. Halliwell had not told us that his *"Rambles in Western Cornwall, by the Footsteps of the Giants,"* had led him to attempt " to remove part of a veil beyond which lies hid a curious episode in the history" of an ancient people.

In writing of the Giants, the fairies, and the spectral bands, I have often asked myself, How is it possible to account for the enduring life of those romantic tales, under the constantly-repressing influences of Christian teaching, and of the advances of civilisation? I have, to some extent, satisfied myself by such a reply as the following:—

Those things which make a strong impression on the mind of the child are rarely obliterated by the education through which he advances to maturity, and they exert their influences upon the man in advanced age. A tale of terror, related by an ignorant nurse, rivets the attention of an infant mind, and its details are engraven on the memory. The " bogle," or " bogie," with which the child is terrified into quiet by some thoughtless servant, remains a dim and unpleasant reality to shake the nerves of the philosopher. Things like these—seeing that existence is surrounded by clouds of mystery—become a Power which will, ever and anon through life, exert considerable control over our actions. As it is with the individual, so is it with the race to which that individual belongs. When our Celtic ancestors—in the very darkness of their ignorance—were taught, through their fears, a Pantheistic religion, and saw a god in every grand phenomenon :—when not merely the atmospheric changes—the aspects of the starry sky—and the peculiarities apparent in the sun and moon, were watched with fearful anxiety ; but when the trembling of a rock—the bubbling of a spring—the agitation of the forest leaves—and the flight of a bird, were charged with sentences of life and death .—then was moulded the Celtic mind, and the early impressions have never been entirely obliterated. " There were maddening orgies amongst the sacred rites of the Britons ; orgies that, whilst they reminded one writer of the Bacchic dances, reminded another of the worship of Demeter." [*]

The Romans came and possessed the land. Even to the most westerly promontory, we have evidences of their rule, and indications of their superiority. The Saxons overcame the Danmonii—Athelstane drove the Cornish beyond the Tamar, and planted his banner on the Scilly Islands ;—and this Teutonic people diffused their religion and their customs over the West.[†] The Dane followed upon

[*] Latham.
[†] "Athelstane (937) handled them yet more extremely; for he drove them out of

the Saxon, and he has left his earthworks, in evidence of his possession, upon the Cornish hills.* The Norman conquerors eventually took possession of our island, and several of the existing families of Cornwall can speak of ancestors, who won their lands by favour of William, the Duke of Normandy.

Notwithstanding the influences which can be—not very obscurely —traced of Roman and Saxon, Danish and Norman civilisations, the Celtic superstitions lingered on :—varied perhaps in their clothing, but in all essentials the same. Those wild dreams which swayed with irresistible force the skin-clad Briton of the Cornish hills, have not yet entirely lost their power where even the National and the British Schools are busy with the people, and Mechanics' Institutions are diffusing the truths of science In the infancy of the race, terror was the moving power . in the maturity of the people, the dark shadow still sometimes rises, like a spectre, partially eclipsing the mild radiance of that Christian truth which shines upon the land.

It must not be forgotten that Cornwall has, until a recent period, maintained a somewhat singular isolation. England, with many persons, appeared to terminate on the shores of the river Tamar ; and the wreckers of the coasts, and the miners of the hills, were equally regarded as indicating the semi-civilisation of this county The difficulties of travelling in Cornwall were great. A clergyman writing in 1788, says, " Our object was now to obtain a passage to Loo, without losing sight of the noble sea. Saddle-horses would render the difficulty of this route a pleasure, but with my carriage it is deemed impracticable."† Again, he tells us he was with his guide "five hours coming the eleven miles from Loo to Lostwithiel." Within my own memory, the ordinary means of travelling from Penzance to Plymouth was by a van called a "kitterine," and three days were occupied in the journey. There was in latter years, a mail coach, but the luxury of this conveyance was, even then, reserved for the wealthier classes. This difficulty of transit in a great measure explains the seclusion of the people up to a comparatively recent period ; and to it we certainly owe the preservation of their primitive character, and most of the material to be found in these volumes. At one period indeed—but still earlier than the days of kitterines—we find the Cornish people, as a body,

Excester, where, till then, they bare equal sway with the Saxons, and left them only the narrow angle on the west of Tamar river for their inheritance, which hath ever since beene their fatall bound "—*Carew*, p 96

* " And divers round holds on the tops of hill , some single, some double, and treble trenched, which are termed *Castellan Denis* or *Danis*, as raysed by the Danes when they were destyned to become our scourge "—*Carew*, p 85

† A Tour to the West of England in 1788. By the Rev. S Shaw, M A , London, 1789.

curiously, but completely, cut off by the river Tamar, from their countrymen. They were then informed of the active life of the world beyond them by the travelling historian only, who, as he also sought amuse the people, was called the "droll-teller."

The wandering minstrel, story-teller, and newsmonger appears to have been an old institution amongst the Cornish. Indeed Carew, in his "Survey of Cornwall," tells us that "the last of the Wideslades, whose estates were forfeited in the Rebellion, was called Sir Tristram. He led a walking life with his harp to gentlemen's houses." As the newspaper gradually found its way into this western county (the first one circulated in Cornwall being the *Sherbourne Mercury*), the occupation of this representative of the bards was taken away ; but he has only become extinct within the last twenty years. These old men wandered constantly from house to house, finding a hearty welcome at all. Board and bed were readily found them, their only payment being a song or a droll (story). A gentleman to whom I am under many obligations writes :—

" The only wandering droll-teller whom I well remember was an old blind man, from the parish of Cury,—I think, as he used to tell many stories about the clever doings of the conjurer Luty of that place, and by that means procure the conjurer much practice from the people of the west. The old man had been a soldier in his youth, and had a small pension at the time he went over the country, accompanied by a boy and dog. He neither begged nor offered anything for sale, but was sure of a welcome to bed and board in every house he called at. He would seldom stop in the same house more than one night, not because he had exhausted his stories, or 'eaten his welcome,' but because it required all his time to visit his acquaintances once in the year. The old man was called Uncle Anthony James. (Uncle is a term of respect, which was very commonly applied to aged men by their juniors in Cornwall. Aunt (A'nt or Ann), as A'nt Sally or Ann' Jenney, was used in the same manner when addressing aged women.

" Uncle Anthony James used to arrive every year in St Leven parish about the end of August. Soon after he reached my father's house, he would stretch himself on the 'chimney-stool,' and sleep until supper-time When the old man had finished his frugal meal of bread and milk, he would tune his fiddle and ask if 'missus' would like to hear him sing her favourite ballad As soon as my dear mother told him how pleased she would be, Uncle Anthony would go through the 'woeful hunting' ('Chevy Chase'), from beginning to end, accompanied by the boy and the fiddle.

I expect the air was his own composition, as every verse was a different tune   The young were then gratified by hearing the 'sfreams' (strains) of 'Lovely Nancy,' divided in three parts.*
I never saw this ballad published, yet it is a very romantic old thing, almost as long as 'Chevy Chase.'   Another favourite was .—

> 'Cold blows the wind to-day, sweetheart;
>   Cold are the drops of rain;
> The first truelove that ever I had
>   In the green wood he was slain

> ''Twas down in the garden-green, sweetheart,
>   Where you and I did walk,
> The fairest flower that in the garden grew
>   Is withered to a stalk

> 'The stalk will bear no leaves, sweetheart;
>   The flowers will ne'er return;
> And since my truelove is dead and gone,
>   What can I do but mourn?

> 'A twelvemonth and a day being gone,
>   The spirit rose and spoke—
> "My body is clay cold, sweetheart;
>   My breath smells heavy and strong;
> And if you kiss my lily-white lips,
>   Your time will not be long."'

" Then follows a stormy kind of duet between the maiden and her lover's ghost, who tries to persuade the maid to accompany him to the world of shadows.   Uncle Anthony had also a knack of turning Scotch and Irish songs into Cornish ditties.   'Barbara Allan' he managed in the following way, and few knew but that he had composed the song :—

> 'In Cornwall I was born and bred,
>   In Cornwall was my dwelling,
> And there I courted a pretty maid,
>   Her name was Ann Tremellan

" The old man had the 'Babes in the Wood' for religious folks; but he avoided the 'Conorums,' as he called the Methodists.   Yet the grand resource was the stories in which the supernatural bore great part.   The story I told you about the ancestors of the conjurer Luty finding the mermaid, who gave them the power to break the spell of witchcraft, was one of this old man's tales, which he seemed to believe; and he regarded the conjurer with as much respect as the bard might the priest in olden time.   I have a dim recollection of another old droll-teller, called Billy Frost, in St Just, who used to go round to the feasts in the neighbouring parishes, and be well entertained at the public-houses for the sake of his drolls."

* Carew, in his " Survey of Cornwall," makes especial mention of "three men's songs, as being peculiar to this county

In 1829 there still existed two of those droll-tellers, and from them were obtained a few of the stories here preserved.

These wanderers perpetuated the traditions of the old inhabitants; but they modified the stories, according to the activity of their fancy, to please their auditors. Not merely this . they without doubt introduced the names of people remembered by the villagers; and when they knew that a man had incurred the hatred of his neighbours, they made him do duty as a demon, or placed him in no very enviable relation with the devil. The legends of Tregeagle are illustrations of this. The man who has gained the notoriety of being attached to a tale as old as that of Orestes,— was a magistrate in Cornwall two hundred years since The story of the murderess of Ludgvan and her lover is another, and a very modern, example of the process by which recent events are interwoven with very ancient superstitions.*

When the task of arranging my romances was commenced, I found that the traditions of Devonshire, as far east as Exeter—the tract of country which was known as " Danmonium," or even more recently as " Old Cornwall "—had a striking family resemblance. My collection then received the name it bears, as embracing the district ordinarily known as the West of England. Although I have avoided repeating any of the traditions which are to be found in Mrs Bray's books; I have not altered my title; for the examples of folk-lore given in these volumes belong strictly to " Old Cornwall "

There are some points of peculiar interest connected with the Dartmoor traditions, indicating, as I conceive, a purely Saxon origin, deserving an attention which they have not yet received.

Childe's Tomb, in one of the dreariest portions of the moor, is a large cross of granite. This Childe, lord of the manor of Plymstock, was benighted on the moor in a snowstorm; he killed his horse, and got within its body for warmth, having first written in blood on a granite slab, near which he was found dead,—

> "The first that finds and brings me to my grave,
> The lands of Plymstock he shall have "

The Benedictine monks of Tavistock are said to have found the body, and thus secured their right to the lands. This is without doubt an old Saxon legend, modified, as it has been handed down from age to age. Wistman's Wood, with its "hundred oaks one hundred yards high,"—a remnant of the old Dartmoor Forest,—

---

* I find in Campbell's "Popular Tales of the West Highlands" particular mention made of numerous historical events which have taken the forms of ancient legends. "There is popular history of events which really happened within the last five centuries."

is the very home of the *Wish hounds*, which hunt so fiercely over the Moor; and this Wistman appears to have been some demon creature, whose name alone remains. Mr Kemble gives *Wusc*, or *Wisc*, as one of the names of Odin. Here we have a similar name given to a strange wood in Devonshire, associated with wild superstitions; and *whish*, or *whisht*, is a common term for that weird sorrow which is associated with mysterious causes.

The stone circles, the stone avenues, and the rock tribunals,—of which Crockern Tor furnishes us with a fine example,—have yet tales to tell, which would well repay any labour that might be bestowed upon them. Ancient British rule gave way to Saxon power, and probably there was no tract in England less known to the Romans than Dartmoor. Thus we may expect to find the paganism of the Briton and the rude Christianity of the Saxon, shadowed out in the remaining legends of Dartmoor.

> "Crocker, Conwys, and Coplestone,
> When the Conqueror came, were found at home,"

is an old Devonshire rhyme. Those names are associated with many a moorland tradition, and indicate their Saxon origin.

It may appear strange to many, that having dealt with the superstitions of the Cornish people, no mention has been made of the Divining Rod (the "*Dowzing Rod*," as it is called), and its use in the discovery of mineral lodes. This has been avoided, in the first place, because any mention of the practice of "*dowzing*" would lead to a discussion, for which this work is not intended; and, in the second place, because the use of the hazel-twig is not Cornish. The divining or dowzing rod is certainly not older than the German miners, who were brought over by Queen Elizabeth to teach the Cornish to work their mines, one of whom, called Schutz, was some time Warden of the Stannaries. Indeed, there is good reason for believing that the use of this wand is of more recent date, and, consequently, removed from the periods which are sought to be illustrated by this collection. The Divining Rod belongs no more to them than do the modern mysteries of twirling hats, of teaching tables to turn, and,—in their wooden way,—to talk

The giant stories, prefaced with the often-told tale of Gogmagog, are of a character peculiarly their own. They do not appear to resemble the giants described in Mr Campbell's "Popular Tales of the West Highlands;" but it must be admitted that there are some indications of a common origin between those of Cromarty and of Cornwall. In Mr Dasent's translation of Asbjornsen, and Moe's collection of "Norse Tales," the giant is not like our native friends. May we venture to believe that the

Cornish giant is a true Celt, or may he not belong to an earlier race? He was fond of home, and we have no record of his ever having passed beyond the wilds of Dartmoor. The giants o Lancashire, of Cheshire, and Shropshire have a family likeness, and are, no doubt, closely related; but if they are cousins to the Cornish giants, they are cousins far removed Dr Latham, in his " Ethnology of the British Islands," says " Tradition, too, indicates the existence of an old march or debatable land; for south of Rugby begins the scene of the deeds of Guy, Earl of Warwick, the slayer of the dun cow." The large bone which is shown in Redcliff Church, Bristol, is the last indication of the dun cow in the south. As this marvellous cow moved within prescribed limits, so was it with the giants of old Cornwall.

The fairies of Cornwall do not exhibit the same marked individuality. Allowing for the influences of physical conditions, they are clearly seen to be an offshoot from the common stock. Yet they have several local peculiarities, and possess names which are especially their own.

A few of the more popular legends of the Cornish saints are preserved, for the purpose of showing how enduringly the first impressions of power, as exhibited by the earliest missionaries, have remained fixed amongst the people; this being due mainly to the mental operation of associating mental power and physical strength with external things in the relations of cause and effect.

I cannot but consider myself fortunate in having collected these traditions thirty-five years ago. They could not be collected now. Mr J. O. Halliwell speaks of the difficulties he experienced in his endeavours to obtain a story. The common people think they will be laughed at if they tell their " ould drolls " to a stranger. Beyond this, many of the stories have died out with those who told them. In the autumn of 1862, being very desirous of getting every example of folk-lore which existed in the remote parishes of Zennor and Morva, I employed the late C. Taylor Stephens, " sometime rural postman from St Ives to Zennor," and the author of " The Chief of Barat-Anac," to hunt over the district. This he did with especial care, and the results of his labours are included in those pages. The postman and poet, although he spent many days and nights amidst the peasantry, failed to procure stories which had been told me, without hesitation, thirty years before.

When it was known that I was engaged in preparing for publication a work on the Traditions and Superstitions of Cornwall, numerous contributions, from much-valued friends, and from strangers interested in the preservation of these characteristics of the West of England, were sent to me. From these some stories have been selected, but by far the larger number were modifications of stories already told. My obligations and thanks are, nevertheless, due to all; but there are two gentlemen to whom acknowledgments beyond this are necessary. These are Mr T. Q. Couch, who had already published examples of the folk-lore of Polperro and the neighbourhood, who has communicated several original stories, and Mr W. Botterell of Caerwyn, a native of St Leven, who possesses a greater knowledge of the household stories of the Land's-End district than any man living. Mr Botterell has, with much labour, supplied me with gleanings from his store, and his stories have been incorporated, in most cases, as he told them. Beyond this, it was satisfactory to have the correctness of many in my own collection confirmed by so reliable an authority. Without the assistance which this gentleman has given, the West Cornwall stories would not have possessed the interest which will be found to belong to them

One word on the subject of arrangement. In the First Series are arranged all such stories as appear to belong to the most ancient inhabitants of these islands. It is true that many of them, as they are now told, assume a mediæval, or even a modern character. This is the natural result of the passage of a tradition or myth from one generation to another. The customs of the age in which the story is told are interpolated for the purpose of rendering them intelligible to the listeners, and thus they are constantly changing their exterior form I am, however, disposed to believe that the spirit of all the romances included in this series shows them to have originated before the Christian era. The romances of the Second Series belong certainly to the historic period, though the dates of many of them are exceedingly problematical.

All the stories given in these volumes are the genuine household tales of the people. The only liberties which have been taken with them has been to alter them from the vernacular—in which they were for the most part related—into modern language. This applies to every romance but one. "The Mermaid's Vengeance" is a combination of three stories, having no doubt a common origin, but·varying considerably in their details. They were too much alike to bear repeating, consequently it was thought best to throw them into one tale, which should preserve the peculiarities of all. This has been done with much care, and even the songs given preserve lines which are said by the fisherman—from whom the stories were obtained—to have been sung by the mermaids.

The traditions which are told, the superstitions which are spoken of, and the customs which are described in these volumes, may be regarded as true types of the ancient Cornish mythology, and genuine examples of the manners and customs of a people who will not readily deviate from the rules taught them by their fathers.   .

Romances such as these have floated down to us as wreck upon the ocean.   We gather a fragment here and a fragment there, and at length, it may be, we learn something of the name and character of the vessel when it was freighted with life, and obtain a shadowy image of the people who have perished.

Hoping to have been successful in saving a few interesting fragments of the unwritten records of a peculiar race, my labours are submitted to the world.   The pleasure of recalling the past has fully repaid me for the labour of arranging the *Traditions of Old Cornwall.*

ROBERT HUNT.

ROMANCES AND SUPERSTITIONS

OF THE

MYTHIC AGES.

THE GIANTS.

" Of Titan's monstrous race
Only some few disturb'd that happy place.
Raw hides they wore for clothes, their drink was blood,
Rocks were their dining-rooms, their prey their food,
Caverns their lodging, and their bed their grove,
Their cup some hollow trunk."

—*Havilan's* " *Architrenium*,"
translated in Gough's " *Camden* "

POPULAR ROMANCES OF THE
WEST OF ENGLAND.

THE AGE OF THE GIANTS.

" Eald enta geweorc
Idlu stodon "—*The Wanderer. Exeter Book.*

" The old works of giants
Stood desolate "—THOMAS WRIGHT

IN wandering over some of the uncultivated tracts which still maintain their wildness, austerely and sullenly, against the march of cultivation, we are certain of finding rude masses of rock which have some relation to the giants. The giant's hand, or the giant's chair, or, it may be, the giant's punch-bowl, excites your curiosity. What were the mental peculiarities of the people who fixed so permanently those names on fantastic rock-masses? What are the conditions—mental or otherwise—necessary for the preservation of these ideas? are questions which I have often asked myself when wandering amidst the Tors of Dartmoor, and when seated upon the granite masses which spread themselves so strangely, yet so picturesquely, over Carn Brea and other rocky hills in Cornwall. When questions of this kind are continually recurring, the mind naturally works out some reply, which satisfies at least itself; and it consequently not unfrequently reposes contentedly on a fallacy as baseless as the giant-spectre of the mountain mists. This may possibly be the condition at which I have arrived, and many of my readers may smile at my dreams. It is not in my nature to work without some hypothesis; but I endeavour to hold it as loosely as possible, that it may be yielded up readily the moment a more promising theory is born, whoever may be its parent—wherever its birthplace

Giants, and every form of giant-idea, belong to the wilds of nature. I have never discovered the slightest indication of the existence of a tradition of giants, of the true legendary type, in a fertile valley or in a well-cultivated plain. Wherever there yet linger the faint shadows of the legendary giant, there the country still retains much of its native wildness, and the inhabitants have, to a great extent, preserved their primitive character In other words, they have nurtured a gloomy imagination, and permitted ignorance to continue its melancholy delusions. The untaught mind, in every age, looks upon the grander phenomena of nature with feelings of terror, and endeavours to explain them by the aid of those errors which have been perpetuated from father to son since the days when the priests of superstition sought to rule the minds of men by exciting their fears.

I shall have to tell, by and by, the story of a so-called giant, who could bestride the lovely river which flows through the luxuriant valley of Tavistock, where, also, the inquiring traveller is shown his grave. The giant's grave in Penrith churchyard is familiar to me; and in or near many a picturesque village, shadowed by noble trees, and surrounded by richly-clothed fields, I can point to mounds, and to stones, which are said to be the resting-places of giants. These, however, will invariably be found to be rude monuments to ordinary men, who were possessed of more wealth, intelligence, courage, or strength than their fellows. men who have been the objects of hero-worship, but whose names have perished amidst the wrecks of time. It may be argued that these village giants are creations of the same character as those of the true legendary type, and that both result from analogous operations in the human mind. It may be so ; but how vastly different must have been the constitution of those minds to which we owe the creations of the Titans of our mountains and the large men of our lowlands. Had I the learning necessary for the task of showing that our legendary giant is of Oriental origin, I have not the required leisure to pursue that inquiry to its end ; and I leave it to abler men, contenting myself, and, let me hope, satisfying my readers, by studying the subject in its more simple aspects.

I find, over a tract of country extending from the eastern edge of Dartmoor to the Land's End—and even beyond it, to the Scilly Islands—curious relics of the giants. This district is in many respects a peculiar one. The physical features of the country are broadly marked ; and, even after the civilising influences of centuries, wild nature contests with man, and often maintains her supremacy. On one hand we see industry taking possession of the hills, and holding them firm in its ameliorating grasp ; on the other, we find the sterile moor and the rock-spread region still resisting successfully the influences of man and his appliances. When I travel into other parts of the British Isles, and reach a district having the same general features, I usually discover some outstanding memory of the giants, often, it must be admitted, faint and ill-defined. The giant Tarquin, almost forgotten amidst the whir of spindles, " who had his dwelling in a well-fortified castle near Manchester, on the site of what is yet known by the name of Castlefield," and Carados—

> " A mighty giant, just pull'd down,
> Who lived near Shrewsbury's fair town "—

may be quoted as examples of the fading myths.*

I therefore draw the conclusion that those large masses of humanity—of whom Saturn devouring his own children would seem to be the parental type—can exist only in the memories of those races who are born and live amidst the sublime phenomena of nature.

On the rugged mountain, overspread with rocks which appear themselves to be the ruins of some Cyclopean hall, amidst which the tempests play, still harmless in their fury ;—here, where the breezes of spring and summer whistle as with some new delight—where the autumnal winds murmur the wildest music, or make the saddest wail ; and the winter storms, as if joyous in their strength, shout in voices of thunder from cairn to cairn ;—here does the giant dwell ! On the beetling cliff, where coming tempests delight to send those predicating moanings, which tell of the coming war of winds and waves ;—on rocks which have frowned for ages on the angry sea, and in caverns which mock, by repeating, the sounds of air and water—be they joyous as the voice of birds, or wild and solemn as the howl of savages above the dead , —here does the giant dwell !

In the valley, too, has he sometimes fixed his home ; but the giant has usually retired from business when he leaves the hills Even here we miss not the old associations Huge boulders are spread on every side ; rock-masses are overgrown with furze, ferns, mosses, and heaths ; and torrents rush from the hills, bringing, as it were, their native music with them. Wherever, indeed, the giants have made a home, we find a place remarkable for the grand scale on which the works of nature are displayed.

* See " Popular Traditions of Lancashire," by J Roby, Esq , M R S L Bohn, 1843

The giants of Danmonium—as that region was once named to which I have confined my inquiries—will be found to be a marked race. They appear to bear about them the characteristics of the giants of the East. They have the peculiarities which may be studied in those true Oriental Titans, Gog and Magog, who still preside so grimly and giantly at our City feasts. They have none of that stony, cold-hearted character which marks the giants of Scandinavia; and although Mr Keightley* would connect the mighty Thor with the no less mighty giants of the Arabian stories, I think it can be shown that all those of the West of England resemble their Northern brethren only in the manner in which the sensual monsters succumb to the slightest exercise of thought.

Mr J O Halliwell appears to have been a little surprised at discovering, during a very short residence in the West of Cornwall, that the Land's End district was "anciently the chosen land of the giants;" that it was "beyond all other the favourite abode and the land of the English giants." Peculiarly fitted for the inquiry as Mr Halliwell is, by his life-long studies, it is to be regretted that he spent so brief a period amidst "what still remains of these memorials of a Titan race." †

Who were the giants? Whence came they? ‡ I asked myself these questions when, seated in the Giant's Chair, I have looked down upon a wide expanse of "furzy downs," over which were scattered in picturesque confusion vast masses of granite rocks, every one of them standing in monumental grandeur, inscribed by the finger of tradition with memorials of this mighty race. Did Cormelian and Cormoran really build St Michael's Mount? Did Thunderbore walk the land, inspiring terror by his extreme ugliness? Did Bolster persecute the blessed St Agnes, until she was compelled by stratagem to destroy him? Did, indeed, our British Titans play at quoits and marbles with huge rocks? Is it a fact that all the giants died of grief after Corineus overthrew Gog Magog on Plymouth Hoe? Let us, if only for amusement—and to give to a light work some appearance of

---

* Tales and Popular Fictions : their Resemblance and Transmission from Country to Country. By Thomas Keightley 1834

† Rambles in Western Cornwall by the Footsteps of the Giants, with Notes on the Celtic Remains of the Land's End District, and the Islands of Scilly. By J O Halliwell, F R S 1861.

‡ That these Titans lived down to historic times is suggested by the following :—

"Guy, Earl of Warwick, fought at the request of Athelstan a combat with Colbrand, a Danish giant, and slew him."—*Gilbert*, quoting Carew, who again quotes Walter of Exeter. Vol iv., p. 111.

research—examine a few antiquated authorities, who may be said —in their own way—indirectly to answer those questions.

M. Pezron, D.D., and abbot of *La Charmoye,* wrote a strange book, "The Antiquities of Nations," which in 1706 was "Englished by Mr Jones."*

In his Epistle Dedicatory to Charles Lord Halifax, speaking of the "Famous Pezron," Mr Jones asks, "Was there ever any before him that attempted to Trace the Origin of the *Celtæ,* who with Great Probability of Truth, were the same People, and spoke the same Language, as our Ancient *Britains* did, and their Descendants continue to do to this Day, so high as *Gomer* and the *Gomarians ?*"

This authority, with a great display of learning, proves that Gomer, the eldest son of Japhet, was the chief of the Gomarians, and that these Gomarians afterwards were called Galatians, or Gauls. We further learn from him that a section of the Gomarians were called Sacæ, and that the Sacæ went into Phrygia, and afterwards assumed 'the name of TITANS This race, "and especially the Princes that commanded them, exceeded all others in Bulk and Strength of Body ; and hence it is that they have been looked upon to be terrible people, and, as it were, Giants. The Scripture itself, the Rule of Truth, even gives such an Idea as this, of those famous and potent men, who, according to it, ruled over all the Earth. *Judith,* speaking of them in her fine Song, called them *Giants* the sons of the *Titans.*† And the Prophet Isaiah informs us, also, that these Giants were anciently Masters of the World."

This mighty race dwelt in mountains, woods, and rough and inaccessible places, and "they lay in the Hollows of Valleys, and the like Places of Shelter and retirement, because they had no Houses in those Times." The learned abbot proceeds, exerting all his powers to prove that the Titans were the true Celtæ—that a people of Greece were the descendants of the Titans—that Gomer was "the true stock of the Gauls "—and that Magog, his brother, "is also looked upon to be the Origin of the *Scythians,* or People of *Great Tartary.*"‡

To seize on another authority, who appears to connect the Oriental with the British cromlech, and through those the people

---

* The Antiquities of Nations more particularly of the Celtæ or Gauls, taken to be originally the same People as our Ancient Britains

† Judith xvi. 7 . "Neither the sons of the Titans smite him, nor high giants set upon him "

‡ Those who are curious in this matter may examine also, "Gomer, or, A Brief Analysis of the Language and Knowledge of the Ancient Cymry By John Williams, A.M., Oxen., Archdeacon of Cardigan "

whose remains they cover, we will quote Dr E. D. Clarke, who describes* a Cyclopean structure visited by him near Kiel, consisting of three upright stones, supporting horizontally an enormous slab of granite. After mentioning several cromlechs of a similar character, and other "stupendous vestiges of Cyclopean architecture," he says—"There is nothing *Gothic* about them—nothing denoting the *Cimbri* or the *Franks*, or the old *Saxons*—but rather the ancient *Gaulish*, the ancient *British*, and the ancient *Irish;* and if this be admitted, they were *Titan-Celts:* the GIANTS of the *sacred*, and the CYCLOPS of the *heathen* historians." I am informed that Mr Christy has lately examined several cromlechs in Algeria; beneath each he found a human skeleton.

Such may be presumed to be the sources from which sprang the giants of Cornwall, whose labours—of which relics still remain—prove them to have been a race by the side of whom

> "In stature the tall Amazon
> Had stood a pigmy's height."

Everything they have left us informs us that they were men who

> "Would have ta'en
> Achilles by the hair, and bent his neck,
> Or with a finger stay'd Ixion's wheel." †

With these evidences, who then dares say that the *Samotheans*, who, under the reign of *Bardus*, people this island, were not subdued by *Albion*, a giant son of Neptune, "who called the land after his own name, and reigned forty-four years."‡ Let us not forget the evidence also given by Milton in his "Lycidas," when he asks, in his poetic sorrow, if his friend

> "Sleep'st by the fable of Bellerus old,
> Where the great Vision of the guarded Mount
> Looks towards Namancos and Bayona's hold "

Bellerian was the name formerly given to the promontory of the Land's End. It was the home of a mighty giant, after whom, in all probability, the headland was called §

---

* Travels in Various Countries of Europe, Asia, and Africa, vol ix., p 59
† Hyperion By John Keats
‡ The History of Britain By John Milton Second edition, 1678.
§ Keightley, who of all men should have traced this Bellerus to his home, in his "Life of Milton" confuses St Michael's Mount and the Land's End, and "conceives the giant Bellerus to have been an invention of Milton's" The evidence of the "History

Tradition throws a faint light back into those remote ages, and informs us that Cyclopean walls, vast earthworks, and strangely-piled masses of rock, which still remain, imperishable monuments of animal power, in various parts of the ancient Danmonium, were the works of the giants. With the true history of Jack the Giant-Killer—of him of the Bean-Stalk—and some others, we are all acquainted. We listened to those histories ere yet the dark seed of that troublesome weed—doubt—had germinated. They were poured forth from loving lips into believing ears ; and often in the sleep of innocency have we buried our heads in the maternal bosom to hide the horrid visage of some Cormoran Blunderbore, or Thunderbore, and escape the giant's toils. By this process the stories were imprinted on memory's tablets with an indelible ink, and for long years, the spunge and water—which is employed by the pioneers in the great March of Intellect—has been used almost in vain. Notwithstanding the influences which have been brought to bear, with no kindly spirit, upon the old-world tales, we have still lingering, though in ruins, the evidences by which they were supported. Mr Thomas Wright, in his " Memoir on the Local Legends of Shropshire," quotes from (and translates his quotation) an Anglo-Saxon poem, which bears the title of " The Ruin," in the " Exeter Book . "—

> " Wondrous is this wall-stone,
> The fates have broken it,
> Have burst the burgh-place ,
> The work of giants is perishing "

From the Land's End[*] to the eastern edge of Dartmoor, the perishing works of the giants—wondrous wall-stones—are yet to be found. In many instances the only records by which we can mark the homes of the giants are the names which yet cling to the rocks on the hills where they dwelt. The Giant's Cradle, on Trecrobben Hill, reminds us of the great man's infancy, as does also the Giant's Spoon, which is near it. The giant of Trecrobben

of Britain " shows with how much diligence the legendary lore which existed in 1678 had been sought out by the poet, and his grand epic proves with how much reverence Milton studied our own mythology. I could lead the reader to twenty places around the Land's End which were not discovered even by Mr J O Halliwell when rambling " In Western Cornwall by the Footsteps of the Giants," upon which Bellerus, although he has not left his name, has left a long-enduring record   See Appendix A.

* "Not far from the land's ende there is a little village called *Trebegean*—in English, *the towne of the Giant's Grave,*—near whereunto, and within memory (as I have been was, beyond question, a temperate one, as the Giant's Well, without the walls of his castle, incontestibly proves. But what shall we say of his neighbour, who dwelt at Beersheba, where the Giant's Bowl is still suggestive of imbibitions deep. The monumental mass of granite on Dartmoor, known as *Bowerman's Nose*, may hand down to us the resting-place and name of a giant whose nose was the index of his vice; though Carrington, in his poem of " Dartmoor," supposes these rocks to be

"A granite god,—
To whom, in days long flown, the suppliant knee
In trembling homage bow'd "

Let those, however, who are curious in this problem visit the granite idol; when, as Carrington assures us, he will find that the inhabitants of

" The hamlets near
Have legends rude connected with the spot
(Wild swept by every wind), on which he stands,
The Giant of the Moor."

Of the last resting-places of the giants there are many. Mardon, on Dartmoor, has a *Giant's Grave,** and from that rude region, travelling westward, we find these graves—proving the mortality of even this Titan race—rising on many a moor and mountain, until, crossing the sea, we see numerous giants' graves in the Scilly Islands; as though they had been the favourite resting-places of the descendants of those who dreamed of yet more western lands, beneath the setting sun, which were, even to them, "the Islands of the Blest." †

* See Shortt's Collection, p 28

† Mr Augustus Smith, in the Reports of the Royal Institution of Cornwall, has described one of the graves opened by him during a visit paid by the Cambrian Archæological Society to the Scilly Isles.

Hugh Miller, in his " Scenes and Legends of the North of Scotland," tells us a story of the giants of Cromarty, which shows us that they were intimately related to the giants of Cornwall Moreover, from him we learn something of the parentage of our giants, for we presume the Scottish myth may be applied with equal truth to the Titans of the south " Diocletian, king of Syria, say the historians, had thirty-three daughters, who, like the daughters of Danaus, killed their husbands on their wedding-night The king, their father, in abhorrence of their crime, crowded them all into a ship, which he abandoned to the mercy of the waves, and which was drifted by tides and winds, until it arrived on the coast of Britain, then an uninhabited island There they lived solitary, subsisting on roots and berries, the natural produce of the soil, until an order of demons, becoming enamoured of them, took them for their wives, and a tribe of giants, who must be regarded as the true aborigines of the country, if indeed the demons have not a prior claim, were the fruits of those marriages Less fortunate, however, than even their prototypes, the Cyclops, the whole tribe was extirpated a few years after by Brutus, the

There is scarcely a pile of rocks around our western shore upon which the giants have not left their impress. At Tol-Pedden-Penwith we have the Giant's Chair ; at Carn Boscawen we see the Giant's Pulpit. If we advance nearer to the towns, even the small mass of rocks behind Street-an-Noan, near Penzance, called Tolcarne, has the mark of the Giant's Foot. The priests, however, in the season of their rule, strove to obliterate the memories of those great pagans. They converted the footprint at Tolcarne—and similar indentations elsewhere—into the mark of the devil's hoof, when he stamped in rage at the escape of a sinner, who threw himself from the rock, strong in faith, into the arms of the Church. In more recent times, this footmark has been attributed to the devil jumping with joy, as he flew off, from this spot, with some unfortunate miller, who had lost his soul by mixing china clay with his flour The metamorphosis of ancient giants into modern devils is a curious feature in our inquiry. At Lemorna we have the Giant's Cave. On Gulval Cairn we find also the giant's mark, which the magic of Sir H. Davy's science could not dispel.* On Carn Brea are no end of evidences of these Titans—the Giant's Hand rivalling in size any of the monstrous monuments of the Egyptian gods Thus, in nearly every part of the country where granite rocks prevail, the monuments of the giants may be found. Why do the giants show such a preference for granite ? At Looe, indeed, the Giant's Hedge is a vast earthwork; but this is an exception,† unless the Bolster in St Agnes is a giant's work. In pursuing the dim lights which yet remain to guide us to the history of the giants, we must not forget the record of the *Fatal Wrestling* on Plymouth Hoe. ·

parricide, who, with a valour to which mere bulk could render no effectual resistance, overthrew Gog, Magog, and Termagol, and a whole host of others with names equally terrible The Cromarty legends give accounts of a ponderous stone flung from the point of a spindle across Dornoch Firth , and of another yet larger, still to be seen, a few miles from Dingwall, which was thrown equally far, and which bears the impress of the giant's finger and thumb Also, they tell us of the *cailliach-more*, or great woman, who "from a pannier filled with earth and stones, which she carried on her back, formed almost all the hills of Ross-shire " The Sutars, as the promontories of Cromarty are named, served as the work-stools of two giants, who were shoemakers, or soutars, and hence, says Hugh Miller, " in process of time the name soutar was transferred by a common metonymy from the craftsmen to their stools, the two promontories, and by this name they have ever since been distinguished "

* Sir H Davy, when a youth, would frequently steal to Gulval Cairn, and in its solitude pursue his studies

† See Davies Gilbert's History, vol. iv , p 29

CORINEUS AND GOGMAGOG.

WHO can dare question such an authority as John Milton? In his "History of Britain, that part especially now called England. From the first Traditional beginning continued to the Norman Conquest. Collected out of the antientest and best authors thereof," he gives us the story of Brutus and of Corineus, "who with the battele Ax which he was wont to manage against the *Tyrrhen Giants,* is said to have done marvells." With the adventures of these heroes in *Africa* and in *Aquitania* we have little concern. They suffer severe defeats; and then "Brutus, finding now his powers much lessn'd, and this not yet the place foretold him, leaves Aquitain, and with an easy course arriving at Totness in *Dev'nshire,* quickly perceivs heer to be the promis'd end of his labours." The following matters interest us more closely :*—

"The Iland, not yet *Britain,* but *Albion,* was in a manner desert and inhospitable, kept only by a remnant of *Giants,* whose excessive Force and Tyrannie had consumed the rest Them Brutus destroies, and to his people divides the land, which, with some reference to his own name, he thenceforth calls *Britain.* To *Corineus, Cornwall,* as now we call it, fell by lot , the rather by him lik't, for that the hugest Giants in Rocks and Caves were said to lurk still there; which kind of Monsters to deal with was his old exercise.

"And heer, with leave bespok'n to recite a grand fable, though dignify'd by our best Poets : While *Brutus,* on a certain Festival day, solemnly kept on that shoar where he first landed (*Totness*), was with the People in great jollity and mirth, a crew of these savages, breaking in upon them, began on the sudden another sort of Game than at such a meeting was expected. But at length by many hands overcome, *Gocmagog,* the hugest, in hight twelve cubits, is reserved alive; that with him Corineus, who desired nothing more, might try his strength, whom in a Wrestle the Giant catching aloft, with a terrible hugg broke three of his Ribs Nevertheless Corineus, enraged, heaving him up by main force, and on his shoulders bearing him to the next high rock, threw him hedlong all shatter'd into the sea, and left his name on the cliff, called ever since *Langoemagog,* which is to say, the Giant's Leap." The same story has been somewhat differently told, although there is but little variation in the main incidents. When Brutus and

---

* For a discussion of the question relative to Brutus, see Gough s "Camden's Britannia," vol. i., pp xlix. to lv

Corineus, with their Trojan hosts, landed at Plymouth, these chiefs wisely sent parties into the interior to explore the country, and to learn something of the people. At the end of the first day, all the soldiers who had been sent out as exploring parties, returned in great terror, pursued by several terrific giants. Brutus and Corineus were not, however, to be terrified by the immense size of their enemies, nor by the horrid noises which they made, hoping to strike terror into the armed hosts. These chieftains rallied their hosts and marched to meet the giants, hurling their spears and flinging their darts against their huge bodies. The assault was so unexpected that the giants gave way, and eventually fled to the hills of Dartmoor. Gogmagog, the captain of the giants, who was sadly wounded in the leg, and, unable to proceed, hid himself in a bog, but there, by the light of the moon, he was found by the Trojan soldiers, bound with strong cords, and carried back to the Hoe at Plymouth, where the camp was. Gogmagog was treated nobly by his victors, and his wounds were speedily healed. Brutus desired to make terms with the giants; and it was at length proposed by Gogmagog to try a fall with the strongest in the host, and that whoever came off the conqueror should be proclaimed king of Cornwall, and hold possession of all the western land. Corineus at once accepted the challenge of the monster. Notwithstanding, the giant,

> "Though bent with woes,
> Full eighteen feet in height he rose,
> His hair, exposed to sun and wind,
> Like wither'd heath, his head entwined,"

and that Corineus was but little above the ordinary size of man, the Trojan chief felt sure of a victory. The day for the wrestling was fixed. The huge Gogmagog was allowed to send for the giants, and they assembled on one side of a cleared space on Plymouth Hoe, while the Trojan soldiers occupied the other. All arms were thrown aside; and fronting each other, naked to the waist, stood the most lordly of the giants, and the most noble of men. The conflict was long, and it appeared for sometime doubtful. Brute strength was exerted on one side, and trained skill on the other. At length Corineus succeeded in seizing Gogmagog by the girdle, and by regularly-repeated impulses he made the monster undulate like a tree shaken by a winter storm, until at length, gathering all his strength into one effort, the giant was forced to his back on the ground, the earth shaking with his weight, and the air echoing with the thunder of his mighty groan, as the breath was forced from his body by the terrible momentum of his fall. There lay the giant, and there were all the other giants, appalled at the power which they could not understand, but which convinced them that there was something superior to mere animal strength. Corineus breathed for a minute, then he rushed upon his prostrate foe, and seizing him by the legs, he dragged him to the edge of the cliff, and precipitated him into the sea. The giant fell on the rocks below, and his body was broken into fragments by the fall; while the

> "Fretted flood
> Roll'd frothy waves of purple blood."

"Gogmagog's Leap" has been preserved near the spot which now presents a fortress to the foes of Britain; and there are those "who say that, at the last digging on the Haw for the foundation of the citadel of Plymouth, the great jaws and teeth therein found were those of Gogmagog." *

THE GIANTS OF THE MOUNT

THE history of the redoubtable Jack proves that St Michael's Mount was the abode of the giant Cormelian, or, as the name is sometimes given, Cormoran. We are told how Jack destroyed the giant, and the story ends. Now, the interesting part, which has been forgotten in the narrative, is not only that Cormoran lived *on*, but that he built the Mount, his dwelling-place. St Michael's Mount, as is tolerably well known, is an island at each rise of the tide—the distance between it and the mainland being a little more than a quarter of a mile. In the days of the giants, however, it was some six miles from the sea, and was known as *the White Rock in the wood*, or in Cornish, "Carreg luz en kuz." Of the evidences in favour of this, more will be said when the traditions connected with physical phenomena are dealt with. In this wood the giant desired to build his home, and to rear it above the trees, that he might from the top keep watch over the neighbouring country. Any person carefully observing the structure of the granite rocks will notice their tendency to a cubical form. These stones were carefully selected by the giant from the granite of the neighbouring hills, and he was for a long period employed in carrying and piling those huge masses, one on the other, in which labour he compelled his wife to aid him. It has been suggested, with much show of probability, that the confusion of the two name:

* See Appendix B for the "Poem of the Wrestling," &c

alluded to has arisen from the fact that the giant was called Cormoran, and that the name of his wife was Cormelian ; at all events, there is no harm in adopting this hypothesis. The toil of lifting those granitic masses from their primitive beds, and of carrying them through the forest, was excessive. It would seem that the heaviest burthens were imposed upon Cormelian, and that she was in the habit of carrying those rocky masses in her apron. At a short distance from the "White Rock," which was now approaching completion, there exists large masses of greenstone rock. Cormelian saw no reason why one description of stone would not do as well as another, and one day, when the giant Cormoran was sleeping, she broke off a vast mass of the greenstone rock, and taking it in her apron, hastened towards the artificial hill with it, hoping to place it without being observed by Cormoran. When, however, Cormelian was within a short distance of the " White Rock," the giant awoke, and presently perceived that his wife was, contrary to his wishes, carrying a green stone instead of a white one. In great wrath he arose, followed her, and, with a dreadful imprecation, gave her a kick. Her apron-string broke, and the stone fell on the sand. There it has ever since remained, no human power being sufficient to remove it. The giantess died, and the mass of greenstone, resting, as it does, on clay slate rocks, became her monument In more recent days, when the light of Christianity was dawning on the land, this famous rock was still rendered sacred : "a lytle chapel"* having been built on it ; and to this day it is usually known as the " The Chapel Rock."†

THE KEY OF THE GIANT'S CASTLE.

THE giant's castle at Treryn, remarkable as a grand example of truly British Cyclopean architecture, was built by the power of enchantment. The giant to whom all the rest of his race were indebted for this stronghold was in every way a remarkable mortal. He was stronger than any other giant, and he was a mighty necromancer. He sat on the promontory of Treryn, and by the power of his will he compelled the castle to rise out of the sea. It is only kept in its present position by virtue of a magic key. This the giant placed in a holed rock, known as the Giant's Lock, and whenever this key, a large round stone, can be taken out of the lock, the promontory of Treryn and its castle will disappear beneath the waters. There are not many people who obtain even a sight of this wonderful key. You must pass at low

---

* Leland   † See Appendix C for the Irish legend of Shara and Sheela.

tide along a granite ledge, scaicely wide enough for a goat to
stand on. If you happen to make a false step, you must be dashed
to pieces on the rocks below. Well, having got over safely, you
come to a pointed rock with a hole in it; this is the castle lock.
Put your hand deep into the hole, and you will find at the bottom
a large egg-shaped stone, which is easily moved in any direction.
You will feel certain that you can take it out,—but try ! Try as you
may, you will find it will not pass through the hole; yet no one can
doubt but that it once went in

Lieutenant Goldsmith dissolved one bit of superstition by foolishly
throwing the fatal Logan Stone from off its bearing ; but no one
has ever yet succeeded in removing the key of the giant's castle
from the hole in which the neciomancer is said to have placed it
when he was dying.

THE RIVAL GIANTS.

THOSE who have visited the Logan Rock will be familiar with
the several groups which form the Treryn promontory.
Treryn Castle, an ancient British fortress, the Cyclopean walls of
which, and its outer earthwork, can still be traced, was the dwelling of a famous giant and his wife. I have heard it said that he
gave his name to this place, but that is, of course, doubtful. This
giant was chief of a numerous band, and by his daring he held
possession, against the giants of the Mount, of all the lands west
of Penzance. Amongst the hosts who owned allegiance to him,
was a remaikable fine young fellow, who had his abode in a cave,
in the pile of rocks upon which the Logan Rock stands. This
young giant grew too fond of the giantess, and it would appear
that the lady was not unfavourably inclined towards him. Of
their love passes, howevei, we know nothing. Tradition has only
told us that the giantess was one day reclining on the rock still
known as the Giant Lady's Chair, while the good old giant was
dosing in the Giant's Chair which stands near it, when the young
and wicked lover stole behind his chief and stabbed him in the
belly with a knife * The giant fell over the rocks to the level
ridge below, and there he lay, iapidly pouring out his life-blood.
Fiom this spot the young muidei kicked him into the sea, ere
yet his life was quite extinct, and he perished in the waters.

The guilty pair took possession of Treryn Castle, and, we are
told, lived happily for many years.

* Mr Halliwell infers from this that the story is Sixon　See "Wanderings in the
Footsteps of the Giants."

THE GIANTS OF TRENCROM, OR TRECROBBEN.

THE rough granite hill of Trecrobben rises in almost savage grandeur from the wooded lands which form the park of Trevetha, close by the picturesque village of Lelant. From the summit of this hill may be surveyed one of the most striking panoramic views in Cornwall. The country declines, rather rapidly, but still with a pleasing contour, towards the sea on the southern side. From the sandy plain, which extends from Marazion to Penzance, there stretch out two arms of land, one on the eastern side, towards the Lizard Point, and the other on the western side towards Mousehole and Lemorna, which embrace as it were that fine expanse of water known as the Mount's Bay. The most striking object, "set in the silver sea," is the pyramidical hill St Michael's Mount, crowned with the "castle," an unhappy mixture of church, castle, and modern dwelling-house, which, nevertheless, from its very incongruities, has a picturesque appearance when viewed from a distance. Nestling amidst the greenstone rocks, sheltered by "the Holy Mount," is the irregular town of Marazion, or Market-Jew, and, balancing this, on the western side of "the Green," Penzance displays her more important buildings, framed by the beautifully fertile country by which the town is surrounded.

The high lands to the westward of Penzance, with the fishing villages of Newlyn and Mousehole, the church of Paul on the summit of the hill, and the engine-house belonging to a mine at its base, have much quiet beauty under some aspects of light,— the yet more western hills shutting out the Land's End from the observer's eye   .

Looking from Trencrom (this is the more common name) to the south-east, the fine hills of Tregoning and Godolphin,—both of which have given names to two ancient Cornish families,— mark the southern boundary of a district famed for its mineral wealth. Looking eastward, Carn Brea Hill, with its ancient castle and its modern monument, stands up from the tableland in rugged grandeur. This hill, "a merry place, 'tis said, in days of yore,"—when British villages were spread amidst the mighty cairns, and Cyclopean walls sheltered the inhabitants,—rises to mark the most productive piece of mining-ground, of the same area, to be found in the world. Around the towns of Camborne and Redruth are seen hundreds of miners' cottages, and scores of tall chimneys, telling of the mechanical appliances which are

D

brought to bear upon the extraction of tin and copper from the earth   Beyond this thickly-peopled region the eye wanders yet eastward, and eventually reposes on the series of granite hills which rise beyond St Austell and stretch northward,—the two highest hills in Cornwall, which are known as Roughtor and Brownwhilly,* being in this range

Let the observer now turn his face northward, and a new and varied scene lies before him.   Within two miles the waters of St Ives' Bay break against the cliffs   On the left is the creek of Hayle, which has been fashioned by the energy of man into a useful harbour, and given rise to the foundation of two extensive iron-foundries   Between those and the sea are the hills of blown sand, which have ever been the homes of the Fairy people.   The lighthouse of Godrevy stands, a humble companion, to balance in this bay the "Mount," which adorns the bay, washing the southern slope of this "narrow neck of land."   Godrevy marks the region of sand extending to the eastward   To the north the shores become more and more rugged, culminating in St Agnes' Beacon,—a hill of graceful form rising somewhat rapidly to a considerable elevation.   From this the "beetling cliffs" stretch away northward, until the bold promontory Trevose Head closes the scene, appropriately displaying another of those fine examples of humanity—a lighthouse.

To the left, towards the sea, rises the cenotaph of Knill, an eccentric man, who evidently sought to secure some immortality by this building, and the silly ceremonials carried on around it ; the due performance of which he has secured by bequests to the Corporation of St Ives.   Around this the mining district of St Ives is seen, and her fishing-boats dotting the sea give evidence of another industry of vast importance to the town and neighbourhood.   Westward of St Ives, hills more brown and rugged than any which have yet been viewed stretch away to Zennor, Morva, and St Just, and these, girding the scene beneath our feet, shut out from us the region of the Land's End.

On the summit of this hill, which is only surpassed in savage grandeur by Carn Brea, the giants built a castle—the four entrances to which still remain in Cyclopean massiveness to attest the Herculean powers by which such mighty blocks were piled upon each other.   There the giant chieftains dwelt in awful state   Along the serpentine road, passing up the hill to the principal gateway, they dragged their captives, and on the great flat rocks within the castle they sacrificed them   Almost every rock still bears some name connected with the giants—" a race may perish,

* *Bryn whella*, the highest hill, according to Mr Bellows.

but the name endures." The treasures of the giants who dwelt here are said to have been buried in the days of their troubles, when they were perishing before the conquerors of their land. Their gold and jewels were hidden deep in the granite caves of this hill, and secured by spells as potent as those which Merlin placed upon his "hoarded treasures" They are securely preserved, even to the present day, and carefully guarded from man by the Spriggans, or Trolls, of whom we have to speak in another page.

THE GIANTS AT PLAY.

IN several parts of Cornwall there are evidences that these Titans were a sportive race. Huge rocks are preserved to show where they played at trap-ball, at hurling, and other athletic games. The giants of Trecrobben and St Michael's Mount often met for a game at bob-buttons. The Mount was the " bob," on which flat masses of granite were placed to serve as buttons, and Trecrobben Hill was the " mit," or the spot from which the throw was made. This order was sometimes reversed. On the outside of St Michael's Mount, many a granite slab which had been knocked off the " bob" is yet to be found; and numerous piles of rough cubical masses of the same rock, said to be the granite of Trecrobben Hill,* show how eagerly the game was played.

Trecrobben Hill was well chosen by the giants as the site of their castle. From it they surveyed the country on every side , and friend or enemy was seen at a considerable distance as he approached the guarded spot. It is as clear as tradition can make it, that Trecrobben was the centre of a region full of giants. On Lescudjack Hill, close to Penzance, there is " The Giant's Round," evidently the scene of many a sanguinary conflict, since the Cornish antiquarian authority Borlase informs us, that Lesgudzhek signifies the " Castle of the Bloody Field." On the cairn at Gulval are several impressions on the rocks, all referable to the giants. In Madron there is the celebrated " Giant's Cave;" and the well-known Lanyon cromlech is reported by some to be the " Giant's Coit," while others declare it to be the " Giant's Table." Cairn Galva, again, is celebrated for its giant , and, indeed, every

* Mr O Halliwell, who carefully followed in the " Footsteps of the Giants," referring to this game as played by them, says —

" Doubtlessly the Giant's Chair on Trink Hill was frequently used during the progress of the game, nor is it improbable that the Giant's Well was also in requisition Here, then, were at hand opportunities for rest and refreshment—the circumstances of the various traditions agreeing well with, and, in fact, demonstrating the truth of each other " hill within sight has some monument preserving the memory of those, " the Titans fierce."

HOLIBURN OF THE CAIRN.*

HOLIBURN, according to tradition, was a very amiable and somewhat sociable gentleman ; but, like his brethren, he loved to dwell amongst the rocks of Cairn Galva He made his home in this remote region, and relied for his support on the gifts of sheep and oxen from the farmers around—he, in return, protecting them from the predatory incursions of the less conscientious giants of Trecrobben. It is said that he fought many a battle in the defence of his friends, and that he injured but one of his neighbours during his long lifetime This was, however, purely an accident The giant was at play with the human pigmies, and in the excitement of the moment, being delighted at the capital game made by a fine young peasant, he tapped him on the head, and scattered his brains on the grass. I once heard that Holiburn had married a farmer's daughter, and that a very fine race, still bearing a name not very dissimilar, was the result of this union Holiburn, like his brethren, was remarkably fond of quoits ; indeed, go where we will within the Land's End district, the " Giant's Quoit " is still shown. Other—shall we call them *household*—relics of the giants occur. From Cairn Galva to Zennor we find a series of " Giant's Chairs ;" and, careful to preserve each remarkable relic of this interesting race, here is also the " Giant's Dinner-plate." That St Ives, too, was not without its giant, although the record of his name is lost, is evident from the fact that a tooth, an inch broad, was taken from a " Giant's Grave." †

* " Somewhere amongst the rocks in this cairn is the Giant's Cave—in ages long gone by the abode of a giant named Holiburn "—HALLIWELL Mr Halliwell was fortunate in securing a name I have often heard of the giant in question, but I never heard his name

† The following extract from a note written by the late Zennor postman and poet, shows how enduringly the giants have left their names on the rocks of Cornwall :—

" Some districts in Cornwall were said to have been peopled in olden times by giants, and even Zennor district possesses the largest quoit—three Logan rocks—whilst Trecrobben Hill still exhibits the Bowl in which the giants of the west used to wash The large granite boulder near to the residence of the Rev Mr S——, curate of Morva, is said to be the Giant's Dinner-plate Farther down the hill, and hard by the Zennor vicarage, the seats of the giants are still shown by the inhabitants Indeed, so strong is the belief that giants inhabited the hills of the west, that a young lady in this neighbourhood assayed, a month or two ago, to deliver a lecture, or address, on the subject, taking for her text, ' There were giants in those days ' But the giants were not immortal, colossal as were their frames, they too had to ' sleep with their fathers.' Whether Jack the Giant-killer took any part in ridding the earth of this wonderful race of men

THE GIANT OF NANCLEDRY.*

IN Nancledry Bottoms, about a mile from the famous hill Castle-an-Dinas, there stood at one time a thatched house near the brook which runs murmuring down the valley. Rather more than thirty years since, some mouldering " clob " (mud) walls, indicating the existence at one time of a large dwelling, were pointed to as the former residence of a terrible giant. He appears to have led a solitary life, and to have lived principally on little children, whom he is said to have swallowed whole. His strength was indicated by several huge masses of granite which were scattered around the Bottoms, and in the neighbouring fields. These were carried by him in his pockets, to defend himself from the giants of Trecrobben, with whom he appears to have been on unfriendly terms. This giant is noteworthy as the only one recorded who lived in a house.

TREBIGGAN THE GIANT.*

TREBEGEAN is the name of a village near the Land's End This name, as we have already stated, signifies the town of the giant's grave The giant's existence was confirmed by the discovery of a vault and some large bones in it, on this spot.†

Trebiggan divides with Tregeagle the honourable immortality of being employed to frighten children into virtue. Often have I heard the unruly urchins of this neighbourhood threatened with Trebiggan. They are told that Trebiggan was a vast man, with arms so long that he could take men out of the ships passing by the Land's End, and place them on the Longships ; but that sometimes he would, having had his fun with them, good-humouredly place them on board their ships or boats again. He is said to have dined every day on little children, who were generally fried on a large flat rock which stood at a little distance from his cave.

THE LORD OF PENGERSWICK AND THE GIANT OF ST MICHAEL'S MOUNT.

THE giant who dwelt on St Michael's Mount had grown very old, and had lost all his teeth; still he was the terror of the neighbouring villages. The horrid old monster—who had but one

we cannot positively state , but thus much is certain, the giants were succeeded by a numerous race of small people, and so small as not to be observable by the eye ''

* See Appendix D.   † See Heath's Description of Cornwall, 1750

eye, and that one in the middle of his forehead—would, whenever
he required food—which was pretty often—walk or wade across
to Market-Jew, as the tide might be, select the best cow in the
neighbourhood, and, swinging it over his shoulders, return to his
island.   This giant had often taken cattle from the Pengerswick
estate ; and one day he thought he should like another of this
choice breed.   Accordingly, away he went, across the sea, to
Pengerswick Cove.   The giant did not know that the lord of
Pengerswick had returned from the East, a master of " white-
witchcraft," or magic   The lord had seen the giant coming, and
he began to work his spells.   The giant was bewildered, yet he
knew not how.   At last, after much trouble, he caught a fine calf,
tied its four feet together, passed his great head between the fore and
hind legs, and, with the calf hanging on his shoulders, he trod in
joy towards the shore.   He wandered on in perfect unconsciousness
of the path, and eventually he found himself on the precipitous
edge of the great black rock which still marks the western side of
Pengerswick Cove   As if the rock had been a magnet, the giant
was chained fast   He twisted, turned, and struggled in vain.
He found himself gradually becoming stiff, so that at last he could
neither move hand nor foot ; yet were his senses more keenly alive
than ever   The giant had to remain thus, during a long winter's
night, with the calf bleating, as never calf bleated before, into his
ear.   In the morning when the enchanter thought he had punished
the giant sufficiently, he mounted his mare, and rode down to the
shore.   He disenchanted the giant, by giving him a severe horse-
whipping, and he then made him drop the calf.   He continued to
flog the giant until he leaped off the rock into the sea, through
which in great agony he waded to the Mount ; and from that day
to this he has never ventured on the mainland.

We learn, however, from undoubted authority, that some time
after this, Tom, the giant of Lelant, visited the giant on the Mount,
and, finding him half starved, he took his aunt Nancy from Gulval
to see his friend, with a large supply of butter and eggs.   The old
giant was exceedingly glad to see the farmer's wife, bought all her
store at a very extravagant price, and bargained and paid in
advance for more   He had a store of wealth in the caverns of the
Mount.   The knowing old woman kept him well supplied as long
as the giant had money to pay her ; and aunt Nancy's family
became the wealthiest in the parish of Gulval.

THE GIANT OF ST MICHAEL'S MOUNT LOSES HIS WIFE.

THE giant on the Mount and the giant on Trecrobben Hill were very friendly. They had only one cobbling-hammer between them, which they would throw from one to the other, as either required it One day the giant on the Mount wanted the hammer in a great hurry, so he shouted, " Holloa, up there ! Trecrobben, throw us down the hammer, woost a'?"

" To be sure," sings out Trecrobben ; " here ! look out, and catch 'm."

Now, nothing would do but the giant's wife, who was very near-sighted, must run out of her cave to see Trecrobben throw the hammer. She had no hat on ; and coming at once out into the light, she could not distinguish objects. Consequently, she did not see the hammer coming through the air, and received it between her eyes. The force with which it was flung was so great that the massive bone of the forehead of the giantess was crushed, and she fell dead at the giant's feet. You may be sure there was a great to-do between the two giants. They sat wailing over the dead body, and with their sighs they produced a tempest. These were unavailing to restore the old lady, and all they had to do was to bury her. Some say they lifted the Chapel Rock and put her under it, others, that she is buried beneath the castle court, while some—no doubt the giants' detractors—declare that they rolled the body down into the sea, and took no more heed of it.

TOM AND THE GIANT BLUNDERBUSS; OR, THE WHEEL AND EXE FIGHT *

A YOUNG giant, who does not appear to have been known by any other name than Tom, lived somewhere westward of Hayle, probably in Lelant. Tom would eat as much meat as

---

* The similarity of this story to the well-known tale of " Tom Hickathrift " will strike every one. It might be supposed that the old story of the strong man of the Isle of Ely had been read by some Cornish man, and adapted to the local peculiarities This may possibly have been the case, but I do not think it probable. I first heard the story from a miner, on the floors of Ding-Dong Mine, during my earliest tour in search of old stories I have since learned that it was a common story with the St Ives nurses, who told it to amuse or terrify their children. Recently, I have had the same tale communicated to me by a friend, who got it from a farmer living in Lelant. This story is confined to the parishes of Lelant, St Ives, Sancreed, Towednach, Morva, and Zennor.

three men, and when he was in the humour he could do as much work as half a dozen Howbeit, Tom was a lazy fellow, and spent most of his time wandering about the parish with his hands in his pockets. Occasionally Tom would have an industrious fit ; then, if he found any of his neighbours hedging, he would turn to and roll in all the largest rocks from over the fields, for " grounders." * This was the only work Tom took delight in ; he was won't to say, he could feel his strength about such work as that. Tom didn't appear so very big a man in those days, when all men were twice the size they are now He was about four feet from shoulder to shoulder, square built, and straight all the way down from shoulder to cheens (loins).

Tom's old mother was constantly telling her idle son to do something to earn his food, but the boy couldn't find any job to his mind for a long time. At last he undertook to drive a brewer's wain, in the hope of getting into plenty of strong drink, and he went to live in Market-Jew, where the brewery was. The first day he was so employed, he was going to St Ives with his load of beer, and on the road he saw half a score of men trying to lift a fallen tree on to a " draw " It was, however, more than the whole of them could do.

" Stand clear ! " shouts Tom.

He put his hands, one on each side of the tree, and lifted it on the " draw," without so much as saying " Ho ! " to his oxen, or looking behind him The feat was performed in Ludgvan Lees, and a little farther on was a giant's place diverting the road, which should have gone straight to St Ives but for it This place was hedged in with great rocks, which no ten men of these times could move. They call them the Giant's Hedges to the present day. There was a gate on that side of the giant's farm which was nearest Market-Jew, and another on that side which joined the highway leading on to St Ives. Tom looked at the gate for some time, half disposed to drive through, but eventually he decided on proceeding by the ordinary road. When, however, Tom was coming

---

Mr Halliwell thinks the adventures of Tom Hickathrift are connected with " some of the insurrections in the Isle of Ely, such as that of Herewood, described in Wright's ' Essays,' ii 91." Now, Herewood the Saxon is said to have taken refuge in the extreme part of Cornwall, and we are told of many romantic adventures, chiefly in connection with the beautiful daughter of Alef, a Cornish chief. May it not be, that here we have tho origin of the story as it is told in Lincolnshire and in Cornwall ?

* In making the really Cyclopean hedges which prevail in some parts of Cornwall, the large boulders of granite, or other stones, which lie scattered on the moors are used for the foundation Indeed, one purpose, and a very important one, served by those hedges, has been the removal of the stones from the ground which has been enclosed, and the disposal of the stones so removed.

back from St Ives with his empty wain, his courage screwed up by the influence of some three or four gallons of strong beer which he had drunk, he began to reason with himself thus .—

" The king's highway ought not to be twisting and turning like an angle-twitch.* It should go straight through here What right has the giant to keep his place closed, stopping honester men than he ever was longer on the road home ? If everybody were of my mind, the road would soon be opened. Faith, I'll drive through. He wouldn't eat me, I suppose. My old mammy never told me I was to come to my end that way. They say the giant has had scores of wives. What becomes of them nobody can tell ; yet there are always more ready to supply their place Well, that's no business of mine. I never met the man to make me turn back yet ; so come along, Neat and Comely," shouts Tom to the oxen, opening the great gate for them to pass through. On went Tom, without seeing anything of the giant or of anybody else, except the fat cattle of all sorts in the fields. After driving about a mile, Tom came to a pair of gates in a high wall, which was close to and surrounding the giant's castle. There was no passing round those, as deep ditches, full of water, were on either side of these gates. So at them went Tom. The huge gates creaked on their hangings, and the wheels of Tom's wain rattled on over the causey.† A little ugly midgan of a cur began to bark, and out tore the giant, a great ugly unshapely fellow, all head and stomach.

" You impudent little villain," roared the giant, " to drive into my grounds, disturbing my afternoon's nap. What business have you here ? "

" I am on the road," says Tom, " and you—nor a better man than you—shan't put me back. You ha' no right to build your hedges across what used to be the king's highway, and shall be again."

" I shan't bemean myself to talk with such a little saucy black-guard as thee art," said the giant ; " I 'll get a twig, and drive thee out faster than thee came in."

" Well," says Tom, " you may keep your breath to cool your porridge ; but, if that's the game you are up to, I can play at that as well as you."

The giant had pulled up a young elm-tree, about twenty feet high or so, and he began stripping the small branches from the head of the tree, as he came up the hill, gaping (yawning) all the time, as if he were half asleep. Tom, seeing what he was up to,

---

* A worm.   † Causeway, pavement

upset his wain. This he did without the oxen moving, as the
tuntsy (pole) turned round in the ring of the yoke He then
slipped off the further wheel in a wink, hauled out the exe (axle-
tree) fast in the other wheel, against the giant came up. (In old
time the axle was made to work in gudgeons under the carts or
wains.)

"Now then," says Tom, "fair play for the buttons. If you
can beat me, I'll go back The exe and wheel is my sword and
buckler, which I'll match against your elm-tree" Then Tom
began whistling.

The giant got round the uphill side, lifted his tree, and tore
towards Tom without saying a word, as if he would cleave him
from head to heel

Tom lifted the axle-tree, with the wheel, up, to guard off the
blow of the giant's twig—the giant being in such a towering
passion to hear Tom coolly whistling all the time, that he couldn't
steady himself He missed Tom's head, struck the edge of the
wheel, and, the ground being slippery, the giant fell upon his face
on the ground Tom might have driven the "exe" through him
as he lay sprawling in the mud, and so have nailed him to the
earth ; but no, not he ! Tom would rather be killed than not
fight fair, so he just tickled the giant under the ribs with the end
of the "exe." "Come, get up," says Tom, "let's have another
turn " The giant rose very slowly, as if he were scarcely able to
stand, bent double, supporting himself on his twig He was only
dodging—the great cowardly skulk—to get the uphill side again,
and take Tom unawares ; but he was waiting with his right hand
grasping the "exe," the wheel resting on the ground. Quick as
lightning the giant raised his tree Tom fetched him a heavy kick
on the shins, he slipped, fell forward, and Tom so held the "exe,"
that it passed through his body like a spit Good Lord, how the
giant roared !

"Thee stop thy bleating," says Tom. "Stand quiet a moment.
Let's draw the exe out of thy body, and I'll give thee a chance
for another round. Thee doesn't deserve it, because thee aren't
playing fair."

Tom turned the giant over, laid hold of the wheel, and dragged
out the "exe." In doing this he was nearly blinded with the
blood that spouted out of the hole Blunderbuss rolled on the
ground like an empty sack, roaring amain all the time in great
agony.

"Stop thy bleating," says Tom, "and put thy hands in the
hole the 'exe' has made in thee, to keep in the blood, until I

can cut a turf to stop up the place, and thee will'st do again yet."

As Tom was plugging the wound with the turfs, the giant groaned and said, "It's all no good; I shall kick the bucket I feel myself going round land ; but with my last breath I 'll do thee good, because I like thee better than anybody else I ever met with, for thy fair play and courage. The more thee wouldst beat me, the better I should like thee. I have no near relations. There is heaps of gold, silver, copper, and tin down in the vaults of the castle, guarded by two dogs. Mind there names are Catchem and Tearem. Only call them by these names and they 'll let thee pass The land from this to the sea is all mine There is more head of oxen, cows, sheep, goats, and deer, than thee canst count. Take them all, only bury me decent "

"Did you kill all your wives ? " asked Tom.

"No," sighed the giant, "they died natural. Don't let them abuse me after death I like thee as a brother "

"Cheer up," says Tom, " you 'll do again."

He then tried to raise the giant up, but the plug of turf slipped from the wound, and all was over.

Tom put the wheel and axle in order, turned over the wain, and drove home to Market-Jew. The brewer was surprised and well pleased to see Tom back so early, and offered him good wages to stop for the year.

" I must leave this very night," says Tom, "for my old granfer, who lived up in the high countries, is dead. I am his nearest relation. He lived all alone. He 's left me all his money and lands, so I must go and bury my old granfer this very night " The brewer was about to pay him for his day's work—" Oh, never mind that," says Tom ; " I 'll give up that for as much beer as I can drink with supper "

After supper Tom went and took possession of the giant's castle and lands—nobody the wiser except a little woman, the giant's last wife, who came from some place not far from the castle. Some name Crowlas, some Tregender, others Bougiehere, as the place where she dwelt. Howbeit, she knew all about the giant's overthrow, and thought it the wisest course to "take up" at once with Tom ; and she being a tidy body, Tom was by no means unwilling. Tom and this woman took possession of the castle. They buried the giant down in the bottom, and placed a block of granite to keep him down. They gave the carcass of a sheep to Catchem and Tearem, visited the caves of the castle, found lots of treasure, and fairly got into the giant's shoes.

TOM THE GIANT, HIS WIFE JANE, AND JACK THE TINKEARD, AS TOLD BY THE "DROLLS."*

WHEN Tom and his wife had settled themselves in the giant's castle, they took good care not to allow any one to make a king's highway across their grounds. Tom made the hedges higher, and the gates stronger than ever, and he claimed all the run of land on the sea-side, and enclosed it. Tom's wife, Jane, was a wonderful cleanly body—the castle seemed to be always fresh swept and sanded, while all the pewter plates and platters shone like silver. She never quarrelled with Tom, except when he came in from hedging covered with mud; then in a pet she would threaten to go home to her mother. Jane was very famous for her butter and cheese, and Tom became no less so for his fine breed of cattle, so that he fared luxuriously, and all went on happily enough with Tom and his wife. They had plenty of children, and these were such fine healthy babies, that it took two or three of the best cows to feed them, when but a few weeks old. Tom and Jane thought that they had all that part of the world to themselves, and that no one could scale their hedges or break through their gates. They soon found their mistake. Tom was working one morning, not far from the gate, on the Market-Jew side of his property, when he heard a terrible rattle upon the bars. Running up, he saw a man with a hammer smashing away, and presently down went the bars, and in walked a travelling tinkeard, with his bag of tools on his back.

"Holla! where are you bound for?" says Tom.

"Bound to see if the giant, whom they say lives up here, wouldn't let a body pass through where the road ought to be," says the tinkeard.

"Oh, ay! are you?" says Tom.

"He must be a better man than I am who stops me," says the tinkeard. "As you are a fine stout chap, I expect you are the giant's eldest son. I see you are hedging. That's what all the people complain of. You are hedging in all the country."

---

* In some of the old *geese dances* (guise dances, from *danse déguisé*) the giant Blunderbuss and Tom performed a very active part Blunderbuss was always a big-bellied fellow—his smoke-frock being well stuffed with straw. He fought with a tree, and the other giant with the wheel and axle The giant is destroyed, as in the story, by falling on the axle. The tinker, of whom we have yet to tell, with his unfailing coat of darkness, comes in and beats Tom, until Jane comes out with the broom and beats the tinker, and then,—as in nearly all these rude plays,—St George and the Turkish knight come in, but they have no part in the real story of the drama.—See note, page 66 Appendix E

" Well," says Tom, " if I am his son, I can take my dad's part
any way ; and we'll have fair play too.   I don't desire better fun
than to try my strength with somebody that is a man.   Come on.
Any way you like—naked fists, single-stick, wrestling, bowling,
slinging, or throwing the quoits."

" Very well," says the tinkeard, " I'll match my blackthorn
stick against anything in the way of timber that you can raise on
this place."

Tom took the bar which the tinker had broken from the gate, and
said, " I'll try this piece of elm if you don't think it too heavy."

" Don't care if it's heavier.   Come on !"

The tinkeard took the thorn-stick in the middle, and made it
fly round Tom's head so fast that he couldn't see it.   It looked
like a wheel whizzing round his ears, and Tom soon got a bloody
nose and two black eyes.   Tom's blows had no effect on the tinkeard,
because he wore such a coat as was never seen in the West Country before   It was made out of a shaggy black bull's hide, dressed
whole with the hair on.   The skin of the forelegs made the sleeves,
the hind quarters only were cut, pieces being let in to make the
spread of the skirts, while the neck and skin of the head formed a
sort of hood.   The whole appeared as hard as iron ; and when
Tom hit the tinkeard, it sounded, as if the coat roared, like
thunder.   They fought until Tom got very hungry, and he found
he had the worst of it.   " I believe thee ait the devil, and no
man," says Tom.   " Let's see thy feet before thee dost taste any
more of my blood."

The tinkeard showed Tom that he had no cloven foot, and told
him that it depended more on handiness than strength to conquer
with the single-stick ; and that a small man with science could
beat a big man with none   The tinkeard then took the clumsy
bar of the gate from Tom, gave him his own light and tough
blackthorn, and proceeded to teach him to make the easiest
passes, cuts, &c   Whilst the two men were thus engaged, Jane
had prepared the dinner, and called her husband three times.   She
wondered what could be keeping Tom, as he was always ready to
run to his dinner at the first call.   At length she went out of the
castle to seek for him, and surprised she was, and—if truth must
be told—rather glad to see another man inside the gates, which
no one had passed for years.   Jane found Tom and the tinkeard
tolerable friends by this time, and she begged them both to come
into dinner, saying to the tinkeard that she wished she had something better to set before him.   She was vexed that Tom hadn't
sent her word, that she might have prepared something better

than the everlasting beef and pease ; and vowed she would give him a more savoury mess for supper, if she had to go to the hills for a sheep or a kid herself.

At length the men were seated at the board, which groaned beneath the huge piece of boiled beef, with mountains of pease-pudding, and they soon got fairly to work. Jane then went to the cellar, and tapped a barrel of the strongest beer, which was intended to have been kept for a tide (feast). Of the meat, Tom ate twice as much as the tinkeard, and from the can of ale he took double draughts. The tinkeard ate heartily, but not voraciously ; and, for those days, he was no hard drinker. Consequently, as soon as dinner was over, Tom fell back against the wall, and was quickly snoring like a tempest. His custom was to sleep two or three hours after every meal. The tinkeard was no sleepy-head, so he told Jane to bring him all her pots and pans which required mending, and he would put them in order. He seated himself amidst a vast pile, and was soon at work The louder Tom snored, the more Jack rattled and hammered away at the kettles ; and ere Tom was awake, he had restored Jane's cooking vessels to something like condition.

At length Tom awoke, and, feeling very sore, he begged the tinkeard to put off until to-morrow a wrestling-match which they had talked of before dinner. The tinkeard, nothing loath, agreed ; so Tom took him up to the topmost tower of the castle, to show him his lands and his cattle. For miles and miles, farther over the hill than the eye could reach, except on the southern side, everything belonged to Tom. In this tower they found a long and strong bow. Tom said none but the old giant could bend it. He had often tried, and fretted because he could not bring the string to the notch. The tinkeard took the bow ; he placed one end to his toe, and, by what appeared like sleight-of-hand to Tom, he bent the bow, brought the string to the notch, sent the arrow off —thwang,—and shot a hare so far away that it could hardly be seen from the heath and ferns. Tom was surprised, until the tinkeard showed him how to bend the bow, more by handiness than strength, and again he killed a kid which was springing from rock to rock on the cairns far away. The hare and kid were brought home, cooked for supper, and the tinkeard was invited to stop all night.

The story ordinarily rambles on, telling of the increasing friendship between the three, and giving the tinkeard's story of himself, which was so interesting to Tom and Jane that they stayed up nearly all night to hear it. He told how he was born and bred in a country far away—more than a score days' journey from this land, far to the north and east of this, from which it was divided by a large river. This river the tinkeard had swam across ; then there was a week's journey in a land of hills and cairns, which were covered with snow a great part of the year. In this land there were many giants, who digged for tin and other treasures. With these giants he had lived and worked,—they always treated him well ; indeed, he always found the bigger the man the more gentle. Half the evil that's told about them by the cowardly fools who fear to go near them is false. Many, many more strange things did the tinkeard tell. Amongst other matters, he spoke of wise men who came from a city at no great distance from this land of tin for the purpose of buying the tin from the giants, and they left them tools, and other things, that the diggers required in exchange. One of these merchants took a fancy to the tinkeard, named him Jack—he had no name previously —and removed him to the city, where Jack was taught his trade, and many other crafts. The tinkeard had left that city four months since, and worked his way down to Market-Jew. Being there, he heard of the giant, and he resolved to make his acquaintance. The rest has been told.

While this, which was a long story, was being told, Jack the Tinkeard was enjoying Jane's new barley-bread, with honey and cream, which he moistened with metheglin. " Good night, Tom," says he at last ; " you see you have lived all your days like a lord on his lands, and know nothing. I never knew father or mother, never had a home to call my own All the better for me, too If I had possessed one, I would never have known one-thousandth part of what I have learned by wandering up and down in the world."

Morning came ; and, after breakfast, Tom proposed to try " a hitch " on the grass in the castle court. Jack knew nothing of wrestling ; so he told Tom he had never practised, but still he would try his strength. Tom put the tinkeard on his back at every " hitch," but he took all the care he could not to hurt him. At last the tinkeard cried for quarter, and declared Tom to be best man.

Jane had made a veal-and-parsley pie, and put it down to bake, when, being at leisure, she came out to see the sport. Now, it must be remembered the tinkeard had broken down the gate, and no one had thought of repairing it, or closing the opening. Two men of Tregender were coming home from Bal,* and passing the

---

* Popular name for a mine · " *Bal*, a place of digging—*Balas*, to dig "—PRYCE·

giant's gate, they thought it very strange that it should be broken down. After consulting for some time, they summoned all their courage, and—it must be confessed, with fear and trembling— they crawled into the grounds, and proceeded towards the castle. Now, no one in that country except Tom and Jane knew that the old giant was dead.

The two men turned round a corner, and saw three very large children playing The baby, a year old, was riding an old buck-goat about the field. The two elder children, Tom Veān* and young Jane, were mounted on a bull, back to back, one holding on by the horns, and the other by the tail, galloping round the field like mad, followed by the cows and dogs,—a regular " cow's courant."

" Lord, you," says one of the men to the other, "what dost a' think of that for a change ?"

" But to think," says the other, " that the old giant should ever have a wife and young chil'ien here, and the people knaw nothing about it."

" Why, don't everybody say that he ate all his wives and chil'-ren too. What lies people tell, don't they, you ?"

" Le's go a little farther ; he won't eat we, I suppose."

" I'll throw my pick and sho'el down the throat of an, as soon as a' do open as [his] jaws "

" Look you," now shouts the other, " you come round a little farther . just peep round the corner and thee meest see two fellows wrestling, and a woman looking on."

" Can I believe my eyes, you ? Don't that woman look some-thing like Jane I used to be courson of ?"

The miners satisfied themselves that it was Jane, sure enough, and quietly beat a retreat. Soon was St Ives in a state of excite-ment, and all Jane's cousins, believing from the accounts given by the miners that Jane was well off, resolved to pay her a visit. These visits worked much confusion in Tom's castle and family. He and his wife quarrel, but the tinkeard is the never-failing friend All this part of the story is an uninteresting account of fair-weather friends.

Jack the Tinkeard taught Tom how to till his ground in a proper manner He had hitherto contented himself with gatheiing wild herbs,—such as nettles, wild beet, mallows, elecampane, various kinds of lentils, and chick or cat-peas Jack now planted a gaiden for his friends,—the first in Cornwall,—and they grew all kinds of good vegetables. The tinkeard also taught Jane to make mait and

* *Veān*, a term of endearment.

to brew beer; hitherto they had been content with barley-wort, which was often sour. Jack would take the children and collect bitter herbs to make the beer keep, such as the alehoof (ground ivy), mugwort, bannell (the broom), agrimony, centuary, woodsage, bettony, and pellitory. Jane's beer was now amongst the choicest of drinks, and her St Ives cousins could never have enough of it. Tom delighted in it, and often drank enough to bewilder his senses.

Tom had followed the example of the old giant, and killed his cattle by flinging rocks at them. The giant's "bowls" are seen to this day scattered all over the country. Jack gave Tom a knife of the keenest edge and finest temper, and taught him how to slaughter the beasts. When a calf was to be skinned, he instructed Tom how to take the skin off whole from the fore legs, by unjointing the shoulders, and to remove it entirely clear of grain, and without the smallest scratch. In addition to all this, Tomy Veān (who was now a boy four years old, but bigger than many at ten) must have a coat possessing all the virtues which belonged to the tinkeard's. So a bull-calf's skin was put on to the boy, and Jane had special instructions how she was to allow the coat to dry on his back, and tan and dress it in a peculiar way. The skin thus treated would shrink and thicken up until it came to his shape. Nobody can tell how proud the young Tom was of his coat when all was done, though the poor boy suffered much in the doing.

Now Jack the Tinkeard desired the intrusion of strangers as little as did Tom and Jane, so he set to work to repair the gate which he had broken down. He not only did this, but he constructed a curious latch with the bobbin; it was so contrived that no stranger could find the right end of it, and if they pulled at any other part, the latch was only closed the tighter. While he was at work a swarm of Jane's St Ives cousins came around him; they mistook Jack for Tom, and pointed out how the children, who were playing near him, were like their father. Jack "parlayed" with them until he had completed his task, and then he closed the gate in their faces.

Much more of this character is related by the "drolls," but with the exception of constant alternations of feasting and fighting, there is little of novelty in the story, until at last a grand storm arises between Tom and his wife, who is believed by the husband to be on too intimate terms with Jack the Tinkeard. The result of this is, that Jane goes home to Crowlas, fights with her mother, old Jenny, because old Jenny abuses Tom, which Jane will not allow in her presence. While yet at Crowlas another boy is born, called Honey;

E

and, as the cow was not at hand as when she was in the castle, he was nursed by a goat, and it is said a class of his descendants are yet known as the Zennor goats.

HOW TOM AND THE TINKEARD* FOUND THE TIN, AND HOW IT LED TO MORVA FAIR.

WHEN Tom had fairly thrown the tinkeard in the wrestling match, which, it must be remembered, was seen by the miners of Tregender, at which Tom was much pleased, although he did not express his pleasure, it was settled that Tom was the best man. This was sealed over a barrel of strong ale, and a game of quoits was proposed, while Jane was taking up the dinner. Tom had often wished, but never more so than now, that the green sloping banks against the inside of the castle walls had not been there, that he might have a fair fling of the quoits from end to end of the court. Tom's third throw in this game was a very strong one, and the quoit cut a great piece of turf from the banks, laying bare many gray-looking stones, small rounded balls, and black sandy stuff.

"Look here you, Jack," says Tom; "whatever could possess the old fools of giants to heap up such a lot of black and gray mining-stones against the wall? wherever could they have found them all?"

Jack carefully looked at the stuff thus laid bare, clapped his hands together, and shouted—

* I have preserved the pronunciation of this word, which was common in Cornwall between twenty and thirty years since, and which still prevails in some of the outlying districts.

In Webster's English Dictionary we find tinker oddly enough derived from the Welsh *tincerz*, the ringer, from *tinciaw*, to ring, "a mender of brass kettles, pans, and the like." The word being so obviously *tin-ceard*, or *tin-cerdd*,—the original having been in all probability *staen*, or *ystaen-cerdd*, a worker in tin The Gaelic still retains "ceard" and "caird" to represent the English smith *

In the present case, we have to deal, there can be little doubt, not with the modern tinker, but the ancient worker in tin, as is shown in this division of the legend, although the story has suffered some modern corruption, and Jack is made to mend Jane's pots and pans

The old Cornish saying—

    Stean San Agnes an quella stean in Kernow,

    St Agnes' tin is the best tin in Cornwall—

gives the original Cornish term for tin

Jack the Tinkeard partakes of the character of Wayland Smith in many of his peculiarities See Appendix F

* Gomer; or, A Brief Analysis of the Language and Knowledge of the Ancient Cymry. By John Williams, A.M., Oxon.

" By the gods, it 's all the richest tin ! "

Now Tom, poor easy-going soul, " didn't knaw tin ; " so he could scaicely believe Jack, though Jack had told him that he came from a tin country.

" Why, Tom," says Jack, " thee art a made man. If these banks are all tin, there is enough here to buy all the land, and all the houses, from sea to sea."

" What do I care for the tin ; haven't I all a man can desire ? My lands are all stocked with sheep and horned cattle. We shall never lack the best beef and mutton, and we want no better than our honest homespun."

Jane now made her appearance, announcing that dinner was ready. She was surprised at seeing so much tin, but she didn't say anything. She thought maybe she would get a new gown out of it, and go down to St Ives Fair. Notwithstanding that Tom and Jane professed to treat lightly the discovery of the tin, it was clear they thought deeply about it, and their thoughts spoiled their appetites. It was evidently an accession of wealth which they could not understand

Tom said he didn't know how to diess tin, it was of little use to him. Jack offered to dress it for the market on shares. Tom told him he might take as much as he had a mind to for what he cared. After dinner, the giant tried to sleep, but could not get a snore for the soul of him. Therefoie, he walked out into the court, to get some fresh air, as he said, but in reality to look at the tin. Jane saw how restless Tom was, so she unhung his bows and arrows, and told him he must away to the hills to get some kids and hares.

" I shan't trouble myself with the bows and arrows," says Tom ; "all I want are the slings Jack and I have in our pockets. Stones are plenty enough, hit or miss, no matter ; and we needn't be at the trouble to gather up the stones again "

Off went Tom and Jack, followed by young Tom and Jane, to the Towednack and Zennor hills. They soon knocked down as many kids, hares, and rabbits as they desired ;—they caught some colts, placed the children on two of them and the game on the others, and home they went. On their return, whilst waiting for supper, Jack wandered around the castle, and was struck by seeing a window which he had not before observed Jack was resolved to discover the room to which this window belonged, so he very carefully noticed its position, and then threw his hammer in through it, that he might be certain of the spot when he found the tool inside of the castle. The next day, after dinner, when

Tom was having his snooze, Jack took Jane with him, and they commenced a search for the hammer near the spot where Jack supposed the window should be, but they saw no signs of one in in any part of the walls. They discovered, however, a strangely-fashioned, worm-eaten oak hanging-press. They carefully examined this, but found nothing. At last Jack, striking the back of it with his fist, was convinced, from the sound, that the wall behind it was hollow. He and Jane went steadily to work, and with some exertion they moved the press aside, and disclosed a stone door. They opened this, and there was Jack's hammer lying amidst a pile of bones, evidently the relics of some of old Blunderbuss's wives, whom he had imprisoned in the wall, and who had perished there. Jane was in a great fright, and blessed her good fortune that she had escaped a similar end. Jack, however, soon consoled her by showing her the splendid dresses which were here, and the gold chains, rings, and bracelets, with diamonds and other jewels, which were scattered around It was agreed that Tom for the present should be kept in ignorance of all this. Tom awoke, his head full of the tin. He consulted with Jack and Jane. They duly agreed to keep their secret, and resolved that they would set to work the very next day to prepare some of the tin stuff for sale. Tom as yet scarcely believed in his wealth, which was magnified as much as possible by Jack, to bewilder him. However, several sacks of tin were duly dressed, and Tom and Jack started with them for Market-Jew, Tom whispering to Jack before he left the castle, that they would bring home a cask of the brewer's best ale with 'em. "It is a lot better than what Jane brews with her old-fashioned yerbes ; but don't 'e tell her so."

The brewer of Market-Jew was also mayor, and, as it appears, tin-smelter, or tin merchant. To him, therefore, Tom went with his black tin,* and received not only his cask of beer, but such an amount of golden coin—all of it being a foreign coinage—as convinced him that Jack had not deceived him This brewer is reputed to have been an exceedingly honest and kind-hearted man, beloved by all It was his practice, when any of the townspeople came before him, begging him to settle their disputes,—even when they "limbed" one another,—to shut them up in the brewery-yard, give them as much beer as they could drink, and keep them there until they became good friends Owing to this practice he seldom had enough beer to sell, and was frequently troubled to pay for his barley. This brewer, who was reputed to be " the best mayor

* "*Black tin,*" tin ore ; oxide of tin

that ever was since the creation of gray cats," gave rise, from the above practice of his, to the proverb still in daily use, " Standing, like the mayor of Market-Jew, in his own light."

The mayor was always fat and jolly. He was an especial favourite, too, with the Lord of Pengerswick, who is believed to have helped him out of many troubles. He had bought his tin of Tom and Jack, such a bargain, that he resolved to have some sport, so a barrel of beer was broached in the yard, and the crier was sent round the town to call all hands to a " courant " (merry-making) They came, you may be certain, in crowds. There was wrestling, hurling,—the length of the Green from Market-Jew to Chyandour, and back again,—throwing quoits, and slinging. Some amused themselves in pure wantonness by slinging stones over the Mount , so that the old giant, who lived there, was afraid to show above ground, lest his only eye should get knocked out. The games were kept up right merrily until dusk ; when in rode the Lord of Pengerswick on his enchanted mare, with a colt by her side. The brewer introduced Tom and Jack, and soon they became the best of friends. Tom invited Pengerswick to his castle, and they resolved to go home at once and make a night of it. Pengerswick gave Tom the colt, and, by some magic power, as soon as he mounted this beautiful animal, he found himself at home, and the lord, the brewer, and Jack with him. How this was brought about Tom could never tell, but Jack appeared to be in the secret. Tom was amazed and delighted to find Jane dressed like a queen, in silks and diamonds, and the children arrayed in a manner well becoming the dignity of their mother.

Jane, as soon as Tom and Jack had left her, had proceeded to the room in the wall, and with much care removed the jewels, gold, and dresses, caring little, as she afterwards said, for the dead bones, although they rattled as she shook them out of the robes In a little time she had all the dresses in the main court of the castle, and having well beaten and brushed them, she selected the finest—those she now wore—and put the rest aside for other grand occasions.

The condescension of the great Lord of Pengerswick was some-thing wonderful He kissed Jane until Tom was almost jealous, and the great lord romped about the court of the castle with the children. Tom was, on the whole, however, delighted with the attention paid to his wife by a real lord, but our clear-headed Jack saw through it all, and took measures accordingly

Pengerswick tried hard to learn the secret of the stores of tin, but he was foiled by the tinkeard on every tack. You may well suppose how desirous he was of getting Jack out of the way, and eventually he began to try his spells upon him. The power of his necromancy was such, that all in the castle were fixed in sleep as rigid as stones, save Jack. All that the enchanter could do produced no effect on him. He sat quietly looking on, occasionally humming some old troll, and now and then whistling to show his unconcern. At last Pengerswick became enraged, and he drew from his breast a dagger and slyly struck at Jack. The dagger, which was of the finest Eastern steel, was bent like a piece of soft iron against Jack's black hide.

"Art thou the devil?" exclaimed Pengerswick

"As he's a friend of yours," says Jack, "you should know his countenance."

"Devil or no devil," roared Pengerswick, "you cannot resist this," and he held before Jack a curiously-shaped piece of polished steel.

Jack only smiled, and quietly unfastening his cow's hide, he opened it. The cross, like a star of fire, was reflected in a mirror under Jack's coat, and it fell from Pengerswick's grasp. Jack seized it, and turning it full upon the enchanter, the proud lord sank trembling to the ground, piteously imploring Jack to spare his life and let him go free Jack bade the prostrate lord rise from the ground. He kicked him out of the castle, and sent the vicious mare after him. Thus he saved Tom and his family from the power of this great enchanter. In a little time the sleep which had fallen upon them passed away, and they awoke, as though from the effects of a drunken frolic The brewer hurried home, and Tom and Jack set to work to dress their tin. Tom and Jane's relations and friends flocked around them, but Jack said, "Summer flies are only seen in the sunshine," and he shortly after this put their friendship to the test, by conveying to them the idea that Tom had spent all his wealth These new friends dropped off when they thought they could get no more, and Tom and Jane were thoroughly disgusted with their summer friends and selfish relations. The tinkeard established himself firmly as an inmate of the castle. No more was said about the right of the public to make a king's highway through the castle grounds. He aided Tom in hedging in the waste lands, and very carefully secured the gates against all intruders. In fact, he also quite altered his politics.

Jack had a desire to go home to Dartmoor to see his mother, who had sent to tell him that the old giant Dart was near death. He started at once, on foot. Tom wished him to have Pengerswick's colt, but Jack preferred his legs. It would be too long a tale to tell the story of his travels. He killed serpents and wild beasts in the woods, and when he came to rivers, he had but to take off his coat, gather up the skirts of it with a string, and stretch out the body with a few sticks,—thus forming a cobble,—launch it on the water, and paddle himself across. He reached home. The old giant was at his last gasp. Jack made him give everything to his mother before he breathed his last. When he died, Jack carefully buried him. He then settled all matters for his mother, and returned to the West Country again.

Tom's daughter became of marriageable years, and Jack wished to have her for a wife. Tom, however, would not consent to this, unless he got rid of a troublesome old giant who lived on one of the hills in Morva, which was the only bit of ground between Hayle and St Just which Tom did not possess. The people of Morva were kept in great fear by this giant, who made them bring him the best of everything. He was a very savage old creature, and took exceeding delight in destroying every one's happiness Some of Tom's cousins lived in Morva, and young Tom fell in love with one of his Morva cousins seven times removed, and by Jack's persuasion, they were allowed by Tom and Jane to marry. It was proclaimed by Jack all round the country that great games would come off on the day of the wedding. He had even the impudence to stick a bill on the giant's door, stating the prizes which would be given to the best games. The happy day arrived, and, as the custom then was, the marriage was to take place at sundown. A host of people from all parts were assembled, and under the influence of Jack and Tom, the games were kept up in great spirit. Jack and Tom, by and by, amused themselves by pitching quoits at the giant's house on the top of the hill. The old giant came out and roared like thunder. All the young men were about to fly, but Jack called them a lot of scurvy cowards, and stayed their flight. Jack made faces at the giant, and challenged him to come down and fight him. The old monster thought he could eat Jack, and presently began to run down the hill,—when, lo ! he disappeared. When the people saw that the giant was gone, they took courage, and ran up the hill after Jack, who called on them to follow him.

There was a vast hole in the earth, and there, at the bottom of it, lay the giant, crushed by his own weight, groaning like a volcano and shaking like an earthquake.

Jack knew there was an adit level driven into the hill, and he had quietly, and at night, worked away the roof at one particular part, until he left only a mere shell of rock above, so it was, that, as the giant passed over this spot, the ground gave way. Heavy rocks were thrown down the hole on the giant, and there his bones are said to lie to this day.

Jack was married at once to young Jane, her brother Tom to the Morva girl, and great were the rejoicings. From all parts of the country came in the wrestlers, and never since the days of Gogmagog had there been such terrific struggles between strong men. Quoits were played ; and some of the throws of Tom and the tinkeard are still shown to attest the wonderful prowess of this pair. Hurling was played over the wild hills of those northern shores, and they rung and echoed then, as they have often rung and echoed since, with the brave cry, "*Guare wheag yw guare teag,*" which has been translated into " Fair play is good play," *
—an honourable trait in the character of our Celtic friends. All this took place on a Sunday, and was the origin of Morva Feast and Morva Fair. We are, of course, astonished at not finding some evidence of direct punishment for these offences, such as that which was inflicted on the hurlers at Padstow. This has, however, been explained on the principle that the people were merely rejoicing at the accomplishment of a most holy act, and that a good deed demanded a good day.†

THE GIANT OF MORVA.‡

IN the Giant's Field in Morva still stand some granite fragments which once constituted the Giant's House. From this we see the Giant's Castle at Bosprenis, and the Giant's Cradle, thus perpetuating the infancy of the great man, and his subsequent power The quoits used by this giant are numerous indeed. This great man, on the 1st day of August, would walk up to Bosprenis Croft, and there perform some magical rites, which were either never known, or they have been forgotten. On this day,—for when thus engaged the giant was harmless,—thousands of people would congregate to get a glimpse of the monster ; and as he passed them,—all being seated on the stone hedges,—every one drank "to the health of Mr Giant " At length the giant died, but the gathering on the 1st of August has never been given up,

---

* Or, " Sweet play is fair play," *i e* , it is not fair to play roughly
† See Appendix G for Mr Wright's story of "The Wonderful Cobbler of Wellington '
‡ The above notices were collected for me in Morva by the late C Taylor Stephens, author of "The Chief of Barat-Anac," and "some time rural postman from St Ives to Zennor " Their connection with the traditions of Jack and Tom will be evident to every reader

or rather, the day shifts, and is made to agree with Morva Feast, which is held on the first Sunday in August.

A Morva farmer writes —"A quarter of an acre would not hold the horses ridden to the fair,—the hedges being covered by the visitors, who drink and carouse as in former times. Morva Fair is, however, dying out."

The parish-clerk informed me that the giant had twenty sons ; that he was the first settler in these parts ; and that he planted his children all round the coast. It was his custom to bring all his family together on the 1st of August, and hence the origin of the fair. Whichever may be the true account of the cause which established the fair and the feast, these romances clearly establish the fact that the giants were at the bottom of it.

THE GIANT BOLSTER.

THIS mighty man held especial possession of the hill formerly known as *Carne Bury-anacht* or *Bury-anack*,* " the spar-stone grave," sometimes called *St Agnes' Ball* and *St Agnes' Pestis*, but which is now named, from the use made of the hill during the long war, St Agnes' Beacon. He has left his name to a very interesting, and undoubtedly most ancient earthwork, which still exists at the base of the hill, and evidently extended from Trevaunance Porth to Chapel Porth, enclosing the most important tin district in St Agnes. This is constantly called " The Bolster."

Bolster must have been of enormous size . since it is stated that he could stand with one foot on St Agnes' Beacon and the other on Carn Brea; these hills being distant, as the bird flies, six miles,† his immensity will be clear to all. In proof of this, there still exists, in the valley running upwards from Chapel Porth, a stone in which may yet be seen the impression of the giant's fingers. On one occasion, Bolster, when enjoying his usual stride from the Beacon to Carn Brea, felt thirsty, and stooped to drink out of the well at Chapel Porth, resting, while he did so, on the above-mentioned stone We hear but little of the wives of our giants; but Bolster had a wife, who was made to labour hard by her tyrannical husband. On the top of St Agnes' Beacon there yet exist the evidences of the useless labours to which this unfortunate giantess was doomed, in grouped masses of small stones. These, it is said, have all been gathered from an estate at the foot of the hill, immediately adjoining the village of St Agnes. This farm is to

* *Bury*, Saxon for *grave* Th s does not appear to be Cornish, which is *bedh*, Welsh, *bedd*

† See Appendix H.

the present day remarkable for its freedom from stones, though situated amidst several others, which, like most lands reclaimed from the moors of this district, have stones in abundance mixed with the soil. Whenever Bolster was angry with his wife, he compelled her to pick stones, and to carry them in her apron to the top of the hill. There is some confusion in the history of this giant, and of the blessed St Agnes to whom the church is dedicated. They are supposed to have lived at the same time, which, according to our views, is scarcely probable, believing, as we do, that no giants existed long after their defeat at Plymouth by Brutus and Corineus. There may have been an earlier saint of the same name; or may not Saint Enns or Anns, the popular name of this parish, indicate some other lady?

Be this as it may, the giant Bolster became deeply in love with St Agnes, who is reputed to have been singularly beautiful, and a pattern woman of virtue. The giant allowed the lady no repose. He followed her incessantly, proclaiming his love, and filling the air with the tempests of his sighs and groans. St Agnes lectured Bolster in vain on the impropriety of his conduct, he being already a married man. This availed not; her prayers to him to relieve her from his importunities were also in vain. The persecuted lady, finding there was no release for her, while this monster existed, resolved to be rid of him at any cost, and eventually succeeded by the following stratagem :—Agnes appeared at length to be persuaded of the intensity of the giant's love, but she told him she required yet one small proof more. There exists at Chapel Porth a hole in the cliff at the termination of the valley. If Bolster would fill this hole with his blood the lady would no longer look coldly on him. This huge bestrider-of-the-hills thought that it was an easy thing which was required of him, and felt that he could fill many such holes and be none the weaker for the loss of blood Consequently, stretching his great arm across the hole, he plunged a knife into a vein, and a torrent of gore issued forth. Roaring and seething the blood fell to the bottom, and the giant expected in a few minutes to see the test of his devotion made evident, in the filling of the hole. It required much more blood than Bolster had supposed; still it must in a short time be filled, so he bled on. Hour after hour the blood flowed from the vein, yet the hole was not filled. Eventually the giant fainted from exhaustion. The strength of life within his mighty frame enabled him to rally, yet he had no power to lift himself from the ground, and he was unable to stanch the wound which he had made. Thus it was, that after many throes, the giant Bolster died!

The cunning saint, in proposing this task to Bolster, was well aware that the hole opened at the bottom into the sea, and that as rapidly as the blood flowed into the hole it ran from it, and did

> "The multitudinous seas incarnadine,
> Making the green one red."

Thus the lady got rid of her hated lover ; Mrs Bolster was released, and the district freed from the presence of a tyrant. The hole at Chapel Porth still retains the evidences of the truth of this tradition, in the red stain which marks the track down which flowed the giant's blood.

There is another tradition, in some respects resembling this one, respecting a giant who dwelt at Goran, on the south coast.

THE HACK AND CAST.

IN the parish of Goran is an intrenchment running from cliff to cliff, and cutting off about a hundred acres of coarse ground This is about twenty feet broad, and twenty-four feet high in most places.

Marvellous as it may appear, tradition assures us that this was the work of a giant, and that he performed the task in a single night. This fortification has long been known as *Thica Vosa*, and the Hack and Cast.

The giant, who lived on the promontory, was the terror of the neighbourhood, and great were the rejoicings in Goran when his death was accomplished through a stratagem by a neighbouring doctor.

The giant fell ill through eating some food—children or otherwise—to satisfy his voracity, which had disturbed his stomach. His roars and groans were heard for miles, and great was the terror throughout the neighbourhood. A messenger, however, soon arrived at the residence of the doctor of the parish, and he bravely resolved to obey the summons of the giant, and visit him. He found the giant rolling on the ground with pain, and he at once determined to rid the world, if possible, of the monster.

He told him that he must be bled. The giant submitted, and the doctor moreover said that, to insure relief, a large hole in the cliff must be filled with the blood. The giant lay on the ground, his arm extended over the hole, and the blood flowing a torrent into it. Relieved by the loss of blood, he permitted the stream to flow on, until he at last became so weak, that the doctor kicked him over the cliff, and killed him. The well-known promontory of The Dead Man, or Dodman, is so called from the dead giant. The spot on which he fell is the " Giant's House," and the hole has ever since been most favourable to the growth of ivy.

THE GIANT WRATH, OR RALPH.

NOT far from Portreath there exists a remarkable fissure, or gorge, on the coast, formed by the wearing out, through the action of the sea, of a channel of ground softer than that which exists on either side of it. This is generally known as Ralph's Cupboard ; and one tale is, that Ralph was a famous smuggler, who would run his little vessel, even in dark nights, into the shelter afforded by this gorge, and safely land his goods. Another is, that it was formerly a cavern in which dwelt Wrath— a huge giant—who was the terror of the fishermen. Sailing from St Ives, they ever avoided the Cupboard; as they said, " Nothing ever came out of it which was unfortunate enough to get into it." Wrath is reputed to have watched for those who were drifted towards his Cupboard by currents, or driven in by storms. It is said that wading out to sea, he tied the boats to his girdle, and quietly walked back to his den, making, of course, all the fishermen his prey. The roof of the cavern is supposed to have fallen in after the death of the giant, leaving the open chasm as we now see it.

ORDULPH THE GIANT.

THIS *Tavistock* Sampson is far removed from our fine old legendary giant ; yet we perceive in the stories of Ordulph precisely the same process as that which has given immortality to Blunderbuss and others. In the church of the monastery of Tavistock, built by Orgar in 960, and consecrated by St Rumon, was buried Orgar, and also his son Edulf, or Ordulph, to whom, by some writers, the foundation of the abbey is attributed. Ordulph was a man of giant size, and possessing most remarkable strength. He once appeared before the gates of the city of Exeter in company with King Edward, and demanded admission. His demand was not immediately complied with He tore away the bars of the portcullis with his hands—burst open the gates with his foot—rent the locks and bolts asunder—and broke down a considerable portion of the wall—walking into the city over the ruins, and occasioning great alarm amidst the inhabitants

The king is said to have attributed this extraordinary feat of strength to the chieftain's having entered into a compact with the devil ; and the people generally believed the king to be correct.

At Tavistock, it was the custom of Ordulph to stand with one foot on either side of the Tavy, which is about twenty feet wide, and having the wild beasts driven in from the Dartmoor forests, he would—with the seemingly insignificant blows of a small knife —strike their heads off into the stream.*

* William of Malmesbury tells us that both father and son were buried at Tavistock, which is thus described —" Est in Domnonia cænobium monachorum, juxta Tau fluvium, quod Tavistock vocator , quod per Ordgarum, comitem Domnoniensem, patrem Elfrida, qui fuit uxor regis Edgari, surgendi exordium, per Livingum episcopum, cresendi accepit auspicium ; locus, amænus opportunitate nemorum, captura copiosa piscum, Ecclesiæ congruente fabrica, fluvialibus rivis per officinas monachorum de-currentibus, qui suo impetu effusi, quidquid invenerint superflum, portant in exitum " Quoted by Pedler in his " Episcopate of Cornwall."

Mrs Bray, in her " Traditions, Legends, Superstitions, and Sketches of Devonshire," says,—" But notwithstanding the superiority of his strength and stature, Ordulph died in the flower of his age. He gave orders to be buried at his abbey at Horton, in Dorsetshire , but was interred in or near the Abbey Church of Tavistock, where a mausoleum or tomb of vast dimensions was erected to his memory, which is represented to have been visited as a wonder ' The thigh-bone of Ordulph is still preserved in Tavistock Church ' "

THE FAIRIES.

"Elves, urchins, goblins all, and little fairyes"—*Mad Prankes.*

"I do wander everywhere,
Swifter than the moone's sphere;
And I serve the fairy queen,
To dew her orbs upon the green."—SHAKESPEARE

"By the moon we sport and play;
With the night begins our day;
As we dance the dew doth fall—
Trip it little urchins all;
Lightly as the little bee,
Two by two, and three by three,
And about go we, and about go we."
—LYLIE, *Maydes' Metamorphoses.*

ROMANCES OF THE FAIRIES.

THE ELFIN CREED OF CORNWALL.

> "To thee the fairy state
> I with discretion dedicate,
> Because thou prizest things that are
> Curious and unfamiliar "
>
> *Oberon's Feast.*—ROBERT HERRICK.

TO the " Fairy Mythology" of Thomas Keightley, I must refer all those who are desirous of examining the metamorphoses which this family of spiritual beings undergo, in passing from one country to another. My business is with the Cornish branch of this extensive family, and I shall be in a position to show that, notwithstanding Mr Keightley has entirely excluded Cornwall from consideration, there exists, even to the present day, a remarkable fairy mythology in that county. Between thirty and forty years since, ere yet the influences of our practical education had disturbed the poetical education of the people, every hill and valley, every tree, shrub, and flower was peopled with spiritual creations, deriving their characteristics from the physical peculiarities amidst which they were born. Extending over the whole district which was formerly known as Danmonium,*—embracing not only Cornwall, but Devonshire, to the eastern edge of Dartmoor,—we find a mythology, which varies but little in its main features. Beyond an imaginary line, drawn in a north-westerly direction from the mouth of the Teign to the rise of the Torridge, the curiously wild and distinguishing superstitions of the "Cornwallers"† fade away, and we have those which are common to Somersetshire and the more fertile counties of mid-England.

---

* " If Alfred, as is probable, fixed the limits of Devon where the ancient eastern boundary was, between the Belgæ and Durotriges on the east, and Danmonii on the west, ancient Cornwall will have included all Devon, as well as what is west of the Tamar "—*Camden's Britannia* Gough, vol i, p 1

† "The 'Cornwallers' overpowered by the Saxons."—*Camden's Britannia*, vol. i, p. cxxxix.

The Piscy or Pixy of East Devon and Somersetshire is a different creature from his cousin of a similar name in Cornwall. The former is a mischievous, but in all respects a very harmless creation, who appears to live a rollicking life amidst the luxuriant scenes of those beautiful counties   The latter, the piskies of Cornwall, appear to have their wits sharpened by their necessities, and may be likened to the keen and cunning "Arab" boy of the London streets, as seen in contrast with the clever child who has been reared in every comfort of a well-regulated home.   A gentleman, well known in the literary world of London, very recently told me, that he once saw in Devonshire a troop of fairies.   It was a breezy summer afternoon, and these beautiful little creatures were floating on the circling zephyrs up the side of a sunlit hill, and fantastically playing

> "Where oxlips and the nodding violet grow"

They are truly the fairies of "Midsummer Night's Dream"   They haunt the most rural and romantic spots, and they gather

> "On hill, in dale, forest, or mead,
> By paved fountain, or by rushy brook,
> Or on the beached margent of the sea,
> To dance their ringlets to the whistling wind."

No such fairies are ever met with on Dartmoor.   A few, judging from Mrs Bray's tales,* may have been tempted into the lovely valley of the Tavy, but certainly they never crossed the Tamar. The darker shades in the character of the Cornish fairy almost dispose me to conclude that they belong to an older family than those of Devonshire.

It should be understood that there are in Cornwall five varieties of the fairy family, clearly distinguishable—

1. The Small People.
2. The Spriggans.
3 Piskies, or Pigseys.
4. The Buccas, Bockles, or Knockers.
5. The Browneys.

Of the *Small People* I have heard two accounts.   Indeed, it is by no means clear that the tradition of their origin does not apply to the whole five branches of this ancient family   The Small People are believed by some to be the spirits of the people who

---

*   aditions, Legends, Superstitions, and Sketches of Devonshire, on the Borders of the Tamar and the Tavy, by Mrs Bray

inhabited Cornwall many thousands of years ago—long, long be-fore the birth of Christ. That they were not good enough to in-herit the joys of heaven, but that they were too good to be condemned to eternal fires. They were said to be "poor innocents" (this phrase is now applied to silly children). When they first came into this land, they were much larger than they are now, but ever since the birth of Christ they have been getting smaller and smaller. Eventually they will turn into muryans (ants), and at last be lost from the face of the earth. These Small People are exceedingly playful amongst themselves, but they are usually demure when they know that any human eye sees them. They commonly aid those people to whom they take a fancy, and, frequently, they have been known to perform the most friendly acts towards men and women. The above notion corresponds with the popular belief in Ireland, which is, "that the fairies are a portion of the fallen angels, who, being less guilty than the rest, were not driven to hell, but were suffered to dwell on earth."* In Cornwall, as in Wales, another popular creed is, that the fairies are Druids becom-ing—because they will not give up their idolatries—smaller and smaller. These Small People in many things closely resemble the Elves of Scandinavia.

The *Spriggans* are quite a different class of beings. In some respects they appear to be offshoots from the family of the Trolls of Sweden and Denmark. The Spriggans are found only about the cairns, coits, or cromlechs, burrows, or detached stones, with which it is unlucky for mortals to meddle. A correspondent writes "This is known, that they were a remarkably mischievous and thievish tribe. If ever a house was robbed, a child stolen, cattle carried away, or a building demolished, it was the work of the Spriggans. Whatever commotion took place in earth, air, or water, it was all put down as the work of these spirits Wherever the giants have been, there the Spriggans have been also. It is usually considered that they are the ghosts of the giants; certainly, from many of their feats, we must suppose them to possess a giant's strength. The Spriggans have the charge of buried trea-sure."

The *Piskie.*—This fairy is a most mischievous and very un-sociable sprite. His favourite fun is to entice people into the bogs by appearing like the light from a cottage window, or as a man carrying a lantern. The Piskie partakes, in many respects, of the character of the Spriggan So wide-spread were their depreda-tions, and so annoying their tricks, that it at one time was neces-

See Keightley's "Fairy Mythology"

F

sary to select persons whose acuteness and ready tact were a match for these quick-witted wanderers, and many a clever man has become famous for his power to give charms against Pigseys. It does not appear, however, that anything remarkable was required of the clever man. " No Pigsey could harm a man if his coat were inside-out, and it became a very common practice for persons who had to go from village to village by night, to wear their jacket or cloak so turned, ostensibly to prevent the dew from taking the shine off the cloth, but in reality to render them safe from the Pigseys " *

They must have been a merry lot, since to " laugh like a Piskie " is a popular saying. These little fellows were great plagues to the farmers, riding their colts and chasing their cows.

The Buccas or Knockers.—These are the sprites of the mines, and correspond to the Kobals of the German mines, the Duergars, and the Trolls They are said to be the souls of the Jews who formerly worked the tin-mines of Cornwall. They are not allowed to rest because of their wicked practices as tinners, and they share in the general curse which ignorant people believe still hangs on this race.

The Browney.—This spirit was purely of the household. Kindly and good, he devoted his every care to benefit the family with whom he had taken up his abode. The Browney has fled, owing to his being brought into very close contact with the schoolmaster, and he is only summoned now upon the occasion of the swarming of the bees When this occurs, mistress or maid seizes a bell-metal, or a tin pan, and, beating it, she calls " Browney, Browney ! " as loud as she can until the good Browney compels the bees to settle

Mr Thoms has noticed that in Cornwall " the moths which some regard as departed souls, others as fairies, are called *Pisgies.*" This is somewhat too generally expressed , the belief respecting the moth, so far as I know, is confined to one or two varieties only Mr Couch informs us that the local name, around Polperro, of the weasel is *Fairy*. So that we have evidence of some sort of metempsychosis amongst the elf family. Moths, ants, and weasels it would seem are the forms taken by those wandering spirits.

* The Cornish had formerly a great belief in piskays or fairies If a traveller happened to lose his way, he immediately concluded he was "piskay led " To dispel the charm with which the "piskay-led" traveller was entangled, nothing was deemed sufficient but that of his turning one of his garments inside out This generally fell upon one of his stockings , and if this precaution had been taken before the commencement of the journey, it was fully believed that no such delusion would have happened.—*Drew and Hitchins' History of Cornwall*, p. 97

We read in Bishop Corbet, whose work was published in 1648, and was reprinted many years after by Bishop Percy—

> "The fairies
> Were of the old profession;
> Their songs were *Ave Maries,*
> Their dances were procession.
> But now, alas! they all are dead,
> Or gone beyond the seas,
> Or, further, for religion fied,
> Or else they take their ease."

Other writers have supposed that at the time of the Reformation the fairies departed from the land. This hypothesis is not warranted by evidence. It is possible that they may have taken possession of some of the inferior creatures, but they are certainly still to be found in those regions which lie beyond the reach of the railway-giant, with his fiery mouth, or of that electric spirit who, travelling on his mysterious wires, can beat the wildest elf that ever mounted "night-steeds."

NURSING A FAIRY.

A THRIFTY housewife lived on one of the hills between Zennor Church-town and St Ives. One night a gentleman came to her cottage, and told her he had marked her cleanliness and her care : that he had a child whom he desired to have brought up with much tenderness, and he had fixed on her. She should be very handsomely rewarded for her trouble, and he showed her a considerable quantity of golden coin. Well, she agreed, and away she went with the gentleman to fetch this child. When they came to the side of Zennor hill, the gentleman told the woman he must blindfold her, and she, good, easy soul, having heard of such things, fancied this was some rich man's child, and that the residence of its mother was not to be known, so she gave herself great credit for cunning in quietly submitting. They walked on some considerable distance. When they stopped the handkerchief was taken from her eyes, and she found herself in a magnificent room, with a table spread with the most expensive luxuries, in the way of game, fruits, and wines. She was told to eat, and she did so with some awkwardness, and not a little trembling. She was surprised that so large a feast should have been spread for so small a party,—only herself and the master. At last, having enjoyed luxuries such as she never tasted before or since, a

silver bell was rung, and a troop of servants came in, bearing a
cot covered with satin, in which was sleeping the most beautiful
babe that human eyes ever gazed on.   She was told this child
was to be committed to her charge , she should not want for anything ; but she was to obey certain laws.   She was not to teach
the child the Lord's Prayer ; she was not to wash it after sun-
down : she was to bathe it every morning in water, which she
would find in a white ewer placed in the child's room · this was
not to be touched by any one but herself, and she was to be careful not to wash her own face in this water.   In all other respects
she was to treat the child as one of her own children   The woman
was blinded again, and the child having been placed in her arms,
away she trudged, guided by the mysterious father.   When out
on the road, the bandage was removed from her eyes, and she
found she had a small baby in her arms, not remarkably good-
looking, with very sharp, piercing eyes, and but ordinarily dressed.
However, a bargain is a bargain ; so she resolved to make the
best of it, and she presented the babe to her husband, telling him
so much of the story as she thought it prudent to trust him with.
For years the child was with this couple.   They never wanted for
anything ; meat, and even wines, were provided,—as most people
thought,—by wishing for them ; clothes, ready-made, were on the
child's bed when required ; and the charmed water was always in
the magic ewer.   The little boy grew active and strong.   He was
remarkably wild, yet very tractable, and he appeared to have a
real regard for his "big mammy," as he called the woman.
Sometimes she thought the child was mad.   He would run, and
leap, and scream, as though he were playing with scores of boys,
when no soul was near him.   The woman had never seen the
father since the child had been with them ; but ever and anon,
money was conveyed to them in some mysterious manner   One
morning, when washing the boy, this good woman, who had often
observed how bright the water made the face of the child, was
tempted to try if it would improve her own beauty.   So directing
the boy's attention to some birds singing on a tree outside the
window, she splashed some of the water up into her face.   Most
of it went into her eye   She closed it instinctively, and upon
opening it, she saw a number of little people gathered round her
and playing with the boy   She said not a word, though her fear
was great ; and she continued to see the world of small people
surrounding the world of ordinary men and women, being with
them, but not of them.   She now knew who the boy's playmates
were, and she often wished to speak to the beautiful creatures of the

invisible world who were his real companions ; but she was discreet, and kept silence.

Curious robberies had been from time to time committed in St Ives Market, and although the most careful watch had been kept, the things disappeared, and no thief detected One day our good housewife was at the market, and to her surprise she saw the father of her nursling. Without ceremony she ran up to him,— at a moment when he was putting some choice fruit by stealth into his pocket,—and spoke to him. " So, thou seest me, dost thou ? " " To be sure I do, and know 'ee too," replied the woman. " Shut this eye," putting his finger on her left eye. " Canst see me now ? " " Yes, I tell 'ee, and know 'ee too," again said the woman.

> " Water for elf, not water for self ;
> You 've lost your eye, your child, and yourself,"

said the gentleman. From that hour she was blind in the right eye. When she got home the boy was gone. She grieved sadly, but she never saw him more, and this once happy couple became poor and wretched.

CHANGELINGS.

A CORRESPONDENT, to whom I am much indebted for many curious examples of the folk-lore of the people in the remote districts to the west of Penzance, says, in reference to some stories of fairy changelings—" I never knew but one child that had been kept by the Spriggans more than three days. It was always complaining, sickly, and weakly, *and had the very face of a changeling.*"

It has been my fortune, some thirty or forty years since, to have seen several children of whom it had been whispered amongst the peasantry that they were changelings. In every case they have been sad examples of the influence of mesenteric disease—the countenance much altered—their eyes glassy and sunk in their sockets—the nose sharpened—the cheeks of a marble whiteness, unless when they were flushed with hectic fever—the lips sometimes swollen and of a deep, red colour, and small ulcers not unfrequently at the angles of the mouth The wasted frame, with sometimes strumous swellings, and the unnatural abdominal enlargement which accompanies disease of mesenteric glands, gives a very sad, and often a most unnatural appearance to the sufferer The intense ignorance which existed in many of the districts visited by me, at the period named, has been almost dispelled by the civilising influences of Wesleyanism. Consequently, when a scrofulous child is found in a family, we no longer hear of its being a changeling ; but, within a very recent period, I have heard it said that such afflicted children had been "ill-wished."

THE LOST CHILD.

IN the little hamlet of Treonike, in the parish of St Allen, has long lingered the story of a lost child, who was subsequently found. All the stories agree in referring the abduction of the child to supernatural agency, and in some cases it is referred to the "Small People or Piskies,"—in others, to less amiable spiritual creatures. Mr Hals* has given one version of this story, which differs in some respects from the tale as I heard it, from an old woman some thirty years since, who then lived in this parish. Her tale was to the following effect. It was a lovely evening, and the little boy was gathering flowers in the fields, near a wood. The child was charmed by hearing some beautiful music, which he at first mistook for the song of birds ; but, being a sharp boy, he was not long deceived, and he went towards the wood to ascertain from whence the melodious sounds came. When he reached the verge of the wood, the music was of so exquisite a character, that he was compelled to follow the sound, which appeared to travel before him. Lured in this way, the boy penetrated to the dark centre of the grove, and here, meeting with some difficulties, owing to the thick growth of underwood, he paused and began to think of returning. The music, however, became more ravishing than before, and some invisible being appeared to crush down all the low and tangled plants, thus forming for him a passage, over which he passed without any difficulty. At length he found himself on the edge of a small lake, and, greatly to his astonishment, the darkness of night was around him, but the heavens were thick with stars. The music ceased, and, wearied with his wanderings, the boy fell asleep on a bed of ferns. He related, on his restoration to his parents, that he was taken by a beautiful lady through palaces of the most gorgeous description. Pillars of glass supported arches which glistened with every colour, and these were hung with crystals far exceeding anything which were ever seen in the caverns of a Cornish mine. It is, however, stated that many days passed away before the child was found by his friends, and that at length he was discovered, one lovely morning, sleeping on the bed of ferns, on which he was supposed to have

* See Davies Gilbert's Parochial History of Cornwall

fallen asleep on the first adventurous evening. There was no reason given by the narrator why the boy was " spirited away " in the first instance, or why he was returned. Her impression was, that some sprites, pleased with the child's innocence and beauty, had entranced him. That when asleep he had been carried through the waters to the fairy abodes beneath them , and she felt assured that a child so treated would be kept under the especial guardianship of the sprites for ever afterwards. Of this, however, tradition leaves us in ignorance.

A NATIVE PIGSEY STORY.

" D'YE see that 'ere hoss there ? " said a Liskeard farmer to a West-Country miner.

" What ov it ? " asked the miner.

" Well, that 'ere hoss he 'n been ridden to death a'most by the pigsies again."

" Pigsies ! " said the miner ; " thee don't b'leve in they, do 'ee ? "

" Ees I do ; but I specks you 're a West-Country bucca, ain't 'ee ? If you 'd a had yourn hosses wrode to death every nite, you 'd tell another tayl, I reckon But as sure as I 'se living the pigsies do ride on 'em whenever they 've a mind to."

THE NIGHT-RIDERS.

I WAS on a visit when a boy at a farmhouse situated near Fowey river. Well do I remember the farmer with much sorrow telling us one morning at breakfast, that " the piskie people had been riding Tom again ; " and this he regarded as certainly leading to the destruction of a fine young horse. I was taken to the stable to see the horse. There could be no doubt that the animal was much distressed, and refused to eat his food. The mane was said to be knotted into fairy stirrups ; and Mr —— told me that he had no doubt at least twenty small people had sat upon the horse's neck. He even assured me that one of his men had seen them urging the horse to his utmost speed round and round one of his fields.

THE FAIRY TOOLS; OR, BARKER'S KNEE.

THE buccas or knockers are believed to inhabit the rocks, caves, adits, and wells of Cornwall.   In the parish of Towednack there was a well where those industrious small people might every day be heard busy at their labours—digging with pickaxe and shovel.   I said, every day.   No; on Christmas-day —on the Jews' Sabbath—on Easter-day—and on All-Saints' day— no work was done.   Why our little friends held those days in reverence has never been told me.   Any one, by placing his ear on the ground at the mouth of this well, could distinctly hear the little people at work.

There lived in the neighbourhood a great, hulking fellow, who would rather do anything than work, and who refused to believe anything he heard.   He had been told of the Fairy Well—he said it was "all a dream."   But since the good people around him reiterated their belief in the fairies of the well, he said he'd find it all out.   So day after day, Barker—that was this hulk's name— would lie down amidst the ferns growing around the mouth of the well, and, basking in the sunshine, listen and watch.   He soon heard pick and shovel, and chit-chat, and merry laughter.   Well, "he'd see the out of all this," he told his neighbours.   Day after day, and week after week, this fellow was at his post.   Nothing resulted from his watching.   At last he learned to distinguish the words used by the busy workers.   He discovered that each set of labourers worked eight hours, and that, on leaving, they hid their tools.   They made no secret of this ; and one evening he heard one say, he should place his tools in a cleft in the rock ; another, that he should put his under the ferns ; and another said, he should leave his tools on *Barker's knee*.   He started on hearing his own name.   At that moment a heavy weight fell on the man's knee ; he felt excessive pain, and roared to have the cursed things taken away.   His cries were answered by laughter.   To the day of his death Barker had a stiff knee; he was laughed at by all the parish ; and " Barker's knee " became a proverb.

THE PISKIES IN THE CELLAR.

THE following story, for which I am indebted to Mr T. Q. Couch, will remind the reader of " The Cluricaun "* and " The Haunted Cellar," in " Fairy Legends and Traditions of the South of Ireland " By T. Crofton Croker, Esq.

On the Thursday immediately preceding Christmas-tide (year

not recorded), were assembled at "The Rising Sun" the captain
and men of a stream work* in the Couse below. This Couse
was a flat, alluvial moor, broken by gigantic mole-hills, the work
of many a generation of tinners. One was half inclined, on looking at the turmoiled ground, to believe with them that the tin grew
in successive crops, for, after years of turning and searching, there
was still enough left to give the landlord his dole, and to furnish
wages to some dozen streamers. This night was a festival
observed in honour of one *Picrous*,† and intended to celebrate the
discovery of tin on this day by a man of that name. The feast is
still kept, though the observance has dwindled to a supper and its
attendant merrymaking.

Our story has especially to do with the adventures of one of the
party, John Sturtridge, who, well primed with ale, started on his
homeward way for Luxulyan Church-town. John had got as far
as Tregarden Down without any mishap worth recording, when,
alas! he happed upon a party of the little people, who were at their
sports in the shelter of a huge granite boulder. Assailed by shouts
of derisive laughter, he hastened on frightened and bewildered, but
the Down, well known from early experience, became like ground
untrodden, and after long trial no gate or stile was to be found.
He was getting vexed, as well as puzzled, when a chorus of tiny
voices shouted, "Ho! and away for Par Beach!" John repeated
the shout, and was in an instant caught up, and in a twinkling
found himself on the sands of Par. A brief dance, and the cry
was given, "Ho! and away for Squire Tremain's cellar!" A
repetition of the Piskie cry found John with his elfish companions
in the cellars at Heligan, where was beer and wine galore. It
need not be said that he availed himself of his opportunities. The
mixture of all the good liquors so affected him that, alas! he forgot in time to catch up the next cry of "Ho! and away for Par
Beach!" In the morning John was found by the butler, groping
and tumbling among butts and barrels, very much muddled with
the squire's good drink. His strange story, very incoherently told,
was not credited by the squire, who committed him to jail for
the burglary, and in due time he was convicted and sentenced to
death.

The morning of his execution arrived; a large crowd had
assembled, and John was standing under the gallows-tree, when a
commotion was observed in the crowd, and a little lady of com-

---

* A "stream work" is a place where tin is obtained from the drift deposits
"Streamers" are the tinners who wash out the tin.

† Picrous day is still kept up in Luxulyan   See Appendix I.

manding mien made her way through the opening throng to the scaffold. In a shrill, sweet voice, which John recognised, she cried, "Ho! and away for France!" Which being replied to, he was rapt from the officers of justice, leaving them and the multitude mute with wonder and disappointment.

THE SPRIGGANS OF TRENCROM HILL.

IT is not many years since a man, who thought he was fully informed as to the spot in which a crock of the giant's gold was buried, proceeded on one fine moonlight night to this enchanted hill, and with spade and pick commenced his search. He proceeded for some time without interruption, and it became evident to him that the treasure was not far off. The sky was rapidly covered with the darkest clouds, shutting out the brilliant light o the moon—which had previously gemmed each cairn—and leaving the gold-seeker in total and unearthly darkness. The wind rose, and roared terrifically amidst the rocks; but this was soon drowned amidst the fearful crashes of thunder, which followed in quick succession the flashes of lightning. By its light the man perceived that the spriggans were coming out in swarms from all the rocks. They were in countless numbers; and although they were small at first, they rapidly increased in size, until eventually they assumed an almost giant form, looking all the while, as he afterwards said, "as ugly as if they would eat him." How this poor man escaped is unknown, but he is said to have been so frightened that he took to his bed, and was not able to work for a long time.

THE FAIRY MINERS—THE KNOCKERS.

AT Ransom Mine the "Knockers" were always very active in their subterranean operations. In every part of the mine their "knockings" were heard, but most especially were they busy in one particular "end." There was a general impression that great wealth must exist at this part of the "lode." Yet, notwithstanding the inducements of very high "tribute" were held out to the miners, no pair of men could be found brave enough to venture on the ground of the "Bockles." An old man and his son, called Trenwith, who lived near Bosprenis, went out one midsummer eve, about midnight, and watched until they saw the "Smae People" bringing up the shining ore. It is said they were possessed of some secret by which they could communicate with the fairy people. Be this as it may, they told the little miners that they would save them all the trouble of breaking down the ore, that they would bring "to grass" for them, one-tenth of the "richest stuff," and leave it properly dressed, if they would quietly give them up this end. An agreement of some kind was come to The old man and his son took the "pitch," and in a short time realised much wealth. The old man never failed to keep to his bargain, and leave the tenth of the ore for his friends. He died. The son was avaricious and selfish He sought to cheat the Knockers, but he ruined himself by so doing. The "lode" failed; nothing answered with him; disappointed, he took to drink, squandered all the money his father had made, and died a beggar.

THE SPRIGGAN'S CHILD,

AS TOLD BY A CORNISH DROLL.

I 'LL tell you a tale, an you 've patience to hear an,
'Bout the Spriggans, that swarm round Partinney still—
You knew Janey Tregeer, who lives in Brea Vean,
In the village just under the Chapel-Hill.

One afternoon she went out for to reap,
And left the child in the cradle asleep :
Janey took good care to cover the fire ;—
Turn'd down the brandis on the baking-ire (iron),
Swept up the ashes on the hearthstone,
And so left the child in the house all alone—
The boys had all on 'em gone away,
Some to work and some to play
Janey work'd in the field as gay as a lark,
And when she came home it was nearly dark ;
The first thing she saw when she open'd the door
Was the cradle upset—all the straw on the floor.

But no child in sight—
She search'd all round—
Still no child was found :
And it got dark night
So great was Jane's fright,
That for more than an hour
She hadn't the power
To strike a light.

However, she kindled the fire at last,
And threw in a faggot to make a blast.

As she stoop'd over the wood-corner stone,
She heard a sound 'tween a cry and a moan—
  It clearly came from a bundle of ferns—
    The two bigger boy's bed—
  And there, sure enough, as frighten'd she turns,
    Janey saw the child's head.

'Twas very queer. How the child got there,
      Nobody could say ;
Yet ever since that day, the babe pined away—
It was at all times crying, or sucking, or eating,
And blinking and peeping, when it ought to be sleeping,
    But seldom it closed its eyes.
    Jane said for a child it look'd too wise—
    That she thought it a changeling
    She didn't disguise—
    And often and often she gave it a beating,
    To stop—but she couldn't—its cussed bleating.

      Janey resolved to work the spell,
        And whene'er she could stay,
      She bath'd the brat in the Chapel Well—
        Which he thought rare play.

On the three first Wednesdays in flow'ry May
She plunged it deep at the dawn of day—
Pass'd it slowly three times against the sun,
Went three times round,—and when all was done,
The imp of a child roar'd aloud for fun.
        No tongue can tell
          The trouble it gave her
          To dip the shaver,
        And work the spell.

From Brea to Chapel-Uny is a mile or more,
And surely it tried Janey's patience sore
To trudge forth and back from the Chapel Well,
With this brat on her back, to work the spell.

She wish'd it dead ; but it wouldn't die ·
It ate its bread, it would pine and cry ;
And Janey was nearly beside herself
With this plague of her life—this wicked elf.

    Well, one rainy day,—as it rains in May,—
      Janey set out with the child in her arms
      Once more to work the holy charms

When very close to the top of the hill,
    Where she was sure there was nobody near,
    She heard the strangest voice in her ear,
    Saying these words, quite clear and shrill—
" *Tredrill, Tredrill ! thy wife and children greet thee well.*"

    Oh, Janey's heart-strings were like to crack,
    When up spake the thing in her arms, good lack !—
        " For wife or child little care I,
        They may laugh,
        Or they may cry,—
        While milk I quaff,
        When I am dry—
        Get of my pap my fill
        Whenever I will,
        On the dowdy's back ride,
        With my legs astride,
        When we work the spell
        At the Chapel Well "

Janey dropp'd the cussed thing on the ground,
And turn'd round, and round, and round ;
You may be sure she was in a fright
To hear the sound, and nobody in sight,
And to hear a child talk
Months before it could walk.
    She has said o'er and o'er,
        And I am sure you can't wonder,
    'Twouldn't frighten her more,
        Had the rocks burst asunder,
        And the earth belch'd forth thunder.

When Janey at length got over the fright
From hearing the sound and nobody in sight,
And the brat which lay crying, as if it was dying,
Talking out like a man of his wife and his child,
She felt all bedazzled as if she was wild—
Took the brat by the arm, flung it over her shoulder—
Wouldn't believe it her child if the parson had told her—
        Thought the devil was in it,
          As she ran the hill down,
        Without stopping a minute
          Till she came to Brea town.

The old women came out, and all on 'em agreed
'Twas the strangest thing that ever they seed ,
They stood in a row, and each one had a word—
'Twas the wonderfull'st story that ever they heard ;
'Twas a Spriggan's brat—they were all sure of that—
No more like Jane's child than an old ram-cat.
She must beat it black, she must beat it blue,
Bruise its body all o'er with the heel of her shoe—
Then lay it alone beneath the church stile,
And keep out of hearing and sight for a while—
When every one said, as every one thought,
That Janey's child would again be brought :
Some said 'twould be living—some said 'twould be dead—
But the Spriggan's base brat she no longer need dread.

* Jane beat the babe black,
  And she beat the babe blue,
    On the ashes' pile before the door ;
    And she would have beaten it ten times more,
  But out of her hand she lost her shoe,
  Struck away all at once—by she couldn't tell who.

The brat had roar'd—it could roar no more—
  So they carried it off to the old church stile,
And laid it under the stones—some swore
  That when placed on the earth it was seen to smile—
Then all turn'd back, and kept far out of sight :—
  And Janey declared she was almost wild ·
But they kept her back till the turn o' the night,
  When she rush'd to the stile and found her own child.

'Twas there, sure enough, her own dear child :—
  But when first she saw it,
  She did not know it—
It look'd so frighten'd—it seem'd so wild.

    Then the old women said,
      If it keeps its wits,
    We 're sadly afraid
      The poor babe will have fits.

A friend writes me .—" I saw an account in a newspaper the
other day of an Irishwoman who was brought before the magistrates, in New York, for causing the death of a child by making it
stand on *hot coals*, to try if it were her own truly-begotten child,
or a changeling. I think the notion was, that her own child

would stand fire, but an imp would either die, to all *appearance*, or be spirited away   This is much worse than the plan of the woman of Brea Vean, who put the brat on the ashes' pile, and beat it black with the broom." *

THE PISKIES' CHANGELING.

THIS story is told by Mr T. Q. Couch, as an example of the folk-lore of a Cornish village, in "Notes and Queries," under the name of " Coleman Gray . "—

" There is a farmhouse of some antiquity with which my family have a close connection ; and it is this circumstance, more than any other, that has rendered this tradition concerning it more interesting to us, and better remembered than many other equally romantic and authentic.   Close to this house, one day, a little miserable-looking bantling was discovered alone, unknown, and incapable of making its wants understood.   It was instantly remembered by the finder, that this was the way in which the piskies were accustomed to deal with those infants of their race for whom they sought human protection ; and it would have been an awful circumstance if such a one were not received by the individual so visited.   The anger of the piskies would be certain, and some dreful calamity must be the result , whereas, a kind welcome would probably be attended with great good fortune. The miserable plight of this stranger, therefore, attracted attention and sympathy.   The little unconscious one was admitted as one of the family.   Its health was speedily restored, and its renewed strength, activity, intelligence, and good-humour, caused it to become a general favourite   It is true the stranger was often found to indulge in odd freaks ; but this was accounted for by a recollection of its pedigree, which was not doubted to be of the piskie order.   So the family prospered, and had banished the thought that the foundling would ever leave them   There was to the front door of this house, a hatch, which is a half-door, that is kept closed when the whole door behind it is open, and it then serves as a guard against the intrusion of dogs, hogs, and ducks, while air and light are freely admitted.   This little being was one day leaning over the top of this hatch, and looking wistfully outward, when a clear voice was heard to proceed from a neigh-

* " The Father of Eighteen Elves," in " Legends of Iceland," is, in all its chief features, similar to this story, even to the beating him without mercy   " Icelandic Legends. Collected by John Arnason . Translated by George E J Powell and Eiríkur Magnússon " Bentley, 1864

bouring part of the *townplace*, calling, ' Coleman Gray, Coleman Gray ! ' The piskie immediately started up, and with a sudden laugh, clapped its hands, exclaiming, ' Aha ! my daddy is come ! ' It was gone in a moment, never to be seen again."

THE PIXIES OF DARTMOOR.

THERE is a celebrated piskie haunt at Costellas in Cornwall (says Mrs Bray), where they have been seen sitting in a ring —the men smoking after the most approved fashion of the Dutch burgomaster, and the women spinning, perhaps in emulation of the frugal vrow.

I never heard of this place. Like the rest of the "good people," piskies are fond of music, and the sound of their "harp and pipe and symphony," is occasionally heard at nightfall. It is said that a man once passing one of the piskie rings, and hearing them dancing and singing within it, threw a large stone into the midst of the circle, when the music at once ceased and a dreadful shriek arose.

The appearance of the *pixies* of Dartmoor is said to resemble that of a bale or bundle of rags. In this shape they decoy children to their unreal pleasure. A woman, on the northern borders of the moor, was returning home late on a dark evening, accompanied by two children, and carrying a third in her arms, when, on arriving at her own door, she found one missing. Her neighbours, with lanthorns, immediately set out in quest of the lost child; whom they found sitting under a large oak-tree, well known to be a favourite haunt of the pixies. He declared that he had been led away by two large bundles of rags, which had remained with him until the lights appeared, when they immediately vanished *

The pixies of Dartmoor, notwithstanding their darker character, aided occasionally in household work. A washerwoman was one morning greatly surprised, on coming down-stairs, to find all her clothes neatly washed and folded. She watched the next evening, and observed a pixie in the act of performing this kind office for her . but she was ragged and mean in appearance, and Betty's gratitude was sufficiently great to induce her to prepare a yellow petticoat and a red cap for the obliging pixie.

* For additional information respecting the pixies of the banks of the Tamar and the Tavy, the reader is referred to Mrs Bray s " Traditions, Legends, Superstitions, and Sketches of Devonshire."

THE FAIRY FAIR IN GERMOE.

BAL LANE in Germoe was a notorious place for piskies. One night Daniel Champion and his comrade came to Godolphin Bridge,—they were a little bit " overtook " with liquor. They said that when they came to " Bal Lane," they found it covered all over from end to end, and the Small People holding a fair there with all sorts of merchandise—the prettiest sight they ever met with. Champion was sure he saw his child there ; for a few nights before, his child in the evening was as beautiful a one as could be seen anywhere, but in the morning was changed ·for one as ugly and wizened as could be ; and he was sure the Small People had done it. Next day, telling the story at Croft Gothal, his comrade was knocked backward, thrown into the bob-pit, and just killed. Obliged to be carried to his home, Champion followed, and was telling of their adventure with the Small People, when one said, " Don't speak about them , they 're wicked, spiteful devils " No sooner were the words uttered than the speaker was thrown clean over stairs and bruised dreadfully, —a convincing proof to all present of the reality of the existence of the Small Folks.

ST MARGERY AND THE PISKIES.

WE have no reliable information of the birth, parentage, or education of Margery Daw, but we have a nursery rhyme which clearly indicates that she must have been a sloven—perhaps an ancient picture of a literary lady, who was by her sad habit reduced to extreme necessity

See saw, Margery Daw,

clearly indicates a lazy woman rocking herself, either in deep thought, or for want of thought.

Sold her bed and lay on the straw ;

this was stage the first of her degradation.

She sold her straw and lay in the smut,

the second and final stage, which may well induce the poet to inquire—

Was not she a dirty slut ?

Another version of Margery's story is more distinct as to her end :—

G

See saw,
Margery Daw,
Sold her bed
And lay on the straw ;
She sold her straw,
And lay upon hay,
So *piskies* came
And carried her away.

A friend, in writing to me on this dirty Cornish saint, is disposed to regard St Margery Daw as a very devout Roman Catholic, and to refer the version of her story which I have given first to the strong feeling shown by many Protestants against those pious women who rejected the finery of the world, and submitted for the sake of their souls to those privations which formed at one time the severe rule of conventual life. Margery and the fairies are supposed to have left England together at the time of the Reformation, but she has left her name to several Cornish mines.

THE FAIRY REVELS ON THE "GUMP," ST JUST.

LONG has the Gump been the reputed playground of the Small People. Many of the good old people were permitted to witness their revels, and for years they delighted their grandchildren with tales of the songs they have heard, and of the sights they have seen. To many of their friends those fairies have given small but valuable presents ; but woe to the man or woman who would dare to intrude upon the ground occupied by them at the time of their high festivals. There was a covetous old hunks in St Just—never mind his name, he was severely punished, let that suffice—well, this old fellow had heard so much of the riches displayed by the little people, when holding holiday on the Gump, that he resolved to get some of the treasures. He learned all he could learn from his neighbours, but kept his intention to himself. It was during the harvest-moon—the night was a softened day—and everything abroad on such a night should have been in harmony with its quiet brilliancy. But here was a dark soul passing along, making a small eclipse with his black shadow. The old man stole towards the rendezvous of the " good people," as some were fond of calling them, anxiously looking out for the treasures which he coveted. At length, when he had not advanced far on the Gump, he heard music of the most ravishing kind. Its influence was of a singularly mysterious character. As the notes were

solemn and slow, or quick and gay, the old man was moved from
tears to laughter ; and on more than one occasion he was compelled to dance in obedience to the time. Notwithstanding that
he was almost bewildered by the whirling motion to which he was
compelled, the old man " kept his wits awake," and waited his
opportunity to seize some fairy treasure ; but as yet nothing
remarkable had presented itself   The music appeared to surround
him, and, as he thought, to come closer to him than it was at first ;
and although its sound led him to believe that the musicians were
on the surface, he was impressed with an idea that they were
really beneath the earth   Eventually there was a crash of sound,
startling beyond description, and the hill before him opened.   All
was now ablaze with variously-coloured lights.   Every blade of
grass was hung with lamps, and every furze bush was illuminated
with stars   Out from the opening in the hill marched a host of
spriggans, as if to clear the road.   Then came an immense number of musicians playing on every kind of instrument.   These were
followed by troop after troop of soldiers, each troop bearing aloft
their banner, which appeared to spread itself, to display its
blazonry, without the assistance of any breeze.   All these arranged
themselves in order over the ground, some here and some there.
One thing was not at all to our friend's liking ; several hundreds
of the most grotesque of the spriggans placed themselves so as to
enclose the spot on which he was standing.   Yet, as they were
none of them higher than his shoe-tie, he thought he could
" squash " them easily with his foot if they were up to any mischief, and so he consoled himself.   This vast array having disposed
of themselves, first came a crowd of servants bearing vessels of silver
and vessels of gold, goblets cut out of diamonds, rubies, and other
precious stones.   There were others laden, almost to overflowing,
with the richest meats, pastry, preserves, and fruits.   Presently the
ground was covered with tables and everything was arranged in
the most systematic order,—each party falling back as they disposed of their burdens.

The brilliancy of the scene nearly overpowered the old man ;
but, when he was least prepared for it, the illumination became a
thousand times more intense.   Out of the hill were crowding
thousands upon thousands of lovely ladies and gentlemen, arrayed
in the most costly attire.   He thought there would be no end to
the coming crowd.   By and by, however, the music suddenly
changed, and the harmonious sounds which fell upon his ears
appeared to give new life to every sense   His eyes were clearer,
his ears quicker, and his sense of smell more exquisite.

The odours of flowers, more delicious than any he had ever smelt, filled the air. He saw, without any disturbing medium, the brilliant beauty of the thousands of ladies who were now upon the Gump ; and their voices were united in one gush of song, which was clear as silver bells—a hymeneal symphony of the utmost delicacy. The words were in a language unknown to him, but he saw they were directed towards a new group now emerging from the hill.

First came a great number of female children clothed in the whitest gauze, strewing flowers on the Gump. These were not dead or cut flowers, for the moment they touched the ground they took root and grew. These were followed by an equally large number of boys, holding in their hands shells which appeared to be strung like harps, and from which they brought forth murmurs of melody, such as angels only could hope to hear and live. Then came—and there was no end to their coming—line upon line of little men clothed in green and gold, and by and by a forest of banners, which, at a signal, were all furled. Then, seated on thrones, carried upon a platform above the heads of the men, came a young prince and princess who blazed with beauty and jewels, as if they were suns amidst a skyey host of stars. There was much ceremonial marching to and fro, but eventually the platform was placed upon a mound on the Gump, which was now transformed into a hillock of roses and lilies ; and around this all the ladies and gentlemen walked, bowing, and each one saying something to the princess and the prince,—passing onward and taking their seats at the tables. Although no man could count the number of this fairy host, there was no confusion; all the ladies and gentlemen found, as if by instinct, their places. When all were seated, a signal was given by the prince ; servants in splendid liveries placed tables crowded with gold-plate and good things on the platform, and every one, the prince and princess included, began to feast with a will. Well, thought the old man, now is my time ; if I could only crawl up to the prince's table, I should have a catch sure enough, and become a rich man for life. With his greedy mind fixed on this one object, and unobservant of everything else, he crouched down, as though by so doing he could escape observation, and very slowly and stealthily advanced amongst the revellers. He never saw that thousands of spriggans had thrown little strings about him, and that they still held the ends of the threads. The presence of this selfish old mortal did not in any way discompose the assembly ; they ate and drank and were as merry as though no human eye was looking on them. The old man was wondrous cautious lest he should disturb the feasters, consequently a long time was spent in getting, as he desired, to the back of the mound At length he reached the desired spot, and, to his surprise, all was dark and gloomy behind him, but in front of the mound all was a blaze of light Crawling like a serpent on his belly, trembling with anxiety, the old man advanced close to the prince and princess. He was somewhat startled to find, as he looked out over the mound, that every one of the thousands of eyes in that multitude was fixed on his He gazed a while, all the time screwing his courage up ; then, as a boy who would catch a butterfly, he took off his hat and carefully raised it, so as to cover the prince, the princess, and their costly table, and, when about to close it upon them, a shrill whistle was heard, the old man's hand was fixed powerless in the air, and everything became dark around him.

Whir ! whir ! whir ! as if a flight of bees were passing him, buzzed in his ears. Every limb, from head to foot, was as if stuck full of pins and pinched with tweezers. He could not move, he was changed to the ground. By some means he had rolled down the mound, and lay on his back with his arms outstretched, arms and legs being secured by magic chains to the earth ; therefore, although he suffered great agony, he could not stir, and, strange enough, his tongue appeared tied by cords, so that he could not call. He had lain, no one can tell how long, in this sad plight, when he felt as if a number of insects were running over him, and by the light of the moon he saw standing on his nose one of the spriggans, who looked exceedingly like a small dragon-fly. This little monster stamped and jumped with great delight ; and having had his own fun upon the elevated piece of humanity, he laughed most outrageously, and shouted, " Away, away, I smell the day ! " Upon this the army of small people, who had taken possession of the old man's body, moved quickly away, and left our discomfited hero alone on the Gump Bewildered, or, as he said, bedevilled, he lay still to gather up his thoughts. At length the sun arose, and then he found that he had been tied to the ground by myriads of gossamer webs, which were now covered with dew, and glistened like diamonds in the sunshine.

He shook himself, and was free. He rose wet, cold, and ashamed. Sulkily he made his way to his home. It was a long time before his friends could learn from the old man where he had passed the night, but, by slow degrees, they gathered the story I have related to you.

THE FAIRY FUNERAL.

THIS and two or three other bits of folk-lore were communicated to the *Athenæum* by me, when Ambrose Merton (Mr
Thoms) solicited such contributions.

The parish church of Lelant is curiously situated amidst hills
of blown sand, near the entrance of the creek of Hayle. The
sandy waste around the church is called the Towen ; and this
place was long the scene of the midnight gambols of the Small
People. In the adjoining village—or, as it is called in Cornwall,
the " church-town "—lived an old woman who had been, according to her own statement, a frequent witness to the use made by
the fairies of the Towen Her husband, also, had seen some
extraordinary scenes on the same spot. From her—to me, oft-
repeated description—I get the following tale :—It was the fishing season ; and Richard had been to St Ives for some fish. He
was returning, laden with pilchards, on a beautiful moonlight
night , and as he ascended the hill from St Ives, he thought he
heard the bell of Lelant Church tolling. Upon a nearer approach,
he saw lights in the church , and most distinctly did the bell
toll—not with its usual clear sound, but dull and heavy, as
if it had been muffled, scarcely awakening any echo. Richard
walked towards the church, and cautiously, but not without fear,
approaching one of the windows, looked in. At first he could not
perceive any one within, nor discover whence the light came by
which everything was so distinctly illuminated. At length he
saw, moving along the centre aisle, a funeral procession. The
little people who crowded the aisle, although they all looked very
sorrowful, were not dressed in any mourning garments—so far
from it, they wore wreaths of little roses, and carried branches of
the blossoming myrtle. Richard beheld the bier borne between
six—whether men or women he could not tell—but he saw that
the face of the corpse was that of a beautiful female, smaller than
the smallest child's doll. It was, Richard said, " as if it were a
dead seraph,"—so very lovely did it appear to him. The body
was covered with white flowers, and its hair, like gold threads,
was tangled amongst the blossoms. The body was placed within
the altar ; and then a large party of men, with picks and spades,
began to dig a little hole close by the sacramental table. Their
task being completed, others, with great care, removed the body
and placed it in the hole The entire company crowded around,
eager to catch a parting glimpse of that beautiful corpse, ere yet
it was placed in the earth As it was lowered into the ground,

they began to tear off their flowers and break their branches of myrtle, crying, " Our queen is dead ! our queen is dead ! " At length one of the men who had dug the grave threw a shovelful of earth upon the body ; and the shriek of the fairy host so alarmed Richard, that he involuntarily joined in it. In a moment, all the lights were extinguished, and the fairies were heard flying in great consternation in every direction. Many of them brushed past the terrified man, and, shrieking, pierced him with sharp instruments. He was compelled to save his life *by the most rapid flight.*

THE FAIRY REVEL.

R ICHARD also once witnessed a fairy revel in the Towen— upon which tables were spread, with the utmost profusion of gold and silver ornaments, and fruits and flowers. Richard, however, according to the statement of " Aunt Alcey " (the name by which his wife was familiarly called), very foolishly interrupted the feast by some exclamation of surprise ; whereas, had he but touched the end of a table with his finger, it would have been impossible for the fairy host to have removed an article, as that which has been touched by mortal fingers becomes to them accursed. As it was, the lovely vision faded before the eyes of the astonished labourer.

BETTY STOGS AND JAN THE MOUNSTER.

I N the " high counties," as the parishes of Morva, Zennor, and Towednack are called, there has long existed a tradition that the children of dirty, lazy, " courseying " women are often taken away by the Small People, carefully cleansed, and then returned—of course all the more beautiful for being washed by the fairies in morning-dew. This notion has evidently prevailed for many ages, and, like many an old tradition, it has been remodelled in each generation to adapt it to the conditions of the time. The following is but slightly modified in its principal characteristics from a story somewhat coarsely told, and greatly extended, by an old woman in Morva. A woman, up the higher side, called Betty Stogs, very nearly lost her baby a few months ago. Stogs was only a nickname, but every one knew her by that and no other. It was given to her because she was so untidy about the feet and legs She could not darn a hole in her stocking—the lazy slut could never knit one. Betty was always pulling the legs of her stockings down under her feet, that the holes in her heels might not be seen—as long as the tops would come under the garter—and she often gartered half-way down the leg to meet the necessities of the case. Betty was reared up in Towednack, at no great distance from Wheal Reeth, at which Bal the old man, her father, worked. He also farmed a few acres of land, and, " out of core," he and his daughter worked on it. The old people used to say—they wouldn't put the poor innocent chield to work to Bal, for fear the great rough heathens from Lelant might overcome her ; so they kept her at home, and the old man would brag how his Betty could cut furze and turf. Instead of staying at home in the evenings, Betty was always racing round the lanes to class-meetings ; for she had been a "professor ever since she was a chield." Betty was an only child, and the old people had saved a little money, and they hoped some one "above the. common " would marry her. In Higher Side there lived a man called Jan the Mounster (monster), and, tempted by the bit of money, he resolved to lay himself out to catch Betty. Jan became a converted character—he met in the same class with Betty, and expressed himself as being "so fond of the means of grace." Things went on in this way for some time, and it was found that Betty " had met with a misfortune." The old people were now in a great hurry to marry their daughter, and promised Jan money enough to buy a set of cheene (china), and lots of beautiful clome (earthenware) ; but Mounster required more than this, and fought off He left the "people," that he mightn't be read out. He said he was heartily sick of the lot, told strange stories about their doings, and became as bad a character as ever. Time advanced, and Betty's mother —who was herself a wretchedly dirty woman, and, as people said, too fond of the " drop of drink"—saw that she must lose no chance of making her daughter an honest woman So she went to Penzance and bought a new bed—a real four-poster—a new dresser, painted bright lead and liver colour—an eight-day clock, in a painted mahogany case—a mass of beautiful clome—and a glass milk-cup. When all these things were ranged in a cottage, Jan was well enough pleased with them, and hung his " great turnip of a watch " up in the middle of the dresser, to see how it would look. When he had satisfied himself, he told the old woman he would marry Betty out of hand, if she would give them their great pretty, bright, warming-pan to hang opposite the door. This was soon settled, and Jan the Mounster and Betty Stogs were married.

In a little time the voice of a baby was heard in Jan's cottage, but the poor child had no cradle, only a " costan" (a straw and bramble basket) ; and, in addition to the ordinary causes of neglect, another cause was introduced—Betty took to diink. A great, nasty suss of a woman, who went about pretending to sell crochet-work, but in reality to sell gin—which she kept in a bottle under the dirty rags, which she called " the most beautiful croshar-work collars and cuffs, that all the ladies in the towns and up the country wear on Sundays and high holidays "—formed a close acquaintance with Jan's wife. The result was, things went from bad to worse. Jan was discontented, and went to Bal, and returned from Bal always a sullen man. One day Betty had to bake some bread— she had never before done so, as her mother had always attended to that job. Jan had left his watch hanging to the dresser, that Betty might know the time All went well till the middle of the day, and, just as the bread was ready to put down, in came the crochet-woman First Betty had a noggin of gin—she then had her fortune told—and because she was promised no end of good luck and the handsomest children in the country, and Jan the best luck in tribute-pitches, the kettle was boiled, and some pork fried for the fortune-teller.

All this time the dough was forgotten, and it was getting sour and heavy. At last, when the woman went away, the lump of sour " leven " was put down to bake. The neglected child got troublesome, and as Jan would be home early to supper, Betty was in a great hurry to get things done To quiet the child, she gave it Jan's watch ; and, that it might be the better pleased, she opened it, " that the dear chield might see the pretty little wheels spinning round." In a short time the " machine " was thrown down in the ashes, and it, of course, stopped. Betty, at last, wished to know the time ; she then found the watch clogged full of dirt. To put the thing to rights she washed it out in the kettle of dish-water, which had not been changed for two or three days, and was thick with salt pilchard-bones, and potato-skins. She did her best to clean the watch, for she was now terribly afraid of Jan, and she wiped all the little wheels, as far as she could reach, with the corner of the dishcloth, but the confounded thing would not go. She had to bake the bread by guess; and, therefore, when she took it up, it was as black as soot, and as hard as a stone.

Jan came home ; and you may judge the temper he was in at finding things as they were, and his watch stopped. Betty swore to the deepest that she had never taken the thing into her hands. Next morning Jan got up early to go to Bal; and taking the burnt loaf, he tried to cut it with a knife, but it was in vain—as well try to cut a stone ; next he tried the dag (axe), and Mounster said it strook fire, and the dag never made the least mark in the crust.

The poor fellow had to go to his work without his breakfast, and to depend upon the share of a comrade's fuggun for dinner.

Next day, Friday, was pay-day, and Jan having got his pay, went to St Ives for bread, and took the precious watch with him to be set to rights. The watchmaker soon found out the complaint; here was a bit of fish-bone, there a piece of potato-paring; in one tooth a piece of worsted from a dishcloth, in another a particle of straw, and ashes everywhere

The murder was out; and that night Jan, having first drunk to excess in St Ives, went home and nearly murdered his wife. From this time Jan was drunk every day, and Betty was so as often as she could get gin. The poor child was left half the day to suck his thumbs, and to tumble and toss on the filthy rags in the old costan, without any one to look after it.

One day Betty was in a "courseying" mood, and went from house to house, wherever she could find a woman idle enough to gossip with her. Betty stayed away till dark—it was Jan's last core by day—and the poor child was left all alone

When she came home she was surprised not to hear the child, but she thought it might have cried itself to sleep, and was not concerned. At last, having lit the candle, she looked in the costan, and there was no child to be seen. Betty searched about, in and out, every place she could think of; still there were no signs of the child. This pretty well sobered Betty, and she remembered that she had to unlock the door to get into the cottage.

While yet full of fear and trembling to meet her husband, Jan came home from Bal. He was, of course, told that his "croom of a chield was lost." He didn't believe a word of what Betty told him, but he went about and called up all the neighbours, who joined him in the search. They spent the night in examining every spot around the house and in the village—all in vain.

After daybreak they were all assembled in deep and earnest consultation, when the cat came running into the house, with her tail on end, and mewing anxiously. She ran forth and back round a brake of furze, constantly crying, as if she wished the people to follow her. After a long time some one thought of going after the cat, and in the middle of the furze-brake, on a beautiful green, soft spot of mossy grass, was the baby sleeping, "as sweet as a little nut," wrapped carefully up in some old dry gowns, and all its clothes clean and dry. When they unwrapped the child, they found he was covered over with bright flowers, as we place them round a babe in the coffin. He had a bunch of violets in his dear little hands, and there were wallflowers and primroses, and balm and mint spread over his body. The furze was high all around, so that no cold wind could reach the infant Every one declared that the child never looked so handsome before. It was plain enough, said the old women, that the Small People had taken the child and washed it from top to toe ; that their task of cleansing the babe was a long one, and that the sun arose before they could finish it , that they had placed the child where it was found, intending to take it away the next night

They were never known to come for the babe, but every one said that this affair worked a great change in Betty Stogs and in Jan the Mounster. The cottage was kept tidy, the child clean ; and its father and mother drank less, and lived happier, for ever afterwards.

THE FOUR-LEAVED CLOVER.

NOT many years since a farmer lived in Bosfrancan in St Burrien, who had a very fine red-and-white cow called Daisey. The cow was always fat, with her dewlaps and udder sweeping the grass. Daisey held her milk from calf to calf; had an udder like a bucket, yet she would never yield more than a gallon or so of milk, when one might plainly see that she had still at least two gallons more in her udder. All at once, when the milk was in full flow, she would give a gentle bleat, *cock up* her ears, and the milk would stop at once If the milkmaid tried to get any more from her after that, she would up foot, kick the bucket, and spill all the milk, yet stand as still as a stock, and keep chewing her cud all the time Everybody would have thought the cow bewitched, if she hadn't been always fat and held her milk all the year round , besides, everything prospered with the farmer, and all the other cows had more milk than any of the neighbours'. No one could tell what the deuce could be the matter with Daisey ; and they tried to drive her to Burrien Church-town fair, that they might be rid of her, as she was always fit for the butchers. All the men and boys on the farm couldn't get her to Church-town. As fast as they drove her up Alsie Lane, she would take down Cotneywilley, through by the Crean, down the Bottoms, and up the Gilley, and be in the field again before the men and boys would be half way home.

One midsummer's day in the evening, the maid was later than usual milking, as she had been down to Penberth to the *games*. The stars were beginning to blink when she finished her task. Daisey was the last cow milked, and the bucket was so full she could scarcely lift it to her head. Before rising from the

milking-stool, the maid plucked up a handful of grass and clover
to put in the head of her hat, that she might carry the bucket the
steadier   She had no sooner placed the hat on her head, than
she saw hundreds and thousands of Small People swarming in all
directions about the cow, and dipping their hands into the milk,
taking it out on the clover blossoms and sucking them   The grass
and clover, all in blossom, reached to the cow's belly.   Hundreds
of the little creatures ran up the long grass and clover stems, with
buttercups, lady's smocks, convolvuluses, and foxglove flowers,
to catch the milk that Daisey let flow from her four teats, like a
shower, among them.   Right under the cow's udder the maid
saw one much larger than the others lying on his back, with his
heels cocked up to the cow's belly.   She knew he must be a
Piskie, because he was laughing, with his mouth open from ear to
ear   The little ones were running up and down his legs, filling
their cups, and emptying them into the Piskie's mouth.   Hundreds
of others were on Daisey's back, scratching her rump, and tickling
her round the horns and behind the ears.   Others were smooth-
ing down every hair of her shining coat into its place
    The milkmaid wasn't much startled to see them, as she had
so often heard of fairies, and rather wished to see them.   She
could have stayed for hours, she said, to look at them dancing
about among the clover, which they hardly bent any more than
the dew-drops.
    The cows were in the field called Park-an-Ventan, close under
the house.   Her mistress came out into the garden between the
field and the house, and called to know what was keeping the
maid so long.   When the maid told what she had seen, her mistress said she couldn't believe her unless she had found a four-leaved
grass.   Then the maid thought of the handful of grass in the
head of her hat.   In looking it over by the candlelight, she found
a bunch of three-leaved grass, and one stem with four leaves.
They knew that it was nothing strange that she should see the
Small People, but they didn't know what plan to take to get rid
of them, so that they might have the whole of Daisey's milk, till the
mistress told her mother about it.   Her mother was a very notable
old dame, who lived in Church-town.   The old woman knew all
about witches, fairies, and such things ; was noted for being a
sharp, careful old body ; for when she happened to break the eye
of her stocking darning-needle, she would take it to the blacksmith
that he might put a new eye to it.   The smith always charged her
twopence.   She would rather pay that than throw it away.
    Our Betty told her daughter that everybody knowed that the

Small People couldn't abide the smell of fish, nor the savour of salt or grease ; and advised her to rub the cow's udder with fish brine to drive the Small People away. Well, she did what her mammy told her to do. Better she had let it alone. From that time Daisey would yield all her milk, but she hadn't the half, nor quarter, so much as before, but took up her udder, so that one could hardly see it below her flanks. Every evening, as soon as the stars began to twinkle, the cow would go round the fields bleating and crying as if she had lost her calf; she became hair-pitched, and pined away to skin and bone before the next Burrien fair, when she was driven to Church-town and sold for next to nothing. I don't know what became of her afterwards ; but nothing throve with the farmer, after his wife had driven the Small People away, as it did before.

THE FAIRY OINTMENT.

MANY years since, there lived as housekeeper with a cele-brated squire, whose name is associated with the history of his native country, one Nancy Tregier There were many peculiarities about Nancy , and she was, being a favourite with her master, allowed to do much as she pleased. She was in fact a petted, and, consequently, a spoiled servant Nancy left Pen-deen one Saturday afternoon to walk to Penzance, for the purpose of buying a pair of shoes. There was an old woman, Jenny Trayer, living in Pendeen Cove—who had the reputation of being a witch—or, as some people mildly put it, "who had strange dealings ; " and with her Nancy desired, for sundry reasons best known to herself, to keep on the closest of terms So on this Saturday, Nancy first called on the old woman to inquire if she wished to have anything brought home from Penzance. Tom, the husband of Nancy's friend, did no work , but now and then he would go to sea for an hour or two and fish. It is true everybody gave Jenny just what she asked for her fish, out of pure fear. Sometimes they had a "venture" with the smugglers, who, in those days, carried on a roaring trade in Pendeen Cove. The old Squire was a justice ; but he winked very hard, and didn't know anything about the smugglers. Indeed, some ill-natured people—and there are always such to be found in any nook or corner—said Nancy often took her master home a choice bottle of Cogniac , even a case of " Hollands " now and then ; and, especially when there was to be a particularly "great run," there were some beau-tiful silk handkerchiefs to be seen at the Squire's. But this is

beyond our story. When Nancy went into Jenny's cottage, Tom
was there, and right busy was she in preparing some ointment,
and touching her husband's eyes with it. this Jenny tried to hide
in the mouth of the oven at the side of the chimney. Tom got up
and said he must be off, and left the two women together. After
a few idle compliments, Jenny said that Nancy must have something to drink before she started for Penzance, and she went
to the *spence* for the bottles. Nancy, ever curious, seized the
moment, dipped her finger into the pot of green ointment, and,
thinking it was good for the eyes, she just touched her right eye
with it before Jenny returned. They then took a horn or two
together, and being thus spliced, Nancy started for Penzance.

Penzance Market was in those days entirely in the street; even
the old market-house had not yet an existence. Nancy walked
about doing a little business and a great deal of gossiping; when
amongst the standings in Market-Jew Street, whom should Nancy
see but Tom Trayer, picking off the standings, shoes, stockings,
hanks of yarn, and pewter spoons—indeed, some of all the sorts
of things which were for sale Nancy walked up to him, and,
taking him by the arm, said, " Tom! ar'then't ashamed to be here
carrying on such a game? However thee canst have the impudence, I can't think, to be picking the things from the standings
and putting them in thy pocket in broad daylight, and the people
all around thee." Tom looked very much surprised when Nancy
spoke to him. At last he said, " Is that you, Nancy?—which eye
can you see me upon?" Nancy shut her left eye, this made no
difference; she then shut her right eye, and, greatly to her surprise, she saw all the people, but she no longer saw Tom She
opened her right eye, and there was Tom as before She winked,
and winked, and was surprised, you may be sure, to find that she
could not see Tom with either eye. " Now, Nancy," said Tom,
" right or left." " Well," said Nancy, " 'tis strange; but there is
something wrong with my left eye." *

" Oh, then, you see me with the right, do you?"

Then Tom put his finger on her right eye, and from that
moment she was blind on that side.

On her way home, Nancy was always going off the road on
her blind side, but the hedges kept her from wandering far away.
On the downs near Pendeen there were no hedges, so Nancy
wandered into a furze brake,—night came on, she could not find
her way out, and she was found in it the next morning fast asleep.

* The tale, " Nursing a Fairy," p. 83, where a similar incident occurs, will be
remembered.

The old Squire was out hunting in the early morning, according to his usual custom.   In passing along the road leading to Carn-yorth, he saw a woman's knitting-work hanging on a bramble, and the yarn from the stocking leading away into the brake.   He took the yarn in his hand and followed it until he came to the old woman, who had the ball in her pocket.   When the Squire awakened the old woman, she told him the story which I have told you.   Her master, however, said that he didn't believe she had been into Penzance at all, but that she had stayed in the Cove and got drunk . that when dark night came, she had endeavoured to find her way home,—lost her road,—fallen down, and probed her eye out on a furze bush, and then gone off in drunken unconsciousness   Nancy told her master that he was no better than an unbelieving heathen ; and to the day of her death she protested that Tom Trayer put her eye out.   Jenny's ointment is said to have been made with a four-leaved clover, gathered at a certain time of the moon.   This rendered Fairyland visible, and made men invisible

Another version of this story, varying in a few details, was given me by a gentleman, a native of St Levan.   It is as follows ·—

HOW JOAN LOST THE SIGHT OF HER EYE.

JOAN was housekeeper to Squire Lovell, and was celebrated for her beautiful knitting.   One Saturday afternoon Joan wished to go to Penzance to buy a pair of shoes for herself, and some things for the Squire   So the weather being particularly fine, away she trudged.

Joan dearly loved a bit of gossip, and always sought for company.   She knew Betty Trenance was always ready for a jaunt : to be sure, everybody said Betty was a witch ; but, says Joan, " Witch or no witch, she shall go ; bad company is better than none."

Away went Joan to Lemorna, where Betty lived   Arrived at Betty's cottage, she peeped through the latch-hole (the finger-hole), and saw Betty rubbing some green ointment on the children's eyes.   She watched till Betty Trenance had finished, and noticed that she put the salve on the inner end of the chimney stool, and covered it over with a rag.

Joan went in, and Betty was delighted, sure enough, to see her, and sent the children out of the way   But Betty couldn't walk to Penzance, she was suffering pain, and she had been taking milk and suet, and brandy and rue, and she must have some more   So away went Betty to the other room for the bottle.

Joan seized the moment, and taking a very small bit of the ointment on her finger, she touched her right eye with it   Betty came with the bottle,

and Joan had a drink ; when she looked round she was surprised to see
the house swarming with small people. They were playing all sorts of
planks on the key-beams and rafters　Some were swinging on cobwebs,
some were riding the mice, and others were chasing them into and out of
the holes in the thatch　Joan was surprised at the sight, and thought she
must have a four-leaved clover about her

However, without stopping to take much drink, she started alone for
Penzance. She had wasted, as it was, so much time, that it was nearly
dark when she reached the market

After having made her purchases, and as she was about to leave the
market, who should Joan spy but Betty's husband, Tom Trenance　There
he was, stealing about in the shadows, picking from the standings, shoes
and stockings from one, hanks of yarn from another, pewter spoons from a
third, and so on　He stuffed these things into capacious pockets, and yet
no one appeared to notice Tom.

Joan went forth to him.

" Aren't ye ashamed to be here in the dark carrying on such a game ?"

" Is that you, Dame Joan, ' says Tom ; " which eye can you see me
upon ?"

After winking, Joan said she could see Tom plain enough with her
right eye.

She had no sooner said the word than Tom Trenance pointed his finger
to her eye, and she lost the sight of it from that hour.

" The work of the world " had Joan to find her way out of Penzance.
She couldn't keep the road, she was always tumbling into the ditch on her
blind side　When near the Fawgan, poor Joan, who was so weary that she
could scarcely drag one leg after the other, prayed that she might find a
quiet old horse on which she might ride home

Her desire was instantly granted. There, by the roadside, stood an old,
bony white horse, spanned with its halter.

Joan untied the halter from the legs and placed it on the head of the
horse ; she got on the hedge, and seated herself on the horse's back.

There she was mounted, " Gee wup, gee wup . k'up, k'up, k'up "
The horse would not budge. Busy were Joan's heels rattling against the
ribs of the poor horse, and thwack, thwack went a thorn-stick over his tail,
and by and by the old blind brute began to walk.　Joan beat, and kicked,
and k'uped, and coaxed, the horse went but little faster until it got to the
top of the hill

Then away, away, like the wind it went through Toldava Lanes, and it
swelled out until the horse became as high as the tower.　Over hedges and
ditches, across all the corners that came into the road, on went the horse.
Joan held on by the mane with both hands, and shouted, " Woa ! woa !
woey '" until she could shout no longer.

At length they came to Toldava Moor ; the " ugly brute " took right away down towards the fowling-pool, when Joan, fearing he might plunge in and drown her, let go her hold.

The wind was blowing so strong, and the pair were going so fast against it, that Joan was lifted off, over the hindquarters of the horse, and by luck she fell soft on the rushes at the very edge of the fowling-pool.

When she looked up, Joan saw whatever she had been riding going down the "bottom" in a blaze of fire, and the devil riding after, with lots of men, horses, and hounds, all without heads. All the marketing was lost , and in getting through the bogs, Joan had her shoes dragged from her feet. At last she got to Trove Bottoms, and seeing the Bougé (sheep-house), she clambered over the hedge as she best could ; got into it, and laying herself down amongst the sheep, she soon fell fast asleep, thoroughly wearied out.

She would have slept for a week, I believe, if she had not been disturbed But, according to custom on Sunday morning, the Squire and his boys came out to the Downs to span the sheep, and there, greatly to their surprise, they found her.

They got the miserable woman home between them. The Squire charged her with having got drunk, and said her eye had been scratched out by a furze-bush ; but Joan never wandered from her story, and to the day of her death she told it to all young women, warning them never to meddle with "Fairy Salve "

THE OLD WOMAN WHO TURNED HER SHIFT.

IN a lone house—situated not far from the hill on which now stands Knill's Steeple, as it is called—which was then known as Chyanwheal, or the *House on the Mine*, lived a lone woman, the widow of a miner, said to have been killed in one of the very ancient " coffens," as the open mine-workings existing in this hill are termed. A village now bears this name, but it has derived it from this lone house. Whether it was that they presumed upon her solitude, or whether the old lady had given them some inducement, is not now known, but the spriggans of Trencrom Hill were in the habit of meeting almost every night in her cottage to divide their plunder. The old woman usually slept, or at least she pretended to sleep, during the visit of the spriggans. When they left, they always placed a small coin on the table by her bedside, and with this indeed the old woman was enabled to provide herself with not merely the necessaries of life, but to add thereto a few of those things which were luxuries to one in her position. The old lady, however, was not satisfied with this. She resolved to bide her time, and when the spriggans had an unusually large amount

H

of plunder, to make herself rich at once and for ever at their expense. Such a time at last arrived. The spriggans had gathered, we know not how much valuable gold and jewellery. It gleamed and glistened on the floor, and the old woman in bed looked on with a most covetous eye. After a while, it appears, the spriggans were not able to settle the question of division with their usual amicability. The little thieves began to quarrel amongst themselves.

Now, thought the old woman, is my time. Therefore huddling herself up under the bedclothes, she very adroitly contrived to turn her shift, and having completed the unfailing charm, she jumped from her bed, placed her hand on a gold cup, and exclaimed, " Thee shusn't hae one on 'em ! "

In affright the spriggans all scampered away, leaving their stolen treasure behind them The last and boldest of the spriggans, however, swept his hand over the old woman's only garment as he left the house. The old woman, now wealthy, removed in a little time from Chyanwheal to St Ives, and, to the surprise of every one, purchased property and lived like a gentlewoman. Whenever, however, she put on the shift which had secured her her wealth, she was tortured beyond endurance. The doctors and all the learned people used hard names to describe her pains, but the wise women knew all along that they came of the spriggans.

THE FAIRY WIDOWER.

NOT many years since a very pretty girl called Jenny Permuen lived in Towednack. She was of poor parents, and lived in service. There was a good deal of romance, or what the old people called nonsense, in Jenny She was always smartly dressed, and she would arrange wildflowers very gracefully in her hair. As a consequence, Jenny attracted much of the attention of the young men, and again, as a consequence, a great deal of envy from the young women. Jenny was, no doubt, vain , and her vanity, which most vain persons will say is not usual, was accompanied by a considerable amount of weakness on any point connected with her person. Jenny loved flattery, and being a poor, uneducated girl, she had not the genius necessary to disguise her frailty. When any man told her she was lovely, she quite admitted the truth of the assertion by her pleased looks. When any woman told her not to be such a fool as to believe such nonsense, her lips, and eyes too, seemed to say you are only jealous of me, and if there was a pool of water near, nature's mirror was speedily consulted to prove to herself that she was really the best-looking girl in the parish. Well, one day Jenny, who had been for some time out of a situation, was sent by her mother down to the lower parishes to "look for a place." Jenny went on merrily enough until she came to the four cross roads on the Lady Downs, when she discovered that she knew not which road to take. She looked first one way and then another, and she felt fairly puzzled, so she sat down on a boulder of granite, and began, in pure want of thought, to break off the beautiful fronds of ferns which grew abundantly around the spot she had chosen. It is hard to say what her intentions were, whether to go on, to return, or to remain where she was, so utterly indifferent did Jenny appear. Some say she was entirely lost in wild dreams of self-glorification. However, she had not sat long on this granite stone, when hearing a voice near her, she turned round and saw a young man.

"Well, young woman," says he, "and what are you after?"

"I am after a place, sir," says she.

"And what kind of a place do you want, my pretty young woman?" says he, with the most winning smile in the world.

"I am not particular, sir," says Jenny; "I can make myself generally useful."

"Indeed," says the stranger; "do you think you could look after a widower with one little boy?"

"I am very fond of children," says Jenny.

"Well, then," says the widower, "I wish to hire for a year and a day a young woman of your age, to take charge of my little boy."

"And where do you live?" inquired Jenny.

"Not far from here," said the man; "will you go with me and see?"

"An it please you to show me," said Jenny.

"But first, Jenny Permuen,"—Jenny stared when she found the stranger knew her name. He was evidently an entire stranger in the parish, and how could he have learnt her name, she thought. So she looked at him somewhat astonished. "Oh! I see, you suppose I didn't know you; but do you think a young widower could pass through Towednack and not be struck with such a pretty girl? Beside," he said, "I watched you one day dressing your hair in one of my ponds, and stealing some of my sweet-scented violets to put in those lovely tresses. Now, Jenny Permuen, will you take the place?"

"For a year and a day?" asked Jenny.

"Yes, and if we are pleased with each other then, we can renew the engagement."

"Wages," said Jenny.

The widower rattled the gold in his breeches-pocket.

"Wages! well, whatever you like to ask," said the man.

Jenny was charmed; all sorts of visions rose before her eyes, and without hesitation she said—

"Well, I'll take the place, sir; when must I come?"

"I require you now—my little boy is very unhappy, and I think you can make him happy again. You'll come at once?"

"But mother"——

"Never mind mother, I'll send word to her."

"But my clothes"——

"The clothes you have will be all you require, and I'll put you in a much gayer livery soon."

"Well, then," says Jane, "'tis a bargain"——

"Not yet," says the man; I've got a way of my own, and you must swear my oath."

Jenny looked frightened.

"You need not be alarmed," said the man, very kindly; "I only wish you to kiss that fern-leaf which you have in your hand, and say, 'For a year and a day I promise to stay.'"

"Is that all?" said Jenny; so she kissed the fern-leaf and said—

> "For a year and a day
> I promise to stay"

Without another word he walked forward on the road leading eastward Jenny followed him—she thought it strange that her new master never opened his lips to her all the way, and she grew very tired with walking. Still onward and onward he went, and Jenny was sadly weary and her feet dreadfully sore. At last poor Jenny began to cry. He heard her sob and looked round.

"Tired are you, poor girl? Sit down—sit down," says the man, and he took her by the hand and led her to a mossy bank. His kindness completely overcame her, and she burst into a flood of tears. He allowed her to cry for a few minutes, then taking a bunch of leaves from the bottom of the bank, he said, "Now I must dry your eyes, Jenny."

He passed the bunch of leaves rapidly first over one and then over the other eye.

The tears were gone. Her weariness had departed. She felt herself moving, yet she did not know that she had moved from the bank The ground appeared to open, and they were passing very rapidly under the earth. At last there was a pause.

" Here we are, Jenny," said he, "there is yet a tear of sorrow on your eyelids, and no human tears can enter our homes, let me wipe them away." Again Jenny's eyes were brushed with the small leaves as before, and, lo ! before her was such a country as she had never seen previously. Hill and valley were covered with flowers, strangely varied in colour, but combining into a most harmonious whole ; so that the region appeared sown with gems which glittered in a light as brilliant as that of the summer sun, yet as mild as the moonlight. There were rivers clearer than any water she had ever seen on the granite hills, and waterfalls and fountains ; while everywhere ladies and gentlemen dressed in green and gold were walking, or sporting, or reposing on banks of flowers, singing songs or telling stories. Oh ! it was a beautiful world

" Here we are at home," said Jenny's master ; and strangely enough he too was changed ; he was the most beautiful little man she had ever seen, and he wore a green silken coat covered with ornaments of gold. " Now," said he again, " I must introduce you to your little charge." He led Jenny into a noble mansion in which all the furniture was of pearl and ivory, inlaid with gold and silver, and studded with emeralds. After passing through many rooms, they came at length to one which was hung all over with lace, as fine as the finest cobweb, most beautifully worked with flowers ; and, in the middle of this room was a little cot made out of some beautiful sea-shell, which reflected so many colours that Jenny could scarcely bear to look at it She was led to the side of this, and she saw, as she said, " One of God's sweetest angels sleeping there " The little boy was so beautiful that she was ravished with delight.

" This is your charge," said the father ; " I am the king in this land, and I have my own reasons for wishing my boy to know something of human nature. Now you have nothing to do but to wash and dress the boy when he wakes, to take him to walk in the garden, and to put him to bed when he is weary."

Jenny entered on her duties, and gave, and continued to give, satisfaction. She loved the darling little boy, and he appeared to love her, and the time passed away with astonishing rapidity.

Somehow or other she had never thought of her mother. She had never thought of her home at all. She was happy and in luxury, and never reckoned the passing of time.

Howsoever happiness may blind us to the fact, the hours and days move onward. The period for which Jenny had bound herself was gone, and one morning she awoke and all was changed. She was sleeping in her own bed in her mother's cottage. Everything was strange to her, and she appeared strange to everybody. Numerous old gossips were called in to see Jenny, and to all Jenny told her strange tale alike. One day, old Mary Calineck of Zennor came, and she heard, as all the others had done, the story of the widower, and the baby, and the beautiful country. Some of the old crones who were there at the time said the girl was "gone clean daft." Mary looked very wise—"Crook your arm, Jenny," said she.

Jenny sat up in the bed and bent her arm, resting her hand on her hip.

" Now say, I hope my arm may never come uncrooked if I have told ye a word of a lie."

" I hope my arm may never come uncrooked if I have told ye a word of a lie," repeated Jenny

" Uncrook your arm," said Mary

Jenny stretched out her arm.

" It is truth the girl is telling," said Mary; "and she has been carried by the Small People to some of their countries under the hills."

" Will the girl ever come right in her mind?" asked her mother.

" All in good time," said Mary; "and if she will but be honest, I have no doubt but her master will take care that she never wants."

. Howbeit, Jenny did not get on very well in the world. She married and was discontented and far from happy Some said she always pined after the fairy widower. Others said they were sure she had misbehaved herself, or she would have brought back lots of gold. If Jenny had not dreamt all this, while she was sitting picking ferns on the granite boulder, she had certainly had a very strange adventure.

THE SMALL PEOPLE'S GARDENS.

IF the adventurous traveller who visits the Land's End district will go down as far as he can on the south-west side of the Logan Rock Cairn, and look over, he will see, in little sheltered places between the cairns, close down to the water's edge, beautifully green spots, with here and there some ferns and cliff-pinks These are the gardens of the Small People, or, as they are called by the natives, Small Folk. They are beautiful little creatures, who appear to pass a life of constant enjoyment amongst their own favourite flowers. They are harmless ; and if man does not meddle with them when they are holding their fairs—which are indeed high festivals—the Small Folk never interfere with man or anything belonging to him. They are known to do much good, especially when they discover a case of oppressed poverty; but they do it in their own way. They love to do good for its own sake, and the publication of it in any way draws down their censure, and sometimes severe anger, on the object whom it was their purpose to serve. To prove that those lovely little creatures are no dream, I may quote the words of a native of St Levan :—

"As I was saying, when I have been to sea close under the cliffs, of a fine summer's night, I have heard the sweetest of music, and seen hundreds of little lights moving about amongst what looked like flowers. Ay! and they are flowers too, for you may smell the sweet scent far out at sea. Indeed, I have heard many of the old men say, that they have smelt the sweet perfume, and heard the music from the fairy gardens of the Castle, when more than a mile from the shore." Strangely enough, you can find no flowers but the sea-pinks in these lovely green places by day, yet they have been described by those who have seen them in the midsummer moonlight as being covered with flowers of every colour, all of them far more brilliant than any blossoms seen in any mortal garden.

ST LEVAN FAIRIES.

YEARS since—the time is past now—the green outside the gate at the end of Trezidder Lane was a favourite place with the Small Folks on which to hold their fairs. One might often see the rings in the grass which they made in dancing, where they footed it. Mr Trezillian was returning late one night from Penzance ; when he came near the gate, he saw a number of little creatures spinning round and round. The sight made him lightheaded, but he could not resist the desire to be amongst them, so he got off his horse. In a moment they were all over him like a swarm of bees, and he felt as if they were sticking needles and pins into him His horse ran off, and he didn't know what to do, till, by good luck, he thought of what he had often heard, so he turned his glove inside out, threw it amongst the Small Folk, and ere the glove reached the ground they were all gone Mr Trezillian had now to find his horse, and the Small Folk, still determining to lead him a dance, bewildered him. He was piskie-led, and he could not find out where he was until broad daylight. Then he saw he was not a hundred yards from the place at which he had left his horse.   On looking round the spot where he had seen the Small Folk dancing, he found a pair of very small silver knee-buckles of a most ancient shape, which, no doubt, some little gentleman must have lost when he was punishing the farmer. Those who knew the families will well remember the little silver buckles, which were kept for some time at Trezidder and some time at Raftra.

Down in Penberth Cove lived an old woman who was an especial favourite with these little people.   She was a good old creature, and had been for many years bedridden.   These Small Folk were her only company   Her relations dropped in once a day, rendered her the little aid she required, and left food by the bedside.   But day by day, and all the day long, the Small Folk vied with each other to amuse her   The men, she related, were for the most part dressed in green, with a red or a blue cap and a feather—"They look for all the world like little sodgers."   As for the ladies—you should have heard the old woman tell of the gay ladies, with their feathers, hooped petticoats with furbelows, trains, and fans, and what saucy little creatures they were with the men ! No sooner was the old woman left alone than in they came and began their frolics, dancing over the rafters and key-beams, swinging by the cobwebs like rope-dancers, catching the mice and riding them in and out through the holes in the thatch.   When one party got tired another party came, and by daylight, and even by moonlight, the old bedridden creature never wanted amusement.

THE ADVENTURE OF CHERRY OF ZENNOR.

THIS may be regarded as another version of the story of the Fairy Widower ·—Old Honey lived with his wife and family in a little hut of two rooms and a "talfat," [*] on the cliff side of Trereen in Zennor.   The old couple had half-a-score of children, who were all reared in this place.   They lived as they best could on the produce of a few acres of ground, which were too poor to keep even a goat in good heart.   The heaps of crogans (limpet-shells) about the hut, led one to believe that their chief food was limpets and gweans (periwinkles).   They had, however, fish and potatoes most days, and pork and broth now and then of a Sunday.   At Christmas and the Feast they had white bread.   There was not a healthier nor a handsomer family in the parish than Old Honey's.   We are, however, only concerned with one of them—his

---

[*] *Talfat* is a half-floor at one end of a cottage on which a bed is placed.

daughter Cherry. Cherry could run as fast as a hare, and was ever full of frolic and mischief

Whenever the miller's boy came into the " town," tied his horse to the furze-rick and called in to see if any one desired to send corn to the mill, Cherry would jump on to its back and gallop off to the cliff. When the miller's boy gave chase, and she could ride no further over the edge of that rocky coast, she would take to the cairns, and the swiftest dog could not catch her, much less the miller's boy

Soon after Cherry got into her teens she became very discontented, because year after year her mother had been promising her a new frock that she might go off as smart as the rest, " three on one horse to Morva Fair." * As certain as the time came round the money was wanting, so Cherry had nothing decent She could neither go to fair, nor to church, nor to meeting.

Cherry was sixteen. One of her playmates had a new dress smartly trimmed with ribbons, and she told Cherry how she had been to Nancledry to the preaching, and how she had ever so many sweethearts who brought her home. This put the volatile Cherry in a fever of desire. She declared to her mother she would go off to the " low countries " † to seek for service, that she might get some clothes like other girls.

Her mother wished her to go to Towednack, that she might have the chance of seeing her now and then of a Sunday.

" No, no ! " said Cherry, " I 'll never go to live in the parish where the cow ate the bell-rope, and where they have fish and taties (potatoes) every day, and conger-pie of a Sunday for a change."

One fine morning Cherry tied up a few things in a bundle and prepared to start She promised her father that she would get service as near home as she could, and come home at the earliest opportunity. The old man said she was bewitched, charged her to take care she wasn't carried away by either the sailors or pirates, and allowed her to depart. Cherry took the road leading to Ludgvan and Gulval When she lost sight of the chimneys of Trereen, she go out of heart, and had a great mind to go home again. But she went on.

At length she came to the four cross roads on the Lady Downs, sat herself down on a stone by the roadside, and cried to think of her home, which she might never see again

* A Cornish proverb

† The terms "high" and "low countries;" are applied respectively to the hills and the valleys of the country about Towednack and Zennor

Her crying at last came to an end, and she resolved to go home and make the best of it

When she dried her eyes and held up her head she was surprised to see a gentleman coming towards her;—for she couldn't think where he came from ; no one was to be seen on the Downs a few minutes before

The gentleman wished her " Good morning," inquired the road to Towednack, and asked Cherry where she was going.

Cherry told the gentleman that she had left home that morning to look for service, but that her heart had failed her, and she was going back over the hills to Zennor again

"I never expected to meet with such luck as this," said the gentleman.   " I left home this morning to seek for a nice clean girl to keep house for me, and here you are."

He then told Cherry that he had been recently left a widower, and that he had one dear little boy, of whom Cherry might have charge.   Cherry was the very girl that would suit him.   She was handsome and cleanly   He could see that her clothes were so mended that the first piece could not be discovered ; yet she was as sweet as a rose, and all the water in the sea could not make her cleaner.   Poor Cherry said " Yes, sir," to everything, yet she did not understand one quarter part of what the gentleman said. Her mother had instructed her to say " Yes, sir," to the parson, or any gentleman, when, like herself, she did not understand them. The gentleman told her he lived but a short way off, down in the low countries ; that she would have very little to do but milk the cow and look after the baby , so Cherry consented to go with him.

Away they went, he talking so kindly that Cherry had no notion how time was moving, and she quite forgot the distance she had walked

At length they were in lanes, so shaded with trees that a checker of sunshine scarcely gleamed on the road.   As far as she could see, all was trees and flowers   Sweetbriars and honeysuckles perfumed the air, and the reddest of ripe apples hung from the trees over the lane.

Then they came to a stream of water as clear as crystal, which ran across the lane.   It was, however, very dark, and Cherry paused to see how she should cross the river.   The gentleman put his arm around her waist and carried her over, so that she did not wet her feet.

The lane was getting darker and darker, and narrower and narrower, and they seemed to be going rapidly down-hill

Cherry took firm hold of the gentleman's arm, and thought, as he had been so kind to her, she could go with him to the world's end

After walking a little farther, the gentleman opened a gate which led into a beautiful garden, and said, " Cherry, my dear, this is the place we live in."

Cherry could scarcely believe her eyes   She had never seen anything approaching this place for beauty.   Flowers of every dye were around her ; fruits of all kinds hung above her ; and the birds, sweeter of song than any she had ever heard, burst out into a chorus of rejoicing.   She had heard granny tell of enchanted places.   Could this be one of them ?   No.   The gentleman was as big as the parson ; and now a little boy came running down the garden-walk shouting, " Papa, papa."

The child appeared, from his size, to be about two or three years of age ; but there was a singular look of age about him.   His eyes were brilliant and piercing, and he had a crafty expression. As Cherry said, " He could look anybody down."

Before Cherry could speak to the child, a very old, dry-boned, ugly-looking woman made her appearance, and seizing the child by the arm, dragged him into the house, mumbling and scolding. Before, however, she was lost sight of, the old hag cast one look at Cherry, which shot through her heart " like a gimblet."

Seeing Cherry somewhat disconcerted, the master explained that the old woman was his late wife's grandmother ; that she would remain with them until Cherry knew her work, and no longer, for she was old and ill-tempered, and must go.   At length, having feasted her eyes on the garden, Cherry was taken into the house, and this was yet more beautiful.   Flowers of every kind grew everywhere, and the sun seemed to shine everywhere, and yet she did not see the sun.

Aunt Prudence—so was the old woman named—spread a table in a moment with a great variety of nice things, and Cherry made a hearty supper   She was now directed to go to bed, in a chamber at the top of the house, in which the child was to sleep also. Prudence directed Cherry to keep her eyes closed, whether she could sleep or not, as she might, perchance, see things which she would not like.   She was not to speak to the child all night. She was to rise at break of day; then take the boy to a spring in the garden, wash him, and anoint his eyes with an ointment, which she would find in a crystal box in a cleft of the rock, but she was not, on any account, to touch her own eyes with it.   Then Cherry was to call the cow ; and having taken a bucket full of milk, to draw a bowl of the last milk for the boy's breakfast. Cherry was dying with curiosity. She several times began to question the child, but he always stopped her with, " I'll tell Aunt Prudence " According to her orders, Cherry was up in the morning early. The little boy conducted the girl to the spring, which flowed in crystal purity from a granite rock, which was covered with ivy and beautiful mosses. The child was duly washed, and his eyes duly anointed. Cherry saw no cow, but her little charge said she must call the cow.

" Pruit ! pruit ! pruit ! " called Cherry, just as she would call the cows at home ; when, lo ! a beautiful great cow came from amongst the trees, and stood on the bank beside Cherry.

Cherry had no sooner placed her hands on the cow's teats than four streams of milk flowed down and soon filled the bucket The boy's bowl was then filled, and he drank it. This being done, the cow quietly walked away, and Cherry returned to the house to be instructed in her daily work

The old woman, Prudence, gave Cherry a capital breakfast, and then informed her that she must keep to the kitchen, and attend to her work there—to scald the milk, make the butter, and clean all the platters and bowls with water and gard (gravel sand). Cherry was charged to avoid curiosity. She was not to go into any other part of the house , she was not to try and open any locked doors.

After her ordinary work was done on the second day, her master required Cherry to help him in the garden, to pick the apples and pears, and to weed the leeks and onions.

Glad was Cherry to get out of the old woman's sight. Aunt Prudence always sat with one eye on her knitting, and the other boring through poor Cherry. Now and then she'd grumble, " I knew Robin would bring down some fool from Zennor—better for both that she had tarried away "

Cherry and her master got on famously, and whenever Cherry had finished weeding a bed, her master would give her a kiss to show her how pleased he was.

After a few days, old Aunt Prudence took Cherry into those parts of the house which she had never seen. They passed through a long dark passage. Cherry was then made to take off her shoes ; and they entered a room, the floor of which was like glass, and all round, perched on the shelves, and on the floor, were people, big and small, turned to stone. Of some, there were only the head and shoulders, the arms being cut off ; others were perfect. Cherry told the old woman she " wouldn't cum ony furder for the wurld." She thought from the first she was got into a land of Small People underground, only master was like other men ; but now she know'd she was with the conjurois, who had turned all these people to stone. She had heard talk on 'em up in Zennor, and she knew they might at any moment wake up and eat her.

Old Prudence laughed at Cherry, and drove her on, insisted upon her rubbing up a box, "like a coffin on six legs," until she could see her face in it. Well, Cherry did not want for courage, so she began to rub with a will ; the old woman standing by, knitting all the time, calling out every now and then, "Rub ! rub ! rub ! harder and faster !" At length Cherry got desperate, and giving a violent rub at one of the corners, she nearly upset the box. When, O Lor ! it gave out such a doleful, unearthly sound, that Cherry thought all the stone-people were coming to life, and with her fright she fell down in a fit The master heard all this noise, and came in to inquire into the cause of the hubbub. He was in great wrath, kicked old Prudence out of the house for taking Cherry into that shut-up room, carried Cherry into the kitchen, and soon, with some cordial, recovered her senses. Cherry could not remember what had happened ; but she knew there was something fearful in the other part of the house But Cherry was mistress now—old Aunt Prudence was gone. Her master was so kind and loving that a year passed by like a summer day. Occasionally her master left home for a season ; then he would return and spend much time in the enchanted apartments, and Cherry was certain she had heard him talking to the stone-people. Cherry had everything the human heart could desire, but she was not happy, she would know more of the place and the people. Cherry had discovered that the ointment made the little boy's eyes bright and strange, and she thought often that he saw more than she did, she would try, yes, she would !

Well, next morning the child was washed, his eyes anointed, and the cow milked ; she sent the boy to gather her some flowers in the garden, and taking a "crum" of ointment, she put it into her eye Oh, her eye would be burned out of her head ! Cherry ran to the pool beneath the rock to wash her burning eye ; when lo ! she saw at the bottom of the water, hundreds of little people, mostly ladies, playing,—and there was her master, as small as the others, playing with them Everything now looked different about the place. Small people were everywhere, hiding in the flowers sparkling with diamonds, swinging in the trees, and run-

ning and leaping under and over the blades of grass.   The master
never showed himself above the water all day ; but at night he rode
up to the house like the handsome gentleman she had seen before.
He went to the enchanted chamber and Cherry soon heard the
most beautiful music.

In the morning, her master was off, dressed as if to follow the
hounds.   He returned at night, left Cherry to herself, and proceeded at once to his private apartments.   Thus it was day after
day, until Cherry could stand it no longer.   So she peeped through
the keyhole, and saw her master with lots of ladies, singing ;
while one dressed like a queen was playing on the coffin.   Oh,
how madly jealous Cherry became when she saw her master kiss
this lovely lady !   However, the next day, the master remained at
home to gather fruit   Cherry was to help him, and when, as usual,
he looked to kiss her, she slapped his face, and told him to kiss
the Small People, like himself, with whom he played under the
water.   So he found out that Cherry had used the ointment.
With much sorrow he told her she must go home,—that he would
have no spy on his actions, and that Aunt Prudence must come
back.   Long before day, Cherry was called by her master.   He
gave her lots of clothes and other things ;—took her bundle in one
hand, and a lantern in the other, and bade her follow him.   They
went on for miles on miles, all the time going up hill, through
lanes, and narrow passages.   When they came at last on level
ground, it was near daybreak.   He kissed Cherry, told her she
was punished for her idle curiosity ; but that he would, if she behaved well, come sometimes on the Lady Downs to see her.   Saying this, he disappeared.   The sun rose, and there was Cherry
seated on a granite stone, without a soul within miles of her,—a
desolate moor having taken the place of a smiling garden.   Long,
long did Cherry sit in sorrow, but at last she thought she would
go home

Her parents had supposed her dead, and when they saw her,
they believed her to be her own ghost.   Cherry told her story,
which every one doubted, but Cherry never varied her tale, and
at last every one believed it   They say Cherry was never afterwards right in her head, and on moonlight nights, until she died,
she would wander on to the Lady Downs to look for her master.

ANNE JEFFERIES AND THE FAIRIES.

A NNE JEFFERIES was the daughter of a poor labouring man, who lived in the parish of St Teath. She was born in 1626, and is supposed to have died in 1698.

When she was nineteen years old, Anne, who was a remarkably sharp and clever girl, went to live as a servant in the family of Mr Moses Pitt. Anne was an unusually bold girl, and would do things which even boys feared to attempt. Of course, in those days every one believed in fairies, and everybody feared those little airy beings. They were constantly the talk of the people, and this set Anne longing anxiously to have an interview with some of them. So Anne was often abroad after sundown, turning up the fern leaves, and looking into the bells of the foxglove to find a fairy, singing all the time—

> " Fairy fair and fairy bright ;
> Come and be my chosen sprite."

She never allowed a moonlight night to pass without going down into the valley, and walking against the stream, singing—

> " Moon shines bright, waters run clear,
> I am here, but where 's my fairy dear ? "

The fairies were a long time trying this poor girl ; for, as they told her afterwards, they never lost sight of her ; but there they would be, looking on when she was seeking them, and they would run from frond to frond of the ferns, when she was turning them up in her anxious search

One day Anne, having finished her morning's work, was sitting in the arbour in her master's garden, when she fancied she heard some one moving aside the branches, as though endeavouring to look in upon her ; and she thought it must be her sweetheart, so she resolved to take no notice. Anne went on steadily with her work, no sound was heard but the regular beat of the knitting-needles one upon the other. Presently she heard a suppressed laugh, and then again a rustle amidst the branches. The back of the arbour was towards the lane, and to enter the garden it was necessary to walk down the lane to the gate, which was, however, not many yards off.

Click, click went the needles, click, click, click At last Anne began to feel vexed that the intruder did not show himself, and she pettishly said, half aloud—

" You may stay there till the kueney* grows on the gate, ere
1 'll come to 'ee "

There was immediately a peculiar ringing and very musical
laugh. Anne knew this was not her lover's laugh, and she felt
afraid. But it was bright day, and she assured herself that no
one would do her any mischief, as she knew herself to be a general
favourite in the parish. Presently Anne felt assured that the garden
gate had been carefully opened and again closed, so she waited
anxiously the result. In a few moments she perceived at the
entrance of the arbour six little men, all clothed very handsomely
in green. They were beautiful little figures, and had very charming faces, and such bright eyes. The grandest of these little
visitors, who wore a red feather in his cap, advanced in front of
the others, and, making a most polite bow to Anne, addressed her
familiarly in the kindest words.

This gentleman looked so sweetly on Anne that she was
charmed beyond measure, and she put down her hand as if to
shake hands with her little friend, when he jumped into her palm,
and she lifted him into her lap. He then, without any more ado,
clambered upon her bosom and neck, and began kissing her
Anne never felt so charmed in her life as while this one little gentleman was playing with her ; but presently he called his companions,
and they all clambered up by her dress as best they could, and kissed
her neck, her lips, and her eyes One of them ran his fingers over
her eyes, and she felt as if they had been pricked with a pin.
Suddenly Anne became blind, and she felt herself whirled through
the air at a great rate. By and by, one of her little companions
said something which sounded like " Tear away," and lo ' Anne
had her sight at once restored She was in one of the most
beautiful places—temples and palaces of gold and silver. Trees
laden with fruits and flowers. Lakes full of gold and silver fish,
and the air full of birds of the sweetest song, and the most
brilliant colours Hundreds of ladies and gentlemen were walking about. Hundreds more were idling in the most luxuriant
bowers, the fragrance of the flowers oppressing them with a
sense of delicious repose. Hundreds were also dancing, or
engaged in sports of various kinds Anne was, however, surprised to find that these happy people were no longer the small
people she had previously seen. There was now no more than the
difference usually seen in a crowd, between their height and her
own. Anne found herself arrayed in the most highly-decorated
clothes. So grand, indeed, did she appear, that she doubted her

* Moss, or mildew; properly, *curney*

identity. Anne was constantly attended by her six friends; but the finest gentleman, who was the first to address her, continued her favourite, at which the others appeared to be very jealous. Eventually Anne and her favourite contrived to separate themselves, and they retired into some most lovely gardens, where they were hidden by the luxuriance of the flowers. Lovingly did they pass the time, and Anne desired that this should continue for ever. However, when they were at the happiest, there was heard a great noise, and presently the five other fairies at the head of a great crowd came after them in a violent rage. Her lover drew his sword to defend her, but this was soon beaten down, and he lay wounded at her feet. Then the fairy who had blinded her again placed his hands upon her eyes, and all was dark. She heard strange noises, and felt herself whirled about and about, and as if a thousand flies were buzzing around her.

At length her eyes were opened, and Anne found herself on the ground in the arbour where she had been sitting in the morning, and many anxious faces were around her, all conceiving that she was recovering from a convulsion fit.[*]

THE PISKIE THRESHERS.

MANY an industrious farmer can speak of the assistance which he has received from the piskies. Mr T. Q Couch tells a story of this kind so well that no other is required.[†] Long, long ago, before threshing-machines were thought of, the farmer who resided at C——, in going to his barn one day, was surprised at the extraordinary quantity of corn that had been threshed the previous night, as well as to discover the mysterious agency by which it was effected. His curiosity led him to inquire into the matter; so at night, when the moon was up, he crept stealthily to the barn-door, and looking through a chink, saw a little fellow, clad in a tattered suit of green, wielding the " dreshel " (flail) with astonishing vigour, and beating the floor with blows so rapid that the eye could not follow the motion of the implement. The farmer slunk away unperceived, and went to bed, where he lay a long while awake, thinking in what way he could best show his gratitude to the piskie for such an important service. He came to the conclusion at length, that, as the little fellow's clothes were getting very old and ragged, the gift of a new suit would be a proper way to lessen the obligation; and, accordingly, on the morrow he had a suit of green made, of what was supposed to be the proper

---

* See Moses Pitt's Letter, Appendix K.   † See *Notes and Queries.*

size, which he carried early in the evening to the barn, and left for the piskie's acceptance. At night the farmer stole to the door again to see how his gift was taken. He was just in time to see the elf put on the suit, which was no sooner accomplished than, looking down on himself admiringly, he sung—

> " Piskie fine, and piskie gay,
> Piskie now will fly away."

THE MURYANS' BANK.*

THE ant is called by the peasantry a Muryan. Believing that they are the Small People in their state of decay from off the earth, it is deemed most unlucky to destroy a colony of ants. If you place a piece of tin in a bank of Muryans at a certain age of the moon, it will be turned into silver.

* *Murrian*, Welsh, " Crig murrian," the hill of ants.

TREGEAGLE.

"In Cornwaile's fair land, bye the poole on the moore,
Tregeagle the wicked did dwell."
  — *Tregeagle; or, Dozmare Pool.*
          By JOHN PENWARNE.

ROMANCES OF TREGEAGLE.

THE DEMON TREGEAGLE.

"Thrice he began to tell his doleful tale,
And thrice the sighs did swallow up his voice."
—Thomas Sackville.

WHO has not heard of the wild spirit Tregeagle? He haunts equally the moor, the rocky coasts, and the blown sand-hills of Cornwall. From north to south, from east to west, this doomed spirit is heard of, and to the day of judgment he is doomed to wander, pursued by avenging fiends. For ever endeavouring to perform some task by which he hopes to secure repose, and being for ever defeated Who has not heard the howling of Tregeagle? When the storms come with all their strength from the Atlantic, and urge themselves upon the rocks around the Land's End, the howls of the spirit are louder than the roaring of the winds. When calms rest upon the ocean, and the waves can scarcely form upon the resting waters, low wailings creep along the coast. These are the wailings of this wandering soul. When midnight is on the moor or on the mountains, and the night winds whistle amidst the rugged cairns, the shrieks of Tregeagle are distinctly heard. We know, then, that he is pursued by the demon dogs, and that till daybreak he must fly with all speed before them. The voice of Tregeagle is everywhere, and yet he is unseen by human eye. Every reader will at once perceive that Tregeagle belongs to the mythologies of the oldest nations, and that the traditions of this wandering spirit in Cornwall, which centre upon one tyrannical magistrate, are but the appropriation of stories which belong to every age and country. Tradition thus tells Tregeagle's tale.

There are some men who appear to be from their births given over to the will of tormenting demons. Such a man was Tregeagle. He is as old as the hills, yet there are many circumstances in the story of his life which *appear* to remove him from this remote antiquity. Modern legends assert him to belong to comparatively modern times, and say that, without doubt, he was one of the Tregeagles who once owned Trevorder near Bodmin. We have not, however, much occasion to trouble ourselves with the man or his life ; it is with the death and the subsequent existence of a myth that we are concerned.

Certain it is that the man Tregeagle was diabolically wicked. He seems to have been urged on from one crime to another until the cup of sin was overflowing.

Tregeagle was wealthy beyond most men of his time, and his wealth purchased for him that immunity, which the Church, in her degenerate days, too often accorded to those who could aid, with their gold or power, the sensual priesthood As a magistrate, he was tyrannical and unjust, and many an innocent man was wantonly sacrificed by him for the purpose of hiding his own dark deeds As a landlord, he was rapacious and unscrupulous, and frequently so involved his tenants in his toils, that they could not escape his grasp. The stain of secret murder clings to his memory, and he is said to have sacrificed a sister whose good-ness stood between him and his demon passions ; his wife and children perished victims to his cruelties. At length death drew near to relieve the land of a monster whose name was a terror to all who heard it. Devils waited to secure the soul they had won, and Tregeagle in terror gave to the priesthood wealth, that they might fight with them and save his soul from eternal fire Desperate was the struggle, but the powerful exorcisms of the banded brotherhood of a neighbouring monastery, drove back the evil ones, and Tregeagle slept with his fathers, safe in the custody of the churchmen, who buried him with high honours in St Breock Church. They sang chants and read prayers above his grave, to secure the soul which they thought they had saved. But Tregeagle was not fated to rest. Satan desired still to gain possession of such a gigantic sinner, and we can only refer what ensued to the influence of the wicked spiritings of his ministers.

A dispute arose between two wealthy families respecting the ownership of extensive lands around Bodmin. The question had been rendered more difficult by the nefarious conduct of Tregeagle, who had acted as steward to one of the claimants, and who had destroyed ancient deeds, forged others, and indeed made it appear that he was the real proprietor of the domain. Large portions of the land Tregeagle had sold, and other parts were leased upon long terms, he having received all the money and appropriated it. His death led to inquiries, and then the transactions were gradually

brought to light. Involving, as this did, large sums of money—
and indeed it was a question upon which turned the future well-
doing or ruin of a family—it was fought by the lawyers with great
pertinacity. The legal questions had been argued several times
before the judges at the assizes The trials had been deferred,
new trials had been sought for and granted, and every possible
plan known to the lawyers for postponing the settlement of a suit
had been tried. A day was at length fixed, upon which a final
decision must be come to, and a special jury was sworn to admin-
ister justice between the contending parties. Witnesses innumerable were examined as to the validity of a certain deed, and the
balance of evidence was equally suspended. The judge was about
to sum up the case and refer the question to the jury, when the
defendant in the case, coming into court, proclaimed aloud that
he had yet another witness to produce. There was a strange
silence in the judgment-hall. It was felt that something chilling
to the soul was amongst them, and there was a simultaneous
throb of terror as Tregeagle was led into the witness-box.

When the awe-struck assembly had recovered, the lawyers for
the defendant commenced their examination, which was long and
terrible. The result, however, was the disclosure of an involved
system of fraud, of which the honest defendant had been the
victim, and the jury unhesitatingly gave a verdict in his favour.

The trial over, every one expected to see the spectre-witness
removed. There, however, he stood, powerless to fly, although
he evidently desired to do so. Spirits of darkness were waiting
to bear him away, but some spell of holiness prevented them from
touching him. There was a struggle with the good and the evil
angels for this sinner's soul, and the assembled court appeared
frozen with horror. At length the judge with dignity commanded
the defendant to remove his witness

" To bring him from the grave has been to me so dreadful a
task, that I leave him to your care, and that of the Prior's, by
whom he was so beloved." Having said this, the defendant left
the court.

The churchmen were called in, and long were the deliberations
between them and the lawyers, as to the best mode of disposing
of Tregeagle.

They could resign him to the devil at once, but by long trial
the worst of crimes might be absolved, and as good churchmen
they could not sacrifice a human soul. The only thing was to
give the spirit some task, difficult beyond the power of human
nature, which might be extended far into eternity. Time might

thus gradually soften the obdurate soul, which still retained all the black dyes of the sins done in the flesh, that by infinitely slow degrees repentance might exert its softening power. The spell therefore put upon Tregeagle was, that as long as he was employed on some endless assigned task, there should be hope of salvation, and that he should be secure from the assaults of the devil as long as he laboured steadily A moment's rest was fatal— labour unresting, and for ever, was his doom.

One of the lawyers, remembering that Dosmery Pool* was bottomless, and that a thorn-bush which had been flung into it, but a few weeks before, had made its appearance in Falmouth Harbour, proposed that Tregeagle might be employed to empty this profound lake Then one of the churchmen, to make the task yet more enduring, proposed that it should be performed by the aid of a limpet-shell having a hole in it.

This was agreed to, and the required incantations were duly made. Bound by mystical spells, Tregeagle was removed to the dark moors and duly set to work. Year after year passed by, and there, day and night, summer and winter, storm and shine, Tregeagle was bending over the dark water, working hard with his perforated shell , yet the pool remained at the same level.

His old enemy the devil kept a careful eye on the doomed one, resolving, if possible, to secure so choice an example of evil. Often did he raise tempests sufficiently wild, as he supposed, to drive Tregeagle from his work, knowing that if he failed for a season to labour, he could seize and secure him. These were long tried in vain ; but at length an auspicious hour presented itself.

Nature was at war with herself, the elements had lost their balance, and there was a terrific struggle to recover it. Lightnings flashed and coiled like fiery snakes around the rocks of Roughtor. Fire-balls fell on the desert moors and hissed in the accursed lake. Thunders peeled through the heavens, and echoed from hill to hill ; an earthquake shook the solid earth, and terror was on all living The winds arose and raged with a fury which was irresistible, and hail beat so mercilessly on all things, that it spread death around. Long did Tregeagle stand the " pelting of the pitiless storm," but at length he yielded to its force and fled. The demons in crowds were at his heels. He doubled, however, on his pursuers, and returned to the lake ; but so rapid were they, that he could not rest the required moment to dip his shell in the now seething waters.

* Or *Dozmare* Unfortunately for its bottomless character, in a recent hot and rainless summer, this little lake became dry.

Three times he fled round the lake, and the evil ones pursued him. Then, feeling that there was no safety for him near Dosmery Pool, he sprang swifter than the wind across it, shrieking with agony, and thus,—since the devils cannot cross water, and were obliged to go round the lake,—he gained on them and fled over the moor.

Away, away went Tregeagle, faster and faster the dark spirits pursuing, and they had nearly overtaken him, when he saw Roach Rock and its chapel before him. He rushed up the rocks, with giant power clambered to the eastern window, and dashed his head through it, thus securing the shelter of its sanctity. The defeated demons retired, and long and loud were their wild wailings in the air. The inhabitants of the moors and of the neighbouring towns slept not a wink that night.

Tregeagle was safe, his head was within the holy church, though his body was exposed on a bare rock to the storm. Earnest were the prayers of the blessed hermit in his cell on the rock to be relieved from his nocturnal and sinful visitor.

In vain were the recluse's prayers. Day after day, as he knelt at the altar, the ghastly head of the doomed sinner grinned horridly down upon him. Every holy ejaculation fell upon Tregeagle's ear like molten iron. He writhed and shrieked under the torture; but legions of devils filled the air, ready to seize him, if for a moment he withdrew his head from the sanctuary. Sabbath after Sabbath the little chapel on the rock was rendered a scene of sad confusion by the interruptions which Tregeagle caused. Men trembled with fear at his agonising cries, and women swooned. At length the place was deserted, and even the saint of the rock was wasting to death by the constant perturbation in which he was kept by the unholy spirit, and the demons who, like carrion birds, swarmed around the holy cairn. Things could not go on thus. The monks of Bodmin and the priests from the neighbouring churches gathered together, and the result of their long and anxious deliberations was, that Tregeagle, guarded by two saints, should be taken to the north coast, near Padstow, and employed in making trusses of sand, and ropes of sand with which to bind them. By powerful spell, Tregeagle was removed from Roach, and fixed upon the sandy shores of the Padstow district. Sinners are seldom permitted to enjoy any peace of soul. As the ball of sand grew into form, the tides rose, and the breakers spread out the sands again a level sheet; again was it packed together and again washed away. Toil! toil! toil! day and night unrestingly, sand on sand grew with each hour, and ruthlessly the ball was swept, by one blow of a sea wave, along the shore.

The cries of Tregeagle were dreadful ; and as the destruction of the sand heap was constantly recurring, a constantly increasing despair gained the mastery over hope, and the ravings of the baffled soul were louder than the roarings of the winter tempest.

Baffled in making trusses of sand, Tregeagle seized upon the loose particles and began to spin them into a rope. Long and patiently did he pursue his task, and hope once more rose like a star out of the midnight darkness of despair. A rope was forming, when a storm came up with all its fury from the Atlantic, and swept the particles of sand away over the hills.

The inhabitants of Padstow had seldom any rest. At every tide the howlings of Tregeagle banished sleep from each eye. But now so fearful were the sounds of the doomed soul, in the madness of the struggle between hope and despair, that the people fled the town, and clustered upon the neighbouring plains, praying, as with one voice, to be relieved from the sad presence of this monster.

St Petroc, moved by the tears and petitions of the people, resolved to remove the spirit ; and by the intense earnestness of his prayers, after long wrestling, he subdued Tregeagle to his will. Having chained him with the bonds which the saint had forged with his own hands, every link of which had been welded with a prayer, St Petroc led the spirit away from the north coast, and stealthily placed him on the southern shores.

In those days Ella's Town, now Helston, was a flourishing port. Ships sailed into the estuary, up to the town, and they brought all sorts of merchandise, and returned with cargoes of tin from the mines of Breage and Wendron.

The wily monk placed his charge at Bareppa, and there condemned him to carry sacks of sand across the estuary of the Loo, and to empty them at Porthleven, until the beach was clean down to the rocks. The priest was a good observer. He knew that the sweep of the tide was from Trewavas Head round the coast towards the Lizard, and that the sand would be carried back steadily and speedily as fast as the spirit could remove it.

Long did Tregeagle labour ; and, of course, in vain. His struggles were giant-like to perform his task, but he saw the sands return as regularly as he removed them. The sufferings of the poor fishermen who inhabited the coast around Porthleven were great. As the howlings of Tregeagle disturbed the dwellers in Padstow, so did they now distress those toil-worn men.

> " When sorrow is highest,
> Relief is nighest."

And a mischievous demon-watcher, in pure wantonness, brought that relief to those fishers of the sea.

Tregeagle was laden with a sack of sand of enormous size, and was wading across the mouth of the estuary, when one of those wicked devils, who were kept ever near Tregeagle, in very idleness tripped up the heavily-laden spirit. The sea was raging with the irritation of a passing storm ; and as Tregeagle fell, the sack was seized by the waves, and its contents poured out across this arm of the sea.

There, to this day, it rests a bar of sand, fatally destroying the harbour of Ella's Town. The rage of the inhabitants of this seaport,—now destroyed,—was great ; and with all their priests, away they went to the Loo Bar, and assailed their destroyer. Against human anger Tregeagle was proof. The shock of tongues fell harmlessly on his ear, and the assault of human weapons was unavailing.

By the aid of the priests, and faith-inspired prayers, the bonds were once more placed upon Tregeagle ; and he was, by the force of bell, book, and candle, sent to the Land's End. There he would find no harbour to destroy, and but few people to terrify. His task was to sweep the sands from Porthcurnow Cove round the headland called Tol-Peden-Penwith, into Nanjisal Cove. Those who know that rugged headland, with its cubical masses of granite, piled in Titanic grandeur one upon another, will appreciate the task ; and when to all the difficulties are added the strong sweep of the Atlantic current,—that portion of the Gulf-stream which washes our southern shores,—it will be evident that the melancholy spirit has, indeed, a task which must endure until the world shall end.

Even until to-day is Tregeagle labouring at his task. In calms his wailing is heard ; and those sounds which some call the " soughing of the wind," are known to be the moanings of Tregeagle ; while the coming storms are predicated by the fearful roarings of this condemned mortal.

JAHN TERGAGLE THE STEWARD.

THERE are numerous versions of this legend, and sundry statements made as to the man who is supposed to have achieved the no very envious immortality which he enjoys

One or two of these may interest the reader.

The following very characteristic narrative, from a much-esteemed correspondent, gives several incidents which have not a place in the legend as I have related it, which comprehends the explanation given for the appearance of Tregeagle at so many different parts of the county.

The Tregeagle, of whom mention occurs in the writings of Cornish legendary authors, was a real person: a member of a respectable family, resident during the seventeenth century at Trevorder, in the parish of St Breock, and identical probably with a John Tregeagle whose tombstone may yet be seen in the parish church there, close to the chancel.

Lingering one day amid the venerable arches of that same church, the narrator, a native of the parish, encountered, near a small transept called the Trevorder aisle, the sexton, a man then perhaps of about eighty years of age. The conversation turning not unnaturally on the "illustrious dead," the narrator was gratified in receiving from the lips of the old man the following characteristic specimen of folk-lore, the greater part of which has remained clearly imprinted in his memory after a lapse of many years ; though [he thinks he has had to supply the very last sentence of all from the general popular tradition] here and there he may have had to supply a few expressions :—

"Theess Jahn Tergagle, I've a heeid mun tell, sir, he was a steward to a lord.*

"And a man came fore to the court and paid az rent and Jahn Tergagle didn't put no cross to az name in the books

"And after that Tergagle daied : and the lord came down to look after az rents : and when he zeed the books, he zeed this man's name that there wasn't no cross to ut.

"And he zent for the man, and axed 'n for az rent · and the man zaid he'd apaid az rent : and the lord said he hadn't, there wain't no cross to az name in the books, and he tould 'n that he'd have the law for 'n if he didn't pay.

"And the man, he didn't know what to do : and he went voie to the minister of Simonward ; † and the minister axed 'n if he'd a got faith : and the man, he hadn't got faith, and he was obliged for to come homewards again.

"And after that the 'Zaizes was coming naigh, and he was becoming afeerd, sure enough · and he went vore to the minister again, and tould 'n he'd a got faith ; the minister might do whatever a laiked.

"And the minister draed a ring out on the floor : and he caaled out dree times, Jahn Tergagle, Jahn Tergagle, Jahn Tergagle ! and (I've a heeid the ould men tell ut, sir) theess Jahn Tergagle stood before mun in the middle of the ring.

"And he went vore wi' mun to the Ezaizes, and gave az evidence and tould how this man had a paid az rent ; and the lord he was cast.

"And after that they was come back to their own house, theess Jahn

---

Teigagle he gave mun a brave deal of trouble ; he was knackin' about the place, and wouldn't laive mun alone at all.

"And they went vore to the minister, and axed he for to lay un.

"And the minister zaid, thicky* was their look-out ; they'd a brought'n up, and they was to gett 'n down again the best way they could. And I 've a heerd the ould men tell ut, sir The minister he got dree hunderd pound for a layin' of un again.

"And first, a was bound to the old epping-stock † up to Churchtown ; ‡ and after that a was bound to the ould oven in T'evurder , James Wyatt down to Wadebridge, he was there when they did open ut.

"And after that a was bound to Dozmary Pool ; and they do say that there he ez now emptying of it out with a lampet-shell, with a hole in the bottom of ut "

This is a very ancient idea, and was one of the torments of the classical Tartarus. The treacherous daughters of Danaus being condemned therein to empty Lethe with a bottomless vessel :—

> " Et Danai proles Veneris quæ numma læsit,
>   In cava Lethæas solia portat aquas."

Dosmare Pool is a small lake or tarn on the Bodmin Moors, a fit repre-sentative of Lethe, with its black water and desolate environs.—J. C. H.

Another correspondent to whom I am much indebted for valuable notes on the folk-lore of the Land's End district, sends me the following version :—

You may know the story better than I do ; however, I 'll give you the west-country version. A man in the neighbourhood of Redruth, I think (I have almost forgotten the story), lent a sum of money to another without receiving bond or note, and the transaction was witnessed by Tregagle, who died before the money was paid back. When the lender demanded the money, the borrower denied having received it. He was brought into a court of justice, when the man denied on oath that he ever borrowed the money, and declared that if Tregagle saw any such thing take place, he wished that Tregagle would come and declare it. The words were no sooner out of his mouth than Tregagle stood before him, and told him that it was easy to bring him, but that he should not find it so easy to put him away. Tregagle followed the man day and night, wouldn't let him have a moment's rest, until he got all the parsons, conjurors, and other wise men together, to lay him. The wise ones accomplished this for a short time by binding the spirit to empty Dosmery (or Dorsmery) Pool with a crogan (limpet-shell). He soon finished the job and came to the man

---

* Thicky, correctly written thilke—i e , the ilka, a true word frequent in Chaucer.

† Perhaps Uppingstock, an erection of stone steps for the farmers' wives to get on their horses by

‡ Not Chúrchtown, but Churchtówn

again, who sent for Parson Corker, of Burian, who was a noted hand for laying spirits, driving the devil from the bedside of old villains, and other kinds of jobs of the same kind. When the parson came into the room with the spirit and the man, the first thing the parson did was to draw a circle and place the man to stand within it; the spirit took the form of a black bull, and (roared as you may still hear Tregagle roar in Genvor Cove before a northerly storm) did all he could to get at the man with his horns and hoofs. The parson continued reading all the time. At first the reading seemed to make him more furious, but little by little he became as gentle as a lamb, and allowed the parson to do what he would with him, and consented at last to go to Genvor Cove (in Escols Cliff), and make a truss of sand, which he was to carry above a certain rock in Escols Cliff. He was many years trying, without being able to accomplish this piece of work, until it came to a very cold winter, when Tregagle, by taking water from the stream near by, and pouring over the sand, caused it to freeze together, so that he finished the task, came back to the man, and would have torn him in pieces, but the man happened to have a child in his arms, so the spirit couldn't harm him. The man sent for the parson without delay; Parson Corker couldn't manage him alone, this time; had to get some more parsons to help,—very difficult job;—bound Tregagle at last to the same task, and not to go near the fresh water. He is still there, making his truss of sand and spinning sand ropes to bind it. What some people take to be the *"calling of the northern cleves"* (cliffs) is the roaring of Tregagle because there is a storm coming from the north to scatter his sand.* W. B.

---

* In connection with the incident given of Tregeagle and the child, the following is interesting :—

I find in the *Temple Bar Magazine* for January 1862, "The Autobiography of an Evil Spirit," professing to be an examination of a strange story related by Dr Justinus Kerner. In this a woman is possessed by a devil or sometimes by devils "Sometimes a legion of fiends appeared to take possession of her, and the clamour on such occasions is compared to that of a pack of hounds. Amid all these horrors her confinement occurred, which was the means of procuring her some respite, as the demon appeared to have no power over her while her innocent babe was in her arms." To this the author adds the following note —

This ancient general and beautiful superstition is graphically illustrated in the legend of Swardowski, the Polish Faust. Satan, weary of the services the magician is continually requiring at his hands, decoys him to a house in Cracow, where, for some unexplained reason, he expects to have him at a disadvantage. Put on his guard by the indiscretion of a flock of ravens and owls, who cannot suppress their satisfaction at seeing him enter the house, Swardowski snatches a new-born child from the cradle and paces the room with it in his arms. In rushes the devil, as terrible as horns, tail, and hoofs can make him, but confronted with the infant, recoils and collapses *instanter*. This suggests to him the propriety of resorting to "moral suasion," and after a while he thus addresses the magician,—"Thou art a gentleman and knowest that *verbum nobile debet esse stabile*". Swardowski feels that he cannot break his word of honour as a gentleman, replaces the child in the cradle, and flies up the chimney with his companion. In the confusion of his faculties, however, the demon would seem to have mistaken the way,

DOSMERY POOL.

MR BOND, in his "Topographical and Historical Sketches of the Boroughs of East and West Looe," writes— " This pool is distant from Looe about twelve miles off. Mr Carew says :—

> 'Dosmery Pool amid the moores,
>   On top stands of a hill ;
> More than a mile about, no streams
>   It empt, nor any fill.'

It is a lake of fresh water about a mile in circumference, the only one in Cornwall (unless the Loe Pool near Helston may be deemed such), and probably takes its name from *Dome-Mer*, sweet or fresh-water sea. It is about eight or ten feet deep in many parts. The notion entertained by some, of there being a whirlpool in its middle, I can contradict, having, some years ago, passed all over in a boat then kept there."

Such is Mr Bond's evidence ; but this is nothing compared with the popular belief, which declares the pool to be bottomless ; and beyond this, is it not known to every man of faith, that a thorn-bush thrown into Dosmery Pool has sunk in the middle of it, and after some time has come up in Falmouth Harbour ?

Notwithstanding that Carew says that " no streams it empt, nor any fill," James Michell, in his parochial history of St Neot's, says,—" It is situate on a small stream called St Neot's River, a branch of the Fowey, which rises in Dosmare Pool."

There is a ballad, " *Tregeagle; or, Dozmaré Poole: an Anciente Cornishe Legende, in two parts,*" by John Penwarne. He has given a somewhat different version of the legend from any I have heard, and in the ballad very considerable liberties have been taken. It must, however, be admitted, that nearly all the incidents intro-duced in the poem are to be found in some of the many stories current amongst the peasantry.

Speaking of Dozmaré Pool, Mr Penwarne says :—

" There is a popular story attached to this lake, ridiculous enough, as most of those tales are. It is, that a person of the name of Tregeagle, who had been a rich and powerful man, but very

at all events, the pair fly upwards instead of downwards,—Swardowski lustily intoning a hymn till suddenly he finds his companion gone, and himself fixed at an immeasurable height in the air, and hears a voice above him saying, " Thus shalt thou hang until the day of judgment !" He has, however, changed one of his disciples into a spider, and is in the habit of letting him down to collect the news of earth   When, therefore, we see any floating threads of gossamer, we may suspect that "a chiel's amang us taking notes," though it is not equally probable that he will ever "prent them " wicked, guilty of murder and other heinous crimes, lived near this place ; and that, after his death, his spirit haunted the neighbourhood, but was at length exorcised and laid to rest in Dozmaré Pool. But having in his lifetime, in order to enjoy the good things of this world, disposed of his soul and body to the devil, his infernal majesty takes great pleasure in tormenting him, by imposing on him difficult tasks ; such as spinning a rope of sand, dipping out the pool with a limpet-shell, &c., and at times amuses himself with hunting him over the moors with his hell-hounds, at which time Tregeagle is heard to roar and howl in a most dreadful manner, so that 'roaring or howling like Tregeagle,' is a common expression amongst the vulgar in Cornwall. Such is the foundation on which is built the following tale. The author has given it an ancient dress, as best suited to the subject."

Tregeagle, in the ballad, is a shepherd dwelling "by the poole on the moore." He was ambitious and unscrupulous. " I wish for all that I see ! " was his exclamation, when "a figure gigantick" is seen "midst the gloom of the night "

This spirit offers Tregeagle, in exchange for his soul, all that he desires for one hundred years. Tregeagle does not hesitate.—

> "'A bargaine ! a bargaine !' he said aloude ;
>   'At my lot I will never repine ;
>   I sweare to observe it, I sweare by the roode.
>   And am readye to seale and to sygne with my bloode,
>   Both my soul and my body are thine.' "

Tregeagle is thrown into a trance, from which he awakes to find himself "cloathed in gorgeous attyre," and master of a wide domain of great beauty :—

> " Where Dozmare lake its darke waters did roll,
>   A castle now reared its heade,
>   Wythe manye a turrete soe statelye and talle ;
>   And many a warden dyd walke on its walle,
>   All splendidly cloathed in redde."

Surrounded with all that is supposed to minister to the enjoyment of a sensual life, time passes on, and " Tregeagle ne'er notyc'd its flyghte." Yet we are told " he marked each day with some damnable deed." In the midst of his vicious career he is returning home through a violent storm, and he is accosted by a damsel on a white horse and a little page by her side, who craves his protection Tregeagle takes this beautiful maiden to his castle. The page is made to tell the lady's story ; she is called Goonhylda,

and is the daughter of " Earl Cornwaill," living in Launceston, or,
as it was then called, " Dunevyd Castle "   Engaged in the pleasures of the hunt, the lady and her page are lost and overtaken
by the storm.   Tregeagle, as the storm rages savagely, makes
them his " guests for the nyghte," promising to send a " quicke
messenger " to inform her father of her whereabouts.   At the
same time—

>   *   " If that the countenance speaketh the mynde,*
>   *Dark deeds he revolved in hys breaste."*

The earl hears nothing of his daughter ; and having passed a
miserable night, he sets forth in the morning, " wyth hys knyghtes,
and esquyers, and serving-men all," in search of his child ; and—

> *" At length to the plaine he emerged from the woode,*
>   *For a father, alas, what a syghte !*
> *There lay her fayre garments all drenched in blood,*
> *Her palfreye all torn in the dark crimson floode,*
>   *By the ravenous beasts of the nyghte."*

This is a delusion caused by enchantment ; Goonhylda still lives.
Tregeagle offers himself to Goonhylda, who rejects his suit with
scorn, and desires to leave the castle.   Tregeagle coolly informs
her that she cannot quit the place ; Goonhylda threatens him with
her father's vengeance.   She is a prisoner, but her page contrives to
make his escape, and in the evening arrives at Launceston Castle
gate.   The Earl of Cornwall, hearing from the page that his
daughter lives and is a prisoner, arms himself and all his retainers—

> *" And ere the greye morne peep'd the eastern hills o'er,*
>   *At Tregeagle's gate sounded hys horne."*

Tregeagle will not obey the summons, but suddenly " they hearde
the Black Hunter's dread voyce in the wynde ! "

> *" They heard hys curste hell-houndes runn yelping behynde,*
>   *And his steede thundered loude on the eare ! "*

This gentleman in black shakes the castle with his cry, " Come
forth, Sir Tregeagle ! come forth and submit to thy fate !'"   Of
course he comes forth, and " the rede bolte of vengeaunce shot
forth wyth a glare, and strooke him a corpse to the grounde ! "

> *" Then from the black corpse a pale spectre appear'd,*
>   *And hyed him away through the night."*

Goonhylda is of course found uninjured, and taken home by the
earl.   The castle disappears and Dozmare Pool re-appears ; but—

" Stylle as the traveller pursues hys lone waye,
    In horroure at nyghte o'er the waste,
    He hears Syr Tregeagle with shrieks rushe awaye,
    He hears the Black Hunter pursuing his preye,
    And shrynkes at hys bugle's dread blaste."

THE WISH HOUNDS.

THE tradition of the Midnight Hunter and his headless hounds
—always, in Cornwall, associated with Tregeagle—prevails
everywhere.

The Abbot's Way on Dartmoor, an ancient road which extends
into Cornwall, is said to be the favourite coursing ground of " the
wish or wisked hounds of Dartmoor," called also the "yell-
hounds," and the " yeth-hounds." The valley of the Dewerstone is
also the place of their midnight meetings. Once I was told at
Jump, that Sir Francis Drake drove a hearse into Plymouth at
night with headless horses, and that he was followed by a pack of
" yelling hounds " without heads. If dogs hear the cry of the
wish hounds they all die May it not be that "wish" is connected
with the west-country word " whist," meaning more than ordinary
melancholy, a sorrow which has something weird surrounding it ?

" And then he sought the dark-green lane,
    Whose willows mourn'd the faded year,
    Sighing (I heard the love-lorn swain),
    '*Wishness!* oh, *wishness!* walketh here.' "
    — *The Wishful Swain of Devon.* By POLWHELE.

The author adds in a note, " An expression used by the vulgar
in the north of Devon to express local melancholy. There is
something sublime in this impersonation of *wishness.*" The expression is as common in Cornwall as it is in Devonshire.

Mr Kemble has the following incorrect remarks on this word :—
" In Devonshire to this day all magical or supernatural dealings go
under the common name of wishtness. Can this have any
reference to Woden's name ' wysc ? '" Mr Polwhele's note gives
the true meaning of the word Still Mr Kemble's idea is supported
by the fact that " there are *Wishanger* (Wisehangre or Woden's
Meadow), one about four miles south-west of Wanborough in
Surrey, and another near Gloucester." * And we find also, "south-

* Kemble's " Saxons in England," vol. i , p 346. Wistman's Wood on Dartmoor, no

K

east of Pixhill in Tedstone, Delamere, there are *Wishmoor* and Inksmoor near Sapey Bridge in Whitbourn." *

CHENEY'S HOUNDS.

IN the parish of St Teath, a pack of hounds was once kept by an old squire named Cheney. How he or they died I cannot learn ; but on "Cheney Downs" the ghosts of the dogs are sometimes seen, and often heard, in rough weather.

In the western parishes of the county, I can name several places which are said to be haunted by the "wish hounds." †

doubt derives it name from its extraordinary character. Carrington, in his "Dartmoor," well describes its oaks —

　　　　　"But of this grove,
This pigmy grove, not one has climb'd the air,
So emulously that its loftiest branch
May brush the traveller's brow. The twisted roots
Have clasp'd, in search of nourishment, the rocks,
And straggled wide, and pierced the stony soil"
　　　　　"Around the boughs
Hoary and feebly, and around the trunks
With grasp destructive feeding on the life
That lingers yet, the ivy winds, and moss
Of growth enormous "

　　　　　　　　—*Dartmoor, a descriptive poem.*
　　　　　　By N T CARRINGTON, 1826 Murray.

* " The British, Roman, and Saxon Antiquities and Folk-lore of Worcestershire ' By Jabez Allies
† See *Athenæum*, No 1013, March 27, 1847 See Appendix L for Notes on the BARGEST

THE MERMAIDS.

" One Friday morning we set sail,
    And when not far from land,
We all espied a fair mermaid
    With a comb and glass in her hand.
The stormy winds they did blow," &c.
                                    —*Old Song*

ROMANCES OF THE MERMAIDS.

MORVA OR MORVETH (Sea-daughters).

" You dwell not on land, but in the flood,
Which would not with me agree "
—Duke Magnus and the Mermaid —SMALAND.

THE parish of this name is situated on the north-west coast ot Cornwall,—the parish of St Just being on its western borders, and that of Zennor on the east, between it and St Ives. The Cornish historian Tonkin says, " *Morva* signifies Locus Maritimus, a place near the sea, as this parish is. The name is sometimes written *Morveth*, implying much the same sense."

The similarity of this name to " Morgan," *sea-women*, and " Morverch," *sea-daughters*, which Mr Keightley has shown us is applied to the mermaids of the Breton ballads, is not a little curious. There are several stories current in this parish of *ladies seen on the rocks*, of *ladies going off from the shore to peculiar isolated rocks at special seasons*, and of *ladies sitting weeping and wailing on the shore*. Mr Blight, in his " Week at the Land's End," speaking of the church in the adjoining parish, Zennor, which still remains in nearly its primitive condition, whereas Morva church is a modern structure, says—" Some of the bench ends were carved ; on one is a strange figure of a *mermaid*, which to many might seem out of character in a church." (Mr Blight gives a drawing of this bench end.) This is followed by a quotation bearing the initials R. S. H., which, it is presumed, are those of the Rev. R. S Hawker, of Morwenstow.—

" The fishermen who were the ancestors of the Church, came from the Galilean waters to haul for men. We, born to God at the font, are children of the water. Therefore, all the early symbolism of the Church was of and from the sea. The carvure of the early arches was taken from the sea and its creatures. Fish, dolphins, mermen, and mermaids abound in the early types, transferred to wood and stone."

Surely the poet of "the Western Shore" might have explained the fact of the figures of mermaids being carved on the bench ends of some of the old churches with less difficulty, had he remembered that nearly all the churches on the coast of Cornwall were built by and for fishermen, to whom the superstitions of mermen and mermaidens had the familiarity of a creed.

The intimate connection between the inhabitants of Brittany, of Cornwall, and of Wales, would appear to lead to the conclusion that the Breton word *Morverch*, or mermaid, had much to do with the name of this parish, Morva,—of Morvel, near Liskeard,—and probably of Morwenstow, of which the vicar, Mr Hawker, writes— " My glebe occupies a position of wild and singular beauty. Its western boundary is the sea, skirted by tall and tremendous cliffs, and near their brink, with the exquisite taste of ecclesiastical antiquity, is placed the church. The original and proper designation of the parish is *Morwen*-stow—that is, Morwenna's Stow, or station ; but it has been corrupted by recent usage, like many other local names."

MERRYMAIDS AND MERRYMEN.

THE "merry-maids" of the Cornish fishermen and sailors possess the well-recognised features of the mermaid. The Breton ballad, quoted by Mr Keightley, relating to the Morgan (*sea-women*) and the Morverch (sea-daughters), peculiarly adapts itself to the Cornish merry-maid.

" Fisher, hast thou seen the mermaid combing her hair, yellow as gold, by the noontide sun, at the edge of the water ? "

" I have seen the fair mermaid ; I have also heard her singing her songs plaintive as the waves."

The Irish legends make us acquainted with the amours of men with those sea-sirens We learn that the Merrows, or Moruachs, came occasionally from the sea, and interested themselves in the affairs of man Amongst the fragments which have been gathered, here a pebble and there a pebble, along the Western coast, will be found similar narratives.

The sirens of the Ægean Sea—probably the parents of the mediæval mermaid—possess in a pre-eminent degree the beauty and the falsehood of all the race Like all other things, even those mythical creations take colour from that they work in, like the dyer's hand The Italian mermaid is the true creature of the romance of the sunny South ; while the lady of our own southern seas, although she possesses much in common with her Mediterranean sister, has less poetry, but more human sympathy. The following stories, read in connection with those given by Mr Keightley and by Mr Croker, will show this.*

When, five-and-thirty years since, I spent several nights in a fisherman's cottage on a south-western coast, I was treated to many a "long yarn" respecting mermaids seen by the father and his sons in the southern ocean The appearance of those creatures on our own shores, they said, was rare; but still they knew they had been seen. From them I learned of more than one family who have received mysterious powers from the sea-nymphs; and I have since heard that members of those families still live, and that they intimate to their credulous friends their firm belief that this power, which they say has been transmitted to them, was derived, by some one of their ancestors, from merman or mermaiden.

Usually those creatures are associated with some catastrophe; but they are now and then spoken of as the benefactors of man.

One word more. The story of "*The Mermaid's Vengeance*" has been produced from three versions of evidently the same legend, which differed in many respects one from the other, yet' agreeing in the main with each other. The first I heard at the Lizard, or rather at Coverach; the second in Sennen Cove, near the Land's End; the third at Perranzabaloe. I have preferred the last locality, as being peculiarly fitted for the home of a mermaid story, and because the old man who told the tale there was far more graphic in his incidents; and these were strung more closely together than either of the other stories.†

* See "The Fairy Family a Series of Ballads and Metrical Tales Illustrating the Fairy Mythology of Europe," Longman, 1857, "The Fairy Mythology, Illustrative of the Romance and Superstitions of Various Countries," by Thomas Keightley; and "Irish Fairy Legends," by Crofton Croker.

† The following extract from a letter from an esteemed correspondent shows the existence of a belief in those fabled creations of the ocean amongst an extensive class of the labouring population of Cornwall There is so much that is characteristic in my correspondent's letter that it is worth preserving as supporting the evidence of the existing belief.—

"I had the chance of seeing what many of our natives firmly believed to be that family Some fourteen years ago I found myself, with about fifty emigrants, in the Gulf of St Lawrence, on board the old tub *Resolution*, Captain Davies, commander. We were shrouded in a fog so thick that you might cut it like a cheese, almost all the way from the Banks to Anticosti. One morning, soon after sunrise, when near that island, the fog as thick as night overhead, at times would rise and fall on the shore like the tantalising stage curtain All at once there was a clear opening right through the dense clouds which rested on the water, that gave us a glimpse of the shore, with the rocks covered with what to us appeared very strange creatures In a minute, the hue and cry from

THE MERMAID OF PADSTOW.

THE port of Padstow has a good natural harbour, so far as rocky area goes, but it is so choked up with drifting sands as to be nearly useless. A peasant recently thus explained the cause. He told how "it was once deep water for the largest vessel, and under the care of a *merry-maid*—as he called her; but one day, as she was sporting on the surface, a fellow with a gun shot at her. "She dived for a moment; but re-appearing, raised her right arm, and vowed that henceforth the harbour should be desolate." "And," added the old man, "it always will be so. We have had commissions, and I know not what, about converting this place into a harbour of refuge. A harbour of refuge would be a great blessing, but not all the Government commissions in the world could keep the sand out, or make the harbour deep enough to swim a frigate, unless the parsons can find out the way to take up the merry-maid's curse."

Another tale refers the choking up of this harbour to the bad spirit Tregeagle.

THE MERMAID'S ROCK.

TO the westward of the beautiful Cove of Lemorna is a rock which has through all time borne the above name. I have never been enabled to learn any special story in connection with this rock. There exists the popular fancy of a lady showing herself here previous to a storm—with, of course, the invariable comb and glass. She is said to have been heard singing most plaintively before a wreck, and that, all along the shore, the spirits have echoed her in low moaning voices.[*] Young men are

stem to stern, among all the cousin Johnnys, was 'What are they, you? What are they, you?' Somebody gave the word mermaids. Old men, women, and children, that hadn't been out of their bunks for weeks, tore on deck to see the mermaids; when, alas! the curtain dropped, or rather closed, and the fair were lost to sight, but to memory dear, for, all the way to Quebec, those not lucky enough to see the sight bothered the others out of their lives to know how they looked, and if we saw the comb and glass in their hands. The captain might as well save his breath as tell them that the creatures they saw on the rocks were seals, walruses, and sea-calves 'Not *yet*, *Captain* dear, you won't come that over me at all; no, not by a long chalk! no, not at all, I can tell 'e! I know there are mermaids in the sea, have heard many say so who have seen them too! but as for sea-calves, I ain't such a calf nor donkey neither as to believe it There may be a few of what we call soils (seals) for all I know, perhaps so, but the rest were mermaidens' No doubt, centuries hence, this story of the mermaidens will be handed down with many additions, in the log-huts of the Western States"

* The undulations of the air, travelling with more rapidity than the currents, reach our shores long before the tempest by which they have been established in the centre of

said to have swam off to the rock, lured by the songs which they heard, but they have never returned.   Have we not in this a dim shadow of the story of the Sirens?

THE MERMAID OF SEATON.

NEAR Looe,—that is, between Down Derry and Looe,—there is a little sand-beach called " Seaton."

Tradition tells us that here once stood a goodly commercial town bearing this name, and that when it was in its pride, Plymouth was but a small fishing-village.

The town of Seaton is said to have been overwhelmed with sand at an early period, the catastrophe having been brought about,—as in the case of the filling up of Padstow harbour,—by the curse of a mermaid, who had suffered some injury from the sailors who belonged to this port.   Beyond this I have been unable to glean any story worth preserving.

THE OLD MAN OF CURY.

MORE than a hundred years since, on a fine summer day, when the sun shone brilliantly from a cloudless sky, an old man from the parish of Cury, or, as it was called in olden time, Corantyn, was walking on the sands in one of the coves near the Lizard Point.   The old man was meditating, or at least he was walking onward, either thinking deeply, or not thinking at all—that is, he was " lost in thought "—when suddenly he came upon a rock on which was sitting a beautiful girl with fair hair, so long that it covered her entire person.   On the in-shore side of the rock was a pool of the most transparent water, which had been left by the receding tide in the sandy hollow the waters had scooped out.   This young creature was so absorbed in her occupation,—arranging her hair in the watery mirror, or in admiration of her own lovely face, that she was unconscious of an intruder

The old man stood looking at her for some time ere he made up his mind how to act   At length he resolved to speak to the maiden.   " What cheer, young one ? " he said ; " what art thee doing there by thyself, then, this time o' day ? "   As soon as she heard the voice, she slid off the rock entirely under the water.

the Atlantic, and by producing a low moaning sound, " the soughing of the wind," predicates the storms.   The "moans of Tregeagle " is another expression indicating the same phenomenon

The old man could not tell what to make of it. He thought the girl would drown herself, so he ran on to the rock to render her assistance, conceiving that in her fright at being found naked by a man she had fallen into the pool, and possibly it was deep enough to drown her. He looked into the water, and, sure enough, he could make out the head and shoulders of a woman, and long hair floating like fine sea-weeds all over the pond, hiding what appeared to him to be a fish's tail. He could not, however, see anything distinctly, owing to the abundance of hair floating around the figure. The old man had heard of mermaids from the fishermen of Gunwalloe; so he conceived this lady must be one, and he was at first very much frightened. He saw that the young lady was quite as much terrified as he was, and that, from shame or fear, she endeavoured to hide herself in the crevices of the rock, and bury herself under the sea-weeds.

Summoning courage, at last the old man addressed her, " Don't 'e be afraid, my dear. You needn't mind me. I wouldn't do ye any harm. I'm an old man, and wouldn't hurt ye any more than your grandfather."

After he had talked in this soothing strain for some time, the young lady took courage, and raised her head above the water. She was crying bitterly, and, as soon as she could speak, she begged the old man to go away.

" I must know, my dearie, something about ye, now I have caught ye. It is not every day that an old man catches a merry-maid, and I have heard some strange tales of you water-ladies Now, my dear, don't 'e be afraid, I would not hurt a single hair of that beautiful head. How came ye here?" After some further coaxing she told the old man the following story :—She and her husband and little ones had been busy at sea all the morning, and they were very tired with swimming in the hot sun, so·the merman proposed that they should retire to a cavern, which they were in the habit of visiting in Kynance Cove. Away they all swam, and entered the cavern at mid-tide. As there was some nice soft weed, and the cave was deliciously cool, the merman was disposed to sleep, and told them not to wake him until the rise of the tide. He was soon fast asleep, snoring most lustily. The children crept out and were playing on the lovely sands; so the mermaid thought she should like to look at the world a little She looked with delight on the children rolling to and fro in the shallow waves, and she laughed heartily at the crabs fighting in their own funny way. " The scent from the flowers came down over the cliffs so sweetly," said she, " that I longed to get nearer the lovely things which yielded those rich odours, and I floated on from rock to rock until I came to this one ; and finding that I could not proceed any further, I thought I would seize the opportunity of dressing my hair." She passed her fingers through those beautiful locks, and shook out a number of small crabs, and much broken sea-weed. She went on to say that she had sat on the rock amusing herself, until the voice of a mortal terrified her, and until then she had no idea that the sea was so far out, and a long dry bar of sand between her and it. " What shall I do ? what shall I do ? Oh ! I 'd give the world to get out to sea ! Oh ! oh ! what shall I do ? "

The old man endeavoured to console her ; but his attempts were in vain. She told him her husband would " carry on " most dreadfully if he awoke and found her absent, and he would be certain of awaking at the turn of the tide, as that was his dinner-time. He was very savage when he was hungry, and would as soon eat the children as not, if there was no other food at hand. He was also dreadfully jealous, and if she was not at his side when he awoke, he would at once suspect her of having run off with some other merman. She begged the old man to bear her out to sea. If he would but do so, she would procure him any three things he would wish for. Her entreaties at length prevailed ; and, according to her desire, the old man knelt down on the rock with his back towards her. She clasped her fair arms around his neck, and locked her long finny fingers together on his throat. He got up from the rock with his burthen, and carried the mermaid thus across the sands. As she rode in this way, she asked the old man to tell her what he desired.

" I will not wish," said he, " for silver and gold, but give me the power to do good to my neighbours . first, to break the spells of witchcraft ; next, to charm away diseases , and thirdly, to discover thieves, and restore stolen goods."

All this she promised he should possess ; but he must come to a half-tide rock on another day, and she would instruct him how to accomplish the three things he desired. They had reached the water, and taking her comb from her hair, she gave it to the old man, telling him he had but to comb the water and call her at any time, and she would come to him The mermaid loosened her grasp, and sliding off the old man's back into the sea, she waved him a kiss and disappeared. At the appointed time the old man was at the half-tide rock,—known to the present time as the Mermaid's Rock,—and duly was he instructed in many mysteries. Amongst others, he learned to break the spells of witches from man or beast ; to prepare a vessel of water, in which to show to any one who had property stolen the face of the thief ; to charm shingles, tetters, St Antony's fire, and St Vitus's dance , and he learnt also all the mysteries of bramble leaves, and the like.

The mermaid had a woman's curiosity, and she persuaded her old friend to take her to some secret place. from which she could see more of the dry land, and of the funny people who lived on it, "and had their tails split, so that they could walk." On taking the mermaid back to the sea, she wished her friend to visit her abode, and promised even to make him young if he would do so, which favour the old gentleman respectfully declined. A family, well known in Cornwall, have for some generations exercised the power of charming, &c They account for the possession of this power in the manner related. Some remote great-grandfather was the individual who received the mermaid's comb, which they retain to the present day, and show us evidence of the truth of their being supernaturally endowed. Some people are unbelieving enough to say the comb is only a part of a shark's jaw. Sceptical people are never lovable people.

THE MERMAID'S VENGEANCE.*

IN one of the deep valleys of the parish of Perranzabuloe, which are remarkable for their fertility, and especially for the abundance of fruit which the orchards produce, lived in days long ago, amidst a rudely-civilised people, a farmer's labourer, his wife, with one child, a daughter The man and woman were equally industrious. The neatly white-washed walls of their mud-built cottage, the well-kept gravelled paths, and carefully-weeded beds of their small garden, in which flowers were cultivated for ornament, and vegetables for use, proclaimed at once the character of the inmates. In contrast with the neighbouring cottages, this one, although smaller than many others, had a superior aspect, and the occupiers of it exhibited a strong contrast to those peasants and miners amidst whom they dwelt.

Pennaluna, as the man was called, or Penna the Proud, as he was, in no very friendly spirit, named by his less thoughtful and more impulsive fellows, was, as we have said, a farmer's labourer.

---

* Several versions of the following story have been given me The general idea of the tale belongs to the north coast ; but the fact of mermaidens taking innocents under their charge-was common around the Lizard, and in some of the coves near the Land's End

His master was a wealthy yeoman, and he, after many years' experience, was so convinced of the exceeding industry and sterling honesty of Penna, that he made him the manager of an outlying farm in this parish, under the hind (or hine—the Saxon pronunciation is still retained in the West of England), or general supervisor of this and numerous other extensive farms.

Penna was too great a favourite with the Squire to be a favourite of the hind's ; he was evidently jealous of him, and from not being himself a man of very strict principles, he hated the unobtrusive goodness of his underling, and was constantly on the watch to discover some cause of complaint. It was not, however, often that he was successful in this. Every task committed to the care of Penna, —and he was often purposely overtasked,—was executed with great care and despatch. With the wife of Penna, however, the case was unfortunately different. Honour Penna was as industrious as her husband, and to him she was in all respects a helpmate. She had, however, naturally a proud spirit, and this had been encouraged in her youth by her parents. Honour was very pretty as a girl, and, indeed, she retained much beauty as a woman. The only education she received was the wild one of experience, and this within a very narrow circle. She grew an ignorant girl, amongst ignorant men and women, few of them being able to write their names, and scarcely any of them to read. There was much native grace about her, and she was flattered by the young men, and envied by the young women, of the village,—the envy and the flattery being equally pleasant to her. In the same village was born, and brought up, Tom Chenalls, who had, in the course of years, become hind to the Squire. Tom, as a young man, had often expressed himself fond of Honour, but he was always distasteful to the village maiden, and eventually, while yet young, she was married to Pennaluna, who came from the southern coast, bringing with him the recommendation of being a stranger, and an exceedingly hard-working man, who was certain to earn bread, and something more, for his wife and family. In the relations in which these people were now placed towards each other, Chenalls had the opportunity of acting ungenerously towards the Pennas. The man bore this uncomplainingly, but the woman frequently quarrelled with him whom she felt was an enemy, and whom she still regarded but as her equal. Chenalls was a skilled farmer, and hence was of considerable value to the Squire , but although he was endured for his farming knowledge and his business habits, he was never a favourite with his employer. Penna, on the contrary, was an especial favourite, and the evidences of this were so often brought strikingly under the observation of Chenalls, that it increased the irritation of his hate, for it amounted to that. For years things went on thus. There was the tranquil suffering of an oppressed spirit manifested in Penna—the angry words and actions of his wife towards the oppressor,—and, at the same time, as she with much fondness studied to make their humble home comfortable for her husband, she reviled him not unfrequently for the meek spirit with which he endured his petty, but still trying, wrongs. The hind dared not venture on any positive act of wrong towards those people, yet he lost no chance of annoying them, knowing that the Squire's partiality for Penna would not allow him to venture beyond certain bounds, even in this direction.

Penna's solace was his daughter. She had now reached her eighteenth year, and with the well-developed form of a woman, she united the simplicity of a child. Selina, as she was named, was in many respects beautiful. Her features were regular, and had they been lighted up with more mental fire, they would have been beautiful ; but the constant repose, the want of animation, left her face merely a pretty one. Her skin was beautifully white, and transparent to the blue veins which traced their ways beneath it, to the verge of that delicacy which indicates disease ; but it did not pass that verge Selina was full of health, as her well-moulded form at once showed, and her clear blue eye distinctly told. At times there was a lovely tint upon the cheek—not the hectic of consumptive beauty,—but a pure rosy dye, suffused by the healthy life stream, when it flowed the fastest.

The village gossips, who were always busy with their neighbours, said strange things of this girl. Indeed, it was commonly reported that the real child of the Pennas was a remarkably plain child, in every respect a different being from Selina. The striking difference between the infant and the woman was variously explained by the knowing ones. Two stories were, however, current for miles around the country. One was, that Selina's mother was constantly seen gathering dew in the morning, with which to wash her child, and that the fairies on the Towens had, in pure malice, aided her in giving a temporary beauty to the girl, that it might lead to her betrayal into crime. Why this malice, was never clearly made out.

The other story was, that Honour Penna constantly bathed the child in a certain pool, amidst the arched rocks of Perran, which was a favourite resort of the mermaids ; that on one occasion the child, as if in a paroxysm of joy, leapt from her arms into the

water, and disappeared.   The mother, as may well be supposed,
suffered a momentary agony of terror ; but presently the babe
swam up to the surface of the water, its little face more bright and
beautiful than it had ever been before.   Great was the mother's
joy, and also—as the gossips say—great her surprise at the sudden
change in the appearance of her offspring.   The mother knew no
difference in the child whom she pressed lovingly to her bosom,
but all the aged crones in the parish declared it to be a changeling.   This tale lived its day ; but, as the girl grew on to womanhood, and showed none of the special qualifications belonging
either to fairies or mermaids, it was almost forgotten.   The un-
complaining father had solace for all his sufferings in wandering
over the beautiful sands with his daughter.   Whether it was when
the summer seas fell in musical undulations on the shore, or when,
stirred by the winter tempests, the great Atlantic waves came up
in grandeur, and lashed the resisting sands in giant rage, those two
enjoyed the solitude.   Hour after hour, from the setting sun time,
until the clear cold moon flooded the ocean with her smiles of light,
would the father and child walk these sands.   They seemed never
to weary of them and the ocean.

Almost every morning, throughout the milder seasons, Selina
was in the habit of bathing, and wild tales were told of the frantic
joy with which she would play with the breaking billows.   Sometimes floating over, and almost dancing on the crests of the waves,
at other times rushing under them, and allowing the breaking waters
to beat her to the sands, as though they were loving arms, endeavouring to encircle her form.   Certain it is, that Selina greatly
enjoyed her bath, but all the rest must be regarded as the creations
of the imagination.   The most eager to give a construction unfav-
ourable to the simple mortality of the maiden was, however, compelled to acknowledge that there was no evidence in her general conduct to support their surmises.   Selina, as an only child, fared the fate
of others who are unfortunately so placed, and was, as the phrase
is, spoiled   She certainly was allowed to follow her own inclinations
without any check.   Still her inclinations were bounded to working in the garden, and to leading her father to the sea-shore.
Honour Penna, sometimes, it is true, did complain that Selina
could not be trusted with the most ordinary domestic duty.   Beyond this, there was one other cause of grief, that was, the increasing dislike which Selina exhibited towards entering a church.   The
girl, notwithstanding the constant excuses of being sick, suffering
from headache, having a pain in her side, and the like, was often
taken, notwithstanding, by her mother to the church.   It is said

that she always shuddered as she passed the church-stile, and again on stepping from the porch into the church itself. When once within the house of prayer she evinced no peculiar liking or disliking, observing respectfully all the rules during the performance of the church-service, and generally sleeping, or seeming to sleep, during the sermon. Selina Pennaluna had reached her eighteenth year; she was admired by many of the young men of the parish, but, as if surrounded by a spell, she appeared to keep them all at a distance from her. About this time, a nephew to the Squire, a young soldier,—who had been wounded in the wars, —came into Cornwall to heal his wounds, and recover health, which had suffered in a trying campaign.

This young man, Walter Trewoofe, was a rare specimen of manhood. Even now, shattered as he was by the combined influences of wounds, an unhealthy climate, and dissipation, he could not but be admired for fineness of form, dignity of carriage, and masculine beauty. It was, however, but too evident, that this young man was his own idol, and that he expected every one to bow down with him, and worship it. His uncle was proud of Walter, and although the old gentleman could not fail to see many faults, yet he regarded them as the follies of youth, and trusted to their correction with the increase of years and experience. Walter, who was really suffering severely, was ordered by his surgeon, at first, to take short walks on the sea-shore, and, as he gained strength, to bathe. He was usually driven in his uncle's ponycarriage to the edge of the sands. Then dismounting he would walk for a short time, and quickly wearing, return in his carriage to the luxuriant couches at the manor-house.

On some of those occasions Walter had observed the father and daughter taking their solitary ramble. He was struck with the quiet beauty of the girl, and seized an early opportunity of stopping Penna to make some general inquiry respecting the bold and beautiful coast. From time to time they thus met, and it would have been evident to any observer that Walter did not so soon weary of the sands as formerly, and that Selina was not displeased with the flattering things he said to her. Although the young soldier had hitherto led a wild life, it would appear as if for a considerable period the presence of goodness had repressed every tendency to evil in his ill-regulated heart. He continued, therefore, for some time playing with his own feelings and those of the childlike being who presented so much of romance, combined with the most homely tameness, of character. Selina, it is true, had never yet seen Walter except in the presence of her father, and it is questionable if she had ever for one moment had a warmer feeling than that of the mere pleasure—a silent pride—that a gentleman, at once so handsome, so refined, and the nephew of her father's master, should pay her any attention. Evil eyes were watching with wicked earnestness the growth of passion, and designing hearts were beating quicker with a consciousness that they should eventually rejoice in the downfall of innocence. Tom Chenalls hoped that he might achieve a triumph, if he could but once asperse the character of Selina. He took his measures accordingly. Having noticed the change in the general conduct of his master's nephew, he argued that this was due to the refining influence of a pure mind, acting on one more than ordinarily impressionable to either evil or good.

Walter rapidly recovered health, and with renewed strength the manly energy of his character began to develop itself. He delighted in horse-exercise, and Chenalls had always the best horse on the farms at his disposal. He was a good shot, and Chenalls was his guide to the best shooting-grounds. He sometimes fished, and Chenalls knew exactly where the choicest trout and the richest salmon were to be found. In fact, Chenalls entered so fully into the tastes of the young man, that Walter found him absolutely necessary to him to secure the enjoyments of a country life.

Having established this close intimacy, Chenalls never lost an opportunity of talking with Walter respecting Selina Penna. He soon satisfied himself that Walter, like most other young men who had led a dissipated life, had but a very low estimate of women generally. Acting upon this, he at first insinuated that Selina's innocence was but a mask, and at length he boldly assured Walter that the cottage girl was to be won by him with a few words, and that then he might put her aside at any time as a prize to some low-born peasant. Chenalls never failed to impress on Walter the necessity of keeping his uncle in the most perfect darkness, and of blinding the eyes of Selina's parents. Penna was,—so thought Chenalls,—easily managed, but there was more to be feared from the wife. Walter, however, with much artifice, having introduced himself to Honour Penna, employed the magic of that flattery, which, being properly applied, seldom fails to work its way to the heart of a weak-minded woman. He became an especial favourite with Honour, and the blinded mother was ever pleased at the attention bestowed with so little assumption,—as she thought,—of pride, on her daughter, by one so much above them. Walter eventually succeeded in separating occasionally, though not often, Penna and his daughter. The witching whispers of unholy love were poured into the trusting ear. Guileless herself, this child-woman suspected no guile in others, least of all in one whom she had been taught to look upon as a superior being to herself. Amongst the villagers, the constant attention of Walter Trewoofe was the subject of gossip, and many an old proverb was quoted by the elder women, ill-naturedly, and implying that evil must come of this intimacy. Tom Chenalls was now employed by Walter to contrive some means by which he could remove Penna for a period from home. He was not long in doing this. He lent every power of his wicked nature to aid the evil designs of the young soldier, and thus he brought about that separation of father and child which ended in her ruin.

Near the Land's End the squire possessed some farms, and one of them was reported to be in such a state of extreme neglect, through the drunkenness and consequent idleness of the tenant, that Chenalls soon obtained permission to take the farm from this occupier, which he did in the most unscrupulous disregard for law or right. It was then suggested that the only plan by which a desirable occupier could be found, would be to get the farm and farm-buildings into good condition, and that Penna, of all men, would be the man to bring this quickly about. The squire was pleased with the plan. Penna was sent for by him, and was proud of the confidence which his master reposed in him. There was some sorrow on his leaving home. He subsequently said that he had had many warnings not to go, but he felt that he dared not disoblige a master who had trusted him so far—so he went.

Walter needed not any urging on the part of Chenalls, though he was always ready to apply the spur when there was the least evidence of the sense of right asserting itself in the young man's bosom. Week after week passed on. Walter had rendered himself a necessity to Selina. Without her admirer the world was cold and colourless With him all was sunshine and glowing tints.

Three months passed thus away, and during that period it had only been possible for Penna to visit his home twice. The father felt that something like a spirit of evil stood between him and his daughter. There was no outward evidence of any change, but there was an inward sense—undefined, yet deeply felt—like an overpowering fear—that some wrong had been done. On parting, Penna silently but earnestly prayed that the deep dread might be removed from his mind. There was an aged fisherman, who resided in a small cottage built on the sands, who possessed all the superstitions of his class. This old man had formed a father's liking for the simple-hearted maiden, and he had persuaded

L

himself that there really was some foundation for the tales which the gossips told. To the fisherman, Walter Trewoofe was an evil genius. He declared that no good ever came to him, if he met Walter when he was about to go to sea. With this feeling he curiously watched the young man and maiden, and he, in after days, stated his conviction that he had ·seen " merry maidens " rising from the depth of the waters, and floating under the billows, to watch Selina and her lover. He has also been heard to say, that on more than one occasion Walter himself had been terrified by sights and sounds. Certain, however, it is, these were insufficient, and the might of evil passions were more powerful than any of the protecting influences of the unseen world.

Another three months had gone by, and Walter Trewoofe had disappeared from Perranzabuloe. He had launched into the gay world of the metropolis, and rarely, if ever, dreamed of the deep sorrow which was weighing down the heart he had betrayed. Penna returned home—his task was done—and Chenalls had no reason for keeping him any longer from his wife and daughter. Clouds gathered slowly but unremittingly around him. His daughter retired into herself, no longer as of old reposing her whole soul on her father's heart. His wife was somewhat changed too—she had some secret in her heart which she feared to tell. The home he had left was not the home to which he had returned. It soon became evident that some shock had shaken the delicate flame of his daughter. She pined rapidly ; and Penna was awakened to a knowledge of the cause by the rude rejoicing of Chenalls, who declared " that all people who kept themselves so much above other people were sure to be pulled down." On one occasion he so far tempted Penna with sneers, at his having hoped to secure the young squire for a son-in-law, that the long-enduring man broke forth and administered a severe blow upon his tormentor. This was duly reported to the squire, and added thereto was a magnified story of a trap which had been set by the Pennas to catch young Walter ; it was represented that even now they intended to press their claims, on account of grievous wrongs upon them, whereas it could be proved that Walter was guiltless—that he was indeed the innocent victim of designing people, who thought to make money out of their assumed misfortune. The squire made his inquiries, and there were not a few who eagerly seized the opportunity to gain the friendship of Chenalls by representing this family to have been hypocrites of .the deepest dye ; and the poor girl especially was now loaded with a weight of iniquities of which she had no knowledge. All this ended in the dismissal of Penna from the Squire's service, and in his being deprived of the cottage in which he had taken so much pride. Although thrown out upon the world a disgraced man, Penna faced his difficulties manfully. He cast off, as it were, the primitive simplicity of his character, and evidently worked with a firm resolve to beat down his sorrows. He was too good a workman to remain long unemployed; and although his new home was not his happy home as of old, there was no repining heard from his lips. Weaker and weaker grew Selina, and it soon became evident to all, that if she came from a spirit-world, to a spirit-world she must soon return. Grief filled the hearts of her parents—it prostrated her mother, but the effects of severe labour, and the efforts of a settled mind, appeared to tranquillise the breast of her father. Time passed on, the wounds of the soul grew deeper, and there lay, on a low bed, from which she had not strength to move, the fragile form of youth with the countenance of age. The body was almost powerless, but there beamed from the eye the evidences of a spirit getting free from the chains of clay

The dying girl was sensible of the presence of creations other than mortal, and with these she appeared to hold converse, and to derive solace from the communion. Penna and his wife alternately watched through the night hours by the side of their loved child, and anxiously did they mark the moment when the tide turned, in the full belief that she would be taken from them when the waters of the ocean began to recede from the shore. Thus days passed on, and eventually the sunlight of a summer morning shone in through the small window of this humble cottage,—on a dead mother—and a living babe.

The dead was buried in the churchyard on the sands, and the living went on their ways, some rejoicingly and some in sorrow.

Once more Walter Trewoofe appeared in Perran-on-the-sands. Penna would have sacrificed him to his hatred; he emphatically protested that he had lived only to do so; but the good priest of the Oratory contrived to lay the devil who had possession, and to convince Penna that the Lord would, in His own good time, and in His own way, avenge the bitter wrong. Tom Chenalls had his hour of triumph; but from the day on which Selina died everything went wrong. The crops failed, the cattle died, hay-stacks and corn-ricks caught fire, cows slipped their calves, horses fell lame, or stumbled and broke their knees,—a succession of evils steadily pursued him. Trials find but a short resting-place with the good, they may be bowed to the earth with the weight of a sudden sorrow, but they look to heaven, and their elasticity is restored. The evil-minded are crushed at once, and grovel on the ground in irremediable misery. That Chenalls fled to drink in his troubles appeared but the natural result to a man of his character. This unfitted him for his duties, and he was eventually dismissed from his situation. Notwithstanding that the Squire refused to listen to the appeals in favour of Chenalls, which were urged upon him by Walter, and that indeed he forbade his nephew to countenance " the scoundrel " in any way, Walter still continued his friend. By his means Tom Chenalls secured a small cottage on the cliff, and around it a little cultivated ground, the produce of which was his only visible means of support. That lonely cottage was the scene, however, of drunken carousals, and there the vicious young men, and the no less vicious young women, of the district, went after nightfall, and kept " high carnival " of sin. Walter Trewoofe came frequently amongst them ; and as his purse usually defrayed the costs of a debauch, he was regarded by all with especial favour.

One midnight, Walter, who had been dancing and drinking for some hours, left the cottage wearied with his excesses, and although not drunk, he was much excited with wine. His pathway lay along the edge of the cliffs, amidst bushes of furze and heath, and through several irregular, zigzag ways. There were lateral paths striking off from one side of the main path, and leading down to the sea-shore. Although it was moonlight, without being actually aware of the error, Walter wandered into one of those ; and before he was awake to his mistake, he found himself on the sands. He cursed his stupidity, and, uttering a blasphemous oath, he turned to retrace his steps.

The most exquisite music which ever flowed from human lips fell on his ear ; he paused to listen, and collecting his unbalanced thoughts, he discovered that it was the voice of a woman singing a melancholy dirge .—

> " The stars are beautiful, when bright
> They are mirror'd in the sea ;
> But they are pale beside that light
> Which was so beautiful to me.
> My angel child, my earth-born girl,
> From all your kindred riven,
> By the base deeds of a selfish churl,
> And to a sand-grave driven !
> How shall I win thee back to ocean?
> How canst thou quit thy grave,
> To share again the sweet emotion
> Of gliding through the wave ?"

Walter, led by the melancholy song, advanced slowly along the sands. He discovered that the sweet, soft sounds proceeded from the other side of a mass of rocks, which project far out over the sands, and that now, at low-water, there was no difficulty in walking around it. Without hesitation he did so, and he beheld, sitting at the mouth of a cavern, one of the most beautiful women he had ever beheld. She continued her song, looking upwards to the stars, not appearing to notice the intrusion of a stranger. Walter stopped, and gazed on the lovely image before him with admiration and wonder, mingled with something of terror. He dared not speak, but fixed, as if by magic, he stood gazing on. After a few minutes, the maiden, suddenly perceiving that a man was near her, uttered a piercing shriek, and made as if to fly into the cavern. Walter sprang forward and seized her by the arm, exclaiming, "Not yet, my pretty maiden, not yet."

She stood still in the position of flight, with one arm behind her, grasped by Walter, and turning round her head, her dark eyes beamed with unnatural lustre upon him. Impressionable he had ever been, but never had he experienced anything so entrancing, and at the same time so painful, as that gaze. It was Selina's face looking lovingly upon him, but it seemed to possess some new power—a might of mind from which he felt it was impossible for him to escape. Walter slackened his hold, and slowly allowed the arm to fall from his hand. The maiden turned fully round upon him. "Go!" she said. He could not move. "Go, man!" she repeated. He was powerless.

> "Go to the grave where the sinless one sleepeth!
> Bring her cold corse where her guarding one weepeth;
> Look on her, love her again, ay! betray her,
> And wreath with false smiles the pale face of her slayer!
> Go, go! now, and feel the full force of my sorrow!
> For the glut of my vengeance there cometh a morrow."

Walter was statue-like, and he awoke from this trance-like state only when the waves washed his feet, and he became aware that even now it was only by wading through the waters that he could return around the point of rocks. He was alone. He called; no one answered. He sought wildly, as far as he now dared, amidst the rocks, but the lovely woman was nowhere to be discovered.

There was no real danger on such a night as this; therefore Walter walked fearlessly through the gentle waves, and recovered the pathway up from the sands. More than once he thought he heard a rejoicing laugh, which was echoed in the rocks, but no one was to be seen. Walter reached his home and bed, but he found no sleep ; and in the morning he arose with a sense of wretchedness which was entirely new to him. He feared to make any one of his rough companions a confidant, although he felt this would have relieved his heart. He therefore nursed the wound which he now felt, until a bitter remorse clouded his existence. After some days, he was impelled to visit the grave of the lost one, and in the fulness of the most selfish sorrow, he sat on the sands and shed tears. The priest of the Oratory observed him, and knowing Walter Trewoofe, hesitated not to inquire into his cause of sorrow. His heart was opened to the holy man, and the strange tale was told—the only result being, that the priest felt satisfied it was but a vivid dream, which had resulted from a brain over-excited by drink. He, however, counselled the young man, giving him some religious instruction, and dismissed him with his blessing. There was relief in this. For some days Walter did not venture to visit his old haunt, the cottage of Chenalls. Since he could not be lost to his companions without greatly curtailing their vicious enjoyments, he was hunted up by Chenalls, and again enticed within the circle. His absence was explained on the plea of illness. Walter was, however, an altered man ; there was not the same boisterous hilarity as formerly. He no longer abandoned himself without restraint to the enjoyments of the time. If he ever, led on by his thoughtless and rough-natured friends, assumed for a moment his usual mirth, it was checked by some invisible power. On such occasions he would turn deadly pale, look anxiously around, and fall back, as if ready to faint, on the nearest seat. Under these influences, he lost health. His uncle, who was really attached to his nephew, although he regretted his dissolute conduct, became now seriously alarmed Physicians were consulted in vain ; the young man pined, and the old gossips came to the conclusion that Walter Trewoofe was ill-wished, and there was a general feeling that Penna or his wife was at the bottom of it. Walter, living really on one idea, and that one the beautiful face which was, and yet was not, that of Selina, resolved again to explore the spot on which he had met this strange being, of whom nothing could be learned by any of the covert inquiries he made. He lingered long ere he could resolve on the task ; but wearied, worn by the oppression of one undefined idea, in which an intensity of love was mixed with a shuddering fear, he at last gathered sufficient courage to seize an opportunity for again going to the cavern. On this occasion, there being no moon, the night was dark, but the stars shone brightly from a sky, cloudless, save a dark mist which hung heavily over the western horizon. Every spot of ground being familiar to him, who, boy and man, had traced it over many times, the partial darkness presented no difficulty. Walter had scarcely reached the level sands, which were left hard by the retiring tide, than he heard again the same magical voice as before. But now the song was a joyous one, the burthen of it being—

> " Join all hands—
> Might and main,
> Weave the sands,
> Form a chain,
> He, my lover,
> Comes again ! "

He could not entirely dissuade himself but that he heard this repeated by many voices ; but he put the thought aside, referring it, · as well he might, to the numerous echoes from the cavernous openings in the cliffs.

He reached the eastern side of the dark mass of rocks, from the point of which the tide was slowly subsiding. The song had ceased, and a low moaning sound—the soughing of the wind—passed along the shore. Walter trembled with fear, and was on the point of returning, when a most flute-like murmur rose from the other side of the rocky barrier, which was presently moulded into words :—

> " From your couch of glistening pearl,
> Slowly, softly, come away ;
> Our sweet earth-child, lovely girl,
> Died this day,—died this day."

Memory told Walter that truly was it the anniversary of Selina Pennaluna's death, and to him every gentle wave falling on the shore sang, or murmured—

> " Died this day,—died this day."

The sand was left dry around the point of the rocks, and Walter, impelled by a power which he could not control, walked onward. The moment he appeared on the western side of the rock, a wild laugh burst into the air, as if from the deep cavern before him, at the entrance of which sat the same beautiful being whom he had formerly met. There was now an expression of rare joy on her face, her eyes glistened with delight, and she extended her arms, as if to welcome him.

" Was it ever your wont to move so slowly towards your loved one ? "

Walter heard it was Selina's voice. He saw it was Selina's features ; but he was conscious it was not Selina's form.

" Come, sit beside me, Walter, and let us talk of love." He sat down without a word, and looked into the maiden's face with a vacant expression of fondness. Presently she placed her hand upon his heart ; a shudder passed through his frame ; but having passed, he felt no more pain, but a rare intensity of delight. The maiden wreathed her arm around his neck, drew Walter towards her, and then he remembered how often he had acted thus towards Selina. She bent over him and looked into his eyes. In his mind's mirror he saw himself looking thus into the eyes of his be-trayed one.

" You loved her once ? " said the maiden.

" I did indeed," answered Walter, with a sigh.

" As you loved her, so I love you," said the maiden, with a smile which shot like a poisoned dart through Walter's heart. She lifted the young man's head lovingly between her hands, and bending over him, pressed her lips upon and kissed his forehead, Walter curiously felt that although he was the kissed, yet that he was the kisser.

" Kisses," she said, " are as true at sea as they are false on land. You men kiss the earth-born maidens to betray them. The kiss of a sea-child is the seal of constancy. You are mine till death."

" Death ! " almost shrieked Walter.

A full consciousness of his situation now broke upon Walter. He had heard the tales of the gossips respecting the mermaid origin of Selina ; but he had laughed at them as an idle fancy. He now felt they were true. For hours Walter was compelled to sit by the side of his beautiful tormentor, every word of assumed love and rapture being a torture of the most exquisite kind to him. He could not escape from the arms which were wound around him. He saw the tide rising rapidly. He heard the deep voice of the winds coming over the sea from the far west. He saw that which appeared at first as a dark mist, shape itself into a dense black mass of cloud, and rise rapidly over the star-bedecked space above him. He saw by the brilliant edge of light which occasion? be fringed the clouds that they were deeply charged with th . long There was something sublime in the steady motion of the by the and now the roll of the waves, which had been disturb cy of love Atlantic, reached our shores, and the breakers fell red sufficient within a few feet of Walter and his companion to the cavern. terror shook him, and with each convulsion h night was dark, but with still more ardour, and pressed so closely to the maiden's bosom, that he heard her heart dancing of joy

At length his terrors gave birth to words, and he implored her to let him go.

" The kiss of the sea-child is the seal of constancy." Walter vehemently implored forgiveness. He confessed his deep iniquity. He promised a life of penitence.

" Give me back the dead," said the maiden bitterly, and she planted another kiss, which seemed to pierce his brain by its coldness, upon his forehead.

The waves rolled around the rock on which they sat ; they washed their seat. Walter was still in the female's grasp, and she lifted him to a higher ledge. The storm approached. Lightnings struck down from the heavens into the sands, and thunders roared along the iron cliffs. The mighty waves grew yet more rash, and washed up to this strange pair, who now sat on the highest pinnacle of the pile of rocks. Walter's terrors nearly overcame him ; but he was roused by a liquid stream of fire, which positively hissed by him, followed immediately by a crash of thunder, which shook the solid earth. Tom Chenall's cottage on the cliff burst into a blaze, and Walter saw, from his place amidst the raging waters, a crowd of male and female roisterers rush terrified out upon the heath, to be driven back by the pelting storm. The climax of horrors appeared to surround Walter. He longed to end it in death, but he could not die. His senses were quickened. He saw his wicked companion and evil adviser struck to the ground, a blasted heap of ashes, by a lightning stroke, and at the same moment he and his companion were borne off the rock on the top of a mountainous wave, on which he floated ; the woman holding him by the hair of his head, and singing in a rejoicing voice, which was like a silver bell heard amidst the deep base bellowings of the storm—

> " Come away, come away,
> O'er the waters wild !
> Our earth-born child
> Died this day, died this day.

> " Come away, come away !
> The tempest loud
> Weaves the shroud
> For him who did betray.

> " Come away, come away !
> Beneath the wave
> th the grave
> we slay, him we slay.

> " Come away, come away !
>   He shall not rest
>   In earth's own breast
> For many a day, many a day.
>
> " Come away, còme away !
>   By billows tost
>   From coast to coast,
>   Like deserted boat
>   His corse shall float
> Around the bay, around the bay."

Myriads of voices on that wretched night were heard amidst the roar of the storm. The waves were seen covered with a multitudinous host, who were tossing from one to the other the dying Walter Trewoofe, whose false heart thus endured the vengeance of the mermaid, who had, in the fondness of her soul, made the innocent child of humble parents the child of her adoption. Appendix M.

THE ROCKS.

" Among these rocks and stones, methinks I see
More than the heedless impress that belongs
To lonely nature's casual work : they bear
A semblance strange of power intelligent,
And of design not wholly worn away."
　　　　　　—The Excursion.—WORDSWORTH.

ROMANCES OF THE ROCKS.

CROMLECH AND DRUID STONES.

" Surely there is a hidden power that reigns.
'Mid the lone majesty of untamed nature,
Controlling sober reason "
—*Caractacus.*—WILLIAM MASON.

IT is a common belief amongst the peasantry over every part of
Cornwall, that no human power can remove any of those
stones which have been rendered sacred to them by traditionary
romance.   Many a time have I been told that certain stones had
been removed by day, but that they always returned by night to
their original positions, and that the parties who had dared to
tamper with those sacred stones were punished in some way.
When the rash commander of a revenue cutter landed with a
party of his men and overturned the Logan Rock, to prove the
folly of the prevalent superstition, he did but little service in dispelling an old belief, but proved himself to be a fool for his pains.

I could desire, for the preservation of many of our Celtic remains, that we could impress the educated classes with a similar
reverence for the few relics which are left to us of an ancient and
a peculiar people, of whose history we know so little, and from
whose remains we might, by careful study, learn so much.   Those
poised stones and perforated rocks must be of high antiquity, for
we find the Anglo-Saxons making laws to prevent the British people
from pursuing their old pagan practices.*

The geologist, looking upon the Logan stones and other
curiously-formed rock masses, dismisses at once from his mind
the idea of their having been formed by the hand of man, and
hastily sets aside the tradition that the Druid ever employed them,
or that the old Celt ever regarded them with reverence.   There

* " Perforated stones must once have been common in England, and probably in
Scotland also, as the Anglo-Saxon laws repeatedly denounce similar superstitious
practices."—*The Archæology and Prehistoric Annals of Scotland*, p 97   DANIEL
WILSON.

cannot be a doubt but that many huge masses of granite are, by atmospheric causes, now slowly passing into the condition required for the formation of a Logan rock. It is *possible* that in some cases the "weathering" may have gone on so uniformly around . the stone, as to poise it so exactly that the thrust of a child will shake a mass many tons in weight.

The result, however, of my own observations, made with much curiosity and considerable care, has been to convince me, that in by far the greatest number of instances the disintegration, though general around the line of a "bed-way" or horizontal joint, has gone on rapidly on the side exposed to the beat of the weather, while the opposite extremity has been but slightly worn ; consequently, the stones have a tendency to be depressed on the sheltered side. With a little labour man could correct this natural defect, and with a little skill make a poised stone. We have incontrovertible evidence that certain poised stones have been regarded, through long periods of time, as of a sacred character. Whether these stones were used by the Druids, or merely that the ignorant people supposed them to have some peculiar virtue, I care not. The earliest inhabitants of Cornwall, probably Celts,* were possessed with some idea that these stones were connected with the mysteries of existence ; and from father to son, for centuries, notwithstanding the introduction of Christianity, these stones have maintained their *sacred character.* Therefore, may we not infer that the leaders of the people availed themselves of this feeling ; and finding many rocks of a gigantic size, upon which nature had begun the work, they completed them, and used the mighty moving masses to impress with terror—the principle by which they ruled—the untaught, but poetically constituted, minds of the people. Dr Borlase has been laughed at for finding rock-basins, the works of the Druids, in every granitic mass. At the same time, those who laugh have failed to examine those rock-masses with unprejudiced care, and hence they have erred as wildly as did the Cornish antiquary, but in a contrary direction. Hundreds of depressions are being formed by the winds and rains upon the faces of the granite rocks. With these no Druid ever perplexed himself or his people But there are numerous hollows to be found in large flat rocks which have unmistakably been formed, if not entirely, partly by the hands of man. The Sacrificing Rock, or Carn Brea, is a remarkable example. The larger

---

* "A Celtic race, however, continued to occupy the primeval districts of Cornwall, and preserved, almost to our own day, a distinct dialect of the Celtic tongue "—*Prehistoric Annals of Scotland*, p 195 DANIEL WILSON *See* Appendix N, *The Celts.*

hollows on the Men-rock, in Constantine, several basins in the Logan Rock group, and at Carn Boscawen, may be referred to as other examples. With these remarks, I proceed to notice a few of the most remarkable rock-masses with which tradition has associated some tale.

THE LOGAN OR LOGING ROCK.*

M ODRED, in Mason's " Caractacus," addressing Vellinus and Elidurus, says—

> '' Thither, youths,
> Turn your astonish'd eyes ; behold yon huge
> And unhewn sphere of living adamant,
> Which, poised by magic, rests its central weight
> On yonder pointed rock : firm as it seems,
> Such is the strange and virtuous property,
> It moves obsequious to the gentlest touch
> Of him whose breath is pure ; but to a traitor,
> Though even a giant's prowess nerved his arm,
> It stands as fixed as Snowdon.''

This faithfully preserves the traditionary idea of the purposes to which this in every way remarkable rock was devoted.

Up to the time when Lieutenant Goldsmith, on the 8th of April 1824, slid the rock off from its support, to prove the falsehood of Dr Borlase's statement, that " it is morally impossible that any lever, or, indeed, force, however applied in a mechanical way, can remove it from its present position," the Logan Rock was believed to cure children, who were rocked upon it at certain seasons, of several diseases ; but the charm is broken, although the rock is restored †

* " It may be observed that I have always used the words Loging Rock for the cele-brated stone at Trereen Dinas. Much learned research seems to have been idly expended on the supposed name, ' Logan Rock ' *To log* is a verb in general use throughout Cornwall for vibrating or rolling like a drunken man , and *an* is frequently heard in provincial pronunciation for *ing*, characteristic of the modern present participle The Loging Rock is, therefore, strictly descriptive of its peculiar motion "—*Davies Gilbert*

† When this great natural curiosity was, as it was thought, destroyed, the public wrath was excited, and appeased only by the conciliatory spirit manifested by Mr Davies Gilbert, who persuaded the Lords of the Admiralty to lend Lieutenant Goldsmith the required apparatus for replacing it Mr D Gilbert found the money , and after making the necessary arrangements, on the 2d of November 1824, Goldsmith "had the glory of replacing this immense rock in its natural position " The glory of Goldsmith and of Shrubsall, who overturned another large Logan Rock, is certainly one not to be desired.

MINCAMBER, MAIN-AMBER, OR AMBROSE'S STONE.

A MIGHTY Logan Stone was poised and blessed by Ambrose Merlin, not far from Penzance. " So great," says Drayton, in his " Polyalbion," " that many men's united strength cannot remove it, yet with one finger you may wag it."

Merlin proclaimed that this stone should stand until England had no king ; and Scawen tells us—

" Here, too, we may add what wrong another sort of strangers have done to us, especially in the civil wars, and in particular by the destroying of Mincamber, a famous monument, being a rock of infinite weight, which, as a burden, was laid upon other great stones, and yet so equally thereon poised up by nature only, that a little child could instantly move it, but no one man, or many, remove it. This natural monument all travellers that came that way desired to behold ; but in the time of Oliver's usurpation, when all monumental things became despicable, one Shrubsall, one of Oliver's heroes, then Governor of Pendennes, by labour and much ado, caused to be undermined and thrown down, to the great grief of the country, but to his own great glory, as he thought ; doing it, as he said, with a small cane in his hand. I myself have heard · him to boast of this act, being a prisoner under him." *

So was Merlin's prophecy fulfilled.

ZENNOR COITS.

C. TAYLOR STEPHENS, lately deceased, who was for some time the rural postman of Zennor, sought, in his poem, " The Chief of Barat-Anac," to embody in a story some descriptions of the Zennor coits and other rock curiosities.

I employed this man for some weeks to gather up for me all that remained of legendary lore in Zennor and Morva. He did his work well ; and from his knowledge of the people, he learned more from them than any other man could have done. The results of his labours are scattered through these volumes.

C. Taylor Stephens wrote me on the subject of the cromlechs as follows :—

* " *Ambers* or *Main Ambers*, which signify anointed or consecrated stones ' —*C. S. Gilbert, Historical Survey* See also Scawen's " Dissertation on the Cornish Language," Stukeley's " Stonehenge," and Jabez Allies's " Worcestershire " Appendix O, *Ambrosiæ Petræ.*

Superstitious Belief respecting the Quoits.

" I was in the neighbourhood of Zennor in 1859, and by accident came across the Zennor cromlech, and was struck with the mode of its construction (not having heard of its existence before), and thinking it bore some resemblance to the Druidical altars I had read of, I inquired of a group of persons who were gathered round the village smithery, whether any one could tell me anything respecting the heap of stones on the top of the hill. Several were in total ignorance of their existence. One said, 'Tes caal'd the gient's kite ; thas all I knaw.' At last, one more thoughtful, and one who, I found out, was considered the wiseacre and oracle of the village, looked up and gave me this important piece of information,—'Them ere rocks were put there afore you nor me was boern or thoft ov ; but who don it es a puzler to everybody in *Sunnur* (Zennor) I de bleve theze put up theer wen thes ere wurld wus maade ; but wether they wus or no don't very much mattur by hal akounts. Thes I'd knaw, that nobody caant take car em awa ; if anybody was too, they'd be brot there agin. Hees an ef they wus tuk'd awa wone nite, theys shur to be hal rite up top o' th hil fust thing in morenin. But I caant tel ee s' much as Passen can ; ef you 'd zea he, he 'd tel he hal about et ' "

In one of the notes received from the poet and postman he gives a curious instance of the many parts a man played in those remote districts but a few years since :—

" My venerable grandpapa was well known by all the old people, for he was not only a local preacher, but a charmer, a botanist, a veterinary surgeon, a secretary to a burial and sick benefit society, and, moreover, the blacksmith of the neighbourhood."

THE MÊN-AN-TOL.

NOT more than two miles from Penzance stands the celebrated cromlech of Lanyon—often pronounced Lanine. This, like all the other cromlechs, marks, no doubt, the resting-place of a British chieftain, many of whose followers repose within a short distance of this, the principal monument.

Beyond the village of Lanyon, on a " furzy down," stands the Mên-an-tol, or the " holed stone." For some purpose—it is in vain to speculate on it now—the bardic priesthood employed this stone, and probably the superstition which attaches to it may indicate its ancient uses.

If scrofulous children are passed *naked* through the Mên-an-tol three times, and then drawn on the grass three times *against the sun*, it is felt by the faithful that much has been done towards insuring a speedy cure Even men and women who have been afflicted with spinal diseases, or who have suffered from scrofulous taint, have been drawn through this magic stone, which all declare still retains its ancient virtues.

If two brass pins are carefully laid across each other on the top edge of this stone, any question put to the rock will be answered, by the pins acquiring, through some unknown agency, a peculiar motion.

THE CRICK STONE IN MORVA.

IF any one suffering from a "crick in the back" can pass through this forked rock, on the borders of Zennor and Morva, without touching the stone, he is certain of being cured. This is but a substitute for the holed stone, which, it is admitted, has much more virtue than the forked stone.

In various parts of the county there are, amongst the granitic masses, rocks which have fallen across each other, leaving small openings, or there are holes, low and narrow, extending under a pile of rocks. In nearly every case of this kind, we find it is popularly stated, that any one suffering from rheumatism or lumbago would be cured if he crawled through the openings. In some cases, nine times are insisted on " to make the charm complete."

Mrs Bray, in her "Traditions of Devonshire," gives several examples of the prevalence of this superstition over the granitic district of Dartmoor.*

THE DANCING STONES, THE HURLERS, &c.

IN many parts of Cornwall we find, more or less perfect, circles of stones, which the learned ascribe to the Druids Tradition, and the common people, who have faith in all that their fathers have taught them, tell us another tale. These stones are everlasting marks of the Divine displeasure, being maidens or men, who were changed into stone for some wicked profanation of the Sabbath-day. These monuments of impiety are scattered over the county ; they are to be found, indeed, to the extremity of *Old* Cornwall, many of those circles being upon Dartmoor. It is not necessary to name them all. Every purpose will be served if the tourist is directed to those which lie more directly in the route which is usually prescribed. In the parish of Burian are the " *Dawns Myin* " or *Mên*—the dancing stones—commonly called " The Merry Maidens ; " and near them are two granite pillars, named the " Pipers " One Sabbath evening some of the thoughtless maidens of the neighbouring village, instead of attending

* " Creeping under tolmens for the cure of diseases is still practised in Ireland, and also in the East, as is shown by Mrs Colonel Elwood in her Travels "—*Gentleman's Magazine*, July 1831

vespers, strayed into the fields, and two evil spirits, assuming the guise of pipers, began to play some dance tunes. The young people yielded to the temptation ; and, forgetting the holy day, commenced dancing. The excitement increased with the exercise, and soon the music and the dance became extremely wild ; when, lo ! a flash of lightning from the clear sky transfixed them all, the tempters and the tempted, and there in stone they stand.

The celebrated circle of nineteen stones,—which is seen on the road to the Land's End,—known as the " Boscawen-ûn Circle," is another example. The " Nine Maids," or the " Virgin Sisters," in Stithians, and other " Nine Maids," or, as called in Cornish, Naw-whoors, in St Colomb-Major parish, should also be seen, in the hope of impressing the moral lesson they convey yet more strongly on the mind.*

The three circles, which are seen on the moors not far from the Cheesewring, in the parish of St Cleer, are also notable examples of the punishment of Sabbath-breaking. These are called the " Hurlers," and they preserve the position in which the several parties stood in the full excitement of the game of hurling, when, for the crime of profaning the Sabbath, they were changed into stone.†

* The following quotations are from Davies Gilbert It must not be forgotten that this gentleman was President of the Royal Society, and *therefore* a sceptic in local traditionary story :—

" On the south-west part of the parish of Stithians, towards Gwendron, are still to be seen nine stones set perpendicularly erect in the earth, in a direct manner, about ten feet apart, called the Nine Maids, probably set up there in memory of nine religious sisters or nuns in that place before the fifth century , not women turned into stone, as the English name implies, and as the country people thereabout will tell you."

" The Nine Maids—in Cornish, Naw-voz, *alias* the nine sisters—in Cornish, Naw-whoors—which very name informs us that they were sepulchral stones, erected in memory either of nine natural or spiritual sisters of some religious house, and not so many maids turned into stones for dancing on the Sabbath-day, as the country people will tell you. Those stones are set in order by a line, as is such another monument, also called the Nine Maids, in Gwendron, by the highway, about twenty-five feet distance from each other."

† " With respect to the stones called the 'Hurlers' being once men, I will say with Hals, 'Did but the ball which these Hurlers used when flesh and blood appear directly over them, immovably pendant in the air, one might be apt to credit some little of the tale ,' but as this is not the case, I must add my belief of their being erected by the Druids for some purpose or other—probably a court of justice , long subsequent to which erection, however, they may have served as a goal for hurl-players "—*Topographical and Historical Sketches of the Boroughs of East and West Love, by Thomas Bond*.

May we not address Mr Bond, " O ye of little faith ?" A very small amount of which would have found the ball, fixed as a boulder of granite, not as it passed through the air, but as it rolled along the ground

That an ancient priesthood, endeavouring to reach the minds of an ignorant people through their sensations, should endeavour to persuade the old Celtic population that

THE NINE MAIDS, OR VIRGIN SISTERS.

NINE " Moor Stones " are set up near the road in the parish of Gwendron, or Wendron, to which the above name is given. The perpendicular blocks of granite have evidently been placed with much labour in their present position. Tradition says they indicate the graves of nine sisters. Hals appears to think some nuns were buried here. From one person only I heard the old story of the stones having been metamorphosed maidens. Other groups of stone might be named, as Rosemedery, Tregaseal, Boskednan, Botallack, Tredinek, and Crowlas, in the west, to which the same story extends, and many others in the eastern parts of the county ; but it cannot be necessary.

THE TWELVE-O'CLOCK STONE.

NUMBERS of people would formerly visit a remarkable Logan stone, near Nancledrea, which had been, by supernatural power, impressed with some peculiar sense at midnight. Although it was quite impossible to move this stone during daylight, or indeed by human power at any other time, it would rock like a cradle exactly at midnight. Many a child has been cured of rickets by being placed naked at this hour on the twelve-o'clock stone. If, however, the child was " misbegotten," or, if it was the offspring of dissolute parents, the stone would not move, and consequently no cure was effected. On the Cuckoo Hill, eastward of Nancledrea, there stood, but a few years since, two piles of rock about eight feet apart, and these were united by a large flat stone carefully placed upon them,—thus forming a doorway which was, as my informant told me, " large and high enough to drive a horse and cart through " It was formerly the custom to march in procession through this " doorway" in going to the twelve-o'clock stone.

The stone-mason has, however, been busy hereabout ; and every mass of granite, whether rendered notorious by the Giants or holy by the Druids, if found to be of the size required, has been removed.*

God's vengeance had fallen on the Sabbath-breaker, is not to be wondered at. Up to a very recent period, hurling matches usually came off on the Sunday —See " Hurling," in the chapter on Cornish Customs.

* The following are a few of the interesting remains of old Cornwall which have entirely disappeared from this neighbourhood within a few years —

Between St Ives and Zennor, on the lower road over Tregarthen Downs, stood a Logan

THE MEN-SCRYFA.

AT the entrance to Penzance rises, rather abruptly, a hill, crowned with a very remarkable earthwork. It is known as Castle Lesgudzhek, or, the " Castle of the Bloody Field," to this day.

Tradition, our only guide, tells us that this castle was one of the strong places of a British king, in the third or fourth century ; that a rival chieftain, from the eastern part of Danmonium, besieged him. The defence was long and desperate The besiegers, wearying of the unsuccessful toil, retired at length to the plains of Gulval ; and that the besieged left his castle, and gave his enemies battle on the plain which extends from Penzance to Marazion The "bloody field" remained in possession of the chieftain of Lesgudzhek, and the leader of the eastern men was killed near where he was buried. The *Men-Scryfa*, or inscribed stone, was raised over his grave,—its height, nine feet, being the exact height of the defeated warrior ?

RIALOBRAN CUNOVAL FIL

is engraven on the block ; thus handing to us the name of the unfortunate warrior, who was probably the son of the hero from whom Gulval draws its name ; and if so, may we not suppose that he was but endeavouring to recover the possessions which once belonged to his parent.

TABLE-MÊN.

THE SAXON KINGS' VISIT TO THE LAND'S END.

AT a short distance from Sennen church, and near the end of a cottage, is a block of granite, nearly eight feet long, and about three feet high. This rock is known as the Table-mên, or

rock. An old man, perhaps ninety years of age, told me he had often logged it, and that it would make a noise which could be heard for miles.

At Balnoon, between Nancledrea and Knill's Steeple, some miners came upon "two slabs of granite cemented together," which covered a walled grave three feet square—an ancient kistvean In it they found an earthenware vessel containing some black earth, and a leaden spoon The spoon was given to Mr Praed of Trevetha, and may possibly be in the possession of the present proprietor The kistvean was utterly destroyed

At Brunnion, not far from St Ives, in the garden attached to the house which is occupied by the Hoskings, is an arched doorway of carefully-worked granite Tradition saith this doorway belonged to an ancient church, and that the present garden was the burial-ground Close by, at Treverrack, is a field known as the "Chapel Field," in which the plough is constantly turning up stones which have been carefully chiselled

In Bosprenis Croft there was a very large coit or cromlech. It is said to have been fifteen feet square, and not more than one foot thick in any part This was broken in two parts some years since, and taken to Penzance to form the beds for two ovens.

Table-*main*, which appears to signify the stone-table. At Bosavern, in St Just, is a somewhat similar flat stone ; and the same story attaches to each.

It is to the effect that some Saxon kings used the stone as a dining-table. The number has been variously stated ; some traditions fixing on three kings, others on seven. Hals is far more explicit ; for, as he says, on the authority of the chronicle of Samuel Daniell, they were—

Ethelbert, 5th king of Kent ;
Cissa, 2d king of the South Saxons ;
Kingills, 6th king of the West Saxons ;
Sebert, 3d king of the East Saxons ;
Ethelfred, 7th king of the Northumbers ;
Penda, 5th king of the Mercians ;
Sigebert, 5th king of the East Angles,—who all flourished about the year 600.

At a point where the four parishes of Zennor, Morvah, Gulval, and Madron meet, is a flat stone with a cross cut on it. The Saxon kings are also said to have dined on this.

The only tradition which is known amongst the peasantry of Sennen is, that Prince Arthur and the kings who aided him against the Danes, in the great battle fought near Vellan-Drucher, dined on the Table-mên, after which they defeated the Danes.

MERLYN'S PROPHECIES.

PROPHECIES by Merlyn are tolerably prevalent in Cornwall. The character of these may be known by one or two examples—

> " Aga syth tyer, war and meyne Merlyn
> Ara neb syth Leskey Paul, Penzance hag Newlyn."

This has been translated—

> " There shall land on the stone of Merlyn,
> Those who shall burn Paul, Penzance, and Newlyn."

This prophecy is supposed to have been accomplished when the Spaniards, in the reign of Elizabeth, landed at Mousehole, a fishing village in the Mount's Bay. Near the pier at Mousehole is still a rock called " Merlyn Car," or " Meilyn's Rock," and not far from it another, called " the Spaniard."

THE LEVAN STONE.

This bisected mass of granite has been already noticed in connection with St Levan.

> " When, with panniers astride,
>   A pack-horse can ride
>   Through the Levan Stone,
>   The world will be done."

THE RAME HEAD AND THE DODMAN.

Merlyn is said to have pronounced the following prophecy, standing near St German's Grotto on the shores of Whitsand Bay :—

> " When the Rame Head and Dodman meet,
>   Man and woman will have cause to greet."

THE ARMED KNIGHT.

" AT low water there is to be seen, off the Land's End, towards the Scilly Island (probably so called from the abundance of eel or conger fishes caught there, which are called sillys, or lillis), for a mile or more, a dangerous strag of ragged rocks, amongst which the Atlantic Sea and the waves of St George's and the British Channel meeting, make a dreadful bellowing and rumbling noise at half-ebb and half-flood, which let seamen take notice of to avoid them.

" Of old, there was one of those rocks more notable than the rest, which tradition saith was ninety feet above the flux and reflux of the sea, with an iron spire at the top thereof, which was overturned or thrown down in a violent storm, 1647, and the rock was broken in three pieces.   This iron spire, as the additions to Camden's " Britannia " inform us, was thought to have been erected by the Romans, or set up as a trophy there by King Athelstan, when he first conquered the Scilly Islands (which was in those parts) ; but it is not very probable such a piece of iron, in this salt sea and air, without being consumed by rust, could endure so long a time.   However, it is or was, certain I am it commonly was called in Cornish, An Marogeth Arvowed, *i.e.*, the Armed Knight ; for what reason I know not, except erected by or in memory of some armed knight ; as also Carne-an-peul, *i e.*, the spile, spire, or javelin rock.   Again, remember silly lilly, is in Cornish and Armoric language a conger fish or fishes, from whence Scilly Islands is probably denominated, as elsewhere noted." [*]
Mr Blight says this rock is also called *Guela*, or *Guelaz*,—the " rock easily seen."

[*] Hals, in Gilbert's "History of Cornwall," vol iii p 43.

THE IRISH LADY.

NEAR *Pedn-men-dw*, the "*Headland of Black Rock*," is a curiously-shaped rock, known as the *Irish Lady*. In days long ago some adventurous sailors from Ireland were shipwrecked at night on this rock, and every soul perished, save a lady, who was seen in the morning sitting on the top of the rock. The storm was still raging, and it was quite impossible to render this solitary sufferer any assistance. Days and nights passed away ; the people watched the dying woman from the shore, but they could not reach her. At length they saw that her sufferings were at an end ; and at last the dead body was washed into the sea. Often, when the winds and waves are high, the fishermen see a lady tranquilly sitting on this rock, *with a rose in her mouth ;* to show, it may be presumed, her perfect indifference to the ragings of tempests.*

Sir Humphrey Davy wrote a poem on this tradition. The following is an extract from it :—

> " Where yon dark cliff † o'ershadows the blue main,
> Theora died amidst the stormy waves,
> And on its feet the sea-dews wash'd her corpse,
> And the wild breath of storms shook her black locks.
> Young was Theora ; bluer was her eye
> Than the bright azure of the moonlight night ;
> Fair was her cheek, as is the ocean cloud
> Red with the morning ray.
>
> " Amidst the groves,
> And greens, and nodding rocks that overhang
> The gray Killarney pass'd her morning days,
> Bright with the beams of joy.

---

* This kind of tradition is not uncommon   The following is a Welsh form of it —

GWENNO'S STEEPLE.

Among the numerous irregular caves at the western end of Ogofau is one which has derived the name of Ffynnon Gwenno (the Well of Gwenno), from the following tradition, kindly given to us by Mr Johnes   The water which still occupies its lower part, was, in days of yore, reputed to possess medicinal qualities, which attracted numerous bathers from the surrounding districts   Among these a fair maid, named Gweulhan, or, for brevity, Gwenno, was induced, on an unfortunate day, to explore the recesses of the cavern beyond a frowning rock, which had always been the prescribed limit to the progress of the bathers. She passed beneath it, and was no more seen. She had been seized by some superhuman power, as a warning to others not to invade those mysterious penetralia.   And still, on stormy nights, the spirit of Gweulhan is seen to hover over a lofty crag which rises near the entrance of the now deserted cave, and bears the name of Cloch ty Gwenno, or Gwenno's Steeple *—Note on the Gogofau, or Ogofau Mine.* Memoirs of Geological Survey, vol 1 p 482

† A rock near the Land's End called the " Irish Lady "

" To solitude,
To nature, and to God, she gave her youth ;
Hence were her passions tuned to harmony.
Her azure eye oft glisten'd with the tear
Of sensibility, and her soft cheek
Glow'd with the blush of rapture.   Hence she loved
To wander 'midst the green wood silver'd o'er
By the bright moonbeam.   Hence she loved the rocks,
Crown'd with the nodding ivy, and the lake
Fair with the purple morning, and the sea
Expansive, mingling with the arched sky.

" Dark in the midnight cloud,
When the wild blast upon its pinions bore
The dying shrieks of Erin's injured sons,
She 'scaped the murderer's arm.*

" The British bark
Bore her across the ocean.   From the west
The whirlwind rose, the fire-fraught clouds of heaven
Were mingled with the wave.   The shatter'd bark
Sunk at thy feet, Bolerium, and the white surge
Closed on green Erin's daughter."
—PARIS's *Life of Sir Humphrey Davy*, p. 38.

THE DEVIL'S DOORWAY.

IN the slate (Killas) formations behind Polperro is a good
example of a *fault*.   The geologist, in the pride of his knowledge, refers this to some movement of the solid mass—a rending
of the rocks, produced either by the action of some subterranean
force lifting the earth-crust, or by a depression of one division of
the rocks.   The gray-bearded wisdom of our grandfathers led
them to a conclusion widely different from this.

The mighty ruler of the realms of darkness, who is known to
have an especial fondness for rides at midnight, " to see how his
little ones thrive," ascending from his subterranean country, chose
this spot as his point of egress.

As he rose from below in his fiery car, drawn by a gigantic jet
black steed, the rocks gave way before him, and the rent at Polperro remains to this day to convince all unbelievers.   Not only
this, as his Satanic majesty burst through the slate rocks, his
horse, delighted with the airs of this upper world, reared in wild
triumph, and, planting again his hoof upon the ground, made these

* The Irish lady was shipwrecked at the Land's End about the time of the massacre
of the Irish Protestants by the Catholics, in the reign of Charles the First.   So says Davy
—the tradition is very old.

islands shake as with an earthquake ; and he left the deep impression of his burning foot behind. There, any unbeliever may see the hoof-shaped pool, unmistakable evidence of the wisdom of the days gone by.

PIPER'S HOLE, SCILLY.

ON the banks of Peninnis, in St Mary's, is Piper's Hole, which communicates, as tradition saith, with the island of Tresco, where another orifice known by the same name is seen. Going in at the orifice at Peninnis Banks in St Mary's, it is above man's height, and of as much space in its breadth, but grows lower and narrower farther in : a little beyond which entrance appear rocky basins, or reservoirs, continually running over with fresh water, descending as it distils from the sides of the rocky passage. By the fall of water heard further in, it is probable there may be rocky descents in the passage. The drippings from the sides have worn the passage, as far as it can be seen, into very various angular surfaces. Strange stories are related of this passage, of men going so far in that they never returned ; of dogs going quite through, and coming out at Tresco, with most of their hair off, and such like incredibles. But its retired situation, where lovers retreat to indulge their mutual passion, has made it almost as famous as the cave wherein Dido and Æneas met of old. Its water is exceeding good.*

THE DEVIL'S COITS, &c.

IN St Columb Major, not far from the ruins of what is generally considered to be a British fortification, Castele-an-Dinas, stands a tumulus known as the Devil's Coit. It is curious to find one tradition directly contradicting another. We are told, on the one hand, that—

The devil never came into Cornwall

Because, when he crossed the Tamar, and made Torpoint for a brief space his resting-place, he could not but observe that everything, vegetable or animal, was put by the Cornish people into a pie.

He saw and heard of fishy pie, star-gazy pie, conger pie, and

---

* Heath's " Scilly Isles " These stories of Piper's Hole are still told, and many of the ignorant inhabitants regard it with superstitious dread. The Fugoe Hole, at the Land's End, has yet to be spoken of in the Witch stories Several who have attempted to penetrate this hole have escaped only by great luck—"by the skin of their teeth," as the saying is

indeed pies of all the fishes in the sea.   Of parsley pie, and herby
pie, of lamy pie, and piggy pie, and pies without number.   Therefore, fearing they might take a fancy to a "devily pie," he took
himself back again into Devonshire.

On the other hand we find, amidst the rocks of the shore and
the hills, numerous devil's coits, plenty of devil's footsteps, with
devil's bellows, devil's frying-pans, devil's ovens, and devil's caves
in abundance.   Of course, on Dartmoor, since the devil remained
in Devonshire, we might expect to find such evidences of his presence.   The devil's frying-pan at Mistor is well known, and nearly
every granite Tor preserves some impression of this melancholy,
wandering wicked one.

KING ARTHUR'S STONE.

IN the western part of Cornwall, all the marks of any peculiar
kind found on the rocks are referred either to the giants or
the devil.   In the eastern part of the county such markings are
almost always attributed to Arthur.   Not far from the Devil's Coit
in St Columb, on the edge of the Gossmoor, there is a large stone,
upon which are deeply-impressed marks, which a little fancy may
convert into the marks of four horse-shoes.   This is "King
Arthur's Stone," and these marks were made by the horse upon
which the British king rode when he resided at *Castle Denis*, and
hunted on these moors.   King Arthur's beds, and chairs, and
caves, are frequently to be met with.   The Giant's Coits,—and
many traditions of these will be found in the section devoted to
the giant romances—are probably monuments of the earliest types
of rock mythology.   Those of Arthur belong to the period when
the Britons were so far advanced in civilisation as to war under
experienced rulers ;   and those which are appropriated by the devil
are evidently instances of the influence of priestcraft on the minds
of an impressible people *

* Another example of like stories in Wales may be interesting —

"Five juvenile saints, on their pilgrimage to the celebrated shrine of St David,
emaciated with hunger, and exhausted with fatigue, here reclined themselves to rest; and
reposed their weary heads on this ponderous pillow , their eyes were soon closed by the
powerful hand of sleep, and they were no longer able to resist, by the force of prayer, the
artifices of their foes   The sky was suddenly overwhelmed with clouds—the thunder
rolled—the lightning flashed, and the rain poured in torrents.   The storm increased in
vehemence ; all nature became chilled with cold, and even Piety and Charity felt its
effects   The drops of rain were soon congealed into enormous hailstones, which, by the
force of the wind, were driven with so much violence against the heads of the weary
pilgrims as to affix them to their pillow, and the vestiges they left are still discernible.
Being borne away in triumph by the malignant sorcerer who inhabits the hollows of

THE COCK-CROW STONE.

A ROCK of white marble (?) with many rock basins on its surface lies in Looe harbour, under Saunder's Lane, and is now
covered by every tide.   This stone once stood on the top of an
elevated rock near it, and when in this position, whenever it heard
a cock crow in the neighbouring farmyard of Hay, it turned round
three times.

The topmost stone of that curious pile of rocks in the parish of
St Cleer known as the Cheesewring is gifted in like manner.
Even now the poultry-yards are very distant, but in ancient days
the cocks must have crowed most lustily, to have produced vibra-
tions on either the sensitive rock or the tympanum of man.

these hills, they were concealed in the innermost recesses of his cavern, where they are
destined to remain asleep, bound in the irrefragable chain of enchantment until that
happy period shall arrive when the diocese shall be blessed with a pious bishop, for when
that happens, no doubt Merlin himself, the enemy of malignant sorcerers, will be disenchanted, and he will come and restore to liberty the dormant saints, when they will
immediately engage in the patriotic work of reforming the Welsh "—*From the English
Works of the late Rev. Eleazor Williams,* quoted by Warington W. Smyth, M A.
Memoirs of the Geological Survey, vol. i. p. 480.

LOST CITIES.

"Between Land's End and Scilly rocks
Sunk lies a town that ocean mocks.
.   .   .   .   .   .   ˋ
Where breathes the man that would not weep
O'er such fine climes beneath the deep?"
Historical Records of Ancient Cornwall.
—THOMAS HOGG.

ROMANCES OF LOST CITIES.

LOST LANDS.

> " And oh I how short are human schemes I
> Here ended all our golden dreams "
> —Jonathan Swift

THE notion of cities and extensive tracts of cultivated country being under the waters of the ocean and of lakes appears to have existed from all time. In the " Arabian Nights," we have constant refeiences to lands under the sea, and in the tiaditionary stories of all Celtic people the same idea presents itself in some form or other. Mr Campbell appears to confound stories of mermaids with those traditions which have their origin in actual physical changes. They appear to me to have little relation to each other.*

In addition to the traditions given of large tracts of land which have been lost in the sea, I have given those which relate to cities, or towns, or churches which have been buried in the sands. These traditions are of the same general character.

This subject deserves a much more careful investigation than it has yet received. I hope simply to diaw attention to the subject, and to show that those dim traditions point to some buried truth. They are like the buried lights which are supposed to indicate the resting-places of the dead.

THE TRADITION OF THE LYONESSE OR LETHOWSOW.

THOSE who may stand on the extreme point of the Land's End, and, looking over that space where the waters of the Atlantic mix with those of the British Channel, see in the far distance the Scilly Islands, will have to call upon their imagina-

* See West Highland Tales, by J F. Campbell. Vol iii. p 410

tion to conceive that these broad waters roll over a country which has existed within historic time.

A region of extreme fertility, we are told, once united the Scilly Islands with Western Cornwall. A people, known as the Silures, inhabited this tract,—which has been called the Lyonesse, or sometimes Lethowsow,—who were remarkable for their industry and their piety. No less than 140 churches stood over that region, which is now a waste of waters ; and the rocks called the Seven Stones are said to mark the place of a large city. Even tradition is silent on the character of this great cataclysm. We have only one hint—and we know not its value—which appears to show that the deluge was comparatively gradual. One of the ancestors of the Trevilians is said to have had time to remove his family and his cattle , but at last he had to fly himself with all the speed which a fleet horse could give him. From this it might appear that, though gradual at first, the waters, having broken down the barriers, burst over the whole at last with uncontrolled fury. A small, but very ancient, oratory, " Chapel Idne," or the " Narrow Chapel," formerly stood in Sennen Cove. It is said to have been founded by one Lord of Goonhilly, who owned a portion of the Lyonesse, on the occasion of his escape from the flood. By this war of waters several large towns were destroyed, and an immense number of the inhabitants perished.

In the absence of full traditional evidence, it will not be un-interesting to gather together the fragmentary statements which exist in the writings of historians and others :—

" The number of parish churches lost is so astonishingly great as to baffle the power of evidence, to preclude the possibility of conviction. I, therefore, take upon me to reduce the number from 140 to 40,—to cut off what any dash of Worcester's pen might casually have created, the first figure "—*Whitaker's Supplement to Polwhele's History of Cornwall.*

The Saxon Chronicle says the Lionesse was destroyed on the 11th of November 1099

" On the third of the Nones of November (1099) the sea overflowed the shore, destroying towns and drowning many persons and innumerable oxen and sheep."—*The Chronicle of Florence of Worcester, translated by Thomas Forester, A.M.* Bohn, 1854.

Solinus (cap 22) applies Silura to the country lying west of the Land's End. His words are, " Siluram quoque insulam ab ora quam gens Britanna Dunmonii tenent, turbidum fretum distinguit "

" There is a tradition that there formerly existed a large track of land between the Land's End and the Scilly Islands, called the Lioness, which was destroyed by an inundation of the sea. One of the family of Trevilian, now residing in Somerset, but originally Cornish, saved himself by the assistance of his horse at the time of this inundation ; and it is reported that the arms of this family were taken from his fortunate escape, to commemorate his providential preservation."—*Drew and Hitchin's Cornwall.*

"A cave is pointed out in Perranuthnoe, where the ancestor of the Trevelyans is said to have been borne on shore, by the strength of his horse, from the destruction of the Lionesse country west of the Land's End. The Trevelyan family are too old, too honourable, and now too much distinguished by science, for them to covet any addition of honour through the medium of fabulous history

"It is recorded in the *Saxon Chronicle* that, in the year 1099, there was so very high a tide, and the damage so great in consequence, that men remembered not the like to have ever happened before, and the same day was the first of the new moon. Stow, who wrote his History of England about the year 1580, notices the great tide of 1099, when he says, 'The sea brake in over the banks of the Thames and other ryvers, drowning many towns and much people, with innumerable numbers of oxen and sheepe ; at which time the lands in Kent, that sometime belonged to Duke Godwyne, Earle of Kent, were covered with sandes and drowned, which are to this day called Godwyne Sandes' On the slender foundation of these alluvial catastrophes, Florence of Worcester either invented, or, with more than monkish credulity, received the tale of a whole district being engulfed, not at some remote geological period, but in what may be considered as the recent times of authentic history, after the existence of systematic registers and records ; a district covered, as he states, by a city and by a hundred and forty churches, with their accompanying villages, farms, &c , an event that must have shaken the whole of Europe ; and, to increase the wonder, a gentleman, accidentally on horseback, is carried by this animal to the neighbouring shore of Whitsand Bay, or twenty miles further off, to Perranuthnoe, through a sea which had swallowed an entire country, and from which the largest of modern vessels could not possibly have escaped. This idle tale, related by one writer after another, has almost reached our own times. The editor remembers a female relation of a former vicar of St Erth who, instructed by a dream, prepared decoctions of various herbs, and, repairing to the Land's End, poured them into the sea, with certain incantations, expecting to see the Lionesse country rise immediately out of the water, having all its inhabitants alive, notwithstanding their long submersion. But

> ' Perchance some form was unobserved,
> Perchance in prayer or faith she swerved.'

No country appeared, and although the love of marvellous events, and of tales exciting the passions, seems not to have diminished in recent times, yet the editor is unaware of any subsequent attempt having been made to rescue those unfortunate people from their protracted state of suspended animation."—*The Parochial History of Cornwall, by Davies Gilbert*, vol. iii. pp 109, 110.

"Although a sweep of ocean twenty-seven miles in breadth, separates at present the Land's End from the Scilly Islands, there can yet be little doubt of their having been heretofore united to each other by the mainland. The records of history indeed do not rise so high as the era when this disjunction was first effected , but we have documents yet remaining which prove to us that this strait must have been considerably widened, and the number of the Scilly Islands greatly increased within the last sixteen or seventeen centuries, by the waters of the Atlantic (receding probably from the coast of America) pressing towards this coast of Britain, accumulating upon Bolerium, and overwhelming part of the western shores of Cornwall.

"Strabo expressly tells us that the Cassiterides (so called from the Greek name of *tin*, there produced) were in his time only ten in number; whereas they are now divided into a hundred and forty rocky islets. Solinus also makes mention of a large and respectable island, called *Silura*, evidently the Scilly of present times, lying on Damnonian or Cornish coast, and separated from the mainland by a strait turbulent and dangerous—a character which sufficiently marks the compression of its waters. And William of Worcester, an author of our own country, thirteen centuries after Solinus, states, with a degree of positive exactness, stamping authenticity upon its recital, that between Mount's Bay and the Scilly Islands there had been woods, and meadows, and arable lands, and a hundred and forty parish churches, which before his time were submerged by the ocean. Uninterrupted tradition since this period, which subsists to the present day vigorous and particular, authenticates his account, and leaves no doubt upon the mind that a vast track of land, which stretched anciently from the eastern shore of Mount's Bay to the north-western rock of Scilly (with the exception of the narrow strait flowing between the Long-ships and Land's End), has, since the age of Strabo and Solinus, and previous to that of William of Worcester, been overwhelmed and usurped by the waves of the sea . . . The depth of the water at the Land's End is about eleven fathoms; at the Long-ships, eight; to the north of them, twenty; to the south, thirty; and twenty-five, twenty, and fifteen fathoms between them and the north-west of Scilly. The shallowest water occurs in the mid-space between Cornwall and the Isles "—*A Tour through Cornwall in the Autumn of* 1808, *by the Rev. Richard Warner.*

"Yet the cause of that inundation, which destroyed much of these Islands (the Scilly Islands), might reach also to the Cornish shores, is extremely probable, there being several evidences of a like subsidence of the land in the Mount's Bay. The principal anchoring-place, called a lake, is now a haven, or open harbour. The Mount, from its Cornish name, we must conclude to have stood formerly in a wood, but now, at full tide, is half a mile from the sea, and not a tree near it; and in the sandy beach betwixt the Mount and Penzance, where the sands have been dispersed by violent high tides, I have seen the trunks of several large trees in their natural position."—*Borlase, Phil. Trans.*, vol. xlviii part 1.

"That Cornwall once extended further west may be inferred from hence, that about midway between the Land's End and Scilly are rocks called in Cornish *Lethowsow*, by the English, *Seven-stones.*

"The Cornish call the places within the stones *Tregva,—t e*, a dwelling; —and it has been reported that windows and other stuff have been fished up, and that fishermen still see tops of houses under water. From the Land's End to Scilly, a tract of thirty miles, is an equal depth of water, and the bottom of the sea a plain, level surface. St Michael's Mount is called in Cornish, *Careg cowse in clowse—t e*, the hoary rock in the wood. Large trees with roots and bodies have been driven in by the sea of late years between St Michael's Mount and Penzance; and tradition says that at the time of the inundation which made the separation, one *Trevelyan* swam from thence on horseback; and in memory thereof the family, now in Somersetshire, bears gules a horse argent, from a less wavy argent, and azure, issuing out of a sea proper."—*Gough's Camden*, vol. i. p. 15.

"The flats, which stretched from one island to another, are plain evidences of a former union subsisting between many now distinct islands. The flats between Trescaw, Bréhar, and Sampson are quite dry at a spring-tide, and men easily pass dry-shod from one island to another over sand-banks (where, upon the shifting of the sands, walls and ruins are frequently discovered), upon which, at full sea, there are ten and twelve feet of water. From the southern side of St Martin there stretches out a large shoal towards Trescaw and St Mary's; and from St Mary's a flat, called Sandy-bar, shoots away to meet it; and between these two shoals there are but four feet of water in the channel called Crow Sound,—all strong arguments that those islands were once one continued tract of land, though now, as to their low lands, overrun with the sea and sand. 'The Isles Cassiterides' (says Strabo, Geo, lib. 5) 'are ten in number, close to one another. One of them is desert and unpeopled; the rest are inhabited.' But see how the sea has multiplied these islands; there are now one hundred and forty. Into so many fragments are they divided; and yet there are but six inhabited."—*An Account of the Great Alteration which the Islands of Scylley have undergone, &c., by the Rev. Wm. Borlase, M.A., F.R S, Phil. Trans.*, vol. xlviii. part 1.

"The Cornish land, from Plymouth, discovers itself to be devoured more and more to the westward, according to the aforesaid tradition of the tract of the Lionesse, being encroached upon above half the present distance from the Land's End to Scilly; whence it is probable that the low isthmus once joining Scilly and the Lionesse was first encroached upon in the same manner. The projecting land being exposed to the concurrence of the tides from the Irish, the Bristol, and British Channels, by whose violence and impetuosity, increased by the winds, the loose earth of the Gulf-rock might be worn away, leaving the resistible substance behind, standing as it is in the middle way betwixt Scilly and Cornwall."—*A Natural and Historical Account of the Islands of Scilly, by Robert Heath.*

The following notices are gathered from other local traditions :—

"From Rame-head to the two Looes very fertile valleys are stated to have extended at least a league southwards, over a tract now covered with sea; and around the coast in many places, we are assured, in twelve feet of water, trees are to be seen in the sea."

"The Black Rock in Falmouth Harbour is stated to have been a large island, which was surrounded by the sea only at high-water."

"Six miles south of St Michael's Mount waved, from Clement's Isle to Cudden Rock, a wood."

CUDDEN POINT AND THE SILVER TABLE

THIS point is situated in the parish of Perranuthnoe ; the parish, it will be remembered, into which Trelawney escaped, aided by the fleetness of his horse, from the deluge which buried the lands between this and the Scilly Isles.

At the low-water of spring-tides, the children from all the neighbourhood flock to the sands around this point, in the hope of finding treasure, which they believe is buried in the sands beneath the sea, and which is, it is said, occasionally discovered. Amongst

N

other things, an especial search is made for a silver table, which was lost by a very wealthy lord, by some said to be the old Lord Pengerswick, who enriched himself by grinding down the poor. On one occasion, when the calmness of summer, the clearness of the skies, and the tranquillity of the waters invited the luxurious to the enjoyments of the sea, this magnate, with a party of gay and thoughtless friends, was floating in a beautiful boat lazily with the tide, and feasting from numerous luxuries spread on a silver table. Suddenly—no one lived to tell the cause—the boat sank in the calm, transparent waters ; and, long after the event, the fishermen would tell of sounds of revelry heard from beneath the waters, and some have said they have seen these wicked ones still seated around the silver table.

THE PADSTOW "HOBBY-HORSE." *

A T the time of the spring festival, which is observed at Helston as a revel in honour, probably, of Flora, and hence called the "Furry-day," and by the blowing of horns and gathering of the "May" in St Ives and other places, the people of Padstow were a few years since in the habit of riding the "hobby-horse" to water. This hobby-horse was, after it had been taken round the town, submerged in the sea. The old people said it was once believed that this ceremony preserved the cattle of the inhabitants from disease and death. The appearance of a white horse escaping from the flood which buried the Lionesse, is told at several points, on both the north and south coast, and the riding of the hobby-horse probably belongs to this tradition. In support of this idea, we must not forget the mermaid story associated with the harbour of Padstow.

The water-horse is a truly Celtic tradition. We have it in the "Arabian Nights," and in the stories of all countries in the south of Europe. Mr Campbell, "West Highland Tales," says he finds the *horse* brought prominently forward in the Breton legends, and that animal figures largely in the traditions of Scotland and Ireland.

Has the miners' phrase—"a horse in the lode," applied to a mass of unproductive ground in the middle of a mineral lode ; or, "Black Jack rides a good horse," signifying that zinc ore gives good promise for copper—anything to do with these traditions ?

* See Appendix P.

ST MICHAEL'S MOUNT—THE WHITE ROCK IN THE WOOD.

"An old legend of St Michael speaketh of a tounelet in this part (between Pensandes and Mousehole), now defaced, and lying under the water."
—*Leland's Itinerary.*

ALREADY it has been told how St Michael's Mount was built by the giants. So much for its Titanic origin. The tradition that the Mount was formerly called in old Cornish, *Careg-luz en kuz,** and that it rose from the midst of an extensive forest, is very prevalent. "A forest is supposed to have extended along the coast to St Michael's Mount, which was described as a 'hoare rock in a wood,' and stood five or six miles from the sea. The bay was said to have been a plain of five or six miles in extent, formed into parishes, each having its church, and laid out in meadows, corn-fields, and woods." † A similar tradition attaches itself to Mont St Michel, in Normandy.

By and by, when the Saxon rule was extended into Cornwall, this remarkable hill is seized upon, in common with many other such hills, as the residence of some anchorite. This holy recluse is visited by St Michael, who had an especial fondness for hill churches, and the hermit is directed to build a church on the summit, and dedicate it to St Michael.

> " In evile howre thou hentst in hond,
>   Thus holy hills to blame ;
> For sacred unto saints they stand,
>   And of them have their name.
> St Michael's Mount, who does not know,
>   That wards the western coast "
>   —SPENSER.

Milton, in his delicately beautiful poem of "Lycidas," makes especial illusion to this monkish legend :—

> " Where'er thy bones are hurl'd,
> Whether beyond the stormy Hebrides,
> Where thou, perhaps, under the whelming tide,
> Visit'st the bottom of the monstrous world,
> Or, whether thou, to our moist vows denied,
> Sleep'st by the fable of Bellerus old, ‡
> Where *the great vision of the guarded mount,*
> Look towards Namancos, and Bayona's hold ;

* Or *Careg Cowes in Clowse*
† T. T. Blight.
‡ The name Bolerium has been especially given to the Land's End, but there is a cove near the Lizard now called Polurnan or Polerium.

Look homeward, angel, now, and melt with ruth,
And, O ye dolphins, waft the hapless youth "
—MILTON'S *Lycidas.*

Warner, in his " Tour through Cornwall," with much assumption
of learning, attempts to explain these lines. He tells us that the
Land's End was called *Bellerium,* " so named from Bellerus, a
Cornish giant. No such giant ever existed in Cornish fable, as
far as can be ascertained. It is far more probable that Milton
used the poet's license, and, from the name of the Land's End,
Bellerium, created ' the fable of Bellerus old.' " What follows in
Warner is worth extracting :—

" We learn from ' Caston's Golden Legende,' under the history of
the Angel Michael, that, ' Th' apparacyon of this angell is many-
fold. The fyrst is when he appeared in Mount of Gargan, &c.,'
(edit. 1493, fol. cclxxxii. a). William of Worcester, who wrote
his travels over England about 1490, says, in describing St
Michael's Mount, there was an ' Apparicio Sancti Michaelis in
monte Tumba antea vocato *Le Hore Rok in the Wodd'* (Itinerar,
edit. Cantab., 1778, p 102). *The Hoar Rock in the Wood* is this
Mount or Rock of St Michael, anciently covered with thick wood,
as we learn from Drayton and Carew. There is still a tradition,
that a vision of St Michael seated on this crag, or St Michael's
Chair, appeared to some hermits ; and that this circumstance
occasioned the foundation of the monastery dedicated to St
Michael. And hence this place was long renowned for its sanctity,
and the object of frequent pilgrimages. Carew quotes some old
rhymes much to our purpose, p. 154, *ut supra :*—

' Who knows not Mighel's Mount and Chaire,
The pilgrim's holy vaunt ? '

Nor should it be forgot that this monastery was a cell to another
on a St Michael's Mount in Normandy, where was also a vision
of St Michael. But to apply what has been said to Milton.
This great vision is the famous apparition of St Michael, whom
he, with much sublimity of imagination, supposes to be still
throned on this lofty crag of St Michael's Mount in Cornwall,
looking towards the Spanish coast The guarded mount on which
this great vision appeared is simply the *fortified* mount, implying
the fortress above mentioned. And let us observe, that *Mount* is
the peculiar appropriated appellation of this promontory. So in
Daniel's Panegyricke on the King, st. 19, ' From Dover to the
Mount.' "—P. 180.

" In the very corner is *Michael's Mount*, which gives name to the bay (the Mount's Bay) anciently called *DINSOL*, as in the book of Landaff, called by the inhabitants *Careg-Cowse*, or the Gray Rock—in Saxon, *Mychelyroz*, or Michael's Place." *

From Hals, Tonkin, and Gilbert, we learn yet further that " St Michael's Mount is so called, because our fathers, the Britons, believed that the appearance of the archangel St Michael in the year of our Lord 495 was in this place ; though in other countries they believe differently."

" Edward the Confessor, finding the place already celebrated for its holiness, founded an abbey of Benedictine monks, A.D. 1044, and also a chapel, which still stand, part of which is now converted into a dwelling-house. Upon the tower of the chapel is the celebrated Kader Migell,—*i.e.*, Michael's Chair,—a seat artificially cut in the stone, very dangerous in the access, therefore holy for the adventure.

> " ' Who knows not Mighel's Mount and Chaire,
>   The pilgrim's holy vaunt ;
> Both land and island twice a day,
> Both fort and port of haunt ? ' "

It is supposed by many persons to have been placed there for the pilgrims to complete their devotions at the Mount, by sitting in this chair, and showing themselves to the country around as pilgrims. St Kenna, doubtless the same as St Keyna, once visited this Mount,—although the time of her visitation is not precisely known,—and she imparted the very same virtue to the chair as she bestowed on St Keyna's Well. It is whichever, man or wife, sits in this chair first shall rule through life, and as it requires great resolution and steadiness of head to obtain the seat, one may be inclined to anticipate the supposed effect with greater certainty from its achievement, than from drinking water from St Keyna's Well.

It is not pleasant to destroy the romance of ages, but honesty compels me to pronounce this so-called chair to be nothing more than the remains of a stone lantern, built at the south-western angle of the tower. The good monks, without doubt, placing a light therein, it could be seen by the fishermen far off at sea ; and probably they received some tribute of either fish or money for the support of this useful guide to the shore.

It is evident, from the following passage in Carew's Survey, that the " chair " formerly was not within the building at all, but on some rocks without the walls :—

* Gough's Camden's Britannia, vol. 1. p 4

" A little without the castle there is a bad seat in a craggy place called St Michael's Chaire, somewhat dangerous for accesse, and therefore holy for the adventure." *

GWAVAS LAKE.

ON the western side of the Mount's Bay, between the fishing-towns of Newlyn and Mousehole, is the well-known anchoring-place known by the above name. It is not a little curious that any part of the ocean should have been called a lake. Tradition, however, helps us to an explanation. Between the land on the western side of the bay, and St Michael's Mount on the eastern side, there, at one time, extended a forest of beech-trees. Within this forest, on the western side, was a large lake, and on its banks a hermitage. The saint of the lake was celebrated far and near for his holiness, and his small oratory was constantly resorted to by the diseased in body and the afflicted in mind. None ever came in the true spirit who failed to find relief. The prayers of the saint and the waters of the lake removed the severest pains from the limbs and the deepest sorrows from the mind. The young were strengthened and the old revived by their influences. The great flood, however, which separated the Islands of Scilly from England, submerged the forest, and destroyed the lands enclosing this lovely and almost holy lake, burying beneath the waters church and houses, and destroying alike the people and the priest. Those who survived this sad catastrophe built a church on the hill and dedicated it to the saint of the lake—or in Cornish, St Pol—modernised into St Paul.†

In support of this tradition, we may see, of a fine summer day, when the tide is low and the waters clear, the remains of a forest in the line passing from St Michael's Mount to Gwavas. At neap-tides the author has gathered beech-nuts from the sands below Chyandour, and cut the wood from the trees embedded in the sand. ‡

---

* Carew, p 154.

† Gwavas Lake It is said that within historic times, tithes, or an equivalent for them, were collected from the land which surrounded this lake. I have been informed that the parish books of St Paul record the collection of tithes from lands which have disappeared. I applied for information on this point to the rector of the parish, but he has not yet favoured me with a reply.

‡ I have passed in a boat from St Michael's Mount to Penzance on a summer day, when the waters were very clear, and the tide low, and seen the black masses of trees in the white sands extending far out into the bay. On one occasion, while I was at school at Penzance, after a violent equinoctial gale, large trunks of trees were thrown up on the shore, just beyond Chyandour, and then with the other boys I went, at the lowest of

THE CITY OF LANGARROW OR LANGONA.*

WE cannot say how many years since, but once there stood on the northern shores of Cornwall, extending over all that country between the Gannell and Perranporth, a large city called Langarrow or Langona.   The sand-hills which now extend over this part of the coast cover that great city, and the memory of the sad and sudden catastrophe still lingers among the peasantry.   So settled is tradition, that no other time than 900 years since is ever mentioned as the period at which Langarrow was buried.   This city in its prime is said to have been the largest in England, and to have had seven churches, which were alike remarkable for their beauty and their size.   The inhabitants were wealthy, and according to received accounts, they drew their wealth from a large tract of level land, thickly wooded in some parts, and highly cultivated in others—from the sea, which was overflowing with fish of all kinds—and from mines, which yielded them abundance of tin and lead.

To this remote city, in those days, criminals were transported from other parts of Britain.   They were made to work in the mines on the coast, in constructing a new harbour in the Gannell, and clearing it of sand, so that ships of large burden could in those days sail far inland   Numerous curious excavations in the rocks, on either side of this estuary, are still pointed out as being evidences of the works of the convicts.   This portion of the population of Langarrow were not allowed to dwell within the city. The convicts and their families had to construct huts or dig caves on the wild moors of this unsheltered northern shore, and to this day evidences of their existence are found under the sand, in heaps of wood-ashes, amidst which are discovered considerable quantities of mussel and cockle shells, which we may suppose was

the tide, far out over the sands, and saw scores of trees embedded in the sands   We gathered nuts—they were beech-nuts—and leaves in abundance.   It is not a little re-markable,—if it be true, as I am informed it is,—that the trees found in the Pentuan Stream Works, under some fifty or sixty feet of sand and silt, are beech-trees, and that they were destroyed when the fruit was upon them   I learn, that not far from Hull in Yorkshire there exists a submerged forest, where also the beech-trees evidently perished in the autumn.   In Cardigan Bay a large tract of country is said to have been lost. May not all these traditions and evidences relate to one great cataclysm?   See "A Week at the Land's End," by J T. Blight, for an account of the submerged wood near Lariggan Rocks, between Penzance and Newlyn.

* "The vicarage church of Crantock is commonly called Languna or Langona,—that is to say, the hay temple or church,—and is suitable to its name, situate in a large hay meadow of rich land, containing about three acres, where, by ancient custom, the vicar's cattle all pasture over the dead bodies interred thereinto "—*Hals, as given by Gilbert.*   See Appendix Q

their principal food.   As far as I know, these are the first indications of anything resembling the Kjokkenmöddings, or refuse-heaps
of Denmark, which have been discovered in this country.

For a long period this city flourished in its prime, and its inhabitants were in the enjoyment of every luxury which industry
could obtain or wealth could purchase.   Sin, in many of its worst
forms, was however present amongst the people.   The convicts
sent to Langarrow were of the vilest.   They were long kept widely
separated ; but use breeds familiarity, and gradually the more
designing of the convicts persuaded their masters to employ them
within the city.   The result of this was, after a few years, an
amalgamation of the two classes of the population.   The
daughters of Langarrow were married to the criminals, 'and
thus crime became the familiar spirit of the place.   The progress
of this may have been slow—the result was, however, sure ; and
eventually, when vice was dominant, and the whole population
sunk in sensual pleasures, the anger of the Lord fell upon them.
A storm of unusual violence arose, and continued blowing, without intermitting its violence for one moment, for three days and
nights.   In that period the hills of blown sand, extending, with
few intervals, from Crantock to Perran were formed, burying the
city, its churches, and its inhabitants in a common grave.   To the
present time those sand-hills stand a monument of God's wrath ;
and in several places we certainly find considerable quantities of
bleached human bones, which are to many strong evidence of the
correctness of tradition.

Crantock was, according to tradition, once a trading town, and
it then had a religious house, with a dean and nine prebends.
The Gannell filling up ruined the town.   This must have happened when Langarrow was destroyed

On Gwithian Sands the remains of what is supposed to have
been a church has been discovered, and according to Hals and
Gilbert, a similar tradition exists here of a buried town.   Gilbert
writes thus .—

"There has always existed a traditional account of the inundation of
sand in this parish, corroborated by the ecclesiastical valuations, which are
far too high for the actual extent of the land, and also said to be confirmed
by documents preserved in the Arundel family, carrying back the commencement of the evil nearly to the period of their acquiring the property.

" With respect to more recent inundations, Mr Hockin states to Mr
Lysons, that the Barton of Upton, one of the principal farms, was suddenly overwhelmed ; that his great-grandfather remembered the occupier
residing in the farmhouse, which was nearly buried in one night, the
family being obliged to make their escape through the chamber windows ;

and that in consequence of the wind producing a shifting of the sand, in the winter of 1808-9, the house, after having disappeared for more than a century, came again to view.

" The rector further stated that he himself remembered two fields being lost at Gwithian, and that they are now covered with sand to the depth of ten or twelve feet, and that the church-town would have been also lost, if the parish officers had not promptly resorted to the expedient of planting rushes. These stop the complete progress of sand, and greatly facilitate the growth of other vegetation on the surface, so as to create a thin turf, The hillocks of sand exhibit a model in miniature of the Alps."—*Gilbert*, vol. ii. p. 149.

THE SANDS AT LELANT AND PHILLACK.

THERE is a tradition that Lelant and Phillack towns were all meadow land, and that the whole was covered with sand in a single night. Also that the low tract of land extended on both sides of Hayle far beyond the present bar, so that the sea has swallowed up some hundreds of acres. The people say that the sight of the ancient church and village of Lelant was some-where seaward of the Black Rock ;—the ancient burial-ground has been long washed away,—and that human teeth are still fre-quently found on the shore after a great *undertoe*, that takes the sand out to sea. Many circumstances seem to confirm the pro-bability of the tradition. The sand was drifting inland at such a rate before the reed-like plant called by the present inhabitants *the spire* was planted, that the whole of the land about the village would have been rendered worthless ere this, but for the stability given to it The land from which the sand has been cleared, on the sea side of the church, has evidently been ploughed, as the furrows are quite apparent between the ridges. They say that there was a market held in Lelant when St Ives was scarcely a village. Lelant being the mother church, would seem to prove this. One can easily understand how a large tract of land of the nature of that under Lelant sand-hills would be washed away in a comparatively short time, as the soil at the low-water level is a marly clay. This is constantly being washed down by high tides, and carried away by the undercurrent, as it contains no stone to form a pebbly beach, and therefore there is nothing left to protect the shore.

" THE ISLAND," ST IVES.

THE so-called island is now a peninsular mass of clay slate rocks, interpenetrated by very hard trappean masses. Between this and the town of St 'Ives is a low neck of land, which consists chiefly of sand and gravel, with some masses of clay slate broken into small angular fragments. On either side of this neck of land are good examples of raised beaches. Everything, therefore, favours the tradition which is preserved in the name.

One statement is, that " The Island " was *brought in from the sea ;* another, that it *rose out of the sea :—*

"This town, as Mr Camden saith, was formerly called Pendenis or Pendunes, the head fort, fortress, or fortified place, probably from the little island here, containing about six acres of ground, on which there stands the ruins of a little old fortification and a chapel "—*Hals's Cornwall.*

"On the island (or peninsula) work of St Ives standeth the ruins of an old chapel, wherein God was duly worshipped by our ancestors the Britons, before the Church of St Ives was erected or endowed."—*Tonkin's Cornwall.*

The beach on one side of the peninsula is called Porthmew, that on the other Porthgwidden ; and the name of the street between them is " Chyranchy," said to signify "the place of the breach," pointing, it might appear, to the action of the sea in wearing out the softer ground.

" Chyanchy" is another mode of pronouncing this name, " Chyan " signifying a house. Hence the name, it is thought by some, was given when two houses (chy-an-chy) stood alone on the spot.*

THE CHAPEL ROCK, PERRAN-PORTH.

THIS is one of the rocks—of which many exist—around the Cornish coast, upon which, at one time, there stood, in all probability, a small chapel or oratory. This rock is left dry at every tide, but stands far out in the sea at high-water. A curious fancy exists with respect to it. It is said that this rock can be approached on dry sand every day at eleven o'clock throughout the year. There is no truth in this statement, but strangers are gravely assured that this is the fact. From this rock to the sandy peninsula which runs out in the " porth," or port, is about five hundred yards—those, it is said, were, at one time, connected by cultivated land. From the circumstance that the evidences of a burial-place have been found on the little peninsula, it appears highly probable

---

* *Chyanwheal,* the house on the mine, is near St Ives. *Chyandour,* the house by the water, adjoins Penzance *Chyangarrach,* the house on the road. The water-elder is called *skow-dower.*

that the island and it have been closely connected as church and graveyard. Tradition refers the destruction of the land to certain storms or convulsions which swept away the country, for a mile or two out at sea, marked by a line drawn from the rocks off St Agnes, known as " The Man and his Man," and " Carters' Rock," which is off Penhale Point.

FIRE WORSHIP.

"Safely hid
Beneath the purple pall of sacrifice
Did sleep our holy fire, nor saw the air,
Till to that pass we came, where whilom Brute
Planted his five hoar altars.   To our rites
Then swift we hasted, and in one short moment
The rocky piles were clothed with livid flame."
                    Caractacus—WM. MASON, M.A.

ROMANCES OF FIRE WORSHIP.

'An angel who at last in sight
Of both my parents all in flames ascended
From off the altar, where an offering burn d,
As in a fiery column charioting
His god-like presence."
—*Samson Agonistes*—MILTON.

IT would not be profitable to pursue the inquiry into the value
of the numerous hypotheses which have been from time to
time raised in support of the assertion that a system of Fire Worship prevailed amongst the Britons of old Cornwall.

There can be no doubt but that the writings of Borlase, and
other earnest thinkers of his class, have done much to perpetuate
the belief in the existence of a Druidical priesthood in Cornwall,
who had their altars on the hills,—who made the huge piles of
granite rocks the instruments of their worship,—and who availed
themselves of the hollows formed in those rocks by nature, to
procure the unpolluted waters from heaven, with which to wash
away sins.

The antiquary has too frequently placed himself in the unfortunate position of Jonathan Oldbuck amidst the ancient fortifications at the Kaim of Kinprunes, when he was so rudely checked
in his theory by Edie Ochiltree, who would insist on it that he did
"mind the biggin' o' 't." But the modern historian and philosopher has gone as far wrong in the contrary direction. The
antiquaries formerly insisted that all the natural basins formed in
the granite rocks were of Druidic origin, and all the Logan stones
the result of Druid labours. The geologists and historians now
declare them, one and all, to be the result of disintegration, produced by ordinary atmospheric causes. Both are, I presume to
think, wrong. I am quite satisfied that I can point to rock-basins
upon which the hands of man have been busy, and to Logan stones
in which he has, for his own purposes, aided nature.

In the Sacrificing Rock on Carn Brae are a series of hollows so deeply cut, and so entirely unlike anything seen on any of the other rocks on that remarkable hill, although ordinary rock-basins are numerous, that I am disposed to believe in the tradition which gives it its name. On the Main or Men Rock in Constantine, I see, in like manner, evidences of the works of man, side by side with those of nature. The disintegration produced by the accumulation of water, at first in small quantities in a little hollow on the face of a rock, is a curious process. The first action is the separation of a few particles, or small crystals, of quartz or mica. These repose beneath the small deposit of water, until, by the beating of the rains and the action of the winds, they are made to serve as grinding materials, and carry on the work of weathering. The basins thus formed have a regular curvature, which does not belong to those deeper basins to which I have referred. The question, however, before us is, Have we any evidences, traditional or otherwise, which go to support the belief that the Phœnicians, or any other people, introduced the worship of fire into this country?

The influences of education, and the zeal with which religious teachers have penetrated into the remotest districts and taught the truth, have banished nearly every relic of this ancient idolatry. But still amidst the dead ashes a faint spark occasionally appears, to tell us that at one time our forefathers did use the rocks as altars, on which they kindled sacrificial fires; and that they had their periods of solemn feast, when every hill blazed with the emblem of life and dissolution. A few examples of these pale sparks will not be without value.

BAAL FIRES.

OF these Cornish Midsummer fires an account is given by a correspondent in Hone's " Year Book," which I quote entire, not because I can agree with the writer in all his views, but because he places the main question in a fair light .—

" An immemorial and peculiar custom prevails on the sea-coast of the western extremity of Cornwall, of kindling large bonfires on the Eve of June 24; and on the next day the country people, assembling in great crowds, amuse themselves with excursions on the water. I cannot help thinking it the remains of an ancient Druidical festival, celebrated on Midsummer-day, to implore the friendly influence of Heaven on their fields, compounded with that of the first of May, when the Druids kindled large fires on all their sacred places, and on the tops of all their cairns, in honour of Bel, or Belinus, the name by which they distinguished the sun, whose revolving course had again clothed the earth with beauty, and diffused joy and gladness through the creation. Their water parties on the 24th prove that they consider the summer season as now so fully established that they are not afraid to commit themselves to the mercy of the waves. If we reflect on the rooted animosity which subsisted between the Romans and the Druids, and that the latter, on being expelled from their former residences, found, together with the miserable remnants of the Britons, an asylum in the naturally fortified parts of the island, we shall not be surprised at their customs having been faintly handed down through such a long succession of ages. That Cornwall was one of their retreats is sufficiently proved by the numerous remains of their circular temples, cromlechs, cairns, &c. Even in the eleventh century, when Christianity was become the national religion, the people were so attached to their ancient superstitions, that we find a law of Canute the Great strictly prohibiting all his subjects from paying adoration to the sun, moon, sacred groves and woods, hallowed hills and fountains. If, then, this propensity to idolatry could not be rooted out of those parts of the kingdom exposed to the continual influx of foreigners, and the horrors of frequent war, how much more must it have flourished in Cornwall and those parts where the Druids long preserved their authority and influence? It may therefore be fairly inferred that, from their remote situation, and comparative insignificancy with the rest of England, they preserved those religious ceremonies unmolested ; and, corrupted as they must naturally be by long usage and tradition, yet are handed down to us to this to-day with evident marks of a Druidical origin." *

In Hone's " Every-Day Book " will be found several accounts of festivals which may be referred to Baal worship.

Mr Richard Edmonds, a native of Penzance, has given us a very faithful description of the proceedings at Penzance on Midsummer-eve. Although that gentleman states his belief in the true Celtic origin of this remarkable mode of celebrating the Midsummer festival, his description leads us to suppose that it is distinctly Roman :—

" It is the immemorial usage in Penzance and the neighbouring towns and villages to kindle bonfires and torches on Midsummer-eve ; and on Midsummer-day to hold a fair on Penzance quay, where the country folks assemble from the adjoining parishes in great numbers to make excursions on the water. St Peter's-eve is distinguished by a similar display of bonfires and torches, although the ' quay-fair ' on St Peter's-day has been discontinued upwards of forty years.

" On these eves a line of tar-barrels, relieved occasionally by large bonfires, is seen in the centre of each of the principal streets in Penzance. On either side of this line young men and women pass up and down swinging round their heads heavy torches made of large pieces of folded canvas steeped in tar, and nailed to the ends of sticks between three and four feet long; the flames of some of these almost equal those of the tar-barrels.

* In Ireland, May-day is called *la na Bealtina,* and the eve of May is *neen na Bealtina,* —the day and eve of Baal fires. Seeing the intimate relation of the inhabitants of Cornwall and those of Ireland, especially of the southern counties, may we not infer that the bonfires of May and those of Midsummer have a similar origin?

Rows of lighted candles also, when the air is calm, are fixed outside the windows or along the sides of the streets. In St Just and other mining parishes the young miners, mimicking their fathers' employments, bore rows of holes in the rocks, load them with gunpowder, and explode them in rapid succession by trains of the same substance. As the holes are not deep enough to split the rocks, the same little batteries serve for many years On these nights Mount's Bay has a most animating appearance, although not equal to what was annually witnessed at the beginning of the present century, when the whole coast, from the Land's End to the Lizard, wherever a town or village existed, was lighted up with these stationary or moving fires. In the early part of the evening, children may be seen wearing wreaths of flowers,—a custom in all probability originating from the ancient use of these ornaments when they danced around the fires. At the close of the fireworks in Penzance, a great number of persons of both sexes, chiefly from the neighbourhood of the quay, used always, until within the last few years, to join hand in hand, forming a long string, and run through the streets, playing 'thread the needle,' heedless of the fireworks showered upon them, and oftentimes leaping over the yet glowing embers. I have on these occasions seen boys following one another, jumping through flames higher than themselves. But whilst this is now done innocently in every sense of the word, we all know that the passing of children through fire was a very common act of idolatry; and the heathen believed that all persons, and all living things, submitted to this ordeal, would be preserved from evil throughout the ensuing year. A similar blessing was supposed to be imparted to their fields by running around them with flaming torches."—*Richard Edmonds—The Land's End District*, p. 66.

THE GARRICK ZANS, OR HOLY ROCK.

A FEW years—really but a few years—since, the stone altars on which the first inhabitants of these islands lit their holy fires had yet a place amongst us. In the village of Roskestall stood one such altar; in Treen was to be found another. These huge masses of rock, rendered sacred by the memories surrounding them, have been wantonly removed, and employed in most cases in furnishing pillars at the " grand entrances " of the houses of the squire farmers of the Land's End district; or they have been yet more rudely served, and are to be found at the entrance to a pigsty, or in the gate-posts to a potato-field.

The extinction of several of the old families is, to the present day, ascribed by the peasantry to the unholy act of removing or breaking up of the Garrick Zans in the village of Escols. The rock in the village of Mayon was called indifferently *table-mayon* (mōn), or the Garrack Zans. Within our memory is the gathering of the villagers around the Holy Rock. It was their custom, when anything was stolen, or a misdemeanour committed, to light a fire on this altar, and when the fagots were in full blaze, all those who sought to prove their innocence took a burning stick from the rock and spat on the blazing end. If they could extinguish the fire by spitting on the stick, they were declared innocent; but if the mouth was so dry as not to generate sufficient moisture to be heard " frizzing " on it, that unfortunate individual was suspected,·if not declared, to be guilty.* The Midsummer bonfire was first lighted on the rock in Escols, next on the Chapel Hill ; then all the other beacon hills were soon ablaze. Many superstitious rites were formerly performed on the Garrack Zans, which are only found now as the amusements of young people on the eves of St Agnes and Midsummer.

FIRE ORDEAL FOR THE CURE OF DISEASE.

A MINER, who was also a small farmer, living in Zennor, once consulted me on the condition of his daughter, a little girl about five or six years of age. This child was evidently suffering from some scrofulous taint. She was of a delicate complexion, with, usually, a hectic flush on her cheeks ; the skin being particularly fine, and so transparent that the course of the veins was marked by deep blue lines. This little girl had long suffered from indolent tumours, forming on the glands in various parts of the body ; and, as her father said, " they had taken her to all the doctors in the country round, and the child got worse and worse."

I prescribed for this child ; and for two or three weeks she was brought into Penzance on the market-day, that I might observe the influence of the remedial agent which I was employing. Right or wrong, however, the little girl was evidently benefited by the medicine I recommended.

Suddenly my patient was removed from my care, and many months passed away without my seeing either the child or the father. Eventually I met the parent in the market-place, and after some commonplace remarks, he informed me, on my inquiring for his daughter, that she was cured. I expressed satisfaction at hearing this, and inquired why he had not brought the child to me again. After some hesitation he said he had discovered what ailed the child—" *she was overlooked.*" Requiring some explanation of this, I got possession of his story, which was to the following purpose .—

* Boys at school, to prove the truth or falsehood of any charge, will take a stick from the fire and practise upon it in the same manner May not the custom of joining hands and passing through the embers of a dying bonfire, for good luck, be a vestige of the same ritual ?

O

At a short distance from their farm there resided an old woman who was feared by her neighbours, owing to her savage and un-controllable temper, and who hated all around her in consequence of the system of ill-usage to which during a long life she had been subjected.

I have visited this miserable creature in her home. A stone-built hut in the wildest part of the bleak coast, forming but one room, was her dwelling. The door was rotten through age, and the two small windows, neither of them more than eighteen inches long by twelve inches wide, which had once been glazed, had been broken to pieces, and the holes were filled in with old rags. Consequently, when the door was closed, the hovel would have been dark, but for the light which descended through the hole in the roof, which we must call a chimney, and that which gained admission through the cracks in the door—these gave a tolerable amount of illumination.

A low truckle-bed in one corner, with very scanty, dirty, and ragged covering,—a small round table, roughly made and standing on four square legs,—a log of wood, and a three-legged stool, formed, with one exception, all the furniture in the place. This exception was the "dresser." Those who are not acquainted with western England will require to be told that no dwelling, however poor, is regarded as complete without the set of framed shelves and drawers which constitute the dresser.

This old woman's dresser was painted white and blue, and on its shelves were cups and saucers, a few plates, one or two dishes, and some mugs. Here was an orderly arrangement, and a tolerably clean display, strangely contrasting with the dirt and dis-order of everything around. At the period of my visit this old woman was seated on the block of wood, with her naked arms folded before her, rocking herself to and fro. Margery Penwarne, for so she was called, though usually spoken of as "An'," or Aunt "Madge," must have been nearly eighty years old. Her hair was an iron gray, and it struggled out from under a cotton cap, which had once been white, in long thin locks. Her eyebrows were long enough to fall over her disagreeable gray eyes; and this, with the accumulation of long hair around her toothless mouth, gave her a most repulsive appearance. There were still living two or three old people who had known Margery in her youth, and they spoke of her as having been a pretty girl. The general idea evidently being that she had sold her soul to the devil, and that it was the influence of her evil mind which gave her so wretched an aspect.

From Margery I had a long story of the wrongs she suffered, and I believe this sad example of humanity may be regarded as an instance of the reaction of uncontrolled passion. ·Ignorant in the extreme herself, and dwelling amongst a class of people who were at that time but little superior to her in any respect, Margery succeeded in exerting much power over them by her violence. In addition to this, she was more industrious than her neighbours, of which her small farm bore the evidences. Violence begat its like, and where Margery, by her energy, became the apparent conqueror, she called into play all kinds of low cunning against herself, and was always, in the end, the sufferer. Her crops were injured, her pigs died suddenly, her fowls were killed, and even her donkeys were lamed.

As age crept on, the power to provide the necessities of life failed her, and she had, at the time I speak of, been receiving pay from the parish for many years. With age Margery's infirmities of temper increased. She had long been used by the mothers of the parish as a means for frightening the children. Their tears were stopped more readily by a threat, " I 'll give 'e to An' Madge," than by any other means ; and good conduct was insured if An' Madge was to be sent for " to tak 'e away." From this state she passed into another stage. Margery, from being a terror to the young, became the fear of the old. No one would dare refuse her a drop of milk, a few potatoes, or any of those trifles which she almost demanded from her neighbours, every one trembling lest she should exert her evil eye, or vent her curses upon them.

This was the being who had "overlooked" the miner's daughter. He told me that the cause of this was that he caught Margery stealing some straw, and that he " kicked her out of the yard."

The gossips of the parish had for some time insisted upon the fact that the child had been ill-wished, and that she never would be better until " the spell was taken off her." The father, who was in many respects a sensible man, would not for a long period hear of this, but the reiteration of the assertion at length compelled him to give way, and he consulted some " knowing man " in the parish of St Just.

It was then formally announced that the girl could never recover unless three burning sticks were taken from the hearth of the " overlooker," and the child was made to walk three times over them when they were laid across on the ground, and then quench the fire with water.

The father had no doubt respecting the " overlooker," his

quarrel with Madge determined this in his mind; but there were many difficulties in carrying out the prescribed means for effecting the cure. Without exposing themselves to the violence of the old woman it was impossible, and there was some fear that in forcibly entering her dwelling they might be brought "under the law," with which Margery had often threatened the people.

It was found, however, that nothing could be done for the child if they neglected this, and the father and two or three friends resolved to brave alike the old woman and the law.

One evening, the smoke, mixed with sparks, arising from the hole in the roof of Margery's cottage, informed them that the evil crone was preparing her supper, and as she evidently was burning dry furze, now was the time to procure the three blazing sticks. Accordingly three men and the little girl hurried to the hovel. The door was closed, but, not being secured on the inside, the father opened it. As they had planned, his two companions rushed in, and, without a word, seized the old woman, who fell from her block to the floor, to which, with unnecessary violence, they pinned her, she screaming with "the shriek of a goshawk." In the meantime the parent dragged three blazing pieces of furze from the hearth, hastened to the door, laid them one across the other, and then, without losing a moment, forced the trembling child across the fire three times, and compelled her to perform the other necessary portion of the ordeal by which the spell was to be broken.

Margery, weak, aged, and violent, was soon exhausted, and she probably fainted. I was, however, informed by the man, that as the fire was quenched in the sticks, the flames which appeared to kindle in her eyes gradually died away; that all the colour forsook her lips, and that at last she murmured, "My heart! my heart! bring me the girl, and I'll purge her of the spell;" upon which they left her as though dead upon the rough earth floor on which she had fallen.

Many other examples might have been given of the existence of a belief in the "virtue of fire," as I have heard it expressed.

BURNING ANIMALS ALIVE.

THERE can be no doubt but that a belief prevailed, until a very recent period, amongst the small farmers in the districts remote from towns, in Cornwall, that a living sacrifice appeased the wrath of God. This sacrifice must be by fire ; and I have heard it argued that the Bible gave them warranty for this belief.

The accompanying notes, from Hone's "Every-Day Book," and from Drew and Hitchen's "Cornwall," prove the prevalence—at least at the commencement of this century—of this idea. I have lately been informed that within the last few years a calf has been thus sacrificed by a farmer, in a district where churches, chapels, and schools abound.

The burning of blood, drawn from a deceased animal, has been a very common mode of appeasing the spirits of disease.

"There are too many obvious traces of the fact to doubt its truth, that the making of bonfires, and the leaping through them, are vestiges of the ancient worship of the heathen god Bal, and therefore it is, with propriety, that the editor of "Time's Telescope" adduces a recent occurrence from Drew and Hitchin's "History of Cornwall," as a probable remnant of pagan superstition in that country. He presumes that the vulgar notion which gave rise to it was derived from the Druidical sacrifice of beasts : ' An ignorant old farmer in Cornwall, having met with some severe losses in his cattle about the year 1800, was much afflicted with his misfortunes. To stop the growing evil, he applied to the fairiers in his neighbourhood, but unfortunately he applied in vain. The malady still continuing, and all remedies failing, he thought it necessary to have recourse to some extraordinary measure. Accordingly, on consulting with some of his neighbours, equally ignorant with himself, and evidently not less barbarous, they recalled to their recollections a tale, which tradition had handed down from remote antiquity, that the calamity would not cease until he had actually *burned alive the finest calf which he had upon his farm*, but that, when this sacrifice was made, the murrain would afflict his cattle no more. The old farmer, influenced by this counsel, resolved immediately on reducing it to practice ; that, by making the detestable experiment, he might secure an advantage which the whisperers of tradition and the advice of his neighbours had conspired to assure him would follow. He accordingly called several of his friends together on an appointed day, and having lighted a large fire, brought forth his best calf, and without ceremony or remorse, pushed it into the flames. The innocent victim, on feeling the intolerable heat, endeavoured to escape ; but this was in vain. The barbarians that surrounded the fire were armed with pitchforks, or *pikes*, as in Cornwall they are generally called ; and, as the burning victim endeavoured to escape from death, with these instruments of cruelty the wretches pushed back the tortured animal into the flames. In this state, amidst the wounds of pitchforks, the shouts of unfeeling ignorance and cruelty, and the corrosion of flames, the dying victim poured out its expiring groan, and was consumed to ashes. It is scarcely possible to reflect on this instance of superstitious barbarity without tracing a kind of resemblance between it and the ancient sacrifices of the Druids. This *calf* was *sacrificed to fortune*, or *good luck*, to avert impending calamity, and to insure future prosperity, and was selected by the farmer as the finest among his herd' Every intelligent native of Cornwall will perceive that this extract from the history of his county is here made for the purpose of shaming the brutally ignorant, if it be possible, into humanity." *

The remarks in Drew and Hitchin are as follows :—

"There is a tradition in Cornwall, which has been handed down from remote antiquity, that farmers may prevent any calamity by burning alive the finest calf they possess. This was so fully believed, that even as late as the year 1800, an ignorant old farmer, having met with some severe losses in his cattle, determined on being advised by some neighbours, not less barbarous than himself, to try this remedy. He accordingly, on an appointed day, called his friends together, lighted a large fire, brought forth his best calf, and without ceremony or remorse, pushed it into the flames."

[While correcting these sheets, I am informed of two recent instances of this superstition. One of them was the sacrifice of a calf by a farmer near Portreath, for the purpose of removing a disease which had long followed his horses and his cows. The other was the burning of a living lamb, to save, as the farmer said, "his flock from spells which had been cast on 'em."]

* Burning a Calf Alive.—Hone's " Every-Day Book," June 24, p. 431

DEMONS AND SPECTRES.

> " A ghost, shrouded and folded up
> In its own formless horror."
>
> *The Cenci*—SHELLEY.

> " I woke ; it was the midnight hour,
> The clock was echoing in the tower ;
> But though my slumber was gone by,
> This dream it would not pass away—
> It seems to live upon my eye ! "
>
> *Christabel*—COLERIDGE.

ROMANCES OF DEMONS, SPECTRES, ETC.

THE HOOTING CAIRN.

" On either hand, to left to right,
　　Heath, pasture, stream, and lake,
　Glanced dazzling by, too swift for sight;
　　The thundering bridges quake
　' Dost fear, my love ?　The moon shines bright,
　Hurrah !　The dead ride swift to-night,
　And art thou of the dead afraid ?'
　' Oh no !　but name them not—the dead.' "
　　　　　—BURGER'S *Leonora, Herschel's Translation.*

CAIRN Kenidzhek, pronounced Kenidjack, signifying Hooting Cairn, is on the north road from St Just to Penzance, and is strikingly distinguished from other hills by its rugged character. Hoary stones, bleached by the sunshine of ages, are reared in fantastic confusion. The spirits of the Celts, possibly the spirits of a yet older people, dwell amidst those rocks. Within the shadow of this hill are mounds and barrows, and mystic circles, and holed stones, and rude altars, still telling of the past. The dead hold undisputed possession of all around ; no ploughshare has dared to invade this sacred spot, and every effort made by modern man to mark his sway is indicated by its ruin. Nothing but what the Briton planted remains, and, if tales tell true, it is probable long years must pass before the Englishman can banish the Celtic powers who here hold sovereign sway.

" A weird tract is that of Kenidzhek and the Gump, and of ill repute. The old, half-starved horses on the common, with their hides grown rusty brown, like dried and withered grass, by exposure, are ridden by the archfiend at night. He is said to hunt lost souls over this heath ; and an old stile hard by bears an evil name, for there the souls are sure to be caught, none being able

to get over it. The people tell of midnight fights by demons, and of a shadowy form holding a lantern to the combatants."
—*Blight.*

One of the tales which I have heard may be given as a strange mixture of the Celtic and the monastic legend.

Two miners who had been working in one of the now abandoned mines in Morvah, had, their labours being over, been, as was common, "half-pinting" in the public-house in Morvah Church-town. It was after dark, but not late; they were very quiet men, and not drunk. They had walked on, talking of the prospects of the mine, and speculating on the promise of certain "pitches," and were now on the Common, at the base of the Hooting Cairn. No miner ever passed within the shadow of Cairn Kenidzhek who dared to indulge in any frivolous talk : at least, thirty years since, the influence akin to fear was very potent upon all.

Well, our two friends became silent, and trudged with a firm, a resolved footstep onward.

There was but little wind, yet a low moaning sound came from the cairn, which now and then arose into a hoot. The night was dark, yet a strange gleaming light rendered the rocks on the cairn visible, and both the miners fancied they saw gigantic forms passing in and about the intricate rocks. Presently they heard a horse galloping at no great distance behind them. They turned and saw, mounted on a horse which they knew very well, since the bony brute had often worked the "whim" on their mine, a dark man robed in a black gown, and a hood over his head, partly covering his face.

"Hallo! hallo!" shouted they, fearing the rider would ride over them.

"Hallo to you," answered a gruff voice.

"Where be'st goen then?" asked the bravest of the miners.

"Up to the cairn to see the wrastling," answered the rider; "come along! come along!"

Horse and rider rushed by the two miners, and, they could never tell why, they found themselves compelled to follow.

They did not appear to exert themselves, but without much effort they kept up with the galloping horse. Now and then the dark rider motioned them onward with his hand, but he spoke not. At length the miners arrived at a mass of rocks near the base of the hill, which stopped their way; and, since it was dark, they knew not how to get past them. Presently they saw the rider ascending the hill, regardless of the masses of rock; passing unconcernedly over all, and, as it seemed to them, the man, the horse, and the rocks were engaged in a " three man's song," * the chorus to which was a piercing hoot. A great number of uncouth figures were gathering together, coming, as it seemed, out of the rocks themselves. They were men of great size and strength, with savage faces, rendered more terrible by the masses of uncombed hair which hung about them, and the colours with which they had painted their cheeks. The plain in front of the rocks which had checked the miners' progress was evidently to be the wrestling ground. Here gathered those monstrous-looking men, all anxiety, making a strange noise. It was not long ere they saw the rider, who was now on foot, descending the hill with two giants of men, more terrible than any they had yet seen.

A circle was formed ; the rider, who had thrown off his black gown, and discovered to the miners that he was no other than Old Nick, placed the two men, and seated himself in a very odd manner upon the ground.

The miners declared the wrestlers were no other than two devils, although the horns and tail were wanting. There was a shout, which, as if it indicated that the light was insufficient, was answered by the squatting demon by flashing from his eyes two beams of fire, which shed an unearthly glow over everything. To it the wrestlers went, and better men were never seen to the west of Penzance. At length one of them, straining hard for the mastery, lifted his antagonist fairly high in the air, and flung him to the ground, a fair back fall. The rocks trembled, and the ground seemed to thunder with the force of the fall. Old Nick still sat quietly looking on, and notwithstanding the defeated wrestler lay as one dead, no one went near him. All crowded around the victor, and shouted like so many wild beasts. The love of fair play was strong in the hearts of the miners ; they scorned the idea of deserting a fallen foe ; so they scrambled over the rocks, and made for the prostrate giant, for so, for size, he might well be called. He was in a dreadful strait. Whether his bones were smashed or not by the fall, they could not tell, but he appeared " passing away." The elder miner had long been a pro-fessor of religion. It is true he had fallen back ; but still he knew the right road. He thought, therefore, that even a devil might repent, and he whispered in the ear of the dying man the Christian's hope.

If a thunderbolt had fallen amongst them, it could not have

* " They have also *Cornish* three men's songs, cunningly contrived for the ditty, and pleasaut for the note "—*Carew*, p 72

produced such an effect as this. The rocks shook with an earth-quake; everything became pitchy dark; there was a noise of rushing hither and thither, and all were gone, dying man and all, they knew not whither. The two miners, terrified beyond mea-sure, clung to each other on their knees; and, while in this posi-tion, they saw, as if in the air, the two blazing eyes of the demon passing away into the west, and at last disappear in a dreadfully black cloud. These two men were, although they knew the ground perfectly well, inextricably lost; so, after vainly endea-vouring to find the right road off the Common, they lay down in each other's arms under a mass of granite rock, praying that they might be protected till the light of day removed the spell which was upon them.

JAGO'S DEMON.

THE vicar of Wendron, who bore the name of Jago, appears to have had strange intercourse with the invisible world; or, rather, the primitive people of this district believe him to have possessed supernatural powers. Any one visiting the parish of Wendron will be struck with many distinguishing features in its inhabitants. It would appear as if a strange people had settled down amidst the races already inhabiting the spot, and that they had studiously avoided any intimate connection with their neigh-bours. The dialect of the Wendron people is unlike any other in Cornwall, and there are many customs existing amongst them which are not found in any other part of the county. Until of late years, the inhabitants of Wendron were quite uneducated;—hence the readiness with which they associate ancient superstitions with comparatively modern individuals.

The Reverend Mr Jago was no doubt a man who impressed this people with the powers of his knowledge. Hence we are told that no spirit walking the earth could resist the spells laid upon him by Jago. By his prayers—or powers—many a night wanderer has been put back into his grave, and so confined that the poor ghost could never again get loose. To the evil-disposed Mr Jago was a terror. All Wendron believed that every act was visible to the parson at the moment it was done—day or night it mattered not. He has been known to pick a thief at once out of a crowd, and criminal men or women could not endure the glance of his eye. Many a person has at once confessed to guilty deeds of which they have been suspected the moment they have been brought before Mr Jago.

We are told that he had spirits continually waiting upon him, though invisible until he desired them to appear. The parson rode far and wide over the moorland of his parish. He never took a groom with him; for, the moment he alighted from his horse, he had only to strike the earth with his whip, and up came a demon-groom to take charge of the steed.

PETER THE DEVIL.

THE church at Altarnun is said to have been built from the remains of an ancient nunnery which had been founded in the early days of Christianity by the saint to whom it was dedicated.

There was a peculiar sanctity about all that surrounded this little church and its holy well, and few were unfaithful enough to scoff at any of the holy traditions of the sacred place.

About the time of Charles II., an under-clerk or deacon of this church was called Peter, and he is said to have been a man of exceedingly bad character. He scoffed at holy things, and—unless he was belied—he made use of his position for merely temporal benefit, and was not remarkable for his honesty. He was, moreover, the terror of the neighbourhood. Common report insisting on it that Peter had been known to disentomb the dead, whether for the purpose of stealing rings and other trinkets which may have been buried, as some said, or for the purpose of renewing his youth, as others suggested, by mysterious contact with the dead, was not clearly made out. He was invariably called Peter Jowle, or Joule—that is, Peter the Devil. At the age of a hundred he was a gray-headed, toothless man; but then, by some diabolical incantation, he is said to have caused new black hairs to spring forth amongst those which were white with age, and then also new teeth grew in his jaws. Peter is said to have died when he was more than a hundred and fifty years old.

DANDO AND HIS DOGS.

IN the neighbourhood of the lovely village of St Germans formerly lived a priest connected with the old priory church of this parish, whose life does not appear to have been quite consistent with his vows.

He lived the life of the traditional "jolly friar." He ate and drank of the best the land could give him, or money buy; and it is said that his indulgences extended far beyond the ordinary limits of good living. The priest Dando was, notwithstanding all his vices, a man liked by the people. He was good-natured, and therefore blind to many of their sins. Indeed, he threw a cloak over his own iniquities, which was inscribed "charity," and he freely forgave all those who came to his confessional.

As a man increases in years he becomes more deeply dyed with the polluted waters through which he may have waded. It rarely happens that an old sinner is ever a repentant one, until the decay of nature has reduced him to a state of second childhood. As long as health allows him to enjoy the sensualities of life, he continues to gratify his passions, regardless of the cost. He becomes more selfish, and his own gratification is the rule of his existence. So it has ever been, and so was it with Dando.

The sinful priest was a capital huntsman, and scoured the country far and near in pursuit of game, which was in those days abundant and varied, over this well-wooded district. Dando, in the eagerness of the chase, paid no regard to any kind of property. Many a corn-field has been trampled down, and many a cottage garden destroyed by the horses and dogs which this impetuous hunter would lead unthinkingly over them. Curses deep, though not loud, would follow the old man, as even those who suffered by his excesses were still in fear of his priestly power.

Any man may sell his soul to the devil without going through the stereotyped process of signing a deed with his blood. Give up your soul to Satan's darling sins, and he will help you for a season, until he has his chains carefully wound around you, when the links are suddenly closed, and he seizes his victim, who has no power to resist.

Dando worshipped the sensual gods which he had created, and his external worship of the God of truth became every year more and more a hypocritical lie. The devil looked carefully after his prize. Of course, to catch a dignitary of the church was a thing to cause rejoicings amongst the lost ; and Dando was carefully lured to the undoing of his soul. Health and wealth were secured to him, and by and by the measure of his sins was full, and he was left the victim to self-indulgences—a doomed man. With increasing years, and the immunities he enjoyed, Dando became more reckless. Wine and wassail, a board groaning with dishes which stimulated the sated appetite, and the company of both sexes of dissolute habits, exhausted his nights. His days were devoted to the pursuits of the field ; and to maintain the required excitement, ardent drinks were supplied him by his wicked companions. It mattered not to Dando,—provided the day was an auspicious one, if the scent would lie on the ground,—even on the Sabbath, horses and hounds were ordered out, and the priest would be seen in full cry.

One Sabbath morning, Dando and his riotous rout were hunting over the Earth estate ; game was plenty, and sport first-rate. Exausted with a long and eager run, Dando called for drink. He had already exhausted the flasks of the attendant hunters.

"Drink, I say ; give me drink," he cried.

"Whence can we get it ?" asked one of the gang.

"Go to hell for it, if you can't get it on Earth," said the priest, with a bitter laugh at his own joke on the Earth estate.

At the moment, a dashing hunter, who had mingled with the throng unobserved, came forward, and presented a richly-mounted flask to Dando, saying,—

"Here is some choice liquor distilled in the establishment you speak of. It will warm and revive you, I'll warrant. Drink deep, friend, drink."

Dando drank deep ; the flask appeared to cling to his lips. The strange hunter looked on with a rejoicing yet malignant expression, a wicked smile playing over an otherwise tranquil face.

By and by Dando fetched a deep sigh, and removed the flask, exclaiming, "By hell ! that was a drink indeed. Do the gods drink such nectar ?"

"Devils do," said the hunter.

"An they do, I wish I were one," said Dando, who now rocked to and fro in a state of thorough intoxication ; "methinks the drink is very like "—— The impious expression died upon his lips.

Looking round with a half-idiotic stare, Dando saw that his new friend had appropriated several head of game. Notwithstanding his stupid intoxication, his selfishness asserted its power, and he seized the game, exclaiming, in a guttural, half-smothered voice, "None of these are thine"

"What I catch I keep," said the hunter.

"By all the devils they're mine," stammered Dando.

The hunter quietly bowed.

Dando's wrath burst at once into a burning flame, uncontrolled by reason. He rolled himself off his horse, and rushed, staggering as he went, at the steed of his unknown friend, uttering most frightful oaths and curses.

The strange hunter's horse was a splendid creature, black as night, and its eyes gleamed like the brightest stars with unnatural lustre. The horse was turned adroitly aside, and Dando fell to the earth with much force. The fall appeared to add to his fury, and he roared with rage. Aided by his attendants, he was speedily on his legs, and again at the side of the hunter, who shook with laughter, shaking the game in derision, and quietly uttering, "They're mine."

"I'll go to hell after them, but I'll get them from thee," shouted Dando.

"So thou shalt," said the hunter; and seizing Dando by the collar, he lifted him from the ground, and placed him, as though he were a child, before him on the horse.

With a dash, the horse passed down the hill, its hoofs striking fire at every tread, and the dogs, barking furiously, followed impetuously. These strange riders reached the banks of the Lynher, and with a terrific leap, the horse and its riders, followed by the hounds, went out far in its waters, disappearing at length in a blaze of fire, which caused the stream to boil for a moment, and then the waters flowed on as tranquilly as ever over the doomed priest. All this happened in the sight of the assembled peasantry. Dando never more was seen, and his fearful death was received as a warning by many, who gave gifts to the church. One amongst them carved a chair for the bishop, and on it he represented Dando and his dogs, that the memory of his wickedness might be always renewed. There, in St German's Church, stands to this day the chair, and all who doubt the truth of this tradition may view the story carved in enduring oak. If they please, they can sit in the chair until their faith is so far quickened that they become true believers. On Sunday mornings early, the dogs of the priest have been often heard as if in eager pursuit of game. Cheney's hounds and the Wish hounds of Dartmoor are but other versions of the same legend.[*]

Mr T. Q. Couch, in his "Folk Lore of a Cornish Village," tells the story in a somewhat different form .—

THE DEVIL AND HIS DANDY-DOGS.

"A POOR herdsman was journeying homeward across the moors one windy night, when he heard at a distance among the Tors the baying of hounds, which he soon recognised as the dismal chorus of the dandy-dogs. It was three or four miles to his house; and very much alarmed, he hurried onward as fast as the treacherous nature of the soil and the uncertainty of the path would allow; but, alas! the melancholy yelping of the hounds, and the dismal holloa of the hunter came nearer and nearer. After a considerable run, they had so gained upon him, that on looking back,—oh horror! he could distinctly see hunter and dogs. The

[*] See page 145, and Appendix (H), *The Bargest.*

former was terrible to look at, and had the usual complement of *saucer-eyes,* horns, and tail, accorded by common consent to the legendary devil. He was black, of course, and carried in his hand a long hunting-pole. The dogs, a numerous pack, blackened the small patch of moor that was visible ; each snorting fire, and uttering a yelp of indescribably frightful tone. No cottage, rock, or tree was near to give the herdsman shelter, and nothing apparently remained to him but to abandon himself to their fury, when a happy thought suddenly flashed upon him and suggested a resource. Just as they were about to rush upon him, he fell on his knees in prayer. There was strange power in the holy words he uttered ; for immediately, as if resistance had been offered, the hell-hounds stood at bay, howling more dismally than ever, and the hunter shouted, ' Bo Shrove,' which (says my informant) means in the old language, '*The boy prays,*' at which they all drew off on some other pursuit and disappeared."

THE SPECTRAL COACH.*

"You have heard of such a spirit, and well you know
The superstitions, idle-headed eld
Received and did deliver to our age
This tale of Herne the Hunter for a truth."
—MERRY WIVES OF WINDSOR.

THE old vicarage-house at Talland, as seen from the Looe road, its low roof and gray walls peeping prettily from between the dense boughs of ash and elm that environed it, was as picturesque an object as you could desire to see. The seclusion of its situation was enhanced by the character of the house itself. It was an odd-looking, old-fashioned building, erected apparently in an age when asceticism and self-denial were more in vogue than at present, with a stern disregard of the comfort of the inhabitant, and in utter contempt of received principles of taste. As if not secure enough in its retirement, a high wall, enclosing a courtelage in front, effectually protected its inmates from the prying passenger, and only revealed the upper part of the house, with its small Gothic windows, its slated roof, and heavy chimneys partly hidden by the evergreen shrubs which grew in the enclosure. Such was it until its removal a few years since ; and such was it as it lay sweetly in the shadows of an autumnal evening one hundred and thirty years ago, when a stranger in the garb of a country labourer knocked hesitatingly at the wicket-gate which conducted to the court. After a little delay a servant-girl appeared, and finding that the countryman bore a message to the vicar, admitted him within the walls, and conducted him along a paved passage to the little, low, damp parlour where sat the good man. The Rev. Mr Dodge was in many respects a remarkable man.

* Contributed by T. Q. Couch, Esq.

You would have judged as much of him as he sat before the fire in his high-back chair, in an attitude of thought, arranging, it may have been, the heads of his next Sabbath's discourse. His heavy eyebrows throwing into shade his spacious eyes, and indeed the whole contour of his face, marked him as a man of great firmness of character and of much moral and personal courage. His suit of sober black and full-bottomed periwig also added to his dignity, and gave him an appearance of greater age. He was then verging on sixty. The time and the place gave him abundant exercise for the qualities we have mentioned, for many of his parishioners obtained their livelihood by the contraband trade, and were mostly men of unscrupulous and daring character, little likely to bear with patience reflections on the dishonesty of their calling. Nevertheless, the vicar was fearless in reprehending it, and his frank exhortations were, at least, listened to on account of the simple honesty of the man, and his well-known kindness of heart. The eccentricity of his life, too, had a wonderful effect in procuring him the respect, not to say the awe, of a people superstitious in a more than ordinary degree. Ghosts in those days had more freedom accorded them, or had more business with the visible world, than at present; and the parson was frequently required by his parishioners to draw from the uneasy spirit the dread secret which troubled it, or by the aid of the solemn prayers of the Church to set it at rest for ever. Mr Dodge had a fame as an exorcist, which was not confined to the bounds of his parish, nor limited to the age in which he lived.

"Well, my good man, what brings you hither?" said the clergyman to the messenger.

"A letter, may it please your reverence, from Mr Mills of Lanreath," said the countryman, handing him a letter.

Mr Dodge opened it and read as follows :—

"MY DEAR BROTHER DODGE,—I have ventured to trouble you, at the earnest request of my parishioners, with a matter, of which some particulars have doubtless reached you, and which has caused, and is causing, much terror in my neighbourhood. For its fuller explication, I will be so tedious as to recount to you the whole of this strange story as it has reached my ears, for as yet I have not satisfied my eyes of its truth. It has been told me by men of honest and good report (witnesses of a portion of what they relate), with such strong assurances that it behoves us to look more closely into the matter There is in the neighbourhood of this village a barren bit of moor which had no owner, or rather more than one, for the lords of the adjoining manors debated its ownership between themselves, and both determined to take it from the poor, who have for many years past regarded it as a common. And truly, it is little to the credit of these gentlemen, that they should strive for a thing so worthless as scarce to bear the cost of law, and yet of no mean value to poor labouring people. The two litigants, however, contested it with as much violence as if it had been a field of great price, and especially one, an old man (whose thoughts should have been less set on earthly possessions, which he was soon to leave), had so set his heart on the success of his suit, that the loss of it, a few years back, is said to have much hastened his death. Nor, indeed, after death, if current reports are worthy of credit, does he quit his claim to it ; for at night-time his apparition is seen on the moor, to the great terror of the neighbouring villagers. A public path leads by at no great distance from the spot, and on divers occasions has the labourer, returning from his work, been frightened nigh unto lunacy by sight and sounds of a very dreadful character. The appearance is said to be that of a man habited in black, driving a carriage drawn by headless horses. This is, I avow, very marvellous to believe, but it has had so much credible testimony, and has gained so many believers in my parish, that some steps seem necessary to allay the excitement it causes. I have been applied to for this purpose, and my present business is to ask your assistance in this matter, either to reassure the minds of the country people, if it be only a simple terror ; or, if there be truth in it, to set the troubled spirit of the man at rest. My messenger, who is an industrious, trustworthy man, will give you more information if it be needed, for, from report, he is acquainted with most of the circumstances, and will bring back your advice and promise of assistance.

"Not doubting of your help herein, I do, with my very hearty commendation, commit you to God's protection and blessing, and am,

"Your very loving brother,
"ABRAHAM MILLS."

This remarkable note was read and re-read, while the countryman sat watching its effects on the parson's countenance, and was surprised that it changed not from its usual sedate and settled character. Turning at length to the man, Mr Dodge inquired, "Are you, then, acquainted with my good friend Mills ? "

"I should know him, sir," replied the messenger, "having been sexton to the parish for fourteen years, and being, with my family, much beholden to the kindness of the rector."

"You are also not without some knowledge of the circumstances related in this letter. Have you been an eye-witness to any of those strange sights ? "

"For myself, sir, I have been on the road at all hours of the night and day, and never did I see anything which I could call worse than myself One night my wife and I were awoke by the rattle of wheels, which was also heard by some of our neighbours, and we are all assured that it could have been no other than the black coach. We have every day such stories told in the villages by so many creditable persons, that it would not be proper in a plain, ignorant man like me to doubt it."

" And how far," asked the clergyman, " is the mooi from Lanreath ? "

" About two miles, and please your reverence. The whole parish is so frightened, that few will venture far aftei nightfall, for it has of late come much nearer the village. A man who is esteemed a sensible and pious man by many, though an Anabaptist in principle, went a few weeks back to the moor ('tis called Blackadon) at midnight, in order to lay the spirit, being requested thereto by his neighbours, and he was so alarmed at what he saw, that he hath been somewhat mazed ever since."

" A fitting punishment foi his presumption, if it hath not quite demented him," said the parson. " These persons are like those addressed by St Chrysostom, fitly called the golden-mouthed, who said, ' Miserable wretches that ye be ' ye cannot expel a flea, much less a devil ! ' It will be well if it serves no other purpose but to bring back these stray sheep to the fold of the Church. So this story has gained much belief in the parish ? "

" Most believe it, sir, as rightly they should, what hath so many witnesses," said the sexton, " though there be some, chiefly young men, who set up for being wiser than their fathers, and refuse to credit it, though it be sworn to on the book."

" If those things are disbelieved, friend," said the parson, " and without inquiry, which your disbeliever is ever the first to shrink from, of what worth is human testimony ? That ghosts have returned to the earth, either for the discovery of murder, or to make restitution for other injustice committed in the flesh, or compelled thereto by the incantations of sorcery, or to communicate tidings from another world, has been testified to in all ages, and many are the accounts which have been left us both in sacred and profane authors. Did not Brutus, when in Asia, as is related by Plutarch, see "———

Just at this moment the paison's handmaid announced that a person waited on him in the kitchen,—or the good clergyman would probably have detailed all those cases in history, general and biblical, with which his reading had acquainted him, not much, we fear, to the edification and comfort of the sexton, who had to return to Lanreath, a long and dreary road, after nightfall. So, instead, he directed the girl to take him with her, and give him such refreshment as he needed, and in the meanwhile he prepared a note in answer to Mr Mills, informing him that on the morrow he was to visit some sick persons in his parish, but that on the following evening he should be ready to proceed with him to the moor.

On the night appointed the two clergymen left the Lanreath rectory on horseback, and reached the moor at eleven o'clock. Bleak and dismal did it look by day, but then there was the distant landscape dotted over with pretty homesteads to relieve its desolation. Now, nothing was seen but the black patch of sterile moor on which they stood, nothing heard but the wind as it swept in gusts across the bare hill, and howled dismally through a stunted grove of trees that grew in a glen below them, except the occasional baying of dogs from the farmhouses in the distance. That they felt at ease, is more than could be expected of them ; but as it would have shown a lack of faith in the protection of Heaven, which it would have been unseemly in men of their holy calling to exhibit, they managed to conceal from each other their uneasiness. Leading their horses, they trod to and fro through the damp fern and heath with firmness in their steps, and upheld each other by remarks on the power of that Great Being whose ministers they were, and the might of whose name they were there to make manifest. Still slowly and dismally passed the time as they conversed, and anon stopped to look through the darkness for the approach of their ghostly visitor. In vain   Though the night was as dark and murky as ghost could wish, the coach and its driver came not.

After a considerable stay, the two clergymen consulted together, and determined that it was useless to watch any longer for that night, but that they would meet on some other, when perhaps it might please his ghostship to appear. Accordingly, with a few words of leave-taking, they separated, Mr Mills for the rectory, and Mr Dodge, by a short ride across the moor, which shortened his journey by half a mile, for the vicarage at Talland.

The vicar rode on at an ambling pace, which his good mare sustained up hill and down dale without urging. At the bottom of a deep valley, however, about a mile from Blackadon, the animal became very uneasy, pricked up her ears, snorted, and moved from side to side of the road, as if something stood in the path before her. The parson tightened the reins, and applied whip and spur to her sides, but the animal, usually docile, became very unruly, made several attempts to turn, and, when prevented, threw herself upon her haunches. Whip and spur were applied again and again, to no other purpose than to add to the horse's terror. To the rider nothing was apparent which could account for the sudden restiveness of his beast. He dismounted, and attempted in turns to lead or drag her, but both were impracticable, and attended with no small risk of snapping the reins. She was remounted with great difficulty, and another attempt was made to urge her forward, with the like want of success. At length the eccentric clergyman, judging it to be some special signal from Heaven, which it would be dangerous to neglect, threw the reins on the neck of his steed, which, wheeling suddenly round, started backward in a direction towards the moor, at a pace which rendered the parson's seat neither a pleasant nor a safe one. In an astonishingly short space of time they were once more a Blackadon.

By this time the bare outline of the moor was broken by a large black group of objects, which the darkness of the night prevented the parson from defining. On approaching this unaccountable appearance, the mare was seized with fresh fury, and it was with considerable difficulty that she could be brought to face this new cause of fright. In the pauses of the horse's prancing, the vicar discovered to his horror the much-dreaded spectacle of the black coach and the headless steeds, and, terrible to relate, his friend Mr Mills lying prostrate on the ground before the sable driver. Little time was left him to call up his courage for this fearful emergency; for just as the vicar began to give utterance to the earnest prayers which struggled to his lips, the spectre shouted, " Dodge is come! I must begone!" and forthwith leaped into his chariot, and disappeared across the moor.

The fury of the mare now subsided, and Mr Dodge was enabled to approach his friend, who was lying motionless and speechless, with his face buried in the heather.

Meanwhile the rector's horse, which had taken fright at the apparition, and had thrown his rider to the ground on or near the spot where we have left him lying, made homeward at a furious speed, and stopped not until he had reached his stable door The sound of his hoofs as he galloped madly through the village awoke the cottagers, many of whom had been some hours in their beds. Many eager faces, staring with affright, gathered round the rectory, and added, by their various conjectures, to the terror and apprehensions of the family.

The villagers, gathering courage as their numbers increased, agreed to go in search of the missing clergyman, and started off in a compact body, a few on horseback, but the greater number on foot, in the direction of Blackadon. There they discovered their rector, supported in the arms of Parson Dodge, and recovered so far as to be able to speak. Still there was a wildness in his eye, and an incoherency in his speech, that showed that his reason was, at least, temporarily unsettled by the fright. In this condition he was taken to his home, followed by his reverend companion.

Here ended this strange adventure; for Mr Mills soon completely regained his reason, Parson Dodge got safely back to Talland, and from that time to this nothing has been heard or seen of the black ghost or his chariot.*

SIR FRANCIS DRAKE AND HIS DEMON.

SIR FRANCIS DRAKE—who appears to have been especially befriended by his demon—is said to drive at night a black hearse drawn by headless horses, and urged on by running devils and yelping, headless dogs, through Jump, on the road from Tavistock to Plymouth.

Sir Francis, according to tradition, was enabled to destroy the Spanish armada by the aid of the devil. The old admiral went to Devil's Point, a well-known promontory jutting into Plymouth Sound. He there cut pieces of wood into the water, and by the power of magic and the assistance of his demon these became at once well-armed gunboats.

The Queen, Elizabeth, gave Sir Francis Drake Buckland Abbey; and on every hand we hear of Drake and his familiars.

An extensive building attached to the abbey—which was no doubt used as barns and stables after the place had been deprived of its religious character—was said to have been built by the devil in three nights. After the first night, the butler, astonished at the work done, resolved to watch and see how it was performed. Consequently, on the second night, he mounted into a large tree, and hid himself between the forks of its five branches. At midnight the devil came, driving several teams of oxen; and as some of them were lazy, he plucked this tree from the ground and used

---

* The Parson Dodge, whose adventure is related, was vicar of Talland from 1713 till his death. So that the name as well as the story is true to tradition. Bond ("History of East and West Love") says of him: "About a century since the Rev. Richard Dodge was vicar of this parish of Talland, and was, by traditionary account, a very singular man   He had the reputation of being deeply skilled in the black art, and would raise ghosts, or send them into the Dead Sea, at the nod of his head   The common people, not only in his own parish, but throughout the neighbourhood, stood in the greatest awe of him, and to meet him on the highway at midnight produced the utmost horror, he was then driving about the evil spirits; many of them were seen, in all sorts of shapes, flying and running before him, and he pursuing them with his whip in a most daring manner.   Not unfrequently he would be seen in the churchyard at dead of night to the terror of passers-by.   He was a worthy man, and much respected, but had his eccentricities."

it as a goad. The poor butler lost his senses, and never recovered them.

Drake constructed the Channel, carrying the waters from Dartmoor to Plymouth. Tradition says he went with his demon to Dartmoor, walked into Plymouth, and the waters followed him * Even now,—as old Betty Donithorne, formerly the housekeeper at Buckland Abbey, told me,—if the warrior hears the drum which hangs in the hall of the abbey, and which accompanied him round the world, he rises and has a revel.

Some few years since a small box was found in a closet which had been long closed, containing, it is supposed, family papers. This was to be sent to the residence of the inheritor of this property. The carriage was at the abbey door, and a man easily lifted the box into it. The owner having taken his seat, the coachman attempted to start his horses, but in vain. They would not—they could not move. More horses were brought, and then the heavy farm-horses, and eventually all the oxen. They were powerless to start the carriage. At length a mysterious voice was heard, declaring that the box could never be moved from Buckland Abbey. It was taken from the carriage easily by one man, and a pair of horses galloped off with the carriage.

THE PARSON AND CLERK.

NEAR Dawlish stand, out in the sea, two rocks, of red sandstone conglomerate, to which the above name is given.

Seeing that this forms a part of Old Cornwall, I do not go beyond my limits in telling the true story of these singular rocks

The Bishop of Exeter was sick unto death at Dawlish. An ambitious priest, from the east, frequently rode with his clerk to make anxious inquiries after the condition of the dying bishop. It is whispered that this priest had great hopes of occupying the bishop's throne in Exeter Cathedral.

The clerk was usually the priest's guide ; but somehow or other, on a particularly stormy night, he lost the road, and they were wandering over Haldon. Excessively angry was the priest, and very provoking was the clerk. He led his master this way and that way, but they were yet upon the elevated country of Haldon.

* "Here Sir Francis Drake first extended the point of that liquid line wherewith (as an emulator of the sunnes glorie) he encompassed the world."—*The Survey of Cornwall, Carew.*

At length the priest, in a great rage, exclaimed, " I would rather have the devil for a guide than you." Presently the clatter of horse's hoofs were heard, and a peasant, on a moor pony, rode up. The priest told of his condition, and the peasant volunteered to guide them. On rode peasant, priest, and clerk, and presently they were at Dawlish. The night was tempestuous, the ride had quickened the appetite of the priest, and he was wet through, —therefore, when his friend asked him to supper, as they approached an old ruined house, through the windows of which bright lights were shining, there was no hesitation in accepting the invitation.

There were a host of friends gathered together—a strange, wild-looking lot of men. But as the tables were laden with substantial dishes, and black-jacks were standing thick around, the parson, and the clerk too, soon made friends with all.

They ate and drank, and became most irreligiously uproarious. The parson sang hunting songs, and songs in praise of a certain old gentleman, with whom a priest should not have maintained any acquaintance These were very highly appreciated, and every man joined loudly in the choruses. Night wore away, and at last news was brought that the bishop was dead. This appeared to rouse up the parson, who was only too eager to get the first intelligence, and go to work to secure the hope of his ambition. So master and man mounted their horses, and bade adieu to their hilarious friends.

They were yet at the door of the mansion—somehow or other the horses did not appear disposed to move. They were whipped and spurred, but to no purpose.

" The devil's in the horses," said the priest.

" I b'lieve he is," said the clerk.

" Devil or no devil, they shall go," said the parson, cutting his horse madly with his heavy whip

There was a roar of unearthly laughter.

The priest looked round—his drinking friends were all turned into demons, wild with glee, and the peasant guide was an arch little devil, looking on with a marvellously curious twinkle in his eyes. The noise of waters was around them ; and now the priest discovered that the mansion had disappeared, and that waves beat heavy upon his horse's flanks, and rushed over the smaller horse of his man.

Repentance was too late.

In the morning following this stormy night, two horses were

found straying on the sands at Dawlish ; and clinging with the grasp of death to two rocks, were found the parson and the clerk. There stand the rocks to which the devil had given the forms of horses—an enduring monument to all generations.

THE HAUNTED WIDOWER.

A LABOURING man, very shortly after his wife's death, sent to a servant girl, living at the time in a small shipping port, requesting her to come to the inn to him. The girl went, and over a " ha' pint " she agreed to accept him as her husband.

All went on pleasantly enough for a time. One evening the man met the girl. He was silent for some time and sorrowful, but at length he told her his wife had come back.

" What do'st mean ? " asked the girl ; " have 'e seen hur ? "

" Naw, I han't seed her."

" Why, how do'st knaw it is her then ? "

The poor man explained to her, that at night, when in bed, she would come to the side of it, and " flop " his face ; and there was no mistaking her " flop."

" So you knawed her flop, did 'e ? " asked the girl.

" Ay, it couldn't be mistook."

" If she do hunt thee," said the girl, " she 'll hunt me ; and if she do flop 'e, she 'll flop me,—so it must be off atween us."

The unfortunate flop of the dead wife prevented the man from securing a living one.

THE SPECTRE BRIDEGROOM.

LONG, long ago a farmer named Lenine lived in Boscean. He had but one son, Frank Lenine, who was indulged into waywardness by both his parents. In addition to the farm servants, there was one, a young girl, Nancy Trenoweth, who especially assisted Mrs Lenine in all the various duties of a small farmhouse

Nancy Trenoweth was very pretty, and although perfectly uneducated, in the sense in which we now employ the term education, she possessed many native graces, and she had acquired much knowledge, really useful to one whose aspirations would probably never rise higher than to be mistress of a farm of a few acres Educated by parents who had certainly never seen the world beyond Penzance, her ideas of the world were limited to a few miles around the Land's End. But although her book of nature was a small one, it had deeply impressed her mind with its influences. The wild waste, the small but fertile valley, the rugged hills, with their crowns of cairns, the moors rich in the golden furze and the purple heath, the sea-beaten cliffs, and the silver sands, were the pages she had studied, under the guidance of a mother who conceived, in the sublimity of her ignorance, that everything in nature was the home of some spirit form. The soul of the girl was imbued with the deeply religious dye of her mother's mind, whose religion was only a sense of an unknown world immediately beyond our own. The elder Nancy Trenoweth exerted over the villagers around her considerable power. They did not exactly fear her. She was too free from evil for that ; but they were conscious of a mental superiority, and yielded without complaining to her sway.

The result of this was, that the younger Nancy, although compelled to service, always exhibited some pride, from a feeling that her mother was a superior woman to any around her.

She never felt herself inferior to her master and mistress, yet she complained not of being in subjection to them. There were so many interesting features in the character of this young servant girl that she became in many respects like a daughter to her mistress. There was no broad line of division in those days, in even the manorial hall, between the lord and his domestics, and still less defined was the position of the employer and the employed in a small farmhouse. Consequent on this condition of things, Frank Lenine and Nancy were thrown as much together as if they had been brother and sister. Frank was rarely checked in anything by his over-fond parents, who were especially proud of their son, since he was regarded as the handsomest young man in the parish. Frank conceived a very warm attachment for Nancy, and she was not a little proud of her lover. Although it was evident to all the parish that Frank and Nancy were seriously devoted to each other, the young man's parents were blind to it, and were taken by surprise when one day Frank asked his father and mother to consent to his marrying Nancy.

The Lenines had allowed their son to have his own way from his youth up ; and now, in a matter which brought into play the strongest of human feelings, they were angry because he refused to bend to their wills.

The old man felt it would be a degradation for a Lenine to marry a Trenoweth, and, in the most unreasoning manner, he resolved it should never be.

The first act was to send Nancy home to Alsia Mill, where

her parents resided ; the next was an imperious command to his son never again to see the girl.

The commands of the old are generally powerless upon the young where the affairs of the heart are concerned. So were they upon Frank. He, who was rarely seen of an evening beyond the garden of his father's cottage, was now as constantly absent from his home. The house, which was wont to be a pleasant one, was strangely altered. A gloom had fallen over all things ; the father and son rarely met as friends—the mother and her boy had now a feeling of reserve. Often there were angry altercations between the father and son, and the mother felt she could not become the defender of her boy in his open acts of disobedience, his bold defiance of his parents' commands.

Rarely an evening passed that did not find Nancy and Frank together in some retired nook. The Holy Well was a favourite meeting-place, and here the most solemn vows were made. Locks of hair were exchanged ; a wedding-ring, taken from the finger of a corpse, was broken, when they vowed that they would be united either dead or alive ; and they even climbed at night the granite-pile at Treryn, and swore by the Logan Rock the same strong vow.

Time passed onward thus unhappily, and, as the result of the endeavours to quench out the passion by force, it grew stronger under the repressing power, and, like imprisoned steam, eventually burst through all restraint.

Nancy's parents discovered at length that moonlight meetings between two untrained, impulsive youths, had a natural result, and they were now doubly earnest in their endeavours to compel Frank to marry their daughter.

The elder Lenine could not be brought to consent to this, and he firmly resolved to remove his son entirely from what he considered the hateful influences of the Trenoweths. He resolved to go to Plymouth, to take his son with him, and, if possible, to send him away to sea, hoping thus to wean him from his folly, as he considered this love-madness. Frank, poor fellow, with the best intentions, was not capable of any sustained effort, and consequently he at length succumbed to his father ; and, to escape his persecution, he entered a ship bound for India, and bade adieu to his native land.

Frank could not write, and this happened in days when letters could be forwarded only with extreme difficulty, consequently Nancy never heard from her lover.

A baby had been born into a troublesome world, and the infant became a real solace to the young mother. As the child grew, it became an especial favourite with its grandmother ; the elder Nancy rejoiced over the little prattler, and forgot her cause of sorrow. Young Nancy lived for her child, and on the memory of its father. Subdued in spirit she was, but her affliction had given force to her character, and she had been heard to declare that wherever Frank might be she was ever present with him ; whatever might be the temptations of the hour, that her influence was all-powerful over him for good. She felt that no distance could separate their souls, that no time could be long enough to destroy the bond between them   .

A period of distress fell upon the Trenoweths, and it was necessary that Nancy should leave her home once more, and go again into service   Her mother took charge of the babe, and she found a situation in the village of Kimyall, in the parish of Paul. Nancy, like her mother, contrived by force of character to main- tain an ascendancy amongst her companions   She had formed an acquaintance, which certainly never grew into friendship, with some of the daughters of the small farmers around. These girls were all full of the superstitions of the time and place.

The winter was coming on, and nearly three years had passed away since Frank Lenine left his country. As yet there was no sign. Nor father, nor mother, nor maiden had heard of him, and they all sorrowed over his absence. The Lenines desired to have Nancy's child, but the Trenoweths would not part with it. They went so far even as to endeavour to persuade Nancy to live again with them, but Nancy was not at all disposed to submit to their wishes.

It was All-hallows Eve, and two of Nancy's companions per- suaded her—no very difficult task—to go with them and sow hemp-seed.

At midnight the three maidens stole out unperceived into Kim- yall town-place to perform their incantation. Nancy was the first to sow, the others being less bold than she.

Boldly she advanced, saying, as she scattered the seed,—

> " Hemp-seed I sow thee,
> Hemp-seed grow thee ;
> And he who will my true love be,
> Come after me
> And shaw thee "

This was repeated three times, when, looking back over her left shoulder, she saw Lenine ; but he looked so angry that she shrieked with fear, and broke the spell. One of the other girls, however, resolved now to make trial of the spell, and the result of her labours was the vision of a white coffin. Fear now fell on all, and they went home sorrowful, to spend each one a sleepless night.

November came with its storms, and during one terrific night a large vessel was thrown upon the rocks in Bernowhall Cliff, and, beaten by the impetuous waves, she was soon in pieces. Amongst the bodies of the crew washed ashore, nearly all of whom had perished, was Frank Lenine. He was not dead when found, but the only words he lived to speak were begging the people to send for Nancy Trenoweth, that he might make her his wife before he died.

Rapidly sinking, Frank was borne by his friends on a litter to Boscean, but he died as he reached the town-place. His parents, overwhelmed in their own sorrows, thought nothing of Nancy, and without her knowing that Lenine had returned, the poor fellow was laid in his last bed, in Burian Churchyard.

On the night of the funeral, Nancy went, as was her custom, to lock the door of the house, and as was her custom too, she looked out into the night. At this instant a horseman rode up in hot haste, called her by name, and hailed her in a voice that made her blood boil.

The voice was the voice of Lenine. She could never forget that; and the horse she now saw was her sweetheart's favourite colt, on which he had often ridden at night to Alsia.

The rider was imperfectly seen; but he looked very sorrowful, and deadly pale, still Nancy knew him to be Frank Lenine.

He told her that he had just arrived home, and that the first moment he was at liberty he had taken horse to fetch his loved one, and to make her his bride.

Nancy's excitement was so great, that she was easily persuaded to spring on the horse behind him, that they might reach his home before the morning.

When she took Lenine's hand a cold shiver passed through her, and as she grasped his waist to secure herself in her seat, her arm became as stiff as ice. She lost all power of speech, and suffered deep fear, yet she knew not why. The moon had arisen, and now burst out in a full flood of light, through the heavy clouds which had obscured it. The horse pursued its journey with great rapidity, and whenever in weariness it slackened its speed, the peculiar voice of the rider aroused its drooping energies. Beyond this no word was spoken since Nancy had mounted behind her lover. They now came to Trove Bottom, where there was no bridge at that time ; they dashed into the river. The moon shone full in their faces. Nancy looked into the stream, and saw that the rider was in a shroud and other grave-clothes. She now knew that she was being carried away by a spirit, yet she had no power to save herself; indeed, the inclination to do so did not exist.

On went the horse at a furious pace, until they came to the blacksmith's shop near Burian Church-town, when she knew by the light from the forge fire thrown across the road that the smith was still at his labours. She now recovered speech. " Save me ! save me ! save me !" she cried with all her might. The smith sprang from the door of the smithy, with a red-hot iron in his hand, and as the horse rushed by, caught the woman's dress and pulled her to the ground. The spirit, however, also seized Nancy's dress in one hand, and his grasp was like that of a vice. The horse passed like the wind, and Nancy and the smith were pulled down as far as the old Almshouses, near the churchyard. Here the horse for a moment stopped. The smith seized that moment, and with his hot iron burned off the dress from the rider's hand, thus saving Nancy, more dead than alive ; while the rider passed over the wall of the churchyard, and vanished on the grave in which Lenine had been laid but a few hours before.

The smith took Nancy into his shop, and he soon aroused some of his neighbours, who took the poor girl back to Alsia. Her parents laid her on her bed. She spoke no word, but to ask for her child, to request her mother to give up her child to Lenine's parents, and her desire to be buried in his grave. Before the morning light fell on the world, Nancy had breathed her last breath.

A horse was seen that night to pass through the Church-town like a ball from a musket, and in the morning Lenine's colt was found dead in Bernowhall Cliff, covered with foam, its eyes forced from its head, and its swollen tongue hanging out of its mouth. On Lenine's grave was found the piece of Nancy's dress which was left in the spirit's hand when the smith burnt her from his grasp.

It is said that one or two of the sailors who survived the wreck related after the funeral, how, on the 30th of October, at night, Lenine was like one mad ; they could scarcely keep him in the ship. He seemed more asleep than awake, and, after great excite-ment, he fell as if dead upon the deck, and lay so for hours. When he came to himself, he told them that he had been taken to the village of Kimyall, and that if he ever married the woman who had cast the spell, he would make her suffer the longest day she had to live for drawing his soul out of his body.

Poor Nancy was buried in Lenine's grave, and her companion in sowing hemp-seed, who saw the white coffin, slept beside her within the year.

This story bears a striking resemblance to the "Lenore" of Burger, which remarkable ballad can scarcely have found its way, even yet, to Boscean.

DUFFY AND THE DEVIL.*

MANY of the superstitions of our ancestors are preserved in quaint, irregular rhymes, the recitation of which was the amusement of the people in the long nights of winter. These were sung, or rather said, in a monotone, by the professional Drolls, who doubtless added such things as they fancied would increase the interest of the story to the listeners. Especially were they fond of introducing known characters on the scene, and of mixing up events which had occurred within the memory of the old people, with the more ancient legend. The following story, or rather parts of it, formed the subject of one of the Cornish Christmas plays. When I was a boy, I well remember being much delighted with the coarse acting of a set of Christmas players, who exhibited in the "great hall" of a farmhouse at which I was visiting, and who gave us the principal incidents of Duffy and the Devil Terrytop; one of the company doing the part of Chorus, and filling up by rude descriptions—often in rhyme—the parts which the players could not represent.

It was in cider-making time. Squire Lovel of Trove, or more correctly, Trewoof, rode up to Burian Church-town to procure help. Boys and maidens were in request, some to gather the

---

* The incidents of this story are strikingly similar to those in "*Rumpel-stilzchen*" The maiden in that tale has to spin straw into gold thread, and she, like Duffy, has to discover the name of the spirit who has befriended her.

Mr Robert Chambers, in his "Popular Rhymes of Scotland," has a fairy tale in which the fairy threatens the mother that she will have her "lad bairn" unless "ye can tell me my right name." The anxious mother takes a walk in the wood, and she hears the fairy singing—

> "Little kens our gude dame at hame
> That 'Whuppity Stoorie' is my name"

Of course, when the fairy comes to claim the "lad bairn," she is addressed as "Whuppity Stoorie," and she at once disappears.

In "Who Built Reynir Church?" in the "Icelandic Legends" of Jon Arnason, the story turns on the discovery of the name of the builder.—*Icelandic Legends*, p. 49

apples from the trees, others to carry them to the cider-mill. Passing along the village as hastily as the dignity of a squire would allow him, his attention was drawn to a great noise—scolding in a shrill treble voice, and crying—proceeding from Janey Chygwin's door. The squire rode up to the cottage, and he saw the old woman beating her step-daughter Duffy about the head with the skirt of her swing-tail gown, in which she had been carrying out the ashes. She made such a dust, that the squire was nearly choked and almost blinded with the wood ashes.

"What cheer, Janey?" cries the squire; "what's the to-do with you and Duffy?"

"Oh, the lazy hussy!" shouts Janey, "is all her time courseying and courranting with the boys! she will never stay in to boil the porridge, knit the stockings, or spin the yarn."

"Don't believe her, your honour," exclaims Duffy; "my knitting and spinning is the best in the parish"

The war of tongues continued in this strain for some time, the old squire looking calmly on, and resolving in his mind to take Duffy home with him to Trove, her appearance evidently pleasing him greatly. Squire Lovel left the old and young woman to do the best they could, and went round the village to complete his hiring. When he returned, peace had been declared between them; but when Lovel expressed his desire to take Duffy home to his house to help the housekeeper to do the spinning, "A pretty spinner she is!" shouted old Janey at the top of her voice. "Try me, your honour," said Duffy, curtsying very low; "my yarns are the best in the parish."

"We'll soon try that," said the squire; "Janey will be glad to get quits of thee, I see, and thou 'lt be nothing loath to leave her; so jump up behind me, Duffy."

No sooner said than done. The maid Duffy, without ceremony, mounted behind the squire on the horse, and they jogged silently down to Trove.

Squire Lovel's old housekeeper was almost blind—one eye had been put out by an angry old wizard, and through sympathy she was rapidly losing the power of seeing with the other.

This old dame was consequently very glad of some one to help her in spinning and knitting.

The introduction over, the housekeeper takes Duffy up into the garret where the wool was kept, and where the spinning was done in the summer, and requests her to commence her work.

The truth must be told; Duffy was an idle slut, she could

neither knit nor spin. Well, heie she was left alone, and, of course, expected to produce a good specimen of her work.

The garret was piled from the floor to the key-beams with fleeces of wool. Duffy looked despairingly at them, and then sat herself down on the "turn"—the spinning-wheel—and cried out,

" Curse the spinning and knitting ! The devil may spin and knit for the squire for what I care."

Scarcely had Duffy spoken these words than she heard a rustling noise behind some woolpacks, and forth walked a queer-looking little man, with a remarkable pair of eyes, which seemed to send out flashes of light. There was something uncommonly knowing in the twist of his mouth, and his curved nose had an air of curious intelligence. He was dressed in black, and moved towards Duffy with a jaunty air, knocking something against the floor at every step he took.

" Duffy dear," said this little gentleman, " I 'll do all the spinning and knitting for thee."

"Thank 'e," says Duffy, quite astonished.

" Duffy dear, a lady shall you be."

" Thank 'e, your honour," smiled Duffy.

" But, Duffy dear, remember," coaxingly said the queer little man,—" remember, that for all this, at the end of three years, you must go with me, unless you can find out my name."

Duffy was not the least bit frightened, nor did she hesitate long, but presently struck a bargain with her kind but unknown friend, who told her she had only to wish, and her every wish should be fulfilled ; and as for the spinning and knitting, she would find all she required under the black ram's fleece.

He then departed. How, Duffy could not tell, but in a moment the queer little gentleman was gone.

Duffy sung in idleness, and slept until it was time for her to make her appearance. So she wished for some yarns, and looking under the black fleece she found them.

Those were shown by the housekeeper to the squire, and both declared "they had never seen such beautiful yarns."

The next day Duffy was to knit this yarn into stockings. Duffy idled, as only professed idlers can idle ; but in due time, as if she had been excessively industrious, she produced a pair of stockings for the old squire.

If the yarn was beautiful, the stockings were beyond all praise. They were as fine as silk, and as strong as leather.

Squire Lovel soon gave them a trial ; and when he came home at night after hunting, he declared he would never wear any

Q

other than Duffy's stockings. He had wandered all day through brake and briar, furze and brambles ; there was not a scratch on his legs, and he was as dry as a bone. There was no end to his praise of Duffy's stockings.

Duffy had a rare time of it now—she could do what she pleased, and rove where she willed.

She was dancing on the mill-bed half the day, with all the gossiping women who brought their grist to be ground.

In those "good old times" the ladies of the parish would take their corn to mill, and serge the flour themselves. When a few of them met together, they would either tell stories or dance whilst the corn was grinding. Sometimes the dance would be on the mill-bed, sometimes out on the green. On some occasions the miller's fiddle would be in request, at others the "crowd" * was made to do the duty of a tambourine.

So Duffy was always finding excuses to go to mill, and many "a round" would she dance with the best people in the parish.

Old Bet, the miller's wife, was a witch, and she found out who did Duffy's work for her. Duffy and old Bet were always the best of friends, and she never told any one about Duffy's knitting friend, nor did she ever say a word about the stockings being unfinished. *There was always a stitch down.*

On Sundays the people went to Burian Church, from all parts, to look at the squire's stockings ; and the old squire would stop at the Cross, proud enough to show them. He could hunt

> "Through brambles and furze in all sorts of weather ;
> His old shanks were as sound as if bound up in leather."

Duffy was now sought after by all the young men of the country ; and at last the squire, fearing to lose a pretty girl, and one who was so useful to him, married her himself, and she became, according to the fashion of the time and place, Lady Lovel ; but she was commonly known by her neighbours as the Duffy Lady.

Lady Lovel kept the devil hard at work. Stockings, all sorts of fine underclothing, bedding, and much ornamental work, the like of which was never seen, was produced at command, and passed off as her own.

Duffy passed a merry time of it, but somehow or other she was never happy when she was compelled to play the lady. She passed much more of her time with the old crone at the mill, than in the drawing-room at Trove. The squire sported and

* Crowd,—a sieve covered with sheep-skin.

drank, and cared little about Duffy, so long as she provided him with knitted garments.

The three years were nearly at an end. Duffy had tried every plan to find out the devil's name, but had failed in all.

She began to fear that she should have to go off with her queer friend, and Duffy became melancholy. Old Bet endeavoured to rouse her, persuading her that she could from her long experience and many dealings with the imps of darkness, at the last moment put her in the way of escaping her doom.

Duffy went day after day to her garret, and there each day was the devil gibing and jeering till she was almost mad.

There was but another day. Bet was seriously consulted now, and, as good as her word, she promised to use her power.

Duffy Lady was to bring down to the mill that very evening a jack of the strongest beer she had in the cellar. She was not to go to bed until the squire returned from hunting, no matter how late, and she was to make no remark in reply to anything the squire might tell her.

The jack of beer was duly carried to the mill, and Duffy returned home very melancholy to wait up for the squire.

No sooner had Lady Lovel left the mill than old Bet came out with the "crowd" over her shoulders, and the blackjack in her hand. She shut the door, and turned the water off the mill-wheel,—threw her red cloak about her, and away.

She was seen by her neighbours going towards Boleit. A man saw the old woman trudging past the Pipers, and through the Dawnse Main into the downs, but there he lost sight of her, and no one could tell where old Bet was gone to at that time of night.

Duffy waited long and anxiously. By and by the dogs came home alone. They were covered with foam, their tongues were hanging out of their mouths, and all the servants said they must have met the devil's hounds without heads.

Duffy was seriously alarmed. Midnight came but no squire. At last he arrived, but like a crazy, crack-brained man, he kept singing,—

> "Here's to the devil,
> With his wooden pick and shovel."

He was neither drunk nor frightened, but wild with some strange excitement. After a long time Squire Lovel sat down, and began, "My dear Duffy, you haven't smiled this long time ; but now I'll tell 'e something that would make ye laugh if ye're dying. If you'd seen what I've seen to-night, ha, ha, ha !

> ' Here's to the devil,
> With his wooden pick and shovel.' "

True to her orders, Duffy said not a word, but allowed the squire to ramble on as he pleased. At length he told her the following story of his adventures, with interruptions which have not been retained, and with numerous coarse expressions which are best forgotten .—

THE SQUIRE'S STORY OF THE MEETING OF THE WITCHES IN THE FUGOE HOLE.

" Duffy dear, I left home at break of day this morning. I hunted all the moors from Trove to Trevider, and never started a hare all the livelong day. I determined to hunt all night, but that I'd have a brace to bring home. So, at nightfall I went down Lemorna Bottoms, then up Brene Downses, and as we passed the Dawnse Main up started a hare, as fine a hare as ever was seen. She passed the Pipers, down through the Reens, in the mouth of the dogs half the time, yet they couldn't catch her at all. As fine a chase as ever was seen, until she took into the Fugoe Hole.* In went the dogs after her, and I followed, the owls and bats flying round my head. On we went, through water and mud, a mile or more, I'm quite certain. I didn't know the place was so long before. At last we came to a broad pool of water, when the dogs lost the scent, and ran back past me howling and jowling, terrified almost to death ! A little farther on I turned round a corner, and saw a glimmering fire on the other side the water, and there were St Leven witches in scores. Some were riding on ragwort, some on brooms, some were floating on their three-legged stools, and some, who had been milking the little good cows in Wales, had come back astride of the largest leeks they could find. Amongst the rest there was our Bet of the Mill, with her ' crowd' in her hand, and my own blackjack slung across her shoulders.

" In a short time the witches gathered round the fire, and blowed it up, after a strange fashion, till it burned up into a

---

* There is a tradition, firmly believed on the lower side of Burian, that the Fugoe Hole extends from the cliffs underground so far that the end of it is under the parlour of the Tremewen's house in Trove, which is the only remaining portion of the old mansion of the Lovels

Here the witches were in the habit of meeting the devil, and holding their Sabbath. Often his dark Highness has been heard piping, while the witches danced to his music.

A pool of water some distance from the entrance prevents any adventurer from exploring the "Hole" to its termination.

Hares often take refuge in the Fugoe Hole, from which they have never been known to return orilliant blue flame. Then I saw amongst the rest a queer little man in black, with a long forked tail, which he held high in the air, and twirled around. Bet struck her 'crowd' as soon as he appeared, and beat up the tune,—

> 'Here's to the devil,
> With his wooden pick and shovel,
> Digging tin by the bushel,
> With his tail cock'd up!'

Then the queer little devil and all danced like the wind, and went faster and faster, making such a clatter, 'as if they had on each foot a pewter platter.'

"Every time the man in black came round by old Bet, he took a good pull from my own blackjack, till at last, as if he had been drinking my best beer, he seemed to have lost his head, when he jumped up and down, turned round and round, and roaring with laughter, sung,—

> 'Duffy, my lady, you'll never know—what?—
> That my name is Terrytop, Terrytop—top!'"

When the squire sung those lines, he stopped suddenly, thinking that Duffy was going to die. She turned pale and red, and pale again. However, Duffy said nothing, and the squire proceeded.—

"After the dance, all the witches made a ring around the fire, and again blew it up, until the blue flames reached the top of the 'Zawn.'* Then the devil danced through and through the fire, and springing ever and anon amongst the witches, kicked them soundly. At last—I was shaking with laughter at the fun—I shouted, 'Go it, Old Nick!' and, lo, the lights went out, and I had to fly with all my speed, for every one of the witches were after me. I scampered home somehow, and here I am. Why don't you laugh, Duffy?" Duffy did laugh, and laugh right heartily now, and when tired of their fun, the squire and the lady went to bed.

The three years were up within an hour. Duffy had willed for an abundant supply of knitted things, and filled every chest in the house. She was in the best chamber trying to cram some more stockings into a big chest, when the queer little man in black appeared before her.

"Well, Duffy, my dear," said he, "I have been to my word, and served you truly for three years as we agreed, so now I hope you will go with me, and make no objection." He bowed very

---

* Zawn,—a cavernous gorge.

obsequiously, almost to the ground, and regarded Duffy Lady with a very offensive leer.

" I fear," smiled Duffy, " that your country is rather warm, and might spoil my fair complexion."

" It is not so hot as some people say, Duffy," was his reply ; " but come along, I 've kept my word, and of course a lady of your standing will keep your word also. Can you tell me my name ? "

Duffy curtsied, and smilingly said, " You have behaved like a true gentlemen ; yet I wouldn't like to go so far." The devil frowned, and approached as if he would lay forcible hands upon her. " Maybe your name is Lucifer ? "

He stamped his foot and grinned horridly " Lucifer ! Lucifer ! He 's no other than a servant to me in my own country." Suddenly calming again, he said, quietly, " Lucifer ! I would scarcely be seen speaking to him at court. But come along. When I spin for ladies I expect honourable treatment at their hands. You 've two guesses more. But they 're of little use ; my name is not generally known on earth."

" Perhaps," smiled Duffy again, " my lord's name is Beelzebub ? "

How he grinned, and his sides shook with convulsive joy. " Beelzebub ! " says he ; " why, he 's little better than the other, a common devil he. I believe he 's some sort of a cousin—a Cornish cousin, you know."

" I hope your honour," curtsied Duffy, " will not take offence. Impute my mistake to ignorance."

Our Demon was rampant with joy ; he danced around Duffy with delight, and was, seeing that she hesitated, about to seize her somewhat roughly.

" Stop ! stop ! " shouts Duffy ; " perhaps you will be honest enough to admit that your name is Terrytop."

The gentleman in black looked at Duffy, and she steadily looked him in the face. " Terrytop ! deny it if you dare," says she.

" A gentleman never denies his name," replied Terrytop, drawing himself up with much dignity. " I did not expect to be beaten by a young minx like you, Duffy ; but the pleasure of your company is merely postponed." With this Terrytop departed in fire and smoke, and all the devil's knitting suddenly turned to ashes.

Squire Lovel was out hunting, away far on the moors ; the day was cold and the winds piercing. Suddenly the stockings dropped from his legs and the homespun from his back, so that he came home with nothing on but his shirt and his shoes, almost dead with cold. All this was attributed by the squire to the influence of old Bet, who, he thought, had punished him for pursuing her with his dogs when she had assumed the form of a hare.

The story, as told by the Drolls, now rambles on. Duffy cannot furnish stockings. The squire is very wroth. There are many quarrels—mutual recriminations. Duffy's old sweetheart is called in to beat the squire, and eventually peace is procured, by a stratagem of old Bet's, which would rather shock the sense of propriety in these our days.

THE LOVERS OF PORTHANGWARTHA.*

THE names of the youth and maiden who fixed the term of the Lover's Cove upon this retired spot have passed from the memory of man. A simple story, however, remains, the mere fragment, without doubt, of a longer and more ancient tale.

The course of love with this humble pair did not run smooth. On one side or the other the parents were decidedly opposed to the intimacy which existed, and by their persecutions, they so far succeeded, that the young man was compelled to emigrate to some far distant land

In this cove the lovers met for the last time in life, and vowed under the light of the full moon, that living or dead they would meet at the end of three years

The young woman remained with her friends—the young man went to the Indies. Time passed on, and the three years, which had been years of melancholy to both, were expiring

One moonlight night, when the sea was tranquil as a mirror, an old crone sat on the edge of the cliff " making her charms " She saw a figure—she was sure it was a spirit, very like the village maiden—descend into the cove, and seat herself upon a rock, round two-thirds of which the light waves were rippling. On this rock sat the maiden, looking anxiously out over the sea, until, from the rising of the tide, she was completely surrounded. The old woman called ; but in vain—the maiden was unconscious of any voice. There she sat, and the tide was rising rapidly around her. The old woman, now seeing the danger in which she was, resolved to go down into the cove, and, if possible, awaken the maiden to a sense of her danger. To do this, it was necessary to go round a projecting pile of rocks. While doing this, she lost sight of the object of her interest, and much was her surprise, when she again saw the maiden, to perceive a young sailor by her side, with his

* This is said to mean the Lover's Cove.

arm around her waist. Conceiving that help had arrived, the old woman sat herself down on the slope of the descending path, and resolved patiently to await the arrival of the pair on shore, and then to rate the girl soundly.

She sat watching this loving and lovely pair, lighted as they were on the black rock by a full flood of moonshine. There they sat, and the tide rose and washed around them. Never were boy and girl so mad, and at last the terrified old woman shrieked with excitement. Suddenly they appeared to float off upon the waters. She thought she heard their voices; but there was no sound of terror. Instead of it a tranquil murmuring music, like the voice of doves, singing,—

> " I am thine,
>   Thou art mine,
>   Beyond control ;
>   In the wave
>   Be the grave
>   Of heart and soul."

Down, down into the sea passed the lovers. Awestruck, the old woman looked on, until, as she said, " At last they turned round, looked me full in the face, smiling like angels, and, kissing each other, sank to rise no more."

They tell us that the body of the young woman was found a day or two after in a neighbouring cove, and that intelligence eventually reached England that the young man had been killed on this very night.

THE GHOST OF ROSEWARNE.

"EZEKIEL GROSSE, gent., attorney-at-law," bought the lands of Rosewarne from one of the De Rosewarnes, who had become involved in difficulties, by endeavouring, without sufficient means, to support the dignity of his family. There is reason for believing that Ezekiel was the legal adviser of this unfortunate Rosewarne, and that he was not over-honest in his transactions with his client. However this may be, Ezekiel Grosse had scarcely made Rosewarne his dwelling-place, before he was alarmed by noises, at first of an unearthly character, and subsequently, one very dark night, by the appearance of the ghost himself in the form of a worn and aged man. The first appearance was in the park, but he subsequently repeated his visits in the house, but always after dark. Ezekiel Grosse was not a man to be terrified at trifles, and for some time he paid but slight attention to his nocturnal visitor. Howbeit, the repetition of visits, and certain mysterious indications on the part of the spectre, became annoying to Ezekiel. One night, when seated in his office examining some deeds, and being rather irritable, having lost an important suit, his visitor approached him, making some strange indications which the lawyer could not understand. Ezekiel suddenly exclaimed, " In the name of God, what wantest thou ? "

" To show thee, Ezekiel Grosse, where the gold for which thou longest lies buried "

No one ever lived upon whom the greed of gold was stronger than on Ezekiel, yet he hesitated now that his spectral friend had spoken so plainly, and trembled in every limb as the ghost slowly delivered himself in sepulchral tones of this telling speech.

The lawyer looked fixedly on the spectre, but he dared not utter a word. He longed to obtain possession of the secret, yet he feared to ask him where he was to find this treasure   The spectre looked as fixedly at the poor trembling lawyer, as if enjoying the sight of his terror. At length, lifting his finger, he beckoned Ezekiel to follow him, turning at the same time to leave the room. Ezekiel was glued to his seat ; he could not exert strength enough to move, although he desired to do so.

" Come ! " said the ghost, in a hollow voice. The lawyer was powerless to come.

·   " Gold ! " exclaimed the old man, in a whining tone, though in a louder key.

" Where ? " gasped Ezekiel.

" Follow me, and 1 will show thee," said the ghost. Ezekiel endeavoured to rise, but it was in vain

" I command thee, come ! " almost shrieked the ghost. Ezekiel felt that he was compelled to follow his friend; and by some super-natural power rather than his own, he followed the spectre out of the room, and through the hall, into the park.

They passed onward through the night—the ghost gliding be-fore the lawyer, and guiding him by a peculiar phosphorescent light, which appeared to glow from every part of the form, until they arrived at a little dell, and had reached a small cairn formed of granite boulders.   By this the spectre rested ; and when Ezekiel had approached it, and was standing on the other side of the cairn, still trembling, the aged man, looking fixedly in his face, said, in low tones—

" Ezekiel Grosse, thou longest for gold, as I did. I won the glittering prize, but I could not enjoy it.   Heaps of treasure are buried beneath those stones ; it is thine, if thou diggest for it.

Win the gold, Ezekiel. Glitter with the wicked ones of the world; and when thou art the most joyous, I will look in upon thy happiness." The ghost then disappeared, and as soon as Grosse could recover himself from the extreme trepidation,—the result of mixed feelings,—he looked about him, and finding himself alone, he exclaimed, " Ghost or devil, I will soon prove whether or not thou liest ! " Ezekiel is said to have heard a laugh, echoing between the hills, as he said those words.

The lawyer noted well the spot; returned to his house; pondered on all the circumstances of his case ; and eventually resolved to seize the earliest opportunity, when he might do so unobserved, of removing the stones, and examining the ground beneath them

A few nights after this, Ezekiel went to the little cairn, and by the aid of a crowbar, he soon overturned the stones, and laid the ground bare. He then commenced digging, and had not proceeded far when his spade struck against some other metal. He carefully cleared away the earth, and he then felt—for he could not see, having no light with him—that he had uncovered a metallic urn of some kind. He found it quite impossible to lift it, and he was therefore compelled to cover it up again, and to replace the stones sufficiently to hide it from the observation of any chance wanderer.

The next night Ezekiel found that this urn, which was of bronze, contained gold coins of a very ancient date. He loaded himself with his treasure, and returned home. From time to time, at night, as Ezekiel found he could do so without exciting the suspicions of his servants, he visited the urn, and thus by degrees removed all the treasure to Rosewarne house. There was nothing in the series of circumstances which had surrounded Ezekiel which he could less understand than the fact that the ghost of the old man had left off troubling him from the moment when he had disclosed to him the hiding-place of this treasure.

The neighbouring gentry could not but observe the rapid improvements which Ezekiel Grosse made in his mansion, his grounds, in his personal appearance, and indeed in everything by which he was surrounded. In a short time he abandoned the law, and led in every respect the life of a country gentleman. He ostentatiously paraded his power to procure all earthly enjoyments, and, in spite of his notoriously bad character, he succeeded in drawing many of the landed proprietors around him.

Things went well with Ezekiel. The man who could in those days visit London in his own carriage and four was not without a laige circle of flatterers. The lawyer who had struggled hard, in the outset of life, to secure wealth, and who did not always employ the most honest means for doing so, now found himself the centre of a circle to whom he could preach honesty, and receive from them expressions of the admiration in which the world holds the possessor of gold. His old tricks were forgotten, and he was put in places of honour. This state of things continued for some time; indeed, Grosse's entertainments became more and more splendid, and his revels more and more seductive to those he admitted to share them with him. The Lord of Rosewarne was the Lord of the West. To him every one bowed the knee : he walked the Earth as the proud possessor of a large share of the planet.

It was Christmas eve, and a large gathering there was at Rosewarne. In the hall the ladies and gentlemen were in the full enjoyment of the dance, and in the kitchen all the tenantry and the servants were emulating their superiors. Everything went joyously; and when mirth was in full swing, and Ezekiel felt to the full the influence of wealth, it appeared as if in one moment the chill of death had fallen over every one. The dancers paused, and looked one at another, each one struck with the other's paleness; and there, in the middle of the hall, every one saw a strange old man looking angrily, but in silence, at Ezekiel Grosse, who was fixed in terror, blank as a statue.

No one had seen this old man enter the hall, yet there he was in the midst of them. It was but for a minute, and he was gone. Ezekiel, as if a frozen torrent of water had thawed in an instant, roared with impetuous laughter.

"What do you think of that for a Christmas play? There was an old Father Christmas for you ! Ha ! ha ! ha ! ha ! How frightened you all look ! Butler, order the men to hand round the spiced wines ! On with the dancing, my friends ! It was only a trick, ay, and a clever one, which I have put upon you. On with your dancing, my friends !"

Notwithstanding his boisterous attempts to restore the spirit of the evening, Ezekiel could not succeed. There was an influence stronger than any which he could command; and one by one, framing sundry excuses, his guests took their departure, every one of them satisfied that all was not right at Rosewarne.

From that Christmas eve Grosse was a changed man. He tried to be his former self; but it was in vain Again and again he called his gay companions around him ; but at every feast there appeared one more than was desired. An aged man—

weird beyond measure—took his place at the table in the middle of the feast; and although he spoke not, he exerted a miraculous power over all. No one dared to move; no one ventured to speak. Occasionally Ezekiel assumed an appearance of courage, which he felt not; rallied his guests, and made sundry excuses for the presence of his aged friend, whom he represented as having a mental infirmity, as being deaf and dumb. On all such occasions the old man rose from the table, and looking at the host, laughed a demoniac laugh of joy, and departed as quietly as he came.

The natural consequence of this was that Ezekiel Grosse's friends fell away from him, and he became a lonely man, amidst his vast possessions—his only companion being his faithful clerk, John Call.

The persecuting presence of the spectre became more and more constant; and wherever the poor lawyer went, there was the aged man at his side. From being one of the finest men in the county, he became a miserably attenuated and bowed old man. Misery was stamped on every feature—terror was indicated in every movement. At length he appears to have besought his ghostly attendant to free him of his presence. It was long before the ghost would listen to any terms; but when Ezekiel at length agreed to surrender the whole of his wealth to any one whom the spectre might indicate, he obtained a promise that upon this being carried out, in a perfectly legal manner, in favour of John Call, that he should no longer be haunted.

This was, after numerous struggles on the part of Ezekiel to retain his property, or at least some portion of it, legally settled, and John Call became possessor of Rosewarne and the adjoining lands. Grosse was then informed that this evil spirit was one of the ancestors of the Rosewarne, from whom by his fraudulent dealings he obtained the place, and that he was allowed to visit the earth again for the purpose of inflicting the most condign punishment on the avaricious lawyer. His avarice had been gratified, his pride had been pampered to the highest; and then he was made a pitiful spectacle, at whom all men pointed, and no one pitied. He lived on in misery, but it was for a short time. He was found dead · and the country people ever said that his death was a violent one; they spoke of marks on his body, and some even asserted that the spectre of De Rosewarne was seen rejoicing amidst a crowd of devils, as they bore the spirit of Ezekiel over Carn Brea.

Hals thus quaintly tells this story .—

"Rosewarne, in this parish, gave to its owner the name of De Rosewarne, one of which tribe sold those lands, temp James I , to Ezekiel Grosse, gent., attorney-at-law, who made it his dwelling, and in this place got a great estate by the inferior practice of the law ; but much more, as tradition saith, by means of a spirit or apparition that haunted him in this place, till he spake to it (for it is notable that sort of things called apparitions are such proud gentry, that they never speak first) ; whereupon it discovered to him where much treasure lay hid in this mansion, which, according to the (honest) ghost's direction, he found, to his great enriching. After which, this phantasm or spectrum became so troublesome and direful to him, day and night, that it forced him to forsake this place (as rich, it seems, as this devil could make him), and to quit his claim thereto, by giving or selling it to his clerk, John Call ; whose son, John Call, gent , sold it again to Robert Hooker, gent , attorney at-law, now in possession thereof. The arms of Call were, in a field three trumpets—in allusion to the name in English ; but in Cornish-British, 'call,' 'cal,' signifies any hard, flinty, or obdurate matter or thing, and 'hirgorue' is a trumpet."*

THE SUICIDE'S SPEARMAN.

A FAMILY of the name of Spearman has lived in Cornwall for many ages, their native centre having been somewhere between Ludgvan and St Ives.

Years long ago, an unfortunate man, weary of life, destroyed himself ; and the rude laws of a remote age. carrying out, as they thought, human punishments even after death, decreed that the body should be buried at the four cross-roads, and quicklime poured on the corpse.

Superstition stepped in, and somewhat changed the order of burial. To prevent the dead man from "walking," and becoming a terror to all his neighbours, the coffin was to be turned upside down, and a spear was to be driven through it and the body, so as to pin it to the ground.

It was with some difficulty that a man could be found to perform this task. At length, however, a blacksmith undertook it. He made the spear ; and after the coffin was properly placed, he drove his spear-headed iron bar through it. From that day he was called "the spearman," and his descendants have never lost the name.

In making a new road not many years since, the coffin and spear were found, and removed. From that time several old men and women have declared that the self-murderer "walks the earth."

* See Gilbert's "Parochial History of Cornwall," 1838, vol. i p. 162

THE SUICIDE'S GHOST.

ON the bleak road between Helston and Wendron Church-town, at its highest and wildest spot, three roads meet about a quarter of a mile from the latter place.   Here, at "Three Cross," as the place is called, years ago, when the Downs being unenclosed, it was more desolate than it is even now, a poor suicide, named "Tucker," was buried.   Few liked to pass up Row's Lane, leading there, after nightfall ; for Tucker's shade had more than once been seen.   One man, however, valiant in his cups, on his return from Helston market, cracked his whip, and shouted lustily, "Arise, Tucker !" as he passed the place   It is said Tucker did arise, and fixed himself on the saddle behind the man as he rode on horseback, and accompanied him—how far it is not said.   This was often repeated, until the spirit, becoming angry, refused any more to quit his disturber, and continued to trouble him, till "Parson Jago" was called in to use his skill, which was found effectual, in "laying" Tucker's spirit to rest.

THE "HA-AF" A FACE.

JAMES BERRYMAN said, " Fa-ather took a house doun to Lelant, whear we lived for a bra' bit.   Very often after I ben in bed, our ould cat wud tear up, coover its ars like a ma-aged thing, jump uppon the bed, and dig her ould hed under the clothes, as if she wud git doun to bottom, and jest after, a man's face, with a light round un, wud cum in ; 'twas ha-af a face like, and it wud stop at the bottom of the bed.   I 've sen it many times ; and fa-ather, though he didn't say nothin', was glad enough to leave the place.   I was tould that the house belonged to an ould man, and that two rich gentlemen, brothers, who lived close by, wanted the place, and put on law, and got the place from the poor ould man.   When they war goin' to turn un out, the poor fellow stopped and looked round crying, and then fell down in a fit, was put to bed, and died in the house ; and 'twas he, they said, that used to come back."

THE WARNING.

THE following instance is given me, as from the party to whom it happened, "a respectable person, of undoubted veracity." " When a young man, fearing and caring for no one, I was in the habit of visiting Sancreed from Penzance, and of returning in the evening. One night I took up my hat to return, and went out at the door. It was a most beautiful night, when, without the most remote assignable reason, I was seized in a manner I never experienced either before or since. I was absolutely 'terror-stricken,' so that I was compelled to turn back to the house, a thing I had never done before, and say, 'I must remain here for the night.' I could never account for it; and without caring to be called superstitious, have regarded it as a special interposition of Providence. It was reported that shortly before, a lad, who had driven home a farmer's daughter to her father's house in the neighbourhood, had suddenly been missed, and no clue to his whereabouts had ever been found About four or six weeks after my adventure, a gang of sheep-stealers who had carried on their depredations for a long time previous, were discovered in the neighbourhood; their abode, indeed, adjoined the road from Sancreed to Penzance, and I cannot help believing it probable, that had I returned that night I should have encountered the gang, and perhaps lost my life. Years afterwards, one of the gang confessed that the boy had come suddenly upon them during one of their nefarious expeditions. He was seized, and injudiciously said, 'Well, you may get off once or twice, but you're sure to be hanged in the end.' 'Thee shan't help to do it,' said one, and the poor boy was murdered, and his body thrown into a neighbouring shaft."

LAYING A GHOST.

" TO the ignorance of men in our age in this particular and mysterious part of philosophy and religion,—namely, the communication between spirits and men,—not one scholar out of ten thousand, though otherwise of excellent learning, knows anything of it, or the way how to manage it. This ignorance breeds fear and abhorrence of that which otherwise might be of incomparable benefit to mankind."

Such is the concluding paragraph of "An Account of an Apparition, attested by the Rev. Wm. Ruddell, Minister at Launceston, in Cornwall," 1665.

A schoolboy was haunted by Dorothy Dingley; we know not why, but the boy pined. He was thought to be in love; but when, at the wishes of his friends, the parson questioned him, he told him of his ghostly visitor, and he took the parson to the field in which he was in the habit of meeting the apparition; and the reverend gentleman himself saw the spectral Dorothy, and afterwards he showed her to the boy's father and mother. Then comes the story of the laying. "The next morning being Thursday, I went out very early by myself, and walked for about an hour's space in meditation and prayer in the field next adjoining to the Quartiles. Soon after five, I stepped over the stile into the disturbed field, and had not gone above thirty or forty paces before the ghost appeared at the further stile. I spoke to it with a loud voice, in some such sentences as the way of these dealings directed me ; whereupon it approached, but slowly, and when I came near it it moved not. I spoke again, and it answered again in a voice which was neither very audible nor intelligible. I was not the least terrified, therefore I persisted until it spake again and gave me satisfaction. But the work could not be finished at this time ; wherefore the same evening, an hour after sunset, it met me again, near the same place, and after a few words on each side *it quietly vanished*, and neither doth appear since, nor ever will more to any man's disturbance." *

A FLYING SPIRIT.

ABOUT the year 1761 a pinnacle was thrown down, by lightning, from the tower of the church at Ludgvan. The effect was then universally imputed to the vengeance of a perturbed spirit, exorcised from Treassow, and passing eastward, towards the usual place of banishment—THE RED SEA.

The following story is given as a remarkable example of the manner in which very recent events become connected with exceedingly old superstitious ideas The tales of Tregeagle have shown us how the name of a man who lived about two centuries since is made to do duty as a demon belonging to the pagan times. In this story we have the name of a woman who lived about the commencement of the present century, associated with a legend belonging to the earliest ages.

THE EXECUTION AND WEDDING.

A WOMAN, who had lived at Ludgvan, was executed at Bodmin for the murder of her husband There was but little doubt that she had been urged on to the diabolical deed by a horse-dealer, known as Yorkshire Jack, with whom, for a long period, she was generally supposed to have been criminally acquainted.

* "Historical Survey of Cornwall," C. S. Gilbert

Now, it will be remembered that this really happened within the present century. One morning, during my residence in Penzance, an old woman from Ludgvan called on me with some trifling message. While she was waiting for my answer, I made some ordinary remark about the weather.

" It's all owing to Sarah Polgrain," said she.

" Sarah Polgrain !" said I ; " and who is Sarah Polgrain ? "

Then the voluble old lady told me the whole story of the poisoning, with which we need not, at present, concern ourselves. By and by the tale grew especially interesting, and there I resume it.

Sarah had begged that Yorkshire Jack might accompany her to the scaffold when she was led forth to execution. This was granted ; and on the dreadful morning, there stood this unholy pair, the fatal beam on which the woman's body was in a few minutes to swing, before them.

They kissed each other, and whispered words passed between them.

The executioner intimated that the moment of execution had arrived, and that they must part. Sarah Polgrain, looking earnestly into the man's eyes, said,

" You will ? "

Yorkshire Jack replied, " I will ! " and they separated. The man retired amongst the crowd, the woman was soon a dead corpse, pendulating in the wind.

Years passed on. Yorkshire Jack was never the same man as before, his whole bearing was altered. His bold, his dashing air deserted him. He walked, or rather wandered, slowly about the streets of the town, or the lanes of the country. He constantly moved his head from side to side, looking first over one, and then over the other shoulder, as though dreading that some one was following him.

The stout man became thin, his ruddy cheeks more pale, and his eyes sunken.

At length he disappeared, and it was discovered—for Yorkshire Jack had made a confidant of some Ludgvan man—that he had pledged himself, " living or dead, to become the husband of Sarah Polgrain, after the lapse of years "

To escape, if possible, from himself, Jack had gone to sea in the merchant service.

Well, the period had arrived when this unholy promise was to be fulfilled. Yorkshire Jack was returning from the Mediterranean in a fruit-ship. He was met by the devil and Sarah Polgrain far out at sea, off the Land's-End. Jack would not accompany them willingly; so they followed the ship for days, during all which time she was involved in a storm. Eventually Jack was washed from the deck, by such a wave as the oldest sailor had never seen ; and presently, amidst loud thunders and flashing lightnings, riding as it were in a black cloud, three figures were seen passing onward. These were the devil, Sarah Polgrain, and Yorkshire Jack; and this was the cause of the storm.

" It is all true, as you may learn if you will inquire," said the old woman ; " for many of her kin live in Church-town."

THE LUGGER OF CROFT PASCO POOL.

IN the midst of the dreary waste of Gornhilly, which occupies a large portion of the Lizard promontory, is a large piece of water known as " Croft Pasco Pool," where it is said at night the form of a ghostly vessel may be seen floating with lug-sails spread. A more dreary, weird spot could hardly be selected for a witches' meeting ; and the Lizard folks were always—a fact—careful to be back before dark, preferring to suffer inconvenience, to risking a sight of the ghostly lugger. Unbelieving people attributed the origin of the tradition to a white horse seen in a dim twilight standing in the shallow water ; but this was indignantly rejected by the mass of the residents.

ROMANCES AND SUPERSTITIONS

OF

HISTORIC TIMES.

SECOND SERIES.

THE SAINTS.

" With great pretended spiritual motions,
  And many fine whimsical notions,
  With blind zeal and large devotions."
                              SAMUEL BUTLER.

A Flight of Witches.

POPULAR ROMANCES AND SUPERSTITIONS OF THE WEST OF ENGLAND.

LEGENDS OF THE SAINTS.

" This ilke monk let olde thingës pace,
And held after the newe world the trace
He gave not of the text a pulled hen,
That saith, that hunters be not holy men,
Ne that a monk, when he is reckeless,
Is like to a fish that is waterless ;
This is to say, a monk out of his cloister,
This ilke text held he not worth an oyster,
And I say his opinion was good "
   —*The Canterbury Tales*—CHAUCER

THE process through which a man, who has made himself re-markable to his ignorant fellow-men, is passed after death —first, into the hero performing fabulous exploits, and eventually into the giant—is not difficult to understand.

The remembrance of great deeds, and the memory of virtues,—even in modern days, when the exaggerations of votaries are sub-dued by the influence of education,—ever tends to bring them out in strong contrast with the surrounding objects. The mass of men form the background, as it were, of the picture, and the hero or the saint stands forth in all his brightness of colour in the fore-ground.

Amidst the uneducated Celtic population who inhabited Old Cornwall, it was the practice, as with the Celts of other countries, to exalt their benefactors with all the adornments of that hyperbole which distinguishes their songs and stories. When the first Christian missionaries dwelt amongst this people, they impressed them with the daring which they exhibited by the persecution which they uncomplainingly endured and the holy lives they led.

Those who were morally so superior to the living men, were

represented as physically so to their children, and every generation adorned the relation which it had received with the ornaments derived from their own imaginations, which had been tutored amidst the severer scenes of nature ; and consequently the warrior, or the holy man, was transmuted into the giant.

If to this we add the desire which was constantly shown by the earlier priesthood to persuade the people of their miraculous powers —of the direct interference of Heaven in their behalf—and of the violent conflicts which they were occasionally enduring with the enemy of the human race, there will be no difficulty in marking out the steps by which the ordinary man has become an extra-ordinary hero. When we hear of the saints to whose memories the parish churches are dedicated, being enabled to hurl rocks of enormous size through the air, to carry them in their pockets, and indeed to use them as playthings, we perceive that the traditions of the legitimate giants have been transferred to, and mixed up with, the memories of a more recent people.

In addition to legends of the Titanic type, this section will include a few of the true monastic character. The only purpose I have in giving these is to preserve, as examples, some curious superstitions which have not yet entirely lost their hold on the people.

THE CROWZA STONES.

ST JUST, from his home in Penwith, being weary of having little to do, except offering prayers for the tinners and fishermen, went on a visit to the hospitable St Keverne, who had fixed his hermitage in a well-selected spot, not far from the Lizard headland. The holy brothers rejoiced together, and in full feeding and deep drinking they pleasantly passed the time. St Just gloried in the goodly chalice from which he drank the richest of wines, and envied St Keverne the possession of a cup of such rare value. Again and again did he pledge St Keverne ; their holy bond of brotherhood was to be for ever, Heaven was to witness the purity of their friendship, and to the world they were to become patterns of ecclesiastical love.

The time came when St Just felt he must return to his flock ; and repeating over again his vows, and begging St Keverne to return his visit, he departed—St Keverne sending many a blessing after his good brother.

The Saint of the west had not left his brother of the south many hours before the latter missed his cup. Diligent search was

made in every corner of his dwelling, but no cup could be found.
At length St Keverne could not but feel that he had been robbed
of his treasure by his western friend. That one in whom he had
placed such confidence—one to whom he had opened his heart,
and to whom he had shown the most unstinting hospitality—should
have behaved so treacherously, overcame the serenity of the good
man. His rage was excessive. After the first burst was over,
and reason reasserted her power, St Keverne felt that his wisest
course was to pursue the thief, inflict summary punishment on him,
and recover his cup. The thought was followed by a firm resolve,
and away St Keverne started in pursuit of St Just. Passing over
Crowza Down, some of the boulders of "Ironstone" which are
scattered over the surface caught his eye, and presently he whipped
a few of these stone pebbles into his pockets, and hastened onward.

When he drew near Tre-men-keverne he spied St Just. St
Keverne worked himself up into a boiling rage, and toiled with increased speed up the hill, hallooing to the saintly thief, who pursued
his way for some time in the well-assumed quiet of conscious
innocence.

Long and loud did St Keverne call on St Just to stop, but the
latter was deaf to all calls of the kind—on he went, quickening,
however, his pace a little.

At length St Keverne came within a stone's throw of the dis-
sembling culprit, and calling him a thief—adding thereto some of
the most choice epithets from his holy vocabulary—taking a stone
from his pocket, he let it fly after St Just.

The stone falling heavily by the side of St Just convinced him
that he had to deal with an awkward enemy, and that he had best
make all the use he could of his legs. He quietly untied the
chalice, which he had fastened to his girdle, and let it fall to the
ground. Then, still as if unconscious of his follower, he set off to
run as fast as his ponderous body would allow his legs to carry
him. St Keverne came up to where his cup glistened in the
sunshine. He had recovered his treasure, he should get no good
out of the false friend, and he was sadly jaded with his long run.
Therefore he took, one by one, the stones from his pockets—he
hurled them, fairly aimed, after the retreating culprit, and cursed
him as he went.

There the pebbles remained where they fell,—the peculiarity of
the stone being in all respects unlike anything around, but being
clearly the Crowza stones,—attesting the truth of the legend ; and
their weights, each one being several hundred pounds, proving the
power of the giant saint.

Many have been the attempts made to remove these stones. They are carried away easily enough by day, but they ever return to the spot on which they now repose, at night.

THE LONGSTONE.

THE GIANT'S HAT AND STAFF.

SOME say it was St Roach, others refer it to St Austell; but all agree in one thing, that the Longstone was once the staff of some holy man, and that its present state is owing to the malignant persecution of the demon of darkness. It happened after this manner. The good saint who had been engaged in some mission was returning to his cell across St Austell Downs. The night had been fine, the clearness of the sky and the brightness of the stars conduced to religious thoughts, and those of the saint fled heavenwards. The devil was wandering abroad that night, and maliciously he resolved to play a trick upon his enemy. The saint was wrapt in thought. The devil was working his dire spells. The sky became black, the stars disappeared, and suddenly a terrific rush of wind seized the saint, whirled him round and round, and at last blew his hat high into the air. The hat went ricochetting over the moor and the saint after it, the devil enjoying the sport The long stick which the saint carried impeded his progress in the storm, and he stuck it into the ground. On went the hat, speedily followed the saint over and round the moor, until thoroughly wearied out, he at length gave up the chase. He, now exposed to the beat of the tempest bareheaded, endeavoured to find his way to his cell, and thought to pick up his staff on the way. No staff could be found in the darkness, and his hat was, he thought, gone irrecoverably. At length the saint reached his cell, he quieted his spirit by prayer, and sought the forgetfulness of sleep, safe under the protection of the holy cross, from all the tricks of the devil. The evil one, however, was at work on the wild moor, and by his incantations he changed the hat and the staff into two rocks. Morning came, the saint went abroad seeking for his lost covering and support. He found them both—one a huge circular boulder, and the other a long stone which remains to this day.*

The Saint's, or, as it was often called, the Giant's Hat was removed in 1798 by a regiment of soldiers who were encamped near it. They felt satisfied that this mysterious stone was the cause of the

---

* Another tradition affirms that one of the sons of Cyrus lies buried beneath the Longstone.

wet season which rendered their camp unpleasant, and consequently they resolved to remove the evil spell by destroying it.

ST SENNEN AND ST JUST.

THESE saints held rule over adjoining parishes; but, like neighbours, not unfrequently they quarrelled. We know not the cause which made their angry passions rise; but no doubt the saints were occasionally exposed to the influences of the evil principle, which appears to be one of the ruling powers of the world. It is not often that we have instances of excess of passion in man or woman without some evidence of the evil resulting from it. Every tempest in the physical world leaves its mark on the face of the earth. Every tempest in the moral world, in a similar manner, leaves some scar to tell of its ravages on the soul. A most enduring monument in granite tells us of the rage to which those two holy men were the victims. As we have said, there is no record of the origin of the duel which was fought between St Just and St Sennen; but, in the fury of their rage, they tore each a rock from the granite mass, and hurled it onwards to destroy his brother. They were so well aimed that both saints must have perished had the rocks been allowed to travel as intended. A merciful hand guided them, though in opposite directions, in precisely the same path. The huge rocks came together; so severe was the blow of impact that they became one mass, and fell to the ground, to remain a monument of the impotent rage of two giants.

LEGENDS OF ST LEVEN.

I.—THE SAINT AND JOHANA.

THE walls of what are supposed to be the hut of St Leven are still to be seen at Bodellen. If you walk from Bodellen to St Leven Church, on passing near the stile in Rospletha you will see a three-cornered garden. This belonged to a woman who is only known to us as Johana. Johana's Garden is still the name of the place. One Sunday morning St Leven was passing over the stile to go as usual to his fishing-place below the church, to catch his dinner. Johana was in the garden picking pot-herbs at the time, and she lectured the holy man for fishing on a Sunday. They came to high words, and St Leven told Johana that there was no more sin in taking his dinner from the sea than she herself committed in taking hers from the garden. The saint called her foolish Johana, and said if another of her name was christened in his well she should be a bigger fool than Johana herself. From that day to this no child called Johana has been christened in St Leven. All parents who desire to give that name to their daughters, dreading St Leven's curse, take the children to Sennen.

II.—THE SAINT'S PATH.

The path along which St Leven was accustomed to walk from Bodellen, by Rospletha, on to St Leven's Rocks, as they are still called, may be yet seen ; the grass grows greener wherever the good priest trod than in any other part of the fields through which the footpath passes.

III.—THE ST LEVEN STONE.

On the south side of the church, to the east of the porch, is a rock known by the above name. It is broken in two, and the fissure is filled in with ferns and wild flowers, while the grass grows rank around it. On this rock St Leven often sat to rest after the fatigue of fishing ; and desiring to leave some enduring memento of himself in connection with this his rude but favourite seat, he one day gave it a blow with his fist and cracked it through. He prayed over the rock and uttered the following prophecy :—

> " When, with panniers astride,
> A pack-horse one can ride
> Through St Leven's Stone,
> The world will be done."

This stone must have been venerated for the saint's sake when the church was built, or it would certainly have been employed for the building. It is more than fifty years since I first made acquaintance, as a child, with the St Leven Stone, and it may be a satisfaction to many to know that the progress of separation is an exceedingly slow one I cannot detect the slightest difference in the width of the fissure now and then. At the present slow rate of opening, the pack-horse and panniers will not be able to pass through the rock for many thousands of years to come. We need not, therefore, place much reliance on those prophecies which give but a limited duration to this planet.[*]

IV.—THE TWO BREAMS.

Although in common with many of the churches in the remote districts of Cornwall, "decay's effacing fingers" have been allowed

* See p 181.

to do their work in St Leven Church, yet there still remains some of the ornamental work which once adorned it. Much of the carving is irremediably gone ; but still the inquirer will find that it once told the story of important events in the life of the good St Leven. Two fishes on the same hook form the device, which appears at one time to have prevailed in this church. These are to commemorate a remarkable incident in St Leven's life. One lovely evening about sunset, St Leven was on his rocks fishing. There was a heavy pull upon his line, and drawing it in, he found two breams on the same hook. The good saint, anxious to serve both alike, to avoid, indeed, even the appearance of partiality, took both the fishes off the hook, and cast them back into the sea. Again they came to the hook, and again were they returned to their native element. The line was no sooner cast a third time than the same two fishes hooked themselves once more. St Leven thought there must be some reason unknown to him for this strange occurrence, so he took both the fishes home with him. When the saint reached Bodellen, he found his sister, St Breage,* had come to visit him with two children. Then he thought he saw the hand of Providence at work in guiding the fish to his hook.

Even saints are blind when they attempt to fathom the ways of the Unseen. The fish were, of course, cooked for supper ; and the saint having asked a blessing upon their savory meal, all sat down to partake of it. The children had walked far, and they were ravenously hungry. They ate their suppers with rapidity, and, not taking time to pick out the bones of the fish, they were both choked. The apparent blessing was thus transformed into a curse, and the bream has from that day forward ever gone by the name, amongst fishermen, of " choke children."

There are many disputes as to the fish concerned in this legend. Some of the fishermen of St Leven parish have insisted upon their

---

* St Breock or Briock, a bishop of a diocese in Armorica, is said to have been the patron saint of St Breage. But there is a Cornish distich, " Germow Mathern, Breaga Lavethas " Germoe was a king, Breaga a midwife, which rather favours the statement that St Breage was a sister of St Leven Breage and Germoe are adjoining parishes, having the shores of the Mount's Bay for their southern boundaries When the uncultivated inhabitants of this remote region regarded a wreck as a "God-send," and plundered without hesitation every body, living or dead, thrown upon the shore, these parishes acquired a melancholy notoriety The sailors' popular prayer being,

" God keep us from rocks and shelving sands,
And save us from Breage and Germoe men's lands "

Happily those days are almost forgotten. The ameliorating influences of the Christian faith, which was let in upon a most benighted people by John Wesley, like a sunbeam, dispelled those evil principles, and gave birth to pure and simple virtues being "chad" (the shad, *clupeida alosa*); while others, with the strong evidence afforded by the bony structure of the fish, will have it to have been the bream (*cyprinus brama*). My young readers, warned by the name, should be equally careful in eating either of those fish.

SAINT KEYNE.

BRAGHAN, or Brechan, was a king in Wales, and the builder of the town of Brecknock. This worthy old king and saint was the happy father of twenty-six children, or, as some say, twenty-four. Of these, fourteen or fifteen were sainted for their holiness, and their portraits are preserved within a fold of the kingly robe of the saint, their father, in the window at St Neot's Church, bearing the inscription, "Sante Brechane, cum omnibus sanctis, ora pro nobis," and known as the young women's window.

Of the holy children settled in Cornwall, we learn that the following gave their names to Cornish churches :—

1. John, giving name to the Church of St Ive.		
2 Endellient,	,,	,,	Endellion
3. Menfre,	,,	,,	St Minver.
4. Tethe,	,,	,,	St Teath.
5 Mabena,	,,	,,	St Mabyn.
6. Merewenna,	,,	,,	Marham.
7. Wenna,	,,	,,	St Wenn
8. KEYNE,	,,	,,	ST KEYNE
9. Yse,	,,	,,	St Issey.
10. Morwenna	,,	,,	Morwinstow.
11 Cleder,	,,	,,	St Clether.
12. Keri,	,,	,,	Egloskerry.
13. Helie,	,,	,,	Egloshayle
14. Adwent,	,,	,,	Advent
15. Lanent,	,,	,,	Lelant.*

Of this remarkable family St Keyne stands out as the brightest star. Lovely beyond measure, she wandered over the country safe, even in lawless times, from insult, by "the strength of her purity"

We find this virtuous woman performing miracles wherever she went. The district now known by the name of Keynsham, in Somersetshire, was in those days infested with serpents. St Keyne, rivalling St Hilda of the Northern Isle, changed them all into coils of stone, and there they are in the quarries at the present time to attest the truth of the legend. Geologists, with more learning

* Leland, cited by William of Worcester from the Cornish Calendar at St Michael's Mount Michell's "Parochial History of Saint Neot's"

than poetry, term them Ammonites, deriving their name from the horn of Jupiter Ammon, as if the Egyptian Jupiter was likely to have charmed serpents in England. We are satisfied to leave the question for the consideration of our readers. After a life spent in the conversion of sinners, the building of churches, and the performance of miracles, this good woman retired into Cornwall, and in one of its most picturesque valleys she sought and found that quiet which was conducive to a happy termination of a well-spent life. She desired, above all things, " peace on earth; " and she hoped to benefit the world, by giving to woman a chance of being equal to her lord and master. A beautiful well of water was near the home of the saint, and she planted, with her blessing, four trees around it—the withy, the oak, the elm, and the ash. When the hour of her death was drawing near, St Keyne caused herself to be borne on a litter to the shade which she had formed, and soothed by the influence of the murmur of the flowing fountain, she blessed the waters, and gave them their wondrous power, thus quaintly described by Carew .—" Next, I will relate to you another of the Cornish natural wonders—viz , St Keyne's Well , but lest you make wonder, first at the sainte, before you notice the well, you must understand that this was not Kayne the Manqueller, but one of a gentler spirit and milder sex—to wit, a woman. He who caused the spring to be pictured, added this rhyme for an explanation —-

> 'In name, in shape, in quality,
>   This well is very quaint ,
> The name to lot of Kayne befell,
>   No over-holy saint
> The shape, four trees of divers kind,
>   Withy, oak, elm, and ash,
> Make with their roots an arched roof,
>   Whose floor this spring does wash.
> The quality, that man or wife,
>   Whose chance or choice attains,
> First of this sacred stream to drink,
>   Thereby the mastery gains'" *

ST DENNIS'S BLOOD.

THE patron saint of the parish church of St Dennis was born in the city of Athens, in the reign of Tiberius. His name and fame have full record in the " History of the Saints of the Church of Rome." How his name was connected with this remote parish is not clearly made out. We learn, however, that the good

---

* Carew's Survey, Lord Dedunstanville's edition, p 305. See "The Well of St

man was beheaded at Montmartre, and that he walked after his execution, with his head under his arm, to the place in Paris which still bears his name. At the very time when the decapitation took place in Paris, *blood fell on the stones of this churchyard* in Cornwall. Previously to the breaking out of the plague in London, the stains of the blood of St Dennis were again seen; and during our wars with the Dutch, the defeat of the English fleet was foretold by the rain of gore in this remote and sequestered place. Hals, the Cornish historian, with much gravity, informs us that he had seen some of the stones with blood upon them. Whenever this phenomenon occurs again we may expect some sad calamity to be near.

Some years since a Cornish gentleman was cruelly murdered and his body thrown into a brook. I have been very lately shown stones taken from this brook with bright red spots of some vegetable growth on them. It is said that ever since the murder the stones in this brook are spotted with gore, whereas they never were so previously to this dreadful deed.

ST KEA'S BOAT.

ST KÊA, a young Irish saint, stood on the southern shores of Ireland and saw the Christian missionaries departing to carry the blessed Word to the heathens of Western England. He watched their barks fade beneath the horizon, and he felt that he was left to a solitude which was not fitted to one in the full energy of young life, and burning with zeal.

The saint knelt on a boulder of granite lying on the shore, and he prayed with fervour that Heaven would order it so that he might diffuse his religious fervour amongst the barbarians of Cornwall. He prayed on for some time, not observing the rising of the tide. When he had poured out his full soul, he awoke to the fact, not only that the waves were washing around the stone on which he knelt, but that the stone was actually floating on the water. Impressed with the miracle, St Kea sprang to his feet, and looking towards the setting sun, with his cross uplifted, he exclaimed, "To Thee, and only to Thee, my God, do I trust my soul!"

Onward floated the granite, rendered buoyant by supernatural power. Floated hither and thither by the tides, it swam on;

Keyne," by Robert Southey, in his "Ballads and Metrical Tales," vol. 1., or of Southey's collected works, vol vi

St Keyne, or St Kenna, is said to have visited St Michael's Mount, and imparted this peculiar virtue to a stone chair on the ower blown sometimes in one direction, and sometimes in another, by the varying winds, days and nights were spent upon the waters. The faith of St Kea failed not; three times a day he knelt in prayer to God. At all other times he stood gazing on the heavens. At length the faith of the saint being fairly tried, the moorstone boat floated steadily up the river, and landed at St Kea, which place he soon Christianised; and there stands to this day this monument of St Kea's sincere belief.

ST GERMAN'S WELL.

THE good St German was, it would appear, sent into Cornwall in the reign of the Emperor Valentinian, mainly to suppress the Pelagian heresy. The inhabitants of the shores of the Tamar had long been schooled into the belief in original sin, and they would not endure its denial from the lips of a stranger. In this they were supported by the monks, who had already a firm footing in the land, and who taught the people implicit obedience to their religious instructors, faith in election, and that all human efforts were unavailing, unless supported by priestly aid. St German was a man with vast powers of endurance. He preached his doctrines of freewill, and of the value of good works, notwithstanding the outcry raised against him. His miracles were of the most remarkable character, and sufficiently impressive to convince a large body of the Cornish people that he was an inspired priest. St German raised a beautiful church, and built a monastic house for the relief of poor people. Yet notwithstanding the example of the pure life of the saint, and his unceasing study to do good, a large section of the priests and the people never ceased to persecute him. To all human endurance there is a limit, and even that of the saint weakened eventually, before the never-ceasing annoyances by which he was hemmed in.

One Sabbath morning the priest attended as usual to his Christian duties, when he was interrupted by a brawl amongst the outrageous people, who had come in from all parts of the country with a determination to drive him from the place of his adoption. The holy man prayed for his persecutors, and he entreated them to calm their angry passions and listen to his healing words. But no words could convey any healing balm to their stormy hearts. At length his brethren, fearing that his life was in danger, begged him to fly, and eventually he left the church by a small door near the altar, while some of the monks endeavoured to tranquillise the people. St German went, a sad man, to the cliffs at the Rame head, and there alone he wept in agony at the failure of his labours. So intense was the soul-suffering of this holy man, that the rocks felt the power of spirit-struggling, and wept with him. The eyes of man, a spiritual creation, dry after the outburst of sorrow, but when the gross forms of matter are compelled to sympathise with spiritual sorrow, they remain for ever under the influence ; and from that day the tears of the cliffs have continued to fall, and the Well of St German attests to this day of the saint's agony. The saint was not allowed to remain in concealment long. The crowd of opposing priests and the peasantry were on his track. Hundreds were on the hill, and arming themselves with stones, they descended with shouts, determined to destroy him. St German prayed to God for deliverance, and immediately a rush, as of thunder, was heard upon the hills——a chariot surrounded by flames, and flashing light in all directions, was seen rapidly approaching. The crowd paused, fell back, and the flaming car passed on to where St German knelt. There were two bright angels in the chariot ; they lifted the persecuted saint from the ground, and placing him between them, ascended into the air.

"Curse your persecutors," said the angels. The saint cursed them , and from that time all holiness left the church he had built. The saint was borne to other lands, and lived to effect great good. On the rocks the burnt tracts of the chariot wheels were long to be seen, and the Well of Tears still flows   .

HOW ST PIRAN REACHED CORNWALL.·

GOOD men are frequently persecuted by those whom they have benefited the most. The righteous Piran had, by virtue of his sanctity, been enabled to feed ten Irish kings and their armies for ten days together with three cows. He brought to life by his prayers the dogs which had been killed while hunting the elk and the boar, and even restored to existence many of the warriors who had fallen on the battle-field. Notwithstanding this, and his incomparable goodness, some of these kings condemned him to be cast off a precipice into the sea, with a millstone around his neck.

On a boisterous day, a crowd of the lawless Irish assembled on the brow of a beetling cliff, with Piran in chains. By great labour they had rolled a huge millstone to the top of the hill, and Piran was chained to it. ·At a signal from one of the kings, the stone and the saint were rolled to the edge of, and suddenly over, the cliff into the Atlantic. The winds were blowing temptestuously, the heavens were dark with clouds, and the waves white with crested foam. No sooner was Piran and the millstone launched into space, than the sun shone out brightly, casting the full lustre of its beams on the holy man, who sat tranquilly on the descending stone. The winds died away, and the waves became smooth as a mirror. The moment the millstone touched the water, hundreds were converted to Christianity who saw this miracle. St Piran floated on safely to Cornwall ; he landed on the 5th of March on the sands which bear his name. He lived amongst the Cornish men until he attained the age of 266 years.*

ST PERRAN, THE MINERS' SAINT.

ST PIRAN, or St Perran, has sometimes gained the credit of discovering tin in Cornwall; yet Usher places the date of his birth about the year 352 ; and the merchants of Tyre are said to have traded with Cornwall for tin as early as the days of King Solomon.

There are three places in Cornwall to which the name of Perran is given ;—

Perran-Aworthall—*i.e, Perran on the noted River.*
Perran-Uthno—*i e., Perran the Little.*
Perran-Zabuloe—*i e, Perran in the Sands.*

This sufficiently proves that the saint, or some one bearing that name, was eminently popular amongst the people ; and in St Perran we have an example—of which several instances are given—of the manner in which a very ancient event is shifted forward, as it were, for the purpose of investing some popular hero with additional reasons for securing the devotion of the people, and of drawing them to his shrine.†

Picrous, or Piccras, is another name which has been floating by tradition, down the stream of time, in connection with the discovery of tin ; and in the eastern portion of Cornwall, Picrous-day, the second Thursday before Christmas-day, is kept as the tinners' holiday.

* See Gilbert, vol. iii. p. 329   See Appendix R   The name of this saint is written Piran, Peran, and Perran

† See Perran-Zabuloe, with an Account of the Past and Present State of the Oratory of St Piran in the Sands, and Remarks on its Antiquity. By the Rev. Wm. Haslam B A., and by the Rev Collins Trelawney.

St Kieran, the favourite Celtic saint, reached Scotland from Ireland, the precursor of St Columba (565 A D). "The cave of St Kieran is still shown in Kintyre, where the first Christian teacher of the Western Highlands is believed to have made his abode "—*Wilson's Prehistoric Annals.*

There is a curious resemblance between the deeds and the names of those two saints.

The popular story of the discovery of tin is, however, given with all its anachronisms.

THE DISCOVERY OF TIN.

St Piran, or St Perran, leading his lonely life on the plains which now bear his name, devoted himself to the study of the objects which presented themselves to his notice. The good saint decorated the altar in his church with the choicest flowers, and his cell was adorned with the crystals which he could collect from the neighbouring rocks. In his wanderings on the sea-shore, St Perran could not but observe the numerous mineral veins running through the slate-rocks forming the beautiful cliffs on this coast. Examples of every kind he collected; and on one occasion, when preparing his humble meal, a heavy black stone was employed to form a part of the fireplace. The fire was more intense than usual, and a stream of beautiful white metal flowed out of the fire. Great was the joy of the saint; he perceived that God, in His goodness, had discovered to him something which would be useful to man. St Perran communicated his discovery to St Chiwidden.* They examined the shores, and Chiwidden, who was learned in the learning of the East, soon devised a process for producing this metal in large quantities. The two saints called the Cornish men together. They told them of their treasures, and they taught them how to dig the ore from the earth, and how, by the agency of fire, to obtain the metal. Great was the joy in Cornwall, and many days of feasting followed the announcement. Mead and metheglin, with other drinks, flowed in abundance; and vile rumour says the saints and their people were rendered equally unstable thereby. "Drunk as a Perraner," has certainly passed into a proverb from that day.

The riot of joy at length came to an end, and steadily, seriously, the tribes of Perran and St Agnes set to work. They soon accumulated a vast quantity of this precious metal; and when they carried it to the southern coasts, the merchants from Gaul eagerly purchased it of them. The noise of the discovery, even in those days, rapidly extended itself; and even the cities of Tyre learned that a metal, precious to them, was to be obtained in a country far to the west. The Phœnician navigators were not long in finding out the Tin Islands; and great was the alarm amidst the Cornish Britons lest the source of their treasure should be discovered. Then it was they intrenched the whole of St Agnes beacon; then it was they built the numerous hill castles which have puzzled the antiquarian; then it was that they constructed the rounds,—

* See Appendix S.

amongst which the Perran Round remains as a remarkable example,—all of them to protect their tin ground. So resolved were
the whole of the population of the district to preserve the tin work-
ings, that they prevented any foreigner from landing on the mainland, and they established tin markets on the islands on the coast.
On these islands were hoisted the standard of Cornwall, a white
cross on a black ground, which was the device of St Perran and
St Chiwidden, symbolising the black tin ore and the white metal.*

ST NEOT, THE PIGMY.

WHENCE came the saint, or hermit, who has given his name
to two churches in England, is not known.

Tradition, however, informs us that he was remarkably small
in stature, though exquisitely formed. He could not, according
to all accounts, have been more than fifteen inches high. Yet,
though so diminutive a man, he possessed a soul which was giant-
like in the power of his faith. The Church of St Neot, which has
been built on the ancient site of the hermit's cell, is situated in a
secluded valley, watered by a branch of the river Fowey. The
surrounding country is, even now, but very partially cultivated,
and it must have been, a few centuries since, a desert waste ; but
the valley is, and no doubt ever has been, beautifully wooded.
Not far from the church is the holy well, in which the pious
anchorite would stand immersed to his neck, whilst he repeated
the whole Book of Psalms. Great was the reward for such an
exercise of devotion and faith. Out of numerous miracles we
select only a few, which have some especial character about them.

ST NEOT AND THE FOX.

One day the holy hermit was standing in his bath chanting the
Psalms, when he heard the sound of huntsmen approaching.
Whether the saint feared ridicule or ill-treatment, we know not ;
but certainly he left some psalms unsung that day, and hastily
gathering up his clothes, he fled to his cell.

In his haste the good man lost his shoe, and a hungry fox
having escaped the hunters, came to the spring to drink. Having
quenched the fever of thirst, and being hungry, he spied the saint's
shoe, and presently ate it. The hermit despatched his servant to
look for his shoe ; and, lo, he found the fox cast into a deep sleep,
and the thongs of the shoe hanging out of his vile mouth. Of

* See Appendix T.

course the shoe was pulled out of his stomach, and restored to the saint.

ST NEOT AND THE DOE.

Again, on another day, when the hermit was in his fountain, a lovely doe, flying from the huntsmen, fell down on the edge of the well, imploring, with tearful eyes and anxious pantings, ·the aid of St Neot. The dogs followed in full chase, ready to pounce on the trembling doe, and eager to tear her in pieces. They saw the saint, and one look from his holy eyes sent them flying back into the wood, more speedily, if possible, than they rushed out of it.

The huntsman too came on, ready to discharge his arrow into the heart of the doe ; but, impressed with the sight he saw, he fell on his knees, cast away his quiver, and became from that day a follower of the saint's, giving him his horn to hang, as a memorial, in the church, where it was long to be seen. The huntsman became eventually one of the monks of the neighbouring house of St Petroch.

ST NEOT AND THE THIEVES.

When St Neot was abbot, some thieves came by night and stole the oxen belonging to the farm of the monastery. The weather was most uncertain,—the seed-time was passing away,—and a fine morning rendered it imperative that the ploughs should be quickly employed. There were no oxen. Great was the difficulty, and earnest were the abbot's prayers. In answer to them, the wild stags came in from the forests, and tamely offered their necks to the yoke When unyoked in the evening, they resorted to their favourite pastures, but voluntarily returned each morning to their work. The report of this event reached the ears of the thieves. They became penitent, and restored the oxen to the monastery. Not only so, but they consecrated their days to devotional exercises. The oxen being restored, the stags were dismissed ; but they bore for ever a white ring, like a yoke about their necks, and they held a charmed life, safe from the shafts of the hunters.

ST NEOT AND THE FISHES.

On one occasion, when the saint was at his devotions, an angel appeared unto him, and showing him three fishes in the well, he said, " These are for thee , take one each day for thy daily food, and the number shall never grow less : the choice of one of three fishes shall be thine all the days of thy life." Long time passed by, and daily a fish was taken from the well, and three awaited his coming every morning. At length the saint, who shared in human suffering, notwithstanding his piety, fell ill; and being confined to his bed, St Neot sent his servant Barius to fetch him a fish for his dinner. Barius, being desirous of pleasing, if possible, the sick man's taste, went to the well and caught two fishes. One of these he broiled, and the other he boiled. Nicely cooked, Barius took them on a dish to his master's bedside, who started up alarmed for the consequences of the act of his servant, in disobedience to the injunctions of the angel. So good a man could not allow wrath to get the mastery of him; so he sat up in his bed, and, instead of eating, he prayed with great earnestness over the cooked fish. At last the spirit of holiness exerted its full power. St Neot commanded Barius to return at once and cast the fish into the well. Barius went and did as his master had told him to do; and, lo, the moment the fishes fell into the water they recovered life, and swam away with the third fish, as if nothing had happened to them.

All these things, and more, are recorded in the windows of St Neot's Church.*

PROBUS AND GRACE.

EVERY one is acquainted with the beautiful tower of Probus Church. If they are not, they should lose no time in visiting it. Various are the stories in connection with those two saints, who are curiously connected with the church, and one of the fairs held in the Church-town. A safe tradition tells us that St Probus built the church, and failing in the means of adding a tower to his building, he petitioned St Grace to aid him. Grace was a wealthy lady, and she resolved at her own cost to build a tower, the like of which should not be seen in the "West Countrie." Regardless of the expense, sculptured stone was worked by the most skilful masons, and the whole put together in the happiest of proportions. When the tower was finished, St Probus opened his church with every becoming solemnity, and took to himself all the praise which was lavished on the tower, although he had built only a plain church. When, however, the praise of Probus was at the highest, a voice was heard slowly and distinctly exclaiming,

> "Saint Probus and Grace,
> Not the first, but the last;"

and thus for ever have Probus and Grace been united as patron saints of this church.

* See Appendix U.

Mr Davies Gilbert remarks, however, in his "Parochial History : " " Few gentlemen's houses in the west of Cornwall were without the honour of receiving Prince Charles during his residence in the county about the middle part of the civil wars ; and he is said to have remained for a time longer than usual with Mr Williams, who, after the Restoration, waited on the king with congratulations from the parish ; and, on being complimented by him with the question whether he could do anything for his friends, answered that the parish would esteem themselves highly honoured and distinguished by the grant of a fair, which was accordingly done for the 17th of September. This fair coming the last in succession after three others, has acquired for itself a curious appellation, derived from the two patron saints, and from the peculiar pronunciation in that neighbourhood of the word 'last,' somewhat like laest,—

> 'Saint Probus and Grace,
> Not the first, but the last,'—

and from this distinction it is usually called Probus and Grace Fair." We are obliged, therefore, to lean on the original tradition for the true meaning of this couplet.

ST NECTAN'S KIEVE AND THE LONELY SISTERS.

FAR up the deep and rocky vale of Trevillet, in the parish of Tintagel,* stands on a pile of rocks the little chapel of the good St Nectan. No holy man ever selected a more secluded, or a more lovely spot in which to pass a religious life. From the chapel rock you look over the deep valley full of trees. You see here and there the lovely trout-stream running rapidly towards the sea ; and, opening in the distance, there rolls the mighty ocean itself. Although this oratory is shut in amongst the woods, so as to be invisible to any one approaching it by land, until they are close upon it, it is plainly seen by the fishermen or by the sailor far off at sea ; and in olden time the prayers of St Nectan were sought by all whose business was in the "deep waters."

The river runs steadily along within a short distance of St Nectan's Chapel, and then it suddenly leaps over the rock—a beautiful fall of water—into St Nectan's Kieve. This deep rock-

---

* TINTAGEL is the usual name. Gilbert, in his "Parochial History," has it "DUNDAGELL, *alias* DYNDAGELL, *alias* BOSITHNEY ," in "Doomsday-book" it is called "DUNECHEINE." Tonkin writes "Dindagel or Daundagel," and sometimes DUNGIOGEL. "A King Nectan, or St Nectan, is said to have built numerous churches in several parts of Scotland, as well as in other parts of the kingdom of the Northern Picts."—*Wilson's Prehistoric Annals of Scotland*

basin, brimming with the clearest water, overflows, and another waterfall carries the river to the lower level of the valley. Standing here within a circular wall of rocks, you see how the falling fluid has worked back the softer slate-rock until it has reached the harder masses, which are beautifully polished by the same agent. Mosses, ferns, and grasses decorate the fall, fringing every rock with a native drapery of the most exquisite beauty. Here is one of the wildest, one of the most untrained, and, at the same time, one of the most beautiful spots in Cornwall, full of poetry, and coloured by legend. Yet here comes prosaic man, and by one stroke of his every-day genius, he adds, indeed, a colour to the violet. You walk along the valley, through paths trodden out of the undergrowth, deviously wandering up hill, or down hill, as rock or tree has interposed. Many a spot of quiet beauty solicits you to loiter, and loitering, you feel that there are places from which the winds appear to gather poetry. You break the spell, or the ear, catching the murmur of the waters, dispels the illusions which have been created by the eye, and you wander forward, anxious to reach the holy " Kieve,"—to visit the saint's hermitage. Here, say you, is the place to hold "commune with Nature's works, and view her charms unrolled," when, lo, a well-made door, painted lead colour, with a real substantial lock, bars your way, and Fancy, with everything that is holy, flies away before the terrible words which inform you that trespassers will be punished, and that the key can be obtained at ————. Well was it that Mr Wilkie Collins gave "up the attempt to discover Nighton's Kieve ;"* for had he, when he had found it, discovered this evidence of man's greedy soul, it would have convinced him that the "evil genius of fairy mythology," who so cautiously hid "the nymph of the waterfall," was no other than the farmer, who, as he told me, "owns the fee," and one who is resolved also to pocket the fee before any pilgrim can see the oratory and the waterfall of St Nectan. Of course this would have turned the placid current of the thoughts of "the Rambler beyond Railways," which now flow so pleasantly, into a troubled stream of biliary bitterness.

St Nectan placed in the little bell-tower of his secluded chapel a silver bell, the notes of which were so clear and penetrating that they could be heard far off at sea. When the notes came through the air, and fell on the ears of the seamen, they knew that St Nectan was about to pray for them, and they prostrated themselves before Heaven for a few minutes, and thus endeavoured to win the blessing.

* It is called indifferently Nectan, Nathan, Nighton, or Knighton's Kieve.

St Nectan was on the bed of death. There was strife in the land. A severe struggle was going on between the Churchmen, and endeavours were being made to introduce a new faith.

The sunset of life gave to the saint the spirit of prophecy, and he told his weeping followers that the light of their religion would grow dim in the land ; but that a spark would for ever live amidst the ashes, and that in due time it would kindle into a flame, and burn more brightly than ever. His silver bell, he said, should never ring for others than the true believer. He would enclose it in the rock of the Kieve ; but when again the true faith revived, it should be recovered, and rung, to cheer once more the land.

One lovely summer evening, while the sun was slowly sinking towards the golden sea, St Nectan desired his attendants to carry him to the bank which overhung the " Kieve," and requested them to take the bell from the tower and bring it to him. There he lay for some time in silent prayer, waiting as if for a sign, then slowly raising himself from the bed on which he had been placed, he grasped the silver bell. He rang it sharply and clearly three times, and then he dropped it into the transparent waters of the Kieve. He watched it disappear, and then he closed his eyes in death. On receiving the bell the waters were troubled, but they soon became clear as before, and the bell was nowhere to be seen.

St Nectan died, and two strange ladies from a foreign land came and took possession of his oratory, and all that belonged unto the holy man. They placed—acting, as it was believed, on the wishes of the saint himself—his body, all the sacramental plate, and other sacred treasures, in a large oak chest. They turned the waters of the fall aside, and dug a grave in the river bed, below the Kieve, in which they placed this precious chest. The waters were then returned to their natural course, and they murmur ever above the grave of him who loved them. The silver bell was concealed in the Kieve, and the saint with all that belonged to his holy office rested beneath the river bed. The oratory was dismantled, and the two ladies, women evidently of high birth, chose it for their dwelling. Their seclusion was perfect. " Both appeared to be about the same age, and both were inflexibly taciturn. One was never seen without the other. If they ever left the house, they only left it to walk in the more unfrequented parts of the wood ; they kept no servant ; they never had a visitor ; no living soul but themselves ever crossed the door of their cottage." * The berries of the wood, a few roots which

* Rambles beyond Railways. By Wilkie Collins. Mr Collins was curiously misled by those who told him the tradition The building which these strange solitary women

they cultivated, with snails gathered from the rocks and walls, and fish caught in the stream, served them for food. Curiosity was excited; the mystery which hung around this solitary pair became deepened by the obstinate silence which they observed in everything relating to themselves. The result of all this was an anxious endeavour, on the part of the superstitious and ignorant peasantry, to learn their secret. All was now conjecture, and the imagination commonly enough filled in a wild picture : devils or angels, as the case might be, were seen ministering to the solitary ones. Prying eyes were upon them, but the spies could glean no knowledge. Week, month, year passed by, and ungratified curiosity was dying through want of food, when it was discovered that one of the ladies had died. The peasantry went in a body to the chapel ; no one forbade their entering it now. There sat a silent mourner leaning over the placid face of her dead sister. Hers was, indeed, a silent sorrow—no tear was in her eye, no sigh hove her chest, but the face told all that a remediless woe had fallen on her heart. The dead body was eventually removed, the living sister making no sign, and they left her in her solitude alone. Days passed on ; no one heard of, no one probably inquired after, the lonely one. At last a wandering child, curious as children are, clambered to the window of the cell and looked in. There sat the lady ; her handkerchief was on the floor, and one hand hung strangely, as if endeavouring to pick it up, but powerless to do so. The child told its story—the people again flocked to the chapel, and they found one sister had followed the other. The people buried the last beside the first, and they left no mark to tell us where, unless the large flat stone which lies in the valley, a short distance from the foot of the fall, and beneath which, I was told, " some great person was buried," may be the covering of their tomb No traces of the history of these solitary women have ever been discovered.

Centuries have passed away, and still the legends of the buried bell and treasure are preserved. Some long time since a party of men resolved to blast the " Kieve," and examine it for the silver bell. They were miners, and their engineering knowledge, though rude, was sufficient to enable them to divert the course of the river above the falls, and thus to leave the " Kieve " dry for them

inhabited was St Nectan's, or, as he and many others write it, St Nighton's, Chapel, and not a cottage They died, as Mr Collins describes it , but either he, or those from whom he learned the tale, has filled in the picture from imagination I perceive, on referring to Mr Walter White's admirable little book, "A Londoner's Walk to the Land's-End," that he has made the same mistake about the cottage to work on when they had emptied it, which was an easy task. The " borer " now rung upon the rock, holes were pierced, and, being charged, they were blasted. The result was, however, anything but satisfactory, for the rock remained intact. Still they persevered, until at length a voice was heard amidst the ring of the iron tools in the holes of the rock. Every hand was stayed, every face was aghast, as they heard distinctly the ring of the silver bell, followed by a clear solemn voice proclaiming, " The child is not yet born who shall recover this treasure."

The work was stopped, and the river restored to its old channel, over which it will run undisturbed until the day of which St Nectan prophesied shall arrive.

When, in the autumn of 1863, I visited this lovely spot, my guide, the proprietor, informed me that very recently a gentleman residing, I believe, in London, dreamed that an angel stood on a little bank of pebbles, forming a petty island, at the foot of a waterfall, and pointing to a certain spot, told him to search there and he would find gold and a mummy. This gentleman told his dream to a friend, who at once declared the place indicated to be St Nectan's waterfall. Upon this, the dreamer visited the West, and, upon being led by the owner of the property to the fall, he at once recognised the spot on which the angel stood.

A plan was then and there arranged by which a search might be again commenced, it being thought that as an angel had indicated the spot, the time for the recovery of the treasure had arrived.

Let us hope that the search may be deferred, lest the natural beauties of the spot should be destroyed by the meddling of men, who can threaten trespassers,—fearing to lose a sixpence,—and who have already endeavoured to improve on nature, by cutting down some of the rock and planting rhododendrons.

The Rev R S Hawker, of Morwenstow, has published in his " Echoes of Old Cornwall " a poem on this tradition, which, as it is but little known, and as it has the true poetic ring, I transcribe to adorn the pages of my Appendix.[*]

THEODORE, KING OF CORNWALL.

RIVIERE, near Hayle, now called Rovier, was the palace of Theodore, the king, to whom Cornwall appears to have been indebted for many of its saints. This Christian king, when the pagan people sought to destroy the first missionaries, gave the saints shelter in his palace, St Breca, St Iva, St Burianna, and many others, are said to have made Riviere their residence. It is not a little curious to find traditions existing, as it were, in a state of suspension between opinions. I have heard it said that there

[*] Appendix X.

was a church at Rovier—that there was once a great palace there; and again, that Castle Cayle was one vast fortified place, and Rovier another. Mr Davies Gilbert quotes Whitaker on this point :—

"Mr Whitaker, who captivates every reader by the brilliancy of his style, and astonishes by the extent of his multifarious reading, draws, however, without reserve, on his fertile imagination, for whatever facts may be requisite to construct the fabric of a theory. He has made Riviere the palace and residence of Theodore, a sovereign prince of Cornwall, and conducts St Breca, St Iva, with several companions, not only into Hayle and to this palace, after their voyage from Ireland, but fixes the time of their arrival so exactly, as to make it take place in the night. In recent times the name of Riviere, which had been lost in the common pronunciation, Rovier, has revived in a very excellent house built by Mr Edwards on the farm, which he completed in 1791." *

* Parochial History, vol. iii p. 423.

HOLY WELLS.

"A well there is in the west country,
  And a clearer one never was seen."
                              ROBERT SOUTHEY.

SUPERSTITIONS OF THE WELLS.

WELL-WORSHIP.

"One meek cell,
Built by the fathers o'er a lonely well,
Still breathes the Baptist's sweet remembrance round
A spring of silent waters"
Echoes from Old Cornwall—R S. HAWKER.

A SPRING of water has always something about it which
gives rise to holy feelings. From the dark earth there
wells up a pellucid fluid, which in its apparent tranquil joyous-
ness gives gladness to all around. The velvet mosses, the sword-
like grasses, and the feathery ferns, grow with more of that light and
vigorous nature which indicates a fulness of life, within the charmed
influence of a spring of water, than they do elsewhere.

The purity of the fluid impresses itself, through the eye, upon
the mind, and its power of removing all impurity is felt to the
soul. "Wash and be clean," is the murmuring call of the waters, as
they overflow their rocky basins, or grassy vases; and deeply sunk
in depravity must that man be who could put to unholy uses one
of nature's fountains. The inner life of a well of waters, bursting
from its grave in the earth, may be religiously said to form a type
of the soul purified by death, rising into a glorified existence and
the fulness of light. The tranquil beauty of the rising waters,
whispering the softest music, like the healthful breathing of a sleeping infant, sends a feeling of happiness through the soul of the
thoughtful observer, and the inner man is purified by its influence,
as the outer man is cleansed by ablution.

Water cannot be regarded as having an inanimate existence.
Its all-pervading character and its active nature, flowing on for
ever, resting never, removes it from the torpid elements, and
places it, like the air, amongst those higher creations which belong

to the vital powers of the earth. The spring of water rises from the cold dark earth, it runs, a silver cord glistening in the sunshine, down the mountain-side. The rill (prettily called by Drayton "a rillet") gathers rejoicingly other waters unto itself, and it grows into a *brooklet* in its course. At. length, flowing onward and increasing in size, the *brook* state of being is fairly won ; and then, by the gathering together of some more dewdrops, the full dignity of a stream is acquired. Onwards the waters flow, still gleaming from every side, and wooing new *ruhlets* to its bosom, eager as it were to assume the state which, in America, would be called a "run" of water. Stream gathers on stream, and run on run ; the union of waters becomes a *river;* rolling in its maturity, swelling in its pride, it seeks the ocean, and there is absorbed in the eternity of waters   Has ever poet yet penned a line which in any way conveys to the mind a sense of the grandeur, the immensity of the sea ?   I do not remember a verse which does not prove the incapacity of the human mind to embrace in its vastness the gathering together of the waters in the mighty sea.   Man's mind is tempered, and his pride subdued, as he stands on the sea-side and looks on the undulating expanse to which, to him, there is no end.   A material eternity of rain-drops gathered into a mass which is from Omnipotence and is omnipotent.   The influences of heaven falling on the sheeted waters, they rise at their bidding and float in air, making the skies more beautiful or more sublime, according to the spirit of the hour.   Whether the clouds float over the earth, illumined by sun-rays, like the cars of loving angels; or rush wildly onward, as if bearing demons of vengeance, they are subdued by the mountains, and fall reluctantly as mists around the rocks, condense solemnly as dews upon the sleeping flowers, sink to earth resignedly as tranquil rains, or splash in tempestuous anger on its surface. The draught, in whatever form it comes, is drunk with avidity, and, circulating through the subterranean recesses of the globe, it does its work of re-creation, and eventually reappears a bubbling spring, again to run its round of wonder-working tasks.

Those minds which saw a God in light, and worshipped a Creator in the sun, felt the power of the universal solvent, and saw in the diffusive nature of that fluid which is everywhere something more than a type of the regenerating Spirit, which all, in their holier hours, feel necessary to clear off the earthiness of life.   Man has ever sought to discover the spiritual in the material, and, from the imperfections of human reason, he has too frequently reposed on the material, and given to it the attributes which are purely spiritual.   Through all ages the fountains of the hills and valleys

have claimed the reverence of men ; and waters presenting themselves, under aspects of beauty, or of terror, have been regarded
with religious feelings of hope or of awe.

As it was of old, so is it to-day. It was but yesterday that I
stood near the font of Royston Church, and heard the minister
read with emphasis, " None can enter into the kingdom of God
except he be regenerate and born anew of water." Surely the
simple faith of the peasant mother who, on a spring morning,
takes her weakly infant to some holy well, and three times dipping
it in its clear waters, uttering an earnest prayer at each immersion,
is but another form of the prescribed faith of the educated church-
man.

Surely the practice of consulting the waters of a sacred spring,
by young men and maidens, is but a traditional faith derived from
the early creeds of Greece—a continuance of the *Hydromancy*
which sought in the Castalian fountain the divination of the
future.

THE WELL OF ST CONSTANTINE.

IN the parish of St Merran, or Meryn, near Padstow, are the
remains of the Church of St Constantine, and the holy well
of that saint. It had been an unusually hot and dry summer, and
all the crops were perishing through want of water. The people
inhabiting the parish had grown irreligious, and many of them
sadly profane. The drought was a curse upon them for their
wickedness. Their church was falling into ruin, their well was
foul, and the arches over it were decayed and broken. In their
distress, the wicked people who had reviled the Word of God,
went to their priest for aid.

" There is no help for thee, unless thou cleansest the holy
well."

They laughed him to scorn.

The drought continued, and they suffered want.

To the priest they went again.

" Cleanse the well," was his command, " and see the power of
the blessing of the first Christian emperor " That cleansing a
dirty well should bring them rain, they did not believe. The
drought continued, the rivers were dry, the people suffered thirst.

" Cleanse the well—wash, and drink," said the priest, when
they again went to him.

Hunger and thirst made the people obedient. They went to
the task. Mosses and weeds were removed, and the filth cleansed.
To the surprise of all, beautifully clear water welled forth. They

drank the water and prayed, and then washed themselves, and were refreshed. As they bathed their bodies, parched with heat, in the cool stream which flowed from the well, the heavens clouded over, and presently rain fell, turning all hearts to the true faith.

THE WELL OF ST LUDGVAN.

ST LUDGVAN, an Irish missionary, had finished his work. On the hill-top, looking over the most beautiful of bays, the church stood with all its blessings. Yet the saint, knowing human nature, determined on associating with it some object of a miraculous character, which should draw people from all parts of the world to Ludgvan. The saint prayed over the dry earth, which was beneath him, as he knelt on the church stile. His prayer was for water, and presently a most beautiful crystal stream welled up from below. The holy man prayed on, and then, to try the virtues of the water, he washed his eyes. They were rendered at once more powerful, so penetrating, indeed, as to enable him to see microscopic objects. The saint prayed again, and then he drank of the water. He discovered that his powers of utterance were greatly improved, his tongue formed words with scarcely any effort of his will. The saint now prayed, that all children baptized in the waters of this well might be protected against the hangman and his hempen cord ; and an angel from heaven came down into the water, and promised the saint that his prayers should be granted. Not long after this, a good farmer and his wife brought their babe to the saint, that it might derive all the blessings belonging to this holy well. The priest stood at the baptismal font, the parents, with their friends around. The saint proceeded with the baptismal ceremonial, and at length the time arrived when he took the tender babe into his holy arms. He signed the sign of the cross over the child, and when he sprinkled water on the face of the infant its face glowed with a divine intelligence. The priest then proceeded with the prayer ; but, to the astonishment of all, whenever he used the name of Jesus, the child, who had received the miraculous power of speech, from the water, pronounced distinctly the name of the devil, much to the consternation of all present. The saint knew that an evil spirit had taken possession of the child, and he endeavoured to cast him out ; but the devil proved stronger than the saint for some time. St Ludgvan was not to be beaten ; he knew that the spirit was a restless soul, which had been exorcised from Treassow, and he exerted all his energies in prayer. At length the spirit became obedient, and left the child.   He was now commanded by the saint to take his flight to the Red Sea.   He rose, before the terrified spectators, into a gigantic size ; he then spat into the well ; he laid hold of the pinnacles of the tower, and shook the church until they thought it would fall.   The saint was alone unmoved.   He prayed on, until, like a flash of lightning, the demon vanished, shaking down a pinnacle in his flight.   The demon, by spitting in the water, destroyed the spells of the water upon the eyes * and the tongue too ; but it fortunately retains its virtue of preventing any child baptized in it from being hanged with a cord of hemp.   Upon a cord of silk it is stated to have no power.

This well had nearly lost its reputation once—a Ludgvan woman was hanged, under the circumstances told in the following narrative .—

A small farmer, living in one of the most western districts of the county, died some years back of what was supposed at that time to be " English cholera."   A few weeks after his decease his wife married again.   This circumstance excited some attention in the neighbourhood.   It was remembered that the woman had lived on very bad terms with her late husband, that she had on many occasions exhibited strong symptoms of possessing a very vindictive temper, and that during the farmer's lifetime she had openly manifested rather more than a Platonic preference for the man whom she subsequently married.   Suspicion was generally excited ; people began to doubt whether the first husband had died fairly.   At length the proper order was applied for, and his body was disinterred.   On examination, enough arsenic to have poisoned three men was found in the stomach.   The wife was accused of murdering her husband, was tried, convicted on the clearest evidence, and hanged.   Very shortly after she had suffered capital punishment horrible stories of a ghost were widely circulated.   Certain people declared that they had seen a ghastly resemblance of the murderess, robed in her winding-sheet, with the black mark of the rope round her swollen neck, standing on stormy nights upon her husband's grave, and digging there with a spade, in hideous imitation of the actions of the men who had disinterred the corpse for medical examination.   This was fearful enough ; nobody dared go near the place after nightfall.   But soon another circumstance was talked of in connection with the poisoner, which affected the tranquillity of people's minds in the village where she had lived, and where it was believed she had been born, more

* It is curious that the farm over which some of this water flows is called " Collurian " to this day

T

seriously than even the ghost story itself. The well of St Ludgvan, celebrated among the peasantry of the district for its one remarkable property, that every child baptized in its water (with which the church was duly supplied on christening occasions) was secure from ever being hanged.

No one doubted that all the babies fortunate enough to be born and baptized in the parish, though they might live to the age of Methuselah, and might during that period commit all the capital crimes recorded in the " Newgate Calendar," were still destined to keep quite clear of the summary jurisdiction of Jack Ketch. No one doubted this until the story of the apparition of the murderess began to be spread abroad; then awful misgivings arose in the popular mind.

A woman who had been born close by the magical well, and who had therefore in all probability been baptized in its water, like her neighbours of the parish, had nevertheless been publicly and unquestionably hanged. However, probability is not always the truth. Every parishioner determined that the baptismal register of the poisoner should be sought for, and that it should be thus officially ascertained whether she had been christened with the well water or not. After much trouble, the important document was discovered—not where it was at first looked after, but in a neighbouring parish. A mistake had been made about the woman's birthplace; she had not been baptized in St Ludgvan Church, and had therefore not been protected by the marvellous virtue of the local water. Unutterable was the joy and triumph at this discovery. The wonderful character of the parish well was wonderfully vindicated; its celebrity immediately spread wider than ever. The peasantry of the neighbouring districts began to send for the renowned water before christenings; and many of them actually continue, to this day, to bring it corked up in bottles to their churches, and to beg particularly that it may be used whenever they present their children to be baptized.*

GULVAL WELL.

A YOUNG woman, with a child in her arms, stands by the side of Gulval Well, in Fosses Moor. There is an expression of extreme anxiety in her interesting face, which exhibits a considerable amount of intelligence. She appears to doubt, and yet be disposed to believe in, the virtues of this remarkable well. She

* See another story of this wretched woman in the section devoted to Demons and Spectres, p 256

pauses, looks at her babe, and sighs. She is longing to know something of the absent, but she fears the well may indicate the extreme of human sorrow. While she is hesitating, an old woman advances towards her, upon whom the weight of eighty years was pressing, but not over-heavily ; and she at once asked the young mother if she wished to ask the well after the health of her husband.

"Yes, Aunt Alcie," she replied ; " I am so anxious. I have not heard of John for six long months. I could not sleep last night, so I rose with the light, and came here, determined to ask the well ; but I am afraid. O Aunt Alcie, suppose the well should not speak, I should die on the spot ! "

" Nonsense, cheeld," said the old woman ; " thy man is well enough ; and the well will boil, if thee 'lt ask it in a proper spirit."

" But, Aunt Alcie, if it sends up puddled water, or if it remains quiet, what would become of me ? "

" Never be foreboding, cheeld ; troubles come quick without running to meet 'em. Take my word for it, the fayther of thy little un will soon be home again. Ask the well ! ask the well ! "

" Has it told any death or sickness lately ? " asked the young mother.

" On St Peter's eve Mary Curnew questioned the water about poor Willy "

" And the water never moved ? "

" The well was quiet ; and verily I guess it was about that time he died."

" Any sickness, Aunt Alcie ? "

" Jenny Kelinach was told, by a burst of mud, how ill her old mother was ; but do not be feared, all is well with Johnny Thomas."

Still the woman hesitated ; desire, fear, hope, doubt, superstition, and intelligence struggled within her heart and brain.

The old creature, who was a sort of guardian to the well, used all her rude eloquence to persuade Jane Thomas to put her question, and at length she consented. Obeying the old woman's directions, she knelt on the mat of bright green grass which grew around, and leaning over the well so as to see her face in the water, she repeated after her instructor,

> "Water, water, tell me truly,
> Is the man I love duly
> On the earth, or under the sod,
> Sick or well,—in the name of God ? "

Some minutes passed in perfect silence, and anxiety was rapidly turning cheeks and lips pale, when the colour rapidly returned.

There was a gush of clear water from below, bubble rapidly followed bubble, sparkling brightly in the morning sunshine. Full of joy, the young mother rose from her knees, kissed her child, and exclaimed, " I am happy now ! " *

THE WELL OF ST KEYNE.

ST KEYNE came to this well about five hundred years before the Norman Conquest, and imparted a strange virtue to its waters—namely, that whichever of a newly-married couple should first drink thereof, was to enjoy the sweetness of domestic sovereignty ever after.

Situated in a thickly-wooded district, the well of St Keyne presents a singularly picturesque appearance. " Four trees of divers kinds" grow over the well, imparting a delightful shade, and its clear waters spread an emerald luxuriance around. Once, and once only, have I paid a visit to this sacred spot. Then and there I found a lady drinking of the waters from her thimble, and eagerly contending with her husband that the right to rule was hers. The man, however, mildly insisted upon it that he had had the first drink, as he had rushed before his wife, and dipping his fingers into the water had sucked them. This the lady contended was not drinking, and she, I have no doubt, through life had the best of the argument.

Tonkin says, in his " History of Cornwall," " Did it retain this wondrous quality, as it does to this day the shape, I believe there would be to it a greater resort of both sexes than either to Bath or Tunbridge ; for who would not be fond of attaining this longed-for sovereignty ? " He then adds, " Since the writing of this, the trees were blown down by a violent storm, and in their place Mr

---

* Hals, speaking of Gulval Well, thus describes it and its virtues :—"In Fosses Moor part of this manor of Lanesly, in this parish, is that well-known fountain called Gulval Well. To which place great numbers of people, time out of mind, have resorted for pleasure and profit of their health, as the credulous country people do in these days, not only to drink the waters thereof, but to inquire after the life or death of their absent friends , where, being arrived, they demanded the question at the well whether such a person by name be living, in health, sick, or dead. If the party be living and in health, the still quiet water of the well-pit, as soon as the question is demanded, will instantly bubble or boil up as a pot, clear crystalline water , if sick, foul and puddled waters , if the party be dead, it will neither bubble, boil up, nor alter its colour or still motion. However, I can speak nothing of the truth of those supernatural facts from my own sight or experience, but write from the mouths of those who told me they had seen and proved the veracity thereof. Finally, it is a strong and courageous fountain of water, kept neat and clean by an old woman of the vicinity, to accommodate strangers, for her own advantage, by blazing the virtues and divine qualities of those waters."—*Hals*, *quoted by Gilbert, Parochial History of Cornwall,* vol. ii p. 121.

Rashleigh, in whose land it is, has planted two oaks, an ash, and an elm, which thrive well; but the wonderful arch is destroyed " The author can add to this that (as he supposes, owing to the alteration made in the trees) the sovereign virtues of the waters have perished.

Southey's ballad will be remembered by most readers ·—

> "A well there is in the west country,
> And a clearer one never was seen ;
> There is not a wife in the west country
> But has heard of the Well of St Keyne.
>
> "An oak and an elm-tree stand beside,
> And behind doth an ash-tree grow,
> And a willow from the bank above
> Droops to the water below "

It has been already stated that, sitting in St Michael's Chair, on the tower of the church of St Michael's Mount, has the same virtue as the waters of this well ; and that this remarkable power was the gift of the same St Keyne who imparted such wonderful properties to this well.

MADDERN OR MADRON WELL.

> "Plunge thy right hand in St Madron's spring,
> If true to its troth be the palm you bring ;
> But if a false digit thy fingers bear,
> Lay them at once on the burning share."

OF the holy well at St Maddern, Carne * writes thus :—
" It has been contended that a virgin was the patroness of this church—that she was buried at Minster—and that many miracles were performed at her grave. A learned commentator, however, is satisfied that it was St Motran, who was one of the large company that came from Ireland with St Buriana, and he was slain at the mouth of the Hayle ; the body was begged, and afterwards buried here. Near by was the miraculous Well of St Maddern, over which a chapel was built. so sacred was it held. (This chapel was destroyed by the fanaticism of Major Ceely in the days of Cromwell) It stood at no great distance on the moor, and the soil around it was black and boggy, mingled with a gray moorstone. . . .

" The votaries bent awfully and tremblingly over its sedgy bank, and gazed on its clear bosom for a few minutes ere they proved the fatal ordeal , then an imploring look was cast towards the

* " Tales of the West," by the author of " Letters from the East "

figure of St Motran, many a crossing was repeated, and at last the pin or pebble held aloof was dropped into the depth beneath. Often did the rustic beauty fix her eye intently on the bubbles that rose, and broke, and disappeared; for in that moment the lover was lost, or the faithful husband gained. It was only on particular days, however, according to the increase or decrease of the moon, that the hidden virtues of the well were consulted." *

MADRON WELL.

Of this well we have the following notice by William Scawen, Esq, Vice-Warden of the Stannaries. The paper from which we extract it was first printed by Davies Gilbert, Esq., F.R.S., as an appendix to his "Parochial History of Cornwall." Its complete title is, "Observations on an Ancient Manuscript, entitled 'Passio Christo,' written in the Cornish Language, and now preserved in the Bodleian Library; with an Account of the Language, Manners, and Customs of the People of Cornwall, (from a Manuscript in the Library of Thomas Artle, Esq, 1777)".—

"Of St Mardren's Well (which is a parish west to the Mount), a fresh true story of two persons, both of them lame and decrepit, thus recovered from their infirmity. These two persons, after they had applied themselves to divers physicians and chirurgeons, for cure, and finding no success by them, they resorted to St Mardren's Well, and according to the ancient custom which they had heard of, the same which was once in a year—to wit, on Corpus Christi evening—to lay some small offering on the altar there, and to lie on the ground all night, drink of the water there, and in the morning after to take a good draught more, and to take and carry away some of the water, each of them in a bottle, at their departure. This course these two men followed, and within three weeks they found the effect of it, and, by degrees their strength increasing, were able to move themselves on crutches. The year following they took the same course again, after which they were able to go with the help of a stick; and at length one of them, John Thomas, being a fisherman, was, and is at this day, able to follow his fishing craft. The other, whose name was William Cork, was a soldier under the command of my kinsman, Colonel William Godolphin (as he has often told me), was able to perform his duty, and died in the service of his majesty King Charles. But herewith take also this :—

"One Mr Hutchens, a person well known in those parts, and now lately dead, being parson of Ludgvan, a near neighbouring parish to St Mardren's Well, he observed that many of his parishioners often frequented this well superstitiously, for which he reproved them privately, and sometimes publicly, in his sermons; but afterwards he, the said Mr Hutchens, meeting with a woman coming from the well with a bottle in her hand, desired her earnestly that he might drink thereof, being then troubled with colical pains, which accordingly he did, and was eased of his infirmity. The latter story is a full confutation of the former; for, if the taking the water accidently thus prevailed upon the party to his cure, as it is likely it did, then the miracle which was intended to be by the ceremony of lying on the ground and offering is wholly fled, and it leaves the virtue of the water to be the true cause of the cure. And we have here, as in many places

* The tale of "The Legend of Pacorra."·

of the land, great variety of salutary springs, which have diversity of operations, which by natural reason have been found to be productive of good
effects, and not by miracle, as the vain fancies of monks and friars have
been exercised in heretofore."

Bishop Hale, of Exeter, in his "Great Mystery of Godliness," says :—
"Of which kind was that noe less than miraculous cure, which, at St
Maddern's Well, in Cornwall, was wrought upon a poore cripple ; where-
of, besides the attestation of many hundreds of the neighbours, I tooke a
strict and impartial examination in my last triennial visitation there. This
man, for sixteen years, was forced to walke upon his hands, by reason of
the sinews of his leggs were soe contracted that he cold not goe or walke
on his feet, who upon monition in a dream to wash in that well, which
accordingly he did, was suddainly restored to the use of his limbs ; and
I sawe him both able to walk and gett his owne maintenance. I found
here was neither art nor collusion,—the cure done, the author our invisible
God," &c.

In Madron Well—and, I have no doubt, in many others —may be found
frequently the pins which have been dropped by maidens desirous of
knowing "when they were to be married" I once witnessed the whole
ceremony performed by a group of beautiful girls, who had walked on a
May morning from Penzance Two pieces of straw, about an inch long
each, were crossed and the pin run through them. This cross was then
dropped into the water, and the rising bubbles carefully counted, as they
marked the number of years which would pass ere the arrival of the happy
day. This practice also prevailed amongst the visitors to the well at the
foot of Monacuddle Grove, near St Austell.

On approaching the waters, each visitor is expected to throw in a crooked
pin ; and, if you are lucky, you may possibly see the other pins rising from
the bottom to meet the most recent offering. Rags and votive offerings to
the genius of the waters are hung around many of the wells. Mr Couch
says :—"At Madron Well, near Penzance, I observed the custom of hanging rags on the thorns which grew in the enclosure "

Crofton Croker tells us the same custom prevails in Ireland ; and Dr
O'Connor, in his "Travels in Persia," describes the prevalence of this
custom.

Mr Campbell,* on this subject, writes :—" Holy healing wells are common all over the Highlands, and people still leave offerings of pins and
nails, and bits of rag, though few would confess it. There is a well in
Islay where I myself have, after drinking, deposited copper caps amongst
a hoard of pins and buttons, and similar gear, placed in chinks in the
rocks and trees at the edge of the 'Witches' Well.' There is another well
with similar offerings freshly placed beside it. in an island in Loch
Maree, in Ross-shire, and many similar wells are to be found in other
places in Scotland For example, I learn from Sutherland that 'a well in
the Black Isle of Cromarty, near Rosehaugh, has miraculous healing powers.
A country woman tells me, that about forty years ago, she remembers it
being surrounded by a crowd of people every first Tuesday in June, who
bathed and drank of it before sunrise. Each patient tied a string or rag to
one of the trees that overhung it before leaving It was sovereign for
headaches Mr —— remembers to have seen a well here, called Mary's
Well, hung round with votive rags.'"

---

* "Popular Tales of the West Highlands," by J F Campbell. (See page 134, vol ii)

Well-worship is mentioned by Martin. The custom, in his day, in the Hebrides, was to walk south round about the well.

Sir William Betham, in his "Gael and Cymbri" (Dublin : W. Curry, Jun , & Co., 1834), says, at page 235 :—" The Celtæ were much addicted to the worship of fountains and rivers as divinities. They had a deity called Divona, or the river-god "

THE WELL AT ALTAR-NUN.

CURE OF INSANITY.

AMONGST the numerous holy wells which exist in Cornwall, that of Alternon, or Altar-Nun, is the only one, as far as I can learn, which possessed the virtue of curing the insane.

We are told that Saint Nunne or Nuanita was the daughter of an Earl of Cornwall, and the mother of St David ; that the holy well, which is situated about a mile from the cathedral of St David, was dedicated to her ; and that she bestowed on the waters of the Cornish well those remarkable powers, which were not given to the Welsh one, from her fondness for the county of her birth.

Carew, in his "Survey of Cornwall," thus describes the practice :—

" The water running from St Nun's well fell into a square and enclosed walled plot, which might be filled at what depth they listed. Upon this wall was the frantic person put to stand, his back towards the pool, and from thence, with a sudden blow in the breast, tumbled headlong into the pond ; where a strong fellow, provided for the nonce, took him, and tossed him up and down, alongst and athwart the water, till the patient, by foregoing his strength, had somewhat forgot his fury. Then was he conveyed to the church, and certain masses said over him ; upon which handling, if his right wits returned, St Nun had the thanks ; but if there appeared small amendment, he was bowssened again and again, while there remained in him any hope of life or recovery."

The 2d of March is dedicated to St Nun, and the influence of the water is greatly exalted on that day.

Although St Nun's well has been long famous, and the celebrity of its waters extended far, yet there was a belief prevailing amidst the uneducated, that the sudden shock produced by suddenly plunging an insane person into water was most effective in producing a return to reason.

On one occasion, a woman of weak mind, who was suffering under the influence of a religious monomania, consulted me on the benefit she might hope to receive from electricity. The burden of her ever-melancholy tale was, that " she had lost her God ; " and she told me, with a strange mixture of incoherence and reason, that her conviction was, that a sudden shock would cure her. She had herself proposed to her husband and fiiends that they should take her to a certain rock on St Michael's Mount, stand her on it, with her back to the sea, when " the waters were the strongest, at the flowing of the tide ; " and after having prayed with her, give her the necessary blow on the chest, and thus plunge her into the waters below. I know not that the experiment was ever made in the case of this poor woman, but I have heard of several instances where this sudden plunge had been tried as a cure for insanity.

Mr. T. Q. Couch thus describes the present condition of this well in a paper on " Well-Worship ; "—*

" On the western side of the beautiful valley through which flows the Trelawney River, and near Hobb's Park, in the parish of Pelynt, Cornwall, is St Nun's, or St Ninnie's Well. Its position was, until lately, to be discovered by the oak-tree matted with ivy, and the thicket of willow and bramble which grew upon its roof. The front of the well is of a pointed form, and has a rude entrance about four feet high, and spanned above by a single flat stone, which leads into a grotto with arched roof. The walls on the interior are draped with luxuriant fronds of spleenwort, hart's-tongue, and a rich undercovering of liverwort. At the further end of the floor is a round granite basin, with a deeply moulded brim, and ornamented on its circumference with a series of rings, each enclosing a cross or a ball. The water weeps into it from an opening at the back, and escapes again by a hole in the bottom. This interesting piece of antiquity has been protected by a tradition which we could wish to attach to some of our cromlechs and circles in danger of spoliation."

According to the narrative given by Mr Bond in his " History of Looe," the sacred protection given must have been limited in time, as the following story will prove :—

" KIPPISCOMBE LANE,

Probably so called from a consecrated well on the right hand side of the road. The titular saint of this well is supposed to have been St Cuby, now corrupted into Keby's Well. The spring flows into a circular basin or reservoir of granite, or of some stone like it, two feet four inches at its extreme diameter at top, and about two feet high. It appears to have been neatly carved and ornamented in its lower part with the figure of a griffin, and round the edge with dolphins, now much defaced The water was formerly

* Notes and Queries.

carried off by a drain or hole at the bottom, like those usually seen in fonts and piscinas. This basin (which I take to be an old font) was formerly much respected by the neighbours, who conceived some great misfortune would befall the person who should attempt to remove it from where it stood, and that it required immense power to remove it. A daring fellow, however (says a story), once went with a team of oxen for the express purpose of removing it. On his arrival at the spot, one of the oxen fell down dead, which so alarmed the fellow that he desisted from the attempt he was about to make. There are several loose stones scattered round this basin or reservoir, perhaps the remains of some building which formerly enclosed it—a small chapel likely. The last time I saw this reservoir, it had been taken many feet from where it used to stand, and a piece of the brim of it had been recently struck off."

ST GUNDRED'S WELL AT ROACH ROCK.

CAREW, in his " Survey of Cornwall," p. 139 (p. 324, Lord Dunstanville's edit.), tells us, " near this rock there is another which, having a pit in it, containeth water which ebbs and flows as the sea does. I was thereupon very curious to inspect this matter, and found it was only a hole artificially cut in a stone, about twelve inches deep and six broad ; wherein after rain, a pool of water stands, which afterwards with fair weather vanisheth away, and is dried up ; and then again, on the falling of rain, water is replenished accordingly, which with dry weather abates as aforesaid (for upon those occasions I have seen it to have water in its pit, and again to be without it), which doubtless gave occasion to the feigned report that it ebbs and flows as the sea ." of all which premisses thus speaks Mr Carew further, out of the Cornish " Wonder Gatherer ".—

> " You neighbour scorners, holy, proud,
>   Goe people Roache's cell,
>   Far from the world and neer to the heavens;
>   There hermitts may you dwell.
>
> " Is 't true the springe in rock hereby
>   Doth tidewise ebb and flowe ?
>   Or have we fooles with lyars met ?
>   Fame says it 's ; be it soe."

The last tradition of this hermitage chapel is, that when it was kept in repair, a person diseased with a grievous leprosy was either placed or fixed himself therein, where he lived until the time of his death, to avoid infecting others. He was daily attended with meat, drink, and washing by his daughter, named Gunnett or Gundred, and the well hereby from whence she fetched water for his use is to this day shown, and called by the name of St Gunnett's Well, or St Gundred's Well.

It is not possible to give even the names of the wells which are still thought to have "some healing virtue" in them. The typical wells have alone been mentioned ; and to these brief notices of a few others may be added.

ST CUTHBERT'S OR CUBERT'S WELL.

HAL thus describes this famous place :—"In this parish is that famous and well-known spring of water called Holy-well (so named, the inhabitants say, for that the virtues of this water was first discovered on All-hallows day). The same stands in a dark cavern of the sea-cliff rocks, beneath full sea-mark on spring tides, from the top of which cavern falls down or distils continually drops of water from the white, blue, red, and green veins of those rocks. And accordingly, in the place where those drops of water fall, it swells to a lump of considerable bigness, and there petrifies to the hardness of ice, glass, or freestone, of the several colours aforesaid, according to the nature of those veins in the rock from whence it proceeds, and is of a hard, brittle nature, apt to break like glass.

"The virtues of this water are very great. It is incredible what numbers in summer season frequent this place and waters from counties far distant." *

RICKETY CHILDREN.

THE practice of bathing rickety children on the first three Wednesdays in May is still far from uncommon in the out-lying districts of Cornwall The parents will walk many miles for the purpose of dipping the little sufferers in some well, from which the "healing virtue" has not entirely departed. Among these holy wells, Cubert, just named, is far-famed. To this well the peasantry still resort, firm in the faith that there, at this especial season, some mysterious virtue is communicated to its waters. On these occasions, only a few years since, the crowd assembled was so large, that it assumed the character of a fair.

* Gilbert, vol i.,p. 291.

CHAPELL UNY.

ON the first three Wednesdays in May, children suffering from mesenteric diseases are dipped three times in this well, *against the sun*, and *dragged* three times around the well on the grass, in the same direction.

PERRAN WELL.

CHILDREN were cured of several diseases by being bathed in this well. They were also carried to the sea-shore, and passed through a cleft in a rock on the shore at Perranzabalo. In the autumn of 1863 I sought for these holy waters. I was informed that some miners, in driving an adit, had tapped the spring and drained it. There is not, therefore, a trace of this once most celebrated well remaining. It was with difficulty that its site could be discovered. I have since learned that the cut stone-work which ornamented this holy place, was removed to Chiverton, for the purpose of preserving it.

REDRUTH WELL.

NO child christened in this well has ever been hanged. Saint Ruth, said to have been called Red Ruth, because she always wore a scarlet cloak, especially blessed, to this extent, those waters. I believe the population in this large parish cares but little now whether their children be baptized with this well water or any other; but, half a century since, it was very different. Then, many a parent would insist on seeing the water taken from the well and carried to the font in the church.

HOLY WELL AT LITTLE CONAN.

ON Palm Sunday the people resorted to the well sacred to "Our Lady of Nants," with a cross of palm, and after making the priest a present, they were allowed to throw the cross into the well; if it swam the thrower was to outlive the year, if it sank he was not.*

THE PRESERVATION OF HOLY WELLS.

IT is a very common notion amongst the peasantry, that a just retribution overtakes those who wilfully destroy monuments, such as stone circles, crosses, wells, and the like. Mr Blight

* Carew.

writes me——" Whilst at Boscaswell, in St Just, a few weeks since, an old man told me that a person who altered an old Holy Well there, was drowned the next day in sight of his home, and that a person who carried away the stones of an ancient chapel, had his house burned down that very night." We hope the certainty of punishment will prevent any further spoliation. Cannot we do something towards the preservation of our antiquities? I quote from a local paper the following :——

"If the attention of the members of the Penzance Antiquarian Society were directed to the state of the 'Holy Well' at Laneast, and the remains of the Old Chapel Park, St Clether, they might perhaps induce the proprietors of these 'remnants of antiquity' to bestow a little care on the same, and arrest their further ruin and destruction. Many other 'objects of interest' are in a sad state of neglect, and fast 'fading away.' Slaughter Bridge, near Camelford, has completely vanished. This is much to be regretted, and is a double loss—first, to those who delight in these 'memorials of the past,' and also to the town and neighbourhood, depriving them of an attraction that has induced many strangers of taste to pay them a visit."

KING ARTHUR.

"There is a place within
    The winding shore of Severne sea
On mids of rock, about whose foote
    The tydes turne—keeping play.
A towery-topped castle here,
    Wide blazeth over all,
Which Corineus ancient broode
    Tintagel Castle call "

Old Poet—Translated by CAMDEN.

ROMANCES OF ARTHUR.

ARTHUR LEGENDS.

" For there was no man knew from whence he came;
But after tempest, when the long wave broke
All down the thundering shores of Bude and Boss,
There came a day as still as heaven, and then
They found a naked child upon the sands
Of wild Dundagil by the Cornish sea;
And that was Arthur "

Idyls of the King—TENNYSON.

THE scarcity of traditions connected with King Arthur is not a little remarkable in Cornwall, where he is said to have been born, and where we believe him to have been killed. In the autumn of last year (1863) I visited Tintagel and Camelford. I sought with anxiety for some stories of the British king, but not one could be obtained The man who has charge of the ruins of the castle was very sorry that he had lent a book which he once had, and which contained many curious stories, but he had no story to tell me.

We hear of Prince Arthur at the Land's-End, and of his fights with the Danes in two or three other places. Merlin, who may be considered as especially associated with Arthur, has left indications of his presence here and there, in prophetic rhymes not always fulfilled ; but of Arthur's chieftains we have no folk-lore. All the rock markings, or rock peculiarities, which would in West Cornwall have been given to the giants, are referred to King Arthur in the eastern districts.

Jack the Giant Killer and Thomas Thumb—the former having been tutor, in his own especial calling, to King Arthur's only son,[*] and the latter the king's favourite dwarf [†]—are, except in story-

---

[*] "Popular Rhymes and Nursery Tales," by James O Halliwell.

[†] See "Thomas of the Thumb, or *Tómas na h'ordaig*," Tale lxix. " Popular Tales of the West Highlands," by J F Campbell.

books, unknown. Jack Hornby,*—if he ever lived near the Land's-End, unless he is the same with " Little Jack Horner,"—has been so long a stranger, that his name is forgotten.

The continuance of a fixed belief in the existence of Arthur is easily explained.   The poets and the romance writers have made the acheivements of a British chieftain familiar to all the people ; and Arthur has not only a name, but a local habitation, given to him equally in Scotland, England, Wales, and Ireland.

Mr Campbell, in his " West Highland Tales," gives a " Genealogy Abridgment of the very ancient and noble family of Argyle, 1779 " The writer says this family began with Constantine, grandfather to King Arthur ; and he informs us that Sir Moroie Mor, a son of King Arthur, of whom great and strange things are told in the Irish Traditions—who was born at Dumbarton Castle, and who was usually known as " The Fool of the Forest"—was the real progenitor of " Mac Callen Mor,"   From this Moroie Mor was derived the mighty Diarmaid, celebrated in many a Gaelic lay —" to whom all popular traditions trace the Campbell clan."

" Arthur and Diarmaid," writes Mr Campbell, " primeval Celtic worthies, whose very existence the historian ignores, are thus brought together by a family genealogist."

" Was the Constantine grandfather to Arthur one of the five tyrants named by Gildas ? "—I quote from Camden† and Milton ‡

Constantinus. son of Cador, Duke of Cornwall, Arthur's half-brother by the mother's side, " a tyrannical and bloody king."

Aurelius Conanus, who " wallowed in murder and adultery."

Vortipore, " tyrant of the Dimeta."

Cuneglas, " the yellow butcher."

Maglocunes, " the island dragon."

It is curious to find a Scotch genealogist uniting in one bond the Arthur of Dundagel and the ancestors of the Argyles of Dumbarton.

May we not after this venture to suggest that, in all probability, the parish of Constantine (pronounced, however, *Cus-ten-ton*), between Helstone and Penryn, may derive its name from this Constantinus, rather than from the first Christian emperor ?

Again, the family of Cossentine has been often said to be offsets

---

* "Popular Rhymes and Nursery Tales," by James O Halliwell

† Camden's " Britannica," by Gough, vol 1 , p 139   From this author we do not learn much.   Indeed he says—"As to that Constantine, whom Gildas calls ' that tyrannical whelp of the impure Danmonian lioness,' and of the disforesting of the whole country under King John, before whose time it was all forest, let historians tell—it is not to my purpose."—Vol. i p 8.

‡ Milton's " History of Britain," edit. 1678, p. 155.

from Constantine, the descendant of the Greek emperors, who was buried in Landulph Church. Seeing that the name has been known for so long a period in Cornwall, may not this family rather trace their origin up to this Constantine the Tyrant?

THE BATTLE OF VELLAN-DRUCHAR.*

THE Sea Kings, in their predatory wanderings, landed in Genvor Cove, and, as they had frequently done on previous occasions, they proceeded to pillage the little hamlet of Escols. On one occasion they landed in unusally large numbers, being resolved, as it appeared, to spoil many of the large and wealthy towns of Western Cornwall, which they were led to believe were unprotected. It fortunately happened that the heavy surf on the beach retarded their landing, so that the inhabitants had notice of their threatened invasion.

That night the beacon-fire was lit on the chapel hill, another was soon blazing on Castle-an-Dinas, and on Trecrobben. Carn Brea promptly replied, and continued the signal-light, which also blazed lustrously that night on St Agnes Beacon. Presently the fires were seen on Belovely Beacon, and rapidly they appeared on the Great Stone, on St Bellarmine's Tor, and Cadbarrow, and then the fires blazed out on Roughtor and Brownwilly, thus rapidly conveying the intelligence of war to Prince Arthur and his brave knights, who were happily assembled in full force at Tintagel to do honour to several native Princes who were at that time on a visit to the King of Cornwall. Arthur, and nine other kings, by forced marches, reached the neighbourhood of the Land's-End at the end of two days. The Danes crossed the land down through the bottoms to the sea on the northern side of the promontory, spreading destruction in their paths. Arthur met them on their return, and gave them battle near Vellan-Druchar. So terrible was the slaughter, that the mill was worked with blood that day. Not a single Dane of the vast army that had landed escaped. A few had been left in charge of the ships, and as soon as they learned the fate of their brethren, they hastened to escape, hoping to return to their own northern land. A holy woman, whose name has not been preserved to us, "brought home a west wind" by emptying the Holy Well against the hill, and sweeping the church from the door to the altar. Thus they were prevented from escaping, and were all thrown by the force of a storm and the currents either on the rocky shore, or on the sands, where they

* Vellan (mill), druchar (wheel)

U

were left high and dry. It happened on the occasion of an extra-ordinary spring-tide, which was yet increased by the wind, so that the ships lay high up on the rocks, or on the sands; and for years the birds built their nests in the masts and rigging.

Thus perished the last army of Danes who dared to land upon our western shores.

King Arthur and the nine kings pledged each other in the holy water from St Sennen's Well, they returned thanks for their victory in St Sennen's Chapel, and dined that day on the Table-men.

Merlin, the prophet, was amongst the host, and the feast being ended, he was seized with the prophetic afflatus, and in the hearing of all the host proclaimed—

> " The northmen wild once more shall land,
> And leave their bones on Escol's sand.
> The soil of Vellan-Druchar's plain
> Again shall take a sanguine stain ;
> And o'er the mill-wheel roll a flood
> Of Danish mix'd with Cornish blood.
> When thus the vanquish'd find no tomb,
> Expect the dreadful day of doom "

ARTHUR AT THE LAND'S-END.

BOLERIUM, or *Bellerium*, is the name given by the ancients to the Land's-End. Diodorus writes Belerium , Ptolemy, Bolerium. Milton adopts this name in his " Lycidas," and leads his readers to infer that it was derived from the Giant Bellerus. It is quite possible that in Milton's time the name of one of the numerous giants who appear to have made the Land's-End district their dwelling-place, might have still lived in the memories of men. Certain it is no such giant is remembered now.[*]

In a map of Saxon England we find the Land's-End called Penn ᵭᵲᶜᵉᵱᵵ, and in some early English books this promontory is named *Penrhin-guard*, and *Penrhen-gard*, said to signify the " Headland of Blood." [†] The old Cornish people called this promontory " Pen-von-las," the " End of the Earth," hence we derive the name of the Land's-End. May not this sanguinary name have been derived from a fact, and that actually several battles were fought by the Britons under the command of Arthur,

---

[*] Carew says, 'a promontory (by *Pomp Mela*, called Bolerium : by *Diodorus*, Velerium , by *Volaterane*, Helenium , by the Cornish, Pedn an laaz , and by the English, the Land's-End) "—*Survey of Cornwall*

[†] Penn ᵭᵲᶜᵉᵱᵵ.—The name of the Land's End in the Saxon map , in the text, Camden prints Pennihtᵲᵲᵉᶘᵱᵵ.

with the Saxons or the Danes, in this neighbourhood? We have not far off the *Field of Slaughter,* "Bollait," where the ancient people of Cornwall made their final stand against the Saxons. On this field flint arrow-heads have frequently been found. The tradition of Vellan-Druchar, which is but one of several I have heard of a similar character, points to the same idea. Arthur, according to one story, held possession of Trereen Castle for some time. Another castle on the north coast is said to have been occupied by him. An old man living in Pendean once told me that the land at one time "swarmed with giants, until Arthur, the good king, vanished them all with his cross-sword."

TRADITIONS OF THE DANES IN CORNWALL.

THE Danes are said to have landed in several places around the coast, and have made permanent settlements in some parts. We have already spoken of the battle of Vellan-Druchar. In Sennen Cove there was for a long period a colony of red-haired people,—indeed, I am informed some of them still live on the spot,—with whom the other inhabitants of the district refused to marry. Up to a very recent period, in several of the outlying villages, a red-haired family was "looked down" upon. "Oh, he or she is a red-haired Daäne," was a common expression of contempt.

There are several hills which bear the names of Danes' Castles —as Castle-an-Dinas, near Penzance, and another in St Columb * Another very remarkable earthwork in Perran-Zabula (*Caer-Dane*) is described by Hals.†

* "CASTLE-AN-DINAS.—In the parish of Colomb Major stands a castle of this name. Near this castle, by the highway, stands the Coyt, a stony tumulus so called, of which sort there are many in Wales and Wiltshire, as is mentioned in the 'Additions to Camden's Britannia,' in these places, commonly called the Devil's Coyts It consists of four long stones of great bigness, perpendicularly pitched in the earth contiguous with each other, leaving only a small vacancy downwards, but meeting together at the top, over all which is laid a flat stone of prodigious bulk and magnitude, bending towards the east in way of adoration (as Mr Lhuyd concludes of all those Coyts elsewhere), as the person therein under it interred did when in the land of the living, but how or by what art this prodigious flat stone should be placed on the top of the others, amazeth the wisest mathematicians, engineers, or architects to tell or conjecture Colt, in Belgic-British, is a cave, vault or cott-house, of which coyt might possibly be a corruption "—*Gilbert's Parochial History*

† In the Manor of Lambourn is an ancient barrow, called Cieeg Mear, the Great Barrow, which was cut open by a labourer in search of stones to build a hedge He came upon a small hollow, in which he found nine urns filled with ashes, the man broke them, supposing they were only old pitchers, good for nothing, but Tonkin, who saw them,

Eventually the Danes are said to have made permanent settlements in Cornwall, and to have lived on friendly terms with the Britons.

The Danes and the Cornish are reported to have concentrated their forces to oppose Egbert the Saxon. In 835 the combined body are reported to have met, and fought a pitched battle on Hengistendane (now Hengistondown), near Callington. The Cornish were so totally routed, that Egbert obliged the Danes to retire to their ships, and passed a law "that no Briton should in future cross the Tamar, or set foot on English ground, on pain of death." *

In 997 the Danes, sailing about Penwrith-steort, landed in several places, foraged the country, burnt the towns, and destroyed the people.†

Many of the traditions which are given in different parts of these volumes have much of the Danish element in them ‡

KING ARTHUR IN THE FORM OF A CHOUGH.

I QUOTE the following as it stands :—§

"In Jarvis's translation of 'Don Quixote,' book ii. chap. v., the following passage occurs :—

"'Have you not read, sir,' answered Don Quixote, 'the annals and histories of England, wherein are recorded the famous exploits of King Arthur, whom, in our Castilian tongue, we always call King Artus, of whom there goes an old tradition, and a common one, all over that kingdom of Great Britain, that this king did not die, but that, by magic art, he was turned into a raven, and that, in process of time, he shall reign again and recover his kingdom and sceptre, for which reason it cannot be proved that, from that time to this, any Englishmen has killed a raven?'

believes them to have been Danish, containing the ashes of some chief commanders slain in battle, and, says he, on a small hill just under this barrow is a Danish encampment, called Castle Caer Dane, *vulgo* Castle Caer Don,—*i e*, the Danes' Camp,—consisting of three entrenchments finished, and another begun, with an intent to surround the inner three, but not completed ; and opposite to this, about a bowshot, the river only running between, on another hill is another camp or castle, called Castle Kaerkief, castrum simile, from Kyfel similis, alike alluding to Castle Caer Dane. But this is but just begun, and not finished in any part, from which I guess there were two different parties, the one attacking the other before the entrenchments were finished.

* C S Gilbert's Historical Survey   † Gilbert.

‡ See Popular Tales from the Norse By George Webbe Dasent, D C L Legends of Iceland, collected by Jón Arnason. Translated by George E J Powell and Eiríkur Magnússo

§ *Note and Queries*, vol viii p 618.

" My reason for transcribing this passage is to record the curious fact that the legend of King Arthur's existence in the form of a raven was still repeated as a piece of folk-lore in Cornwall about sixty years ago. My father, who died about two years since, at the age of eighty, spent a few years of his youth in the neighbourhood of Penzance. One day he was walking along Marazion Green with his fowling-piece on his shoulder, he saw a raven at a distance, and fired at it. An old man who was near immediately rebuked him, telling him that he ought on no account to have shot at a raven, for that King Arthur was still alive in the form of that bird. My father was much interested when I drew his attention to the passage which I have quoted above.

" Perhaps some of your Cornish or Welsh correspondents may be able to say whether the legend is still known among the people of Cornwall or Wales.   EDGAR MACCULLOCH.

"GUERNSEY."

I have been most desirous of discovering if any such legend as the above exists. I have questioned people in every part of Cornwall in which King Arthur has been reported to have dwelt or fought, and especially have I inquired in the neighbourhood of Tintagel, which is reported to have been Arthur's stronghold. Nowhere do I find the raven associated with him, but I have been told that bad luck would follow the man who killed a Chough, for Arthur was transformed into one of these birds.

THE CORNISH CHOUGH.

THE tradition relative to King Arthur and his transformation into a raven, is fixed very decidedly on the Cornish Chough, from the colour of its beak and talons. The—

"Talons and beak all red with blood"

are said to mark the violent end to which this celebrated chieftain came.

SLAUGHTER BRIDGE.

HISTORIANS and poets have made the world familiar with King Arthur. We know how Merlin deceived, by his magic, the beautiful Igerna, so that she received King Uter as her husband. We know also that Uter Pendragon died, and that his son, by Igerna, reigned King of Britain. How Arthur ruled, and how he slaughtered all the enemies of Britain, is told in the chronicles. But even at Tintagel * all is silent respecting the king or his celebrated Round Table.

"In the days of King Arthur the Mount of Cornwall was kept by a monstrous giant," is familiar to us all; and it is curious to find a tradition that the extirpation of these Titans was due to Arthur and Christianity, as already related. At Slaughter Bridge I heard the story, but it did not sound like a tradition; the true native character was not in the narrative,—That in 824 the Cornish and Saxons fought so bloody a battle that the river ran red with blood. On Slaughter Bridge Arthur is said to have killed his nephew, Modred, but that, previously to this last fight, Modred wounded his uncle with a poisoned sword, nearly in front of Worthyvale House. A single stone laid over a stream, having some letters cut on its lower surface, is believed to mark the exact spot where Arthur received his death-wound.

CAMELFORD AND KING ARTHUR.

AT the head of this river Alan is seated Camelford, otherwise written Gallefold, a small town. It was formerly called Kambton, according to Leland, who tells us that "Arthur, the British Hector," was slain here, or in the valley near it. He adds, in support of this, that "pieces of armour, rings, and brass furniture for horses are sometimes digged up here by the countrymen; and after so many ages, the tradition of a bloody victory in this place is still preserved" There are also extant some verses of a Middle Age poet about "Camels" running with blood after the battle of Arthur against Modred.†

"Camulus is another name of the god of war, occurring in two of Gruter's inscriptions." ‡

Seeing that Arthur's great battles were fought near this town, and on the banks of the river, may not the names given to the town and river be derived from Camulus?

* " I shall offer a conjecture touching the name of this place, which I will not say is right, but only probable. *Tin* is the same as *Din, Dinas,* and *Di reth,* deceit, so that *Tindixel,* turned, for easier pronunciation, to *Tintagel, Dindagel,* or *Daundagel,* signifies *Castle of Deceit,* which name might be aptly given to it from the famous deceit practised here by Uter Pendragon by the help of Merlin's enchantment "—*Tonkin.*

"Mr Hals says this place is called *Donechenzv* in 'Domesday Survey' *Dunechine* would mean the fortress of the chasm, corresponding precisely with its situation "— *Davies Gilbert*

† Gilbert, vol ii p 402, *et seq.*

‡ Gruter's Collection of Ancient Inscriptions, quoted by J C Pritchard

" O'er Cornwall's cliffs the tempest roar'd,
High the screaming sea-mew soar'd ;
On Tintagel's topmost tower
Darksome fell the sleety shower ;
Round the rough castle shrilly sung
The whirling blast, and wildly flung
On each tall rampart's thundering side
The surges of the tumbling tide :
When Arthur ranged his red cross ranks
On conscious Camlan's crimson'd banks."
The Grave of King Arthur—WHARTON.

In a Welsh poem it is recited that Arthur, after the battle of
Camlan in Cornwall, was interred in the Abbey of Glastonbury,
before the high altar, without any external mark. Henry II. is
said to have visited the abbey, and to have ordered that the spot
described by the bard should be opened We are told that at
twenty feet deep they found the body deposited under a large stone,
with Arthur's name inscribed thereon.

Glastonbury Abbey is said to have been founded by Joseph of
Arimathea, in a spot anciently called the island or valley of Avolnia
or Avolon.

Bale, in his " Acts of English Votaries," attests to the finding of
the remains of Arthur :—

" In Avallon, anno 1191, there found they the flesh bothe of
Arthur and of hys wyfe Guenever turned all into duste, wythin
theyr coffines of strong oke, the bones only remaynynge. A monke
of the same abbeye, standyng and behouldyng the fine broydinges
of the wommanis heare as *yellow as golde* there still to remayne.
As a man ravyshed, or more than halfe from his wyttes, he leaped
into the graffe, xv fote depe, to have caugte them sodenlye. But
he fayled of his purpose. For so soon as they were touched they
fell all to powder."

DAMELIOCK CASTLE.

THIS ancient British castle once stood in savage grandeur a
rival to Tintagel Its ruins, which can scarcely be traced,
are in the parish of St Tudy. Here Gothlois of the Purple Spear,
Earl of Cornwall, fortified himself against Uter Pendragon's soldiery,
and here he was slain. Gothlois, or Gothlouis, was the husband
of Igerna, who was so cruelly deceived by Uter, and who became
the mother of Arthur.

CARLIAN IN KEA.

ONE of the most celebrated of Arthur's knights, Sir Tristram, is said to have been born in this parish. A tradition of this is preserved in the parish, but it is probably derived from the verses of Thomas of Erceldoune, better known as Thomas the Rhymer.

SORCERY AND WITCHCRAFT.

" And, wow! Tam saw an unco sight—
Warlocks and witches in a dance."
Tam o' Shanter— Burns.

ROMANCES OF WITCHES, ETC.

THE "CUNNING MAN."

"And as he rode over the more,
  Hee see a lady where shee sate
  Betwixt an oke and a greene hollen ;
  She was cladd in red scarlett.

"Then there as sho'd have stood her mouth,
  Then there was sett her eye ,
  The other was in her forehead fast,
  The way that she might see

"Her nose was crook'd and turn'd outward,
  Her mouth stood foule awry ,
  A worse-form'd lady then shee was,
  Never man saw with his eye "
                    The Marriage of Sir Gawaine.

THAT a deep-rooted belief in the power of the witch still
lingers in the remote districts of Cornwall, cannot be denied.
A gentleman, who has for many years been actively engaged in a
public capacity, gives me, in reply to some questions which I put
to him relative to a witch or conjurer, much information, which is
embodied in this section.

A "cunning man" was long resident in Bodmin, to whom the
people from all parts of the country went to be relieved of spells,
under the influence of which either themselves or their cattle were
supposed to be suffering. Thomas ——, who resided at Nans-
tallan, not far from the town of Bodmin, was waylaid, robbed, and
well thrashed on his way home from market. This act, which
was accompanied by some appearance of brutality, was generally
referred to one of the dupes of his cunning. Howbeit, Thomas
—— appears to have felt that the place was getting too hot for
him, for he migrated to one of the parishes on the western side of
the Fowey river. Numerous instances are within my knowledge
of the belief which existed amongst the peasantry that this man
really possessed the power of removing the effects of witchcraft.

Thomas —— took up his abode for some time with a small farmer, who had lost some cattle. These losses were attributed to the malign influences of some evil-disposed person ; but as Thomas —— failed to detect the individual, he with the farmer made many journeys to Exeter, to consult the " White Witch," who resided in that city. Whether the result was satisfactory or otherwise, I have never learned. Thomas ——, it must be remembered, was only a " witch." The term is applied equally to men as to women. I never heard any uneducated person speak of a "wizard." There appears to be, however, some very remarkable distinctions between a male and a female witch. The former is almost always employed to remove the evil influences exerted by the latter. Witches, such as Thomas, had but limited power They could tell who had been guilty of ill-wishing, but they were powerless to break the spell and " unbewitch " the sufferer. This was frequently accomplished by the friends of the bewitched, who, in concert with Thomas ——, would perform certain ceremonies, many of them of an obscene, and usually of a blasphemous character. The " White Witch " was supposed to possess the higher power of removing the spell, and of punishing the individual by whose wickedness the wrong had been inflicted.

Jenny Harris was a reputed witch. This woman, old, poor, and, from the world's ill-usage, rendered malicious, was often charged with the evils which fell upon cattle, children, or, indeed, on men and women. On one occasion, a robust and rough-handed washerwoman, who conceived that she was under the spell of Jenny Harris, laid violent hands on the aged crone, being resolved to " bring blood from her." The witch's arm was scratched and gouged from the elbow to the wrist, so that a sound inch of skin did not exist. This violent assault became the subject of inquiry before the magistrates, who fined the washerwoman five pounds for the assault.

My correspondent writes :—" I was also present at a magistrates' meeting at the Porcupine Inn, near Tywardreath, some years ago, when an old woman from Golant was brought up for witchcraft. One farmer, who appeared against her, stated that he had then six bullocks hanging up in chains in his orchard, and he attributed their disease and death to the poor old woman's influence. The case was dismissed, but it afforded a good deal of merriment. There was a dinner at the inn after the meeting, and some of the farmers present were disposed to ridicule the idea of witchcraft. I said, well knowing their real views and opinions, ' Gentleman, it is all well enough to laugh, but it appears to me to be a serious matter.' Upon which Mr ——, a farmer of ——, said, 'You are right, Mr ——; I'll tell of two cases in which one family suffered severely,' and he gave us the details of the cases. All the others present had a case or two, each one within his own experience to vouch for, and the whole afternoon was spent telling witch stories."

The extent to which this belief was carried within a comparatively recent period, may be inferred from the fact that, on one occasion when the visitors were assembled at the county asylum, a man residing at Callington came with the mother of a poor imbecile patient, and sent his card to the boardroom. This was inscribed with his name and M A. Upon being asked how he became a Master of Arts, he replied that he was a "Master of Black Arts." The object of this fellow's visit was, having persuaded the mother of his power, to propose to the visitors that they should place the imbecile girl in his care, upon his undertaking, on their paying him five pounds, to cure her. Of course this was not listened to. This fellow imposed upon people to such an extent that he was eventually tried at the sessions, under an almost forgotten Act of Parliament, for witchcraft. The impression on the mind of my informant is that the case broke down.

NOTES ON WITCHCRAFT.

IN confirmation of the melancholy facts related of the continuance of the belief in witchcraft, I would give the accompanying cuttings from the *West Briton* newspaper of a very recent date :—

GROSS SUPERSTITION.

"During the week ending Sunday last, a 'wise man' from Illogan has been engaged with about half-a-dozen witchcraft cases, one a young tradesman, and another a sea-captain. It appears that the 'wise man' was in the first place visited at his home by these deluded people at different times, and he declared the whole of them to be spell-bound In one case he said that if the person had not come so soon, in about a fortnight he would have been in the asylum ; another would have had his leg broken ; and in every case something very direful would have happened. Numerous incantations have been performed. In the case of a captain of a vessel, a visit was paid to the sea-side, and while the 'wise man' uttered some unintelligible gibberish, the captain had to throw a stone into the sea. So heavy was the spell under which he laboured, and which immediately fell upon the 'wise man,' that the latter pretended that he could scarcely walk back to Hayle. The most abominable part of the incantations is performed during the hours of midnight, and for that purpose the wretch sleeps with his victims, and for five nights following he had five different bed fellows   Having no doubt reaped a pretty good harvest during the week, he returned to his home on Monday ; but such was the pretended effect produced by the different spells and witchcraft that tell upon him from his many dupes, that two of the young men who had been under his charge were obliged to obtain a horse and cart and carry him to the Hayle station.   One of the men, having had 'two spells' resting on him, the 'wise man' was obliged to sleep with him on Saturday and Sunday nights, having spent the whole of the Sunday in his diabolical work.   It is time that the police, or some other higher authorities, should take the matter up, as the person alluded to is well known, and frequently visited by the ignorant and superstitious."

THE CASE OF GROSS SUPERSTITION AT HAYLE.

" In the *West Briton* of the 27th ult. we gave some particulars of several cases of disgraceful fraud and delusion which had been practised by a pretended 'wise man' from Illogan, and of gross superstition and gullibility on the part of his dupes.   A correspondent has furnished us with the following particulars relative to the antecedents of the pretended conjurer. He states that James Thomas, the conjurer from the parish of Illogan, married some time since the late celebrated Tammy Blee, of Redruth, who afterwards removed to Helston and carried on as a fortune-teller, but parted from her husband, James Thomas, on account of a warrant for his apprehension having been issued against him by the magistrates of St Ives, for attempting to take a spell from Mrs Paynter, through her husband, William Paynter, who stated before the magistrates that he wanted to commit a disgraceful offence.   Thomas then absconded, and was absent from the west of Cornwall for upwards of two years.   His wife then stated that the virtue was in her and not in him , that she was of the real ' Pellar ' blood ; and that he could tell nothing but through her   His greatest dupes have been at St Just and Hayle, and other parts of the west of Cornwall. He has been in the habit of receiving money annually for keeping witchcraft from vessels sailing out of Hayle   He slept with several of his dupes recently ; and about a fortnight since he stated that he must sleep with certain young men at Copperhouse, Hayle, in order to protect them from something that was hanging over them, one of them being a mason and another a miner, the two latter lately from St Just.   He said himself 'his week at Truro that he had cured a young man of St Erth, and was going on Saturday again to take a spell from the father, a tin-smelter.   He has caused a great disturbance amongst the neighbours, by charging some with having bewitched others.   He is a drunken, disgraceful, beastly fellow, and ought to be sent to the treadmill.   One of the young men is now thoroughly ashamed of himself to think he has been duped so by this scoundrel.   We have purposely withheld the names of a number of Thomas's egregious dupes, with which our correspondent has furnished us, believing that the badgering which they have doubtless received from their friends has proved a sufficient punishment to them, and that their eyes are now thoroughly opened to the gross and disgraceful imposture that has been practised upon them."

The following is from the *Western Morning News :—*

CALLING A WOMAN A WITCH.

" At the Liskeard police court, on Monday, Harriet King appeared before the sitting magistrates charged with an assault on Elizabeth Welling-ton. The complainant had called the mother of defendant a witch, and said she had ill-wished a person, and the ill wish fell on the cat, and the cat died. This annoyed the daughter, who retaliated by bad words and blows. The magistrates expressed surprise at the cause of the assault, but as that had been proved, they fined defendant 1s. and the costs, £1 in all."

ILL-WISHING.

I GIVE the following notices as I receive them :—"I caant altogether exackly bleve in wiches at al," said a good dame to us ; "but this I can tell ee, our John's wife quarrelled once with her next door neighbor's wife, and when John come home, like a husband always should, he took up for his wife, 'northin but nat'r'l chiel was a.' Well, the woman took a nif, and for a long time never spoke to our John ; at laast, after a bit, she used to speak to un, and like as if a was all over, and she used to speak quite sochebl' like. Well, John alleas was very well when he used to meet her, but as soon as ever he got underground, he was tooken ill to wonce ; when a dedn't meet her, a was well enuf. Well, John was advised to go to the 'Peller,' and off he went to Helstun sure nuf, and the 'Peller,' towld un to come so many times in three months, and do something anorther, and towld un who a was that hoverlooked un, and a was that vere woman. Well, the 'Peller' towld John that if a dedn't do it, a would very likely die sudden. Our John, dear fellow, came home, and got unbelieving, and dedn't do as a was towld. Wat was the konsi-kense? Why, in less than three months a was a dead man. Not as I believe the woman 's a witch—no, not I ; but she had a evil mind, and what 's so bad as a evil mind ? "

"I used to have a woman meeting me," said a fisherman, "when I went a-fishing ; and she used to wish me 'a good catch' every time she seed me, and I was always sure to have no luck whenever I met her ; luck used to be good enough other times. Well, I went to the 'Peller,' and done what he told me I done, and the woman came and begged my pardon, and my luck was good enough after that." To what purpose he had been lucky I could not divine, for he was miserably clad, and I learned that his family were, like himself, miserable and degraded.

In a certain cordwainer's workshop, which we could name, the following impoitant information was afforded by a lady customer. The worthy tradesman was bewailing the loss of a good-sized pig that had sickened, and being afraid it would die, he had drowned it, to make its death easier :—" If thee 'st only towld me afore, tha peg wud a bean wel enuf in a week, I knaw. That peg wus begruged thee, thas the way a wudn' thrive. I 'll tel ee wat mi faathur dun wonse. He wont hof to pausans * an' bot a bra purty letle peg, an' as a wus cumin hom wed'en, a wumun seed un, an' axed faathur to sell un to hur fur five shelins fur his bargin. Shaan't sell un, saze faathur. Mite sa wel, saze she, an' off she went. Faathur tendud un an' tendud un, an' a wudn' grough a mossel Wy ? A was begruged, thas wot a was. Wel, faathur wen' off, an' he wos towld to go hom an fill a botel with waater, an' beré un in the cawl. Faathur dun so, an' a wuden long afore the wumun caame to faathur an' axed un wat had a dun by hur, for she suffered agonies ; an' if heed only *forgive* hur, she 'd nevur do so nevur no mure. So faathur went to the cawl hus, an' brok the botel. She was at wonse relieved, an' the peg got wel enuf aftur. I can tel ee, ef thee's honle dun that, a wud ben wel enuf, if a wusn'd pisind."

"Well," said one of the company, " I believe I was ill-wished once. I had a great beautiful cage, full of pretty canaries. I hung them out one Sunday morning, and a woman came along and asked me to let her have one of my birds. ' Yes,' said I, ' for half-a-crown.' She said she shouldn't buy none. I told her I would not give her one, and off she went. That day week I had not a bird left ; everybody said they was bethought me, and I suppose they were , but this I do know, I lost all my canaries "

Carne,. in his " Legend of Pacorra," well expresses the belief in the power of ill wishes .—" Thriven ! " said the woman, with a bitter laugh ; " not if my curse could avail, should they thrive ! and it has availed," she continued, in a lower tone. " You know the wasting illness that 's fallen on all that cruel faggot, Dame Tredray's children, that said they ought to thraw me from the head of Tol-y-pedden, and that I should neither be broken nor drowned ; and the hard squire of Pendine, that would ha' had me burned in the great bonfire upon the bicking,† because King Harry had a son born,—has he ever left his bed since, or will he ever again, ken ye ? "

THE "PELLER."

A MAN who has resided at several places on the south coast was known by this name. He is said to be in possession of no end of charms, and to possess powers, of no common order, over this and the other world. " He is able," writes a friend, " to

* The Parson's.   † The Beacon.

put ghosts, hobgoblins, and, I believe, even Satan himself, to rest. I have known farmers well informed in many other matters, and members of religious bodies, go to the ' Peller ' to have the ' spirits that possessed the calves ' driven out ; for they, the calves, ' were so wild, they tore down all the wooden fences and gates, and must be possessed with the devil.'

" The ' Peller ' always performs a cure ; but as the evil spirits must go somewhere, and as it is always to be feared that they may enter into other calves or pigs, or, it may be, even possess the bodies of their owners themselves, the ' Peller ' makes it imperative that a stone wall shall be built around the calves, to confine them for three times seven days, or until the next moon is as old as the present one. This precaution always results in taming the devils and the calves, and consequently in curing them—the ' Peller ' usually sending the spirits to some very remote region, and chaining them down under granite rocks."

An old woman had long suffered from debility ; but she and her friends were satisfied that she had been ill-wished. So she went to the " Peller " He told her to buy a bullock's heart, and get a packet of pound pins. She was to stick the heart as full of pins as she could, and " the body that ill-wished her felt every pin run into the bullock's heart same as if they had been run into her." The spell was taken off, and the old woman grew strong.

An old man living on Lady Downs had a lot of money stolen from his house. He, too, went to the " Peller." In this case the magician performed the spells, and the man was told the money would be returned. After a few days, it was so ; the money, during the night, was tied to the handle of the door, and found there by the owner in the morning.

BEWITCHED CATTLE.

A FARMER, who possessed broad acres, and who was in many respects a sensible man, was greatly annoyed to find that his cattle became diseased in the spring. Nothing could satisfy him but that they were bewitched, and he was resolved to find out the person who had cast the evil eye on his oxen. According to an anciently-prescribed rule, the farmer took one of his bullocks and bled it to death, catching all the blood on bundles of straw. The bloody straw was then piled into a heap, and set on fire. Burning with a vast quantity of smoke the farmer expected to see the witch, either in reality or in shadow, amidst the smoke.

In this particular case he was to some extent gratified. An old woman who lived in the adjoining village noticing the fire and smoke,—with all a woman's curiosity,—went to Farmer ———'s field to see what was going on. She was instantly pounced on by this superstitious man, and he would no doubt have seriously ill-treated her, had not the poor, and now terrified, old soul, who roused her neighbours by her cries, been rescued by them. Every person knew this poor woman to be a most inoffensive and good creature, and consequently the farmer was only laughed at for sacrificing thus foolishly one of his oxen.

Another farmer living in one of the western parishes was constantly losing his cattle in the spring. Many persons said this was because they were nearly starved during the winter, but he insisted upon it that he was ill-wished, and that a blight was upon him.

At length, to break the spell, and discover the witch, he betook himself to a conjurer (white witch) who lived near the Lizard Point. This learned person, of whom several other facts are told in these pages, told the farmer to bleed the next animal when taken ill, and to receive the blood upon straw, being careful not to lose any of it. Then the straw and blood were to be burnt, and whilst the blood was burning he would be certain of seeing the witch pass through the smoke.

A young steer fell ill first ; it was bled as ordered, the blood caught upon the straw, and both carefully burnt. While this was going on, female curiosity induced a poor weak old woman to go into the field and see what was going on. She was well known to all, and as guiltless as a child of ill-wishing anybody, but she was seen through the smoke, darted upon by the farmer, and cruelly ill-treated.

HOW TO BECOME A WITCH.

TOUCH a Logan stone nine times at midnight, and any woman will become a witch. A more certain plan is said to be—To get on the Giant's Rock at Zennor Church-town nine times without shaking it. Seeing that this rock was at one time a very sensitive Logan stone, the task was somewhat difficult.

CORNISH SORCERERS.

THE powers of the sorcerer appear to have been passed on from father to son through a long succession of generations. There are many families—the descendants from the ancient Cornish people—who are even yet supposed to possess remarkable powers of one kind or another. Several families, which have become extinct,

X

are more especially reputed by tradition to have had dealings with the bad spirits, and many of them to have made compacts with the Evil One himself. Amongst the most curious of the stories once told,—I believe they are nearly all forgotten,—are those connected with Pengerswick Castle. A small tower alone remains to note the site of a once famous fortified place. This castle was said to have been occupied, in the time of Henry VIII., by a man who had committed some great crime ; but long previous to that period the place was famous for its wickedness.*

HOW PENGERSWICK BECAME A SORCERER.

THE first Pengerswick, by whom the castle, which still bears his name, was built, was a proud man, and desired to ally himself with some of the best families of Cornwall. He wished his son to wed a lady who was very much older than himself, who is said to have been connected with the Godolphin family. This elderly maiden had a violent desire either for the young man or the castle—it is not very clear which. The young Pengerswick gave her no return for the manifestations of love which she lavished upon him. Eventually, finding that all her attempts to win the young man's love were abortive, and that all the love-potions brewed for her by the Witch of Fraddam were of no avail, she married the old lord—mainly, it is said, to be revenged on the son.

The witch had a niece who, though poor, possessed considerable beauty ; she was called Bitha This young girl was frequently employed by her aunt and the lady of Godolphin to aid them in their spells on the young Pengerswick, and, as a natural conse- quence, she fell desperately in love with him herself. Bitha ingratiated herself with the lady of Pengerswick, now the stepmother of the young man, and was selected as her maid. This gave her many opportunities of seeing and speaking to young Pengerswick, and her passion increased. The old stepdame was still passionately fond of the young man, and never let a chance escape her which she thought likely to lead to the excitement of passion in his heart towards her In all her attempts she failed. Her love was turned to hate ; and having seen her stepson in company with Bitha, this hate was quickened by the more violent jealousy. Every means which her wicked mind could devise were employed to destroy the young man. Bitha had learned from her aunt, the Witch of Fraddam, much of her art, and she devoted herself to counteract the spells of her mistress.

* See Appendix Y.

The stepmother failing to accomplish her ends, resolved to ruin young Pengerswick with his father. She persuaded the old man that his son really entertained a violent passion for her, and that she was compelled to confine herself to her tower in fear. The aged woman prevailed on Lord Pengerswick to hire a gang of outlandish sailors to carry his son away and sell him for a slave, giving him to believe that she should herself in a short time present him with an heir.

The young Pengerswick escaped all their plots, and at his own good time he disappeared from the castle, and for a long period was never heard of.

The mistress and maid plotted and counter-plotted to secure the old Pengerswick's wealth, and when he was on his death-bed, Bitha informed him of the vile practices of his wife, and consoled him with the information that he was dying from the effects of poison given him by her.

The young lord, after long years, returned from some Eastern lands with a princess for his wife, learned in all the magic sciences of those enchanted lands. He found his stepmother shut up in her chamber, with her skin covered with scales like a serpent,* from the effects of the poisons which she had so often been distilling for the old lord and his son. She refused to be seen, and eventually cast herself into the sea, to the relief of all parties.

Bitha fared not much better. She lived on the Downs in St Hilary; and from the poisonous fumes she had inhaled, and from her dealings with the devil, her skin became of the colour of that of *a toad.*

THE LORD OF PENGERSWICK AN ENCHANTER.

THE Lord of Pengerswick came from some Eastern clime, bringing with him a foreign lady of great beauty. She was considered by all an "outlandish" woman; and by many declared to be a "Saracen."† No one, beyond the selected servants, was ever allowed within the walls of Pengerswick Castle; and they, it was said, were bound by magic spells. No one dared tell of anything transacted within the walls, consequently all was conjecture amongst the neighbouring peasantry, miners, and fishermen. Certain it was, they said, that Pengerswick would shut himself up for days together in his chamber, burning strange things, which sent their strong odours,—not only to every part of the castle,—

* See Appendix Z.   † See Appendix AA.

but for miles around the country.   Often at night, and especially
in stormy weather, Pengerswick was heard for hours together
. calling up the spirits, by reading from his books in some unknown
tongue.   On those occasions his voice would roll through the halls
louder than the surging waves which beat against the neighbouring
rocks, the spirits replying like the roar of thunder.   Then would
all the servants rush in fright from the building, and remain crowded
together, even in the most tempestuous night, in one of the open
courts.   Fearful indeed would be the strife between the man and
the demons ; and it sometimes happened that the spirits were too
powerful for the enchanter.   He was, however, constantly and
carefully watched by his wife ; and whenever the strife became too
serious, her harp was heard making the softest, the sweetest music.
At this the spirits fled ; and they were heard passing through the
air towards the Land's-End, moaning like the soughing of a departing storm.   The lights would then be extinguished in the enchanter's
tower, and all would be peace.   The servants would return to their
apartments with a feeling of perfect confidence.   They feared their
master, but their mistress inspired them with love.   Lady Pengerswick was never seen beyond the grounds surrounding the castle.
She sat all day in lonely state and pride in her tower, the
lattice-window of her apartment being high on the seaward side.
Her voice accompanying the music of her harp was rarely heard,
but when she warbled the soft love strains of her Eastern land.
Often at early dawn the very fishes of the neighbouring bay would
raise their heads above the surface of the waters, enchanted by the
music and the voice ; and it is said that the mermaids from the
Lizard, and many of the strange spirits of the waters, would come
near to Pengerswick cove, drawn by the same influence.   On
moonlight nights the air has often seemed to be full of sound,
and yet the lady's voice was seldom louder than that of a warbling
bird.   On these occasions, men have seen thousands of spirits
gliding up and down the moonbeams, and floating idly on the
silvered waves, listening to, and sometimes softly echoing, the
words which Lady Pengerswick sang.   Long did this strange
pair inhabit this lonely castle ; and although the Lord of
Pengerswick frequently rode abroad on a most magnificent horse
—which had the reputation of being of Satanic origin, it was
at once so docile to its master and so wild to any other
person,—yet he made no acquaintance with any of the neighbouring gentry.   He was feared by all, and yet they respected him
for many of the good deeds performed by him.   He completely
enthralled the Giants of the Mount , and before he disappeared

from Cornwall, they died, owing, it was said, to grief and want of food.

Where the Lord of Pengerswick came from, no one knew ; he, with his lady, with two attendants, who never spoke in any but an Eastern tongue, which was understood by none around them, made their appearance one winter's day, mounted on beautiful horses, evidently from Arabia or some distant land.

They soon—having gold in abundance—got possession of a cottage , and in a marvellously short time the castle, which yet bears his name, was rebuilt by this lord. Many affirm that the lord by the force of his enchantments, and the lady by the spell of her voice, compelled the spirits of the earth and air to work for them ; and that three nights were sufficient to rear an enormous pile, of which but one tower now remains.

Their coming was sudden and mysterious ; their going was still more so. Years had rolled on, and the people around were familiarised with those strange neighbours, from whom also they derived large profits, since they paid whatsoever price was demanded for any article which they required. One day a stranger was seen in Market-Jew, whose face was bronzed by long exposure to an Eastern sun. No one knew him ; and he eluded the anxious inquiries of the numerous gossips, who were especially anxious to learn something of this man, who, it was surmised by every one, must have some connection with Pengerswick or his lady ; yet no one could assign any reason for such a supposition. Week after week passed away, and the stranger remained in the town, giving no sign. Wonder was on every old woman's lips, and expressed in every old man's eyes ; but they had to wonder on. One thing, it was said, had been noticed ; and this seemed to confirm the suspicions of the people. The stranger wandered out on dark nights—spent them, it was thought on the sea-shore ; and some fishermen said they had seen him seated on the rock at the entrance of the valley of Pengerswick. It was thought that the lord kept more at home than usual, and of late no one had heard his incantation songs and sounds ; neither had they heard the harp of the lady. A very tempestuous night, singular for its gloom—when even the ordinary light, which, on the darkest night, is evident to the traveller in the open country, did not exist— appears to have brought things to their climax. There was a sudden alarm in Market-Jew, a red glare in the eastern sky, and presently a burst of flames above the hill, and St Michael's Mount was illuminated in a remarkable manner. Pengerswick Castle was on fire ; the servants fled in terror ; but neither the lord nor his lady could be found.   From that day to the present they were lost to all.

The interior of the castle was entirely destroyed ; not a vestige of furniture, books, or anything belonging to the " Enchanter " could be found   He and everything belonging to him had vanished, and, strange to tell, from that night the bronzed stranger was never again seen.   The inhabitants of Market-Jew naturally crowded to the fire ; and when all was over they returned to their homes, speculating on the strange occurrences of the night.   Two of the oldest people always declared that, when the flames were at the highest, they saw two men and a lady floating in the midst of the fire, and that they ascended from amidst the falling walls, passed through the air like lightning, and disappeared.

THE WITCH OF FRADDAM AND THE ENCHANTER OF PENGERSWICK.

AGAIN and again had the Lord of Pengerswick reversed the spells of the Witch of Fraddam, who was reported to be the most powerful weird woman in the west country.   She had been thwarted so many times by this " white witch," that she resolved to destroy him by some magic more potent than anything yet heard of.   It is said that she betook herself to Kynance Cove, and that there she raised the devil by her incantations, and that she pledged her soul to him in return for the aid he promised. The enchanter's famous mare was to be seduced to drink from a tub of poisoned water placed by the road-side, the effect of which was to render her in the highest degree restive, and cause her to fling her rider.   The wounded Lord of Pengerswick was, in his agony, to be drenched by the old witch, with some hell-broth, brewed in the blackest night, under the most evil aspects of the stars ; by this he would be in her power for ever, and she might torment him as she pleased.   The devil felt certain of securing the soul of the witch of Fraddam, but he was less certain of securing that of the enchanter.   They say, indeed, that the sorcery which Pengerswick learned in the East was so potent, that the devil feared him.   However, as the proverb is, he held with the hounds and ran with the hare.   The witch collected with the utmost care all the deadly things she could obtain, with which to brew her famous drink.   In the darkest night, in the midst of the wildest storms, amidst the flashings of lightnings and the bellowings of the thunder, the witch was seen riding on her black ram-cat over the moors and mountains in search of her poisons.   At

length all was complete—the horse-drink was boiled, the hell-
broth was brewed. It was in March, about the time of the
equinox ; the night was dark, and the King of Storms was abroad.
The witch planted her tub of drink in a dark lane, through which
she knew the Lord of Pengerswick must pass, and near to it she
sat, croning over her crock of broth. The witch-woman had not
long to wait ; amidst the hurrying winds was heard the heavy
tramp of the enchanter's mare, and soon she perceived the outline
of man and horse defined sharply against the line of lurid light
which stretched along the western horizon. On they came ; the
witch was scarcely able to contain herself—her joy and her fears,
struggling one with the other, almost overpowered her. On came
the horse and her rider · they neared the tub of drink ; the mare
snorted loudly, and her eyes flashed fire as she looked at the black
tub by the road-side. Pengerswick bent him over the horse's neck
and whispered into her ear ; she turns round, and flinging out
her heels, with one kick she scattered all to the wild winds. The
tub flew before the blow ; it rushed against the crock, which it
overturned, and striking against the legs of the old Witch of
Fraddam, she fell along with the tub, which assumed the shape
of a coffin. Her terror was extreme she who thought to have
unhorsed the conjurer, found herself in a carriage for which she
did not bargain. The enchanter raised his voice and gave utterance to some wild words in an unknown tongue, at which even
his terrible mare trembled. A whirlwind arose, and the devil was
in the midst of it. He took the coffin in which lay the terrified
witch high into the air, and the crock followed them The
derisive laughter of Pengerswick, and the savage neighing of the
horse, were heard above the roar of the winds. At length, with a
satisfied tone, he exclaimed, " She is settled till the day of doom,"
gave the mare the spurs, and rode rapidly home.

The Witch of Fraddam still floats up and down, over the seas,
around the coast, in her coffin, followed by the crock, which seems
like a punt in attendance on a jolly-boat. She still works
mischief, stirring up the sea with her ladle and broom till the
waves swell into mountains, which heave off from their crests so
much mist and foam, that these wild wanderers of the winds can
scarcely be seen through the mist. Woe to the mariner who
sees the witch !

The Lord of Pengerswick alone had power over her. He had
but to stand on his tower, and blow three blasts on his trumpet,
to summon her to the shore, and compel her to peace.

TREWA, OR TREWE, THE HOME OF WITCHES.

A S we walk from Nancledrea Bottoms towards Zennor we pass Trewa (pronounced *Truee*), which is said to have been the place where at Midsummer all the witches of the west met. Here are the remains of very ancient tin stream works, and these, I was informed, " were the remains of bals which had been worked before the deluge ; there was nothing so old anywhere else in Cornwall." Around us, on the hill-sides and up the bottoms, huge boulders of granite are most fantastically scattered. All these rocks sprang from the ground at the call of the giants. At Embla Green we still see the ruins of the Giant's House, but all we know of this Titan is that he was the king. On one side we have the " Giant's Well," and not far off the "Druid's Well," and a little before us is Zennor coit or cromlech.

From this point the scenery is of the wildest description. The granite cairns are spread around in every direction, and many of those masses are so strangely fashioned by the atmospheric influences ever acting on them, that fancy can readily·fashion them into tombs and temples. Rock basins abound on these hills, and of ruined cromlechs there are many. Whatever the local historians may say, local traditions assure us that on Mid-summer Eve all the witches in Penwith gathered here, and that they lit fires on every cromlech, and in every rock basin, until the hills were alive with flame, and renewed their vows to the evil ones from whom they derived their power. Hence, to this day this place is called Burn Downs. Amidst these rock masses there was one pile remarkable amidst all the others for its size, and— being formed of cubical masses—for its square character. This was known as the Witches' Rock, and here it was said they assembled at midnight to carry on their wicked deeds. This rock has been removed, and with it the witches have died ; the last real witch in Zennor having passed away, as I have been told, about thirty years since, and with her, some say, the fairies fled. I have, however, many reasons for believing that our little friends have still a few haunts in this locality. There is but one reason why we should regret the disappearance of the Witches' Rock. *Any one touching this rock nine times at midnight was insured against bad luck.*

KENIDZHEK WITCH.

ON the tract called the "Gump," near Kenidzhek, is a beautiful well of clear water, not far from which was a miner's cot, in which dwelt two miners with their sister. They told her never to go to the well after daylight; they would fetch the water for her. However, on one Saturday night she had forgotten to get in a supply for the morrow, so she went off to the well. Passing by a gap in a broken-down hedge (called a *gurgo*) near the well, she saw an old woman sitting down, wrapped in a red shawl; she asked her what she did there at that time of night, but received no reply; she thought this rather strange, but plunged her pitcher in the well; when she drew it up, though a perfectly sound vessel, it contained no water; she tried again and again, and, though she saw the water rushing in at the mouth of the pitcher, it was sure to be empty when lifted out. She then became rather frightened; spoke again to the old woman, but receiving no answer, hastened away, and came in great alarm to her brothers. They told her that it was on account of this old woman they did not wish her to go to the well at night. What she saw was the ghost of old Moll, a witch who had been a great terror to the people in her lifetime, and had laid many fearful spells on them. They said they saw her sitting in the gap by the wall every night when going to bed.

THE WITCHES OF THE LOGAN STONE.

WHO that has travelled into Cornwall but has visited the Logan Stone? Numerous Logan rocks exist on the granite hills of the county, but that remarkable mass which is poised on the cubical masses forming its Cyclopean support, at Trereen, is beyond all others "The Logan Stone."

A more sublime spot could not have been chosen by the Bardic priesthood for any ordeal connected with their worship; and even admitting that nature may have disposed the huge mass to wear away, so as to rest delicately poised on a pivot, it is highly probable that the wild worship of the untrained tribes, who had passed to those islands from the shores of the Mediterranean Sea, may have led them to believe that some superhuman power belonged to such a strangely-balanced mass of rock

Nothing can be more certain than that through all time, passing on from father to son, there has been a wild reverence of this mass of rock; and long after the days when the Druid ceased to be there is every reason for believing that the Christian priests, if they did not encourage, did not forbid, the use of this and similar rocks to be used as places of ordeal by the uneducated and superstitious people around.

Hence the mass of rock on which is poised the Logan Stone has ever been connected with the supernatural. To the south of the Logan Rock is a high peak of granite, towering above the other rocks ; this is known as the Castle Peak.

No one can say for how long a period, but most certainly for ages, this peak has been the midnight rendezvous for witches. Many a man, and woman too, now sleeping quietly in the church-yard of St Levan, would, had they the power, attest to have seen the witches flying into the Castle Peak on moonlight nights, mounted on the stems of the ragwort (*Senécio Jacobœa Linn.*), and bringing with them the things necessary to make their charms potent and strong.

This place was long noted as the gathering place of the army of witches who took their departure for Wales, where they would luxuriate at the most favoured seasons of the year upon the milk of the Welshmen's cows. From this peak many a struggling ship has been watched by a malignant crone, while she has been brew-ing the tempest to destroy it ; and many a rejoicing chorus has been echoed, in horror, by the cliffs around, when the witches have been croaking their miserable delight over the perishing crews, as they have watched man, woman, and child drowning, whom they were presently to rob of the treasures they were bring-ing home from other lands

Upon the rocks behind the Logan Rock it would appear that every kind of mischief which can befall man or beast was once brewed by the St Levan witches.

MADGY FIGGY'S CHAIR.

ALL those who have visited the fine piles of rocks in the vicinity of the so-called "St Levan," Land's-End, called Tol-Pedden-Penwith,— and infinitely finer than anything immedi-ately surrounding the most western promontory itself,—cannot have failed to notice the arrangement of cubical masses of granite piled one upon the other, known as the *Chair Ladder*.

This remarkable pile presents to the beat of the Atlantic waves a sheer face of cliff of very considerable height, standing up like a huge basaltic column, or a pillar built by the Titans, the hori-zontal joints representing so many steps in the so-called "Ladder."

On the top is placed a stone of somewhat remarkable shape, which is by no great effort of the imagination converted into a chair. There it was that Madgy Figgy, one of the most celebrated of the St Levan and Burian witches, was in the habit of seating herself when she desired to call up to her aid the spirits of the storm. Often has she been seen swinging herself to and fro on this dizzy height when a storm has been coming home upon the shores, and richly-laden vessels have been struggling with the winds. From this spot she poured forth her imprecations on man and beast, and none whom she had offended could escape those withering spells ; and from this " chair," which will ever bear her name, Madgy Figgy would always take her flight. Often, starting like some huge bird, mounted on a stem of ragwort, Figgy has headed a band of inferior witches, and gone off rejoicing in their iniquities to Wales or Spain.

This old hag lived in a cottage not far from Raftra, and she and all her gang, which appears to have been a pretty numerous crew, were notorious wreckers. On one occasion, Madgy from her seat of storms lured a Portuguese Indiaman into Perloe Cove, and drowned all the passengers. As they were washed on shore, the bodies were stripped of everything valuable, and buried by Figgy and her husband in the green hollow, which may yet be seen just above Perloe Cove, marking the graves with a rough stone placed at the head of the corpse. The spoils on this occasion must have been large, for all the women were supplied for years with rich dresses, and costly jewels were seen decking the red arms of the girls who laboured in the fields. For a long time gems and gold continued to be found on the sands. Howbeit, amongst the bodies thrown ashore was one of a lady richly dressed, with chains of gold about her. " Rich and rare were the gems she wore," and not only so, but valuable treasure was fastened around her, she evidently hoping, if saved, to secure some of her property. This body, like the others, was stripped ; but Figgy said there was a mark on it which boded them evil, and she would not allow any of the gold or gems to be divided, as it would be sure to bring bad luck if it were separated. A dreadful quarrel ensued, and bloodshed was threatened ; but the diabolical old Figgy was more than a match for any of the men, and the power of her impetuous will was superior to them all.

Everything of value, therefore, belonging to this lady was gathered into a heap, and placed in a chest in Madgy Figgy's hut. They buried the Portuguese lady the same evening , and after dark a light was seen to rise from the grave, pass along the cliffs, and seat itself in Madgy's chair at Tol-Pedden. Then, after some hours, it descended, passed back again, and, entering the cottage, rested upon the chest. This curious phenomenon continued for more than three months,—nightly,—much to the alarm of all-but Figgy, who said she knew all about it, and it would be all right in time. One day a strange-looking and strangely-attired man arrived at the cottage. Figgy's man (her husband) was at home alone. To him the stranger addressed himself by signs,—he could not speak English, so he does not appear to have spoken at all, —and expressed a wish to be led to the graves. Away they went, but the foreigner did not appear to require a guide. He at once selected the grave of the lady, and sitting down upon it, he gave vent to his pent-up sorrows He sent Figgy's man away, and remained there till night, when the light arose from the grave more brilliant than ever, and proceeded directly to the hut, resting as usual on the chest, which was now covered up with old sails, and all kinds of fishermen's lumber.

The foreigner swept these things aside, and opened the chest. He selected everything belonging to the lady, refusing to take any of the other valuables. He rewarded the wreckers with costly gifts, and left them—no one knowing from whence he came nor whither he went. Madgy Figgy was now truly triumphant. "One witch knows another witch, dead or living," she would say; "and the African would have been the death of us if we hadn't kept the treasure, whereas now we have good gifts, and no gainsaying 'em" Some do say they have seen the light in Madgy Figgy's chair since those times.

OLD MADGE FIGGEY AND THE PIG.

MADGE FIGGEY once lived in St Leven, but she removed to Burian Church-town. She had a neighbour, Tom Trenoweth, who had a very fine sow, and the old creature took it into her head to desire this sow The pig was worth a pound of any man's money, but Madge offered Tom five shillings for it.

"No," says Tom, "I shan't sell the sow to you, nor to anybody else. I am going to put her in the house, and feed her for myself against winter."

"Well," said old Madge, nodding her head, and shaking her finger at Tom, "you will wish you had"

From that time the sow ceased to "goody" (thrive). The more corn the sow ate, the leaner she became. Old Madge came again, "Will ye sell her now, Tom?"

" No ! and be —— to you," said Tom.

" Arreah, Tom ! you will wish you had, before another week is ended, I can tell ye."

By next week the sow was gone to skin and bone, yet eating all the time meat enough for three.

At last Tom took the sow out of the house, and prepared to drive her to Penzance market, and sell her for what she would fetch.

The rope was put round her leg, but more for fashion's sake than anything else. The poor pig could scarcely stand on her legs, consequently there was little chance of her running away. Well, Tom and his pig were no sooner on the highroad than the sow set off like a greyhound, and never stopped, racing over hedges and ditches, until she reached Leah Lanes. Tom kept hold of the rope till his arm was almost dragged from his body, and he was fairly " out of breath." He dropped the rope, piggy went on " as quiet as a lamb," but only the way which pleased her best. At last Tom and the sow arrived at Tregenebris Downs. At the corner of the roads, where they divide,—one going to Sancreed, and the other to Penzance,—Tom again laid hold of the rope, and said to himself, " I 'll surely get thee to Penzance yet."

The moment they came to the market-road, the sow made a bolt, jerked the rope out of Tom's hand, and ran off at full speed, never stopping until she got in under Tregenebris Bridge. Now that bridge is more like a long drain—locally a bolt—than anything else, and is smallest in the middle ; so when the sow got half way in, she stuck fast ; she couldn't go forward—she wouldn't come back. Tom fired all the stones he could find—first at the pig's head, and then at her tail—and all he got for his pains was a grunt. There he stopped, watching the sow till near sunset ; he had eaten nothing since five in the morning, and was starving. He saw no chance of getting the sow out, so he swore at her, and prepared to go home, when who should come by but old Madge Figgey, with her stick in one hand and basket in the other.

" Why, Tom, is that you ? What in the world are ye doing here at this time o' day ? "

" Well," says Tom, " I 'm cussed if I can tell ; look under the bridge, if you 're a mind to know."

" Why, I hear the sow grunting, I declare. What will ye sell her for now? "

" If you can get her out, take her," says Tom ; " but hast anything to eat in your basket ? "

Madge gave him a twopenny loaf.

"Thank ye," says Tom. "Now the devil take the both of ye!"

"Cheat! cheat! cheat!" says Madge. Out came the sow, and followed her home like a dog.

MADAM NOY AND OLD JOAN.

THEY say that, a long time since, there lived an old witch down by Alsia Mill, called Joan. Everybody feared to offend the old woman, and gave her everything she looked for, except Madam Noy, who lived in Pendrea.

Madam Noy had some beautiful hens of a new sort, with "cops" on their heads.

One morning early, Joan comes up to Pendrea, so as to catch Madam Noy going out into the farmyard, with her basket of corn to feed her poultry, and to collect the eggs.

Joan comes up nodding and curtsying every step. "Good morrow to your honour; how well you are looking, Madam Noy! and, oh, what beautiful hens! I've got an old hen that I do want to set; will you sell me a dozen of eggs? Those with the 'cops' I'd like to have best."

Madam turned round half offended, and said, "I have none to sell, neither with the cops nor yet without the cops, whilst I have so many old clucking hens about, and hardly an egg to be found."

"You surely wouldn't send me home empty as I came, madam dear?"

"You may go home the same way you came, for you aren't wanted here"

"Now," croaked Joan, hoarse with passion, "as true as I tell you so, if you don't sell me some eggs, you will wish your cakes dough."

As the old witch said this, she perched herself on the stile, shaking her finger and "nodling" her head.

Madam Noy was a bit of a virago herself, so she took up a stone and flung it at Joan; it hit her in the face, and made her jaws rattle.

As soon as she recovered, she spinned forth ·—

> "Madam Noy, you ugly old bitch,
> You shall have the gout, the palsy, and itch;
> All the eggs your hens lay henceforth shall be addle;
> All your hens have the pip, and die with the straddle;
> And ere I with the mighty fine madam have done,
> Of her favourite 'coppies' she shan't possess one."

From that day forward, madam was always afflicted. The doctor from Penzance could do little for her. The fowls' eggs were always bad; the hens died, and madam lost all her " coppies." This is the way it came about—in the place of cops the brains came out—and all by the spells of old Joan.

This forms the subject of one of the old Cornish drolls, which ran in an irregular jingle, such as the above, and was half sung, half said by the droll-teller.

THE WITCH OF TREVA.

ONCE on a time, long ago, there lived at Treva, a hamlet in Zennor, a wonderful old lady deeply skilled in necromancy. Her charms, spells, and dark incantations made her the terror of the neighbourhood. However, this old lady failed to impress her husband with any belief in her supernatural powers, nor did he fail to proclaim his unbelief aloud.

One day this sceptic came home to dinner, and found, being exceedingly hungry, to his bitter disappointment, that not only was there no dinner to eat, but that there was no meat in the house. His rage was great, but all he could get from his wife was, " I couldn't get meat out of the stones, could I ? " It was in vain to give the reins to passion, the old woman told him, and he must know " that hard words buttered no parsnips." Well, at length he resolved to put his wife's powers to the proof, and he quietly but determinedly told her that he would be the death of her if she did not get him some dinner ; but if in half an hour she gave him some good cooked meat, he would believe all she had boasted of her power, and be submissive to her for ever. St Ives, the nearest market-town, was five miles off; but nothing doubting, the witch put on her bonnet and cloak, and started. Her husband watched her from their cottage door, down the hill ; and at the bottom of the hill, he saw his wife quietly place herself on the ground and disappear. In her place a fine hare ran on at its full speed.

He was not a little startled, but he waited, and within the half-hour in walked his wife with " good flesh and taties all ready for aiting." There was no longer any doubt, and the poor husband lived in fear of the witch of Treva to the day of her death.

This event took place after a few years, and it is said the room was full of evil spirits, and that the old woman's shrieks were awful to hear. Howbeit, peace in the shape of pale-faced death came to her at last, and then a black cloud rested over the house when all the heavens were clear and blue.

She was borne to the grave by six aged men, carried, as is the custom, underhand. When they were about half way between the house and the church, a hare started from the roadside and leaped over the coffin. The terrified bearers let the corpse fall to the ground, and ran away. Another lot of men took up the coffin and proceeded They had not gone far when puss was suddenly seen seated on the coffin, and again the coffin was abandoned. After long consultation, and being persuaded by the parson to carry the old woman very quickly into the churchyard, while he walked before, six others made the attempt, and as the parson never ceased to repeat the Lord's Prayer, all went on quietly. Arrived at the church stile, they rested the corpse, the parson paused to commence the ordinary burial service, and there stood the hare, which, as soon as the clergyman began " I am the resurrection and the life," uttered a diabolical howl, changed into a black, unshapen creature, and disappeared.

HOW MR LENINE GAVE UP COURTING.

MR LENINE had been, as was his wont, spending his evening hours with the lady of his love. He was a timid man, and always returned to Tregenebris early. Beyond this, as the lady was alone, she deemed it prudent to let the world know that Mr Lenine left her by daylight.

One evening, it was scarcely yet dark, and our lover was returning home through Leah Lanes. His horse started at an old woman, who had crept under the hedge for shelter from a passing shower. As Mr Lenine saw a figure moving in the shade he was terrified.

" Tu-whit, tu-whoo, ho," sang an owl.

" It 's only me—Mr Lenine of Tregenebris," said he, putting the spurs to his horse

Something followed him, fast as he might go, and he forced his horse up the hill by Leah vean.

" Tu-whit, tu-whoo, ho," sang the owl.

" It 's only me—Aunt Betty Foss," screamed the old woman.

" Tu-whit, tu-whoo, ho, ho," sang the owl again.

" Don't ye be afeared, Mr Lenine," shrieked Aunt Betty, almost out of breath.

" Tu-whit, tu-whoo, ho, ho, ho," also shrieked the owl.

"Oh, it's only John Lenine of Tregenebris," stammered the frightened lover, who had, however, reached home

He went no more a-courting. He was fully persuaded that either a highwayman and his crew, or the devil and his imps, were upon him. He died a bachelor, and the charming lady became a peevish old maid, and died in solitude ; all owing to the hooting owl

Some do say Betty Foss was a witch, and the owl her familiar.

THE WITCH AND THE TOAD.

AN old woman called Alsey—usually Aunt Alsey—occupied a small cottage in Anthony, one of a row which belonged to a tradesman living in Dock—as Devonport was then designated to distinguish it from Plymouth. The old woman possessed a very violent temper, and this, more than anything else, fixed upon her the character of being a witch. Her landlord had frequently sought his rent, and as frequently he received nothing but abuse. He had, on the special occasion to which our narrative refers, crossed the Tamar and walked to Anthony, with the firm resolve of securing his rent, now long in arrear, and of turning the old termagant out of the cottage. A violent scene ensued, and the vicious old woman, more than a match for a really kind-hearted and quiet man, remained the mistress of the situation. She seated herself in the door of her cottage and cursed her landlord's wife, "the child she was carrying," and all belonging to him, with so devilish a spite that Mr —— owned he was fairly driven away in terror.

On returning home, he, of course, told his wife all the circumstances ; and while they were discoursing on the subject,—the whole story being attentively listened to by their daughter, then a young girl, who is my informant,—a woman came into the shop requiring some articles which they sold.

"Sit still, father," said Mrs —— to her husband ; "you must be tired I will see to the shop."

So she went from the parlour into the shop, and, hearing the wants of her customer, proceeded to supply them ; gossiping gaily, as was her wont, to interest the buyer.

Mrs —— was weighing one of the articles required, when something falling heavily from the ceiling of the shop, struck the beam out of her hand, and both—the falling body and the scales—came together with much noise on to the counter. At the same instant

Y

both women screamed;—the shopkeeper calling also " Father ! father ! "—meaning her husband thereby—with great energy.

Mr —— and his daughter were in the shop instantly, and there, on the counter, they saw an enormous and most ugly toad sprawling amidst the chains of the scales.   The first action of the man was to run back to the parlour, seize the tongs, and return to the shop.   He grasped the swollen toad with the tongs, the vicious creature spitting all the time, and, without a word, he went back and flung it behind the block of wood which was burning in the grate.   The object of terror being removed, the wife, who was shortly to become the mother of another·child, though usually a woman who had great command over her feelings, fainted.

This circumstance demanding all their attention, the toad was forgotten.   The shock was a severe one ; and although Mrs ——was restored in a little time to her senses, she again and again became faint.   Those fits continuing, her medical attendant, Dr —— was sent for, and on his arrival he ordered that his patient should be immediately placed in bed, and the husband was informed that he must be prepared for a premature birth.

The anxiety occasioned by these circumstances, and the desire to afford every relief to his wife, so fully occupied Mr ——, that for an hour or two he entirely forgot the cause of all this mischief ; or, perhaps satisfying himself that the toad was burnt to ashes, he had no curiosity to look after it.   He was, however, suddenly summoned from the bedroom, in which he was with his wife, by his daughter calling to him, in a voice of terror—

" O father, the toad, the toad ! "

Mr —— rushed down-stairs, and he then discovered that the toad, though severely burnt, had escaped destruction   It must have crawled up over the log of wood, and from it have fallen down amongst the ashes.   There it was now making useless struggles to escape, by climbing over the fender.

The tongs were again put in requisition, with the intention this time of carrying the reptile out of the house   Before, however, he had time to do so, a man from Anthony came hastily into the shop with the information that Aunt Alsey had fallen into the fire, as the people supposed, in a fit, and that she was nearly burnt to death.   This man had been sent off with two commissions— one to fetch the doctor, and the other to bring Mr —— with him, as much of the cottage had been injured by fire, communicated to it by the old woman's dress

In as short a time as possible the parish surgeon and Mr —— were at Anthony, and too truly they found the old woman most severely burnt—so seriously, indeed, there was no chance that one so aged could rally from the shock which her system must have received. However, a litter was carefully prepared, the old woman was placed in it, and carried to the workhouse. Every attention was given to her situation, but she never recovered perfect consciousness, and during the night she died.

The toad, which we left inside the fender in front of a blazing fire, was removed from a position so trying to any cold-blooded animal, by the servant, and thrown, with a " hugh " and a shudder, upon one of the flower-beds in the small garden behind the house.

There it lay the next morning dead, and when examined by Mr ——, it was found that all the injuries sustained by the toad corresponded with those received by the poor old wretch, who had no doubt fallen a victim to passion.

As we have only to deal with the mysterious relation which existed between the witch and the toad, it is not necessary that we should attend further to the innocent victim of an old woman's vengeance, than to say that eventually a babe was born—that that babe grew to be a handsome man, was an officer in the navy, and having married, went to sea, and perished, leaving a widow with an unborn child to lament his loss. Whether this was a result of the witch's curse, those who are more deeply skilled in witchcraft than I am may perhaps tell.

THE SAILOR WIZARD.

THIS appears to have been, and it may still be, a very common superstition. I have lately received from Mr T. Q Couch of Bodmin the story of some sailors, who had reason to suspect that one of their body was a wizard. This was eventually proved to have been the case, by circumstances in every way resembling those of our old witch. There had been a quarrel, and revenge had been talked of. The sailors were all grouped together in the forepart of the ship, except the suspected one, and a toad fell sprawling amongst them. One of the men flung the creature into the fire in the caboose. It struggled for a moment in the fire, and then by a convulsive effort flung itself out. Immediately the toad was caught up by one of the men, and flung into the sea.

In the course of some little time the absent sailor made his appearance dripping wet. In a drunken frolic he had first fallen into the fire at a low beer shop or " Kiddle-e-wink," and subsequently he fell out of the boat into the sea.

THE MINERS.

" To us our Queen, who, in the central earth,
  Midst fiery lavas or basaltine seas,
  Deep-throned the illimitable waste enjoys,
  Enormous solitude, has given these
  Her subterraneous realms ; bids us dwell here,
  In the abyss of darkness, and exert
  Immortal alchymy.

" Each devious cleft, each secret cell explore,
  And from its fissures draw the ductile ore."
            The Mine: a Dramatic Poem—
                   JOHN SARGENT.

ROMANCES OF THE MINERS.

TRADITIONS OF TINNERS.

"An ancient story I'll tell you anon,
Which is older by far than the days of King John;
But this you should know, that that red-robed sinner
Robb'd the Jew of the gold he had made as a tinner"
Old Cornish Song.

THERE is scarcely a spot in Cornwall where tin is at present found, that has not been worked over by the "old men," as the ancient miners are always called.

Every valley has been "streamed"—that is, the deposits have been washed for tin ; over every hill where now a tin mine appears, there are evidences, many of them most extensive, of actual mining operations having been carried on to as great a depth as was possible in the days when the appliances of science were unknown.

Wherever the "streamer" has been, upon whatever spot the old miner has worked, there we are told the "Finician" (*Phœnician*) has been, or the Jew has mined.*

There is much confusion in these traditions. The Jew, and the Saracen, and the Phœnician are regarded as terms applied to the same people. Whereas the Phœnicians, who are recorded to have traded with the Cornish Britons for tin, and the Jews, who were the great tin miners and merchants in the days of King John, are separated by wide periods of time ; and the "Saracens," whom some suppose to have been miners who came from Spain when that country was under the dominion of the Moors, occupy a very undefined position. Tradition, however, tells us that the old Cornish miners shipped their tin at several remarkable islands

---

* "They maintaine these works to have been veric auncient, and first wrought by the *Jewes* with Pickaxes of Holme-Boxe and Hartshorne   They prove this by the name of those places yet enduring, to wit, *Attall Sarazin*, in English, the *Jewes Offcast*, and by those tooles daily found amongst the rubble of such workes."—*Survey of Cornwall,* Carew. (Appendix, AA)

round the coast. St Michael's Mount has been especially noticed, but this arises from the circumstance that it still retains the peculiar character which it appears to have possessed when Diodorus wrote. But Looe Island, St Nicholas's Island in Plymouth Sound, the island at St Ives, the Chapel Rock at Perran, and many other insular masses of rock, which are at but a short distance from the coast, are said to have been shipping-places.

Tradition informs us that the Christian churches upon Dartmoor, which are said to have been built about the reign of John, were reared by the Jews. Once, and once only, I heard the story told in more detail. They, the Jews, did not actually work in the tin streams and mines of the Moor, but they employed tinners, who were Christians ; and the king imposed on the Jew merchants the condition that they should build churches for their miners.

That the Phœnicians came to Cornwall to buy tin has been so often told that there is little to be added to the story. It was certainly new, however, to be informed by the miners in Gwennap —that there could be no shade of doubt but that St Paul himself came to Cornwall to buy tin, and that Creekbraws—a mine still in existence—supplied the saint largely with that valuable mineral. Gwennap is regarded by Gwennap men as the centre of Christianity. This feeling has been kept alive by the annual meeting of the Wesleyan body in Gwennap Pit—an old mine-working— on Whitmonday. This high estate and privilege is due, says tradition, to the fact that St Paul himself preached in the parish.*

I have also been told that St Paul preached to the tinners on Dartmoor, and a certain cross on the road from Plympton to Princes-Town has been indicated as the spot upon which the saint stood to enlighten the benighted miners of this wild region. Of St Piran or Perran we have already spoken as the patron saint of the tinners, and of the discovery of tin a story has been told (p. 274) ; and we have already intimated that another saint, whose name alone is preserved, St Picrous, has his feast-day amongst the tinners of eastern Cornwall, on the second Thursday before Christmas.

Amidst the giant stories we have the very remarkable Jack the Tinker, who is clearly indicated as introducing the knowledge of tin, or of the dressing of tin, to the Cornish. This is another version of Wayland Smith, the blacksmith of Berkshire. The blacksmith of the Berkshire legend reappears in a slightly altered

---

* Is this supported by the statement of Dr Stillingfleet, Bishop of Worcester, who says, "The Christian religion was planted in the Island of Great Britain during the time of the apostles, and probably by St Paul"?

character in Jack the Tinker. In Camden's " Britannia " we read, relative to Ashdown, in Berkshire :—

" The burial-place of Baereg, the Danish chief who was slain in this fight (the fight 'between Alfred and the Danes), is distinguished by a parcel of stones, less than a mile from the hill, set on edge, enclosing a piece of ground somewhat raised. On the east side of the southern extremity stand three squarish flat stones, of about four or five feet over either way, supporting a fourth, and now called by the vulgar, WAYLAND SMITH, from an idle tradition about an invisible smith replacing lost horse-shoes there."— *Gough's Camden.*

See " Kenilworth," by Sir Walter Scott, who has appropriated Wayland Smith with excellent effect

" The Berkshire legend of Wayland Smith ('Wayland Smith,' by W S. Singer) is probably but a prototype of Dædalus, Tubal Cain, &c "—*Wilson's Prehistoric Annals of Scotland.*

See also Mr Thomas Wright's Essay on Wayland Smith.

The existence of the terms " Jews' houses," " Jews' tin," " Jews' leavings," or " attall," and " attall Saracen," prove the connection of strangers with the Cornish tin mines. The inquiry is too large to be entered on here. I reserve it for another and more fitting place. I may, however, remark in passing, that 1 have no doubt the Romans were active miners during the period of their possession ; and many relics which have been found and ascribed to the Britons are undoubtedly Roman. See further remarks on p. 346, " Who are the Knockers ? "

Mr Edmonds supposes that he found in a bronze vessel discovered near Marazion a caldron in which tin was refined. In the first place, a bronze vessel would never have been used for that purpose—chemical laws are against it ; and in the second place, it is more than doubtful if ever the " Jews' tin " was subjected to this process. In all probability, the bronze vessel discovered was a " Roman camp-kettle." A very full description of bronze caldrons of this description will be found in " The Archæology and Prehistoric Annals of Scotland," by Daniel Wilson, p 274

It may not be out of place to insert here the tradition of a very important application of this metal

The use of tin as a mordant, for which very large quantities are now used, is said to have been thus discovered .—

Mr Crutchy, Bankside, married a Scotchwoman. This lady often told her husband that his scarlet was not equal to one she could dye. He set her to work. She dyed a skein of worsted in a saucepan, using the same material as her husband, but produced a better colour. She did not know this was owing to the saucepan's being tinned, but he detected the fact, and made his fortune as a dyer of scarlet and Turkey-red. The most important Turkey-red dye-

works are even now in the neighbourhood of Lochlomond ; therefore, this Scotchwoman may have been better acquainted with the
process than the story tells.

THE TINNER OF CHYANNOR.*

THE village of Treieen, near the Logan Stone, was at one time an
important market-town.   Here came all the tin-streamers who
worked from Penberth to the hills, and to protect the place and
the valuable property which was accumulated here, Castle Treereen
was built.   Here came—or rather into the cove near it came—
the Tyrian merchants.   They were not allowed to advance beyond
the shores, lest they should discover the country from which the
tin was brought   But it is not of them that we have now to tell,
but of a knot of tinners who came from the low country between
Chyannor and Trengothal.   These were assembled round the
Garrack Zans, which then stood in the centre of the market-place
of Treereen.   Times had been bad, and they were consulting
together what they had better do.   The " streams " had failed them,
and they believed all the tin was worked out.   Some of them
had heard that there was tin in " the country a long way off," some
miles beyond Market-Jew; but they had but a very dim idea of
the place or of the people.   One of them, who, though an old man,
was more adventurous than any of his comrades, said he would
travel there and see what could be done.   It was then determined
that Tom Trezidder should try his fortune, and the others would
wait until he came home again, or sent for them to come to him.
This was soon noised about, and all the women, old and young,
came to say " Good-bye " to Tom.   His parting with his wife was
brief but bitter.   He bore up well, and with a stout heart started
on his adventure.   Tom Trezidder arrived at length at a place not
far from Goldsythney, and here he found one of the Jew merchants, who farmed the tin ground, and sold the tin at St Michael's
Mount ; and the Jew was very anxious to engage so experienced a
" streamer " as Tom was.   Tom, nothing loath, took service for a
year.   He was to have just enough to live on, and a share of
profits at the year's end.   Tom worked diligently, and plenty of
tin was the result of his experienced labour.   The year expired,
and Tom looked for his share of the profits.   The Jew contrived
to put Tom off, and promised Tom great things if he would stop
for another year, and persuaded him to send for some of his old
comrades, clenching every argument which he employed with a
small piece of advice, " Never leave an old road for a new one."

* See Appendix BB

The other tinners were shy of venturing so far, so that two or three only could be persuaded to leave the West Country. With Tom and with his brethren the year passed by, and at the end he got no money, but only the same piece of advice, " Never leave an old road for a new one " This went on for a third year, when all of them, being naturally tired of this sort of thing, resolved to go home again.

Tom Trezidder was a favourite with his master, and was greatly esteemed for his honesty and industry by his mistress.

When they left she gave Tom a good currant cake to take home to his old woman, and told him to remember the advice, " Never leave an old road for a new one."

The tinners trudged on together until they were on the western side of Penzance. They were weary, and they found that since they had left home a new road had been made over the hills, which saved them a considerable distance—in fact it was a " short cut." On they went. " No," says Tom ; " never leave an old road for a new one." They all laughed at him, and trudged on. But Tom kept in the old road along the valley round the hill. When Tom reached the other end of the " short cut " he thought he would rest a bit, and he sat down by the road-side and ate his *fuggan.* This his mistress had given him, that he might not break his cake until he got home.

He had not sat long when he heard a noise, and, looking up the hill, he saw his comrades, who he thought were miles in advance of him, slowly and sorrowfully descending it. They came at last to where Tom was seated, and a sad tale had they to tell. They had scarcely got into the new road when they were set upon by robbers, who took from them " all their little bit of money," and then beat them because they had no more.

Tom, you may be sure, thought the piece of advice worth something now, as it had saved his bacon.

Tom arrived home at last, and glad was the old woman to see her old man once again ; so she made him some " herby tea" at once. He showed his wife the cake, and told her that all he had recieved for his share of profits was the piece of advice already given.

The ladies who read this story will understand how vexed was Tom's wife,—there are but few of them who would not have done as she did, that was to seize the cake from the table and fling it at her husband's head, calling him an old fool. Tom Trezidder stooped to avoid the blow. Slap against the corner of the dresser went the cake, breaking in pieces with the blow, and out on the lime-ash floor rolled a lot of gold coins.

This soon changed the aspect of things ; the storm rolled back, and sunshine was once more in the cottage. The coins were all gathered up, and they found a scrap of paper, on which, when they got the priest to read it, they discovered was written an exact account of each year's profits, and Tom's share. The three years' shares had been duly hoarded for him by his master and mistress ; and now this old couple found they had enough to make them comfortable for the rest of their days. Many were the prayers said by Tom and his wife for the happiness and health of the honest Jew tin merchant and his wife.

" WHO ARE THE KNOCKERS ? "

CHARLES KINGSLEY in his " Yeast : a Problem," asks this question—Tregarra answers,—

" They are *the ghosts,* the miners hold, *of the old Jews that crucified our Lord, and were sent for slaves by the Roman emperors to work the mines ·* and we find their old smelting-houses, which we call *Jews' houses,* and their blocks at the bottom of the great bogs, which we call *Jews' tin :* and then a town among us too, which we call *Market Jew,* but the old name was Marazion, that means the bitterness of Zion, they tell me ; and bitter work it was for them, no doubt, poor souls ! We used to break into old shafts and adits which they had made, and find fine old stag's-horn pick-axes, that crumbled to pieces when we brought them to grass. And they say that if a man will listen of a still night about these shafts, he may hear the ghosts of them at work, knocking and picking, as clear as if there was a man at work in the next level."

In *Notes and Queries* will be found some learned discussions on the question of the Jews working the Cornish tin mines, as though it were merely one of tradition. That the Jews farmed the tin mines of Cornwall and Devonshire is an historical fact, of which we have evidence in charters granted by several of our kings, especially by King John. Carew in his " Survey of Cornwall" gives some account of their mode of dealing with the tinners. Hence the terms " Jews' houses," given to old and rude smelting-works,—many of which I have seen,—and hence the name of " Jews' tin," given to the old blocks of tin, specimens of which may be seen in the *Museum of Practical Geology,* and in the museum of the *Royal Institution of Cornwall,* at Truro. " *Atall Sarazin*" is another term applied to some of the old waste-heaps of the ancient tin mines.

" The Jews," says Whitaker (" Origin of Arianism," p. 334),

" denominated themselves, and were denominated by the Britons of Cornwall, *Saracens*, as the genuine progeny of Sarah " Be this as it may, I have often heard in the mining villages—from twenty to thirty years since—a man coming from a distant parish, called *" a foreignerer ; "* a man from a distant country, termed *" an outlandish man ; "* and any one not British born, designated as *" a Saracen."*

But this has led me away from the knockers, who are in some districts called also *" the buccas."* Many a time have I been seriously informed by the miners themselves that these sprites have been heard working away in the remote parts of a lode, repeating the blows of the miner's pick or sledge with great precision. Generally speaking, the knockers work upon productive lodes only ; and they have often kindly indicated to the trusting miners, where they might take good tribute pitches.

To Wesley, Cornwall owes a deep debt. He found the country steeped in the darkness of superstitious ignorance, and he opened a new light upon it. Associated with the spread of Wesleyan Methodism, has been the establishment of schools ; and under the influence of religion and education, many of the superstitions have faded away. We rarely hear of the knockers now ; but the following occurrence will show that the knockers have not entirely left the land :—

One Saturday night I had retired to rest, having first seen that all the members of the household had gone to their bedrooms. These were my daughters, two female servants, and an old woman, named Mary, who was left, by the proprietor, in charge of the house which I occupied.

I had been some time in bed, when I distinctly heard a bedroom door open, and footsteps which, after moving about for some time in the passage or landing, from which the bedrooms opened, slowly and carefully descended the stairs. I heard a movement in the kitchen below, and the footsteps again ascended the stairs, and went into one of the bedrooms This noise continued so long, and was so regularly repeated, that I began to fear lest one of the children were taken suddenly ill. Yet I felt assured, if it was so, one of the servants would call me. Therefore I lay still and listened until I fell asleep.

On the Sunday morning, when I descended to the breakfast-room, I asked the eldest of the two servants what had occasioned so much going up and down stairs in the night. She declared that no one had left their bedrooms after they had retired to them. I then inquired of the younger girl, and of each of my daughters as they made their appearance. No one had left their rooms—they had not heard any noises. My youngest daughter, who had been, after this inquiry of mine, for some minutes alone with the youngest servant, came laughing to me,—

"Papa, Nanny says the house is haunted, and that they have often heard strange noises in it"

So I called Nancy; but all I could learn from her was that noises, like that of men going up and down stairs,—of threshing corn, and of "beating the borer" (a mining operation), were not uncommon.

We all laughed over papa's ghost during the breakfast, and by and by old Mary made her appearance.

"Yes," she said, "it is quite true, as Nanny as a told you. I have often heard all sorts of strange noises ; but I b'lieve they all come from the lode of tin which runs under the house. *Wherever there is a lode of tin, you are sure to hear strange noises.*"

"What, Mary ! was it the knockers I heard last night ?"

"Yes ; 'twas the knackers, down working upon the tin—no doubt of it."

This was followed by a long explanation, and numerous stories of mines in the Lelant and St Ives district, in which the knockers had been often heard.

After a little time, Mary, imagining, I suppose, that the young ladies might not like to sleep in a house beneath which the knockers were at work, again came with her usual low courtesy into the parlour.

"Beg pardon, sir," says she ; "but none of the young ladies need be afraid. There are no spirits in the house , it is very nearly a new one, and no one has ever died in the house."

This makes a distinct difference between the ghost of the departed and those gnomes who are doomed to toil in the earth's dark recesses.[*] The Cornish knocker does not appear to be the

---

[*] " Some are sent, like the spirit Gathon in Cornwall, to work the will of his master in the mines "—*Mrs Bray's Traditions of Devonshire.*

Who was the spirit Gathon ?

" The miner starts as he hears the mischievous Gathon answering blow for blow the stroke of his pickaxe, or deluding him with false fires, noises, and flames."—*A Guide to the Coasts of Devon and Cornwall. Mackenzie Walcott, M A*

Carne, in his " Tales of the West," alludes to this —" The miners have their full share of the superstitious feelings of the country, and often hear with alarm the noises, as it were, of other miners at work deep underground, and at no great distance The rolling of the barrows, the sound of the pickaxes, and the fall of the earth and stones, are distinctly heard through the night,—often, no doubt, the echo of their own labours ; but sometimes continued long after that labour has ceased, and occasionally voices seem to mingle with them. Gilbert believed that he was peculiarly exposed to these visitations ;

"*cobal*" of German miners. The former are generally kindly, and often serve the industrious miner; the latter class are always malicious, and, I believe, are never heard but when mischief is near.

MINERS' SUPERSTITIONS.

MINERS say they often see little imps or demons underground. Their presence is considered favourable; they indicate the presence of lodes, about which they work during the absence of the miners. A miner told my informant that he had often seen them, sitting on pieces of timber, or tumbling about in curious attitudes, when he came to work.

Miners do not like the form of the cross being made underground. A friend of my informant, going through some "levels" or "adits," made a + by the side of one, to know his way back, as he would have to return by himself. He was compelled to alter it into another form.

If miners see a snail when going to "bal" in the morning, they always drop a piece of tallow from their candles by its side.

CHRISTMAS-EVE IN THE MINES.

ON Christmas-eve, in former days, the small people, or the spriggans, would meet at the bottom of the deepest mines, and have a midnight mass. Then those who were in the mine would hear voices, melodious beyond all earthly voices, singing, " Now well ! now well , " * and the strains of some deep-toned organ would shake the rocks. Of the grandeur of those meetings, old stories could not find words sufficiently sonorous to speak , it was therefore left to the imagination But this was certain, the temple

he had an instinctive shrinking from the place where the accident had happened ; and, when left alone there, it was in vain that he plied his toil with desperate energy to divert his thoughts. Another person appeared to work very near him he stayed the lifted pick and listened. The blow of the other fell distinctly, and the rich ore followed it in a loud rolling, he checked the loaded barrow that he was wheeling , still that of the unknown workman went on, and came nearer and nearer, and then there followed a loud, faint cry, that thrilled through every nerve of the lonely man, for it seemed like the voice of his brother These sounds all ceased on a sudden, and those which his own toil caused were the only ones heard, till, after an interval, without any warning, they began again at times more near, and again passing away to a distance "—*The Tale of the Miner.*

    * " Now well ! now well ' the angel did say
        To certain poor shepherds in the fields who lay
        Late in the night, folding their sheep ,
        A winter's night, both cold and deep.
          Now well ! now well ' now well !
          Born is the King of Israel !"

formed by the fairy bands in which to celebrate the eve of the birth of a Saviour, in whose mercy they all had hope, was of the most magnificent description.

Midsummer-eve and new-year's day and eve are holidays with the miners. It has been said they refuse to work on those days from superstitious reasons. I never heard of any.

WARNINGS AND "TOKENS."

AMONGST the mining population there is a deeply-rooted belief in warnings. The following, related by a very respectable man, formerly a miner, well illustrates this :—

"My father, when a lad, worked with a companion (James or 'Jim,' as he was called) in Germo. They lived close by Old Wheal Grey in Breage. One evening, the daughter of the person with whom they lodged came in to her mother, crying, ' Billy and Jim ben out theer for more than a hour, and I ben chasin them among the Kilyur banks, and they waan't ler me catch them. As fast as I do go to one, they do go to another.' ' Hould your tongue, child,' said the mother ; ' 'twas their forenoon core, and they both ben up in bed this hours.' ' I 'm sure I ben chasin them,' said the girl. The mother then went up-stairs and awoke the lads, telling them the story. One of them said, ' 'Tis a warning ; somethin will happen in un old end, and I shan't go to mine this core.' ' Nonsense,' said the other ; ' don't let us be so foolish ; the child has been playing with some strangers, and it isn't worth while to be spaled for any such foolishness.' ' I tell you,' replied the other, ' I won't go.' As it was useless for one man to go alone, both remained away. In the course of the night, however, a run took place in the end they were working in, and tens of thousands of kibblefuls came away. Had they been at work, it was scarcely possible for them to have escaped."

At Wheal Vor it has always been and is now believed that a fatal accident in the mine is presaged by the appearance of a hare or white rabbit in one of the engine-houses. The men solemnly declare that they have chased these appearances till they were hemmed in apparently, without being able to catch them. The white rabbit on one occasion being *run into a " windbore"* lying on the ground, *and, though stopped in,* escaped.

In this mine there appears to be a general belief among the men in " tokens" and supernatural appearances. A few months since, a fine old man reported, on being relieved from his turn as watcher, that during the night he heard a loud sound like the emptying of a cartload of rubbish in front of the account-house, where he was staying. On going out, nothing was to be seen. The poor fellow, considering the strange sound as a "warning," pined away and died within a few weeks.

THE GHOST ON HORSEBACK.

BILLY —— and John ——, working at Wheal Vor, were in the habit, early in the morning, of calling out a dog or two, kept by the occupier of an adjoining farm, and with them hunt over the Godolphin warren adjoining. One morning, while thus engaged, one of them gave the alarm that a man on horseback was coming down the road. "'Tisn't possible," said the other; "no horse can ever come over that road" "There is a horse, and old Cap'n T. is upon it," replied the first. "Hold thy tongue," rejoined his comrade; "he's dead months ago." "I know that; but 'tis he, sure enough." Both crouched down behind a bush; and my informant, whose father was one of the parties, declared that the appearance of Capt. T., on a black horse, passed noiselessly down the road immediately before them, but without noticing their presence.

THE BLACK DOGS.

ABOUT thirty years since, a man and a lad were engaged in sinking a shaft at Wheal Vor Mine, when the lad, through carelessness or accident, missed in charging a hole, so that a necessity arose for the dangerous operation of picking out the charge. This they proceeded to do, the man severely reprimanding the carelessness of his assistant Several other miners at the time being about to change their core, were on the plat above, calling down and conversing occasionally with man and boy. Suddenly the charge exploded, and the latter were seen to be thrown up in the midst of a volume of flame. As soon as help could be procured, a party descended, when the remains of the poor fellows were found to be shattered and scorched beyond recognition. When these were brought to the surface, the clothes and a mass of mangled flesh dropped from the bodies. A bystander, to spare the feelings of the relatives, hastily caught up the revolting mass in a shovel, and threw the whole into the blazing furnace of Woolf's engine, close at hand From that time the engineman declared that troops of little black dogs continually haunted the place, even when the doors were shut. Few of them liked to talk about it; but it was difficult to obtain the necessary attendance to work the machine.

PITMEN'S OMENS AND GOBLINS.

IT is curious to notice the correspondence between the superstitions of the coal-miner and those employed in the metalliferous mines. The following comes very opportunely to our hand :—

The superstitions of pitmen were once many and terrible ; but so far from existing now-a-days, they are only matters of tradition among the old men. One class only of superstitions does exist among a few of the older and less-educated pitmen—namely, the class of omens, warnings, and signs. If one of these pitmen meet or see a woman, if he catch but a glimpse of her draperies, on his way, in the middle of the night to the pit, the probability is that he returns home and goes to bed again. The appearance of a woman at this untimely hour has often materially impeded the day's winning, for the omen is held not to be personal to the individual perceiving it, but to bode general ill luck to all. The walk from home to pit mouth, always performed at dead of the night, was the period when omens were mostly to be looked for. The supernatural appearance of a little white animal like a rabbit, which was said to cross the miner's path, was another warning not to descend. Sometimes the omens were rather mental than visual. The pitmen in the midland counties have, or had, a belief, unknown in the north, in aerial whistlings, warning them against the pit. Who, or what the invisible musicians were, nobody pretended to know ; but for all that, they must have been counted and found to consist of seven, as "The Seven Whistlers" is the name they bear to this day. Two goblins were believed to haunt the northern mines. One was a spiteful elf, who indicated his presence only by the mischief he perpetrated. He rejoiced in the name of "Cutty Soams," and appears to have employed himself only in the stupid device of severing the rope-traces or soams, by which an assistant-putter—honoured by the title of "the fool"—is yoked to the tub. The strands of hemp which were left all sound in the board at "kenner-time," were found next morning severed in twain. "Cutty Soams" has been at work, would the fool and his driver say, dolefully knotting the cord. The other goblin was altogether a more sensible, and, indeed, an honest and hard-working bogie, much akin to the Scotch brownie, or the hairy fiend, whom Milton rather scurvily apostrophises as a lubber. The supernatural personage in question was no other than a ghostly putter, and his name was "Bluecap." Sometimes the miners would perceive a light blue flame flicker through the air, and settle on a full coal-tub, which immediately moved towards the rolley-way, as though impelled by the sturdiest sinews in the working. Industrious Bluecap was at his vocation ; but he required, and rightly, to be paid for his services, which he modestly rated as those of an ordinary average putter ; therefore once a fortnight Bluecap's wages were left for him in a solitary corner of the mine. If they were a farthing below his due, the indignant Bluecap would not pocket a stiver ; if they were a farthing above his due, indignant Bluecap left the surplus revenue where he found it. The writer asked his informant, a hewer, whether, if Bluecap's wages were now-a-days to be left for him, he thought they would be appropriated ; the man shrewdly answered, he thought they would be taken by Bluecap, or by somebody else. Of the above notions it must be understood that the idea of omens is the only one still seriously entertained, and even its hold upon the popular mind, as has been before stated, is becoming weaker and weaker.—
Colliery Guardian, May 23, 1863

THE DEAD HAND.

" I'VE seen it—I've seen it !" exclaimed a young woman, pale with terror, approaching with much haste the door of a cottage, around which were gathered several of the miners' wives inhabiting the adjoining dwellings.

" God's mercy be with the chield !" replied the oldest woman of the group, with very great seriousness.

" Aunt Alice," asked one of the youngest women, " and do 'e b'lieve any harm will come o' seeing it ? "

" Mary Doble saw it and pined ; Jinny Trestrail was never the same woman after she seed the hand in Wheal Jewel ; and I knows ever so many more ; but let us hope, by the blessing o' the Lord, no evil will come on Mary."

Mary was evidently impressed with a sense of some heavy trouble. She sighed deeply, and pressed her hand to her side, as if to still the beating of her heart. The thoughtless faith of the old woman promised to work out a fulfilment of her fears in producing mental distress and corporeal suffering in the younger one.

While this was passing in the little village, a group of men were gathered around a deserted shaft, which existed in too dangerous proximity with the abodes of the miners. They were earnestly discussing the question of the reality of the appearance of the *dead hand*—those who had not seen it expressing a doubt of its reality, while others declared most emphatically, " that in that very shaft they had seed un with a lighted candle in his hand, moving up and down upon the ladders, as though he was carried by a living man."

It appears that some time previously to the abandonment of the mine, an unfortunate miner was ascending from his subterranean labours, carrying his candle in his hand. He was probably seized with giddiness, but from that or some other cause, he fell away from the ladders, and was found by his comrades a bleeding corpse at the bottom. The character of this man was not of the best ; and after his burial, it was stated by the people that *he had been seen.* From a vague rumour of his spectral appearance on the surface, the tale eventually settled itself into that of the dead hand moving up and down in the shaft.

By the spectral light of the candle, the hand had been distinctly visible to many, and the irregular motion of the light proved that the candle was held in the usual manner between the thumb and finger in its ball of clay, while the fingers were employed in grasping stave after stave of the ladder. The belief in the evil attendant on being unfortunate enough to see this spectral hand, prevailed very generally amongst the mining population about twenty years since.   The dead hand was not, however, confined to one shaft or mine.   Similar narrations have been met with in several districts.

DORCAS, THE SPIRIT OF POLBREEN MINE.

POLBREEN MINE is situated at the foot of the hill known as St Agnes Becon.   In one of the small cottages which immediately adjoins the mine once lived a woman called Dorcas.

Beyond this we know little of her life ; but we are concerned chiefly with her death, which, we are told, was suicidal.

From some cause, which is not related, Dorcas grew weary of life, and one unholy night she left her house and flung herself into one of the deep shafts of Polbreen Mine, at the bottom of which her dead and broken body was discovered.   The remnant of humanity was brought to the surface ; and after the laws of the time with regard to suicides had been fulfilled, the body of Dorcas was buried.

Her presence, however, still remained in the mine.   She appears ordinarily to take a malicious delight in tormenting the industrious miner, calling him by name, and alluring him from his tasks. This was carried on by her to such an extent, that when a "tributer" had made a poor month, he was asked if he had " been chasing Dorcas." *

Dorcas was usually only a voice.   It has been said by some that they have seen her in the mine, but this is doubted by the miners generally, who refer the spectral appearance to the fears of their " comrade."

But it is stated as an incontrovertible fact, that more than one man who has met the spirit in the levels of the mine has had his clothes torn off his back ; whether in anger or in sport, is not clearly made out.   On one occasion, and on one occasion only, Dorcas appears to have acted kindly.   Two miners, who for distinction's sake we will call Martin and Jacky, were at work in their end, and at the time busily at work " beating the borer."

The name of Jacky was distinctly uttered between the blows. He stopped and listened—all was still.   They proceeded with their task . a blow on the iron rod.—" Jacky."   Another blow.—

* A tributer is a man who agrees with the adventurers in a mine to receive a certain share of the profits on the ore raised by him in lieu of wages   This account is settled monthly or bi-monthly, which will explain the phrase a ' poor month "

"Jacky." They pause—all is silent. "Well, thee wert called, Jacky," said Martin, "go and see."

Jacky was, however, either afraid, or he thought himself the fool of his senses.

Work was resumed, and "Jacky ! Jacky ! Jacky !" was called more vehemently and distinctly than before.

Jacky threw down his heavy hammer, and went from his companion, resolved to satisfy himself as to the caller.

He had not proceeded many yards from the spot on which he had been standing at work, when a mass of rock fell from the roof of the level, weighing many tons, which would have crushed him to death. Martin had been stooping, holding the borer, and a projecting corner of rock just above him turned off the falling mass. He was securely enclosed, and they had to dig him out, but he escaped without injury. Jacky declared to his dying day that he owed his life to Dorcas.

Although Dorcas's shaft remains a part of Polbieen Mine, I am informed by the present agent that her presence has departed.

HINGSTON DOWNS.

"Hengsten Down, well ywrought,
Is worth London town dear ybought."
CAREW—*Lord De Dunstanville's Edition.*

IT may be worthy of consideration whether we have not evidence in this distich of the extent to which mining operations were carried on over this moorland and the adjoining country by the ancient Cornish miners.

It is said that this moorland was originally Hengiston ; and tradition affirms that the name preserves the memory of a severe contest, when the Welsh joined Egbright, a king of the West Saxons, and defeated the host of Danes, who had come over to "West Wales," meaning thereby Cornwall. On this waste Hengist had his fenced camp, and here the Cornish and the Welsh attacked and entirely overthrew him. It is evident, if tradition is to be believed, that the struggle was to gain possession of a valuable tin ground.

FISHERMEN AND SAILORS.

"I was saying to Jack, as we talk'd t' other day
 About lubbers and snivelling elves,
That if people in life did not steer the right way,
 They had nothing to thank but themselves.
Now, when a man's caught by those mermaids the girls
 With their flattering palaver and smiles ;
He runs, while he's list'ning to their fal de rals,
 Bump ashore on the Scilly Isles."

                                        TOM DIBDIN.

ROMANCES OF FISHERMEN
AND SAILORS.

THE PILOT'S GHOST STORY.

" On a sudden shrilly sounding,
Hideous yells and shrieks were heard ;
Then each heart with fear confounding,
A sad troop of ghosts appear'd,
All in dreary hammocks shrouded,
Which for winding-sheets they wore "
Admiral Hosier's Ghost.

I PREFER giving this story in the words in which it was communicated. For its singular character, it is a ghost story
well worth preserving :—" Just seventeen years since, I went
down on the wharf from my house one night about twelve and one
in the morning, to see whether there was any ' hobble,' and found
a sloop, the *Sally* of St Ives (the *Sally* was wrecked at St Ives
one Saturday afternoon in the spring of 1862), in the bay, bound
for Hayle. When I got by the White Hart public-house, I saw a
man leaning against a post on the wharf,—I spoke to him, wished
him good morning, and asked him what o'clock it was, but to no
purpose. I was not to be easily frightened, for I didn't believe in
ghosts ; and finding I got no answer to my repeated inquiries, I
approached close to him and said, ' Thee 'rt a queer sort of fellow,
not to speak ; I 'd speak to the devil, if he were to speak to me.
Who art a at all ? thee 'st needn't think to frighten me ; that thee
wasn't do, if thou wert twice so ugly ; who art a at all ? ' He
turned his great ugly face on me, glared abroad his great eyes,
opened his mouth, and it was a mouth sure nuff. Then I saw
pieces of sea-weed and bits of sticks in his whiskers ; the flesh of
his face and hands were parboiled, just like a woman's hands after
a good day's washing. Well, I did not like his looks a bit, and
sheered off ; but he followed close by my side, and I could hear
the water squashing in his shoes every step he took. Well, I

stopped a bit, and thought to be a little bit civil to him, and spoke to him again, but no answer. I then thought I would go to seek for another of our crew, and knock him up to get the vessel, and had got about fifty or sixty yards, when I turned to see if he was following me, but saw him where I left him. Fearing he would come after me, I ran for my life the few steps that I had to go. But when I got to the door, to my horror there stood the man in the door grinning horribly. I shook like an aspen-leaf; my hat lifted from my head; the sweat boiled out of me. What to do I didn't know, and in the house there was such a row, as if everybody was breaking up everything. After a bit I went in, for the door was 'on the latch,'—that is, not locked,—and called the captain of the boat, and got light, but everything was all right, nor had he heard any noise. We went out aboard of the *Sally*, and I put her into Hayle, but I felt ill enough to be in bed. I left the vessel to come home as soon as I could, but it took me four hours to walk two miles, and I had to lie down in the road, and was taken home to St Ives in a cart; as far as the Terrace from there I was carried home by my brothers, and put to bed. Three days afterwards all my hair fell off as if I had had my head shaved The roots, and for about half an inch from the roots, being quite white. I was ill six months, and the doctor's bill was £4, 17s 6d. for attendance and medicine. So you see I have reason to believe in the existence of spirits as much as Mr Wesley had. My hair grew again, and twelve months after I had as good a head of dark-brown hair as ever." *

THE PHANTOM SHIP.

YEARS long ago, one night, a gig's crew was called to go off to a "hobble," to the westwards of St Ives Head. No sooner was one boat launched than several others were put off from the shore, and a stiff chase was maintained, each one being eager to get to the ship, as she had the appearance of a foreign trader. The hull was clearly visible, she was a schooner-rigged vessel, with a light over her bows

Away they pulled, and the boat which had been first launched still kept ahead by dint of mechanical power and skill. All the men had thrown off their jackets to row with more freedom. At length the helmsman cried out, " Stand ready to board her " The sailor rowing the bow oar slipped it out of the row-lock, and stood on the forethought, taking his jacket on his arm, ready to spring aboard.

* "The man has still a good thick head of hair —C I. S "

The vessel came so close to the boat that they could see the men, and the bow-oar man made a grasp at her bulwarks. His hand found nothing solid, and he fell, being caught by one of his mates, back into the boat, instead of into the water. Then ship and lights disappeared. The next morning the *Neptune* of London, Captain Richard Grant, was wrecked at Gwithian, and all perished. The captain's body was picked up after a few days, and that of his son also. They were both buried in Gwithian churchyard.

JACK HARRY'S LIGHTS.

THE phantom lights are called, they tell me, "Jack Harry's lights," because he was the first man who was fooled by them. They are generally observed before a gale, and the ship seen is like the ship which is sure to be wrecked. The man who communicated this to me said, "What or how it is we can't tell, but the fact of its being seen is too plain."

The following is another version, which I received from an old pilot —

"Some five years ago, on a Sunday night, the wind being strong, our crew heard of a large vessel in the offing, after we came out of chapel. We manned our big boat, the *Ark*,—she was nearly new then,—and away we went, under close-reefed foresail and little mizen, the sea going over us at a sweet rate. The vessel stood just off the head, the wind blowing W.N.W. We had gone off four or five miles, and we thought we were up alongside, when, lo! she slipped to windward a league or more. Well, off we went after her, and a good beating match we had, too, but the *Ark* was a safe craft, and we neared and neared till, as we thought, we got up close. Away she whizzed in a minute, in along to Godrevy, just over the course we sailed; so we gave it up for "Jack Harry's light," and, with wet jackets and disappointed hopes, we bore up for the harbour, prepared to hear of squalls, which came heavier than ever next day

"Scores of pilots have seen and been led a nice chase after them. They are just the same as the *Flying Dutchman*, seen off the Cape of Good Hope "

Another man informed me that, once coming down channel, they had a phantom ship alongside of them for miles : it was a moonlight night, with a thin rain and mist. They could see several men aboard moving about. They hailed her several times, but could not get an answer, "and we didn't know what to think of her, when all at once she vanished."

THE PIRATE-WRECKER AND THE DEATH SHIP.

ONE lovely evening in the autumn, a strange ship was seen at a short distance from Cape Cornwall The little wind there was blew from the land, but she did not avail herself of it. She was evidently permitted to drift with the tide, which was flowing southward, and curving in round Whitesand Bay towards the Land's-End.   The vessel, from her peculiar rig, created no small amount of alarm amongst the fishermen, since it told them that she was manned by pirates; and a large body of men and women watched her movements from behind the rocks at Caraglose.   At length, when within a couple of pistol-shots off the shore, a boat was lowered and manned.   Then a man, whose limited movements show him to be heavily ironed, was brought to the side of the ship and evidently forced—for several pistols were held at his head— into the boat, which then rowed rapidly to the shore in Priest's Cove.   The waves of the Atlantic Ocean fell so gently on the strand, that there was no difficulty in beaching the boat.   The prisoner was made to stand up, and his ponderous chains were removed from his arms and ankles.   In a frenzy of passion he attacked the sailors, but they were too many and too strong for him, and the fight terminated by his being thrown into the water, and left to scramble up on the dry sands.   They pushed the boat off with a wild shout, and this man stood uttering fearful imprecations on his former comrades.

It subsequently became known that this man was so monstrously wicked that even the pirates would no longer endure him, and hence they had recourse to this means of ridding themselves of him.

It is not necessary to tell how this wretch settled himself at Tregaseal, and lived by a system of wrecking, pursued with un- heard-of cruelties and cunning.   "It's too frightful to tell," says my correspondent, " what was said about his doings   We scarcely believed half of the vile things we heard, till we saw what took place at his death.   But one can't say he died, because he was taken off bodily.   We shall never know the scores, perhaps hundreds, of ships that old sinner has brought on the cliffs, by fastening his lantern to the neck of his horse, with its head tied close to the forefoot.   The horse, when driven along the cliff, would, by its motion, cause the lantern to be taken for the stern- light of a ship; then the vessel would come right in on the rocks, since those on board would expect to find plenty of sea-room; and, if any of the poor sailors escaped a watery grave, the old wretch would give them a worse death, by knocking them on the head with his hatchet, or cutting off their hands as they tried to grasp the ledges of the rocks.

A life of extreme wickedness was at length closed with circum- stances of unusual terror—so terrible, that the story is told with feelings of awe even at the present day. The old wretch fought lustily with death, but at length the time of his departure came. It was in the time of the barley-harvest Two men were in a field on the cliff, a little below the house, mowing. A universal calm prevailed, and there was not a breath of wind to stir the corn. Suddenly a breeze passed by them, and they heard the words, " The time is come, but the man isn't come." These words appeared to float in the breeze from the sea, and consequently it attracted their attention. Looking out to sea, they saw a black, heavy, square-rigged ship, with all her sails set, coming in against wind and tide, and not a hand to be seen on board. The sky became black as night around the ship, and as she came under the cliff—and she came so close that the top of the masts could scarcely be perceived— the darkness resolved itself into a lurid storm-cloud, which extended high into the air. The sun shone brilliantly over the country, except on the house of the pirate at Tregaseal—that was wrapt in the deep shadow of the cloud.

The men, in terror, left their work , they found all the neighbours gathered around the door of the pirate's cottage, none of them daring to enter it. Parson —— had been sent for by the terrified peasants, this divine being celebrated for his power of driving away evil spirits.

The dying wrecker was in a state of agony, crying out, in tones of the most intense terror, " The devil is tearing at me with nails like the claws of a hawk ! Put out the sailors with their bloody hands !" and using, in the paroxysms of pain, the most profane imprecations. The parson, the doctor, and two of the bravest of the fishermen, were the only persons in the room. They related that at one moment the room was as dark as the grave, and that at the next it was so light that every hair on the old man's head could be seen standing on end. The parson used all his influence to dispel the evil spirit His powers were so potent that he reduced the devil to the size of a fly, but he could not put him out of the room. All this time the room appeared as if filled with the sea, with the waves surging violently to and fro, and one could hear the breakers roaring, as if standing on the edge of the cliff in a storm. At last there was a fearful clash of thunder, and a blaze of the intensest lightning The house appeared on fire, and the ground shook, as if with an earthquake. All rushed in terror from the house, leaving the dying man to his fate.

The storm raged with fearful violence, but appeared to contract its dimensions. The black cloud, which was first seen to come in with the black ship, was moving, with a violent internal motion, over the wrecker's house.   The cloud rolled together, smaller and smaller, and suddenly, with the blast of a whirlwind, it passed from Tregaseal to the ship, and she was impelled, amidst the flashes of lightning and roarings of thunder, away over the sea.

The dead body of the pirate-wrecker lay a ghastly spectacle, with eyes expanded and the mouth partly open, still retaining the aspect of his last mortal terror.   As every one hated him, they all desired to remove his corpse as rapidly as possible from the sight of man. A rude coffin was rapidly prepared, and the body was carefully cased in its boards.   They tell me the coffin was carried to the churchyard, but that it was too light to have contained the body, and that it was followed by a black pig, which joined the company forming the procession, nobody knew where, and disappeared nobody knew when.   When they reached the church stile, a storm, similar in its character to that which heralded the wrecker's death, came on.   The bearers of the coffin were obliged to leave it without the churchyard stile, and rush into the church for safety. The storm lasted long and raged with violence, and all was as dark as night.   A sudden blaze of light, more vivid than before, was seen, and those who had the hardihood to look out saw that the lightning had set fire to the coffin, and it was being borne away through the air, blazing and whirling wildly in the grasp of such a whirlwind as no man ever witnessed before or since.

THE SPECTRE SHIP OF PORTHCURNO.

PORTHCURNO COVE is situated a little to the west of the Logan Stone.   There, as in nearly all the coves around the coast, once existed a small chapel * or oratory, which appears to have been dedicated to St Leven.   There exists now a little square enclosure about the size of a (*bougie*) sheep's house, which is all that remains of this little holy place.   Looking up the valley (Bottom), you may see a few trees, with the chimney-tops and part of the roof of an old fashioned house.   That place is Raftra, where they say St Leven Church was to have been built ; but as fast as the stones were taken there by day, they were removed by night to the place of the present church.   (These performances are usually the act of the devil, but I have no information as to the saint or sinner who did this work.)   Raftra House, at the time it was built, was the largest mansion west of Penzance.   It is said to have been erected by the Tresillians, and, ere it was finished, they ap-

* I am informed that there are no less than four of these cliff chapels between St Leven and St Loy, which was a larger building, where mass was probably celebrated.

pear to have been obliged to sell house and lands for less than it had cost them to build the house.

This valley is, in every respect, a melancholy spot, and during a period of storms, or at night, it is exactly the place which might well be haunted by demon revellers. In the days of the saint from whom the parish has its name—St Leven—he lived a long way up from the cove, at a place called Bodelan, and his influence made that, which is now so dreary, a garden. By his pure holiness he made the wilderness a garden of flowers, and spread gladness where now is desolation.

Few persons cared to cross that valley after nightfall; and it is not more than thirty years since that I had a narrative from an inhabitant of Penberth, that he himself had seen the spectre ship sailing over the land.

This strange apparition is said to have been observed frequently, coming in from sea about nightfall, when the mists were rising from the marshy ground in the Bottoms.

Onward came the ill-omened craft. It passed steadily through the breakers on the shore, glided up over the sands, and steadily pursued its course over the dry land, as if it had been water. She is described to have been a black, square-rigged, single-masted affair, usually, but not always, followed by a boat. No crew was ever seen It is supposed they were below, and that the hatches were battened down. On it went to Bodelan, where St Leven formerly dwelt. It would then steer its course to Chygwiden, and there vanish like smoke

Many of the old people have seen this ship, and no one ever saw it, upon whom some bad luck was not sure to fall

This ship is somehow connected with a strange man who returned from sea, and went to live at Chygwiden. It may be five hundred years since—it may be but fifty.

He was accompanied by a servant of foreign and forbidding aspect, who continued to be his only attendant, and this servant was never known to speak to any one save his master. It is said by some they were pirates; others make them more familiar, by calling them privateers; while some insist upon it they were American buccaneers. Whatever they may have been, there was but little seen of them by any of their neighbours. They kept a boat at Porthcurno Cove, and at daylight they would start for sea, never returning until night, and not unfrequently remaining out the whole of the night, especially if the weather was tempestuous. This kind of sea-life was varied by hunting. It mattered not to them whether it was day or night, when the storm was loudest, there was this strange man, accompanied either by his servant or by the devil, and the midnight cry of his dogs would disturb the country.

This mysterious being died, and then the servant sought the aid of a few of the peasantry to bear his coffin to the churchyard. The corpse was laid in the grave, around which the dogs were gathered, with the foreigner in their midst. As soon as the earth was thrown on the coffin, man and dogs disappeared, and, strange to say, the boat disappeared at the same moment from the cove. It has never since been seen; and from that day to this, no one has been able to keep a boat in Porthcurno Cove.

THE LADY WITH THE LANTERN.

THE night was dark and the wind high. The heavy waves rolled round the point of "the Island" into St Ives Bay, as Atlantic waves only can roll. Everything bespoke a storm of no ordinary character There were no ships in the bay—not a fishing-boat was afloat. The few small trading vessels had run into Hayle for shelter, or had nestled themselves within that very unquiet resting-place, St Ives pier. The fishing-boats were all high and dry on the sands

Moving over the rocks which run out into the sea from the eastern side of "the Island," was seen a light. It passed over the most rugged ridges, formed by the intrusive Greenstone masses, and over the sharp edges of the upturned slate-rocks with apparent ease. Forth and back—to and from—wandered the light.

" Ha ! " said an old sailor with a sigh, as he looked out over the sea ; " a sad night ! a sad night ! The Lady and the Lantern is out."

" The Lady and the Lantern," repeated I ; "what do you mean ? "

" The light out yonder "——

" Is from the lantern of some fisherman looking for something he has lost," interrupted I.

" Never a fisherman nor a ' salt ' either would venture there to-night," said the sailor.

" What is it, then ? " I curiously inquired

" Ha'ast never heard of the Lady and the Lantern ? " asked a woman who was standing by.

" Never."

Without any preface, she began at once to enlighten me. I am compelled, however, to reduce her rambling story to something like order, and to make her long-drawn tale as concise as possible.

In the year —— there were many wrecks around the coast. It was a melancholy time. For more than a month there had been a succession of storms, each one more severe than the preceding one. At length, one evening, just about dusk, a large ship came suddenly out of the mist. Her position, it was at once discovered, equally by those on board, and by the people on the shore, was perilous beyond hope. The sailors, as soon as they saw how near they were to the shore, made every effort to save the ship, and then to prepare for saving themselves The tempest raged with such fury from the west, that the ship parted her anchors at the moment her strain came upon them, and she swang round,— her only sail flying into ribbons in the gale—rushing, as it were, eagerly upon her fate. Presently she struck violently upon a sunken rock, and her masts went by the board, the waves sweeping over her, and clearing her decks. Many perished at once, and, as each successive wave urged her onward, others of the hardy and daring seamen were swept into the angry sea.

Notwithstanding the severity of the storm, a boat was manned by the St Ives fishermen, and launched from within the pier. Their perfect knowledge of their work enabled them, by the efforts of willing hearts, anxiously desiring to succour the distressed, to round the pier-head, and to row towards the ship.

These fishermen brought their boat near to the ship. It was impossible to get close to her, and they called to the sailors on board to throw them ropes. This they were enabled to do, and some two or three of the sailors lowered themselves by their aid, and were hauled into the boat.

Then a group appeared on the deck, surrounding and supporting a lady, who held a child in her arms. They were imploring her to give her charge into the strong arms of a man ere they endeavoured to pass her from the ship to the boat.

The lady could not be prevailed on to part with the infant. The ship was fast breaking up, not a moment could be lost So the lady, holding her child, was lowered into the sea, and eagerly the fishermen drew her through the waves towards the boat.

In her passage the lady had fainted, and she was taken into the boat without the infant. The child had fallen from her arms, and was lost in the boiling waters.

Many of the crew were saved by these adventurous men, and

taken safely into St Ives   Before morning the shore was strewed
with fragments of wreck, and the mighty ship had disappeared.

Life returned to the lady ; but, finding that her child was gone,
it returned without hope, and she speedily closed her eyes in death.
In the churchyard they buried her ; but, shortly after her burial, a
lady was seen to pass over the wall of the churchyard, on to the
beach, and walk towards the Island.   There she spent hours amidst
the rocks, looking for her child, and not finding it, she would sigh
deeply and return to her grave.   When the nights were tempestuous
or very dark, she carried a lantern ; but on fine nights she made
her search without a light.   The Lady and the Lantern have ever
been regarded as predictors of disaster on this shore

May not the Lady Sibella, or Sibbets, mentioned by Mr Blight
as passing from the shore to a rock off Morva, be but another
version of this story ?

THE DROWNED "HAILING THEIR NAMES."

THE fishermen dread to walk at night near those parts of the
shore where there may have been wrecks.   The souls of the
drowned sailors appear to haunt those spots, and the " calling of
the dead " has frequently been heard.   I have been told that, under
certain circumstances, especially before the coming of storms, or
at certain seasons, but always at night, these callings are common.
Many a fisherman has declared he has heard the voices of dead
sailors " hailing their own names "

THE VOICE FROM THE SEA.

A FISHERMAN or a pilot was walking one night on the sands
at Porth-Towan, when all was still save the monotonous fall
of the light waves upon the sand.

He distinctly heard a voice from the sea exclaiming,—

"The hour is come, but not the man "

This was repeated three times, when a black figure, like that of a
man, appeared on the top of the hill.   It paused for a moment,
then rushed impetuously down the steep incline, over the sands,
and was lost in the sea

In different forms this story is told all around the Cornish
coast.

THE SMUGGLER'S TOKEN.

UNTIL about the time of the close of the last French war, a large portion of the inhabitants of the south-west coast of Cornwall were in some way or other connected with the practice of smuggling. The traffic with the opposite coast was carried on principally in boats or undecked vessels. The risks encountered by their crews produced a race of hardy, fearless men, a few of whom are still living, and it has been said that the Government of those days winked at the infraction of the law, from an unwillingness to destroy so excellent a school for seamen. Recently the demand for ardent spirits has so fallen off that there is no longer an inducement to smuggle ; still it is sometimes exultingly rumoured that, the " Coast Guard having been cleverly put off the scent, a cargo has been successfully run " The little coves in the Lizard promontory formed the principal trading places, the goods being taken as soon as landed to various places of concealment, whence they were withdrawn as required for disposal. About eighty years since, a boat, laden with " ankers " of spirits, was about, with its crew, to leave Mullian Cove for Newlyn. One of the farmers concerned in the venture, members of whose family are still living, was persuaded to accompany them, and entered the boat for the purpose, but, recollecting he had business at Helston, got out again, and the boat left without him. On his return from Helston, late in the evening, he sat down exclaiming, " The boat and all on board are lost! I met the men as I passed the top of Halzaphron (a very high cliff on the road), with their hair and clothes dripping wet ! " In spite of the arguments of his friends, he persisted in his statement. The boat and crew were never more heard of, and the farmer was so affected by the circumstance, that he pined and died shortly after.

THE HOOPER, OR THE HOOTER, OF SENNEN COVE.

THIS was supposed to be a spirit which took the form of a band of misty vapour, stretching across the bay, so opaque that nothing could be seen through it. It was regarded as a kindly interposition of some ministering spirit, to warn the fishermen against venturing to sea. This appearance was always followed, and often suddenly, by a severe storm It is seldom or never seen now. One profane old fisherman would not be warned by the bank of fog The weather was fine on the shore, and the

waves fell tranquilly on the sands ; and this aged sinner, declaring
he would not be made a fool of, persuaded some young men to
join him.   They manned a boat, and the aged leader, having with
him a threshing-flail, blasphemously declared that he would drive
the spirit away ; and he vigorously beat the fog with the " threshel "
—so the flail is called.

The boat passed through the fog and went to sea.   A severe
storm came on.   No one ever saw the boat or the men again ;
and since that time the Hooper has been rarely seen.

HOW TO EAT PILCHARDS.

IT is unlucky to commence eating pilchards, or, indeed, any kind
of fish, from the head downwards.   I have often heard persons rebuked for committing such a grievous sin, which is " sure
to turn the heads of the fish away from the coasts."

The legitimate process—mark this, all fish-eaters—*is to eat the
fish from the tail towards the head.*   This brings the fish to our
shores, and secures good luck to the fishermen.

PILCHARDS CRYING FOR MORE.

WHEN there is a large catch of fish (pilchards), they are preserved,—put in bulk, as the phrase is,—by being rubbed
with salt, and placed in regular order, one on the other, head and
tails alternately, forming regular walls of fish.

The fish often, when so placed, make a squeaking noise ; this
is called " crying for more," and is regarded as a most favourable
sign   More fish may soon be expected to be brought to the same
cellar.

The noise which is heard is really produced by the bursting of
the air-bladders , and when many break together, which, when
hundreds of thousands are piled in a mass, is not unusual, the
sound is a loud one.

THE PRESSING-STONES.

THOSE who are not familiar with the process of " curing "
(salting) pilchards for the Italian markets, will require a
little explanation to understand the accompanying story.

The pilchards being caught in vast quantities, often amounting
to many thousand hogsheads at a time, in an enclosed net called
a " seine," are taken out of it—the larger net—in a smaller net,

called the " tuck net," and from it loaded into boats and taken to the shore. They are quickly transferred to the fish-sellers, and " put in bulk "—that is, they are well rubbed with salt, and carefully packed up—all interstitial spaces being filled with salt—in a pile several feet in height and depth. They remain in this condition for about six weeks; when they are removed from "the bulk," washed, and put into barrels in very regular order. The barrels being filled with pilchards, pressing-stones,—round masses of granite, weighing about a hundredweight,—with an iron hook fixed into them for the convenience of moving, are placed on the fish. By this they are much compressed, and a considerable quantity of oil is squeezed out of them. This process being completed, the cask is " headed," marked, and is ready for exportation.

Jem Tregose and his old woman, with two sons and a daughter, lived over one of the fish cellars in St Ives. For many years there had been a great scarcity of fish ; * their cellar had been empty; Jem and his boys were fishermen, and it had long been hard times with them. It is true they went out " hook-and-line " fishing now and then, and got a little money. They had gone over to Ireland on the herring-fishing, but very little luck attended them.

Summer had passed away, and the early autumn was upon them. The seine boats were out day after day, but no " signs of fish." One evening, when the boys came home, Ann Jenny Tregose had an unusual smile upon her face, and her daughter Janniper, who had long suffered from the " megrims," was in capital spirits.

" Well, mother," says one of the sons, " and what ails thee a'?"

" The press-stones a bin rolling."

" Haas they, sure enuff," says the old man.

" Ees ! ees !" exclaims Janniper ; "they has been making a skimmage !"

" Hark ye," cries the old woman, " there they go again."

And sure enough there was a heavy rolling of the stones in the cellar below them. It did not require much imagination to image these round granite pebbles sliding themselves down on the " couse," or stone flooring, and dividing themselves up into sets, as if for a dance,—a regular "cows' courant," or game of romps.

" Fish to-morrow !" exclaimed the old woman. The ejaculations of each one of the party showed their perfect faith in the belief, that the stones rolling down from the heap, in which they had been useless for some time, was a certain indication that pilchards were approaching the coast.

Early on the morrow the old man and his sons were on their

---

* Pilchards are called *par excellence* " fish.

2 A

" stem ; " and shortly after daylight the cry of " Heva ! heva ! " *
was heard from the hills ; the seine was shot, and ere night a
large quantity of fish might be seen in the cellar, and every one
joyous.

WHIPPING THE HAKE.

I T is not improbable that the saying applied to the people of one
of the Cornish fishing-towns, of " Who whipped the hake ? "
may be explained by the following :—

" Lastly, they are persecuted by the hakes, who (not long
sithence) haunted the coast in great abundance ; but now being
deprived of their wonted bait, are much diminished, verifying the
proverb, ' *What we lose in hake we shall have in herring.*' "—
Carew, Survey, p. 34.

Annoyed with the hakes, the seiners may, in their ignorance,
have actually served one of those fish as indicated.

* Heva is shouted from the hills, upon which a watch is kept for the approach of pilchards by the " huer," who telegraphs to the boats by means of bushes covered with
white cloth, or, in modern days, with wire frames so covered   These signals are well
understood, and the men in the seine and the other boats act according to the huer's directions   The following song contains all the terms employed in the fishing ; many of them,
especially *Could Roos,* do not appear to have any definite meaning attached to them
    The song is by the late C Taylor Stevens of St Ives, who was for some time the rural
postman to Zennor   I employed Mr Taylor Stevens for some time collecting all that
remains of legendary tales and superstitions in Zennor and Morva   The net is spelled
sometimes *Seine* at others *Sean*

                    " MERRY SEAN LADS
    " With a cold north wind and a cockled sea,
        Or an autumn's cloudless day,
    At the huer's bid, to stem we row,
        Or upon our paddles play.
    All the signs, ' East, West, and Quiet,
        Could Roos,' too well we know ;
    We can bend a stop, secure a cross,
        For brave sean lads are we !
Chorus—We can bend a stop, secure a cross,
        For brave sean lads are we !
    " If we have first stem when heva comes
        We 'll the huer's bushes watch ;
    We will row right off or quiet lie,
        Flying summer sculls to catch.
    And when he winds the towboat round,
        We will all ready be,
    When he gives Could Roos, we 'll shout hurrah !
        Merry sean lads are we '
Chorus—When he gives Could Roos, we 'll shout hurrah !
        Merry sean lads are we !
    " When the sean we've shot, upon the tow,
        We will heave with all our might,
    With a heave ! heave O ! and rouse ! rouse O !
        Till the huer cries, ' All right '
    Then on the bunt place kegs and weights,
        And next to tuck go we
    We 'll dip, and trip, with a ' Hip hurrah ! '
        Merry sean lads are we !
Chorus—We 'll dip, and trip, with a ' Hip hurrah ! '
        Merry sean lads are we ! "

            * See Appendix CC.

DEATH SUPERSTITIONS.

" Continually at my bed's head
   A hearse doth hang, which doth me tell
That I e1e morning may be dead,
   Though now I feel myself full well."
                ROBERT SOUTHWELL.

DEATH TOKENS
AND SUPERSTITIONS.

THE DEATH-TOKEN OF THE VINGOES.

" The messenger of God
With golden trumpe I see,
With many other angels more,
Which sound and call for me.
Instead of musicke sweet,
Go toll my passing bell."

The Bride's Burial.

WHEN you cross the brook which divides St Leven from Sennen, you are on the estate of Treville.

Tradition tells us that this estate was given to an old family who came with the Conqueror to this country. This ancestor is said to have been the Duke of Normandy's wine-taster, and that he belonged to the ancient counts of Treville, hence the name of the estate. Certain it is the property has ever been held without poll deeds. For many generations the family has been declining, and the race is now nearly, if not quite, extinct.

Through all time a peculiar token has marked the coming death of a Vingoe. Above the deep caverns in the Treville cliff rises a carn. On this, chains of fire were seen ascending and descending, and often accompanied by loud and frightful noises.

It is said that these tokens have not been seen since the last male of the family came to a violent end.

THE DEATH FETCH OF WILLIAM RUFUS.

ROBERT, Earl of Moreton, in Normandy,—who always carried the standard of St Michael before him in battle,—was made Earl of Cornwall by William the Conqueror. He was remarkable for his valour and for his virtue, for the exercise of his power, and his benevolence to the priests. This was the Earl of Cornwall who gave the Mount in Cornwall to the monks of Mont St Michel in Normandy. He seized upon the priory of St Petroc at Bodmin, and converted all the lands to his own use.

This Earl of Cornwall was an especial friend of William Rufus. It happened that Robert, the earl, was hunting in the extensive woods around Bodmin—of which some remains are still to be found in the Glyn Valley. The chase had been a severe one ; a fine old red deer had baffled the huntsmen, and they were dispersed through the intricacies of the forest, the Earl of Cornwall being left alone. He advanced beyond the shades of the woods on to the moors above them, and he was surprised to see a very large black goat advancing over the plain. As it approached him, which it did rapidly, he saw that it bore on its back " King Rufus," all black and naked, and wounded through in the midst of his breast. Robert adjured the goat, in the name of the Holy Trinity, to tell what it was he carried so strangely. He answered, " I am carrying your king to judgment ; yea, that tyrant William Rufus, for I am an evil spirit, and the revenger of his malice which he bore to the Church of God. It was I that did cause this slaughter, the protomartyr of England, St Albyn, commanding me so to do, who complained to God of him, for his grievous oppression in this Isle of Britain, which he first hallowed." Having so spoken, the spectre vanished Robert, the earl, related the circumstance to his followers, and they shortly after learned that at that very hour William Rufus had been slain in the New Forest by the arrow of Walter Tirell.

SIR JOHN ARUNDELL.

IN the first year of the reign of Edward IV., the brave Sir John Arundell dwelt on the north coast of Cornwall, at a place called Efford, on the coast near Stratton. He was a magistrate, and greatly esteemed amongst men for his honourable conduct. He had, however, in his official capacity, given offence to a wild shepherd, who had by some means acquired considerable influence over the minds of the people, under the impression of his possessing some supernatural powers. This man had been imprisoned by Arundell, and on his return home he constantly waylaid the knight, and, always looking threateningly at him, slowly muttered,—

> " When upon the yellow sand,
> Thou shalt die by human hand "

Notwithstanding the bravery of Sir John Arundell, he was not free from the superstitions of the period. He might, indeed, have been impressed with the idea that this man intended to murder him. It is, however, certain that he removed from Efford on the sands, to the wood-clad hills of Trerice, and here he lived for some years without the annoyance of meeting his old enemy. In the tenth year of Edward IV., Richard de Vere, Earl of Oxford, seized St Michael's Mount. Sir John Arundell, then sheriff of Cornwall, gathered together his own retainers and a large host of volunteers, and led them to the attack on St Michael's Mount. The retainers of the Earl of Oxford, on one occasion, left the castle, and made a sudden rush upon Arundell's followers, who were encamped on the sands near Marazion. Arundell then received his death-wound. Although he left Efford "to counteract the will of fate," the prophecy was fulfilled ; and in his dying moments, it is said his old enemy appeared, singing joyously,—

> "When upon the yellow sand,
> Thou shalt die by human hand."

PHANTOMS OF THE DYING.

A GAY party were assembled one afternoon, in the latter days of January, in the best parlour of a farmhouse near the Land's-End. The inhabitants of this district were, in many respects, peculiar. Nearly all the land was divided up between, comparatively, a few owners, and every owner lived on and farmed his own land.

This circumstance, amongst others, led to a certain amount of style in many of the old farmhouses of the Land's-End district; and even now, in some of them, from which, alas ! the glory has departed, may be seen the evidences of taste beyond that which might have been expected in so remote a district.

The "best parlour" was frequently panelled with carved oak, and the ceiling, often highly, though it must be admitted, heavily decorated. In such a room, in the declining light of a January afternoon, were some ten or a dozen farmers' daughters, all of them unmarried, and many of them having an eye on the farmer's eldest son, a fine young man about twenty years of age, called Joseph.

This farmer and his wife, at the time of which we speak, had three sons and two daughters. The eldest son was an excellent and amiable young man, possessed of many personal attractions, and especially fond of the society of his sisters and their friends. The next son was of a very different stamp, and was more frequently found in the inn at Church-town than in his father's house;

the younger son was an apprentice at Penzance. The two daughters, Mary and Honour, had coaxed their mother into "a tea and heavy cake" party, and Joseph was especially retained, to be, as every one said he was, "the life of the company."

In those days, when, especially in those parts, every one took dinner at noon, and tea not much after four o'clock, the party had assembled early.

There had been the usual preliminary gossip amongst the young people, when they began to talk about the wreck of a fruit-ship, which had occurred but a few days before, off the Land's-End, and it was said that considerable quantities of oranges were washing into Nangissell Cove. Upon this, Joseph said he would take one of the men from the farm, and go down to the Cove—which was not far off—and see if they could not find some oranges for the ladies.

The day had faded into twilight, the western sky was still bright with the light of the setting sun, and the illuminated clouds shed a certain portion of their splendour into the room in which the party were assembled. The girls were divided up into groups, having their own pretty little bits of gossip, often truly delightful from its entire freedom and its innocence; and the mother of Joseph was seated near the fireplace, looking with some anxiety through the windows, from which you commanded a view of the Atlantic Ocean. The old lady was restless; sometimes she had to whisper something to Mary, and then some other thing to Honour. Her anxiety, at length, was expressed in her wondering where Joseph could be tarrying so long. All the young ladies sought to ease her mind by saying that there were no doubt so many orange-gatherers in the Cove, that Joseph and the man could not get so much fruit as he desired.

Joseph was the favourite son of his mother, and her anxiety evidently increased. Eventually, starting from her chair, the old lady exclaimed, "Oh, here he is; now I'll see about the tea."

With a pleased smile on her face, she left the room, to return, however, to it in deeper sorrow.

The mother expected to meet her son at the door—he came not. Thinking that he might possibly have been wetted by the sea, and that he had gone round the house to another door leading directly into the kitchen, for the purpose of drying himself, or of changing his boots, she went into the dairy to fetch the basin of clotted cream,—which had been "taken up" with unusual care,—to see if the junket was properly set, and to spread the flaky cream thickly upon its surface.

Strange,—as the old lady subsequently related,—all the pans of milk were agitated—" the milk rising up and down like the waves of the sea "

The anxious mother returned to the parlour with her basin of cream, but with an indescribable feeling of an unknown terror. She commanded herself, and, in her usual quiet way, asked if Joseph had been in.   When they answered her " No," she sighed heavily, and sank senseless into a chair.

Neither Joseph nor the servant ever returned alive.   They were seen standing together upon a rock, stooping to gather oranges as they came with each wave up to their feet, when one of the heavy swells—the lingering undulations of a tempest, so well known on this coast—came sweeping onward, and carried them both away in its cave of waters, as the wave curved to engulf them.

The undertow of the tidal current was so strong that, though powerful men and good swimmers, they were carried at once beyond all human aid, and speedily perished.

The house of joy became a house of mourning, and sadness rested on it for years.   Day after day passed by, and, although a constant watch was kept along the coast, it was not until the fated ninth day that the bodies were discovered, and they were then found in a sadly mutilated state.

Often after long years, and when the consolations derivable from pure religious feeling had brought that tranquillity upon the mind of this loving mother,—which so much resembles the poetical repose of an autumnal evening,—has she repeated to me the sad tale.

Again and again have I heard her declare that she saw Joseph, her son, as distinctly as ever she saw him in her life, and that, as he passed the parlour windows, he looked in upon her and smiled.

This is not given as a superstition belonging in any peculiar way to Cornwall.   In every part of the British Isles it exists ; but I have never met with any people who so firmly believed in the appearance of the phantoms of the dying to those upon whom the last thoughts are centred, as the Cornish did.

Another case is within my knowledge.

A lady, the wife of an officer in the navy, had been with her husband's sister, on a summer evening, to church.   The husband was in the Mediterranean, and there was no reason to expect his return for many months.

These two ladies returned home, and the wife, ascending the stairs before her sister-in law, went into the drawing-room—her intention being to close the windows, which, as the weather had been warm and fine, had been thrown open.

She had proceeded about half way across the room, when she shrieked, ran back, and fell into her sister-in-law's arms. Upon recovery, she stated that a figure, like that of her husband, enveloped in a mist, appeared to her to fill one of the windows.

By her friends, the wife's fancies were laughed at ; and, if not forgotten, the circumstance was no longer spoken of.

Month after month glided by, without intelligence of the ship to which that officer belonged. At length the Government became anxious, and searching inquiries were made. Some time still elapsed, but eventually it was ascertained that this sloop of war had perished in a white squall, in which she became involved, near the Island of Mitylene, in the Grecian Archipelago, on the Sunday evening when the widow fancied she saw her husband.

THE WHITE HARE.

IT is a very popular fancy that when a maiden, who has loved not wisely but too well, dies forsaken and broken-hearted, that she comes back to haunt her deceiver in the shape of a white hare.

This phantom follows the false one everywhere, mostly invisible to all but him. It sometimes saves him from danger, but invariably the white hare causes the death of the betrayer in the end.

The following story of the white hare is a modification of several tales of the same kind which have been told me Many, many years have passed away, and all who were in any way connected with my story have slept for generations in the quiet churchyard of ———.

A large landed proprietor engaged a fine, handsome young fellow to manage his farm, which was a very extensive as well as a high-class one When the young farmer was duly settled in his new farmhouse, there came to live with him, to take the management of the dairy, a peasant's daughter. She was very handsome, and of a singularly fine figure, but entirely without education.

The farmer became desperately in love with this young creature, and eventually their love passed all the bounds of discretion It became the policy of the young farmer's family to put down this unfortunate passion, by substituting a more legitimate and endearing object.

After a long trial, they thought they were successful, and the young farmer was married.

Many months had not passed away when the discharged dairy-maid was observed to suffer from illness, which, however, she constantly spoke of as nothing ; but knowing dames saw too clearly the truth. One morning there was found in a field a newly-born babe strangled. The unfortunate girl was at once suspected as being the parent, and the evidence was soon sufficient to charge her with the murder. She was tried, and, chiefly by the evidence of the young farmer and his family, convicted of, and executed for, the murder.

Everything now went wrong in the farm, and the young man suddenly left it and went into another part of the country.

Still nothing prospered, and gradually he took to drink to drown some secret sorrow. He was more frequently on the road by night than by day; and, go where he would, a white hare was constantly crossing his path. The white hare was often seen by others, almost always under the feet of his horse ; and the poor terrified animal would go like the wind to avoid the strange apparition.

One morning the young farmer was found drowned in a forsaken mine ; and the horse, which had evidently suffered extreme terror, was grazing near the corpse Beyond all doubt the white hare, which is known to hunt the perjured and the false-hearted to death, had terrified the horse to such a degree, that eventually the rider was thrown into the mine-waste in which the body was found.

THE HAND OF A SUICIDE.

PLACING the hand of a man who has died by his own act is a cure for many diseases.

The following is given me by a thinking man, living in one of the towns in the west of Cornwall :—

" There is a young man in this town who had been afflicted with running tumours from his birth. When about seventeen years of age he had the hand of a man who had hanged himself, passed over the wounds on his back, and, strange to say, he recovered from that time, and is now comparatively robust and hearty This incident is true; I was present when the charm was performed. It should be observed that the notion appears to be that the ' touch ' is only effectual on the opposite sex ; but in this case they were both, the suicide and the afflicted one, of the same sex."

This is only a modified form of the superstition that a wen, or any strumous swelling, can be cured by touching it with the dead hand of a man who has just been publicly hanged.

I once saw a young woman led on to the scaffold, in the Old Bailey, for the purpose of having a wen touched with the hand of a man who had just been executed.

THE NORTH SIDE OF A CHURCH.*

A STRONG prejudice has long existed against burying on the northern side of the church. In many churchyards the southern side will be found full of graves, with scarcely any on the northern side.

I have sought to discover, if possible, the origin of this prejudice, but I have not been able to trace it to any well-defined feeling I have been answered, " Oh, we like to bury a corpse where the sun will shine on the grave ;" and, " The northern graveyard is in the shadow, and cold ;" but beyond this I have not advanced.

We may infer that this desire to place the remains of our friends in earth on which the sun shines, is born of that love which, forgetting mortality, lives on the pleasant memories of the past, hoping for that meeting beyond the grave which shall know no shadow. The act of planting flowers, of nurturing an evergreen tree, of hanging " eternals " on the tomb, is only another form of the same sacred feeling.

POPULAR SUPERSTITIONS.

I T is, or rather was, believed, in nearly every part of the West of England, that death is retarded, and the dying kept in a state of suffering, by having any lock closed, or any bolt shot, in the dwelling of the dying person.

A man cannot die easy on a bed made of fowls' feathers, or the feathers of wild birds

Never carry a corpse to church by a new road.

Whenever a guttering candle folds over its cooling grease, it is watched with much anxiety. If it curls upon itself it is said to form the " handle of a coffin," and the person towards whom it is directed will be in danger of death.

Bituminous coal not unfrequently swells into bubbles, these bubbles of coal containing carburetted hydrogen gas When the pressure becomes great they burst, and often throw off the upper section with some explosive force. According to the shape of the piece thrown off, so is it named. If it proves round, it is a purse of money ; if oblong, it is a coffin, and the group towards which it flew will be in danger.

* See Appendix DD.

If a cock crows at midnight, the angel of death is passing over the house ; and if he delays to strike, the delay is only for a short season.

The howling of a dog is a sad sign.   If repeated for three nights, the house against which it howled will soon be in mourning.

A raven croaking over a cottage fills its inmates with gloom.

There are many other superstitions and tokens connected with life and death, but those given show the general character of those feelings which I may, I think, venture to call the " inner life" of the Cornish people.   It will be understood by all who have studied the peculiarities of any Celtic race, that they have ever been a peculiarly impressible people.   They have ever observed the phenomena of nature ; and they have interpreted them with hopeful feelings, or despondent anxiety, according as they have been surrounded by cheerful or by sorrow-inducing circumstances.   That melancholy state of mind, which is so well expressed by the word " whisht," leads the sufferer to find a " sign " or a " token " in the trembling of a leaf, or in the lowering of the tempest-clouds.   A collection of the almost infinite variety of these " signs and tokens" which still exist, would form a curious subject for an essay.   Yet this could only now be done by a person who would skilfully win the confidence of the miner or the peasant.   They feel that they might subject themselves to ridicule by an indiscreet disclosure of the religion of their souls.   When, if ever, such a collection is made, it will be found that these superstitions have their origin in the purest feelings of the heart—that they are the shadowings forth of love, tinctured with the melancholy dyes of that fear which is born of mystery.

One would desire that even those old superstitions should be preserved   They illustrate a state of society, in the past, which will never again return   There are but few reflecting minds which do not occasionally feel a lingering regret that times should pass away during which life was not a reflection of cold reason.

But these things must fade as a knowledge of nature's laws is disseminated amongst the people.   Yet there is—

> " The lonely mountains o'er,
>   And the resounding shore,
>   A voice of weeping heard, and loud lament ;
>   From haunted spring and dale,
>   Edged with poplar pale,
>   The parting genius is, with sighing sent."

OLD USAGES.

"The king was to his palace, though the service was ydo,
Yled with his meinie, and the queen to her also ;
For she held *the old usages.*"

ROBERT OF GLOUCESTER.

CUSTOMS OF ANCIENT DAYS.

SANDING THE STEP ON NEW YEAR'S DAY.

"They say, miracles are past, and we have our philosophical persons, to make modern and familiar things supernatural and causeless. Hence is it that we make trifles of terrors, ensconcing ourselves into seeming knowledge."—*All's Well that Ends Well*—SHAKESPEARE.

IN the rural districts of Cornwall, it is thought to be unlucky if a female is the first to enter the house on new-year's morning. To insure the contrary, it was customary to give boys some small reward for placing sand on the door-steps and in the passage.

In many places, not many years since, droves of boys would march through the towns and villages, collecting their fees for "sanding your step for good luck."

This custom prevails over most parts of England. I know a lady who, at the commencement of the present year, sent a cabman into her house before her, upon promise of giving him a glass of spirits, so that she might insure the good luck which depends upon "a man's taking the new year in."

MAY-DAY.

THE first of May is inaugurated with much uproar. As soon as the clock has told of midnight, a loud blast on tin trumpets proclaims the advent of May. This is long continued. At daybreak, with their "tintarrems," they proceed to the country, and strip the sycamore-trees (called May-trees) of all their young branches, to make whistles. With these shrill musical instruments they return home. Young men and women devote May-day to junketing and pic-nics.

It was a custom at Penzance, and probably at many other Cornish towns, when the author was a boy, for a number of young people to sit up until twelve o'clock, and then to march round the town with violins and fifes, and summon their friends to the Maying.

When all were gathered, they went into the country, and were welcomed at the farmhouses at which they called, with some refreshment in the shape of rum and milk, junket, or something of that sort.

They then gathered the " May," which included the young branches of any tree in blossom or fresh leaf. The branches of the sycamore were especially cut for the purpose of making the " May-music " This was done by cutting a circle through the bark to the wood a few inches from the end of the branch. The bark was wetted and carefully beaten until it was loosened and could be slid off from the wood. The wood was cut angularly at the end, so as to form a mouth-piece, and a slit was made in both the bark and the wood, so that when the bark was replaced a whistle was formed. Prepared with a sufficient number of May whistles, all the party returned to the town, the band playing, whistles blowing, and the young people singing some appropriate song.

SHROVE TUESDAY AT ST IVES.

FORMERLY it was customary for the boys to tie stones to cords, and with these parade the town, slinging these stones against the doors, shouting aloud,—

"Give me a pancake, now—now—now,
Or I'll souse in your door with a row—tow—tow."

A genteel correspondent assures me "this is observed now in the lower parts of the town only."

"THE FURRY"—HELSTONE.

THIS ancient custom, which consists in dancing through the streets of the town, and entering the houses of rich and poor alike, is thus well described :—

"On the 8th of May, at Helstone, in Cornwall, is held what is called 'the Furry.' The word is supposed by Mr Polwhele to have been derived from the old Cornish word *fer*, a fair or jubilee. The morning is ushered in by the music of drums and kettles, and other accompaniments of a song, a great part of which is inserted in Mr Polwhele's history, where this circumstance is noticed. So strict is the observance of this day as a general holiday, that should any person be found at work, he is instantly seized, set astride on a pole, and hurried on men's shoulders to the river, where he is sentenced to leap over a wide place, which he, of course, fails in attempting, and leaps into the water. A small contribution towards the good cheer of the day easily compounds for the leap. About nine o'clock the revellers appear before the grammar-school, and demand a holiday for the schoolboys, after which they collect contributions from houses. They then *fade* into the country (fade being an old English word for *go*), and, about the middle of the day, return with flowers and oak-branches in their hats and caps. From this time they dance hand in hand through the streets, to the sound of the fiddle, playing a particular tune, running into every house they pass without opposition. In the afternoon a select party of the ladies and gentlemen make a progress through the street, and very late in the evening repair to the ball-room. A stranger visiting the town on the eighth of May would really think the people mad, so apparently wild and thoughtless is the merriment of the day There is no doubt of 'the Furry' originating from the 'Floralia,' anciently observed by the Romans on the fourth of the calends of May."—*Every-Day Book.*

MIDSUMMER SUPERSTITIOUS CUSTOMS.

I F on midsummer-eve a young woman takes off the shift which she has been wearing, and, having washed it, turns its wrong side out, and hangs it in silence over the back of a chair, near the fire, she will see, about midnight, her future husband, who deliberately turns the garment.

If a young lady will, on midsummer-eve, walk backwards into the garden and gather a rose, she has the means of knowing who is to be her husband. The rose must be cautiously sewn up in a paper bag, and put aside in a dark drawer, there to remain until Christmas-day

On the morning of the Nativity the bag must be carefully opened in silence, and the rose placed by the lady in her bosom. Thus she must wear it to church. Some young man will either ask for the rose, or take it from her without asking. That young man is destined to become eventually the lady's husband.

> " At eve last midsummer no sleep I sought,
> But to the field a bag of hemp-seed brought ;
> I scatter'd round the seed on every side,
> And three times in a trembling accent cried,—
> ' This hemp-seed with my virgin hand I sow,
> Who shall my true love be, the crop shall mow.'
> I straight look'd back, and, if my eyes speak truth,
> With his keen scythe behind me came the youth "
> *Gay's Pastorals.*

The practice of sowing hemp-seed on midsummer-eve is not especially a Cornish superstition, yet it was at one time a favourite practice with young women to try the experiment. Many a strange story have I been told as to the result of the sowing, and many a trick could I tell off, which has been played off by young men who had become acquainted with the secret intention of some maidens. I believe there is but little difference in the rude rhyme used on the occasion,—

" Hemp-seed I sow,
Hemp-seed I hoe,"

(the action of sowing the seed and of hoeing it in, must be deliberately gone through) ;—

" And he
Who will my true love be,
Come after me and mow."

A phantom of the true lover will now appear, and of course the maid or maidens retire in wild affright.

If a young unmarried woman stands at midnight on Midsummer-eve in the porch of the parish church, she will see, passing by in procession, every one who will die in the parish during the year. This is so serious an affair that it is not, I believe, often tried. I have, however, heard of young women who have made the experiment. But every one of the stories relate that, coming last in the procession, they have seen shadows of themselves ; that from that day forward they have pined, and ere midsummer has again come round, that they have been laid to rest in the village graveyard.

CRYING THE NECK.

OWING to the uncertain character of the climate of Cornwall, the farmers have adopted the plan of gathering the sheaves of wheat, as speedily as possible, into " arishmows." These are solid cones from ten to twelve feet high, the heads of the stalks turned inwards, and the whole capped with a sheaf of corn inverted. Whence the term, I know not ; but " arish " is commonly applied to a field of corn recently cut, as, " Turn the geese in upon the ' arish ' "—that is, the short stubble left in the ground.

After the wheat is all cut on most farms in Cornwall and Devon, the harvest people have a custom of " crying the neck." I believe that this practice is seldom omitted on any large farm in these counties. It is done in this way. An old man, or some one else well acquainted with the ceremonies used on the occasion (when the labourers are reaping the last field of wheat), goes round to the shocks and sheaves, and picks out a little bundle of all the best ears he can find ; this bundle he ties up very neat and trim, and plaits and arranges the straws very tastefully. This is called " the neck " of wheat, or wheaten-ears. After the field is cut out, and the pitcher once more circulated, the reapers, binders, and the women stand round in a circle. The person with " the neck " stands in the centre, grasping it with both his hands. He first stoops and holds it near the ground, and all the men forming the ring

2 B

take off their hats, stooping and holding them with both hands towards the ground. They then all begin at once, in a very prolonged and harmonious tone, to cry, " The neck ! " at the same time slowly raising themselves upright, and elevating their arms and hats above their heads ; the person with the neck also raising it on high. This is done three times. They then change their cry to " We yen ! we yen ! " which they sound in the same prolonged and slow manner as before, with singular harmony and effect, three times. This last cry is accompanied by the same movements of the body and arms as in crying " the neck." I know nothing of vocal music, but I think I may convey some idea of the sound by giving you the following notes in gamut :—

Very slow.

We yen! we yen!

Let these notes be played on a flute with perfect *crescendoes* and *diminuendoes*, and perhaps some notion of this wild-sounding cry may be formed. Well, after this they all burst out into a kind of loud, joyous laugh, flinging up their hats and caps into the air, capering about, and perhaps kissing the girls. One of them then gets " the neck," and runs as hard as he can down to the farmhouse, where the dairy-maid, or one of the young female domestics, stands at the door prepared with a pail of water. If he who holds " the neck" can manage to get into the house in any way unseen, or openly by any other way than the door at which the girl stands with the pail of water, then he may lawfully kiss her ; but, if otherwise he is regularly soused with the contents of the bucket. I think this practice is beginning to decline of late, and many farmers and their men do not care about keeping up this old custom. The object of crying " the neck " is to give notice to the surrounding country of the *end* of the harvest, and the meaning of " we yen " is " *we have ended.*" It may probably mean " we end," which the uncouth and provincial pronunciation has corrupted into " we yen." The " neck " is generally hung up in the farmhouse, where it often remains for three or four years.

DRINKING TO THE APPLE-TREES ON TWELFTH-NIGHT-EVE.

IN the eastern part of Cornwall, and in western Devonshire, it was the custom to take a milk-panful of cider, into which roasted apples had been broken, into the orchard This was placed as near the centre of the orchard as possible, and each person, taking a "clomben" cup of the drink, goes to different apple-trees, and addresses them as follows :—

> " Health to the good apple-tree;
> Well to bear, pocketfuls, hatfuls,
> Peckfuls, bushel-bagfuls."

Drinking part of the contents of the cup, the remainder, with the fragments of the roasted apples, is thrown at the tree, all the company shouting aloud.   Another account tells us, " In certain parts of Devonshire, the farmer, attended by his workmen, goes to the orchard this evening ; and there, encircling one of the best-bearing trees, they drink the following toast three times ·—

> ' Here 's to thee, old apple-tree ;
> Hence thou mayst bud, and whence thou mayst blow,
> And whence thou mayst bear apples enow !
> Hats full ! caps full !
> Bushel, bushel-sacks full !
> And my pockets full, too !   Huzza !'

This done, they return to the house, the doors of which they are sure to find bolted by the females, who, be the weather what it may, are inexorable to all entreaties to open them, till some one has guessed what is on the spit, which is generally some nice little thing difficult to be hit on, and is the reward of him who first names it.   The doors are then thrown open, and the lucky clodpole receives the tit-bit as his recompense.   Some are so superstitious as to believe that if they neglect this custom, the trees will bear no apples that year." *

Christmas-eve was selected in some parts of England as the occasion for wishing health to the apple-tree.   Apples were roasted on a string until they fell into a pan of spiced ale, placed to receive them.   This drink was called *lamb's-wool*, and with it the trees were wassailed, as in Devonshire and Cornwall.

Herrick alludes to the custom :—

> " Wassaile the trees, that they may beare
> You many a plum, and many a peare ,
> For moie or lesse fruits they will bring,
> And you do give them wassailing."

May not Shakespeare refer to this ?—

> " Sometimes lurk I in a gossip's bowl,
> In very likeness of a roasted crab ;

---

* Hone's " Every-Day Book "

And when she drinks, against her lips I bob,
And on her wither'd dew-lap pour the ale."
—*Midsummer Night's Dream.*

In some localities apples are blessed on St James's Day, July 25.

ALLHALLOWS-EVE AT ST IVES.

THE ancient custom of providing children with a large apple on Allhallows-eve is still observed, to a great extent, at St Ives. " Allan-day," as it is called, is the day of days to hundreds of children, who would deem it a great misfortune were they to go to bed on " Allan-night " without the time-honoured Allan apple to hide beneath their pillows. A quantity of large apples are thus disposed of, the sale of which is dignified by the term Allan Market.

THE TWELFTH CAKE.

THE custom, apparently a very ancient one, of putting certain articles into a rich cake, is still preserved in many districts. Usually, sixpence, a wedding-ring, and a silver thimble are employed. These are mixed up with the dough, and baked in the cake. At night the cake is divided. The person who secures the sixpence will not want money for that year ; the one who has the ring will be the first married ; and the possessor of the thimble will die an old maid.

" Then also every householder,
    To his abilitie
Doth make a mighty cake, that may
    Suffice his companie :
Herein a pennie doth he put,
    Before it come to fire ;
This he divides according as
    His household doth require,
And every peece distributeth
    As round about they stand,
Which in their names unto the poor
    Is given out of hand.
But who so chanceth on the peece
    Wherein the money lies,
Is counted king amongst them all ;
    And is with shoutes and cries
Exalted to the heavens up "
    —*Naogeorgus's Popish Kingdom.*

OXEN PRAY ON CHRISTMAS-EVE.

I REMEMBER, when a child, being told that all the oxen and cows kept at a farm in the parish of St Germans, at which I was visiting with my aunt, would be found on their knees when the clock struck twelve. This is the only case within my own knowledge of this wide-spread superstition existing in Cornwall. Brand says, "A superstitious notion prevails in the western parts of Devonshire, that at twelve o clock at night on Christmas-eve, the oxen in their stalls are always found on their knees, as in an attitude of devotion; and that (which is still more singular) since the alteration of the style, they continue to do this only on the eve of Old Christmas-day. An honest countryman, living on the edge of St Stephen's Down, near Launceston, Cornwall, informed me, October 28, 1790, that he once, with some others, made a trial of the truth of the above, and, watching several oxen in their stalls at the above time,—at twelve o'clock at night,—they observed the two oldest oxen only, fall upon their knees, and, as he expressed it in the idiom of the country, make 'a cruel moan, like Christian creatures.' I could not, but with great difficulty, keep my countenance; he saw, and seemed angry that I gave so little credit to his tale; and, walking off in a pettish humour, seemed to 'marvel at my unbelief.' There is an old print of the Nativity, in which the oxen in the stable, near the Virgin and the Child, are represented upon their knees, as in a suppliant posture. This graphic representation has probably given rise to the above superstitious notion on this head."

"ST GEORGE"—THE CHRISTMAS PLAYS.

THE Christmas play is a very ancient institution in Cornwall. At one time religious subjects were chosen, but those gave way to romantic plays. The arrangements were tolerably complete, and sometimes a considerable amount of dramatic skill was displayed.

"*St George*, and the other tragic performers, are dressed out somewhat in the style of morris-dancers, in their shirt sleeves and white trousers, much decorated with ribbons and handkerchiefs, each carrying a drawn sword in his hand, if they can be procured, otherwise a cudgel. They wear high caps of pasteboard, adorned with beads, small pieces of looking-glass, coloured paper, &c.; several long strips of pith generally hang down from the top, with small pieces of different coloured cloth strung on them; the whole has a very smart effect.

Father Christmas is personified in a grotesque manner, as an ancient man.

wearing a large mask and wig, and a huge club, wherewith he keeps the bystanders in order.

The *Doctor*, who is generally the merryandrew of the piece, is dressed in any ridiculous way, with a wig, three-cornered hat, and painted face.

The other comic characters are dressed according to fancy.

The *female*, where there is one, is usually in the dress worn half a century ago.

The *hobbyhorse*, which is a character sometimes introduced, wears a representation of a horse's hide

Beside the regular drama of "St George," many parties of mummers go about in fancy dresses of every sort, most commonly the males in female attire, and *vice versâ*.

BATTLE OF ST GEORGE.

[One of the party steps in, crying out,—

Room, a room, brave gallants, room !
Within this court
I do resort,
To show some sport
And pastime,
Gentlemen and ladies, in the Christmas time.

[After this note of preparation, Old Father Christmas capers into the room, saying,—

Here comes I, Old Father Christmas ;
Welcome or welcome not,
I hope Old Father Christmas
Will never be forgot.

I was born in a rocky country, where there was no wood to make me a cradle ; I was rocked in a stouring bowl, which made me round shouldered then, and I am round shouldered still.

[He then frisks about the room, until he thinks he has sufficiently amused the spectators, when he makes his exit, with this speech :—

Who went to the orchard to steal apples to make gooseberry pies against Christmas ?

[These prose speeches, you may suppose, depend much upon the imagination of the actor

Enter Turkish Knight.

Here comes I, a Turkish knight,
Come from the Turkish land to fight ;
And if St George do meet me here,
I 'll try his courage without fear.

Enter St George.

Here comes I, St George,
That worthy champion bold ;
And, with my swoid and spear,
I won three crowns of gold.
I fought the dragon bold,
And brought him to the slaughter ;
By that I gain'd fair Sabra,
The King of Egypt's daughter.

T. K. St George, I pray, be not too bold ;
    If thy blood is hot, I 'll soon make it cold.
St G. Thou Turkish knight, I pray, forbear ;
    I 'll make thee dread my sword and spear.

          [They fight until the Turkish knight falls.

St G. I have a little bottle, which goes by the name of Elicumpane ;
    If the man is alive, let him rise and fight again.

      *[The Knight here rises on one knee, and endeavours to continue the
      fight, but is again struck down*

T. K. Oh, pardon me, St George; oh, pardon me, I crave ;
    Oh, pardon me this once, and I will be thy slave.
St G. I 'll never pardon a Turkish knight ;
    Therefore arise and try thy might.

      *[The knight gets up, and they again fight, till the Knight receives a
      heavy blow, and then drops on the ground as dead.*

St G. Is there a doctor to be found,
    To cure a deep and deadly wound?

          Enter Doctor.

Oh yes, there is a doctor to be found,
To cure a deep and deadly wound.
St G. What can you cure?
Doctor I can cure the itch, the palsy, and gout ;
    If the devil 's in him. I 'll pull him out

      *[The Doctor here performs the cure with sundry grimaces, and St
      George and the knight again fight, when the latter is knocked
      down, and left for dead*
      [Then another performer enters, and, on seeing the dead body, says,—

Ashes to ashes, dust to dust ;
If Uncle Tom Pearce won't have him, Aunt Molly must.

      [The hobbyhorse here capers in, and takes off the body.

          Enter Old Squire

Here comes I, old, Old Squire,
As black as any friar,
As ragged as a colt,
To leave fine clothes for malt.

          Enter Hub Bub.

Here comes I, old Hub Bub Bub Bub ;
Upon my shoulders I carries a club,
And in my hand a frying-pan,
So am I not a valiant man?

      *[These characters serve as a sort of burlesque on St George and the
      other hero, and may be regarded in the light of an anti-masque.*

          Enter the Box-holder.

Here comes I, great head and little wit ;
Put your hand in your pocket, and give what you think fit.
Gentlemen and ladies, sitting down at your ease,
Put your hands in your pockets, and give me what you please.

St G Gentlemen and ladies, the sport is almost ended ;
Come pay to the box, it is highly commended.
The box it would speak, if it had but a tongue ;
Come throw in your money, and think it no wrong.
The characters now generally finish with a dance, or sometimes a song or two is introduced. In some of the performances, two or three other tragic heroes are brought forward, as the King of Egypt and his son, &c., but they are all of them much in the style of that I have just described, varying somewhat in length and number of characters."—*The Every-Day Book.*

Of the Cornish mystery plays which were once acted in the famous " Rounds," it is not necessary, in this place, to say anything The translations by Mr Norris preserve their characteristics, which indeed differ in few respects from the mystery plays of other parts.

The " Perran Round " is fortunately preserved by the proprietor in its original state. Every one must regret the indifference of the wealthy inhabitants of St Just to their " Round," which is now a wretched ruin.

GEESE-DANCING—PLOUGH MONDAY.

THE first Monday after Twelfth-day is Plough Monday, and it is the ploughman's holiday.

At this season, in the Islands of Scilly, at St Ives, Penzance, and other places, the young people exercise a sort of gallantry called " geese-dancing." The maidens are dressed up for young men, and the young men for maidens ; and, thus disguised, they visit their neighbours in companies, where they dance, and make jokes upon what has happened during the year, and every one is humorously " told their own," without offence being taken. By this sort of sport, according to yearly custom and toleration, there is a spirit of wit and drollery kept up among the people. The music and dancing done, they are treated with liquor, and then they go to the next house, and carry on the same sport. A correspondent, writing to the " Table-Book," insists on calling these revels "goose-dancing." The true Cornishman never uses the term, which is, as I have elsewhere shown, derived from *dance deguiser*,—hence guise-dancing, or geese-dancing, by corruption.

CHRISTMAS AT ST IVES.

" THE GUISE-DANCING."

" WE doubt if there is a spot in 'merrie England' where Christmas receives so hearty a welcome, and is 'made so much of,' as in the old-fashioned 'antient borough of beloved St Ives.' It is often said that ' extremes meet ,' but as well might we expect the extremities of

Britain—John o'Groat's and Cape Cornwall—to meet, as that the frolic-loving descendants of Albion will ever imitate the cold, mountain-nurtured Caledonians in their observance of Christmas time. For months previous to the merry-making time, preparations are made for the approaching 'carnival;' we can assure our readers that never were the real 'carnivals' ushered in with greater festivities at Rome or Venice, in the zenith of their glory, than is observed here at Christmas. Were many of the denizens of our large towns to witness the making up of the scores of 'sugar loaf,' 'three-cocked,' and indescribable-shaped hats, caps, bonnets, bloomer skirts, leggings, jackets, &c., numberless *et ceteras* of the most grotesque and pantomimic character, colour, and shape, which goes on in October and November, they would imagine there was to be a *bal masque* on a large scale, or a pantomime at 'the theatre,' of metropolitan proportions. But not so, for there is not even a singing-class in the town, if we except the choirs of the various congregations, and all 'this wilful waste' of long cloth, scarlet, ringstraked, and speckled, is to do honour to King Christmas during the twelve nights which intervene 'twixt the birth of Christmas common and Christmas proper, which said outward manifestations of honour are known in the neighbourhood as 'Christmas geezze-daancing,' or guise-dancing; but of this presently. Not only are the 'lovers of pleasure' on the alert, but the choirs of the different places of worship strive to 'get up' a piece or two to tickle the ears of their hearers on Christmas-night, and the house that boasts the best 'singing seat' is sure to be crammed by persons attracted by the twofold advantage of a short sermon and a good lively tune A pretty brisk trade is carried on by children in the retailing unquenched lime, in small quantities to suit the convenience of purchasers, and few are the domiciles but have had a lick of the lime brush, either on the wall, window-sill, door-post, or chimney 'A slut, indeed,' is she declared who refuses to have a thorough clean out before Christmas New shoes and clothes are worn for the first time on the great holiday; and woe betide the unlucky Crispin who, by some unaccountable oversight, has neglected to make Jennifer's bran new shoes, for her to go and see how smart the church is on Christmas-day. As in other parts of England, a pretty large sum is spent in evergreens, such as holly, or, as it is called here, 'prickly Christmas,' bays, and laurels Of mistletoe and cypress there is very little in the neighbourhood, and the windows of shops and private dwellings, as well as the parish church, are profusely and tastefully decorated. As to provisions, there is no lack. Many a flock of geese has been bespoken and set apart for private customers, whilst the ears of the grocers, who generally do a supplementary trade in swine's flesh, are so accustomed to receive a month's notice for 'a nice bit of flea (spare) rib,' that they are loath to engage any of the porcine fraternity that are not all rib. The Christmas market is not a mean affair at St Ives; if the butchers cannot boast of many prize oxen or 'South Downs,' they generally manage to make the best of their 'home-raised' and well-fed cattle, and the stalls are 'titivated off' nicely too. This year, however, the inspector of nuisances, who is also market-toll collector and police constable, sergeant, and inspector, actually refused to clean, or allow to be cleaned, the St Ives Market on Tuesday for the Christmas-eve market, because there was no extra tolls payable for the Christmas markets, and, as may be expected, the epithets bestowed on him were by no means flattering or complimentary—we did hear of a suggestion to put the 'gentleman' policeman in an aldermanic stall on the 5th of next November, or maybe during the guise-dancing

Tradesmen have for the most part 'cacht their jobs,' and the good house wife 'done her churs in season' on Christmas-eve. In many families, a crock of 'fish and tatees' is discussed in West-Cornwall style before the 'singers' commence their time-honoured carol, 'While Shepherds,' which is invariably sung to 'the same old tune,' struck by some novice in *u* flat. There is usually a host of young men and maidens to accompany the 'singers;' these are composed of the choirs of two or three dissenting bodies, who chiefly select the members of their respective congregations for the honour of being disturbed from a sound nap on the eventful morning. The last two or three years the choirs have done their carolling amongst the most respectable of the inhabitants on the evening of Christmas-day, after divine service.

"On Christmas-day the mayor, aldermen, and councillors walk in procession to church from the house of the mayor for the time being. The church is, as we have before remarked, gaily decked with evergreens Two or three days after the singers make a call 'for something for singing,' the proceeds, which are pretty handsome, being spent in a substantial supper for the choir.

"But of the 'guise-dancing,' which has found a last retreat at St Ives,— this is the only town in the country where the old Cornish Christmas revelry is kept up with spirit. The guise-dancing time is the twelve nights after Christmas, *i.e.,* from Christmas-day to Twelfth-day. Guise-dancing at St Ives is no more nor less than a pantomimic representation or *bal masque* on an extensive scale, the performers outnumbering the audience, who in this case take their stand at the corners of the streets, which are but badly lighted with gas, and rendered still more dismal of late years by the closing of the tradesmen's shops after sunset during this season, on account of the noise and uproar occasioned, the town being literally given up to a lawless mob, who go about yelling and hooting in an unearthly manner, in a tone between a screech and a howl, so as to render their voices as undistinguishable as their buffoon-looking dresses. Here a Chinese is exhibiting 'vite mishe' and 'Dutch dops,' there a turbaned Indian asks you if you 'vant a silver vatch.' A little further on you meet with a Highlander with 'dops to cure the gout.' The home-impoverishing packman, or duffer, has also his representative, urging to be allowed just to leave 'a common low price dress at an uncommon high price, and a quartern of his 6s. sloe-leaves of the best quality.' Faithless swains not unfrequently get served out by the friends of the discarded one at this time, whilst every little peccadillo meets with a just rebuke and exposure. About eighteen years ago, a party of youngsters, to give more variety to the sports, constructed a few nice representations of elephants, horses, and—start not gentle reader—lifelike facsimiles of that proverbially stupid brute, the ass For several seasons it was quite a treat to witness the antics of the self-constituted elephants, horses, and asses, in the thoroughfares of this little town. On the whole, the character of the guise-dancing has degenerated very much this last twenty years. It was formerly the custom for parties to get up a little play, and go from house to house to recite their droll oddities, and levy contributions on their hearers in the form of cake or plum-pudding. Wassailing, as far as I can learn, never obtained much in this neighbourhood. Old Father Christmas and bold King George were favourite characters. It is not uncommon to see a most odiously-disguised person with a bedroom utensil, asking the blushing bystanders if there is 'any need of me.' Some of the dresses are, indeed, very smart, and even costly ; but for the most part they consist of old clothes, arranged in the oddest manner, even fright fully ugly. It is dangerous for children, and aged or infirm persons, to venture out after dark, as the roughs generally are armed with a sweeping-rush or a shillalagh. The uproar at times is so tremendous as to be only equalled in a 'rale Irish row.' As may be anticipated, these annual diversions have a very demoralising influence on the young, on account of the licentious nature of the conversation indulged in, though we really wonder that there are not many more instances of annoyance and insult than now take place, when we consider that but for such times as Christmas and St Ives feast, the inhabitants have no place of amusement, recreation, or public instruction ; there being no library, reading-room, institution, literary or scientific, or evening class ; and unless there is one at the National School room, not a night school or even a working-men's institution is in the town.

"We should not omit that one of the old customs still observed is the giving apprentices three clear holidays (not including Sunday) after Christmas-day, though we hear of attempts being made to lessen this treat to the youngsters. If we don't wish success to these efforts, we do desire those should succeed who will endeavour to impart to our rising population a thorough contempt for guise-dancing and all such unmeaning buffoonery There is one thing which must not be overlooked—viz., the few drunken brawls that occur at such times. Cases of drunkenness certainly occur, but these are far below the average of towns of its size, the population being in 1861 (parliamentary limits) 10,354."—*St Ives Correspondent.*

LADY LOVELL'S COURTSHIP.

BY the especial kindness of one who has a more abundant store of old Cornish stories than any man whom I have ever met, I am enabled to give some portion of one of the old Cornish plays, or guise-dances. Many parts are omitted, as they would, in our refined days, be considered coarse ; but as preserving a true picture of a peculiar people, as they were a century and a half or two centuries since, I almost regret the omissions.

SCENE 1.—*The Squire's Kitchen—Duffy sitting on the chimney-stool—Jane, the housekeeper, half drunk, holding fast by the table.*

Jane Oh, I am very bad, I must go to bed with the wind in my stomach. You can bake the pie, Duffy, and give the Squire his supper. Keep a good waking fire on the pie for an hour or more. Turn the glass again ; when the sand is half down, take the fire from the kettle Mind to have a good blazing fire in the hall, for the Squire will be as wet as a shag. The old fool, to stay out hunting with this flood of rain ! Now, I'll take a cup of still waters, and crawl away to bed.

Duffy. Never fear, I'll bake the pie as well as if you were under the kettle along with it ; so go to bed, Jane.

[*As soon as Jane turns her back, Huey Lenine (Lanyon) comes in with,*—

Huey. What cheer, Duffy, my dear? how dost aw get on, then?

Duffy. Never the better for thee, I bla, Huey. What do bring thee here this time of night?

Huey. Why, thee art never the worse, nan, I'm sure Nor thee cussent say that the lanes are longer than the love neither, when I'm come a-courting to *thee* with this rainy weather.

[*Huey places himself on the chimney-stool, at a good distance from Duffy*

D Why doesn't aw come a little nearer then, Huey?

H. Near enuff, I bla.

D. Nearer the fire, I mean. Why doesn't aw speak to me then, Huey?

H. What shall I say, nan?

D. Why, say thee dost love me, to be sure.

H. So I do.

D. That's a dear. Fine pretty waistcoat on to you, man, Huey.

H. Cost pretty money too

D. What did it cost, man?

H. Two-and-twenty pence, buttons and all.

D Take good care of en, man.

H. So I will.

D. That's a dear.

[*The Squire is heard calling the dogs.*

D. Dost aw hear? there's the Squire close to the door. Where shall I put thee? Oh, I'm in such a fright. Wouldn't for the world that he found thee here this time of night. Get in the wood-corner, quick, out of sight, and I'll cover thee up with the furze.

H. No.

D Then jump into the oven. A little more baking will make thee no worse.

[*Duffy pushes Huey back into the oven with the fire-prong, till he gets out of sight, when the Squire comes in, calling,—*

Squire. Jane, take the hares and rabbits, be sure hang them out of the way of the dogs

D Give them to me, master; Jane is gone to bed. The wind from her stomach is got up in her head, at least so she said.

S. Why, who is here, then? I heard thee speaking to some one as I opened the door.

D I was driving away a great owl, master, that fell out of the ivy-bush on the top of the chimney and came tumbling down through the smoke, perched hisself there on the end of the chimney-stack; there he kept blinking and peeping, like a thing neither waking nor sleeping, till he heard the dogs barking, when he stopped his winking, cried out, "Hoo! hoo!" flapped his wings, and fled up the chimney the same way he came down.

D Now, master, you had better go up in the hall; you will find there a good blazing fire.

[*The Squire examines his legs by the fire-light*

S Well, I declare, these are the very best stockings I ever had in my life. I've been hunting since the break of day, through the bogs and the brambles, the furze and the thorns, in all sorts of weather; and my legs— look, Duffy, look—are still as dry and sound as if they had been bound up in leather.

D. Then take good care of them, master; for I shall soon have a man of my own to knit for. Huey and I are thinking to get married before the next turfey season.

S. You think of having a man' a young girl like you! If I but catch the boy Huey Lenine here, I'll break his neck, I declare. I can never wear old Jane's stockings any more. Why, thee dust ought to be proud to know that the people from all over the parish, who were never to church before in their lives, come, and from parishes round, that they may see my fine stockings. And don't I stop outside the church door—ay, sometimes two hours or more—that the women may see thy fine work? Haven't I stopped at the cross till the parson came out to call the people in, because he and the clerk, he said, wanted to begin?

> [*The Squire places himself beside Duffy on the chimney-stool. The devil comes out of the wood-corner, and ranges himself behind them. Whenever the Squire is backward, the devil tickles him behind the ear or under the ribs His infernal highness is supposed to be invisible throughout Huey shows a wry face now and then, with clenched fist through the oven door.*

The following portion, which is the Squire's courtship of Duffy with the help of the devil, is a sort of duet in the old play. I don't remember the whole, yet sufficient, I think, to give some idea of the way it is intended to be carried out .—

S. No ; I 'll marry thee myself, rather than Huey Lenine
Shall ever wear stockings the equal of mine.
Thou shalt have the silk gowns, all broider'd in gold,
In the old oak chest ; besides jewels and rings,
With such other fine things,
In the old oak chest, as thee didst never behold.
D I 'd rather work all the day by any young man's side,
Than sit in the bower, and be an old man's bride.
S. Thou shalt have silver and gold, and riches untold.
D I 'll buy my true-love his shirt, rather than your silver and gold,
With one like yourself, both feeble and old
S. You must say I 'm old ; though I 'm near sixty,
I 'm stronger still than many a man of twenty.
Thou shalt ride to church behind me, upon a new pillion,
As grand as Madam Noy, or Madam Trezilhan.
D. O master! hold your flattering tongue ;
I 'm very foolish, and very young
But——

> [*Here the devil tickles the Squire sharply under the ribs, when the Squire attempts to hug and kiss Duffy, who takes the fire-prong and brandishes it in the Squire's face. The devil tickles them both*

Stand off, keep your distance, and none of your hugging ;
No man shall kiss me till he takes me to church ;
I,'ll never cry at Michaelmas for Christmas laughing,
Like the poor maid left in the lurch.

Look, the sand is all down, the pie is burn'd black,
And the crust is too hard for your colt s teeth to crack ;
Up to the hall now, and take your supper.

> [*Here Duffy pushes the Squire off the stool The Squire jumps up and begins to dance, singing the old dancing tune, "Here's to the devil, with his wooden pick," &c Duffy and the devil soon join in the dance, and cut all sorts of capers, till the Squire dances off to the hall, followed by the devil, when Huey crawls out of the oven, Duffy opens the kitchen, drives Huey out, saying,—*

Now take thyself outside the door,
And never show thy face here any more ;
Don't think I'd have a poor pityack like thee,
When I may marry a squire of high degree.

> [*Then takes up the pie, and dances away. During the old pitch-and-pass dance, they beat time with the fire-prong and hunting staff.*

SCENE 2.—*The first appearance of Lady Lovell (Duffy) after the wedding. She is seen walking up and down the hall dressed in all sorts of ill-assorted, old-fashioned finery, that might have been forgotten in the old oak chest for many generations of Lovells. The high-heeled shoes, train, fan, ruff, high tête, all sorts of rings on her fingers, and in her ears are de rigeui. Then she sings something like the following.—*

Now I have servants to come at my call,
As I walk in grand state in the hall,
    Deck'd in silks and satins fine ;
But I grieve all the day, and fret the long night away,
    To think of my true love, young Huey Lenine.

Many a weary long hour I sit all alone in my bower,
    Where I do nothing but pine,
Whilst I grieve all the day, and fret the night away,
    To think of my true love, young Huey Lenine.

Would the devil but come at my call, and take the old Squire, siks, satins,
    and all,
    With jewels and rings so fine ;
Then merry and gay I'd work all the day, and pass the night away,
    Kissing my true love, young Huey Lenine.

Another Cornish " Droll " is preserved in part, as an example of the kind of doggerel verse in which many of those stories were told.

Bet of the Mill tells the Squire and company that one Christmas night all the inmates of Trevider House were gone off to a guise-dance, except Madame Pender and herself, and that they agreed to spin for pastime :—

> " One Christmas night, from Trevider Hall
> They were off in a guise-dance, big and small ;
> Nobody home but Madam Pender and I :
> So to pass away time we agreed to try
> Which would spin the finest yarn,
>   The length of the hall,
>   While the holly and bays
>   Deck'd window and wall.

> " We took the rushes up from the floor,
> From up by the chimney down to the door :
> When we had the wool carded, ready to spin,
> It came into our heads, before we'd begin
> We'd have a jug of hot spiced beer,
> To put life in our heels, our hearts to cheer.
> So we drank to the healths of one and all,

      While the holly and bays
      Looked bright on the wall.

" The night was dark, the wind roar'd without,
And whirl'd the cold snow about and about.
      But the best part of that night,
      By the bright fire-light,
      While the Christmas stock did burn,
We danced forth and back as light as a feather,
Spinning and keeping good time together,
      To the music of the ' turn.' *
And we never felt weary that night at all,
      While the holly and bays
      Hung so gay on the wall.

"We pull'd out the yarn as even and fine,
As a spinner can spin the best of twine :
      All the length of the hall,
      From window to wall,
      From up by the chimney
      Down to the door,
Full a dozen good paces and more ;
      And never felt weary at all,
      While the holly and bays
      Were so green on the wall.

" At the turn of the night,
      Old Nick, out of spite,
      To see the log burn,
      And to hear the gay ' turn,'
      Made my yarn to crack ;
      And I fell on my back,
      Down the steps of the door.
I thought I was dead, or, twice as bad,
      Should never be good any more.
If I had broken my bones on the cursed hard stones,
      'Twas no wonder.
But worst of all, with the force of the fall,
      My twadling-string burst asunder.

    .   .   .   .

"Old madam was seized with frights and fears,—
She thought the house falling about her ears ;
And, to save herself, she tore up-stairs,
Where they found her next morning under the bed,
With the brandy-bottle close to her head."

Bet is found in a similar plight, and all is attributed to spinning ;
however, the Squire orders that Madam Pender shall spin no
more,—

      " And dance, one and all,
      With the holly and bays so bright on the wall."

---

         * Spinning wheel.

THE GAME OF HURLING.

THE game of "Hurling" was, until a recent period, played in the parishes to the west of Penzance on the Sunday afternoon. The game was usually between two parishes, sometimes between Burian and Sancreed, or against St Leven and Sennen, or the higher side of the parish played against the lower side.

The run was from Burian Cross in the Church-town, to the Pipers in Boloeit. All the gentry from the surrounding parishes would meet at Boloeit to see the ball brought in.

"Hurling matches" are peculiar to Cornwall. They are trials of skill between two parties, consisting of a considerable number of men, forty to sixty a side, and often between two parishes. These exercises have their name from "hurling" a wooden ball, about three inches in diameter, covered with a plate of silver, which is sometimes gilt, and has commonly a motto, " Gware wheag yeo gware teag," " Fair play is good play." The success depends on catching the ball dexterously when thrown up, or *dealt*, and carrying it off expeditiously, in spite of all opposition from the adverse party ; or, if that be impossible, throwing it into the hands of a partner, who in his turn, exerts his efforts to convey it to his own goal, which is often three or four miles' distance. This sport, therefore, requires a nimble hand, a quick eye, a swift foot, and skill in wrestling ; as well as strength, good wind, and lungs. Formerly it was practised annually by those who attended corporate bodies in surveying the bounds of parishes ; but from the many accidents that usually attended that game, it is now scarcely ever practised. Silver prizes used to be awarded to the victor in the games. A correspondent at St Ives writes :—

HURLING THE SILVER BALL.—This old custom is still observed at St Ives. The custom is also kept up at St Columb and St Blazey, on the anniversary of the dedication of the church St Ives Feast is governed by the Candlemas-day, it being the nearest Sunday next before that day. On the Monday after, the inhabitants assemble on the beach, when the ball, which is left in the custody of the mayor for the time being, is thrown from the churchyard to the crowd. The sides are formed in this way,—

> Toms, Wills, and Jans.
> Take off all's on the san's—

that is, all those of the name of Thomas, John, or William are ranged on one side, those of any other *Christian* name on the other , of late years the odd names outnumbered the Toms, Wills, and Jans. There is a pole erected on the beach, and each side strives to get the oftenest at the "goold," *i e*, the pole ; the other side as manfully striving to keep them out, and to send their opponents as great a distance from the pole as possible. The tradition is, that the contest used to be between the parishes of Ludgvan, Lelant, and St Ives,—St Ives then being part of the *living* of Ludgvan,—and that they used to have a friendly hurling at Ludgvan, and that afterwards the contest was between Lelant and St Ives   A stone near to Captain Peiry's house is shown, where the two parishes used to meet at the feast, and the struggle was to throw the ball into the parish church, the successful party keeping the ball, the unsuccessful buying a new one   St Ives is said to have out-numbered the Lelant folks, so that they gave up the contest, and the ball was left with St Ives.   Thus much is certain—that the feasts of St Ives, Lelant, and Ludgvan fall properly on one Sunday, though a misunderstanding has arisen, Lelant claiming to be governed by the day before Candlemas-day, which will alter the three every seven years.

The game of hurling is now but rarely played, and the Sabbath is never broken by that or by any other game.

SHAM MAYORS.

I.—THE MAYOR OF MYLOR.

THERE was a curious custom in the town of Penryn in Corn-wall, which long outlived all modern innovations.   On some particular day in September or October (I forget the exact date), about when the hazel-nuts are ripe, the festival of nutting-day is kept.   The rabble of the town go into the country to gather nuts, returning in the evening with boughs of hazel in their hands, shouting and making a great noise.   In the meantime the journeymen tailors of the town have proceeded to the adjoining village of Mylor, and elected one of their number "Mayor of Mylor," taking care the selection falls on the wittiest.   Seated in a chair shaded with green boughs, and borne on the shoulders of four stalwart men, the worthy mayor proceeds from his "good town of Mylor" to his "ancient borough of Penryn," the van being led by the "body-guard" of stout fellows well armed with cudgels,—which they do not fail to use should their path be obstructed,—torch-bearers, and two "town serjeants," clad in official gowns and cocked hats, and carrying each a monstrous cabbage on his shoulder in lieu of a mace.   The rear is brought up by the rabble of the "nutters." About mid-day a band of music meets them, and plays them to Penryn, where they are received by the entire population.   The procession proceeds to the town-hall, in front of which the mayor delivers a speech, declaratory of his intended improvements, &c , for the coming year, being generally an excellent sarcastic burlesque on the speeches of parliamentary candidates.   The procession then moves on to each public-house door, where the mayor, his council, and officers, are liberally supplied with liquor, and the speech is repeated with variations. They then adjourn to the "council-chamber," in some public-house, and devote the night to drinking. At night the streets are filled with people bearing torches, throwing fireballs, and discharging rockets; and huge bonfires are kindled on the "Green," and "Old Wall." The legal mayor once made an effort to put a stop to this saturnalia, but his new-made brother issued prompt orders to his body-guards, and the *posse comitatus* had to fly.

The popular opinion is, that there is a clause in the borough charter compelling the legitimate mayor to surrender his power to the "Mayor of Mylor" on the night in question, and to lend the town sergeants' paraphernalia to the gentlemen of the shears.

II.—THE MAYOR OF ST GERMANS.

One of the first objects that attracts attention on entering the village of St Germans is the large walnut-tree, at the foot of what is called Nut-Tree Hill. In the early part of the present century there was a very ancient dwelling a few yards south-east of this tree, which was supposed to have been the residence of some ecclesiastic of former times. Many a gay May-fair has been witnessed by the old tree; in the morning of the 28th of the month, splendid fat cattle, from some of the largest and best farms in the county, quietly chewed the cud around its trunk; in the afternoon the basket-swing dangled from its branches, filled with merry laughing boys and girls from every part of the parish. On the following day, the mock mayor, who had been chosen with many formalities, remarkable only for their rude and rough nature, starting from some "bush-house," where he had been supping too freely of the fair ale, was mounted on wain or cart, and drawn around it, to claim his pretended jurisdiction over the ancient borough, until his successor was chosen at the following fair. Leaving the old nut-tree, which is a real ornament to the town, we pass by a stream of water running into a large trough, in which many a country lad has been drenched for daring to enter the town on the 29th of May without the leaf or branch of oak in his hat.

III.—THE MAYOR OF HALGAVER MOOR.

The people of Bodmin had an old custom of assembling in large numbers on Halgaver Moor in the month of July, and electing a "Mayor of Misrule," for the punishment of petty offenders. Our old historian gives a quaint description. "The youthlyer sort of Bodmin townsmen use sometimes to spolt themselves by playing the box with strangers, whom they summon to Halgaver; the

name signifieth the Goats' Mooie, and such a place it is, lying a
little without the town, and very full of quagmires. When these
mates meet with any raw serving-man or other young master, who
may serve and deserve to make pastime, they cause him to be
solemnly arrested for his appearance before the Mayor of Halgaver,
where he is charged with wearing one spur, or wanting a girdle,
or some such like felony, and after he hath been arraigned and
tiied with all requisite circumstances, judgment is given in formal
terms, and executed in some one ungracious prank or other, more
to the scorn than hurt of the paity condemned. Hence is sprung
the proverb, when we see one slovenly apparelled, to say, 'He
shall be piesented in Halgaver Court.'"

THE FACTION FIGHT AT CURY GREAT TREE.

ON a green knoll in the centre of the intersection of the roads
from Helston to the Lizard, and Mawgan to Cury, flourished
an ash-tree of magnificent dimensions The peculiarity of its
position, together with its unusual size, in the midst of a district
singularly destitute of trees, rendered it famous throughout the
surrounding neighbourhood ; and in designating a special locality,
reference was, and still continues to be, made to " Cury Great
Tree," as a position generally known During the last fifty years
the tree has been gradually decaying, and at present only a portion
of the hollow trunk remains, which is rapidly disappearing. It
stands about half way up a gentle rise facing the noith ; and in
passing over the road, the country people speak of a dim tradition
of a time when the " road ran with blood." The occasion of this,
which is almost forgotten, was a faction fight, on a large scale,
between the men of the paiishes of Wendron and Breage, happen-
ing about a hundred years since. A wreck took place near the
Lizard, and the Wendron-men being nearest, were soon upon the
spot to appropriate whatevei flotsam and jetsam might come in
their way. Returning laden with their spoils, they were encountered at the Great Tree by the Wendron-men bound on a similar
errand, and a fight, as a matter of course, ensued, which was
prolonged till the following day. The contest is said to have been
a most terrible one, each party being armed with staves. The
savage nature of the fight may be infeired from the following
fact :—A Wendron-man named Gluyas, having been disabled, was
put upon the top of the roadside hedge, out of the *mêlée*, when
he was seen by a Breage termagant known as " Prudy the Wicked,"
and by her quickly dragged into the road, " Prudy " exclaiming,

" Ef thee artn't ded, I make thee," suiting the action to the word
by striking Gluyas with her patten iron until he was dead.   There
is some account of Prudy's having been taken before the " Justice,"
but she does not appear to have been punished.   These fights
between parishes were so common in those days that any death
occurring in the fray was quietly passed over as a thing of course,
and soon forgotten.   " So late as thirty years since it was unsafe
to venture alone through the streets of the lower part of this town
(Helston) after nightfall on a market-day owing to the frays of the
Breage, Wendron, and Sithney men."   So writes a friend residing
in Helston.

TOWEDNACK CUCKOO FEAST.

THE parish feast takes place on the nearest Sunday to the 28th
of April.

It happened in very early times, when winters extended further
into the spring than they now do, that one of the old inhabitants
resolved to be jovial, notwithstanding the inclemency of the season;
so he invited all his neighbours, and to warm his house he placed
on the burning faggots the stump of a tree   It began to blaze,
and, inspired by the warmth and light, they began to sing and
drink ; when, lo ! with a whiz and a whir, out flew a bird from the
hollow in the stump, crying, Cuckoo ! cuckoo !   The bird was
caught and kept by the farmer, and he and his friends resolved to
renew the festal meeting every year at this date, and to call it
their " cuckoo feast."   Previous to this event Towednack had no
" feasten Sunday," which made this parish a singular exception
to the rule in Cornwall.

This feast is sometimes called " crowder " feast, because the
fiddler formed a procession at the church door, and led the people
through the village to some tune on his " crowd."

THE DUKE OF RESTORMEL.

A VERY singular custom formerly prevailed at Lostwithiel, in
Cornwall, on Easter Sunday.   The freeholders of the town
and manor having assembled together, either in person or by their
deputies, one among them, each in his turn, gaily attired and
gallantly mounted, with a sceptre in his hand, a crown on his
head, and a sword borne before him, and respectfully attended by
all the rest on horseback, rode through the principal street in
solemn state to the church.   At the churchyard stile, the curate,

or other minister, approached to meet him in reverential pomp, and then conducted him to church to hear divine service. On leaving the church, he repaired, with the same pomp and retinue, to a house previously prepared for his reception. Here a feast, suited to the dignity he had assumed, awaited him and his suite ; and, being placed at the head of the table, he was served, kneeling, with all the rites and ceremonies that a real prince might expect. This ceremony ended with the dinner ; the prince being voluntarily disrobed, and descending from his momentary exaltation, to mix with common mortals On the origin of this custom but one opinion can be reasonably entertained, though it may be difficult to trace the precise period of its commencement. It seems to have originated in the actual appearance of the prince, who re-sided at Restormel Castle in former ages ; but, on the removal of royalty, this mimic grandeur stepped forth as its shadowy repre-sentative, and continued for many generations as a memorial to posterity of the princely magnificence with which Lostwithiel had formerly been honoured.*

This custom is now almost forgotten, and Lostwithiel has little to disturb its quiet.

* " Every-Day Book."

POPULAR SUPERSTITIONS.

"The carrion crow, that loathsome beast,
  Which cries against the rain,
Both for her hue, and for the rest,
  The devil resembleth plain.
And as with guns we kill the crow
  For spoiling our relief,
The devil so must we o'erthrow
  With gunshot of belief."
                    —GEORGE GASCOIGNE,

CHARMING, PROPHETIC POWER, ETC.

CHARMING, AND PROPHETIC POWER.

I CANNOT more appropriately preface this section, than by quoting the remarks of a medical gentleman in large practice, on the subject of charms .—

" In common with most of the lower classes of the West of England, the miner is not free from many absurd superstitions (though I am glad to observe, even in the last few years, a great change has taken place, and such follies are gradually declining). Some think themselves endowed with a species of supernatural agency, and, like the Egyptian alluded to by Othello, call themselves charmers, and profess to stop the flowing of blood (no matter from what cause—a divided artery even), to remove specks from the cornea (which, in the dialect of the country, are called cannons '), and cure erysipelas, by charming. But I have never been able to ascertain by what means the charm is supposed to work. I only know that it is an everyday occurrence for mothers to bring children to the surgery, afflicted with either of the diseases mentioned, and say that they have had them charmed ; but they were no better, such want of improvement having obviously excited the greatest feelings of astonishment I knew a person connected with the mines, who felt himself endowed with prophetic powers ; and in his case the divination was not confined to events momentous and terrible, but extended to the most trifling minutiæ of life.

" He with grave simplicity told me one day, by way of exemplifying the proper estimation in which his prophetic powers were held by his wife, that on one occasion, his pig having wandered from his sty, she came to him to ascertain in what direction it was to be sought for ; and on his professing utter ignorance of the animal's peregrinations, she exclaimed in reproachful tones, ' *Ah ! you are not so pious as you used to be. I remember the time when you could have told me in an instant the exact spot to have found it.*' " *

* "On the Diseases of Cornish Miners " By William Wale Tayler, F.R C.S.

FORTUNE-TELLING, CHARMS, ETC.

IN relation to this subject, and confirming an opinion already expressed in the existence still of a belief in magic and charms, I print the following communication from a lady of considerable literary ability :—

"Every country, it may be safely inferred, has its own individual, perhaps characteristic, Charm-record ; and inquiry into it would more than probably recompense the labour, by the light it would let in on the still but little investigated philosophy of the human mind, and the growth of popular superstitions. The portion of our country best known to the writer of these remarks is Cornwall, remarkable for the picturesque wildness of its scenery, and not less so for its numerous superstitions. The Rev. Charles Kingsley, in his 'Yeast,' has availed himself, with his usual tact and power, of one of the most striking of these, having reference to the cruel treatment of the Jews, who were sold as slaves to work in the mines ; the evil treatment they experienced being avenged on modern miners, by the terrors the souls of the departed Hebrews inflicted, in returning to the scene of their former compulsory toil, and echoing the sounds of the workmen now labouring in flesh and blood. But this is a digression from the main object of this article—viz , the belief in charms. Several years ago, while residing at Falmouth, I remember to have heard of a man in humble life, named Thomas Martin, whose abode was said to be at a village in the neighbourhood of Redruth, and who accomplished wonderful cures of children subject to fits, or personally injured by any deformity, by his power of charming. This man also practised soothsaying to a considerable extent, and revealed, with unquestionable accuracy, where articles mysteriously abstracted were concealed. If a cow suddenly lost her milk, whether witchcraft had exerted its malignant influence on the non-producing animal or no, such a personage could not but exercise an important power over the rustic population of the neighbourhood. But belief in the mysterious intelligence of Martin was by no means confined to the peasant class. A highly-respected and even ladylike person told the writer, with all the gravity becoming such a communication, that she had once made an appointment with Thomas Martin to meet him at a certain stile, for the purpose of receiving from him the prediction of her future lot, —in other words, having her fortune told ; and hastening thither at the time appointed, was horrified to find the stile occupied by a large black snake. As Martin did not make his appearance, she inferred that he had assumed the serpent form, and not being disposed to hold any intercourse with a being of such questionable exterior, she hastened away, determined never more to risk the attainment of the knowledge she coveted through a probably diabolic channel.

"This anecdote is given as veritable experience of the belief which may prevail in a mind fairly intelligent, and generally rational in conducting the ordinary business of life.

"Martin's reputation was disputed by no one, and that it continued unimpaired to the close of his life reflects no inconsiderable credit on the shrewdness and sagacity of his mind and his power of guessing.

"In the town where the writer has been residing for the last four months, there is a female, advanced in years and of good character, who, according to the report of many persons,—one a relative of her own,—

is peculiarly endowed with the power of charming away the disease called the 'kennel,' an affection of the eye which causes extreme pain. A young lady's father was one evening suffering severe pain in the right eye, and after trying various remedies without effect (the agony having greatly increased), in her despair she sought an occasion to leave the house, and hastened at once to the abode of the charmer. She told her errand to the woman, who said that many had come to her for the purpose of ridiculing her, and she did not like to say anything about charming,—she did not wish to be laughed at. On this the young lady assured her that her object in true faith was to obtain relief for her suffering father, and by no means to indulge the spirit of ridicule. On this representation she was satisfied, and desired to know the *kind* of kennel which affected the gentleman's eye. This information the daughter was unable to give her, being unacquainted with their peculiarities ; 'because,' said the charmer, 'there are nine kinds of kennels,' intimating at the same time that a different charm might be said or applied to each,—so that, to avoid omitting any, she must say the charms for all, in order that the one especially affecting the diseased eye should be certainly included in the charm. She went up-stairs, and remained about half an hour. On her return she addressed the young lady, and told her she might go home, where she would learn whether the eye had been relieved. She took no money for her incantation. Any little present might be offered at a subsequent visit, but no direct payment was ever requested, and indeed would have been declined. The amazement and pleasure of the anxious daughter, on her arrival at home, will be imagined, on learning from her father that the intense pain in the eye had ceased during her absence, though he had not been made acquainted with her errand. The influence of the faith of another, in this case. on the relief of the afflicted person, has no verisimilitude save with that of the father of the demoniac in the gospel, or the removal of the son's fever in consequence of the faith of the father. I have no reason whatever to question the truth of this story, which was confirmed by the wife of the gentleman thus relieved.

"A still more curious instance of the effect of charm, though quite of another character, was related to me by the same party. The gentleman referred to being much afflicted with cramp, his wife was earnestly advised, by a country woman to whom she mentioned the circumstance, to request her husband to place his slippers, with the toes turned upward, at the foot of the bed. Half smiling at the wise counsel, yet perhaps not altogether incredulous, he followed the good woman's advice, and to his great comfort found himself unaffected by his dreaded enemy throughout the night. His faith being thus established in the *anti-cramp* influence of upturned slippers, he took care to place them, or to have them placed, in the prescribed attitude on several successive nights. One night, however, he was again seized with some appalling twinges, and bethinking himself of the cause, suddenly recollected that in hastening into bed he had not observed the important rule ; instantly he had the slippers restored to their proper position, and, to his astonishment and delight, the pain ceased, and visited him no more. After this experience of the wonderful effects that followed so simple a specific, it may be easily imagined that he did not again risk the return of the cramp from neglecting it. Such phenomena seem beyond the power of explanation on any known medical principles. If any one more than usually versed in the subtle power exercised on the body by the mind, can throw light on the *slipper* cure of the cramp, he will deserve much at the hands of physiological and mental science." S. E. M.

THE ZENNOR CHARMERS.

BOTH men and women in this parish possessed this power to
a remarkable degree.   They could stop blood, however freely
it might be flowing.   " Even should a pig be sticked in the very
place, if a charmer was present, and *thought* of his charm at the
time, the pig would not bleed."   This statement, made by a Zennor
man, shows a tolerably large amount of faith in their power.   The
charmers are very cautious about communicating their charms.   A
man would not on any account tell his charm to a woman, or a
woman communicate hers to a man.   People will travel many
miles to have themselves or their children charmed for " wildfires "
(erysipelas), ringworms, pains in the limbs or teeth, " kennels " on
the eyes (ulcerations).   A correspondent writes me :—" Near
this lives a lady charmer, on whom I called.   I found her to be a
really clever, sensible woman.   She was reading a learned treatise
on ancient history.   She told me there were but three charmers
left in the west,—one at New Mill, one in Morva, and herself."
Their charm for stopping blood is but another version of one given
on another page.

> " Christ was born in Bethlehem ;
> Baptized in the river Jordan.
> The river stood,—
> So shall thy blood,
> *Mary Jane Polgrain* [*or whatever the person*
>   *may be called*],
> In the name of the Father," &c.

J—— H——, THE CONJURER OF ST COLOMB.

THIS old man was successful in persuading his dupes that he
owed his powers over evil spirits to his superior learning and
his unblemished life.   This assumption of piety was well preserved,
and to the outside world his sanctity was undoubted.   The only
practice which can be named as peculiar to H—— was that of
lighting scores of candles and placing them around the meadow
near his house.   Of course such a display would attract much attention ; and J—— succeeded in conveying an impression to the
minds of the country people that this process was required to
counteract the spells of the witches.   When this old fellow has
been summoned, as he often was, to the houses supposed to be
under the influence of evil, or to be bewitched, his practice was not
a little original, though wanting in all that dignifies the office of
an exorcist.   When he arrived at the house, before speaking to any

one, he would commence operations by beating with a heavy stick on the wooden partitions, screens, or pieces of furniture, so as to make the greatest possible noise, shouting loudly all the time, " Out ! out ! out !—Away ' away ' away !—to the Red Sea—to the Red Sea—to the Red Sea." Frequently he would add, with violent enunciation and much action, a torrent of incoherent and often incomprehensible words (locally, "*gibberish*"). The proceeding being brought to a close, and the spirits of evil flown, every part of the house was ordered to be well cleansed, and the walls and ceilings to be thoroughly lime-washed,—certainly the only sensible part of the whole operation. When J—— H—— was applied to respecting stolen property, his usual practice was to show the face of the thief in a tub of water. J—— drove a considerable trade in selling powders to throw over bewitched cattle.*

CURES FOR WARTS.

I. THE vicar of Bodmin found, not long since, a bottle full of pins laid in a newly-made grave. I have heard of this as an unfailing remedy ; each wart was touched with a new pin, and the pin then dropped into the bottle. I am not quite certain that it was necessary that the bottle should be placed in a newly-made grave , in many cases burying it in the earth, and especially at a " four cross-roads," was quite sufficient. As the pins rust, the warts decay.

II. A piece of string should be taken, and as many knots tied on it as there are warts on the body ; each wart being carefully touched with the knot dedicated to it. The string is then to be buried, and the warts fade away as it decays. A few years since a shipwright in Devonport dockyard professed to cure warts by merely receiving from an indifferent person a knotted string,—the knots of which had been tied by the afflicted. What he did with the string I know not.

III. To touch each wart with a pebble, place the pebbles in a bag, and to lose the bag on the way to church, was for many years a very favourite remedy ; but the unfortunate person who found the bag received the warts. A lady once told me that she picked up such a bag, when a child, and out of curiosity, and in ignorance,

---

* When cattle or human beings have been bewitched, it was very commonly thought that if a bottle of urine from the diseased beast or person was obtained, then corked very tight and buried mouth downwards, that the witch would be afflicted with strangury, and in her suffering confess her crime and beg forgiveness.

examined the contents. The result was that she had, in a short time, as many warts as there were stones in the bag.

IV. Another remedy was to *steal* a piece of meat from a butcher's stall in the public market, and with this to touch the warts, and bury it. As the meat putrefied the warts decayed.

V. I remember, when quite a child, having a very large "seedy wart" on one of my fingers. I was taken by a distant relation, an elderly lady, residing in Gwinear, to some old woman, for the purpose of having this wart charmed. I well remember that two charred sticks were taken from the fire on the hearth, and carefully crossed over the fleshy excrescence, while some words were muttered by the charmer. I know not how long it was before the wart disappeared, but certainly, at some time, it did so.

A CURE FOR PARALYSIS.

MARGERY PENWARNE, a paralysed woman, about fifty years of age, though from her affliction looking some ten years older, sat in the church porch of St——, and presented her outstretched withered arm and open palm to the congregation as they left the house of God after the morning service.

Penny after penny fell into her hand, though Margery never opened her lips. All appeared to know the purpose, and thirty pennies were speedily collected. Presently the parson came with his family, and then she spoke for the first time, soliciting the priest to change the copper coins into one silver one. This wish was readily acceded to, and the paralytic woman hobbled into the church, and up the aisle to the altar rails. A few words passed between her and the clerk; she was admitted within the rails, and the clerk moved the communion-table from against the wall, that she might walk round it, which she did three times.

"Now," said Margery, "with God's blessing, I shall be cured; my blessed bit of silver must be made into a ring" (this was addressed to the clerk, half aside); "and within three weeks after it is on my finger I shall get the use of my limbs again."

This charm is common throughout the three western counties for the cure of rheumatism,—the Devonshire halt,—or for any contraction of the limbs.

A CURE FOR RHEUMATISM.

CRAWL under a bramble which has formed a second root in the ground. Or get a woman who has been delivered of a child feet foremost, to tread the patient.

SUNDRY CHARMS.

THE vicar of a large parish church informs me that a woman came to him some time since for water from the font after a christening; she required it to undo some spell. The vicar states, that all the fonts in the country were formerly locked, to prevent people from stealing the "holy water," as they called it.

CURE FOR COLIC IN TOWEDNACK.

To stand on one's head for a quarter of an hour.

FOR A SCALD OR BURN.

" There came three angels out of the east,
One brought fire and two brought frost;
Out fire and in frost,
In the name of the Father, Son, and Holy Ghost.
                              Amen !"

Bramble-leaves, or sometimes the leaves of the common dock, wetted with spring water, are employed in this charm, as also in the following one.

CHARMS FOR INFLAMMATORY DISEASES.

A similar incantation to that practised for a burn is used. Three angels are invoked to come from the east, and this form of words is repeated three times to each one of nine bramble-leaves immersed in spring water, making passes with the leaves *from* the diseased part.

CHARMS FOR THE PRICK OF A THORN.

I.

"Christ was of a virgin born,
And he was prick'd by a thorn,
And it did never bell* nor swell,
As I trust in Jesus this never will."

II.

"Christ was crown'd with thorns:
The thorns did bleed, but did not rot,
No more shall thy finger.
In the name," † &c.

CHARMS FOR STANCHING OF BLOOD.

" Sanguis mane in te,
Sicut Christus fuit in se;

* Throb.

† The invocation of the " Father, Son, and Holy Ghost," invariably accompanies every form of charm

> Sanguis mane in tuâ venâ,
> Sicut Christus in suâ penâ ;
> Sanguis mane fixus,
> Sicut Christus quando crucifixus."

As this is repeated by ignorant old men or women, it becomes a confused jargon of unmeaning words, but it impresses the still more ignorant sufferer with awe, approaching to fear. The following is more common :—

> "Christ was born in Bethlehem,
> Baptized in the river Jordan ;
> There he digg'd a well,
> And turn'd the water against the hill,
> So shall thy blood stand still.
>   In the name," &c.

CHARM FOR A TETTER.

> "Tetter, tetter, thou hast nine brothers.
> God bless the flesh and preserve the bone ;
> Perish, thou tetter, and be thou gone.
>   In the name, &c.

> "Tetter, tetter, thou hast eight brothers.
> God bless the flesh and preserve the bone ;
> Perish, thou tetter, and be thou gone.
>   In the name, &c.

> "Tetter, tetter, thou hast seven brothers."
>   &c.   &c.

Thus the verses are continued until tetter, having " no brother," is imperatively ordered to begone.

CHARM FOR THE STING OF A NETTLE.

Many a time do I remember, when a child playing in the fields, having suffered from the stings of the nettle, and constantly seeking for the advantages of the charm of the dock-leaf. The cold leaf was placed on the inflamed spot, and the well-known rhyme three times repeated .—

> "Out nettle,
> In dock ;
> Dock shall have
> A new smock."

CHARM FOR TOOTHACHE.

> " Christ pass'd by His brother's door,
> Saw His brother lying on the floor.
> ' What aileth thee, brother ?
> Pain in the teeth ?—
> Thy teeth shall pain thee no more.
>   In the name,' " &c.

CHARM FOR SERPENTS.

The body of a dead serpent bruised on the wound it has occasioned, is said to be an infallible remedy for its bite. Common report is sufficient to warrant a poetical allusion :—

> " The beauteous adder hath a sting,
> Yet bears a balsam too "—*Polwhele's Sketches.*

THE CURE OF BOILS.

The sufferer is to pass nine times against the sun, under a bramble-bush growing at both ends. This is the same as the cure prescribed for rheumatism.

RICKETS, OR A CRICK IN THE BACK.

The holed stone—Mên-an-tol—in Lanyon, is commonly called by the peasantry the crick-stone. Through this the sufferer was drawn nine times against the sun—or, if a man, he was to crawl through the hole nine times.

Strumous children were not unfrequently treated after another fashion.

A young ash-tree was cleft vertically, and the parts being drawn forcibly asunder, the child was passed " three times three times " against the sun through the tree. This ceremony having been performed, the tree was carefully bound together ; if the bark grew together and the tree survived, the child would grow healthy and strong ; if the tree died, the death of the child, it was believed, would surely follow.

THE CLUB-MOSS.

(LYCOPODIUM INUNDATUM.)

IF this moss is properly gathered, it is " good against all diseases of the eyes."

The gathering is regarded as a mystery not to be lightly told ; and if any man ventures to write the secret, the virtues of the moss avail him no more. I hope, therefore, my readers will fully value the sacrifice I make in giving them the formula by which they may be guided.

On the third day of the moon—when the thin crescent is seen for the first time—show it the knife with which the moss is to be cut, and repeat,—

> " As Christ heal'd the issue of blood,
> Do thou cut, what thou cuttest, for good ! "

At sun-down, having carefully washed the hands, the club-moss is to be cut kneeling. It is to be carefully wrapped in a white cloth, and subsequently boiled in some water taken from the spring nearest to its place of growth. This may be used as a fomentation. Or the club-moss may be made into an ointment, with butter made from the milk of a new cow.

MOON SUPERSTITIONS.

THE following superstitions are still prevalent on the north coast of Cornwall :—

"This root (the sea-poppy), so much valued for removing all pains in the breast, stomach, and intestines, is good also for disordered lungs, and is so much better here than in other places, that the apothecaries of Cornwall send hither for it; and some people plant them in their gardens in Cornwall, and will not part with them under sixpence a root. A very simple notion they have with regard to this root, which falls not much short of the Druids' superstition in gathering and preparing their selago and samolus. This root, you must know, is accounted very good both as an emetic and cathartic If, therefore, they design that it shall operate as the former, their constant opinion is that it should be scraped and sliced upwards—that is, beginning from the root, the knife is to ascend towards the leaf;—but if that it is intended to operate as a cathartic, they must scrape the root downwards. The *senecio* also, or groundsel, they strip upwards for an emetic and downwards for a cathartic. In Cornwall they have several such groundless opinions with regard to plants, and they gather all the medicinal ones when the moon is just such an age ; which, with many other such whims, must be considered as the reliques of the Druid superstition." [*]

They, the Druids, likewise used great ceremonies in gathering an herb called *samolus*, marsh-wort, or fen-berries, which consisted in a previous fast, in not looking back during the time of their plucking it, and, lastly, in using their left hand only ; from this last ceremony, perhaps, the herb took the name of *samol*, which, in the Phœnician tongue, means the left hand. This herb was considered to be particularly efficacious in curing the diseases incident to swine and cattle.—(*C. S. Gilbert.*)

CURES FOR WHOOPING-COUGH.

I, GATHER nine spar stones from a running stream, taking care not to interrupt the free passage of the water in doing so. Then dip a quart of water from the stream, which must be taken in the direction in which the stream runs ;—by no means must the vessel be dipped against the stream.

[*] "Borlase's Observations on the Ancient and Present State of the Island of Scilly" "Notes and Queries," vol x p 181 1854.

Then make the nine stones red hot, and throw them into the quart of water. Bottle the prepared water, and give the afflicted child a wine-glass of this water for nine mornings following. If this will not cure the whooping-cough, nothing else can, says the believer.

II. A female donkey of three years old was taken, and the child was drawn naked nine times over its back and under its belly. Then three spoonfuls of milk were drawn from the teats of the animal, and three hairs cut from the back and three hairs cut from the belly were placed in it, this was to stand for three hours to acquire the proper virtue, and then the child drank it in three doses.

This ceremony was repeated three mornings running, and my informant said the child was always cured. I knew of several children who were treated in this manner in one of the small villages between Penzance and Madron Church town, some twenty or thirty years since. There were some doggerel lines connected with the ceremony, which have escaped my memory, and I have endeavoured, in vain, to find any one remembering them. They were to the effect that, as Christ placed the cross on the ass's back when he rode into Jerusalem, and so rendered the animal holy, if the child touched where Jesus sat, it should cough no more.

CURE OF TOOTHACHE.

ONE good man informed me that, though he had no faith in charming, yet this he knew, that he was underground one day, and had the toothache " awful bad, sure enough ; and Uncle John ax'd me, ' What 's the matter ? ' says he ' The toothache,' says I. ' Shall I charm it ? ' says he. ' Ees,' says I. ' Very well,' says he ; and off he went to work in the next pitch. Ho ! dedn't my tooth ache, Lor' bless ee ; a just ded, ye knaw ; just as if the charm were tugging my very life out. At last Uncle John comed down to the soller, and sing'd out, ' Alloa ! how 's your tooth in there,' says he. ' Very bad,' says I. ' How 's a feeling ? ' says he. ' Pulling away like an ould hoss with the " skwitches," ' says I. ' Hal drag my jaw off directly,' says I. ' Ees the charm working ? ' says he. ' Es, a shure enuf,' says I. ' Es,' says he, ' al be better d'rectly.' ' Hope a will,' says I. Goodness gracious ! dedn't a ache , I believe a did you ; then a stopped most to once. ' Es better,' says I ' I thought so,' says he ; ' and you waan't have un no more for a long time,' says he. ' Thank ee, Uncle John,' says I ; ' I 'll give ee a pint o' beer pay-day,' and so I ded ;

an' I haben't had the toothache ever since. Now, if he dedn't charm un, how ded a stop ? and if he dedn't knaw a would be better a long time, how ded he say so ? No, nor I haven't had un never since. So that's a plain proof as he knaw'd all about it, waden't a you ? "

I nodded assent, convinced it was useless to argue against such reasoning as that.

THE CONVALESCENT'S WALK.

I F an invalid goes out for the first time and makes a circuit, this circuit must be with the sun ; if against the sun, there will be a relapse.

ADDERS, AND THE MILPREVE.

THE country people around the Land's End say that in old times no one could live in the low grounds, which were then covered with thickets, and these swarming with adders. Even at a much later period, in the summer-time, it was not safe to venture amongst the furze on the Downs without a *milpreve*. (I have never seen a milpreve , but it is described to me as being about the size of a pigeon's egg, and I am told that it is made by the adders when they get together in great numbers Is it not probable that the milpreve may be one of the madrepore corals— *millepore*—found sometimes on the beaches around Land's End ?)

A friend writes me :—" I was once shown a milpreve ; it was nothing more than a beautiful ball of coralline lime-stone, the section of the coral being thought to be entangled young snakes."

When some old men were streaming the " Bottoms " up near Partimey, they were often obliged to leave work on account of the number of adders that would get together as if by agreement, and advance upon them.

One day one of the tin streamers chanced to leave his pot of milk, uncovered, out of the moor-house, when an adder got into it. The man cut a turf and put over the pot to prevent the reptile from escaping. In a few minutes the tinners saw " the ugly things crawling and leaping from all quarters towards the pot " The streamers were obliged to run, and take which way they would, the adders seemed to be coming from every direction, further and further off

At last " they formed a heap round the pot as large as a pook [cock] of hay." Towards night all the reptiles were quite still then the men gathered together, around the mass of adders, a great quantity of furze (being summer, there was plenty cut and dry close at hand), and piled it up like sheaves to make a mow, laying a circle of well-dried turf without it. They then fired the turf on every side, and when it was well ignited, they fired the furze. "Oh, it was a sight to see the adders when they felt the smoke and the flame! they began to boil, as it were, all in a heap, and fell back into the flaming furze; those which leaped through perishing on the brilliant ring of burning peat. Thus were killed thousands upon thousands of adders, and the moors were clear for a long, long period."

This is related nearly as the story was told; but it appears necessary to make some allowance for that spirit of exaggeration which is a characteristic of all Celtic people, ere they have been tutored to know the dignity of truth.

"The country people retaine a conceite, that the snakes, by their breathing upon a hazel-wand, doe make a stone ring of blew colour, in which there appeareth the yellow figure of a snake, and that beasts which are stung, being given to drink of the water wherein this stone hath bene socked, will there-through recover."[*]

This was clearly one of the so-called "Druidic rings,"—examples of which may be seen in our museums,—which have been found in England and in Ireland. It is curious that at the glassworks of Murano, near Venice, they still make rings, or beads, precisely resembling the ancient ones, and these are used largely as money in Africa.

Snakes were formerly held in great reverence; and Camden asserts that one of the prevailing superstitions concerning them was that, about midsummer-eve, they all met together in companies, and, joining their heads, began a general hiss, which they continued until a kind of bubble was formed, which immediately hardened, and gave to the finder prosperity in all his undertakings.[†]

Lhuyd, in a letter written in 1701, gives a curious account of the then superstitious character of the people in this district. "The Cornish retain variety of charms, and have still towards the Land's End the amulets of *Maen Magal* and *Glain-neider*, which latter they call a *Melprer*, a thousand worms, and have a charm for the snake to make it, when they have found one asleep, and struck a hazel-wand in the centre of its *spiræ*." Camden mentions the use of snake-stones as a Cornish superstition.

"The very same story, in fact, is told of the *Adder-stane* in the

* The Survey of Cornwall By Richard Carew.
† Draw and Hitchin's Cornwall.

popular legends of the Scottish Lowlands, as Pliny records of the origin of the *Ovum Anguinum.* The various names by which these relics are designated all point to their estimation as amulets or superstitious charms ; and the fact of their occurrence, most frequently singly, in the sepulchral cist or urn, seems to prove that it was as such, and not merely as personal ornaments, that they were deposited with the ashes of the dead. They are variously known as adder-beads, serpent-stones, Druidical beads ; and, amongst the Welsh and Irish, by the synonymous terms of *Gleini na Droedh* and *Glaine nan Druidhe,* signifying the magician's or Druid's glass "—*Wilson's Archæology and Prehistoric Annals of Scotland,* p 304.

SNAKES AVOID THE ASH-TREE.

IT is said that no kind of snake is ever found near the " ashen-tree," and that a branch of the ash-tree will prevent a snake from coming near a person.

A child who was in the habit of receiving its portion of bread and milk at the cottage door, was found to be in the habit of sharing its food with one of the poisonous adders. The reptile came regularly every morning, and the child, pleased with the beauty of his companion, encouraged the visits. The babe and adder were close friends.

Eventually this became known to the mother, and, finding it to be a matter of difficulty to keep the snake from the child whenever it was left alone,—and she was frequently, being a labourer in the fields, compelled to leave her child to shift for itself,—she adopted the precaution of binding an " ashen-twig " about its body.

The adder no longer came near the child ; but from that day forward the child pined, and eventually died, as all around said, through grief at having lost the companion by whom it had been fascinated.

TO CHARM A SNAKE.

WHEN an adder or snake is seen, a circle is to be rapidly drawn around it, and the sign of the cross made within it, while the two first verses of the 68th Psalm are repeated :—

" Let God arise, let his enemies be scattered ; let them also that hate him flee before him

" As smoke is driven away, so drive them away ; as wax melteth before the fire, so let the wicked perish at the presence of God."

When a child, I well remember being shown a snake, not yet dead, within a circle of this kind ; the gardener who drew my attention to the reptile informing me that he had charmed it in the manner related.

THE ASH-TREE.*

WEAKLY children—" children that wouldn't goode," or thrive —were sometimes drawn through the cleft ash-tree. I have seen the ceremony performed but in one case.

The tree was young, and it was taken by the two forks,—bifurcation having taken place,—and by force rended longitudinally. The cleft was kept open, and the child, quite naked, was passed head first through the tree nine times. The tree was then closed and carefully tied together. If the severed parts reunited, the child and the tree recovered together ; if the cleft gaped in any part, the operation was certain to prove ineffectual.

I quote another example. A large knife was inserted into the trunk of the young tree, about a foot from the ground, and a vertical rending made for about three feet. Two men then forcibly pulled the parts asunder, and held them so, whilst the mother passed the child through it three times. This "passing" alone was not considered effective ; it was necessary that the child should be washed for three successive mornings in the dew from the leaves of the " charmed ash."

In the *Athenæum* for September 1846, Ambrose Merton—Mr Thoms—has some interesting notices of the wide-spread belief in, and the antiquity of, this superstition.

RHYME ON THE EVEN ASH.

"EVEN ash, I thee do pluck,
　　Hoping thus to meet good luck.
If no luck I get from thee,
I shall wish thee on the tree."

A TEST OF INNOCENCY.

A FARMER in Towednack having been robbed of some property of no great value, was resolved nevertheless, to employ a test which he had heard the " old people " resorted to for the purpose of catching the thief. He invited all his neighbours into his cottage, and when they were assembled, he placed a cock under the "brandice," (an iron vessel formerly much employed by

* See also p 415.

the peasantry in baking, when this process was carried out on the
hearth, the fuel being furze and ferns)   Every one was directed
to touch the brandice with his, or her, third finger, and say, " In
the name of the Father, Son, and Holy Ghost, speak "   Every one
did as they were directed, and no sound came from beneath the
brandice.   The last person was a woman, who occasionally
laboured for the farmer in his fields,   She hung back, hoping to
pass unobserved amidst the crowd   But her very anxiety made
her a suspected person.   She was forced forward, and most un-
willingly she touched the brandice, when, before she could utter the
words prescribed, the cock crew.   The woman fell faint on the
floor, and, when she recovered, she confessed herself to be the
thief, restored the stolen property, and became, it is said, " a
changed character from that day."

THE BONFIRE TEST.

A BONFIRE is formed of faggots of furze, ferns, and the like.
Men and maidens by locking hands form a circle, and commence a dance to some wild native song.   At length, as the
dancers become excited, they pull each other from side to side
across the fire.   If they succeed in treading out the fire without
breaking the chain, none of the party will die during the year.   If,
however, the ring is broken before the fire is extinguished, " bad
luck to the weak hands," as my informant said.

LIGHTS SEEN BY THE CONVERTED.

THERE is, in many parts of the county, a belief, derived no
doubt from the recollection of St Paul's conversion, that,
when sinners are converted, they see shining lights about themselves.   I have many times heard this, but every one seems to have
his own particular mode of describing the phenomenon,—where
they can be prevailed on to describe it at all,—and usually that is
derived from some picture which has made an impression on their
minds . such as, " exactly like the light shining round the angel
appearing to St Peter, in fayther's Bible."

THE MIGRATORY BIRDS.

I FIND a belief still prevalent amongst the people in the outlying districts of Cornwall, that such birds as the cuckoo and
the swallow remain through the winter in deep caves, cracks in the

earth, and in hollow trees ; and instances have been cited of these birds having been found in a torpid state in the mines, and in hollow pieces of wood. This belief appears to be of some antiquity, for Carew writes in his " Survey of Cornwall " as follows ·—

"In the west parts of Cornwall, during the winter season, swallows are found sitting in old deep tynne-works, and holes in the sea cliffes ; but touching their lurking-places, *Olaus Magnus* maketh a far stranger report. For he saith that in the north parts of the world, as summer weareth out, they clap mouth to mouth, wing to wing, and legge to legge, and so, after a sweet singing, fall downe into certain lakes or pools amongst the caves, from whence at the next spring they receive a new resurrection ; and he addeth, for proofe thereof, that the fishermen who make holes in the ice, to dig up such fish in their nets as resort thither for breathing, doe sometimes light on these swallows congealled in clods, of a slymie substance, and that, carrying them home to their stoves, the warmth restored them to life and flight."

A man employed in the granite quarries near Penryn, informed me that he found such a " slymie substance " in one of the pools in the quarry where he was working, that he took it home, warmth proved it to be a bird, but when it began to move it was seized by the cat, who ran out on the downs and devoured it

SHOOTING STARS.

A MUCILAGINOUS substance is found on the damp ground near the granite quarries of Penryn, this is often very phosphorescent at night. The country people regard this as the substance of shooting stars. A tradesman of Penryn once brought me a bottle full of this substance for analysis, informing me that the men employed at the quarries, whenever they observed a shooting star, went to the spot near which they supposed it to fall, and they generally found a hatful of this mucus. It is curious that the Belgian peasants also call it "the substance of shooting stars" ("Phosphorescence," p. 109. By T. L. Phipson). This author says, "I have sketched the history of this curious substance in the *Journal de Médecine et de Pharmacologie* of Bruxelles, for 1855. It was analysed chemically by Mulder, and anatomically by Carus, and from their observations appears to be the peculiar mucus which envelops the eggs of the frog. It swells to an enormous volume when it has free access to water. As seen upon the damp ground in spring, it was often mistaken for some species of fungus ; it is, however, simply the spawn of frogs, which has been swallowed by some large crows or other birds, and afterwards vomited, from its peculiar property of swelling to an immense size in their bodies."

In Mulder's account of its chemical composition given by Berselius in his *Rapport Annual,* he distinguishes it by designation of *mucilage atmosphérique.*

THE SUN NEVER SHINES ON THE PERJURED.

THERE appears to exist a very old superstition, to the effect that when a man has deeply perjured himself,—especially if by his perjury he has sacrificed the life of a friend,—he not merely loses the enjoyment of the sunshine, but he actually loses all consciousness of its light or its warmth. Howsoever bright the sun may shine, the weather appears to him gloomy, dark, and cold.

I have recently been told of a man living in the western part of Cornwall, who is said to have sworn away the life of an innocent person "The face of this false witness is the colour of one long in the tomb; and he has never, since the death of the victim of his forswearing, seen the sun" It must be remembered the perjured man is not blind. All things around him are seen as by other men, but the sense of vision is so dulled that the world is for ever to him in a dark, vapoury cloud.

CHARACTERISTIC.

AN esteemed and learned correspondent, himself a Cornishman, writing to me on the Cornish character, says —

"There are some adages in which beadledom receives various hard knocks—that abstraction mostly taking the shape of some unlucky mayor, and I have heard in Cornwall, but never elsewhere, that the greatest fool in the place for the time being is always made the mayor.

"There is an adage of the Mayor of Calenich (and yet I doubt if ever that hamlet had such an officer) Calenich is one mile from Truro, and the mayor's hackney was pastured two miles from home; so, as his worship would by no means compromise his dignity by walking to Truro, he invariably walked to his horse to ride there, so that it was said of any one who would keep up appearances at great trouble, that he was '*like the Mayor of Calenich, who walked two miles to ride one*'

"The class who never know on which side their bread is buttered, are said to be '*like the Mayor of Market-Jew, sitting in their own light,*' and the stupid man whose moods, whether of sadness or merriment, are inopportune, is, as may be, said to be '*like the Mayor of Falmouth, who thanked God when the town-jail was enlarged.*'

"Many persons are chronicled in the same manner.

"'*Like Nicholas Kemp, he's got occasion for all.*' Nicholas was said to be a voter in a Cornish borough, who was told to help himself (so that no one should have given him a bribe) from a table covered with gold, in the election committee-room. Taking off his hat, he swept the whole mass into it, saying, 'I've occasion for all.'

"'*Like Uncle Acky Stoddern, the picture of ill luck.*' This was always applied to a once well-known Gwennap-man.

"When a boy is asked what he will be, it is sometimes answered on his behalf, '*I'll be like Knuckey, be as I am.*'

"'*Like Nanny Painter's hens, very high upon the legs,*' is applied to a starveling or threadpaper

"'*Like Malachi's cheeld, choke-full of sense,*' applied derisively to any one boasting of himself or of his children. This is, I believe, purely Cornish.

"'*Like a toad under a harrow, I don't know whichee corse to steer*' The first division of this adage is common property, the last is confined to Cornwall.

"'*He's coming home with Penny Liggan,*' sometimes '*Peter Lacken,*' signifies the return of a penniless scapegrace. The term was probably '*penny lacking*' originally.

"Are the Cornish folk given to making 'bulls,' like the Irish?" asks my correspondent. "I have heard of one or two curious inversions of speech.

"Once upon a time a little boy having vainly importuned his seniors for a penny to go and buy sweets, being determined not to be disappointed, went off, exclaiming, 'I don't care; I'll go and *trust* Betty Rule (the sweatmeat vendor). This is native and genuine Gwennapian.

"The common people are fond of figures of speech. Port-wine negus was christened by the miners 'black wine toddy.' They go on Midsummer-day to Falmouth or Penzance, to get '*a pen'ord o' say*'—that is, they go out in a boat on payment of a penny

"With them, when their health is inquired after, every man is '*brave,*' and every woman '*charming,*' and friendship takes dear household names into its mouth for more expressiveness.

"'Well, Billy, my son, how's faether?'

"'Brave, thank ee'

"'How are you, Coden [Cousin] Jann, and how's Betty?'

"'She's charming, thank ee.'

"*Trade* is a word of special application, '*a pa'cel o' trade*'

"A precious mess is '*a brave shape*'

"Of an undecided person it is said, '*He is neither Nim nor Doll.*' Does this mean he is neither Nimrod nor Dorothy?

A phrase descriptive of vacuity of expression is, '*He looks like anybody that has neither got nor lost.*'"

Years since it was a common custom to assign some ridiculous action to the people of a small town or village. For example, the people of one place were called "Buccas," "because some one of them was frightened at his shadow."

Those of another town were named "Gulls," "because two of the townsmen threw a gull over a cliff to break its neck."

The men of a fishing-village were nicknamed "Congers," "because they threw a conger overboard to drown it."

"Who whipped the hake?" was applied to the inhabitants of another town, because hake, it is said, being excessively plenty, the fishermen flogged one of those fish, and flung it back into the sea ; upon which all the hakes left that coast, and kept away for years *

" Who drowned the man in a dry ditch ? " belongs especially to another place.

Certain Cornishmen built a wall around the cuckoo, to prevent that bird from leaving the county, and thus to insure an early spring. When built, the bird flew out, crying " Cuckoo ! cuckoo !" " If we had put one course more on the wall we should a' kept 'n in," said they.

Camborne is so called from *Camburne,* a *crooked well-pit* of water. This crooked well was at one time far famed for the cure of many diseases.

The persons who washed* in this well were called *Merrasicke.* I know not the meaning of the word. According to an old Cornish custom of fixing nicknames on people, the inhabitants of Camborne are called *Mearageeks,* signifying perverse, or obstinate. —(*Lanyon.*)

The Church was anciently called *Mariadoci.* I therefore suspect that the above terms have some connection with this name. By an easy corruption, and the addition of *geeks,* or *gawks* (meaning awkward), either word can be produced.

Of the Gorran men it is asked, " Who tried to throw the moon over the cliffs ? "

THE MUTTON FEAST.

AN old tradition—the particulars of which I have failed to recover—says that a flock of sheep were blown from the Gwithian Sands over into St Ives Bay, and that the St Ives fishermen caught them,—believing them to be a new variety of fish,— either in their nets, or with hook and line, and brought them ashore as their night's catch.

I learn that Mr Fortescue Hitchins, some fifty or sixty years since, wrote a " copy of verses " on this tradition, but I have never seen this production.

THE FLOATING GRINDSTONE.

I HAVE already told of St Piran and his grindstone. I have, however, another and a more modern story, which is told with great glee at some of the social meetings of the fishermen. This is given merely to indicate the simplicity of this honest race.

---

* In Hugh Miller's " Scenes and Legends of the North of Scotland," edit. 1858, pp. 256, 257, will be found some stories of the flight of the " herring drove " from the coast of Cromarty, which are analogous to this

A party was got together on a promontory at the extremity of the bay which enclosed a fishing-town. They were gathered to see a wonder, a *floating grindstone.* Seeing that grindstones were grindstones in those days, and worth many pounds sterling, a boat was manned, and away they went, the mover of the expedition being in the bow of the boat.

As they approached the grindstone, this man planted his foot on the gunwale, ready for a spring. They were close aboard the circular mass,—" All my own, and none for nobody," he cries, and sprang off, as he fancied, on to the grindstone. Lo ! to his great surprise, he sank under water, presently popping up again within his charmed circle, to be greeted with roars of laughter He had leaped into a sheet of "salt sea foam" which had gathered, and was confined within a large hoop.

CELTS—FLINT ARROW-HEADS, ETC.

THE common people believe these to be produced by thunder, and thrown down from the clouds, and that they show what weather will ensue by changing their colour.

I have also found a belief prevailing in many districts, that Celts impart a virtue to water in which they have been soaked, and that diseases have been cured by drinking it.

THE HORNS ON THE CHURCH TOWER.

WHEN the masons were building the tower of Towednack Church, the devil came every night and carried off the pinnacles and battlements. Again and again this work was renewed during the day, and as often was it removed during the night, until at length the builders gave up the work in despair, feeling that it was of no use to contend with the evil one.

Thus it is that Towednack Church stands lonely, with its squat and odd-looking tower, a mark of the power of evil to the present day. Associated with this tower is a proverb : " There are no cuckolds in Towednack, because there are no horns on the church tower."

TEA-STALKS AND SMUT.

STEMS of tea floating in that beverage indicate strangers. Flakes of smut hanging loose to the fire-bars do the same thing.

The time of the stranger's arrival may be known by placing the stem on the back of one hand and smacking it with the other ;

the number of blows given before it is removed indicates the number of days before his arrival.

The flake of carbon is blown upon, and according as it is removed by the first, second, or third blow, so is the time at the end of which the visitor may be expected.

AN OLD CORNISH RHYME.

" WHEN the corn is in the shock,
    Then the fish are on the rock."

The pilchard visits this coast in the early autumn. These are the " fish " *par excellence* of the Cornish, and they are thus distinguished.

TO CHOOSE A WIFE.

ASCERTAIN the day of the young woman's birth, and refer to the last chapter of Proverbs. Each verse from the 1st to the 31st is supposed to indicate, either directly or indirectly, the character, and to guide the searcher—the verse corresponding with her age indicating the woman's character.

THE ROBIN AND THE WREN.

" THOSE who kill a robin or a wran,
    Will never prosper, boy or man."

This feeling is deeply impressed on every young mind ; there are few, therefore, who would injure either of those birds.

I remember that a boy in Redruth killed a robin : the dead robin was tied round his neck, and he was marched by the other boys through the town, all of them singing the above lines.

TO SECURE GOOD LUCK FOR A CHILD.

GIVE the first person whom you meet between your own house and the church to which you are taking the infant to be christened, a piece of bread and salt.

INNOCENCY.

TO wash the hands is an attestation of innocency. To call a man " dirty fingers," is to accuse him of some foul or unjust deed.

RAIN AT BRIDAL OR BURIAL.

"BLESSED is the bride
 Whom the sun shines on,
Blessed is the dead
 Whom the rain rains on."

If it rains while a wedding party are on their way to the church, or on returning from it, it betokens a life of bickering and unhappiness.

If the rain falls on a coffin, it is supposed to indicate that the soul of the departed has "arrived safe."

CROWING HENS, ETC.

A WHISTLING maid and a crowing hen in one house, is a certain sign of a downfall to some one in it. I have known hens killed for crowing by night.

The braying of an ass is a sign of fair weather; so is also the crowing of a cock. The quacking of ducks foretells rain.

THE NEW MOON.

TO see the new moon for the first time through glass, is unlucky; you may be certain that you will break glass before that moon is out I have known persons whose attention has been called to a clear new moon hesitate "Hev I seed her out a' doors afore?" if not, they will go into the open air, and if possible show the moon "a piece of gold," or, at all events, turn their money.

LOOKING-GLASSES.

BREAKING a looking-glass is certain to insure seven years of misfortune.

THE MAGPIE.

"ONE is a sign of anger,
 Two is a sign of mirth,
Three is a sign of a wedding,
 Four is a sign of a { birth.
                      { death.'

A scolding woman is called a magpie. Whenever you see a magpie, take off your hat to it; this will turn away the anger.

THE MONTH OF MAY UNLUCKY.

MAY is regarded by many as an unhealthy and unlucky month

Children born in the month of May are called " May chets," and kittens cast in May are invariably destroyed, for—

> " May chets
> Bad luck begets."

Another rhyme is—

> " A hot May,
> Fat church hay,"

meaning that funerals will be plenty.

ON THE BIRTHS OF CHILDREN.

> " SUNDAY'S child is full of grace,
> Monday's child is full in the face,
> Tuesday's child is solemn and sad,
> Wednesday's child is merry and glad,
> Thursday's child is inclined to thieving,
> Friday's child is free in giving,
> Saturday's child works hard for his living."

ON WASHING LINEN.

> " THEY that wash Monday got all the week to dry,
> They that wash Tuesday are pretty near by,
> They that wash Wednesday make a good housewife,
> They that wash Thursday must wash for their life,
> They that wash Friday must wash in need,
> They that wash Saturday are sluts indeed."

ITCHING EARS.

WHEN the ears are red and itch, it is a sign that some one is talking of the suffering individual. If it is the left ear, they are being scandalised ; if the right ear, they are being praised.

Often have I heard, when the lower and middle class people have been indulging in some gossip of their neighbours or friends, " I 'll bet how their ears do itch "

THE SPARK ON THE CANDLE.

A BRIGHT spark on the candle-wick indicates a letter coming to the house. The person towards whom it shines will receive it. The time of its arrival is determined by striking the bottom of the candlestick on the table. If the spark comes off on the first blow, it will be received to-morrow ; if two blows are required, on the second day,—and so on.

THE BLUE VEIN,

A FOND mother was paying more than ordinary attention to a fine healthy-looking child, a boy about three years old. The poor woman's breast was heaving with emotion, and she struggled to repress her sighs. Upon inquiring if anything was really wrong, she said " the old lady of the house had just told her that the child could not live long, because *he had a blue vein across his nose.*

THE CROAKING OF THE RAVEN.

THERE is a common feeling that the croaking of a raven over the house bodes evil to some member of the family. The following incident, given to me by a really intelligent man, illustrates the feeling .*—

" One day our family were much annoyed by the continued croaking of a raven over our house. Some of us believed it to be a token ; others derided the idea ; but one good lady, our next-door neighbour, said, ' Just mark the day, and see if something does not come of it.' The day and hour were carefully noted. Months passed away, and unbelievers were loud in their boastings and inquiries after the token.

" The fifth month arrived, and with it a black-edged letter from Australia, announcing the death of one of the members of the family in that country. On comparing the dates of the death and the raven's croak, they were found to have occurred on the same day."

WHISTLING.

TO whistle by night is one of the unpardonable sins amongst the fishermen of St Ives. My correspondent says, " I would no more dare go among a party of fishermen at night whistling a popular air than into a den of untamed tigers."

No miner will allow of whistling underground. I could never learn from the miners whether they regarded it as unlucky or not. I rather think they feel that whistling indicates thoughtlessness, and they know their labour is one of danger, requiring serious attention.

* See "Death Tokens."

MEETING ON THE STAIRS.

IT is considered unlucky to meet on the stairs, and often one will retire to his or her room rather than run the risk of giving or receiving ill luck,

I find this superstition prevails also in the Midland counties.

TREADING ON GRAVES.

" TO see a man tread over graves,
  I hold it no good mark ;
'Tis wicked in the sun and moon,
And bad luck in the dark ! "

So sings Coleridge in his ballad of " The Three Graves."

Whenever a person shivers from a sensation of cold down the spine, it is said some one is walking over his or her grave.

Persons believing this, will give directions that they may be buried in some secluded corner of the churchyard, so that their corpse may not be disturbed by unholy footsteps.

A LOOSE GARTER.

IF an unmarried woman's garter loosens when she is walking, her sweetheart is thinking of her.

TO CURE THE HICCOUGH.

WET the forefinger of the right hand with spittle, and cross the front of the left shoe or boot three times, repeating the Lord's Prayer backwards.

THE SLEEPING FOOT.

THIS irregularity in the circulation is at once removed by crossing the foot with saliva.

THE HORSE-SHOE.

TO nail a horse-shoe, which has been cast on the road, over the door of any house, barn, or stable, is an effectual means of preventing the entrance of witches.

THE BLACK CAT'S TAIL.

THOSE little gatherings which occur on the eyelids of children, locally called "whilks," are cured by passing a black cat's tail nine times over the place. If a ram cat, the cure is more certain.

UNLUCKY THINGS.

TO put the loaf on the table upside down—to cut the butter at both ends—to place the bellows on the table—to upset the salt—to cross your knife and fork—to pour gravy out of a spoon backwards (or back-handed), is each unlucky and leads to quarrels. To borrow or lend a bellows is most unlucky, and many would rather give than lend one.

If you are going on an errand, never turn back to your house, it presages ill luck to do so. If, however, you are compelled to it, fail not to sit down. By doing this some mischief may be avoided.

THE LIMP CORPSE.

IF a corpse stiffens shortly after death, all is thought to proceed naturally; but if the limbs remain flexible, some one of the family is shortly to follow. If the eyes of a corpse are difficult to close, it is said "they are looking after a follower."

To find a louse on one's linen, is a sign of sickness. To find two, indicates a severe illness. If three lice are so found within a month, it is a "token to prepare."

Talking backwards, or putting one word incorrectly before another,—"the cart before the horse,"—is considered to foretell that you will shortly see a stranger.

If two young people, in conversation, happen to think of the same thing at the same time, and one of them utters the thought before the other, that one is certain to be married first.

"BY HOOK OR BY CROOK."

IN the parish of Egles-Hayle are two crosses, known as "Peverell's Crosses," and near Mount Charles, also in this parish, is another "moorstone" cross, called the Prior's Cross, whereon is cut the figure of a hook and a crook, in memory of

2 E

the privileges granted by a prior, belonging to the family of the Peverells, who are said to have possessed lands in this parish since the time of Richard II.

The poor of Bodmin were greatly distressed through the scarcity of fuel, the " turf," or peat of the moors, being insufficient to supply their wants. The prior gave " privilege and freedom " to the poor of Bodmin for gathering, for " fire-boote and house-boote," such boughs and branches of oak-trees in his woods of Dunmear, as they could reach to, or come at, with a "hook and a crook," without further damage to the trees.

Hence the proverb concerning filching, " that they will have it by hook or by crook."

WEATHER SIGNS.

THE WEATHER DOG.—It frequently happens in unsettled weather that banks of rain-cloud gather around the horizon, and that, over isolated tracts, the rain falls. If these depositions from this low stratum of clouds occur opposite to the sun, the lower limb of a bow is formed, often appearing like a pillar of decomposed light ; and sometimes two of these coloured bands will be seen, forming indeed the two extremities of the arch. These are " weather dogs," and they are regarded as certain prognostications of showery or stormy weather.*

The usual proverb with regard to the full bow, which prevails generally, is common in Cornwall—

> "The rainbow in the morning
> Is the shepherd's warning ;
> The rainbow at night
> Is the shepherd's delight."

But, as far as I know, the " weather dog" is peculiarly Cornish.

WEATHER AT LISKEARD.

> "THE south wind always brings wet weather ;
> The north wind, wet and cold together
> The west wind always brings us rain ;
> The east wind blows it back again

* " There appeared in the north-east the frustrum of a large rainbow ; all the colours were lively and distinct , and it was three times as wide as the arch of an ordinary complete rainbow, but no higher than it was wide. They call it here, in Cornwall, *a weather dog*, but in the Cornish language, *Lagas-anel*,—that is, the weather's eye,—and pronounce it a certain sign of hard rain."—*Borlase's Natural History of Cornwall.*

If the sun in red should set,
The next day surely will be wet ;
If the sun should set in gray,
The next will be a rainy day."

Bond's Looe.

THE FIRST BUTTERFLY.

" ONE of the superstitions prevailing in Devonshire is, that any individual neglecting to kill the first butterfly he may see for the season, will have ill luck throughout the year." * The following recent example is given by a young lady :—" The other Sunday, as we were walking to church, we met a man running at full speed, with his hat in one hand, and a stick in the other. As he passed us, he exclaimed, ' I shan't hat 'en now, I b'lieve.' He did not give us time to inquire what he was so eagerly pursuing ; but we presently overtook an old man, whom we knew to be his father, and who, being very infirm, and upwards of seventy, generally hobbled about by the aid of two sticks. Addressing me, he observed, ' My *zin* a took away wan a my sticks, miss ; wan't be ebble to kil'n now though, I b'lieve.' ' Kill what ?' said I. ' Why, 'tis a butterfly, miss,—the *furst* hee'th a zeed for the year ; and they zay that a body will have cruel bad luck if a ditn'en kill a *furst* a zeeth.' "

I have found this belief prevailing in the east, but never in the west, of Cornwall.

PECULIAR WORDS AND PHRASES.†

" THE people in the west," writes a correspondent, " have adopted many words from the Danish invaders." Tradition assures us that the sea-rovers of the North frequently landed at Witsand Bay, burned and pillaged the villages of Escols and Mayon, sometimes took off the women, but never made a settlement. Certain red-haired families are often referred to as Danes, and the dark-haired people will not marry with " a red-haired Dane.' He continues :—" If you were in Buryan Church-town this evening, you might probably hear Betty Trenoweth say, ' I 'll take off my *touser* [toute serve], and run up to Janey Angwins to *cousey* [causer] a spell ; there's a lot of boys gone in there, so there 'll be a grand *courant* [de courir], I expect.' In a short time Betty may come back disappointed, saying, ''Twas a mere *cow's courant* after all, cheld vean—all hammer and tongs '"

The *touser* is a large apron or wrapper to come quite round

---

* Hone's Table Book.   † See Appendix EE.

and keep the under garments clean.   By a *courant* with the boys, they mean a game of running romps.   It is not at all uncommon in other parts of the country to hear the people say, " It was a fine *courant*," " We 've had a good *courant*," when they intend to express the enjoyment of some pleasure party.   These are, however, probably more nearly allied to Norman-French.

There are some proverbial expressions peculiar to the west :—

" Sow barley in dree, and wheat in pul." *

" To make an old nail good, right it on wood."

" Fill the sack, then it can stand."

The last meaning that neither man nor beast can work on an empty stomach.

The following are a few of less common expressions, preserving remarkable words :—

'Tis not *bezibd*—It is not allotted me.

He will never *scrip* it—He will never escape it.

He is nothing *pridy*—He is not handsome.

Give her *dule*—Give her some comfort or consolation.

Hark to his *lidden*—Listen to his word or talk.

It was *twenty* or *some*—It was about twenty.

The wind brings the *pilme*—The wind raises the dust.

How thick the *brusse* lies—How thick the dust lies.

He is *throyting*—He is cutting chips from sticks.

He came of a good *havage*— He belongs to a good or respectable family.

Hame—a straw collar with wooden collar-trees, to which are fastened the rope traces.

Scalpions (*buckthorn*, or rather *buckhorn*)—salt dried fish, usually the whiting.

" Eating fair maids, or fermades—(*fumadoes*)—[pilchards], and drinking mahogany [gin and treacle]."

* In pul, meaning in mud.

MISCELLANEOUS STORIES.

"Farewell, rewards and fairies,
　　Good housewives now may say;
For now foul sluts in dairies
　　Do fare as well as they.
　　・　　・　　・　　・　　・
"A tell-tale in their company
　　They never could endure;
And who kept not secretly
　　Their mirth, was punish'd sure."

Farewell to the Fairies.—RICHARD CORBET.

VARIOUS ROMANCES AND SUPERSTITIONS.

THE BELLS OF FORRABURY CHURCH.

"The Cornish drolls are dead, each one ;
The fairies from their haunts have gone ·
There's scarce a witch in all the land,
The world has grown so learn'd and grand."

HENRY QUICK, the Zennor Poet.

TO this day the tower of Forrabury Church, or, as it is called by Mr Hawker, "the silent tower of Bottreaux," remains without bells. "At Forrabury the chimes have never sounded for a marriage, the knell has never been heard for a funeral."—*Collins.*

In days long ago, the inhabitants of the parish of Forrabury—which does not cover a square mile, but which now includes the chief part of the town of Boscastle and its harbour—resolved to have a peal of bells which should rival those of the neighbouring church of Tintagel, which are said to have rung merrily at the marriage, and tolled solemnly at the death, of Arthur.

The bells were cast ; the bells were blessed ; and the bells were shipped for Forrabury. Few voyages were·more favourable ; and the ship glided, with a fair wind, along the northern shores of Cornwall, waiting for the tide to carry her safely into the harbour of Bottreaux.

The vesper bells rang out at Tintagel ; and the pilot, when he heard the blessed sound, devoutly crossed himself, and bending his knee, thanked God for the safe and quick voyage which they had made.

The captain laughed at the superstition of the pilot, as he called it, and swore that they had only to thank themselves for the speedy voyage, and that, with his arm at the helm, and his judgment to guide them, they should soon have a happy landing. The pilot checked this profane speech ; but the wicked captain—and he swore more impiously than ever that all was due to himself and his men—laughed to scorn the pilot's prayer. " May God forgive you !" was the pilot's reply.

Those who are familiar with the northern shores of Cornwall will know that sometimes a huge wave, generated by some mysterious power in the wide Atlantic, will roll on, overpowering everything by its weight and force.

While yet the captain's oaths were heard, and while the inhabitants on the shore were looking out from the cliffs, expecting, within an hour, to see the vessel, charged with their bells, safe in their harbour, one of these vast swellings of the ocean was seen. Onward came the grand billow in all the terror of its might. The ship rose not upon the waters as it came onward. She was overwhelmed, and sank in an instant close to the land.

As the vessel sank, the bells were heard tolling with a muffled sound, as if ringing the death-knell of the ship and sailors, of whom the good pilot alone escaped with life.

When storms are coming, and only then, the bells of Forrabury, with their dull, muffled sound, are heard from beneath the heaving sea, a warning to the wicked ; and the tower has remained to this day silent.

THE TOWER OF MINSTER CHURCH.

"The Minster of the Trees ! a lonely dell,
 Deep with old oaks, and 'mid their quiet shade,
Gray with the moss of years, yon antique cell !
 Sad are those walls , the cloister lowly laid,
Where pacing monks at solemn evening made
 Their chanted orisons . and as the breeze
Came up the vale, by rock and tree delay'd,
 They heard the awful voice of many seas
Blend with thy pausing hymn, thou Minster of the Trees !"

         HAWKER.

ON a visit to this old church, which is allowed to perish under the influences of damp and the accompanying vegetable growth, in a way which is but little creditable to the parishioners, I was struck at the evidence that the tower had either been taken down or that it had fallen   Amidst the long grass of the churchyard I found many remains of carved stones, which clearly belonged at one time to the tower.   I sought for some information, but I could obtain none.   The officiating clergyman, and several gentlemen of Boscastle, were alike ignorant of any tradition connected with the tower—the prevalent idea being that it was left unfinished.

At length, the ostler at the inn informed me that the story of the destruction of the tower ran thus :—

The tower of the church of the ancient abbey was seen through the gorge which now forms the harbour of Boscastle, far out at sea. The monks were in the habit of placing a light in one of the windows of the tower to guide the worshippers at night to the minster.

Frequently sailors mistook this, by day for some land-mark, and at night for a beacon, and were thus led into a trap from which they could not easily extricate themselves, and within which they often perished. This accident occurred so frequently that the sailors began at last to declare their belief that the monks purposely beguiled them to their fate, hinting, indeed, that plunder was their object. Eventually, a band of daring men, who had been thus lured into Boscastle, went to the abbey. and, in spite of the exertions made by the monks, they pulled down the tower, since which time it has never been rebuilt.

TEMPLE MOORS.

THE parish of Temple in 1851 had a population of 24 Yet once the Knights Templar built a church here; and with the purpose of civilising the inhabitants of the moor in the midst of which it was founded, they secured for their temple some special privileges. "Many a bad marriage bargain," says Tonkin, "is there yearly slubbered up , and grass widows with their fatlings put to lie-in and nurse here." "Send her to Temple Moors," implied that any female requiring seclusion might at one time secure it under the charge of these Christian knights in this their preceptory, and be returned to the world again, probably, in all respects, a better woman. At all events, the world, being in ignorance, did not repudiate the erring sister.

Stories linger over this wilderness of mixed good and evil. The church, which was consecrated to the great cause of saving sinners, has perished. No stone remains to tell us where it stood ; and to " send her to Temple moors," is to proclaim a woman an outcast from society.

THE LEGEND OF TAMARA.

THE lovely nymph Tamara was born in a cavern. Although her parents were spirits of the earth, the child loved the light of day. Often had they chided her for yielding to her desires and visiting the upper world ; and often had they warned her against the consequences which would probably arise from her neglect of their advice.

The giants of the moors were to be feared ; and it was from these that the earth spirits desired to protect their child.

Tamara—beautiful, young, heedless—never lost an opportunity of looking on the glorious sun. Two sons of Dartmoor giants—Tavy and Tawrage—had seen the fair maid, and longed to possess her. Long was their toil, and the wild maiden often led them over mountain and moor in playful chase.

Under a bush in Morewinstow, one day, both Tavy and Tawrage came upon Tamara. They resolved now to compel her to declare upon which of them her choice should fall. The young men used every persuasion, and called her by every endearing name. Her parents had missed Tamara, and they sought and found her seated between the sons of the giants whom they hated. The gnome father caused a deep sleep to fall on the eyes of Tavy and Tawrage, and then he endeavoured to persuade his daughter to return to his subterranean cell.

Tamara would not leave her lovers. In his rage the gnome cursed his daughter, and, by the might of his curse, changed her into a river, which should flow on for ever to the salt sea. The lovely Tamara dissolved in tears, and as a crystal stream of exceeding beauty the waters glided onward to the ocean.

At length Tavy awoke. His Tamara was gone ; he fled to his father in the hills. The giant knew of the metamorphosis, and, to ease the anguish of his son, he transformed him into a stream. Rushing over rocks, running through morasses, gliding along valleys, and murmuring amidst the groves, Tavy still goes on seeking for Tamara—his only joy being that he runs by her side, and that, mingling their waters, they glide together to the eternal sea

Tawrage awakened after a long sleep He divined what had taken place, and fled to the hills to an enchanter. At his prayer he, too, was changed to a stream ; but he mistook the road along which Tamara had gone, and onward, ever sorrowing, he flows—away—away—away from his Tamara for ever.

Thus originated the Tamar, the Tavy, and the Taw.

THE CHURCH AND THE BARN.

THE Daunays were great people in their day ; but many of them bore indifferent characters.

Sir John de Daunay was a strange mixture of ostentatious pride and penuriousness. His Lady Emelyn was as proud as her husband, but extravagant to a fault.

The priests of St Germans persuaded Sir John to build a church on his lands at Sheviock. He commenced the work, and, notwithstanding his great wealth, his heart failed him, and he curtailed the fair proportions on which he had at first decided:

Emelyn was enraged at this ; and it is said, that, prompted by the devil in visible presence, she resolved to build a barn which should exceed in beauty the house of God.

The barn rose with astonishing rapidity. Stones were laid at night, and the work proceeded as if the most lavish expenditure had been bestowed upon it. The church progressed but slowly, and was, after all, a very inferior structure to the barn. The devil, without doubt, having assisted Lady Daunay in her wicked work.

" There runneth a tale amongst the parishioners how one of the Daunay family's ancestors undertook to build the church, and the wife the barn adjoining ; and that, casting up accounts on finishing their work, the barn was found to have cost 1½d. more than the church." *

The Daunay aisle in Sheviock Church still preserves the name of this family, who appear to have possessed at one time nearly all this, and much of the adjoining parish.

THE PENRYN TRAGEDY.

"News from Penryn, in Cornwall, of a most bloody and unexampled Murder."

SUCH was the title of a black-letter pamphlet of eight pages referred to by Lysons. This curious book does not appear to be in existence.

Mr Davies Gilbert, who possessed much property in the parish of Gluvias, was especially interested in the farm of Bohelland, the place which has been rendered for ever notorious, as having been the scene of Lillo's tragedy of " Fatal Curiosity."

From a work entitled " The Reign and Death of King James of Great Britain," Mr Gilbert quotes as follows :—

" He had been blessed with ample possessions and fruitful issue, unhappy only in a younger son, who, taking liberty from his father's bounty, and with a crew of like condition, that wearied on land, they went roving to sea, and, in a small vessel southward, took boot from all they could master. And so increasing force and wealth, ventured on a Turk's man in the Streights ; but by mischance their own powder fired themselves, and our

* Davies Gilbert's " Cornwall."

gallant, trusting to his skilful swimming, got on shore upon Rhodes, with the best of his jewels about him ; where, offering some to sale to a Jew, who knew them to be the Governor's of Algier, he was apprehended, and, as a pirate, sentenced to the galleys among other Christians, whose miserable slavery made them all studious of freedom, and with wit and valour took opportunity and means to murder some officers, got on board of an English ship, and came safe to London ; where his misery, and some skill, made him servant to a surgeon, and sudden preferment to the East Indies. There, by this means, he got money ; with which returning back, he designed himself for his native county, Cornwall. And in a small ship from London, sailing to the west, was cast away upon that coast But his excellent skill in swimming, and former fate to boot, brought him safe to shore ; where, since his fifteen years' absence, his father's former fortunes much decayed, now retired him not far off to a country habitation, in debt and danger.

"His sister he finds married to a mercer, a meaner match than her birth promised. To her, at first, he appears a poor stranger, but in private reveals himself, and withal what jewels and gold he had concealed in a bow-case about him ; and concluded that the next day he intended to appear to his parents, and to keep his disguise till she and her husband should meet, and make their common joy complete. Being come to his parents, his humble behaviour, suitable to his suit of clothes, melted the old couple to so much compassion as to give him covering from the cold season under their outward roof , and by degrees his travelling tales, told with passion to the aged people, made him their guest so long by the kitchen fire, that the husband took leave and went to bed. And soon after his true stories working compassion in the weaker vessel, she wept, and so did he ; but compassionate of her tears, he comforted her with a piece of gold, which gave assurance that he deserved a lodging, to which she brought him ; and being in bed, showed her his girdled wealth, which he said was sufficient to relieve her husband's wants, and to spare for himself, and being very weary, fell fast asleep.

"The wife tempted with the golden bait of what she had, and eager of enjoying all, awakened her husband with this news, and her contrivance what to do ; and though with horrid apprehensions he oft refused, yet her puling fondness (Eve's enchantments) moved him to consent, and rise to be master of all, and both of them to murder the man, which instantly they did ; covering the corpse under the clothes till opportunity to convey it out of the way.

"The early morning hastens the sister to her father's house, where she with signs of joy, inquires for a sailor that should lodge there the last night ; the parents slightly denied to have seen any such, until she told them that he was her brother, her lost brother ; by that assured scar upon his arm, cut with a sword in his youth, she knew him ; and were all resolved this morning to meet there and be merry.

"The father hastily runs up, finds the mark, and with horrid regret of this monstrous murder of his own son, with the same knife cuts his own throat.

"The wife went up to consult with him, where, in a most strange manner beholding them both in blood, wild and aghast, with the instrument at hand, readily rips herself up, and perishes on the same spot.

"The daughter, doubting the delay of their absence, searches for them all, whom she found out too soon ; with the sad sight of this scene, and being overcome with horror and amaze of this deluge of destruction, she sank down and died ; the fatal end of that family. The truth of which was frequently known, and flew to court in this guise ; but the imprinted relation conceals their names, in favour to some neighbour of repute and kin to that family. The same sense makes me therein silent also."— *Gilbert*," vol. ii. p. 100.

Mr Harris of Salisbury, in his " Philological Inquiries," says of Lillo's tragedy —

" It is no small praise to this affecting fable that it so much resembles the 'Œdipus Tyrannus' of Sophocles. In both tragedies, that which apparently leads to joy, leads in its completion to misery ; both tragedies concur in the horror of their discoveries, and both in those great outlines of a truly tragic revolution (according to the nervous sentiment of Lillo himself)—

> ' The two extremes of life,
> The highest happiness the deepest woe
> With all the sharp and bitter aggravations
> Of such a vast transition.' "

GOLDSITHNEY FAIR AND THE GLOVE.

ON the 5th of August, St James's day (old style), a fair is held here, which was originally held in the Church-town of Sithney near Helston.

In olden time, the good *St Perran the Little* gave to the wrestlers in his parish a glove as the prize, and the winner of the glove was permitted to collect the market toll on the day of the feast, and to appropriate the money to his own use. The winner of the glove lived in the Church-town of Sithney, and for long long years the right of holding the fair remained undisputed.

At length the miners of Goldsithney resolved to contest the prize, and they won it, since which time the fair has been held in that village, they paying to the poor of the parish of Sithney one shilling as compensation

Gilbert remarks " The displaying of a glove at fairs is an ancient and widely-extended custom. Mr Lysons says it is continued at Chester. The editor has seen a large ornamented glove over the guildhall at Exeter during the fairs." *

THE HARLYN PIE.†

" ADJOINING the Church of Constantine in the parish of St Merryn, was a cottage which a family of the name of Edwards held for generations, under the proprietors of Harlyn, by

* Vol. iii p. 309. † See Appendix FF.

the annual render of a pie, made of limpets, raisins, and various herbs, on the eve of the festival in honour of the saint to whom the church was dedicated. The pie, as I have heard from my family, and from more ancient members of the family, and from old servants, was excellent. The Edwards had pursued for centuries the occupation of shepherds on Harlyn and Constantine Commons. The last died about forty years ago, and the wreck of their cottage is almost buried in the sand."*

PACKS OF WOOL THE FOUNDATION OF THE BRIDGE OF WADEBRIDGE.

LOVEBONE was the vicar of Wadebridge, and there was a ferry across the river. It was a frequent custom for the farmers to ride their horses and to drive their cattle across when the tide was low, and frequently men and beasts were lost in the quicksands formed on the rising of the tide. A sad accident of this kind happened, and Lovebone resolved on building a bridge; as Leland says in his " Itinerary," " Then one Lovebone, vicar of Wadebridge, moved with pitie, began the bridge, and with great paine and studie, good people putting their help thereto, finished it with xvii fair and great uniform arches of stone."

Great was the labour, and frequent the disappointment. Pier after pier were built, and then they were lost in the sands. A "fair structure" was visible at night, in the morning there was no trace of the work of the masons. Lovebone almost despaired of success, indeed he was about to abandon the work, when he dreamed that an angel came with a flock of sheep, that he sheared them, let the wool fall into the water, and speedily built the bridge upon the wool.

Lovebone awoke with a new idea. He gathered from the farmers around, all the wool they would give him, he put it loosely into into packs, placed these thickly upon the sand, and built his piers. The work remains to this day in proof of the engineering skill of the suggesting angel †

Quoting Beaumont and Fletcher's " Knight of the Burning Pestle," we find the Citizen saying to the Prologue :—

" Why could you not be content as well as others, with the Legend of Whittington ? or the Life and Death of Sir Thomas Gresham, with the building of the Royal Exchange ? or the Story of Queen Eleanor, with the rearing of London Bridge upon woolsacks ? "

* Letter from William Peter, Esq, of Harlyn, to Davies Gilbert, vol iii. p 178
† See Keighton's " Tales and Popular Fictions," p. 247.

THE LAST WOLF IN ENGLAND.

THE extirpation of the wolves, which once existed in every part of these islands, is an oft-told story.

But it is not generally known that the last native wolf lived in the forests of Ludgvan, near Penzance. The last of his race was a gigantic specimen, and terrible was the havoc made by him on the flocks. Tradition tells us that at last he carried off a child. This could not be endured, so the peasantry all turned out, and this famous wolf was captured at Rospeith, the name of a farm still existing in Ludgvan

CHURCHES BUILT IN PERFORMANCE OF VOWS.

THERE are several churches which, tradition tells us, owe their origin to vows made by terrified men that they would, if relieved from their dangers, build a temple to God.

Amongst these may be named Brent Tor, thus spoken of by Mr Bray :—

"The church of Brent Tor is dedicated to St Michael. And there is a tradition among the vulgar that its foundation was originally laid at the foot of the hill ; but that the enemy of all angels, the Prince of Darkness, removed the stones by night from the base to the summit,—probably to be nearer his own dominion, the air,—but that, immediately on the church's being dedicated to St Michael, the patron of the edifice hurled upon the devil such an enormous mass of rock that he never afterwards ventured to approach it. Others tell us that it was erected by a wealthy merchant, who vowed, in the midst of a tremendous storm at sea (possibly addressing himself to his patron, St Michael), that if he escaped, he would built a church on the first land he descried " *

Brent Tor is a very remarkable hill, and can be seen far off at sea. This may possibly lend some support to the latter tradition.

St Anthony, in Kerrier, is likewise stated to be the consequence of a vow Soon after the Conquest, as some persons of rank and fortune were coming to England from Normandy, they were overtaken by a violent storm, from which they expected immediate destruction. In the midst of their distress, they directed their prayers to St Anthony, and laid themselves under a solemn vow to erect a church to his memory, if he would save them from shipwreck ; and that this church should be erected on the very spot where they should first get on shore. Driven by the tempest, they were conducted, by a power fully equal to that which St Anthony might be supposed to possess, into St Mawe's harbour, and happily

* " Traditions, Legends, Superstitions, and Sketches of Devonshire," by Mrs Bray, who gives a letter of her husband's, for some time vicar of Tavistock.

landed on that very spot where the church now stands. And it appears that the materials with which the tower is built, and the situation which the church and tower occupy, are calculated to give sanction to this tradition.

BOLAIT, THE FIELD OF BLOOD.

TRADITION asserts that it was on the spot, so called in the parish of Burian, that the last battle was fought between the Cornish Britons and Athelstan. This is, in some measure, confirmed by the discovery of flint arrow-heads, in considerable quantities, from time to time, in and near this "field of slaughter."

We have little beyond the evidence of tradition to guide us in regard to any of the triumphs of Athelstan in Cornwall. It appears tolerably certain that this Saxon king confined the Cornish Britons to the western side of the Tamar; thus breaking up the division known as Danmonium, and limiting the territory over which the kings of the west ruled.

Scattered over Cornwall, we have the evidence, in the names of places, of Saxon possession. In all probability these were the resting-places of portions of the Saxon army, or the district in which fortified camps were placed by Athelstan to restrain a turbulent people. Be this as it may, the battle at Bolait is said to have raged from morning until night, and then, overpowered by numbers, the Cornish who still survived fled to the hills, and thus left Athelstan the conqueror.

It was after this fight that Athelstan, seeing the islands of Scilly illumined by the setting sun, determined, if possible, to achieve their conquest. He then recorded his vow, that he would, if he returned victorious, build a church, which should be dedicated to St Buryana. Of this church Hals writes as follows :—

"BURIAN —This church was founded and endowed by King Athelstan, about the year 930, after such time as he had conquered the Scilly Islands, as also the county of Devon, and made Cornwall tributary to his sceptre. To which church he gave lands and tithes of a considerable value for ever, himself becoming the first patron thereof, as his successors the kings of England have been ever since , for which reason it is still called the royal rectory, or regal rectory, and the royal or regal peculiar ; signifying thereby that this is the church or chapel pertaining to the king, or immediately under the jurisdiction of him, as the supreme ordinary from whom there is no appeal ; whereas other peculiars, though exempt from the visitation or jurisdiction of the diocesan bishop within whose see they stand, yet are always subject to the provincial Archbishops of Canterbury or York, or other persons.

"This church or college consisted of canons, Augustines or regular priests, and three prebendaries, who enjoyed the revenues thereof in common, but might not marry; and the lord chancellors of England of old visited this peculiar—which extended only over the parishes of Burian, Sennen, and St Levan—for the king.

"One of the Popes of Rome, about the time of Edward III., obtruded upon this church, the canons and prebends thereof, a dean to be an inspector and overseer over them,—whom he nominated to be the Bishop of Exon for the time being,—who for some time visited this church as its governor, as the lord chancellor did before; which encroachment of the Pope being observed by Edward III., as appears from the register of the writs, folio 40 and 41, 8 Edward III , rot. 97, this usurpation of the Pope was taken away."

WOEFUL MOOR, AND BODRIGAN'S LEAP.

THE Bodrigans, from a very early period, were connected with the borough of Looe. Otto, or Otho de Bodrigan, was lord of the manor of Pendrim and Looe in the reign of Edward II. Another Otho de Bodrigan was sheriff of Cornwall in the third of Richard II , A D 1400.

Sir Henry Bodrigan was "attaynted for taking part with King Richard III. against Henry VII. ; and, after flying into Ireland, Sir Richard Egecombe, father of Sir Pears Egecombe, had Bodrigan, and other parcels of Bodrigan's lands ; and Trevanion had part of Bodrigan's lands, as Restronget and Newham, both in Falmouth Haven."

On the Barton of Bodrigan there exists what are evidently the remains of ancient fortifications, and near them a piece of waste land known as the *Woeful Moor.*   .

Here Sir Henry Edgecombe and Trevanion defeated the great Bodrigan. He fled, and tradition preserves, on the side of the cliff, the spot known as Bodrigan's Leap, from which he leapt into the sea, and swam to a ship which kept near the shore. As he leapt the precipice, he bequeathed, with a curse, " his extravagance to the Trevanions, and his folly to the Edgecombes."

These families divided between them an estate said to be worth, in those days, £10,000 per annum.

" At that period in our history when the law of the strongest was the rule, three families in Cornwall were engaged in a series of domestic wars ; these were Bodrigan, Trevanion, and Edgecumbe. And when Richard the Third obtained sovereign power, on the division which then took place in the York faction, Bodrigan endeavoured to seize the property of Edgecumbe, with little respect, as it would seem, for the life of the possessor; but in the final struggle at Bosworth Field, where Henry Tudor put an entire end to this contest for power under the guise of property, by seizing the whole to himself, Trevanion and Edgecumbe had the good fortune to appear on the winning side, and subsequently availed themselves to the utmost of belligerent rights against Bodrigan, as he had attempted to do before against them. The last of that family was driven from his home, and seems to have perished in exile. His property was divided between the two families opposed to him, and, after the lapse of three hundred and fifty years, continues to form a large portion of their respective possessions."—*Gilbert,* vol iii., p. 204.

William de Bodrigan was lord of the manor of Restronget, in the 12th of Henry IV. The family possessed it till the beginning of the reign of Henry VII., when, on the attainder of Bodrigan, it was given to William Trevanion.*

PENGERSWICK CASTLE.

THIS castellated building—for it does not now admit of being called a·castle, notwithstanding its embattled turrets and its machicolated gate—is situated in a hollow running down to Pengerswick Cove, in the Mount's Bay, where there never could have been anything to defend, and certainly there is nothing to induce any one to incur the cost of such a building.

Mr Milliton, in the reign of Henry VIII., slew in the streets of London a man in a drunken brawl. He fled, and went to sea. It is not known to what part of the world he went, but we are told that he became excessively rich ; so rich, indeed, that " when he loaded his ass with his gold, the weight was so great as to break the poor animal's back." Returning to his country, and not daring to appear in any of the large towns, he bought the manor of Pengerswick, and built this castle, to defend himself, in the event of his being approached by any of the officers of the law.

A miserable man, Milliton is said to have lived in a secret chamber in this tower, and to have been visited only by his most trusted friends. Deeply deploring the crime that had condemned him to seclusion from the world, he spent his dreary hours in ornamenting his dwelling. His own story is supposed to be told in the painting of an overladen ass in one room, with a black-letter legend, importing that a miser is like an ass loaded with riches, who, without attending to his golden burden, feeds on thistles. There is also a carving of water wearing a hollow in a stone, and under it the word " Perseverance." Of the death of Milliton we have no account.

There is very little doubt but that Pengerswick Castle is very much older than the time of Milliton ; indeed tradition informs us that he purchased the place. The legends previously given, and others in my possession, refer to a much earlier period. The castle

* See Gilbert, vol iii., p 293, and Bond's account of the Trelawnys in Bond's Looe.

was, it is said, surrounded by trees; but John Hals, who inherited the property, had all the timber cut down and sold.

THE CLERKS OF CORNWALL.

I. " IN the last age there was a familiarity between the parson and the clerk and the people which our feelings of decorum would revolt at—*e.g*, 'I have seen the ungodly flourish like a *green bay*-tree.' 'How can that be, maister?' said the clerk of St Clement's. Of this I was myself an ear-witness."

. II. "At Kenwyn, two dogs, one of which was the parson's, were fighting at the west end of the church ; the parson, who was then reading the second lesson, rushed out of the pew and went down and parted them ; returning to his pew, and doubtful where he had left off, he asked the clerk, 'Roger, where was I?' 'Why, down parting the dogs, maister,' said Roger."

III. "At Mevagizzey, when non-resident clergymen officiated, it was usual with the squire of the parish to invite them to dinner. Several years ago, a non-resident clergyman was requested to do duty in the church of Mevagizzey on a Sunday when the Creed of St Athanasius is directed to be read. Before he had begun the service, the parish clerk asked him whether he intended to read the Athanasian Creed that morning. 'Why?' said the clergyman. 'Because if you do, no dinner for you at the squire's, at Penwarne.'"

IV. "A very short time since parish clerks used to read the first lesson. I once heard the St Agnes clerk cry out, 'To the mouth of the burning *very vurnis*, and spake, and said, Shadrac, Meshac, and Abednego, *com voath and com hether*' (Daniel iii)"

V. "The clerk of Lamorran, in giving out the psalm. 'Like a timorous bird to distant mountains fly,' always said, 'Like a timmersum burde,' &c., &c , with a shake of the head, and a quivering voice, which could not but provoke risibility."—*Hone's Table-Book.*

A FAIRY CAUGHT.

THE following, communicated to me on the 8th of August, is too good to be lost. I therefore give it in my correspondent's own words :—

"I heard last week of three fairies having been seen in Zennor very recently. A man who lived at the foot of Trendreen hill, in the valley of Treridge, I think, was cutting furze on the hill. Near the middle of the day he saw one of the small people, not more than a foot long, stretched at full length and fast asleep, on a bank of griglans (heath),* surrounded by high brakes of furze. The man took off his furze cuff, and slipped the little man into it, without his waking up ; went down to the house ; took the little fellow out of the cuff on the hearthstone, when he awakened, and seemed quite pleased and at home, beginning to play with the children, who were well pleased with the small body, and called him Bobby Griglans.

"The old people were very careful not to let Bob out of the house, or be seen by the neighbours, as he promised to show the man where the crocks

* Quite recently I heard, in St Agnes, heath-flowers called "the blowth of the griglans."

of gold were buried on the hill   A few days after he was brought from the hill, all the neighbours came with their horses (according to custom) to bring home the winter's reek of furze, which had to be brought down the hill in trusses on the backs of the horses.   That Bob might be safe and out of sight, he and the children were shut up in the barn.   Whilst the furze-carriers were in to dinner, the prisoners contrived to get out, to have a 'courant' round the furze-reek, when they saw a little man and woman, not much larger than Bob, searching into every hole and corner among the trusses that were dropped round the unfinished reek.   The little woman was wringing her hands and crying, 'O my dear and tender Skillywidden, wherever canst ah (thou) be gone to ? shall I ever cast eyes on thee again?' 'Go 'e back,' says Bob to the children , 'my father and mother are come here too ' He then cried out, 'Here I am, mammy !' By the time the words were out of his mouth, the little man and woman, with their precious Skillywidden, were nowhere to be seen, and there has been no sight nor sign of them since.   The children got a sound thrashing for letting Skillywidden escape."

THE LIZARD PEOPLE.

THERE is a tradition that the Lizard people were formerly a very inferior race.   In fact it is said that they went on all fours, till the crew of a foreign vessel, wrecked on the coast, settled among them, and improved the race so much that they became as remarkable for their stature and physical development as they had been before for the reverse.   At this time, as a whole, the Lizard folks certainly have among them a very large population of tall people, many of the men and women being over six feet in height.

PRUSSIA COVE AND SMUGGLERS' HOLES.

SMUGGLERS' hiding-places (now, of course, unused) are nu-merous.   On the banks of the Helford river are several, and two or three have lately been discovered on the coast about St Keverne by the falling in of their roofs.   In a part of Penzance harbour, nine years ago, a hiding-place of this kind was discovered; it still contained one or two kegs, and the skeleton of a man, with his clothes in good preservation.   It is presumed that the poor fellow while intoxicated was shut in, and the place never more opened by his companions.   Speaking of Penzance,—about fifty years since, in the back of the harbour, was an old adit called "Gurmer's Hole," and in the cliff over its entrance, *on a dark night*, a phosphorescent appearance was always visible from the opposite side.   It could not be seen from beneath, owing to the projection of the face of the cliff.   A fall of the part taking place, the phe-nomenon disappeared.

Sixty or seventy years since, a native of Breage called " Carter," but better known, from a most remarkable personal resemblance to Frederick the Great, as the " King of Prussia," monopolised most of the smuggling trade of the west. By all accounts he was a man of uncommon mental power, and chose as the seat of his business a sequestered rocky cove about two miles east of Marazion, which continues to bear the name of " Prussia Cove," and where deep channels, cut in hard rock, to allow of the near approach of their boats, still show the determination of the illicit traders. Although constantly visited by the excise officers, the " king " rarely failed to remove his goods, the stocks of which were at times very large, suffering for a long period comparatively little from "seizures." On one occasion his boats, while landing a cargo, being hard pressed by the revenue cutter, Carter had some old cannon brought to the edge of the cliff and opened fire on the unwelcome intruder, and after a short but sharp engagement, fairly beat her off. The cutter was, of course, back again early in the morning, and part of the crew, with the captain, landed ; the only traces, however, of the engagement to be seen was the trampled ground. On approaching Carter's house, the officer was met by the " king " himself, with an angry remonstrance about practising the cutter's guns at midnight so near the shore, and disturbing his family at such unseemly hours. Although the principal parties concerned were well known, no evidence could be obtained, and the matter was allowed to drop. Toward the close of his career Carter " ventured " in larger ships, became less successful, and was at last exchequered. He died, at a very advanced age, in poor circumstances.

CORNISH TEENY-TINY.

MR HALLIWELL gives us, in his " Popular Rhymes and Nursery Tales," the story of Teeny-tiny. In this a little old woman takes a bone from the churchyard to make soup She goes to bed, and puts the bone in the cupboard. During the night some one comes demanding the bone, and at length the terrified old woman gives it up.

A similar story is told in Cornwall.

An old lady had been to the church in the sands of Perranzabuloe. She found, amidst the numerous remains of mortality, some very good teeth. She pocketed these, and at night placed them on her dressing-table before getting into bed. She slept, but was at length disturbed by some one calling out, " Give me my teeth—give me my teeth." At first, the lady took no notice of this, but the cry,

"Give me my teeth," was so constantly repeated, that she, at last, in terror, jumped out of bed, took the teeth from the dressing-table, and, opening the window, flung them out, exclaiming, "Drat the teeth, take 'em" They no sooner fell into the darkness on the road than hasty retreating footsteps were heard, and there were no more demands for the teeth.

THE SPANIARD AT PENRYN.

IN the reign of James I. there happened to be upon our coast a Spanish vessel of war. Favoured by the mists of evening and the growing darkness, the ship entered Falmouth Harbour un-seen. The crew armed themselves, and taking to their boats, proceeded with great caution to the town of Penryn, situated at the head of the harbour. There they landed, formed themselves into proper order, and marched into the town, purposing to plunder the inhabitants and burn the town. With steady tramp they cautiously proceeded up the dark main street, resolving to attack the principal dwellings first. Suddenly a great shout was heard, drums and trumpets sounded, the noise of many feet rushing to and fro fell on the ears of the Spaniards. Believing that they were discovered, and that preparations had been made for their reception, fear seized them, and they fled precipitately to their boats and left the town. The martial music proceeded, however, from a temporary theatre, in which a troop of strolling players were entertaining the people.

BOYER, MAYOR OF BODMIN.

IN the reign of Edward VI., Boyer was the mayor of Bodmin, and he appears to have been suspected of aiding in an insur-rection of the men of Devonshire and Cornwall. However this may be, Sir Anthony Kingston, provost-marshal of the king's army, sent orders to Boyer to have a gibbet erected in the street opposite his own house by the next day at noon. He, at the same time, sent his compliments to the mayor, telling him that he should dine with him, in order to be present at the execution of some rebels.

The unsuspecting mayor obeyed the command, and at the time appointed provided an entertainment for his guest. Kingston put about the wine, and when he observed the mayor's spirits were exhilarated, asked him if the gibbet was ready. Being told that it was, with a wanton and diabolical sneer he ordered the mayor to hanged upon it.

At the same time a miller was ordered to be hanged ; his servant was so deeply attached to him, that he went to Kingston and begged him to spare his master's life, even if he hung him in his place. "If you are so fond of hanging," said Kingston, "you shall not be disappointed," and he hanged the miller and his servant together.

A similar story is told of a mayor of St Ives.

THOMASINE BONAVENTURE.

IN the reign of Henry VI., about the year 1450, in the parish of Week St Mary, on the northern coast of Cornwall, was born of humble parents a girl, to whom the name of Thomasine was given.   This child was in no way distinguished from other Cornish children ; they ever have been, and still are, remarkable for their healthful beauty, and Thomasine, like others, was beautiful.   Her father was a small farmer, and the daughter was usually employed in minding the sheep upon Greenamore, or preventing the geese from straying too far from his dwelling.

Thomasine appears to have received no education beyond that which nature gave her   She grew to womanhood a simple, artless maiden, who knew nothing of the world or its cares beyond the few sorrows which found their way into the moorland country of Week and Temple

Thomasine was watching her flocks when a mounted traveller, with well-filled saddle-bags, passing over the moors, observed her. Struck by the young woman's beauty, he halted and commenced a conversation with her. "Her discreet answers, suitable to the beauty of her face, much beyond her rank or degree," says the quaint Hals, "won upon him, and he desired to secure her as a servant in his family." This traveller, who was a draper from London, sought out the parents of the shepherdess, and proposed to relieve them of this daughter, by taking her to the metropolis, promising her good wages and many privileges ; and beyond this he agreed that, in case he should die, seeing she would be so far removed from her friends, she should be carefully provided for.

Having satisfied themselves of the respectability of this merchant traveller, the parents agreed to part with their daughter ; and Thomasine, full of girlish curiosity to see the city, of which she had heard, was willing to leave her home.

We next find Thomasine in London as a respected servant to this city draper   His wife and family are pleased with the inno-cent Cornish girl : and by her gentle manners and great goodness of heart, she won upon all with whom she was brought in contact. Years passed away, and the draper's wife died. In the course of time he proposed to make the faithful Thomasine his wife. The proposal was accepted, and "Thomasine and her master were solemnly married together as man and wife; who then, according to his promise, endowed her with a considerable jointure in case of her survivorship." Within two years of this marriage the draper died, and Thomasine was left sole executrix. The poor servant, who but a few years previous was minding sheep on the moors, was now a rich widow, courted by the wealthy of the metropolis. With that good sense which appears ever to have distinguished her, she improved her mind; and following the examples by which she had been for some time surrounded, she added to her natural graces many acquired elegances of manner.

The youth and beauty of the widow brought her numerous admirers, but all were rejected except Henry Gale, of whom we know little, save that he was "an eminent and wealthy citizen." He was accepted, and Thomasine Gale was the most toasted of all city madams. After a few years passed in great happiness, Thomasine became again a widow. Gale left her all his property, and she became, when not yet thirty years of age, one of the wealthiest women in London. So beautiful, so rich, and being yet young, the widow was soon induced to change her state again. She chose now for her companion John Percivall, who was already high in the honours of the corporation.

At the feast of Sir John Collet, who was Lord Mayor in the second year of the reign of Henry VII, in 1487, Percivall was the mayor's carver, " at which time, according to the custom of that city, Sir John drank to him in a silver cup of wine, in order to make him sheriff thereof for the year ensuing, whereupon he covered his head and sat down at table with the Lord Mayor of London." John Percivall was elected Lord Mayor himself in 1499, and he was knighted in the same year by Henry VII. Sir John Percivall and Dame Thomasine Percivall lived many years happily together; but he died, leaving all his fortune to his widow.

Lady Percivall was now advanced in years. She had had three husbands, but no children. The extraordinary accession of fortune made no change in her simple honest heart; the flattery of the great, by whom she had been surrounded, kindled no pride in the beautiful shepherdess. The home of her childhood, from which she had been so long separated, was dear to her, and she retired in her mourning to the quiet of that distant home.

She spent her declining years in good works. Roads were made and bridges built at her cost; almshouses for poor maids were erected; she relieved prisoners; fed the hungry, and clothed the naked. In Week St Mary, Thomasine founded a chantry and free school "to pray for the souls of her father and mother, and her husbands and relatives" To the school she added a library, and a dwelling for the chanters and others, "and endowed the same with £20 lands for ever." Cholwell, a learned man and great linguist, was master here in Henry VIII.'s time; and here he educated in the "liberal arts and sciences," says Carew, "many gentlemen's sons." Such were a few of the benefits conferred on Week by the girl who once had tended the flocks upon the moors; but who, by great good fortune and more by the exercise of good sense, became Lady Mayoress.

Dame Thomasine Percivall died, respected by all who knew her, in 1530, having then reached the good old age of eighty years.

It appears probable that the name Bonaventure, by which this remarkable female is usually known, was given to her, likely enough, by the linguist Cholwell, to commemorate her remarkable fortune.

Berry Comb, in Jacobstow, was once the residence of Thomasine, and it was given at her death to the poor of St Mary Week.

THE LAST OF THE KILLIGREWS.

LADY JANE, the widow of Sir John Killigrew, sate in one of the windows of Arwenick house, looking out upon the troubled waters of Falmouth Harbour. A severe storm had prevailed for some days, and the Cornish coast was strewn with wrecks. The tempest had abated; the waves were subsiding, though they still beat heavily against the rocks. A light scud was driving over the sky, and a wild and gloomy aspect suffused all things. There was a sudden outcry amongst a group of men, retainers of the Killigrew family, which excited the attention of Lady Jane Killigrew. She was not left long in suspense as to the cause. In a few minutes two Dutch ships were seen coming into the harbour. They had evidently endured the beat of the storm, for they were both considerably disabled; and with the fragments of sail which they carried, they laboured heavily. At length, however, these vessels were brought round within the shelter of Pendennis; their anchors were cast in good anchoring-ground; and they were safe, or at least the crew thought so, in comparatively smooth water.

As was the custom in those days, the boat belonging to the Killigrew family, manned by the group of whom we have already spoken, went off as soon as the ships were anchored and boarded them. They then learnt that they were of the Hanse Towns, laden with valuable merchandise for Spain, and that this was in the charge of two Spanish factors On the return of the boat's crew, this was reported to Lady Killigrew ; and she, being a very wicked and most resolute woman, at once proposed that they should return to the ships, and either rob them of their treasure, or exact from the merchants a large sum of money in compensation. The rude men, to whom wrecking and plundering was but too familiar, were delighted with the prospect of a rare prize ; and above all, when Lady Killigrew declared that she would herself accompany them, they were wild with joy.

With great shouting, they gathered together as many men as the largest boat in the harbour would carry, and armed themselves with pikes, swords, and daggers. Lady Jane Killigrew, also armed, placed herself in the stern of the boat after the men had crowded into their places, and with a wild huzzah they left the shore, and were soon alongside of the vessel nearest to the shore. A number of the men immediately crowded up the side and on to the deck of this vessel, and at once seized upon the captain and the factor, threatening them with instant death if they dared to make any outcry. Lady Jane Killigrew was now lifted on to the deck of the vessel, and the boat immediately pushed off, and the remainder of the crew boarded the other ship.

The Dutch crew were overpowered by the numbers of Cornishmen, who were armed far more more perfectly than they. Taken unawares as they were, at a moment when they thought their troubles were for a season at an end, the Dutchmen were almost powerless.

The Spaniards were brave men, and resisted the demands made to deliver up their treasure. This resistance was, however, fatal to them. At a signal, it is said by some, given by their leader, Lady Jane Killigrew,—although this was denied afterwards,— they were both murdered by the ruffians into whose hands they had fallen, and their bodies cast overboard into the sea.

These wretches ransacked the ships, and appropriated whatsoever they pleased, while Lady Jane took from them " two hogsheads of Spanish pieces of eight, and converted them to her own use."

As one of the Spanish factors was dying, he lifted his hands to heaven, prayed to the Lord to receive his soul, and turning to the vile woman to whose villany he owed his death, he said, " My blood will linger with you until my death is avenged upon your own sons."

This dreadful deed was not allowed to pass without notice even in those lawless times. The Spaniards were then friendly with England, and upon the representation made by the Spanish minister to the existing government, the sheriff of Cornwall was ordered to seize and bring to trial Lady Jane Killigrew and her crew of murderers. A considerable number were arrested with her ; and that lady and several of her men were tried at Launceston.

Since the Spaniards were proved to be at the time of the murder "foreigners under the Queen's protection," they were all found guilty, and condemned to death.

All the men were executed on the walls of Launceston Castle ; but by the interest of Sir John Arundell and Sir Nicholas Hals, Queen Elizabeth was induced to grant a pardon for Lady Jane.

How Lady Jane Killigrew lived, and when she died, are matters on which even tradition, by which the story is preserved, is silent. We know, however, that her immediate descendant, John Killigrew, who married one of the Monks, and his son William Killigrew, who was made a baronet in 1660 by Charles II., were only known for the dissoluteness of character, and the utter regardlessness of every feeling of an exalted character which they displayed. Sir William Killigrew, by his ill conduct and his extravagant habits, wasted all the basely-gotten treasure, and sold the manor and barton of Arwenick to his younger brother, Sir Peter Killigrew. With the son of this Peter the baronetcy became extinct. The last Sir Peter Killigrew, however, improved his fortune by marrying one of the coheirs of Judge Twisden. Sir Peter and his wife, of whom we know nothing, died, leaving one son, George Killigrew, who connected himself with the St Aubyn family by marriage. This man appears to have inherited many of the vices of his family. He was given to low company, and towards the close of his life was remarkable only for his drunken habits.

He was one evening in a tavern in Penryn, surrounded by his usual companions, and with them was one Walter Vincent, a barrister-at-law. The wine flowed freely ; songs and loose conversation were the order of the night. At length all were in a state of great excitement through the extravagance of their libations, and something was said by George Killigrew very insultingly to Walter Vincent.

Walter Vincent does not appear to have been naturally a depraved man, but of violent passions. Irritated by Killidrew, he made some remarks on the great-grandmother being sentenced to be hanged. Swords were instantly drawn by the drunken men. They lunged at each other. Vincent's sword passed directly through Killigrew's body and he fell dead in the midst of his revelries, at the very moment when he was defending the character of her who had brought dishonour upon them.

This Walter Vincent was tried for the murder of George Killigrew, but acquitted. We are told by the Cornish historian, " Yet this Mr Vincent, through anguish and horror at this accident (as it was said), within two years after, wasted of an extreme atrophy of his flesh and spirits ; that, at length, at the table whereby he was sitting, in the Bishop of Exeter's palace, in the presence of divers gentleman, he instantly fell back against the wall and died."

George Killigrew left one daughter ; but of her progress in life we know nothing. Thus the Cornish Killigrews ceased to be a name in the land.

Such a tale as this does not, of course, exist without many remarkable additions. Ghosts and devils of various kinds are spoken of as frequenting Arwenick House, and the woods around it. Those spectral and demoniacal visitations have not, however, any special interest. They are only, indeed, repetitions of oft-told tales.

SAINT GERENNIUS.

THIS reached me at too late a period to be included with the legends of the saints :—

"The beacon at Veryan stands on the highest ground in Roseland, at a short distance from the cliff which overlooks Pendower and Gerrans Bay. Dr Whitaker, in his 'Cathedral of Cornwall,' states it to be one of the largest tumuli in the kingdom. Its present height above the level of the field in which it stands is about twenty-eight feet, and its circumference at the base three hundred and fifty feet ; but it must have been originally much larger, as a considerable portion on one side has been removed, its summit being now about eighty feet from the base on the south side, and only fifty feet on the north, whilst the top of the cairn which was discovered in it, and which was, no doubt, placed exactly in the original centre of the mound, is at least ten feet still farther north than the present summit.

"A tradition has been preserved in the neighbourhood, that Gerennius, an old Cornish saint and king, whose palace stood on the other side of Gerrans Bay, between Trewithian and the sea, was buried in this mound many centuries ago, and that a golden boat with silver oars were used in conveying his corpse across the bay, and were interred with him. Part of this tradition receives confirmation from an account incidentally given of King Gerennius, in an old book called the 'Register of Llandaff.' It is there stated that, A D. 588, Telian, bishop of Llandaff, with some of his suffragan bishops, and many of his followers, fled from Wales, to escape an epidemic called the yellow plague, and migrated to Dole in Brittany, to visit Sampson, the archbishop of that place, who was a countryman and friend of Telian's. 'On his way thither,' says the old record, 'he came first to the region of Cornwall, and was well received by Gerennius, the king of that country, who treated him and his people with all honour. From thence he proceeded to Armorica, and remained there seven years and seven months ; when, hearing that the plague had ceased in Britain, he collected his followers, caused a large bark to be prepared, and returned to Wales.' 'In this,' the record proceeds, 'they all arrived at the port called Din-Gerein, king Gerennius lying in the last extreme of life, who when he had received the body of the Lord from the hand of St Teliau, departed in joy to the Lord.' 'Probably,' says Whitaker, in his remarks on this quotation, 'the royal remains were brought in great pomp by water from Din-Gerein, on the western shore of the port, to Carne, about two miles off on the northern; the barge with the royal body was plated, perhaps, with gold in places; perhaps, too, rowed with oars having equally plates of silver upon them; and the pomp of the procession has mixed confusedly with the interment of the body in the memory of tradition.'"

CORNISH DIALOGUE.

AS the Cornish dialogue peculiarly illustrates a description of literary composition which has no resemblance to that of any county, I think it advisable to give one specimen :—

DIALOGUE BETWEEN MAL TRELOARE AND SAUNDRY KEMP.

'Twas Kendle teening, when jung Mal Treloare
Trudg'd hum from Bal, a bucken copper ore;
Her clathing haid and ruff, black was her eye,
Her face and arms like stuff from Cairn Kye.
Full butt she mit jung Saundry Kemp, who long
She had been token'd to, come from Ding Dong;
Hes jacket wet, his faace rud like his beard,
And through his squarded hat hes hair appeared.
She said, " Oh, Kemp, I thoft of thee well leer,
Thees naw that daay we wor to Bougheehere,
That daay with ale and cakes, at three o'clock,
Thees stuff'd me so, I jist neen crack'd me dock:
Jue said to me, ' Thee mayst depend thee life,
I love thee, Mal, and thee shust be ma wife.'
And to ma semmen, tes good to lem ma naw
Whether the words were aal in jest or no."
   Saundry. Why, truly, Mal, I like a thing did zay,
That I wud have thee next Chewiden daay.
But zence that time I like a think ded hear
Thees went wi' some one down, 'I naw where;'
Now es that fitty, Mal? What dost think?
   Mal. Od rot tha body, Saundry, who said so?
Now, faath and traath, I 'll naw afore I go;
Do lem me naw the Gossenbaiy dog.
   Saundry. Why, then, Crull said jue wor down to Wheal Bog
With he and Tabban, and ded make some tricks
By dabben clay at jungsteis making bricks;
Aand that from theie jue went to Aafe-waye house,
Aand diink 't some leeker   Mal, now there's down souse.
Aand jue to he, like a thing ded zay,
Jue wed have he, and I mait go away.
   Mal. I tell the-lubber so ' I to Wheal Bog I
I 'll scatt his chacks, the emprent, saucy dog.

Now hire me, Saundry Kemp, now down and full,
Ef thee arten hastes, thee shust hire the whole.
Fust jue must naw, tes true as thee art there,
Aant Blanch and I went to Golsinny feer.
Who overtookt us in the doosty road,
In common hum but Crull, the cloppen toad.
Zes he to Aant, "What cheer? Aant Blanch, what cheer ?
Jue makes good coose, suppose jue been to feer."
"Why, hiss," zes Aant, "ben there a pewer spur.
I wedn't a gone ef nawed ed been so fur.
I bawft a pair of shods for Sarah's cheeld."
By this time, lock ! we cum jist to the field.
We went to clemmer up the temberen style.
(Haw kept his eye upon me all the while.)
Zes hem to Aant, "Then whos es thees braa maide?
Come tha wayst long, dasent be afraid."
Then mov'd my side, like a thing,
Aand pull'd my mantle, and just tonch'd my ching,
"How arry, jung woman?" zes haw. "How dost do?"
Zes I, "Jue saucy dog, what's that to jue?
Keep off, jung lad, else thees have a slap."
Then haw fooch'd some great big doat figs in me lap.
So I thoft, as haw had been so kind,
Haw might go by Aant Blanch, ef haw had a mind.
Aand so haw ded, aand tookt Aant Blanch's arm.
"Araeh!" zes haw, "I dedn't mane no harm"
So then Aant Blanch and he ded talk and jest
Bout dabbing clay and bricks at Petran feast.
 Saundry. Ahah then, Mal, 'twas there they dabbed the clay
 Mal. Plaase Father, Kemp, tes true wot I do saay.
And hire me now, pla-sure, haw dedent budge
From Aanty's arm till jest this side Long Brudge.
Aand then zes he to Aant, "Shall we go in
To 'Aafe-waye house, and have a dram of gin
And trickle mixt? Depend ol do es good,
Taake up the sweat, and set to rights the blud."
So Aant did saay, "Such things she dedn't chuse,"
And squeezed my hand, aand loike a thing refuse.
So when we pass'd along by Wheal Bog moor,
Haw jumpt behind, and pok't es in the door
Haw caal'd for gin, aand brandy too, I think.
He clunk'd the brandy, we the gin did drink.
So when haw wish'd good night, as es the caase,
Haw kiss't Aant Blanch, and jist neen touched my face.
Now, Saundry Kemp, there's nothing sure in this,
To my moinde, then, that thee shust take amiss.
 Saundry. No, fath, then Mal, ef this is all aand true,
I had a done the same ef I was jue.
 Mal. Next time in any house I see or near am,
I'll down upon the plancheon, rat am, tear am,
Aand I will so poaw am.
 Saundry. Our Kappen's there, just by thickey bush.
   Hush ! now Mally, hush !
Aand as hes here, so close upon the way,

I wedent wish haw nawed what he did zay,
And jett I dedent care, now fath and soul,
Ef so be our Kappen wor to hire the whole.
How arry, Kappen?   Where be going so fast?
Jure goin' hum, suppose, jure in sich haste.
 Kappen. Who's that than?   Saundry, arten thee ashamed
To coosy so again?   Thee wust be blamed
Ef thees stay here all night to prate wi' Mal!
When tes thy cour, thee wusten come to Bal.
Aand thee art a Cobbe, I tell thee so.
I'll tell the owners ef thee dosent go.
 Saundry. Why, harkee, Kappen, doant skoal poor I.
Touch pipe a crum, jue'll naw the reason why.
Cozen Mal aand I ben courtain bout afe a year.
Hould up tha head, Mal; don't be ashamed, dost hire?
Aand Crull one day made grief 'tween I and she;
But he shall smart for it now, I swear by G—.
Haw told me lies, as round as any cup.
Now Mal and I have mit, we've made it up;
So, Kappen, that's the way I stopt, I vow.
 Kappen. Ahah! I dedent giss the case jist now.
But what dost think of that last batch of ore?
 Saundry Why pewer and keenly gossen, Kappen, shure
I bleeve that day, ef Frankey's pair wornt drunk,
We shuld had pewer stuff too from the sump.
But there, tes all good time, as people saay,
The flooken now, aint throw'd es far away;
So hope to have bra tummills soon to grass.
How did laast batch down to Jandower pass?
 Kappen. Why, hang thy body, Saundry, speed, I saay,
Thees keep thy clacker going till tes day.
Go speak to Mally now, jue foolish toad.
I wish both well, I'll keep my road.
 Saundry. Good nightie, Kappen, then I wishee well.
Where artee, Mally?   Dusten haw hire me, Mal?
Dusent go away, why jue must think of this,
Before we part, shure we must have a kiss.

  She wiped her muzzle from the mundic stuff,
  And he rubb'd his, a little stain'd with snuff.

Now then, there, good night, Mal, there's good night;
But, stop a crum.
 Mally Good night
 Kappen. Good night.

Keendle teening, candle lighting
Squarded hat, broken or cracked hat.
Lem ma naw, let me know, tell me.
Wheal Bog, wheal, or, correctly spelt, huel, is old Cornish, and signifies a mine or work.
Doat figs, broad figs
A cobbe, a cobbler, a bungler.
Bra tummills, brave heaps, large piles of ore.

APPENDIX.

A (p. 41).

BELLERIAN.

SAMUEL BUTLER of Shrewsbury, in his "Ancient and Modern Geography," p. 112, says, "Ocrinum was the Lizard, and Bolerium the Land's End." Ainsworth, Latin Dictionary, 4th edition, has "Balerium—Burien in Cornwall." It is really in the parish of Sennen.

B (p. 46).

THE POEM OF THE WRESTLING.*

IT may be here remarked as something more than accidental, that Magog is a well-known Oriental giant, that Gog and Magog figure in the Guildhall of London, and that Gogmagog was the champion selected for a trial of strength with Corineus.

> "Amongst the ragged Cleeves those monstrous giants sought :
> Who (of their dreadful kind) t' appal the Trojans brought
> Great *Gogmagog*, an oake that by the roots could teare ,
> So mighty were (that time) the men who liv'd there .
> But, for the use of armes he did not understand
> (Except some rock or tree, that coming next to hand,
> He raised out of the earth to execute his rage),
> He challenge makes for strength, and offereth there his gage,
> Which *Corin* taketh up, to answer by and by,
> Upon this sonne of earth his utmost power to try.
> All, doubtful to which part the victory should goe,
> Upon that loftie place at *Plimmouth*, called the *Hoe*,
> Those mightie wrastlers met , with many an irefull looke,
> Who threat'ned as the one hold of the other tooke ·
> But, grappled, glowing fire shines in their sparkling eyes,
> And, whilst at length of arme one from the other lyes,
> Their lusty sinewes swell like cables, as they strive,
> Their feet such trampling make, as though they forced to drive
> A thunder out of earth, which stagger'd with the weight
> Thus either's utmost force urged to the greatest height
> Whilst one upon his hips the other seeks to lift,
> And th' adverse (by a turn) doth from his cunning shift,
> Their short-fetcht troubled breath a hollow noise doth make,
> Like bellows of a forge. Then Corin up doth take
> The giant 'twixt the groins; and voiding of his hold
> (Before his cumbrous feet he well recover could),

* From Drayton's "Polyolbion."

Pitcht headlong from the hill : as when a man doth throw
An axtree, that with slight delivered from the toe
Roots up the yielding earth, so that his violent fall
Shook Neptune with such strength as shoulder'd him withal ;
That where the monstrous waves like mountains late did stand,
They leapt out of the place, and left the barèd sand
To gaze upon wide heaven, so great a blow it gave.
For which the conquering Brute on Corneus brave
This horn of land bestow'd, and markt it with his name
Of Corin, Cornwal call'd to his immortal fame "*

In 1750 Robert Heath published his " Natural and Historical Account of the Islands of Scilly," to which was added " A General Account of Cornwall." From paragraphs in this work it may be inferred that the figures of the wrestlers cut out in the turf on Plymouth Hoe then existed.

" The activity of the *Cornish* and *Devonshire* men, beyond others in the faculty of Wrestling, seems to derive their Pedigree from that grand Wrestler, *Corineus.* That there has been such a giant as Gogmagog, opposed by Corineus, the inhabitants of *Plymouth* show you a Portraiture of two Men, one bigger than the other, with *Clubs* in their hands, cut out upon the *Haw*-ground, which have been renewed by order of the Place, as they wear out ; and a steep cliff being near, over which the giant might be thrown, are said to point out together the Probability of the Fact."

In the " Dissertation on the Cornish Tongue," by William Scawen, Vice-Warden of the Stannaries, we find the following passage : " I cannot affirm with so much reason, as some of our neighbours have done with confidence, who say that at the last digging on the Haw for the foundation of the citadel of *Plymouth*, the great jaws and teeth therein found were those of Gogmagog, who was there said to be thrown down by Corineus, whom some will have to be the founder of the Cornish ; † nor am I able to assert that some instruments of war in brass, and huge limbs and portraitures of persons long ago, as some say that have been in some of the western parishes, were parts of giants or other great men, who had formerly had their being there."

C (p. 47).

SHARA AND SHEELA.

AFTER the meeting of the British Association at Cork, I spent some days visiting, with two friends, the various spots of interest in the south of Ireland. At Fermoy, the name given to a somewhat curious cromlech, " The Hag's Bed," interested me. I was at some trouble to learn the origin of the name, and fortunately our car-driver succeeded in finding an old man, who gave me the desired information. As there is some (although a remote) analogy between this legend and that of the Chapel Rock, I give it as I heard it.

* See also Hogg's " Records of Ancient Cornwall "
† *This note is by the Editor*, Mr Davies Gilbert · "These bones must evidently have been found in a cavern, the nature of which has been most ably ascertained and described by Dr. Buckland and the Rev. Richard Hannah, who examined other caverns of precisely the same nature, comprising bones of various larger mammalia, in the limestone formation not far from Plymouth."
Thus we see the poetical belief of one age destroyed by the positive philosophy of the next Happily, we move in all things by waves , the system of undulations prevails in every operation, mental and physical. Amidst the relics of the mammalia of the Devonshire caves we are now discovering the unmistakable remains of man and his works,—stone knives, spear-heads, axes, and hammers speak of an ancient race; and may there not have been " *giants in the earth in those days, and also after that ?* "

On yonder hill there lived, in days gone by, a giant and a giantess. They were called Shara and Sheela. One day Shara returned from his labours (wood-cutting) in the forest, and finding no dinner ready he was exceeding angry, and in his passion gave Sheela a severe wound with his axe on the shoulder. His passion was assuaged as soon as he saw the blood of his wife, and he carefully bound up the wound and nursed her for many weeks with great care. Sheela did not, however, forgive Shara for the injury he had inflicted on her. She brooded on her wrong. Eventually she was so far recovered that Shara was able to leave her; and their stock of wood having fallen short, he proceeded to the forest for a fresh supply. Sheela watched her husband as he descended the hill, and, full of wrath, she seized her bed, and, as he was wading through the river, she flung it after him with a dreadful imprecation. The devil changed the bed into stone in its passage through the air. It fell on the giant, crushed him, and to this day he rests beneath the Hag's Bed. In the solitude which she had made she repented her crime, but she never forgave herself the sin. She sat on the hill-top, the melancholy monument of desolation, bewailing her husband's loss, and the country around echoed with her lamentations. "Bad as Shara was, it is worse to be without him!" was her constant cry. Eventually she died of excess of grief, her last words being, "Bad as Shara was, it is worse to be without him!" "And," said the old man, finishing his story, "whenever any trouble is coming upon Ireland, the voice of Sheela is heard upon the hill still repeating her melancholy lamentation."

THE HAG'S BED NEAR FERMOY.

"Near Fermoy is a very peculiar variety of these early structures, being an oblong building constructed with large blocks of limestone of the locality. It contains an internal chamber, from twenty to thirty feet long, five feet wide, and at the present time about four feet high; the side walls are near five feet thick, constructed with two rows of upright stones on edge, and the interior is filled with smaller stones, forming a wall; the front has only a row of thin upright stones, but fitting nearly close together; the covering stones rest on rude horizontal stones, which are placed on the wall before described, and which would appear to have been of insufficient height, and on those are three large covering stones, one of which is about eighteen feet long." *

D (p 53).

THE GIANT OF NANCLEDRY; AND TREBIGGAN THE GIANT.

From time to time, in Cornwall and other places, bones of a large size have been found, and very exaggerated accounts of these finds have been published. Some years since it was currently reported that the bones of a giant had been discovered in Wendron, and they were said to be "prodigious."

I have endeavoured to trace this matter. And now I have evidence to show that the whole affair was greatly exaggerated. The following extracts from letters will place the whole matter in its true light :—

"The discovery under the chancel window at Wendron, in the beginning of the year 1855, consisted simply of a *large collection of bones*, plainly

* "Practical Geology and Ancient Architecture of Ireland." By George Wilkinson, architect.

2 G

human, at the depth of less *than two feet* beneath the floor ! This accounted in a great measure for the extraordinary *dampness* of this part of the church, and which it was in part my object to get rid of.

" Many of these bones, especially the femoral and crural, were certainly of an unusual magnitude, as compared with others which from time to time had been disinterred in the churchyard when a grave had been dug. I cannot state with any degree of certainty whether the dimensions of the largest bones were accurately measured.

" Being desirous to re-inter the bones found in the chancel of Wendron as nearly as possible *in the same place*, though at a considerable depth, we came at length (after the removal of much damp soil) to a *perfect stone sarcophagus*, as far as I recollect about six feet in length. The upper lid of this was not to be found. In the said sarcophagus, containing little more than dust, we laid all the gigantic bones which had been discovered."

Another correspondent informs me, that closer inquiry has probably connected these bones with a well-known man.

The curate of the parish informs me " that there is a brass in the church to the memory of ' Metheruny,' attached to the collegiate establishment of Glaseney in the time of Henry VIII., which he supposed to refer to a grave situate in the spot where the relics referred to by Mr. Boraston were found. Mr. Milne also told me, that among the published engravings of Holbein's portraits was a fine one of this ' Metheruny,' respecting whom are some interesting particulars in King's ' Monumenta Antiqua,' Dugdale's ' Monasticon,' and Bulase's ' Cornwall.' "

E (p. 60).

GEESE DANCING—GUISE DANCING—GUIZARDS.

" THE doings of the *guizards*—that is, masquers—form a conspicuous feature in the New Year's proceedings throughout Scotland. The evenings on which these personages are understood to be privileged to appear are those of Christmas, Hogmanay, New-Year's day, and Handsel Monday. Such boys as can pretend to anything like a voice have, for weeks before, been thumbing the collection of excellent new songs which lies like a bunch of rags in the window-sole ; and being now able to screech up ' Barbara Allan,' or the ' Wee cot-house and the wee kail-yardie,' they determine upon enacting the part of guizards. For this purpose they don old shirts belonging to their fathers, and mount casques of brown paper, shaped so like a mitre, that I am tempted to believe them to be borrowed from the Abbot of Unreason ; attached to this is a sheet of the same paper, which, falling down in front, covers and conceals the whole face, except where holes are made to let through the point of the nose, and afford sight to the eyes and breath to the mouth. Each vocal guizard is, like a knight of old, attended by a kind of humble squire, who assumes the habiliments of a girl, with an old woman's cap and a broomstick, and is styled ' Bessie.' Bessie is equal in no respects, except that she shares fairly in the proceeds of the enterprise. She goes before her principal, opens all the doors at which he pleases to exert his singing powers, and busies herself during the time of the song in sweeping the floor with her broomstick, or in playing any other antics that she thinks may amuse the indwellers. The common reward of this entertainment is a halfpenny ; but many churlish persons fall upon the unfortunate guizards and beat them out of the house. Let such persons, however, keep a good watch over their cabbage-gardens next Hallowe'en.

"The more important of the guizards are of a theatrical character. There is one rude and grotesque drama which they are accustomed to perform on each of the four above-mentioned nights, and which, in various fragments or versions, exists in every part of Lowland Scotland. The performers, who are never less than three, but sometimes as many as six, having dressed themselves, proceed in a band from house to house, generally contenting themselves with the kitchen for an arena, whither, in mansions presided over by the spirit of good-humour, the whole family will resort to witness the spectacle. Sir Walter Scott, who delighted to keep up old customs, and could condescend to simple things without losing genuine dignity, invariably had a set of guizards to perform this play before his family both at Ashiestiel and Abbotsford. The editor has with some difficulty obtained what appears a tolerably complete copy." *

" GOOSE-DANCING."

"Of late years, at this season, in the Islands of Scilly, the young people exercise a sort of gallantry called 'goose-dancing.' The maidens are dressed up for young men, and the young men for maidens ; and thus disguised, they visit their neighbours in companies, where they dance and make jokes upon what has happened in the island, and every one is humorously 'told their own,' without offence being taken. By this sort of sport, according to yearly custom and toleration, there is a spirit of wit and drollery kept up among the people. The music and dancing done, they are treated with liquor, and then they go to the next house of entertainment." †

This custom was by no means confined to the Islands of Scilly In nearly every town and large village in Cornwall. *geese-dancing*,—not goose-dancing, —formed one of the Christmas entertainments. The term was applied to the old Christmas plays, and indeed to any kind of sport in which characters were assumed by the performers, or disguises worn.

It should be noted that these sports are never termed *goose*, but always *ge.se* or *guise* dancing

F (p. 66).

WAYLAND SMITH,

" 'WAYLAND SMITH:' a Dissertation on a Tradition of the Middle Ages, from the French of G. B Depping and Francisque Michel, with Additions by S. W. Singer, and the Amplified Legend, by Oehlenschlager " Pickering, 1847.

To this very interesting little volume I would refer those of my readers who feel desirous of tracing the resemblance of our humble "Jack the Tinkeard," with the Icelandic *Vælund*, the English *Velond*, or Sir Walter Scott's *Wayland* in "Kenilworth."

G (p 72).

THE WONDERFUL COBBLER OF WELLINGTON.

THERE is a considerable family likeness between the Tinker in this Cornish tale of the Giants, and the Wonderful Cobbler of Wellington, in Shropshire, as related by Mr. Thomas Wright in his interesting paper "On the Local

---

* Robert Chambers's " Popular Rhymes of Scotland."
† " Strutt's Sports," p 307 " Table Book," p 41.

. Legends of Shropshire." As this story will interest many readers, I quote it, as the original paper is not easily obtained :—

"Now, according to the legend, there lived at this time, somewhere, I believe, in the neighbourhood of Wellington, a wonderful cobbler, who was so skilful in his art that he monopolised the mending of shoes of the inhabitants of Shrewsbury, and he used to come at certain times with sacks to carry home with him the shoes which were in need of his handiwork. Well, the giant set out on his journey, carrying an immense spadeful of earth, which he intended to throw over the devoted town, and bury all its inhabitants alive ; but it happened that he had never seen Shrewsbury, and was not well informed as to the road ; and he had arrived near Wellington when, whom should he overtake but the clever cobbler labouring along under the burden of two great sacks full of worn shoes he was carrying home. The giant entered into conversation with him, told him where he was going, and let out rather indiscreetly the object of his journey, but confessed his ignorance of the road and the distance. The cobbler had a natural sympathy with the town of Shrewsbury, first, because he was on good terms with the inhabitants ; and, secondly, because, if the town were destroyed, his own occupation would be ruined ; so he resolved to outwit the giant. He told him, therefore, that he knew Shrewsbury very well—in fact, that he was then returning from it, and that he, the giant, was in the right track, but added, with a look of discouragement, that it was very far off. The giant, who had already had a long walk, and imagined he must have reached the object of his search, inquired with some surprise how many days more it would take to walk thither. The cobbler said he had not counted the days, but emptying his two sacks on the ground, declared that he had worn out all those shoes on the journey ; upon which the giant, with a movement of disappointment and disgust, threw the earth from his spade on the spot where it now forms the Wrekin ; and seeing that some mould still adhered to the spade, he pushed it off with his foot, and it formed Ercald Hill, which still adjoins its loftier neighbour."

It is curious to trace in every incident of those stories the lesson taught, that trained skill can at all times overcome mere brute force. These stories belong to a very early age, and they have been the winter-evening amusements of a primitive people, down to a very recent period. Jack the Tinker figures in many similar stories ; he is invariably covered with his wonderful coat (similar to the coat of darkness in several of our nursery tales), and not unfrequently he has the shoes of swiftness.

H (p 73).

The following letter, addressed to the publisher of the first and second editions of this book, will be read with interest :—

263 Hampstead Road, N W., *April 18th*, 1865.

Dear Mr Hotten,—I have received your note, in which you express a doubt as to whether some portion of the public will understand my representation of the Giant " Bolster "

To all such persons, I would beg of them to reflect, that if a giant could stride six miles across a country, he must be twelve miles in height, according to the proportions of the human figure In order to get a sight of the *head* of such a giant, the spectator must be distant a mile or two from the figure. This would, by adding half the "*stride*" and above eleven miles perpendicular, place the spectator about fifteen miles distant from the giant's head, which head, in proportion to the other parts of the body, would be about three quarters of a mile, measuring from the chin to the crown of the head Now, let any one calculate, according to the laws of perspective, what size such a head would be at such a distance   To give a little insight into the matter of perspective, let any one imagine that they are looking down a street, fifteen miles long, of large houses, and then calculate what *size* the *last* house would be at the farther end of the street; and it must therefore be recollected that every part of such a huge body must lessen in the same way—body and limbs—smaller by degrees, if not beautifully less

I selected this subject from my friend Robert Hunt's work as one of the numerous proofs, which are shown in both the volumes, of the horrible dark ignorance of the Early Ages—a large amount of which ignorance and darkness, I am sorry to find, still remains

I hope that these few lines will explain satisfactorily why Giant "Bolster" has been thus displayed by,—Yours truly,   GEORGE CRUIKSHANK

P S —The first time that I put a *very large* figure in perspective was about forty years back, in illustrating that part of "Paradise Lost" where Milton describes Satan as

" Prone on the flood, extended long and large,
Lay floating many a rood."

This I never published, but possibly I may do so one of these days.

I (p. 89).

ST PIRAN'S-DAY AND PICROUS-DAY.

HONE, in his "Every-Day Book," has the following remarks on St Piran —

"This saint, anciently of good repute in Cornwall, is not mentioned by Butler   According to Porter, he was born in Ireland, and became a hermit there.   He afterwards came to England, and settling at Cornwall, had a grave made for him, entered into it, and dying on the 6th of March, 'in the glorie of a great light and splendour that appeared at the same instant,' was buried at Padstow.   'He is reported,' says Porter, 'to have wrought manie wonderful miracles in his lifetime, which, because they tend rather to breed an incredulous amazement in the readers than move to anie workes of virtues or pietie, we have willingly omitted.'   We have had a specimen of such miracles as Father Porter deemed worthy of belief; those of St Piran, which would have caused 'incredulous amazement' in Porter's readers, must have been 'passing wonderful '"

"*St Piran's-day* is said to be a favourite with the tinners.   Having a tradition that some secrets regarding the manufacture of tin was communicated to their ancestors by that saint, they leave the manufacture to shift for itself for that day, and keep it as a holiday." *

Mr T. Q. Couch obligingly favours me with the following note on Picrous-day :—

"The second Thursday before Christmas-day is a festival observed by the tinners of the district of Blackmore, and known as *Picrous-day*.   It is not at present marked by any distinctive ceremonies, but it is the occasion of a supper and much merry-making.   The owner of the tin-stream contributes a shilling a man towards it.   *This is said to be the feast of the discovery of tin by a man named Picrous.*   My first impression was that the day took its name from the circumstance of a *pie* forming the *pièce de résistance* of the supper ; but this explanation is not allowed by tinners, nor sanctioned by the usages of the feast.   What truth there may be in the tradition of the first tinner, Picrous, it is now too late to discover, but the notion is worth recording.   It has occurred to me whether, from some similarity between the names (not a close one, I admit it), the honours of Picrous may not have been transferred to St Piran, who is generally said to be the patron saint of tinners.   St Piran is not known in Blackmore, and his festival is on the 5th of March.   The tinners also have a festival to commemorate the discovery of smelting."

* Gilbert's "History."

K (p. 129).

MOSES PITT'S LETTER RESPECTING ANNE JEFFERIES.

" AN account of Anne Jefferies, now living in the county of Cornwall, who was fed for six months by a small sort of airy people, called fairies; and of the strange and wonderful cures she performed with salves and medicines she received from them, for which she never took one penny of her patients. —In a letter from Moses Pitt to the Right Reverend Father in God, Dr. Edward Fowler, Lord Bishop of Gloucester."

Anne Jefferies, who was afterwards married to one William Warren, was born in the parish of St Teath in December 1626, "and she is still living, 1696, being now in the 70th year of her age." From the published narrative, we learn that Mr Humphrey Martin was requested by Mr Moses Pitt to see and examine Anne in 1693. Mr Martin writes, "As for Anne Jefferies, I have been with her the greater part of one day, and did read to her all that you wrote to me; but she would not own anything of it, as concerning the fairies, neither of any of the cures that she did. She answered, that if her own father were now alive, she would not discover to him those things which did happen then to her. I asked her the reason why she would not do it; she replied, that if she should discover it to you, that you would make books or ballads of it; and she said, that she would not have her name spread about the country in books or ballads of such things, if she might have five hundred pounds for it."

Mr Pitt's correspondent goes on to say that Anne was so frightened by the visitors she had in the arbour "that she fell into a kind of convulsion fit. But when we found her in this condition we brought her into the house and put her to bed, and took great care of her. As soon as she recovered out of her fit, she cried out, 'They are just gone out of the window—they are just gone out of the window. Do you not see them?'" Anne recovered, and "as soon as she recovered a little strength, she constantly went to church" "She took mighty delight in devotion, and in hearing the Word of God read and preached, although she herself could not read."

Anne eventually tells some portions of her story, and cures numerous diseases amongst the people, by the powers she had derived from the fairy world. "People of all distempers, sicknesses, sores, and ages, came not only so far off as the Land's End, but also from London, and were cured by her. She took no moneys of them, nor any reward that ever I knew or heard of, yet had she moneys at all times sufficient to supply her wants. She neither made nor bought any medicines or salves that ever I saw or heard of, yet wanted them not as she had occasion. *She forsook eating our victuals, and was fed by these fairies from that harvest time to the next Christmas-day,* upon which day she came to our table and said, because it was that day. she would eat some roast beef with us, the which she did —I myself being then at the table."

The fairies constantly attended upon Anne, and they appear to have vied with each other to win her favour. They fed her, as we have been already told, and the writer says that on one occasion she "gave me a piece of her bread, which I did eat, and I think it was the most delicious bread that ever I did eat, either before or since" Anne could render herself invisible at will. The fairies would come and dance with her in the orchard. She had a silver cup, given at her wish by the fairies to Mary Martyn, when she was about four years of age.

At last, "one John Tregeagle, Esq., who was steward to John Earl of

Radnor, being a justice of peace in Cornwall, sent his warrant for Anne, and sent her to Bodmin jail, and there kept her a long time." The fairies had previously given her notice that she would be apprehended.

"She asked them if she should hide herself. They answered no; she should fear nothing, but go with the constable. So she went with the constable to the justice, and he sent her to Bodmin jail, and ordered the prison-keeper that she should be kept without victuals, and she was so kept, and yet she lived, and that without complaining. But poor Anne lay in jail for a considerable time after, and also Justice Tregeagle, who was her great prosecutor, kept her in his house some time as a prisoner, and that without victuals."

We have a curious example of the fairies quoting Scripture. I am not aware of another instance of this. Anne, when seated with the family was called three times. "Of all these three calls of the fairies, none heard them but Anne. After she had been in her chamber some time, she came to us again, with a Bible in her hand, and tells us that when she came to the fairies, they said to her, 'What! has there been some magistrates and ministers with you, and dissuaded you from coming any more to us, saying, we are evil spirits, and that it was all a delusion of the devil? Pray, desire them to read that place of Scripture, in the First Epistle of St. John, chap. iv. ver. 1, "Dearly beloved, *believe not every spirit, but try the spirits,* whether they are of God;"' and this place of Scripture was turned down so in the said Bible. I told your lordship before, *Anne could not read.*"

Anne was at length liberated from confinement. She lived in service near Padstow, and in process of time married William Warren.

How honestly and simply does Moses conclude his story!

"And now, my lord, if your lordship expects that I should give you an account when, and upon what occasion, these fairies forsook our Anne, I must tell your lordship I am ignorant of that. She herself can best tell, if she would be prevailed upon to do so; and the history of it, and the rest of the passages of her life, would be very acceptable and useful to the most curious and inquisitive part of mankind." *

L (p. 146).

THE BARGEST, OR SPECTRE-HOUND.

In the glossary to the Rev. Mr. Carr's "Horæ Momenta Carvenæ," I find the following. "*Bargest*, a sprite that haunts towns and populous places. Belg. *berg*, and *geest*, a ghost." I really am not a little amused at Mr. Carr's derivation, which is most erroneous. Bargest is not a town-ghost, nor is it a haunter "of towns and populous places;" for, on the contrary, it is said in general to frequent small villages and *hills*. Hence the derivation may be *berg*, Germ a *hill*, and *geest*, a ghost—*i e.*, a hill-ghost; but the real derivation appears to me to be *bar*, Germ. a *bear*, and *geest*, a ghost—*i e.*, a bear-ghost, from its appearing in the form of a bear or large dog, as Billy B——'s narrative shows.

The appearance of the spectre-hound is said to precede a death. Like other spirits, Bargest is supposed to be unable to cross water; and in case any of my craven readers should ever chance to meet with his ghostship, it may be as well to say, that unless they give him the wall, he will tear them in pieces, or otherwise ill-treat them, as he did John Lambert, who, refusing to let him have the wall, was so punished for his want of manners, that he died in a few days.

* "An Historical Survey of the County of Cornwall" C S Gilbert. 1817.

BILLY B——'S ADVENTURE.

" You see, sir, as how I'd been a clock-dressing at Gurston (Grassington), and I'd staid rather lat, and maybe gitten a li'le sup o' spirit; but I war far from being drunk, and knowed everything that passed. It war about eleven o'clock when I left, and it war at back end o' t' year, and a most admirable (beautiful) neet it war. The moon war varra breet, and I nivver seed Kylstone-fell plainer in a' my life. Now, you see, sir, I war passin' down t' mill loine, and I heerd summat come past me,—brush, brush, brush, wi' chains rattling a' the while, but I seed nothing ; and thowt I to mysel, now this is a most mortal queer thing. And I then stuid still, and luik'd about me; but I seed nothing at aw, nobbut the two stane wa's on each o' t' mill loine. Then I heerd again this brush, brush, brush, wi' the chains; for you see, sir, when I stuid still it stopped, and then, thowt I, this mun be a Bargest, that sae much is said about , and I hurried on towards t' wood brig ; for they say as how this Bargest cannot cross a water ; but Lord, sir, when I gat o'er t' brig, I heerd this same thing again ; so it mun either hev crossed t' watter, *or have gane round by t' spring heed!* (about thirty miles ') And then I becam a valliant man, for I war a bit freekn'd afore ; and, thinks I, I'll turn and hev a peep at this thing ; so I went up Greet Bank towards Linton, and heerd this brush, biush, biush, wi' the chains a' the way, but I seed nothing ; then it ceased all of a sudden. So I turned back to go hame ; but I'd hardly reached the door when I heerd again this brush, brush, brush, and the chains going down towards t' Holin House ; and I followed it, and the moon there shone varra breet, and *I seed its tail!* Then, thowt I, thou owd thing, I can say Ise seen thee now ; so, I'll away hame. When I gat to t' door, there war a grit thing like a sheep, but it war larger, ligging across t' threshold of t' door, and it war woolly like ; and says I, ' Git up,' and it wouldn't git up. Then says I, ' Stir thysel,' and it wouldn't stir itsel l And I grew valliant, and I raised t' stick to baste it wi' ; and then it luik'd at me and sich oies (eyes), they did glower, and war as big as saucers, and like a cruelled ball. First there war a red ring, then a blue one, then a white one ; and these rings grew less and less *till they came to a dot!* Now, I war nane feer'd on it, tho' it grin'd at me fearfully, and I kept on saying, ' Git up,' and ' Stir thysel,' and t' wife heerd as how I war at t' door, and she cam to oppen it ; and then this thing gat up and walked off, *for it war mare freet'd o' t' wife than it war o' me ;* and I told the wife, and she said it war Bargest ; but I nivver seed it since—and that's a true story." *

M (p. 170).

THE MERMAID'S VENGEANCE.

" INEVITABLE death awaits the wretch who is seduced by their charms. They seize and drown the swimmer, and entice the child ; and when they anticipate that their malevolence will be gratified, they are seen gaily darting over the surface of the waters."

Since this tale has been in type, my attention has been called to an article on the "Popular Mythology of the Middle Ages," by Sir F. Palgrave, in the *Quarterly Review,* No 44, 1820. The Nixies, to whom the above quotation especially refers, are in most respects like the Cornish mermaids.

* Hone's "Every-Day Book"

N (p. 173).

ROCK MASSES, CELTIC.

"The Celts, or Κελτοί, or Κελται, were a people of the origin of which nothing *positive* is known. They occupied a great part of Western Europe perhaps in times antecedent to the invasion of Indo-Germanic nations.

"The very name *Celt* is of uncertain etymology. Ammian derives it from the king, *Kelta*, or *Celta* ; Leibnitz, from the German *gelt*, or *geld*, money ; Mezerai, from the British *gall*, or *gault*, a forest; Pellontier, from the Tudesk *wallen*, to wander ; Latour d'Auvergne, from *gael*, or *gæll*, yellow, alluding to the light hair of the *Galli*, whom Bochart identifies with *Dodanim* (for Rhodanim) of Gen. x. *

"But the name of *Celt* may probably come, as Camden says, from *gwalth*, a head of hair ; *coma*, and *gwalthay*, *comatus* ; from whence Κελ-ται, Γαλάται, or Γάλλοι. *Galli* or *Gauls*, the *Gædil*, *Cædil*, or *Keile*, and in pl. *Keilt*, or *Keiltiet*, or *Gaels*, *Gædels*, or *Guidhelod*, as the Irish call themselves and their tongue.

"The language called *Celtic* is divided into two principal branches—*viz.*, 1. The *Irish* or *Hibernian*, from which the present *Irish*, or *Erse*, and the *Gaelic* of Scotland are derived. 2. The *British*, to which the primitive Gaellic or Gallic are allied, and from which are derived the *Welsh*, the *Cornish*, and the *Armoric*, or language of Brittany." †

"The Welsh, which is the relic of the language of the inland Britons, or Cæsar's aborigines, is most probably akin to the dialect of *Gallia Celtica*, and the Cornish to the idiom of the Belgæ, who overran the southern district of England, and probably sought refuge in the west when the Saxons were extending themselves from the eastern part of the island " ‡

But surely there are indications of a people inhabiting Cornwall long before the Saxons gained a foot of ground in England ?

O (p. 175).

AMBROSIÆ PETRÆ.

In connection with the Bambury stone in Worcestershire, Mr. Jabez Allies remarks, and Dr Nash is of the same opinion, that it was in all probability originally *Ambury*. He then gives us several examples of the occurrence of this name—as Ambreforde in Yorkshire, Ambrelie in Sussex, Ambresberie in Wilts, Ambresdone in Oxfordshire, and many others. §

"The ancients distinguished stones, erected with a religious view, by the name of *amber*, by which was signified anything solar and divine. ‖

"Respecting the Phœnicians being the founders of the Druidical discipline in Britain, one fact weighs more with me than a thousand arguments. I allude to the Tyrian coin, on which appear the tree, the sacred fire, the two stone pillars of Hercules (Thoth), and the singular legend, Tyr. Col. (Colony of Tyrians), and the still more remarkable words under the erect stones, ΑΜΒΡΟΣΙΕ ΠΕΤΡΕ (Ambrosiæ Petræ), the anointed rocks. Let the reader remember the monkish traditions of Ambrosius, the exact likeness of these pillars on this coin to the stones at Stonehenge, the

---

* " And the sons of Javan : Elishah, and Tarshish, Kittim and Dodanim " (Gen x 4)
† " A History of the Sacred Scriptures in every Language and Dialect into which Translations have been made " Bagster & Sons, 1860.
‡ " Researches into the Physical History of Mankind." By James Cowles Prichard, M D , F A.S , vol iii. § Allies' " Worcestershire "
‖ Bryant's " Ancient Mythology "

Ambrosiæ Petræ; and if he does not think the origin of Ambrosbury, or Amesbury, was derived from the Ambrosiæ Petræ, or anointed rocks of the Tyrian colonists, he will think the coincidence most remarkable." [*]

"*Main Ambres, petræ ambrosiæ,* signify the stones anointed with holy oil, consecrated; or, in a general sense, a temple, altar, or place of worship." [†]

P (p. 194).

PADSTOW HOBBY HORSE.

MR. GEORGE RAWLINGS writes, September 1, 1865:—Formerly all the respectable people kept the anniversary decorated with the choicest flowers, but some unlucky day a number of rough characters from a distance joined it, and committed some sad assaults on old and young—spoiling all their nice summer clothes, and covering their faces and persons with smut. From that time—fifty years since—the procession is formed of the lowest. . . . The Maypole was once decorated with the best flowers—now, with only some elm branches and furze in blossom. The horse is formed as follows:—The dress is made of sailcloth painted black—a fierce mask—eyes red—horse's head—horse-hair mane and tail distended by a hoop. Some would call it very frightful. Carried by a powerful man—they could inflict much mischief with the *snappers,* &c No doubt it is a remnant of the ancient plays, and it represents the Devil, or the power of Darkness. They commence singing at sunrise.

THE MORNING SONG.

Unite and unite and let us all unite,
　For summer it is come unto day;
And whither we are going we all will unite
　In the merry morning of May

Arise up, Mr. ——, and joy you betide,
　For summer is come unto day;
And bright is your bride that lays by your side
　In the merry morning of May

Arise up, Mrs ——, and gold be your ring,
　For summer is come unto day,
And give to us a cup of ale, the merrier we shall sing
　In the merry morning of May.

Arise up, Miss ——, all in your smock of silk,
　For summer is come unto day;
And all your body under as white as any milk,
　In the merry morning of May.

The young men of Padstow might, if they would,
　For summer is come unto day;
They might have built a ship and gilded her with gold
　In the merry morning of May.

Now fare you well, and we bid you good cheer,
　For summer is come unto day,
We will come no more unto your house before another year,
　In the merry morning of May.

THE DAY SONG.

Awake, St. George, our English knight,
　For summer is a-come O, and winter is a go;
And every day God give us His grace
　By day and by night O!

[*] Bowles' "Hermes Britannicus"
[†] Stukeley, Stonehenge. See Akerman "On the Stone Worship of the Ancients, Illustrated by their Coins." "Transactions of the Numismatic Society," January 1838.

Where is St George, where is he O ?
  He is out in his long boat all on the salt sea O !
And in every land O ! the land where'er we go,
  And for to fetch th summer home.
                The summer and the May O,
                For summer is a come,
                And winter is a go.

Where are the French dogs that make such boast O ?
  They shall eat the grey goose feather,
And we will cattle roast O !
  And in every land O ! the land where'er we go,
          The summer and the May O.

Thou mightst have shown thy knavish face !
  Thou mightst have tarried at home O !
But thou shalt be an old cuckold,
  And thou shalt wear the horns O ;
          The summer and the May O.

ADDITIONAL CHORUS.

With hal an-tow * and jolly rumble O,
  For summer is a come O, and winter is a go,
And in every land O, the land where'er we go,
Up flies the kite, and down falls the lark O !
  Aunt Ursula Birdhood she had an old ewe,
And she died in her own park O !
  And for to fetch the summer home.

Q (p. 199.)

THE CITY OF LANGARROW OR LANGONA.—PERRAN CHURCHES.

NEAR the oldest Perran church there formerly existed a lake called the *Vlow*, and across this lake the sand was never blown. The sands encroached rapidly on the first church, and it was resolved by the parish to build a church on the other side of the lake, where it would be quite beyond the reach of the sands. The church was built and remained for a long period free from the effects of the blowing sands. At length a miner, called Roberts, drove an adit in from the cliffs under the lake, to reach the mine now called Huel Vlow, and this carried off all the water from the lake. Then the sands rapidly advanced towards, and at length threatened to bury, the second church. So great was the danger of this, that at length it was resolved to remove the church to the position which it at present occupies. The limits of the lake can be readily traced.

It is now said—and there is much appearance of truth in it—that the sand will not cross the small stream which divides Perranzabuloe from Cubert. Those who have watched the travelling of the sand will understand the influence of running water in checking its progress.

Languna or Langona (p. 220). "Church on the Down."

Lan, a church or enclosure. *Gun*, a down or common. *Gan*, a level plain, a down—same as *Goon*.

R (p. 273).

ST PIRAN—PERRAN ZABULOE.

"IT is rather a curious circumstance," says Davies Gilbert, "that the word *Zabuloe* added to Perran, for the distinction of this parish, is not Celtic, but through the French *sable*, from *sabalum*, a word frequently used by Pliny, as indicative of sand or gravel.

* Cornish, *jollification.*

"The encroachments of the sand have caused no less than three churches to be built, after considerable intervals of time, in this parish. The last was commenced in 1804; and in this year (1835), a building has been discovered more ancient than the first of these churches, and not improbably the Oratory of St Perran himself The length of this chapel within the walls is 25 feet, without, 30 feet; the breadth within, 12½ feet; and the height of the walls the same.

"At the eastern end is a neat altar of stone covered with lime, 4 feet long, by 2½ feet wide, and 3 feet high. Eight inches above the centre of the altar is a recess in the wall, where probably stood a crucifix; and on the north side of the altar is a small doorway, through which the priest may have entered. Out of the whole length, the chancel extended exactly 6 feet. In the centre of what may be termed the nave, in the south wall, occurs a round arched doorway, highly ornamented The building is, how-ever, without any trace of window; and there is only one small opening, apparently for the admission of air.

"The discovery has excited much curiosity throughout the neighbourhood; which has, unfortunately, manifested itself by the demolition of everything curious in this little oratory, to be borne away as relics."—*Gilbert.*

"Very little is known concerning the saint who has given his name to the three Perrans. He is, however, held in great veneration, and esteemed the patron of all Cornwall, or at least of the mining district."—*Hals.*

S (p. 274).

ST CHIWIDDEN.

THE last Thursday—a clear week before Christmas-day—was formerly always claimed by the tinners as a holiday, and was called by them White-Thursday (*Jew-whidn*), because on this day, according to tradition, black tin (tin ore) was first melted and refined into white tin. From *Jew-whidn* to *Chi-widden* is an easy transition. Jew-whidn is a name given to the old furnaces generally called Jews'-houses.

T (p. 275).

THE DISCOVERER OF TIN

BY an anachronism of fifteen hundred years or more, St Perran was con-sidered as the person who first found tin; and this conviction induced the miners to celebrate his day, the 5th of March, with so much hilarity, that any one unable to guide himself along the road has received the appellation of a Perraner; and that, again, has most unjustly reflected as a habit on the saint.

"It may here be worthy of remark, that, as the miners impute the dis-covery of tin to St Perran, so they ascribe its reduction from the ore, in a large way, to an imaginary person, St Chiwidden; but *chi-wadden* is white house, and must, therefore, mean a smelting or blowing-house, where the black ore of tin is converted into a white metal.

"A white cross on a black ground was formerly the banner of St Perran, and the standard of Cornwall; probably with some allusion to the black ore and the white metal of tin."—*Gilbert.*

A college, dedicated to St Perran, once stood in the parish of St Kevern (Dugdale's "Monasticon," vol. vi. p. 1449). This probably had some connection with Perran Uthnoe. The shrine of St Perran was in that parish, which is said to have contained his head, and other relics

Lysons quotes a deed in the registry of Exeter, showing the great resort of pilgrims hither in 1485.

In the will of Sir John Arundell, 1433, occurs this bequest.—"Item, lego ad usum parochie S'c't' Pyerani in Zabulo, ad clandendum capud S. Pierani honorificè et meliori modo quo sciunt xls."—*Collectanea Topogr. et Geneal.*, vol. iii. p 392.

For a full examination of the question, Did the Phœnicians trade with Britain for tin? the following works should be consulted :—"History of Maritime and Inland Discovery," by W. D. Cooley ; "Historical Survey of the Astronomy of the Ancients," by Sir George Cornewall Lewis; "Commerce and Navigation of the Ancients," by W. Vincent, D.D. ; "Phœnicia," by John Kenrick, M.A. ; "The Cassiterides: an Inquiry into the Commercial Operations of the Phœnicians in Western Europe, with Particular Reference to the British Tin Trade," by George Smith, LL D., F.A.S.

U (p. 277).

ST NEOT.

THE following account of this celebrated saint, as given by Mr Davies Gilbert, will not be without interest :—

"Multitudes flocked to him from all parts. He founded a monastery, and repaired to Rome for a confirmation, and for blessing at the hands of the Pope ; these were readily obtained. He returned to his monastery, where frequent visits were made to him by King Alfred, on which occasions he admonished and instructed the great founder of English liberty, and finally quitted this mortal life on the 31st of July about the year 883, in the odour of sanctity so unequivocal that travellers all over Cornwall were solaced by its fragrance. Nor did the exertions of our saint terminate with his existence on earth ; he frequently appeared to King Alfred, and sometimes led his armies in the field. But if the tales of these times are deserving of any confidence, the nation is really and truly indebted to St Neot for one of the greatest blessings ever bestowed on it. To his advice, and even to his personal assistance as a teacher, we owe the foundation by Alfred of the University at Oxford.

"The relics of St Neot remained at his monastery in Cornwall till about the year 974, when Earl Alric, and his wife Ethelfleda, having founded a religious house at Eynesbury, in Huntingdonshire, and being at a loss for some patron saint, adopted the expedient of stealing the body of St Neot ; which was accordingly done, and the town retains his name, thus feloniously obtained, up to this time. The monastery in Cornwall continued feebly to exist after this disaster through the Saxon times ; but having lost its palladium, it felt the ruiner's hand ; and almost immediately after the Norman Conquest it was finally suppressed. Yet the memory of the local saint is still cherished by the inhabitants of the parish and of the neighbourhood—endeared, perhaps, by the tradition of his diminutive stature, reduced in their imagination to fifteen inches of height, and to these feelings we, in all probability, owe the preservation of the painted glass, the great decoration of this church, and one of the principal works of Art to be seen in Cornwall."—*Gilbert's Hist. Corn.*, vol. iii. p. 262.

X (p. 282).

THE SISTERS OF GLEN-NEOT.

BY THE LATE REV. R. S. HAWKER OF MORWENSTOW.

It is from Neot's sainted steep
The foamy waters flash and leap;
It is where shrinking wild-flowers grow,
They lave the nymph that dwells below!

But wherefore in this far-off dell,
The reliques of a human cell?
Where the sad stream and lonely wind
Bring Man no tidings of their kind!

Long years agone! the old man said,
'I was told him by his grandsire dead,
One day two ancient sisters came,
None there could tell their race or name.

Their speech was not in Cornish phrase,
Their garb had marks of loftier days,
Slight food they took from hands of men,
They wither'd slowly in that glen.

One died! the other's shrunken eye
Gush'd till the fount of tears was dry:
A wild and wasting thought had she—
"I shall have none to weep for me!"

They found her silent at the last,
Bent in the shape wherein she pass'd—
Where her lone seat long used to stand,
Her head upon her shrivell'd hand!

Did fancy give this legend birth?
The grandame's tale for winter-hearth,
Or some dead birk, by Neot's stream,
People these banks with such a dream?

We know not! but it suits the scene,
To think such wild things here have been;
What spot more meet could grief or sin
Choose at the last to wither in?
Echoes of Old Cornwall.

Y (p. 322).

MILLINGTON OF PENGERSWICK.

In the reign of Henry VIII., one Militon, or Millington, appears to have purchased Pengerswick Castle. This Millington is said to have retired into the solitude of this place on account of a murder which he had committed. (Mr. Wilkie Collins appears to have founded his novel of "Basil" on this tradition.) In all probability a very much older story is adapted to Mr. Millington So far from his being a recluse, we learn of his purchasing St. Michael's Mount, "whose six daughters and heirs invested their husbands and purchasers therewith."

That Millington was a man of wealth, and that large possessions were held by his family, is sufficiently evident. St. Michael's Mount appears to have been "granted at first for a term of years to different gentlemen of the neighbourhood To Millington, supposed of Pengerswick, in Breage; to Harris, of Kenegie, in Gulval; and, perhaps jointly with Millington, to a Billett or Bennett."—*Hals.*

Z (p. 323.)

PENGERSWICK.

Another legend relates that it was not the stepmother found by Pengerswick whose "skin was covered with scales like a serpent," but that the lady brought home from Palestine by him was an Ophidian—a serpent-worshipper. Hence she became celebrated as a woman possessed by a serpent —having a serpent's power—in fact, a Lamia. This is the only tradition of the kind with which I am acquainted in this county.

AA (p 323).

SARACEN.

The term *Saracen* is always now supposed to apply to the Moors. This is not exactly correct Percy, for example, in his "Essay on the Ancient Minstrels," says, "The old metrical romance of 'Horn Child,' which, although from the mention of Saracens, &c., it must have been written, at least, after the First Crusade in 1096, yet, from its Anglo-Saxon language or idiom, can scarcely be dated later than within a century after the Conquest." I think this ballad, and several others of an early date, prove the application of this term to some Oriental people previous to the Crusades. Soldàin, soldàn, regarded as a corruption of sultan,—

> "Whoever will fight yon grimme soldàn,
> Right fair his meede shall be,"

is clearly a much older term, applied to any grim Eastern tyrant, and especially to the Oriental giants. It would not be a difficult task to show that the word "Saracen," as used in Cornwall,—*"Atal Saracen !" " Oh, he's a Saracen !"* &c., was applied to the foreigners who traded with this country for tin at a very early period.

BB (p. 344).

THE TINNER OF CHYANNOR.

IN Trengothal stood a low hut called the Ram's House. This was said to have been built by the tinners, and called *Chyan nance* or *House in the Valley. Nor*, in Williams's Welsh Dictionary, is *earth*. This makes *Chyan-nor*, or the *House of Earth.*

CC (p. 370).

MERRY SEAN LADS.

Could Roos, or *Cold-ruse*, may, however, signify the original for *"shooting the seine*," or net ; *roos*, or *ruz*, being the Cornish for net, or pilchard *seine*

DD (p. 379).

THE NORTH SIDE OF A CHURCH

I HAVE been favoured with the following remarks on this subject by the Rev. J. C. Atkinson, of Danby, Grosmont :—

I translate the following from Hylten Cuvalliecs' *Warend och Wirdurne*, pp. 287, 288.

"Inasmuch as all light and all vigour springs from the sun, our Swedish forefathers always made their prayers with their faces turned towards that luminary. When any spell or charm in connection with an 'earth-fast stone' is practised, even in the present day, for the removal of sickness, the patient invariably turns his face towards the east, or the sun. When a child is to be carried to church to be baptized, the Warend usage is for the godmother first to make her morning prayer, face towards the east, and then ask the parents three several times what the child's name is to be. The dead are invariably interred with their feet lying eastward, so as to have their faces turned towards the rising sun. *Fransols*, or with or in a northerly direction, is, on the other hand, according to an ancient popular idea, *the home of the evil spirits*. The *Old Northern Hell was placed far away in the North*. When any one desires to remove or break any witch spell, or the like, by means of 'reading' (or charms), it is a matter particularly observed that the stone (*i e.*, an 'earth-fast' one), is sought to the northward of the house. In like manner also the 'bearing tree' (any tree which produces fruit, or quasi fruit, apples, pears, &c., *rowan tree*, especially, and white thorn herbs), or the shrew mouse, by means of which it is hoped to remedy an evil spell, must be met with in a northerly direction from the patient's home. Nay, if one wants to charm away sickness over (or into) a running stream, it must always be one which runs northwards. On the self same grounds it has ever been the practice of the people of the Warend district, even down to the present time, not to bury their dead *fransols*—or to the northward—of the church. In that part of the churchyard the contemned *framlings hogen* (strangers' burial place) always has its site, and in it are buried malefactors, friendless wretches, and utter strangers. A very old idea, in like manner connects the north side of the church with suicides' graves," &c.

EE (p. 435).

PECULIAR WORDS AND PHRASES.

An angry Cornishman would formerly say when in anger, "I shall push a stone in his cairn," meaning he shall see him buried.

" *Curri nu clack er du cuirn* " is the expression of a Scotch Highlander (Labbach's *Prehistoric Times*). This is interpreted as a mark of respect, or, I will do something to build you a monument.

In the parish of Breage, the habit of prefixing names to the people is common. The "Tubby" Prichard's are well known. "Alsie's" children are common. "Scaw" was applied to several families.

FF (p. 444).

THE HARLYN PIE.

The Peter family, who formerly lived at Harlyn, left the place, and sold the estate to a farmer. The common report was that one of the family manured his land with earth from the graves in Constantine churchyard.

A considerable quantity of land formerly said to belong to the poor of the parish cannot now be found, as all the marks are gone.

The gold collar deposited in the Royal Institution at Truro, by H.R.H. the Duke of Cornwall, was found on the Harlyn estate.

PRINTED BY BALLANTYNE, HANSON AND CO.
EDINBURGH AND LONDON

CHATTO & WINDUS'S
LIST OF BOOKS.

New Series of Three-and-Sixpenny Books.
Crown 8vo, cloth extra.

Merrie England in the Olden Time By G. DANIEL. Illust.
Circus Life and Circus Celebrities. By THOMAS FROST
Tavern Anecdotes and Sayings. By CHARLES HINDLEY With Illustrations.
[FROST
The Old Showman and the Old London Fairs. By THOMAS
The Story of the London Parks. By JACOB LARWOOD Illust
The Life and Adventures of a Cheap Jack. By C. HINDLEY.
The Lives of the Conjurors By THOMAS FROST.

Crown 8vo, Coloured Frontispiece and Illustrations, cloth gilt, *7s. 6d.*

Advertising, A History of.
From the Earliest Times. Illustrated by Anecdotes, Curious Specimens, and Notes of Successful Advertisers. By HENRY SAMPSON.

Crown 8vo, cloth extra, with 639 Illustrations, *7s. 6d.*

Architectural Styles, A Handbook of.
Translated from the German of A. ROSENGARTEN by W. COLLETT-SANDARS. With 639 Illustrations.

Crown 8vo, with Portrait and Facsimile, cloth extra, *7s. 6d.*

Artemus Ward's Works:
The Works of CHARLES FARRER BROWNE, better known as ARTEMUS WARD. With Portrait, Facsimile of Handwriting, &c.

Bardsley (Rev. C. W.), Works by:
English Surnames: Their Sources and Significations. By CHARLES WAREING BARDSLEY, M.A. Crown 8vo, cloth extra, *7s 6d*
Curiosities of Puritan Nomenclature By CHARLES W. BARDSLEY. Crown 8vo, cloth extra, *7s 6d.*

Crown 8vo, cloth extra, 6s.

Balzac.—The Comédie Humaine and its

Author. With Translations from Balzac. By H. H. WALKER.

Crown 8vo, cloth extra, 7s. 6d.

Bankers, A Handbook of London;

With some Account of their Predecessors, the Early Goldsmiths: together with Lists of Bankers from 1677 to 1876. By F. G. HILTON PRICE.

A New Edition, crown 8vo, cloth extra, 7s. 6d.

Bartholomew Fair, Memoirs of.

By HENRY MORLEY. New Edition, with One Hundred Illustrations.

Imperial 4to, cloth extra, gilt and gilt edges, 21s. per volume.

Beautiful Pictures by British Artists:

A Gathering of Favourites from our Picture Galleries. In Two Series.

The FIRST SERIES including Examples by WILKIE, CONSTABLE, TURNER, MULREADY, LANDSEER, MACLISE, E. M. WARD, FRITH, Sir JOHN GILBERT, LESLIE, ANSDELL, MARCUS STONE, Sir NOEL PATON, FAED, EYRE CROWE, GAVIN O'NEIL, and MADOX BROWN.

The SECOND SERIES containing Pictures by ARMITAGE, FAED, GOODALL, HEMSLEY, HORSLEY, MARKS, NICHOLLS, Sir NOEL PATON, PICKERSGILL, G. SMITH, MARCUS STONE, SOLOMON, STRAIGHT, E. M WARD, and WARREN.

All engraved on Steel in the highest style of Art. Edited, with Notices of the Artists, by SYDNEY ARMYTAGE, M.A.

" This book is well got up, and good engravings by Jeens, Lumb Stocks, and others, bring back to us Royal Academy Exhibitions of past years "—TIMES

Small 4to, green and gold, 6s. 6d. ; gilt edges, 7s. 6d.

Bechstein's As Pretty as Seven,

And other German Stories. Collected by LUDWIG BECHSTEIN. With Additional Tales by the Brothers GRIMM, and 100 Illustrations by RICHTER.

NEW NOVEL BY THE AUTHOR OF " THE NEW REPUBLIC."

Belgravia for January, 1881,

Price One Shilling, contained the First Parts of Three New Serials, viz. —

1. A ROMANCE OF THE NINETEENTH CENTURY, by W. H. MALLOCK, Author of " The New Republic "
2. JOSEPH'S COAT, by D. CHRISTIE MURRAY, Author of "A Life's Atonement." With Illustrations by F. BARNARD
3. ROUND ABOUT ETON AND HARROW, by ALFRED RIMMER. With numerous Illustrations.

** The FORTY-THIRD Volume of BELGRAVIA, elegantly bound in crimson cloth, full gilt side and back, gilt edges, price 7s 6d., is now ready.—Handsome Cases for binding volumes can be had at 2s each.

Demy 8vo, Illustrated, uniform in size for binding.

Blackburn's (Henry) Art Handbooks:

Academy Notes, 1875	With 40 Illustrations.	1*s*.
Academy Notes, 1876.	With 107 Illustrations.	1*s*.
Academy Notes, 1877.	With 143 Illustrations.	1*s*
Academy Notes, 1878.	With 150 Illustrations.	1*s*
Academy Notes, 1879.	With 146 Illustrations.	1*s*.
Academy Notes, 1880.	With 126 Illustrations.	1*s*.
Grosvenor Notes, 1878	With 68 Illustrations.	1*s*.
Grosvenor Notes, 1879.	With 60 Illustrations.	1*s*.
Grosvenor Notes, 1880.	With 56 Illustrations.	1*s*

Pictures at the Paris Exhibition, 1878.   80 Illustrations

Pictures at South Kensington. (The Raphael Cartoons, Sheepshanks Collection, &c.) With 70 Illustrations. 1*s*.

The English Pictures at the National Gallery. With 114 Illustrations. 1*s*.

The Old Masters at the National Gallery. 128 Illusts. 1*s*. 6*d*.

Academy Notes, 1875–79. Complete in One Volume, with nearly 600 Illustrations in Facsimile   Demy 8vo, cloth limp, 6*s*

A Complete Illustrated Catalogue to the National Gallery. With Notes by HENRY BLACKBURN, and 242 Illustrations. Demy 8vo, cloth limp, 3*s*

UNIFORM WITH "ACADEMY NOTES."

Royal Scottish Academy Notes, 1878.	117 Illustrations.	1*s*.
Royal Scottish Academy Notes, 1879.	125 Illustrations.	1*s*.
Royal Scottish Academy Notes, 1880.	114 Illustrations.	1*s*.
Glasgow Institute of Fine Arts Notes, 1878.	95 Illusts.	1*s*.
Glasgow Institute of Fine Arts Notes, 1879.	100 Illusts	1*s*.
Glasgow Institute of Fine Arts Notes, 1880	120 Illusts	1*s*.
Walker Art Gallery Notes, Liverpool, 1878.	112 Illusts.	1*s*.
Walker Art Gallery Notes, Liverpool, 1879.	100 Illusts.	1*s*.
Walker Art Gallery Notes, Liverpool, 1880	100 Illusts	1*s*.
Royal Manchester Institution Notes, 1878.	88 Illustrations.	1*s*.
Society of Artists Notes, Birmingham, 1878.	95 Illusts.	1*s*.

Children of the Great City. By F. W. LAWSON. With Facsimile Sketches by the Artist   Demy 8vo, 1*s*

Folio, half-bound boards, India Proofs, 21*s*.

Blake (William):

Etchings from his Works. By W B SCOTT. With descriptive Text. *" The best side of Blake's work is given here, and makes a really attractive volume, which all can enjoy   The etching is of the best kind, more refined and delicate than the original work."*—SATURDAY REVIEW

Crown 8vo, cloth extra, gilt, with Illustrations, 7*s*. 6*d*.

Boccaccio's Decameron;

or, Ten Days' Entertainment. Translated into English, with an Introduction by THOMAS WRIGHT, Esq , M.A., F.S.A. With Portrait, and STOTHARD'S beautiful Copperplates.

Bowers' (G.) Hunting Sketches:

Canters in Crampshire. By G. BOWERS. I. Gallops from Gorseborough. II. Scrambles with Scratch Packs III Studies with Stag Hounds Oblong 4to, half-bound boards, 21s.

Leaves from a Hunting Journal. By G. BOWERS. Coloured in facsimile of the originals. Oblong 4to, half-bound, 21s.

Crown 8vo, cloth extra, gilt, 7s. 6d.

Brand's Observations on Popular Antiquities,

chiefly Illustrating the Origin of our Vulgar Customs, Ceremonies, and Superstitions. With the Additions of Sir HENRY ELLIS. An entirely New and Revised Edition, with fine full-page Illustrations.

Bret Harte, Works by:

Bret Harte's Collected Works. Arranged and Revised by the Author. Complete in Five Vols , crown 8vo, cloth extra, 6s each.

Vol I. COMPLETE POETICAL AND DRAMATIC WORKS. With Steel Plate Portrait, and an Introduction by the Author

Vol. II. EARLIER PAPERS—LUCK OF ROARING CAMP, and other Sketches—BOHEMIAN PAPERS—SPANISH and AMERICAN LEGENDS.

Vol. III TALES OF THE ARGONAUTS—EASTERN SKETCHES.

Vol IV. GABRIEL CONROY.

Vol. V. STORIES—CONDENSED NOVELS, &c.

The Select Works of Bret Harte, in Prose and Poetry. With Introductory Essay by J. M BELLEW, Portrait of the Author, and 50 Illustrations Crown 8vo, cloth extra, 7s. 6d.

An Heiress of Red Dog, and other Stories. By BRET HARTE. Post 8vo, illustrated boards, 2s : cloth limp, 2s. 6d.

The Twins of Table Mountain. By BRET HARTE. Fcap. 8vo, picture cover, 1s , crown 8vo, cloth extra, 3s. 6d.

The Luck of Roaring Camp, and other Sketches. By BRET HARTE Post 8vo, illustrated boards, 2s

Jeff Briggs's Love Story. By BRET HARTE. Fcap. 8vo, picture cover, 1s. ; cloth extra, 2s. 6d.

Small crown 8vo, cloth extra, gilt, with full-page Portraits, 4s. 6d.

Brewster's (Sir David) Martyrs of Science.

Small crown 8vo, cloth extra, gilt, with Astronomical Plates, 4s. 6d.

Brewster's (Sir D.) More Worlds than One,

the Creed of the Philosopher and the Hope of the Christian.

THE STOTHARD BUNYAN —Crown 8vo, cloth extra, gilt, 7s. 6d.

Bunyan's Pilgrim's Progress.

Edited by Rev. T. SCOTT. With 17 beautiful Steel Plates by STOTHARD, engraved by GOODALL ; and numerous Woodcuts

Demy 8vo, cloth extra, 7s 6d.

Burton's The Anatomy of Melancholy:

What it is , its Kinds, Causes, Symptoms, Prognostics, and several Cures of it In Three Partitions , with their several Sections, Members, and Sub-sections, Philosophically, Medically, and Historically Opened and Cut-up A New Edition, corrected and enriched by Translations of the Classical Extracts   [*In the press.*

Crown 8vo, cloth extra, gilt, with Illustrations, 7s. 6d.

Byron's Letters and Journals.

With Notices of his Life. By THOMAS MOORE. A Reprint of the Original Edition, newly revised, with Twelve full-page Plates

Demy 8vo, cloth extra, 14s.

Campbell's (Sir G.) White and Black:

The Outcome of a Visit to the United States. By Sir GEORGE CAMPBELL, M P.

" *Few persons are likely to take it up without finishing it.*"—NONCONFORMIST.

Post 8vo, cloth extra, 1s 6d

Carlyle (Thomas) On the Choice of Books.

With Portrait and Memoir.

Crown 8vo, cloth extra, 7s 6d.

Century (A) of Dishonour:

A Sketch of the United States Government's Dealings with some of the Indian Tribes.

Small 4to, cloth gilt, with Coloured Illustrations, 10s. 6d.

Chaucer for Children:

A Golden Key. By Mrs. H. R. HAWEIS With Eight Coloured Pictures and numerous Woodcuts by the Author

Demy 8vo, cloth limp, 2s. 6d.

Chaucer for Schools.

By Mrs. HAWEIS, Author of "Chaucer for Children"

" *We hail with pleasure the appearance of Mrs. Haweis's 'Chaucer for Schools Her account of 'Chaucer the Tale-teller' is certainly the pleasantest, chattiest, and at the same time one of the soundest descriptions of the old master his life and works and general surroundings, that have ever been written The chapter cannot be too highly praised*"—ACADEMY

Crown 8vo, cloth extra, gilt, 7s. 6d

Colman's Humorous Works:

"Broad Grins," "My Nightgown and Slippers," and other Humorous Works, Prose and Poetical, of GEORGE COLMAN. With Life by G. B. BUCKSTONE, and Frontispiece by HOGARTH

Conway (Moncure D.), Works by:

Demonology and Devil-Lore. By MONCURE D. CONWAY, M.A. Two Vols , royal 8vo, with 65 Illustrations, 28s

" *A valuable contribution to mythological literature . . There is much good writing, a vast fund of humanity, undeniable earnestness, and a delicate sense of humour, all set forth in pure English.*"—CONTEMPORARY REVIEW

A Necklace of Stories. By MONCURE D. CONWAY, M.A. Illustrated by W. J. HENNESSY Square 8vo, cloth extra, 6s.

" *This delightful 'Necklace of Stories' is inspired with lovely and lofty sentiments* "—ILLUSTRATED LONDON NEWS.

The Wandering Jew, and the Pound of Flesh By MONCURE D. CONWAY, M A Crown 8vo, cloth extra, 4s 6d [In the press

Crown 8vo, cloth limp, with Map and Illustrations, 2s 6d.

Cleopatra's Needle:

Its Acquisition and Removal to England   By Sir J. E ALEXANDER.

Demy 8vo, cloth extra, with Coloured Illustrations and Maps, 24s.

Cope's History of the Rifle Brigade

(The Prince Consort's Own), formerly the 95th.   By Sir WILLIAM H. COPE, formerly Lieutenant, Rifle Brigade.

Crown 8vo, cloth extra, 7s. 6d.

Cornwall.—Popular Romances of the West

of England ; or, The Drolls, Traditions, and Superstitions of Old Cornwall. Collected and Edited by ROBERT HUNT, F.R.S   New and Revised Edition, with Additions, and Two Steel-plate Illustrations by GEORGE CRUIKSHANK

Crown 8vo, cloth extra, gilt, with 13 Portraits, 7s. 6d.

Creasy's Memoirs of Eminent Etonians;

with Notices of the Early History of Eton College.   By Sir EDWARD CREASY, Author of "The Fifteen Decisive Battles of the World."

Crown 8vo, cloth extra, with Etched Frontispiece, 7s. 6d.

Credulities, Past and Present.

By WILLIAM JONES, F.S.A, Author of "Finger-Ring Lore," &c.

Two Vols., demy 4to, handsomely bound in half-morocco, gilt, profusely Illustrated with Coloured and Plain Plates and Woodcuts, price £7 7s.

Cyclopædia of Costume;

or, A Dictionary of Dress—Regal, Ecclesiastical, Civil, and Military— from the Earliest Period in England to the reign of George the Third, Including Notices of Contemporaneous Fashions on the Continent, and a General History of the Costumes of the Principal Countries of Europe   By J. R PLANCHÉ, Somerset Herald.

The Volumes may also be had *separately* (each Complete in itself) at £3 13s.6d. each:

Vol. I. THE DICTIONARY

Vol. II. A GENERAL HISTORY OF COSTUME IN EUROPE

Also in 25 Parts, at 5s. each.   Cases for binding, 5s. each.

"*A comprehensive and highly valuable book of reference   . . .   We have rarely failed to find in this book an account of an article of dress, while in most of the entries curious and instructive details are given.   . . .   Mr. Planché's enormous labour of love, the production of a text which, whether in its dictionary form or in that of the 'General History,' is within its intended scope immeasurably the best and richest work on Costume in English   . . .   This book is not only one of the most readable works of the kind, but intrinsically attractive and amusing.*"—ATHENÆUM.

"*A most readable and interesting work—and it can scarcely be consulted in vain, whether the reader is in search for information as to military, court, ecclesiastical, legal, or professional costume.   . . .   All the chromo-lithographs, and most of the woodcut illustrations—the latter amounting to several thousands —are very elaborately executed; and the work forms a livre de luxe which renders it especially suited to the library and the ladies' drawing-room.*"—TIMES.

NEW WORK by the AUTHOR OF "PRIMITIVE MANNERS
AND CUSTOMS."—Crown 8vo, cloth extra, 6s.

Crimes and Punishments.

Including a New Translation of Beccaria's " Dei Delitti e delle Pene."
By JAMES ANSON FARRER.

Crown 8vo, cloth gilt, Two very thick Volumes, 7s 6d. each.

Cruikshank's Comic Almanack.

Complete in TWO SERIES: The FIRST from 1835 to 1843; the SECOND
from 1844 to 1853   A Gathering of the BEST HUMOUR of
THACKERAY, HOOD, MAYHEW, ALBERT SMITH, A'BECKETT,
ROBERT BROUGH, &c   With 2,000 Woodcuts and Steel Engravings
by CRUIKSHANK, HINE, LANDELLS, &c.

Square 8vo, cloth gilt, profusely Illustrated.

Dickens.—About England with Dickens.

With Illustrations by ALFRED RIMMER and CHARLES A VANDER-
HOOF.   [In preparation

Second Edition, revised and enlarged, demy 8vo, cloth extra,
with Illustrations, 24s.

Dodge's (Colonel) The Hunting Grounds of

the Great West : A Description of the Plains, Game, and Indians of
the Great North American Desert   By RICHARD IRVING DODGE,
Lieutenant-Colonel of the United States Army.   With an Introduction
by WILLIAM BLACKMORE ; Map, and numerous Illustrations drawn
by ERNEST GRISET

Demy 8vo, cloth extra, 12s. 6d.

Doran's Memories of our Great Towns.

With Anecdotic Gleanings concerning their Worthies and their
Oddities. By Dr. JOHN DORAN, F.S.A.

Two Vols., crown 8vo, cloth extra, 21s.

Drury Lane (Old) :

Fifty Years' Recollections of Author, Actor, and Manager.   By
EDWARD STIRLING.

"*Mr Stirling's two volumes of theatrical recollections contain, apart from
the interest of his own early experiences, when the London stage was a very different thing from what it now is, a quantity of amusing and interesting facts and
anecdotes, new and old. The book is one which may be taken up in a spare quarter
of an hour or half-hour with a tolerable certainty of lighting upon something of
interest*"—SATURDAY REVIEW.

Demy 8vo, cloth, 16s.

Dutt's India, Past and Present;

with Minor Essays on Cognate Subjects. By SHOSHEE CHUNDER
DUTT, Rai Báhádoor.

Crown 8vo, cloth boards, 6s. per Volume.

Early English Poets.

Edited, with Introductions and Annotations, by Rev. A. B. GROSART.

"Mr. Grosart has spent the most laborious and the most enthusiastic care on the perfect restoration and preservation of the text. . . From Mr. Grosart we always expect and always receive the final results of most patient and competent scholarship."—EXAMINER.

1. **Fletcher's (Giles, B D.) Complete Poems:** Christ's Victorie in Heaven, Christ's Victorie on Earth, Christ's Triumph over Death, and Minor Poems. With Memorial-Introduction and Notes   One Vol.

2. **Davies' (Sir John) Complete Poetical Works,** including Psalms I to L. in Verse, and other hitherto Unpublished MSS, for the first time Collected and Edited. Memorial-Introduction and Notes. Two Vols

3. **Herrick's (Robert) Hesperides,** Noble Numbers, and Complete Collected Poems. With Memorial-Introduction and Notes, Steel Portrait, Index of First Lines, and Glossarial Index, &c. Three Vols.

4. **Sidney's (Sir Philip) Complete Poetical Works,** including all those in "Arcadia" With Portrait, Memorial-Introduction, Essay on the Poetry of Sidney, and Notes. Three Vols.

Imperial 8vo, with 147 fine Engravings, half-morocco, 36s.

Early Teutonic, Italian, and French Masters

(The). Translated and Edited from the Dohme Series, by A. H. KEANE, M A I   With numerous Illustrations

"Cannot fail to be of the utmost use to students of art history"—TIMES.

Crown 8vo, cloth extra, gilt, with Illustrations, 6s.

Emanuel On Diamonds and Precious

Stones ; their History, Value, and Properties ; with Simple Tests for ascertaining their Reality. By HARRY EMANUEL, F.R.G.S. With numerous Illustrations, Tinted and Plain.

Demy 4to, cloth extra, with Illustrations, 36s.

Emanuel and Grego.—A History of the Gold-

smith's and Jeweller's Art in all Ages and in all Countries   By E. EMANUEL and JOSEPH GREGO. With numerous fine Engravings.
[*In preparation.*

Crown 8vo, cloth extra, with Illustrations, 7s. 6d.

Englishman's House, The:

A Practical Guide to all interested in Selecting or Building a House, with full Estimates of Cost, Quantities, &c.   By C. J. RICHARDSON. Third Edition. With nearly 600 Illustrations

Crown 8vo, cloth extra, 6s

Evolutionist (The) At Large.

By GRANT ALLEN.

" Mr. Allen's method of treatment, as explanatory of the scientific revolution known as evolution, gives a sort of personality and human character to the front of the strawberry blossom, which invests them with additional charm, and makes many of his pages read more like a fanciful fairy tale than a scientific work . . . Mr. Allen's essays ought to open many a half-closed eye."—MANCHESTER EXAMINER.

Crown 8vo, cloth extra, with nearly 300 Illustrations, 7s. 6d.

Evolution (Chapters on);

A Popular History of the Darwinian and Allied Theories of Development. By ANDREW WILSON, Ph D., F.R S Edin. &c. [*In preparation.*

Abstract of Contents —The Problem Stated—Sketch of the Rise and Progress of Evolution—What Evolution is and what it is not—The Evidence for Evolution—Evidence from Development—Evidence from Rudimentary Organs—Evidence from Geographical Distribution—Evidence from Geology—Evolution and Environments—Flowers and their Fertilisation and Development—Evolution and Degeneration—Evolution and Ethics—The Relations of Evolution to Ethics and Theology, &c. &c.

Two Vols., crown 8vo, cloth extra, 21s.

Ewald.—Stories from the State Papers.

By ALEX. CHARLES EWALD [*In preparation.*

Folio, cloth extra, £1 11s. 6d.

Examples of Contemporary Art.

Etchings from Representative Works by living English and Foreign Artists. Edited, with Critical Notes, by J. COMYNS CARR.

"*It would not be easy to meet with a more sumptuous, and at the same time a more tasteful and instructive drawing-room book.*"—NONCONFORMIST.

Crown 8vo, cloth extra, with Illustrations, 6s.

Fairholt's Tobacco :

Its History and Associations ; with an Account of the Plant and its Manufacture, and its Modes of Use in all Ages and Countries. By F. W. FAIRHOLT, F.S.A. With Coloured Frontispiece and upwards of 100 Illustrations by the Author.

Crown 8vo, cloth extra, with Illustrations, 4s. 6d.

Faraday's Chemical History of a Candle.

Lectures delivered to a Juvenile Audience. A New Edition. Edited by W. CROOKES, F.C S. With numerous Illustrations.

Crown 8vo, cloth extra, with Illustrations, 4s. 6d.

Faraday's Various Forces of Nature.

New Edition. Edited by W. CROOKES. F.C.S. Numerous Illustrations.

Crown 8vo, cloth extra, with Illustrations, 7s. 6d.

Finger-Ring Lore :

Historical, Legendary, and Anecdotal. By WM JONES, F S.A. With Hundreds of Illustrations of Curious Rings of all Ages and Countries.

"*One of those gossiping books which are as full of amusement as of instruction.*"—ATHENÆUM.

NEW NOVEL BY JUSTIN McCARTHY.

Gentleman's Magazine for January, 1881,

Price One Shilling, contained the First Chapters of a New Novel entitled "THE COMET OF A SEASON," by JUSTIN McCARTHY, M.P., Author of "A History of Our Own Times," "Dear Lady Disdain," &c SCIENCE NOTES, by W. MATTIEU WILLIAMS, F.R A.S , will also be continued Monthly

** *Now ready, the Volume for* JULY *to* DECEMBER, 1880, *cloth extra, price* 8s. 6d.; *and Cases for binding, price* 2s. *each.*

THE RUSKIN GRIMM.—Square 8vo, cloth extra, 6s. 6d. ;
gilt edges, 7s. 6d.

German Popular Stories.

Collected by the Brothers GRIMM, and Translated by EDGAR TAYLOR.
Edited with an Introduction by JOHN RUSKIN. With 22 Illustrations
after the inimitable designs of GEORGE CRUIKSHANK. Both Series
Complete.

"*The illustrations of this volume . . . are of quite sterling and admirable
art, of a class precisely parallel in elevation to the character of the tales which
they illustrate; and the original etchings, as I have before said in the Appendix to
my 'Elements of Drawing,' were unrivalled in masterfulness of touch since Rem-
brandt (in some qualities of delineation, unrivalled even by him). . . To make
somewhat enlarged copies of them, looking at them through a magnifying glass,
and never putting two lines where Cruikshank has put only one, would be an exercise in decision and severe drawing which would leave afterwards little to be learnt
in schools.*"—*Extract from Introduction by* JOHN RUSKIN.

Post 8vo, cloth limp, 2s. 6d.

Glenny's A Year's Work in Garden and

Greenhouse Practical Advice to Amateur Gardeners as to the Management of the Flower, Fruit, and Frame Garden. By GEORGE GLENNY.

"*A great deal of valuable information, conveyed in very simple language. The
amateur need not wish for a better guide*"—LEEDS MERCURY.

Crown 8vo, cloth gilt and gilt edges, 7s. 6d.

Golden Treasury of Thought, The:

An ENCYCLOPÆDIA OF QUOTATIONS from Writers of all Times and
Countries. Selected and Edited by THEODORE TAYLOR.

New and Cheaper Edition, demy 8vo, cloth extra, with Illustrations, 7s. 6d.

Greeks and Romans, The Life of the,

Described from Antique Monuments. By ERNST GUHL and W.
KONER Translated from the Third German Edition, and Edited by
Dr. F. HUEFFER. With 545 Illustrations.

Crown 8vo, cloth extra, gilt, with Illustrations, 7s. 6d.

Greenwood's Low-Life Deeps:

An Account of the Strange Fish to be found there. By JAMES GREEN-
WOOD. With Illustrations in tint by ALFRED CONCANEN.

Crown 8vo, cloth extra, gilt, with Illustrations, 7s. 6d.

Greenwood's Wilds of London:

Descriptive Sketches, from Personal Observations and Experience, of
Remarkable Scenes, People, and Places in London. By JAMES GREEN-
WOOD With 12 Tinted Illustrations by ALFRED CONCANEN.

Crown 8vo, cloth extra, gilt, with Illustrations, 4s. 6d.

Guyot's Earth and Man;

or, Physical Geography in its Relation to the History of Mankind.
With Additions by Professors AGASSIZ, PIERCE, and GRAY ; 12 Maps
and Engravings on Steel, some Coloured, and copious Index.

Square 16mo (Tauchnitz size), cloth extra, 2s. per volume.

Golden Library, The :

Ballad History of England. By W. C. BENNETT.

Bayard Taylor's Diversions of the Echo Club.

Byron's Don Juan.

Emerson's Letters and Social Aims.

Godwin's (William) Lives of the Necromancers.

Holmes's Autocrat of the Breakfast Table. With an Introduction by G. A. SALA.

Holmes's Professor at the Breakfast Table.

Hood's Whims and Oddities. Complete. With all the original Illustrations.

Irving's (Washington) Tales of a Traveller.

Irving's (Washington) Tales of the Alhambra.

Jesse's (Edward) Scenes and Occupations of Country Life.

Lamb's Essays of Elia. Both Series Complete in One Vol.

Leigh Hunt's Essays : A Tale for a Chimney Corner, and other Pieces. With Portrait, and Introduction by EDMUND OLLIER.

Mallory's (Sir Thomas) Mort d'Arthur : The Stories of King Arthur and of the Knights of the Round Table. Edited by B. MONTGOMERIE RANKING.

Pascal's Provincial Letters. A New Translation, with Historical Introduction and Notes, by T M'CRIE, D.D.

Pope's Poetical Works. Complete.

Rochefoucauld's Maxims and Moral Reflections. With Notes, and an Introductory Essay by SAINTE-BEUVE.

St. Pierre's Paul and Virginia, and The Indian Cottage Edited, with Life, by the Rev. E CLARKE.

Shelley's Early Poems, and Queen Mab, with Essay by LEIGH HUNT.

Shelley's Later Poems : Laon and Cythna, &c.

Shelley's Posthumous Poems, the Shelley Papers, &c

Shelley's Prose Works, including A Refutation of Deism, Zastrozzi, St Irvyne, &c.

White's Natural History of Selborne. Edited, with additions, by THOMAS BROWN, F L S.

Hake (Dr. Thomas Gordon), Poems by :

Maiden Ecstasy. Small 4to, cloth extra, 8s.
New Symbols. Crown 8vo, cloth extra, 6s
Legends of the Morrow Crown 8vo, cloth extra, 6s.

Medium 8vo, cloth extra, gilt, with Illustrations, 7s. 6d.

Hall's (Mrs. S. C.) Sketches of Irish Character.

With numerous Illustrations on Steel and Wood by MACLISE, GILBERT, HARVEY, and G. CRUIKSHANK.

"*The Irish Sketches of this lady resemble Miss Mitford's beautiful English sketches in 'Our Village,' but they are far more vigorous and picturesque and bright*"—BLACKWOOD'S MAGAZINE.

Post 8vo, cloth extra, 4s. 6d., a few large-paper copies, half-Roxb., 10s. 6d.

Handwriting, The Philosophy of.

By Don FELIX DE SALAMANCA. With 134 Facsimiles of Signatures.

Haweis (Mrs.), Works by :

The Art of Dress   By Mrs. H. R. HAWEIS. Illustrated by the
Author. Small 8vo, illustrated cover, 1s. ; cloth limp, 1s. 6d.

*" A well-considered attempt to apply canons of good taste to the costumes
of ladies of our time. . . . . Mrs. Haweis writes frankly and to the
point, she does not mince matters, but boldly remonstrates with her own sex
on the follies they indulge in. . . . . We may recommend the book to the
ladies whom it concerns."*—ATHENÆUM.

The Art of Beauty. By Mrs. H. R. HAWEIS. Square 8vo,
cloth extra, gilt, gilt edges, with Coloured Frontispiece and nearly 100
Illustrations, 10s 6d.

The Art of Decoration. By Mrs. H. R. HAWEIS. Small 4to,
handsomely bound and profusely Illustrated, 10s. 6d.   [*In the press.*

*** *See also* CHAUCER, *p. 5 of this Catalogue*

SPECIMENS OF MODERN POETS.—Crown 8vo, cloth extra, 6s.

Heptalogia (The); or, The Seven against Sense.

A Cap with Seven Bells.

*" Of really good parodies it would be difficult to name more than half-a-dozen
outside the 'Anti-Jacobin,' the 'Rejected Addresses,' and the 'Ballads of Bon
Gaultier' .   .   It is no slight praise to say that the volume before us bears
comparison with these celebrated collections . . . But the merits of the book
cannot be fairly estimated by means of a few extracts ; it should be read at length
to be appreciated properly, and, in our opinion, its merits entitle it to be very
widely read indeed "*—ST JAMES'S GAZETTE.

Cr 8vo, bound in parchment, 8s ; Large-Paper copies (only 50 printed), 15s.

Herbert.—The Poems of Lord Herbert of

Cherbury. Edited, with an Introduction, by J. CHURTON COLLINS
[*In the press.*

History of Hertfordshire.

By JOHN EDWIN CUSSANS.

This Magnificent Work, ranging with the highest class of County
Histories, the result of many years' labour, is now completed, and in course
of delivery to Subscribers

It is comprised in Eight Parts, imperial quarto, each containing the
complete History of one of the Eight Hundreds into which the County is
divided, with separate Pagination, Title, and Index. Each Part contains
about 350 pages, and is printed in the most careful manner on fine paper,
with full-page Plates on Steel and Stone, and a profusion of smaller Engravings on Wood of objects of interest in the County, and the Arms of
the principal Landowners, together with elaborate Pedigrees (126 in all),
now for the first time printed

The price to Subscribers is Two Guineas each complete Part. Purchasers are guaranteed the possession of a work of constantly increasing
value by the fact that only three hundred and fifty copies are printed, the
greater number of which are already subscribed for.

Seventy-five copies only, numbered and signed by the Author, have
been specially printed on Large Paper (Royal Folio), price Four Guineas
each Part.

Complete in Four Vols., demy 8vo, cloth extra, 12s. each.

History of Our Own Times, from the Accession
of Queen Victoria to the General Election of 1880. By JUSTIN
McCARTHY, M P.

*"Criticism is disarmed before a composition which provokes little but approval.
This is a really good book on a really interesting subject, and words piled on words
could say no more for it."*—SATURDAY REVIEW.

Crown 8vo, cloth extra, 5s

Hobhouse's The Dead Hand:
Addresses on the subject of Endowments and Settlements of Property.
By Sir ARTHUR HOBHOUSE. Q C , K C.S I

Crown 8vo, cloth extra, 4s. 6d.

Hollingshead's (John) Plain English.
*" I anticipate immense entertainment from the perusal of Mr Hollingshead's
'Plain English,' which I imagined to be a philological work, but which I find to
be a series of essays, in the Hollingsheadian or Sledge-Hammer style, on those
matters theatrical with which he is so eminently conversant."*—G. A. S. in the
ILLUSTRATED LONDON NEWS.

Crown 8vo, cloth limp, with Illustrations, 2s. 6d.

Holmes's The Science of Voice Production
and Voice Preservation : A Popular Manual for the Use of Speakers
and Singers By GORDON HOLMES, L.R C.P.E.

Crown 8vo, cloth extra, gilt, 7s. 6d.

Hood's (Thomas) Choice Works,
In Prose and Verse. Including the CREAM OF THE COMIC ANNUALS.
With Life of the Author, Portrait, and Two Hundred Illustrations.

Square crown 8vo, cloth extra, gilt edges, 6s.

Hood's (Tom) From Nowhere to the North
Pole : A Noah's Arkæological Narrative. With 25 Illustrations by
W. BRUNTON and E. C. BARNES.

*" The amusing letterpress is profusely interspersed with the jingling rhymes
which children love and learn so easily Messrs Brunton and Barnes do full
justice to the writer's meaning, and a pleasanter result of the harmonious co-
operation of author and artist could not be desired "*—TIMES.

Crown 8vo, cloth extra, gilt, 7s. 6d.

Hook's (Theodore) Choice Humorous Works,
including his Ludicrous Adventures, Bons-mots, Puns, and Hoaxes.
With a new Life of the Author, Portraits, Facsimiles, and Illustrations.

Crown 8vo, cloth extra, 7s.

Horne's Orion:
An Epic Poem in Three Books By RICHARD HENGIST HORNE.
With a brief Commentary by the Author. With Photographic Portrait
from a Medallion by SUMMERS. Tenth Edition.

Crown 8vo, cloth extra, 7s. 6d.

Howell's Conflicts of Capital and Labour

Historically and Economically considered. Being a History and Review of the Trade Unions of Great Britain, showing their Origin, Progress, Constitution, and Objects, in their Political, Social, Economical, and Industrial Aspects. By GEORGE HOWELL.

"*This book is an attempt, and on the whole a successful attempt, to place the work of trade unions in the past, and their objects in the future, fairly before the public from the working man's point of view.*"—PALL MALL GAZETTE.

Demy 8vo, cloth extra, 12s. 6d.

Hueffer's The Troubadours:

A History of Provencal Life and Literature in the Middle Ages. By FRANCIS HUEFFER.

Crown 8vo, cloth extra, 6s.

Janvier.—Practical Keramics for Students.

By C. A. JANVIER

"*Will be found a useful handbook by those who wish to try the manufacture or decoration of pottery, and may be studied by all who desire to know something of the art*"—MORNING POST.

A NEW EDITION, Revised and partly Re-written, with several New Chapters and Illustrations, crown 8vo, cloth extra, 7s. 6d.

Jennings' The Rosicrucians:

Their Rites and Mysteries. With Chapters on the Ancient Fire and Serpent Worshippers By HARGRAVE JENNINGS. With Five full-page Plates and upwards of 300 Illustrations.

Jerrold (Tom), Works by:

Our Kitchen Garden · The Plants we Grow, and How we Cook Them. By TOM JERROLD, Author of "The Garden that Paid the Rent," &c. Post 8vo, cloth limp, 2s 6d

"*The combination of hints on cookery with gardening has been very cleverly carried out, and the result is an interesting and highly instructive little work. Mr Jerrold is correct in saying that English people do not make half the use of vegetables they might; and by showing how easily they can be grown, and so obtained fresh, he is doing a great deal to make them more popular.*"—DAILY CHRONICLE.

Household Horticulture: A Gossip about Flowers. By TOM JERROLD Post 8vo, cloth limp, 2s 6d   [*In the press.*

Two Vols. 8vo, with 52 Illustrations and Maps, cloth extra, gilt, 14s.

Josephus, The Complete Works of.

Translated by WHISTON. Containing both "The Antiquities of the Jews" and "The Wars of the Jews"

Small 8vo, cloth, full gilt, gilt edges, with Illustrations, 6s.

Kavanaghs' Pearl Fountain,

And other Fairy Stories. By BRIDGET and JULIA KAVANAGH. With Thirty Illustrations by J. MOYR SMITH.

"*Genuine new fairy stories of the old type, some of them as delightful as the best of Grimm's 'German Popular Stories.' . . . . For the most part the stories are downright, thorough-going fairy stories of the most admirable kind. . . . Mr. Moyr Smith's illustrations, too, are admirable*"—SPECTATOR.

Crown 8vo, illustrated boards, with numerous Plates, 2s. 6d.

Lace (Old Point), and How to Copy and

Imitate it. By DAISY WATERHOUSE HAWKINS. With 17 Illustrations by the Author.

Crown 8vo, cloth extra, gilt, with Portraits, 7s. 6d.

Lamb's Complete Works,

In Prose and Verse, reprinted from the Original Editions, with many Pieces hitherto unpublished. Edited, with Notes and Introduction, by R. H. SHEPHERD. With Two Portraits and Facsimile of a Page of the "Essay on Roast Pig."

"*A complete edition of Lamb's writings, in prose and verse, has long been wanted, and is now supplied. The editor appears to have taken great pains to bring together Lamb's scattered contributions, and his collection contains a number of pieces which are now reproduced for the first time since their original appearance in various old periodicals.*"—SATURDAY REVIEW.

Crown 8vo, cloth extra, with numerous Illustrations, 10s. 6d.

Lamb (Mary and Charles):

Their Poems, Letters, and Remains. With Reminiscences and Notes by W. CAREW HAZLITT. With HANCOCK's Portrait of the Essayist, Facsimiles of the Title-pages of the rare First Editions of Lamb's and Coleridge's Works, and numerous Illustrations.

"*Very many passages will delight those fond of literary trifles; hardly any portion will fail in interest for lovers of Charles Lamb and his sister.*"—STANDARD.

Small 8vo, cloth extra, 5s.

Lamb's Poetry for Children, and Prince

Dorus. Carefully Reprinted from unique copies.

"*The quaint and delightful little book, over the recovery of which all the hearts of his lovers are yet warm with rejoicing.*"—A. C. SWINBURNE.

Demy 8vo, cloth extra, with Maps and Illustrations, 18s.

Lamont's Yachting in the Arctic Seas;

or, Notes of Five Voyages of Sport and Discovery in the Neighbourhood of Spitzbergen and Novaya Zemlya. By JAMES LAMONT, F.R.G.S. With numerous full-page Illustrations by Dr. LIVESAY.

"*After wading through numberless volumes of icy fiction, concocted narrative, and spurious biography of Arctic voyagers, it is pleasant to meet with a real and genuine volume. . . . He shows much tact in recounting his adventures, and they are so interspersed with anecdotes and information as to make them anything but wearisome. . . . The book, as a whole, is the most important addition made to our Arctic literature for a long time.*"—ATHENÆUM.

Crown 8vo, cloth, full gilt, 7s. 6d.

Latter-Day Lyrics:

Poems of Sentiment and Reflection by Living Writers; selected and arranged, with Notes, by W. DAVENPORT ADAMS. With a Note on some Foreign Forms of Verse, by AUSTIN DOBSON.

Crown 8vo, cloth extra, 6*s.*

Lares and Penates;

Or, The Background of Life. By FLORENCE CADDY.

" *The whole book is well worth reading, for it is full of practical suggestions.
. . . . We hope nobody will be deterred from taking up a book which teaches a
good deal about sweetening poor lives as well as giving grace to wealthy ones.*"—
GRAPHIC.

Crown 8vo, cloth, full gilt, 6*s.*

Leigh's A Town Garland.

By HENRY S. LEIGH, Author of "Carols of Cockayne."

"*If Mr Leigh's verse survive to a future generation—and there is no reason
why that honour should not be accorded productions so delicate, so finished, and so
full of humour—their author will probably be remembered as the Poet of the
Strand.*"—ATHENÆUM

SECOND EDITION.—Crown 8vo, cloth extra, with Illustrations, 6*s.*

Leisure-Time Studies, chiefly Biological.

By ANDREW WILSON, F.R.S.E , Lecturer on Zoology and Comparative Anatomy in the Edinburgh Medical School.

"*It is well when we can take up the work of a really qualified investigator,
who in the intervals of his more serious professional labours sets himself to impart
knowledge in such a simple and elementary form as may attract and instruct,
with no danger of misleading the tyro in natural science. Such a work is this
little volume made up of essays and addresses written and delivered by Dr.
Andrew Wilson, lecturer and examiner in science at Edinburgh and Glasgow, at
leisure intervals in a busy professional life . . Dr. Wilson's pages teem with
matter stimulating to a healthy love of science and a reverence for the truths
of nature.*"—SATURDAY REVIEW.

Crown 8vo, cloth extra, with Illustrations, 7*s.* 6*d.*

Life in London;

or, The History of Jerry Hawthorn and Corinthian Tom. With the
whole of CRUIKSHANK'S Illustrations, in Colours, after the Originals.

Crown 8vo, cloth extra, 6*s.*

Lights on the Way:

Some Tales within a Tale   By the late J. H. ALEXANDER, B.A.
Edited, with an Explanatory Note, by H. A. PAGE, Author of
"Thoreau : A Study."

Crown 8vo, cloth extra, with Illustrations, 7*s* 6*d.*

Longfellow's Complete Prose Works.

Including "Outre Mer," "Hyperion," " Kavanagh," "The Poets
and Poetry of Europe," and "Driftwood." With Portrait and Illustrations by VALENTINE BROMLEY.

Crown 8vo, cloth extra, gilt, with Illustrations, 7*s.* 6*d.*

Longfellow's Poetical Works.

Carefully Reprinted from the Original Editions.   With numerous
fine Illustrations on Steel and Wood.

Crown 8vo, cloth extra, 5s.

Lunatic Asylum, My Experiences in a.

By a SANE PATIENT.

*" The story is clever and interesting, sad beyond measure though the subject
be. There is no personal bitterness, and no violence or anger. Whatever may
have been the evidence for our author's madness when he was consigned to an
asylum, nothing can be clearer than his sanity when he wrote this book; it is
bright, calm, and to the point."*—SPECTATOR.

Demy 8vo, with Fourteen full-page Plates, cloth boards, 18s.

Lusiad (The) of Camoens.

Translated into English Spenserian verse by ROBERT FFRENCH DUFF,
Knight Commander of the Portuguese Royal Order of Christ.

Macquoid (Mrs.), Works by:

In the Ardennes. By KATHARINE S. MACQUOID. With
50 fine Illustrations by THOMAS R MACQUOID. Uniform with " Pictures
and Legends " Square 8vo, cloth extra, 10s. 6d.

*" This is another of Mrs. Macquoid's pleasant books of travel, full of useful
information, of picturesque descriptions of scenery, and of quaint traditions
respecting the various monuments and ruins which she encounters in her
tour . To such of our readers as are already thinking about the year's
holiday, we strongly recommend the perusal of Mrs Macquoid's experiences
The book is well illustrated by Mr. Thomas R Macquoid "*—GRAPHIC.

Pictures and Legends from Normandy and Brittany By
KATHARINE S. MACQUOID With numerous Illustrations by THOMAS R.
MACQUOID. Square 8vo, cloth gilt, 10s 6d.

*" Mr. and Mrs Macquoid have been strolling in Normandy and Brittany,
and the result of their observations and researches in that picturesque land
of romantic associations is an attractive volume, which is neither a work of
travel nor a collection of stories, but a book partaking almost in equal degree
of each of these characters. . . . The illustrations, which are numerous,
are drawn, as a rule, with remarkable delicacy as well as with true artistic
feeling "*—DAILY NEWS.

Through Normandy. By KATHARINE S. MACQUOID. With
90 Illustrations by T. R. MACQUOID. Square 8vo, cloth extra, 7s 6d

*" One of the few books which can be read as a piece of literature, whilst at
the same time handy in the knapsack."*—BRITISH QUARTERLY REVIEW.

Through Brittany. By KATHARINE S. MACQUOID. With
numerous Illustrations by T R MACQUOID. Sq 8vo, cloth extra, 7s. 6d.

*" The pleasant companionship which Mrs Macquoid offers, while wander-
ing from one point of interest to another, seems to throw a renewed charm
around each oft-depicted scene "*—MORNING POST

Crown 8vo, cloth extra, with Illustrations, 2s. 6d.

Madre Natura v. The Moloch of Fashion.

By LUKE LIMNER. With 32 Illustrations by the Author. FOURTH
EDITION, revised and enlarged.

Handsomely printed in facsimile, price 5s.

Magna Charta.

An exact Facsimile of the Original Document in the British Museum,
printed on fine plate paper, nearly 3 feet long by 2 feet wide, with the
Arms and Seals emblazoned in Gold and Colours

Mallock's (W. H.) Works:

Is Life Worth Living? By WILLIAM HURRELL MALLOCK.
New Edition, crown 8vo, cloth extra, 6s

"*This deeply interesting volume. . . . . It is the most powerful vindication of religion, both natural and revealed, that has appeared since Bishop Butler wrote, and is much more useful than either the Analogy or the Sermons of that great divine, as a refutation of the peculiar form assumed by the infidelity of the present day. . . . . Deeply philosophical as the book is, there is not a heavy page in it. The writer is 'possessed,' so to speak, with his great subject, has sounded its depths, surveyed it in all its extent, and brought to bear on it all the resources of a vivid, rich, and impassioned style, as well as an adequate acquaintance with the science, the philosophy, and the literature of the day.*"—IRISH DAILY NEWS

The New Republic; or, Culture, Faith, and Philosophy in an English Country House. By W. H. MALLOCK. Post 8vo, cloth limp, 2s. 6d.

The New Paul and Virginia; or, Positivism on an Island. By W. H. MALLOCK. Post 8vo, cloth limp, 2s. 6d.

Poems. By W. H. MALLOCK. Small 4to, bound in parchment, 8s.

A Romance of the Nineteenth Century. By W. H. MALLOCK
Two Vols., crown 8vo [*In the press.*

Mark Twain's Works:

The Choice Works of Mark Twain. Revised and Corrected throughout by the Author. With Life, Portrait, and numerous Illustrations. Crown 8vo, cloth extra, 7s. 6d.

The Adventures of Tom Sawyer. By MARK TWAIN. With 100 Illustrations. Small 8vo, cloth extra, 7s. 6d. CHEAP EDITION, illustrated boards, 2s

A Pleasure Trip on the Continent of Europe: The Innocents Abroad, and The New Pilgrim's Progress. By MARK TWAIN. Post 8vo, illustrated boards, 2s.

An Idle Excursion, and other Sketches. By MARK TWAIN. Post 8vo, illustrated boards, 2s.

A Tramp Abroad. By MARK TWAIN. With 314 Illustrations. Crown 8vo, cloth extra, 7s. 6d.

"*The fun and tenderness of the conception, of which no living man but Mark Twain is capable, its grace and fantasy and slyness, the wonderful feeling for animals that is manifest in every line, make of all this episode of Jim Baker and his jays a piece of work that is not only delightful as mere reading, but also of a high degree of merit as literature. . . . The book is full of good things, and contains passages and episodes that are equal to the funniest of those that have gone before.*"—ATHENÆUM.

Milton (J. L.), Works by:

The Hygiene of the Skin. A Concise Set of Rules for the Management of the Skin, with Directions for Diet, Wines, Soaps, Baths, &c. By J. L. MILTON, Senior Surgeon to St. John's Hospital. Small 8vo, 1s.; cloth extra, 1s. 6d.

The Bath in Diseases of the Skin. Small 8vo, 1s.; cloth extra, 1s. 6d.

Post 8vo, cloth limp, 2s. 6d. per vol.

Mayfair Library, The:

The New Republic. By W. H. MALLOCK.

The New Paul and Virginia. By W. H. MALLOCK.

The True History of Joshua Davidson. By E. LYNN LINTON.

Old Stories Re-told. By WALTER THORNBURY.

Thoreau: His Life and Aims. By H. A. PAGE.

By Stream and Sea. By WILLIAM SENIOR.

Jeux d'Esprit. Edited by HENRY S. LEIGH.

Puniana. By the Hon. HUGH ROWLEY.

More Puniana. By the Hon. HUGH ROWLEY.

Puck on Pegasus. By H. CHOLMONDELEY-PENNELL.

The Speeches of Charles Dickens. With Chapters on Dickens as Letter-Writer and Public Reader

Muses of Mayfair. Edited by H. CHOLMONDELEY-PENNELL.

Gastronomy as a Fine Art. By BRILLAT-SAVARIN.

Original Plays. W. S. GILBERT.

Carols of Cockayne. By HENRY S. LEIGH

Literary Frivolities, Fancies, Follies, and Frolics. By WILLIAM T. DOBSON.

Pencil and Palette: Biographical Anecdotes chiefly of Contemporary Painters, with Gossip about Pictures Lost, Stolen, and Forged, also Great Picture Sales. By ROBERT KEMPT.

The Book of Clerical Anecdotes A Gathering of the Antiquities, Humours, and Eccentricities of "The Cloth." By JACOB LARWOOD.

The Agony Column of "The Times," from 1800 to 1870 Edited, with an Introduction, by ALICE CLAY.

The Cupboard Papers. By FIN-BEC. [In the press.

Quips and Quiddities. Selected and Edited by W. DAVENPORT ADAMS. [In the press.

Pastimes and Players. By ROBERT MACGREGOR [In the press.

Melancholy Anatomised A Popular Abridgment of "Burton's Anatomy of Melancholy." [In press

* *Other Volumes are in preparation.*

New Novels.

A VILLAGE COMMUNE. By OUIDA. Two Vols.

TEN YEARS' TENANT. By BESANT and RICE Three Vols.

A CONFIDENTIAL AGENT. By JAMES PAYN Three Vols.

A LIFE'S ATONEMENT. By D. C. MURRAY. Three Vols.

QUEEN COPHETUA. By R. E. FRANCILLON. Three Vols.

THE LEADEN CASKET. By Mrs. HUNT. Three Vols

REBEL OF THE FAMILY. By E. L. LINTON. Three Vols

NEW NOVEL BY MRS. LINTON

MY LOVE. By E LYNN LINTON. Three Vols. [In the press.

NEW NOVEL BY JAMES PAYN

FROM EXILE. By JAMES PAYN, Author of "By Proxy," "A Confidential Agent," &c. Three Vols, crown 8vo [In the press.

MR. MALLOCK'S NEW NOVEL

A ROMANCE OF THE NINETEENTH CENTURY. By W H. MALLOCK. Two Vols, crown 8vo. [In the press.

WILKIE COLLINS'S NEW NOVEL.

THE BLACK ROBE. By WILKIE COLLINS. Three Vols. crown 8vo. [In the press

Small 8vo, cloth limp, with Illustrations, 2s. 6d.

Miller's Physiology for the Young;

Or, The House of Life: Human Physiology, with its Applications to the Preservation of Health. For use in Classes and Popular Reading. With numerous Illustrations. By Mrs. F. FENWICK MILLER.

"*An admirable introduction to a subject which all who value health and enjoy life should have at their fingers' ends.*"—ECHO.

Square 8vo, cloth extra, with numerous Illustrations, 7s. 6d.

North Italian Folk.

By Mrs. COMYNS CARR. Illustrated by RANDOLPH CALDECOTT.

"*A delightful book, of a kind which is far too rare. If anyone wants to really know the North Italian folk, we can honestly advise him to omit the journey, and read Mrs Carr's pages instead. . Description with Mrs. Carr is a real gift. . It is rarely that a book is so happily illustrated.*"—CONTEMPORARY REVIEW.

Crown 8vo, cloth extra, with Vignette Portraits, price 6s. per Vol.

Old Dramatists, The:

Ben Jonson's Works.
With Notes, Critical and Explanatory, and a Biographical Memoir by WILLIAM GIFFORD. Edited by Colonel CUNNINGHAM. Three Vols.

Chapman's Works.
Now First Collected. Complete in Three Vols. Vol. I contains the Plays complete, including the doubtful ones; Vol. II. the Poems and Minor Translations, with an Introductory Essay by ALGERNON CHARLES SWINBURNE. Vol. III. the Translations of the Iliad and Odyssey.

Marlowe's Works.
Including his Translations. Edited, with Notes and Introduction, by Col. CUNNINGHAM. One Vol.

Massinger's Plays.
From the Text of WILLIAM GIFFORD. With the addition of the Tragedy of "Believe as you List." Edited by Col. CUNNINGHAM. One Vol.

Crown 8vo, red cloth extra, 5s. each.

Ouida's Novels.—Library Edition.

Held in Bondage.	By OUIDA.	Dog of Flanders.	By OUIDA.
Strathmore.	By OUIDA.	Pascarel.	By OUIDA.
Chandos.	By OUIDA.	Two Wooden Shoes.	By OUIDA.
Under Two Flags.	By OUIDA.	Signa.	By OUIDA.
Idalia.	By OUIDA.	In a Winter City.	By OUIDA.
Cecil Castlemaine.	By OUIDA.	Ariadne.	By OUIDA.
Tricotrin.	By OUIDA.	Friendship.	By OUIDA.
Puck.	By OUIDA.	Moths	By OUIDA.
Folle Farine.	By OUIDA	Pipistrello	By OUIDA.

. Also a Cheap Edition of all but the last two, post 8vo, illustrated boards, 2s each.

Post 8vo, cloth limp, 1s. 6d.

Parliamentary Procedure, A Popular Handbook of. By HENRY W. LUCY

Crown 8vo, cloth extra, with Portrait and Illustrations, 7s. 6d.

Poe's Choice Prose and Poetical Works.

With BAUDELAIRE'S "Essay."

LIBRARY EDITIONS, mostly Illustrated, crown 8vo, cloth extra, 3s 6d. each.

Piccadilly Novels, The.

Popular Stories by the Best Authors.

Maid, Wife, or Widow? By Mrs. ALEXANDER

Ready-Money Mortiboy. By W BESANT and JAMES RICE

My Little Girl. By W. BESANT and JAMES RICE.

The Case of Mr. Lucraft. By W. BESANT and JAMES RICE

This Son of Vulcan. By W. BESANT and JAMES RICE.

With Harp and Crown. By W. BESANT and JAMES RICE

The Golden Butterfly. By W. BESANT and JAMES RICE

By Celia's Arbour. By W BESANT and JAMES RICE

The Monks of Thelema. By W. BESANT and JAMES RICE

'Twas in Trafalgar's Bay. By W BESANT and JAMES RICE

The Seamy Side. By WALTER BESANT and JAMES RICE

Antonina. By WILKIE COLLINS.

Basil. By WILKIE COLLINS.

Hide and Seek. W. COLLINS.

The Dead Secret. W COLLINS

Queen of Hearts. W. COLLINS.

My Miscellanies. W. COLLINS.

The Woman in White. By WILKIE COLLINS

The Moonstone. W COLLINS

Man and Wife. W. COLLINS.

Poor Miss Finch. W. COLLINS.

Miss or Mrs.? By W COLLINS.

The New Magdalen. By WILKIE COLLINS.

The Frozen Deep. W. COLLINS.

The Law and the Lady. By WILKIE COLLINS.

The Two Destinies. By WILKIE COLLINS.

The Haunted Hotel By WILKIE COLLINS.

The Fallen Leaves. By WILKIE COLLINS

Jezebel's Daughter. W. COLLINS.

Deceivers Ever. By Mrs. H. LOVETT CAMERON

Juliet's Guardian. By Mrs. H. LOVETT CAMERON

Felicia M. BETHAM-EDWARDS.

Olympia. By R. E. FRANCILLON.

The Capel Girls. By EDWARD GARRETT.

Robin Gray. CHARLES GIBBON.

For Lack of Gold By CHARLES GIBBON.

In Love and War. By CHARLES GIBBON.

What will the World Say? By CHARLES GIBBON

For the King CHARLES GIBBON.

In Honour Bound By CHARLES GIBBON.

Queen of the Meadow By CHARLES GIBBON

In Pastures Green By CHARLES GIBBON

Under the Greenwood Tree. By THOMAS HARDY

Garth By JULIAN HAWTHORNE.

Ellice Quentin By JULIAN HAWTHORNE

Thornicroft's Model. By Mrs. A W. HUNT.

Fated to be Free By JEAN INGELOW.

Confidence. HENRY JAMES, Jun.

The Queen of Connaught By HARRIETT JAY

The Dark Colleen. By H JAY

Number Seventeen. By HENRY KINGSLEY

Oakshott Castle H. KINGSLEY

Patricia Kemball. By E. LYNN LINTON

PICCADILLY NOVELS—*continued.*

The Atonement of Leam Dundas. By E. LYNN LINTON.

The World Well Lost. By E. LYNN LINTON.

Under which Lord? By E. LYNN LINTON.

With a Silken Thread. By E. LYNN LINTON.

The Waterdale Neighbours. By JUSTIN MCCARTHY.

My Enemy's Daughter. By JUSTIN MCCARTHY.

Linley Rochford. By JUSTIN MCCARTHY.

A Fair Saxon. By JUSTIN MCCARTHY.

Dear Lady Disdain. By JUSTIN MCCARTHY

Miss Misanthrope. By JUSTIN MCCARTHY.

Donna Quixote. By JUSTIN MCCARTHY.

Quaker Cousins. By AGNES MACDONELL.

Lost Rose. By KATHARINE S. MACQUOID.

The Evil Eye. By KATHARINE S. MACQUOID.

Open! Sesame! By FLORENCE MARRYAT.

Written in Fire. F. MARRYAT

Touch and Go. By JEAN MIDDLEMASS.

Whiteladies. Mrs. OLIPHANT.

The Best of Husbands. By JAMES PAYN.

Fallen Fortunes JAMES PAYN.

Halves. By JAMES PAYN.

Walter's Word. JAMES PAYN.

What He Cost Her. J. PAYN.

Less Black than we're Painted. By JAMES PAYN.

By Proxy. By JAMES PAYN.

Under One Roof. JAMES PAYN.

High Spirits. By JAMES PAYN.

Her Mother's Darling. By Mrs. J H RIDDELL.

Bound to the Wheel By JOHN SAUNDERS.

Guy Waterman J. SAUNDERS.

One Against the World. By JOHN SAUNDERS

The Lion in the Path. By JOHN SAUNDERS.

The Way We Live Now. By ANTHONY TROLLOPE.

The American Senator. By ANTHONY TROLLOPE.

Diamond Cut Diamond. By T A TROLLOPE.

Post 8vo, illustrated boards, 2s. each.

Popular Novels, Cheap Editions of.

[WILKIE COLLINS' NOVELS and BESANT and RICE'S NOVELS may also be had in cloth limp at 2s. 6d. *See, too, the* PICCADILLY NOVELS, *for Library Editions.*]

Maid, Wife, or Widow? By Mrs ALEXANDER.

Ready-Money Mortiboy. By WALTER BESANT and JAMES RICE.

With Harp and Crown. By WALTER BESANT and JAMES RICE.

This Son of Vulcan By W. BESANT and JAMES RICE.

My Little Girl. By the same.

The Case of Mr. Lucraft. By WALTER BESANT and JAMES RICE.

The Golden Butterfly. By W. BESANT and JAMES RICE.

By Celia's Arbour. By WALTER BESANT and JAMES RICE.

The Monks of Thelema. By WALTER BESANT and JAMES RICE.

'Twas in Trafalgar's Bay. By WALTER BESANT and JAMES RICE.

Seamy Side. BESANT and RICE.

Grantley Grange. By S BEAUCHAMP

POPULAR NOVELS—*continued.*

An Heiress of Red Dog. By
BRET HARTE.

The Luck of Roaring Camp.
By BRET HARTE.

Gabriel Conroy. BRET HARTE.

Surly Tim. By F. E. BURNETT.

Juliet's Guardian. By Mrs. H.
LOVETT CAMERON

Deceivers Ever By Mrs L
CAMERON

Cure of Souls. By MACLAREN
COBBAN.

Antonina. By WILKIE COLLINS.

Basil. By WILKIE COLLINS.

Hide and Seek. W. COLLINS.

The Dead Secret. W. COLLINS.

The Queen of Hearts. By
WILKIE COLLINS.

My Miscellanies. W. COLLINS.

The Woman in White. By
WILKIE COLLINS.

The Moonstone. W. COLLINS.

Man and Wife. W. COLLINS.

Poor Miss Finch. W. COLLINS

Miss or Mrs. ? W. COLLINS.

New Magdalen. By W. COLLINS

The Frozen Deep. W. COLLINS.

The Law and the Lady. By
WILKIE COLLINS

The Two Destinies. By WILKIE
COLLINS.

The Haunted Hotel. By WILKIE
COLLINS.

Fallen Leaves. By W. COLLINS.

Felicia. M. BETHAM-EDWARDS.

Roxy. By EDWARD EGGLESTON.

Filthy Lucre. By ALBANY DE
FONBLANQUE.

Olympia. By R. E. FRANCILLON.

The Capel Girls. By EDWARD
GARRETT.

Robin Gray. By CHAS. GIBBON.

For Lack of Gold. By CHARLES
GIBBON

What will the World Say? By
CHARLES GIBBON.

In Honour Bound By CHAS.
GIBBON

In Love and War By CHARLES
GIBBON.

For the King. By CHARLES
GIBBON.

Queen of the Meadow By
CHARLES GIBBON.

Dick Temple. By JAMES
GREENWOOD.

Every-day Papers. By A
HALLIDAY.

Under the Greenwood Tree.
By THOMAS HARDY.

Garth By JULIAN HAWTHORNE

Thornicroft's Model By Mrs
A. HUNT.

Fated to be Free. By JEAN
INGELOW.

Confidence By HENRY JAMES,
Jun.

The Queen of Connaught. By
HARRIETT JAY.

The Dark Colleen. By H JAY

Number Seventeen. By HENRY
KINGSLEY.

Oakshott Castle H. KINGSLEY.

Patricia Kemball. By E. LYNN
LINTON.

The Atonement of Leam Dundas
By E. LYNN LINTON

The World Well Lost. By E.
LYNN LINTON

Under which Lord ? By Mrs
LINTON

The Waterdale Neighbours
By JUSTIN MCCARTHY.

Dear Lady Disdain. By the same.

My Enemy's Daughter. By
JUSTIN MCCARTHY.

A Fair Saxon. J. MCCARTHY

Linley Rochford. MCCARTHY

Miss Misanthrope. MCCARTHY

Donna Quixote. J MCCARTHY.

POPULAR NOVELS—*continued.*

The Evil Eye. By KATHARINE S. MACQUOID.

Lost Rose. K S. MACQUOID.

Open! Sesame! By FLORENCE MARRYAT.

Wild Oats By F. MARRYAT

Little Stepson. F. MARRYAT.

Fighting the Air. F. MARRYAT.

Touch and Go. By JEAN MIDDLEMASS.

Mr. Dorillion J MIDDLEMASS.

Whiteladies ByMrs OLIPHANT

Held in Bondage. By OUIDA.

Strathmore. By OUIDA.

Chandos. By OUIDA.

Under Two Flags. By OUIDA.

Idalia. By OUIDA.

Cecil Castlemaine. By OUIDA.

Tricotrin. By OUIDA.

Puck. By OUIDA.

Folle Farine. By OUIDA.

Dog of Flanders. By OUIDA.

Pascarel. By OUIDA

Two Little Wooden Shoes By OUIDA.

Signa By OUIDA.

In a Winter City By OUIDA.

Ariadne. By OUIDA.

Friendship. By OUIDA.

Walter's Word. By J. PAYN.

Best of Husbands. By J. PAYN.

Halves. By JAMES PAYN.

Fallen Fortunes. By J. PAYN.

What He Cost Her. J. PAYN.

Less Black than We're Painted. By JAMES PAYN.

By Proxy. By JAMES PAYN.

Under One Roof. By J. PAYN.

High Spirits By JAS. PAYN.

The Mystery of Marie Roget. By EDGAR A. POE.

Her Mother's Darling. By Mrs. J. H. RIDDELL.

Gaslight and Daylight. By GEORGE AUGUSTUS SALA.

Bound to the Wheel. By JOHN SAUNDERS.

Guy Waterman. J. SAUNDERS.

One Against the World. By JOHN SAUNDERS.

The Lion in the Path. By JOHN and KATHERINE SAUNDERS.

Match in the Dark. By A. SKETCHLEY.

Tales for the Marines. By WALTER THORNBURY.

The Way we Live Now. By ANTHONY TROLLOPE.

The American Senator. By ANTHONY TROLLOPE.

Diamond Cut Diamond. By T. A. TROLLOPE.

A Pleasure Trip on the Continent of Europe. By MARK TWAIN.

Adventures of Tom Sawyer. By MARK TWAIN.

An Idle Excursion. By MARK TWAIN.

Fcap. 8vo, picture covers, 1*s.* each.

Jeff Briggs's Love Story. By BRET HARTE.

The Twins of Table Mountain. By BRET HARTE.

Mrs. Gainsborough's Diamonds. By JULIAN HAWTHORNE.

Kathleen Mavourneen. By the Author of "That Lass o' Lowrie's."

Lindsay's Luck. By the Author of "That Lass o' Lowrie's."

Pretty Polly Pemberton. By Author of "That Lass o' Lowrie's."

Trooping with Crows By Mrs. PIRKIS.

The Professor's Wife. By LEONARD GRAHAM.

Large 4to, cloth extra, gilt, beautifully Illustrated, 31s 6d
Pastoral Days ;
Or, Memories of a New England Year   By W. HAMILTON GIBSON
With 76 Illustrations in the highest style of Wood Engraving

"*The volume contains a prose poem, with illustrations in the shape of wood engravings more beautiful than it can well enter into the hearts of most men to conceive   Mr. Gibson is not only the author of the text, he is the designer of the illustrations   and it would be difficult to say in which capacity he shows most of the true poet   There is a sensuous beauty in his prose which charms and lulls you. . . . But, as the illustrations are turned to, it will be felt that a new pleasure has been found.   It would be difficult to express too high admiration of the exquisite delicacy of most of the engravings   They are proofs at once of Mr Gibson's power as an artist, of the skill of the engravers, and of the marvellous excellence of the printer's work.*"—SCOTSMAN.

Crown 8vo, cloth extra, 6s
Planché.—Songs and Poems, from 1819 to 1879.
By J. R. PLANCHE.   Edited, with an Introduction, by his Daughter,
Mrs. MACKARNESS.

Two Vols. 8vo, cloth extra, with Illustrations, 10s. 6d.
Plutarch's Lives of Illustrious Men.
Translated from the Greek, with Notes, Critical and Historical, and a
Life of Plutarch, by JOHN and WILLIAM LANGHORNE.   New Edi-
tion, with Medallion Portraits.

Crown 8vo, cloth extra, 7s. 6d
Primitive Manners and Customs.
By JAMES A. FARRER.

Small 8vo, cloth extra, with Illustrations, 3s. 6d.
Prince of Argolis, The :
A Story of the Old Greek Fairy Time.   By J. MOYR SMITH.   With
130 Illustrations by the Author

Proctor's (R. A.) Works :
Easy Star Lessons for Young Learners   With Star Maps for
Every Night in the Year, Drawings of the Constellations, &c   By RICHARD
A. PROCTOR.   Crown 8vo, cloth extra, 6s.   [*In preparation.*
Myths and Marvels of Astronomy.   By RICH. A. PROCTOR,
Author of "Other Worlds than Ours," &c.   Crown 8vo, cloth extra. 6s
Pleasant Ways in Science.   By R. A. PROCTOR   Cr. 8vo, cl. ex. 6s.
Rough Ways made Smooth·   A Series of Familiar Essays on
Scientific Subjects.   By R A. PROCTOR   Crown 8vo cloth extra, 6s
Our Place among Infinities :   A Series of Essays contrasting
our Little Abode in Space and Time with the Infinities Around us.   By
RICHARD A. PROCTOR.   Crown 8vo, cloth extra, 6s.
The Expanse of Heaven : A Series of Essays on the Wonders
of the Firmament.   By RICHARD A. PROCTOR.   Crown 8vo, cloth, 6s
Wages and Wants of Science Workers.   By RICHARD A.
PROCTOR.   Crown 8vo, 1s 6d.
"*Mr. Proctor, of all writers of our time, best conforms to Matthew Arnold's conception of a man of culture, in that he strives to humanise knowledge, to divest it of whatever is harsh, crude or technical, and so makes it a source of happiness and brightness for all*"—WESTMINSTER REVIEW.

Crown 8vo, cloth extra, gilt, 7s. 6d.

Pursuivant of Arms, The;

or, Heraldry founded upon Facts. A Popular Guide to the Science of Heraldry. By J. R. PLANCHE, Somerset Herald. With Coloured Frontispiece, Plates, and 200 Illustrations.

Crown 8vo, cloth extra, with Illustrations, 7s. 6d.

Rabelais' Works.

Faithfully Translated from the French, with variorum Notes, and numerous characteristic Illustrations by GUSTAVE DORE.

Crown 8vo, cloth gilt, with numerous Illustrations, and a beautifully executed Chart of the various Spectra, 7s. 6d.

Rambosson's Astronomy.

By J. RAMBOSSON, Laureate of the Institute of France. Translated by C. B. PITMAN. Profusely Illustrated.

Second Edition, Revised, Crown 8vo, 1,200 pages, half-roxburghe, 12s. 6d.

Reader's Handbook (The) of Allusions, Re-

ferences, Plots, and Stories. By the Rev. Dr. Brewer.

"*Dr. Brewer has produced a wonderfully comprehensive dictionary of references to matters which are always cropping up in conversation and in everyday life, and writers generally will have reason to feel grateful to the author for a most handy volume, supplementing in a hundred ways their own knowledge or ignorance, as the case may be. . It is something more than a mere dictionary of quotations, though a most useful companion to any work of that kind, being a dictionary of most of the allusions, references, plots, stories, and characters which occur in the classical poems, plays, novels, romances, &c., not only of our own country, but of most nations, ancient and modern.*"—TIMES.

Crown 8vo, cloth extra, 6s.

Richardson's (Dr.) A Ministry of Health,

and other Papers. By BENJAMIN WARD RICHARDSON, M.D., &c.

Square 8vo, cloth extra, gilt, profusely Illustrated, 10s. 6d.

Rimmer's Our Old Country Towns.

With over 50 Illustrations. By ALFRED RIMMER.

Two Vols , large 4to, profusely Illustrated, half-morocco, £2 16s.

Rowlandson, the Caricaturist.

A Selection from his Works, with Anecdotal Descriptions of his Famous Caricatures, and a Sketch of his Life, Times, and Contemporaries. With nearly 400 Illustrations, mostly in Facsimile of the Originals. By JOSEPH GREGO, Author of "James Gillray, the Caricaturist; his Life, Works, and Times."

"*Mr. Grego's excellent account of the works of Thomas Rowlandson . . . illustrated with some 400 spirited, accurate, and clever transcripts from his designs. . . The thanks of all who care for what is original and personal in art are due to Mr Grego for the pains he has been at, and the time he has expended, in the preparation of this very pleasant, very careful, and adequate memorial*" –PALL MALL GAZETTE.

Handsomely printed, price 5s.

Roll of Battle Abbey, The;

or, A List of the Principal Warriors who came over from Normandy with William the Conqueror, and Settled in this Country, A.D. 1066-7. Printed on fine plate paper, nearly three feet by two, with the principal Arms emblazoned in Gold and Colours.

Crown 8vo, cloth extra, profusely Illustrated, 4s. 6d. each.

"Secret Out" Series, The.

The Pyrotechnist's Treasury;
or, Complete Art of Making Fireworks. By THOMAS KENTISH. With numerous Illustrations.

The Art of Amusing:
A Collection of Graceful Arts, Games, Tricks, Puzzles, and Charades. By FRANK BELLEW. 300 Illustrations

Hanky-Panky:
Very Easy Tricks, Very Difficult Tricks, White Magic, Sleight of Hand. Edited by W H CREMER. 200 Illusts

The Merry Circle:
A Book of New Intellectual Games and Amusements. By CLARA BELLEW. Many Illustrations.

Magician's Own Book:
Performances with Cups and Balls, Eggs, Hats, Handkerchiefs, &c. All from Actual Experience Edited by W. H. CREMER. 200 Illustrations.

Magic No Mystery:
Tricks with Cards, Dice, Balls, &c., with fully descriptive Directions; the Art of Secret Writing; Training of Performing Animals, &c. Coloured Frontispiece and many Illustrations.

The Secret Out:
One Thousand Tricks with Cards, and other Recreations, with Entertaining Experiments in Drawing-room or "White Magic." By W H. CREMER 300 Engravings

Crown 8vo, cloth extra, 6s

Senior's Travel and Trout in the Antipodes.

An Angler's Sketches in Tasmania and New Zealand. By WILLIAM SENIOR ("Red Spinner"). Author of "Stream and Sea."

Crown 8vo, cloth extra, gilt, with 10 full-page Tinted Illustrations, 7s. 6d.

Sheridan's Complete Works,

with Life and Anecdotes Including his Dramatic Writings, printed from the Original Editions, his Works in Prose and Poetry, Translations, Speeches, Jokes, Puns, &c; with a Collection of Sheridaniana.

Crown 8vo, cloth extra, with Illustrations, 7s. 6d.

Signboards:

Their History. With Anecdotes of Famous Taverns and Remarkable Characters. By JACOB LARWOOD and JOHN CAMDEN HOTTEN. With nearly 100 Illustrations.

"*Even if we were ever so maliciously inclined, we could not pick out all Messrs. Larwood and Hotten's plums, because the good things are so numerous as to defy the most wholesale depredation.*"—TIMES.

Crown 8vo, cloth extra, gilt, 6s. 6d.

Slang Dictionary, The:

Etymological, Historical, and Anecdotal. An ENTIRELY NEW EDITION, revised throughout, and considerably Enlarged.

"*We are glad to see the Slang Dictionary reprinted and enlarged. From a high scientific point of view this book is not to be despised. Of course it cannot fail to be amusing also. It contains the very vocabulary of unrestrained humour, and oddity, and grotesqueness. In a word, it provides valuable material both for the student of language and the student of human nature.*"—ACADEMY.

Shakespeare:

Shakespeare, The First Folio. Mr. WILLIAM SHAKESPEARE'S Comedies, Histories, and Tragedies. Published according to the true Originall Copies. London, Printed by ISAAC IAGGARD and ED. BLOUNT, 1623.—A Reproduction of the extremely rare original, in reduced facsimile by a photographic process—ensuring the strictest accuracy in every detail. Small 8vo, half-Roxburghe, 10s. 6d.

"*To Messrs. Chatto and Windus belongs the merit of having done more to facilitate the critical study of the text of our great dramatist than all the Shakespeare clubs and societies put together. A complete facsimile of the celebrated First Folio edition of 1623 for half-a-guinea is at once a miracle of cheapness and enterprise. Being in a reduced form, the type is necessarily rather diminutive, but it is as distinct as in a genuine copy of the original, and will be found to be as useful and far more handy to the student than the latter*"—ATHENÆUM.

Shakespeare, The Lansdowne. Beautifully printed in red and black, in small but very clear type. With engraved facsimile of DROESHOUT'S Portrait. Post 8vo, cloth extra, 7s. 6d

Shakespeare for Children: Tales from Shakespeare. By CHARLES and MARY LAMB. With numerous Illustrations, coloured and plain, by J MOYR SMITH Crown 4to, cloth gilt, 10s. 6d.

Shakespeare Music, The Handbook of. Being an Account of 350 Pieces of Music, set to Words taken from the Plays and Poems of Shakespeare, the compositions ranging from the Elizabethan Age to the Present Time. By ALFRED ROFFE. 4to, half-Roxburghe, 7s.

Shakespeare, A Study of. By ALGERNON CHARLES SWINBURNE. Crown 8vo, cloth extra, 8s.

Exquisitely printed in miniature, cloth extra, gilt edges, 2s. 6d.

Smoker's Text-Book, The.

By J. HAMER, F.R S.L

Crown 8vo, cloth extra, 5s.

Spalding's Elizabethan Demonology:

An Essay in Illustration of the Belief in the Existence of Devils and the Powers possessed by them. By T. ALFRED SPALDING, LL.B.

Crown 4to, uniform with "Chaucer for Children," with Coloured Illustrations, cloth gilt, 10s. 6d.

Spenser for Children.

By M. H. TOWRY. With Illustrations in Colours by WALTER J. MORGAN.

"*Spenser has simply been transferred into plain prose, with here and there a line or stanza quoted, where the meaning and the diction are within a child's comprehension, and additional point is thus given to the narrative without the cost of obscurity. . . . Altogether the work has been well and carefully done.*"—THE TIMES.

Crown 8vo, cloth extra, 9s.

Stedman's Victorian Poets:

Critical Essays. By EDMUND CLARENCE STEDMAN.

"*We ought to be thankful to those who do critical work with competent skill and understanding Mr Stedman deserves the thanks of English scholars; . . . he is faithful, studious, and discerning*"—SATURDAY REVIEW.

Post 8vo, cloth extra, 5s.

Stories about Number Nip,

The Spirit of the Giant Mountains. Retold for Children, by WALTER GRAHAME. With Illustrations by J MOYR SMITH.

Crown 8vo, with a Map of Suburban London, cloth extra, 7s 6d.

Suburban Homes (The) of London:

A Residential Guide to Favourite London Localities, their Society, Celebrities, and Associations. With Notes on their Rental, Rates, and House Accommodation. *[In the press*.

Crown 8vo, cloth extra, with Illustrations, 7s. 6d.

Swift's Choice Works,

In Prose and Verse. With Memoir, Portrait, and Facsimiles of the Maps in the Original Edition of "Gulliver's Travels."

Demy 8vo, cloth extra, Illustrated, 21s.

Sword, The Book of the:

Being a History of the Sword, and its Use, in all Times and in all Countries. By Captain RICHARD BURTON. With numerous Illustrations *[In preparation.*

Crown 8vo, cloth extra, with Illustrations, 7s 6d.

Strutt's Sports and Pastimes of the People

of England; including the Rural and Domestic Recreations, May Games, Mummeries, Shows, Processions, Pageants, and Pompous Spectacles, from the Earliest Period to the Present Time. With 140 Illustrations. Edited by WILLIAM HONE.

Swinburne's Works:

The Queen Mother and Rosamond. Fcap. 8vo, 5s.

Atalanta in Calydon.
A New Edition. Crown 8vo, 6s.

Chastelard.
A Tragedy. Crown 8vo, 7s.

Poems and Ballads.
FIRST SERIES. Fcap 8vo, 9s Also in crown 8vo, at same price

Poems and Ballads.
SECOND SERIES Fcap 8vo, 9s. Also in crown 8vo, at same price.

Notes on "Poems and Ballads." 8vo, 1s.

William Blake:
A Critical Essay With Facsimile Paintings. Demy 8vo, 16s.

Songs before Sunrise.
Crown 8vo, 10s 6d

Bothwell:
A Tragedy. Crown 8vo, 12s. 6d.

George Chapman:
An Essay Crown 8vo, 7s.

Songs of Two Nations.
Crown 8vo, 6s.

Essays and Studies.
Crown 8vo, 12s.

Erechtheus:
A Tragedy. Crown 8vo, 6s.

Note of an English Republican on the Muscovite Crusade. 8vo, 1s.

A Note on Charlotte Brontë.
Crown 8vo, 6s.

A Study of Shakespeare.
Crown 8vo, 8s.

Songs of the Springtides. Cr. 8vo, 6s.

Studies in Song.
Crown 8vo, 7s.

Medium 8vo, cloth extra, with Illustrations, 7s. 6d.

Syntax's (Dr.) Three Tours,

in Search of the Picturesque, in Search of Consolation, and in Search of a Wife. With the whole of ROWLANDSON's droll page Illustrations, in Colours, and Life of the Author by J. C. HOTTEN.

Crown 8vo, cloth gilt, profusely Illustrated, 6s.

Tales of Old Thule.

Collected and Illustrated by J. MOYR SMITH.

Four Vols. small 8vo, cloth boards, 30s.

Taine's History of English Literature.

Translated by HENRY VAN LAUN.

*** Also a POPULAR EDITION, in Two Vols. crown 8vo, cloth extra, 15s.

One Vol. crown 8vo, cloth extra, 7s. 6d.

Taylor's (Tom) Historical Dramas:

"Clancarty," "Jeanne Darc," "'Twixt Axe and Crown," "The Fool's Revenge," "Arkwright's Wife," "Anne Boleyn," "Plot and Passion."

*** The Plays may also be had separately, at 1s. each.

Crown 8vo, cloth extra, with Coloured Frontispiece and numerous Illustrations, 7s. 6d.

Thackerayana:

Notes and Anecdotes. Illustrated by a profusion of Sketches by WILLIAM MAKEPEACE THACKERAY, depicting Humorous Incidents in his School-life, and Favourite Characters in the books of his everyday reading. With Hundreds of Wood Engravings, facsimiled from Mr. Thackeray's Original Drawings.

Crown 8vo, cloth extra, gilt edges, with Illustrations, 7s. 6d.

Thomson's Seasons and Castle of Indolence.

With a Biographical and Critical Introduction by ALLAN CUNNINGHAM, and over 50 fine Illustrations on Steel and Wood.

Crown 8vo, cloth extra, with numerous Illustrations, 7s. 6d.

Thornbury's (Walter) Haunted London.

A New Edition, Edited by EDWARD WALFORD, M.A., with numerous Illustrations by F. W. FAIRHOLT, F.S.A.

"*Mr. Thornbury knew and loved his London. . . . He had read much history, and every by-lane and every court had associations for him. His memory and his note-books were stored with anecdote, and, as he had singular skill in the matter of narration, it will be readily believed that when he took to writing a set book about the places he knew and cared for, the said book would be charming. Charming the volume before us certainly is It may be begun in the beginning, or middle, or end; it is all one: wherever one lights, there is some pleasant and curious bit of gossip, some amusing fragment of allusion or quotation.*"—VANITY FAIR.

Crown 8vo, cloth extra, with Illustrations, 7s. 6d.

Timbs' Clubs and Club Life in London.

With Anecdotes of its famous Coffee-houses, Hostelries, and Taverns. By JOHN TIMBS, F.S.A. With numerous Illustrations.

Crown 8vo, cloth extra, with Illustrations, 7s. 6d.

Timbs' English Eccentrics and Eccentrici-
ties: Stories of Wealth and Fashion, Delusions, Impostures, and Fanatic Missions, Strange Sights and Sporting Scenes, Eccentric Artists, Theatrical Folks, Men of Letters, &c. By JOHN TIMBS, F.S.A. With nearly 50 Illustrations.

Demy 8vo, cloth extra, 14s.

Torrens' The Marquess Wellesley,
Architect of Empire. An Historic Portrait. *Forming Vol. I. of* PRO-CONSUL and TRIBUNE: WELLESLEY and O'CONNELL. Historic Portraits. By W. M. TORRENS, M.P. In Two Vols.

Crown 8vo, cloth extra, with Coloured Illustrations, 7s 6d.

Turner's (J. M. W.) Life and Correspondence:
Founded upon Letters and Papers furnished by his Friends and fellow-Academicians. By WALTER THORNBURY. A New Edition, considerably Enlarged. With numerous Illustrations in Colours, facsimiled from Turner's original Drawings.

Two Vols., crown 8vo, cloth extra, with Map and Ground-Plans, 14s.

Walcott's Church Work and Life in English
Minsters; and the English Student's Monasticon. By the Rev. MACKENZIE E. C. WALCOTT, B.D.

The Twenty-first Annual Edition, for 1881, cloth, full gilt, 50s.

Walford's County Families of the United
Kingdom. A Royal Manual of the Titled and Untitled Aristocracy of Great Britain and Ireland. By EDWARD WALFORD, M A., late Scholar of Balliol College, Oxford. Containing Notices of the Descent, Birth, Marriage, Education, &c., of more than 12,000 distinguished Heads of Families in the United Kingdom, their Heirs Apparent or Presumptive, together with a Record of the Patronage at their disposal, the Offices which they hold or have held, their Town Addresses, Country Residences, Clubs, &c.

Large crown 8vo, cloth antique, with Illustrations, 7s. 6d.

Walton and Cotton's Complete Angler;
or, The Contemplative Man's Recreation . being a Discourse of Rivers. Fishponds, Fish and Fishing, written by IZAAK WALTON; and Instructions how to Angle for a Trout or Grayling in a clear Stream, by CHARLES COTTON. With Original Memoirs and Notes by Sir HARRIS NICOLAS, and 61 Copperplate Illustrations.

Carefully printed on paper to imitate the Original, 22 in. by 14 in., 2s.

Warrant to Execute Charles I.
An exact Facsimile of this important Document, with the Fifty-nine Signatures of the Regicides, and corresponding Seals.

Beautifully printed on paper to imitate the Original MS., price 2s.

Warrant to Execute Mary Queen of Scots.

An exact Facsimile, including the Signature of Queen Elizabeth, and a Facsimile of the Great Seal.

Crown 8vo, cloth limp, with numerous Illustrations, 4s. 6d.

Westropp's Handbook of Pottery and Porce-

lain; or, History of those Arts from the Earliest Period. By HODDER M. WESTROPP, Author of "Handbook of Archæology," &c. With numerous beautiful Illustrations, and a List of Marks.

SEVENTH EDITION.   Square 8vo, 1s.

Whistler v. Ruskin: Art and Art Critics.

By J. A. MACNEILL WHISTLER.

Crown 8vo, cloth limp, with Illustrations, 2s. 6d.

Williams' A Simple Treatise on Heat.

By W. MATTIEU WILLIAMS, F.R.A S., F.C.S.

"*This is an unpretending little work, put forth for the purpose of expounding in simple style the phenomena and laws of heat. No strength is vainly spent in endeavouring to present a mathematical view of the subject. The author passes over the ordinary range of matter to be found in most elementary treatises on heat, and enlarges upon the applications of the principles of his science—a subject which is naturally attractive to the uninitiated Mr Williams's object has been well carried out, and his little book may be recommended to those who care to study this interesting branch of physics.*"—POPULAR SCIENCE REVIEW

A HANDSOME GIFT-BOOK.— Small 8vo, cloth extra, 6s.

Wooing (The) of the Water-Witch:

A Northern Oddity. By EVAN DALDORNE. With One Hundred and Twenty-five fine Illustrations by J. MOYR SMITH.

Crown 8vo, half-bound, 12s. 6d.

Words and Phrases:

A Dictionary of Curious, Quaint, and Out-of-the-Way Matters. By ELIEZER EDWARDS.   [*In the press.*

Crown 8vo, cloth extra, with Illustrations, 7s. 6d.

Wright's Caricature History of the Georges.

(The House of Hanover.) With 400 Pictures, Caricatures, Squibs, Broadsides, Window Pictures, &c By THOMAS WRIGHT, M.A., F.S.A.

Large post 8vo, cloth extra, gilt, with Illustrations, 7s. 6d.

Wright's History of Caricature and of the

Grotesque in Art, Literature, Sculpture, and Painting, from the Earliest Times to the Present Day. By THOMAS WRIGHT, M.A., F.S.A. Profusely Illustrated by F. W. FAIRHOLT, F.S.A.

J. OGDEN AND CO., PRINTERS, 172, ST. JOHN STREET, E.C.

Lightning Source UK Ltd.
Milton Keynes UK
UKOW06n1524010916

282004UK00001B/123/P